SEETA

MEADOWS TAYLOR

"Let me not to the marriage of true minds
Admit impediments. Love is not love
Which alters when it alteration finds,
Or bends with the remover to remove:
O no; it is an ever-fixed mark,.
That looks on tempests, and is never shaken;
It is the star to every wandering bark,
Whose worth's unknown, although his height be taken
* * * * *
If this be error, and upon me prov'd
I never writ, nor no man ever lov'd"
SHAKESPEARE, Sonnet CXVI

GYAN

Published by

GYAN

Gyan Publishing House
5, Ansari Road
Daryaganj, New Delhi-110002
Phone: 011-47034999, 9811692060
E-mail: books@gyanbooks.com

Distribution Network
gyanbooks.com
India, USA, Canada, UK, Australia, France

ISBN : 978-81-212-3989-9 (PB)
First Published, 1881

2nd Impression 2020

Printed at: Gyan Press, Delhi.

Seeta
Author: Meadows Taylor

SEETA

TO

MY DEAR DAUGHTERS, ALICE AND AMY,

FOR THEIR DEVOTED LOVE

AND VALUABLE PATIENT ASSISTANCE,

I Dedicate this Volume.

INTRODUCTION.

To my Readers.

The present volume, which relates to 1857, is intended to complete the series that I commenced with "Tara" (1657) in the year 1863, and continued in "Ralph Darnell" (1757) in 1865. The historical events which form the foundation of each of these works, are not only of the highest importance and interest, but occurring strangely at almost exact intervals of a hundred years, are not exceeded in dramatic power by any actions in the History of India.

The first tale, "Tara," illustrated the very remarkable epoch of 1657, when the Mahrattas, previously unknown except as ordinary subjects of the Mahomedan Government of the Deccan, cast off their allegiance, rose to power under Rajah Sivajee Bhóslay, and defeated, at first by treachery, the army of Beejapoor. Having thus established the basis of a national independence, the Mahrattas, after a long and harassing war with the Emperor Aurungzebe, which lasted sixteen years, defeated him in 1707; and his death, which occurred in the same year, and the distractions of the Mahomedan Empire which followed that event, enabled them to extend their conquests till, by the year 1757, they became the most powerful State Confederacy in India, and had totally overthrown the once magnificent Empire of Dehly

In that memorable year a new political power arose in the English, heretofore merchants and traders only. On June 23, 1757, Lord Clive won the battle of Plassy, and laid the foundation of the English Empire which now exists. At that time, however, a strange astrological prediction was recorded, that the rule of the English Company would last only one hundred years, that is from Sumbut 1814 to Sumbut 1914 of the Hindoo era.

As regards the history of India, and the condition of the people, the epoch of 1757 was more momentous than that of 1657. The new power, during a century of progression, became dominant over all, Hindoos and Mahomedans alike. It had deprived both the Mahrattas and Mussulmans of independent political existence and influence, it had introduced new and powerful elements of Western civilization, and the struggle of 1857 was a combination to regain what had been lost. In this struggle the native Sepoy army of Bengal, by its revolt and mutiny, took a prominent part.

In my present tale it has not been my purpose to write history; but to give, as it were in an episode, a general impression of the time which, of all others in the history of India, is the most absorbing and interesting to the English reader, and I have purposely avoided the sickening details of pitiless massacre and suffering, which have already been illustrated by many writers, and which, of necessity, must be repeated in Sir John Kaye's history. I have therefore omitted these distressing events, and introduced casual mention of them only where they could not be avoided.

I may seem to some, perhaps, to have laid more stress upon the weird prediction in regard to the events of Sumbut 1914, 1857–58, than it deserves; but those who lived among the people at the time—as I did—felt what power it had gradually assumed over the native mind, among all classes and in all localities of India, and apart from other pretexts for disaffection mutiny, and rebellion, I have always considered, and shall continue to consider it, as one of the most prominent and exciting causes of general combination and action in that year.

No one, previously, dared to mention openly, or attempt to define, what was to happen. The prediction, in the form of an astrological deduction from a conjunction of planets, had been repeated in every Hindoo Almanac for a century; and as the fatal year approached, Englishmen who were popular among the people or had private friends, were, in many instances, warned of coming troubles and dangers, earnestly entreated to leave India, or, at least, to provide for the safety of wives and children. Such warnings extended to localities far removed from the actual scene of disturbance; while even to the Government itself, very solemn and impressive intimations and counsels were not omitted.

The Sumbut year 1914 commenced on March 25, 1857, and closed on March 19, 1858, before the war had come to an end. It had been preceded by deadly epidemics and disastrous floods, and in addition to these, tumult and massacre, as predicted, had marked its course. Finally, the deposition of the East India Company from power, held to signify the expulsion of the English from India, was literally fulfilled. But, while the Company died, the Queen of England ruled in its stead!

In Azráel Pandé* I have endeavoured to depict the character of the rebel and treasonable emissaries of the time. Malignant and persistent, they were led on by blind hatred and religious fanaticism, to the instigation and commission of crimes at which humanity shudders; and in Azráel's address to the Sepoy delegates at Barrackpoor I think I have included all the "wrongs" under which the Bengal Sepoys professed to suffer.

* Pandé is not, as might be imagined, a surname. It is one of the divisions of Brahmins of Oudh and Bahar, as Doobé, Chowbé, Tewarree, Misser, etc., etc., which are very numerous.

The case of Dacoity with which my tale opens, was an actual one, tried by me in my district court in 1855.

My readers need not look in the map for Noorpoor and Shah Gunje, nor in the civil or military lists for my English characters, for they will not find them.

MEADOWS TAYLOR.

CONTENTS.

SEETA

PART THE FIRST.

CHAPTER I.

ON HOLY GROUND.

It was nearly midnight. A slight passing shower had just fallen, and the moon, nearly at its full, shone out with brilliant lustre over a scene at once strikingly beautiful and impressive. At the head of one of the long ravines which descend westwards from the plateau of Central India, was a deep, lonely glen, the upper end of which was closed by one of those abrupt precipices of basalt, which everywhere mark the boundary of the table-land above, and over which a small stream, swelled somewhat beyond its wont by the showers of the rainy season, now poured a considerable body of water with a dull continuous roar. The moonlight fell directly upon the precipice and fall, and lighted them up with vivid effect. As the waters rushed downwards, at first through a narrow gully at the summit of the precipice, they threw up ever-changing jets of spray, flashing for a moment like molten silver as they caught the light, and then disappeared. Then, as the stream spread out over the nearly perpendicular rock, it became a sheet of dazzling foam, till it reached a deep, dark pool at the foot of the fall, and flowed over its margin tumultuously down the glen. The monotonous dull colour of the rock was relieved by luxuriant creepers, and wild shrubs and flowers, many of which, now in full bloom, loaded the air with rich odours. Above, and on both sides of the glen downwards, rugged hills rose to a considerable height, and it was only by one rocky path near the fall that the glen could be entered easily. At the foot of the fall, and bordering part of the pool, was however an open space, now covered with soft green sward, the only level spot in the glen for some miles of its course, where, on one occasion in each year, the people of the country round held a kind of fair, bathed in the waters of the pool, and worshipped the local deities to whom it was held sacred. At other times, indeed, the place had an evil reputation, and was carefully avoided.

At the back of this level spot, grew a vast peepul tree of enormous size and remarkably picturesque though peculiar character. One half of it still flourished luxuriantly, and its dark glossy foliage, still wet from the shower, and trembling with every breath of wind, sparkled in the strong light. The rest of the tree was dead; and its long, gaunt branches, bleached white by the sun and wind of many centuries, stretched upwards to the precipice, and partly over the pool, in weird, ghastly forms.

As is usual in most parts of India, the tree was held sacred; and some votary perhaps, in times forgotten, might have planted the Neemtree which grew with it, and married them with great ceremony. Such at least was the legend. This was, however, only a modern Hindoo observance, and the sacred character of the tree reached far beyond that, to a period when it was probably adored, together with the image of the rudely carved twisted snakes which lay at its foot, by the ancient tree and snake worshipping tribes of the country. By the side of the snake-image, too, rested a pile of stones, smeared with vermilion and lampblack. This had existed from rude times, even beyond those of the snake-worshippers; and as a part of the dim, aboriginal belief that still lingers among Hindoos, was held in reverence as representing the deities of the place—the spirits, whose goodwill was to be secured by annual sacrifices and oblations, and whose neglect brought with it sore penalties of sickness, and failure of harvests.

Nor was the spot destitute of other ancient religious associations. Two thousand years ago, perhaps, a Boodhist fraternity of monks or devotees had selected this spot, as they did hundreds of others, for its wild beauty and absolute seclusion, and with infinite pains and labour had excavated from the trap-rock a small Vihara or monastery, complete in itself, though roughly executed and ornamented. It consisted of a wide square hall, at the end of which, in an apse or recess, was a large statue of Boodh in a sitting posture, carved out of the rock, with its open palms resting on its thighs; and it seemed as if the mild, placid features ever looked out benignly into the beautiful glen, and over the sparkling waters of the stream. On each side of the hall were rows of small dark chambers, once the dwelling-places of the monks who lived there: and except some mutilation of the face of the image, and a deep deposit of earth on the rock floor, the cave-temple was as perfect as ever.

Standing on its threshold by the two massive pillars which formed the entrance, and looking down the glen, the view was eminently lovely by day, when a soft blue haze trembled over the distance, disclosing the forms of high, rugged hills, covered with wood, lying range upon range till they disappeared in the dim horizon; while the splendour of sunlight rested upon the precipitous sides and rock promontories of the glen, and glinted upon the clear rushing water as it flung itself over cascades and jutting rocks in its downward headlong course. By night, perhaps, under the softer moonlight, the scene was even more beautiful, because more tender in effect; for the grander forms of the picture were hardly less distinct in their nearest portions than by day, though infinitely softened, while the more distant faded gradually into a dim, mysterious haze, blending with the sky.

It was not without cause that this place had earned an evil reputation by night as well as by day. Inside the old Boodhist temple were the ashes of fires, with broken earthen vessels strewed about them; and among these were coarse earthen crucibles in which the booty of many a Pindharee foray, or Dacoity, had been melted down. Sometimes the discordant sounds of midnight revelry and the light of blazing fires had been seen and heard by belated shepherds; and though such tales were believed in the adjacent towns and villages, they excited no particular interest, for they were renewed only perhaps on rare occasions.

Such an one was the present. Inside the cave was now a blazing fire, the smoke of which, striking the low roof, curled up the sides of the precipice in thick wreaths, and around it were seated a company of about twenty men, whose savage appearance betokened a hard, lawless life. The fire was fed from time to time with dry sticks and thorns: and as the flames leaped high, occasionally almost to the roof, they lighted up the fierce faces around, and the great image behind with its soft, placid features, in strange contrast with each other. Some of the men were drinking raw spirits from a copper cup which was passed round, and several of them already showed signs of partial intoxication, which vented itself in snatches of rude songs; while, from the conversation which passed among them, and the joyful anticipation of a division of booty, the occupation of those assembled admitted of no doubt. Finally, a quarrel had arisen between two of the men, and the noise and confusion it had occasioned had been heard even over the monotonous roar of the waterfall; and, as the disputants were still wrangling, a tall figure suddenly presented itself at the entrance of the temple, whose presence caused instant silence, and some of the men slunk backwards into the gloom.

"Again drinking and quarrelling?" cried the new-comer, striking the staff of the broad heavy spear he carried sharply on the ground. "Cannot I trust ye for an hour? Bring me the spirits;" and two men lifted a copper vessel from a dark corner and placed it before him. Stepping aside, he overturned it with his foot, and part of the contents running into the fire, caused it to blaze up fiercely. "See what ye drink, O fools!" he continued with a contemptuous gesture. "Fire to fire, and so to quarrelling, and too often treachery. But no more to-night; we may have other work to do. Can I trust ye?"

The only answer to this was a shout of "Jey Kalee!" "Victory to Kalee," which had only just ceased, when two men entered hastily, and saluting their leader with a low reverence, said, "He is here, master; we have brought him safely."

"And the money?"

"Yes, master, the bags were slung on his pony, and we carried them down the path. They are beside the tree where he sits."

"And he is alone?"

"Yes; he would have brought a servant, but we did not permit him. He is alone."

"Then wait patiently, my sons," said the leader, "I will return soon. No one must follow me; I must speak with this person myself."

We shall see much of this man in our history. A tall commanding figure, with a great breadth of chest and strength of limb, showing the constant use of athletic exercises. His features were regular, and would have been handsome but for his mouth which, when he spoke, disclosed jagged, irregular teeth; and, together with some projection of the lower jaw, gave him, when excited, the expression of a wild beast. The coal-black eyes were large, deep set, and fierce in expression. On his forehead, which was high and smooth, a strange knot of wrinkles would often arise suddenly, and those who knew him best feared him most when these appeared. For a native of India, his complexion might be called fair—a bright olive, which sometimes flushed into dark red. His thick moustache was streaked with grey, and his age might be forty years, while his powerful frame and soldier-like carriage betokened no decay of power in what was evidently the prime of his life. By caste he was a Brahmin, and was well read in the sacred Hindoo books; and when he chose to exercise his powers, his recitations to village assemblies during his wanderings were eagerly welcomed and well rewarded. Some of his men knew him as Moolráj, others as Azráel. His real name had never been avowed, but it was, in truth, Azráel Pandé. No one knew of his antecedents; but among his men he was considered the prince of Dacoity leaders, the most unceasing in devising projects, and the most merciless in their execution. Alike in the Deccan, in Central India and Bengal, had his terrible crimes been committed, and English magistrates and police, and in some instances native princes also, were alike helpless to trace the perpetrators.

Such an affair had been the present. In a far-off district of Western India, one evening not many days before, as the sun went down, a band of men entered a quiet village, possessed themselves of the house of a rich banker, murdered him and several members of his family, and breaking open his strong closet with an axe, deliberately carried off all the valuables it contained. There were no police in the village, and the ordinary watchmen dare not show themselves. The Dacoits were heard to speak in a strange tongue, and no clue whatever was obtained of them. Separating at once, however, the gang had proceeded singly or in pairs to the place where we find them. It was afterwards remembered by the banker's family, that a Brahmin of Upper India, going, as he said, to Raméshwur, had been allowed to recite some of the Pooráns, and had rested with them two days unsuspected.

Such frightful crimes are happily becoming rare in India in comparison to what they used to be; and the humane efforts of the British Government have, to a great extent, been as successful in the extirpation of Dacoity, as they were in the suppression of the even more hideous crime of Thuggee.

On this occasion the amount to be divided was considerable. Some of the most valuable of the booty the leader had concealed about his person; but with the rest there was ample to satisfy his men. It was impossible that such transactions could be completed without confederates, and one of these was Ram Das, who had just arrived. This man was a Sahoukar, or trader in money, of the village of Gokulpoor, about four miles from the glen, with whom Azráel Pandé's dealings had been long and regular, and who, as part of his compact, had now brought the proceeds of the last affair to be divided. Ram Das had, however, a project of his own, long meditated and arranged, to discuss with the Dacoit leader, on the issue of which much of this history will depend.

CHAPTER II.

A BARGAIN AND AN OMEN.

"Ram! Ram! Maharaj! You are welcome though late. We have long expected you," said Azráel to the man, who rose up from the carpet on which he had been sitting. "Be seated—what detained you?"

"Nay, be seated yourself, Jemadar," answered the other, rising and addressing the leader by the title by which only he knew him; and as Azráel threw himself carelessly on the carpet, he settled himself into a more ceremonious posture with his heels under him, and his hands joined before him on his knees.

"Did it rain as you came? you must be wet," said Azráel, by way of opening the colloquy.

"No, I did not leave home till it was fine, and the moon shone out; and I had besides some business to do. I knew my lord would not depart without me. He! he! he!"

"Hardly," replied Azráel; "my Sahoukars (bankers) sometimes try to cheat me; and indeed I seldom trust them. And now, friend, what have you brought? I have your memorandum of what was sent to you."

"Ah! Jemadar!" replied the man in a whining tone, "it is all very well to make valuations, but who can realise them? And I had so little time, your worship was in such a hurry. Who could sell all that gold and silver in my poor village?—and the pearls remain."

"Well, well," said Azráel sharply, "what have you brought? My people are impatient, and have been drinking themselves into a passion, and are not to be trusted. Be quick, good fellow."

The merchant had misinterpreted the apparently calm demeanour of his companion, and replied with cheerful animation, and a slight attempt to laugh—

"Yes, Jemadar Sahib, here is the account, and the money is in the bags; will you have it counted?"

"Enough!" cried the other impatiently, and snatching the paper out of the merchant's hand. "I dare say you know it by heart, so proceed."

"Well, then, Jemadar," replied Ram Das, after a detail which need not be followed; "you see the things that were sold produced altogether two thousand six hundred and forty rupees, which are in these four bags."

"Oh, liar and thief!" cried Azráel, who had with difficulty restrained his passion while the particulars of the sales were being recited. "By your own showing, there should have been upwards of a thousand rupees more, and that thou hast stolen. Now, what prevents me from flinging you as you are into yonder pool, or giving you up to my people, to get what they could out of you? It would not be a thousand, methinks, nor twice that; will you take the risk of a bargain with them, or shall we make it without them?"

"Oh, Jemadar—Maharaj! Oh, my lord! Do not terrify me," exclaimed the man; "I am but a poor weak creature, earning my bread penny by penny, and you are a great leader, of whom all are afraid. I swear by my children, by Krishna, by your neck and feet, that what I have said is the truth. Do not doubt your slave who has been always so faithful."

"Now, Ram Das, listen," said Azráel, "listen carefully to my words. They will be few, for it is useless to waste any on such as you, and you know well that I always do what I say. I do not want much this time. The men have behaved well, and shall have all that is here, but I must have a note of hand for a thousand rupees, and a receipt for the things that have not been sold."

"My lord! my lord, consider how poor I am, consider—— Here is the receipt for the articles still with me," he continued rapidly, observing Azráel's impatience. "O my Jemadar! do not wrong me, and have pity on my poverty."

"I am not deceived, my friend," replied Azráel, calmly. "I remember something of the place where you keep your hoards, and I could take them to-night when, as I hinted to you before, you were lying at the bottom of yonder pool. Have you brought pen and paper?"

"They are here, my lord," said the merchant, trembling, and he produced a writing-case from his pocket.

"Write, then, a promissory note for a thousand rupees. I will come for it when I need it."

"My lord will be merciful: think of the risk I run. Were the English police to know of what I have done, what could save me from the black waters?" said Ram Das, writhing with fear.

"Or me from being hanged, perhaps," returned Azráel, grimly; "but so long as we are alive, good friend, and have our little affairs to transact, we must cheat each other as little as possible. Therefore write the bond, and make no fuss about it. Or else," and he turned his deep eyes on the man with a savage scowl, "I must go and help myself, while the fishes eat thee at the bottom of that dark water. Ha! does that touch thee! O thief and miser!"

Ram Das saw he had fallen into a trap, and he felt that any resistance or delay would be fatal. The merciless character of his companion was known to him, and that human life with him was a thing of no value or moment whatever, when it crossed his objects. Even as it was, the deposit of pearls and the necklace would be security, and the profit on the sales had been large. Not only was all his wealth at the robber's mercy, with his own life; but he had to disclose his private projects, which he knew would be acceptable.

"Make it five hundred, Jemadar," he said, as he took out the paper to write, for even in the peril he was, he could not resist the habit of his trade.

There was no reply.

"Six hundred—six hundred and fifty, payable to the bearer on demand; that will be better, and safer than writing your name on it. My bills are known everywhere, and any banker will cash the order."

"I believe I am a soft fool," cried Azráel, laughing; "and now see how merciful I can be. Write seven hundred and fifty, payable to the bearer. Why, man, the pearls are worth more than that."

Ram Das hesitated no longer; his pen ran rapidly over the paper, and the order was worded as Azráel had said; but his hand still trembled; the document was not so regular in form as one of his clerks would have written, and might be refused if his handwriting were not known. For the time, however, it would stave off danger. When it was finished, he took up a pinch of the white sand near the carpet, dried, and presented it.

"And now, what is thy will, friend?" said Azráel, quietly folding up the paper. "Thou art alive, well for thee; speak, good man, and I will listen."

The merchant looked right and left, forwards and backwards, into the deep shadow, to see if any one were within hearing. Before him was the soft green sward, glistening in the moonlight; by his side the dark pool which he had perhaps narrowly escaped, covered with creamy foam. Behind, the foliage of the peepul, through which the water of the fall flashed brightly. He saw no one; and yet, hidden in the hollow trunk of the tree, two of the gang sat crouching and listening to every word. They had suspected their leader's private conference with the merchant, and had already learned one valuable secret. What was next to follow?

"Ah! thou art afraid of listeners, it seems, Ram Das? but take heart, man; none of my people dare come near us, except I call them," said Azráel; "and the waterfall drowns all noise of voices. I tell thee there is no one near us, except perhaps the spirits of the stones there. They may listen; who knows? Speak!"

The merchant shuddered visibly as he cast a furtive glance on the pile near him, for he believed in the spirits to whom they were sacred; but he had long considered the means to an end which lay at his heart, and by Azráel Pandé's help he might attain his devilish objects.

"The devils may listen if they please, and help what I have to tell if they can," he replied, with a gesture of reverence to the stones; "but thou canst help me more, Jemadar; only swear to me that thou wilt keep my secret. Put thy hand on my head and swear to me."

"I never swear to be true, because I am never false like a miserly merchant, and my honour is in my own keeping," said Azráel, scornfully; "but if thou wilt have it so, then I swear by thy head to be true. Now speak freely and briefly, for the night passes, and we must be far from hence ere morning breaks."

"It is a family matter, and were I to tell all, the night would hardly suffice; but all of it need not concern you," replied the man. "Listen. My uncle Ram Das held the office of Putwary of Gokulpoor, of which he was also Zemindar, and he is dead. His son Huree Das succeeded him in the office and in the estate that belongs to it, and he married Seeta, the grand-daughter of Narendra, the banker and goldsmith of Shah Gunje, who ought to have been given to me. Now of the inheritance, I claim a large part; but Huree Das refuses to give me a cowrie of it: and there are, too, family jewels of great value, other lands, and the office, of which my present share is only a trifle. I have tried my claim in the courts, and spent much money in vain; but the suit has been decided against me. I have only one chance more, they say—to appeal to the Court in Calcutta;

but that would cost thousands. I am poor, and my cousin is rich and prosperous, and I hate him—I hate him, Jemadar—even unto death, and thou canst revenge me."

"Good," replied Azráel calmly; "but look you, I never commit murder. Thou couldst get him killed for a trifle; but were he dead, wouldst thou succeed?"

"No. He has a son, an infant at the breast; and so long as he lived, I should be as helpless as I am now."

"Then why not have them both disposed of in the same way? If thou wert liberal, my friend, which thou art not, I think some of my brave fellows could help thee. Say a thousand rupees, now; it would be worth that. Shall I call some of them, or wilt thou go to them and make the bargain after thine own fashion?"

"Oh no, no!" cried the merchant imploringly, and stretching out his joined hands; "that would be murder. The English police would surely discover it, and thy people and I myself would surely be hanged—but——"

"I see," replied the leader, interrupting him; "thou art a coward! Go thy way, in the name of the devils who have been listening to thee, and be thankful that I do not tell Huree Das what thou hast told me. Begone! I will have none of thy murder plots."

"I am no coward, Jemadar," returned the merchant, "else I should not have come to thee to-night. I can do my part if thou wilt do the rest. Art thou so dull, so careless of good booty, as not to see what I mean?"

"How much didst thou say was in thine enemy's house?" asked Azráel, after a long silence. "He is a money-dealer like thyself, is he not?"

"Yes, yes," returned the other, eagerly, "and a goldsmith also, and works at his trade. How much? Well, it was only a week ago that he received two thousand rupees of silver and gold to make up marriage ornaments, and he has other work in hand. Then the jewels of his house are worth ten thousand; and again, his wife Seeta wears gold bangles and anklets which are worth a thousand. There are valuable copper vessels, and chests full of valuable cloths, besides the gold and silver in the oratory. Besides——"

"Enough!" cried Azráel. "If this is all true, it would be a rare booty, and better than the last. But what I cannot understand is, that thou, with thy miserly nature, shouldst let me take it, for thou wouldst get none back, friend. And if I did take it, thou wouldst be no nearer to the inheritance than now."

"But—but—he might be slain if he resisted," said the merchant in a hoarse whisper, and bending forward; "and I think I know what would happen."

"Would he resist?"

"I think so; nay, I am sure. He is a strong, active man, perfect in athletic exercises, a wrestler, and of good practice with the sword."

"Ha! Is it so?"

"By your head and eyes, Jemadar, I speak the truth. Every one knows him."

"Then, indeed," said Azráel, drawing a deep breath, while the knot of wrinkles gathered together on his forehead, "he might die. Kalee does not suffer resistance to chosen votaries like me. Those who oppose her die; she never spares them. So, in her name, I spare none—nor man, nor woman——"

"Nor child, Jemadar?"

"Silence! or I will strike thee down," cried Azráel, savagely. "Do children fight or carry weapons, that such as I should kill them? And yet—and yet—," he continued, musingly, "it might be in the *mêlée* that that child were slain too."

"Yes, yes," said the merchant, in an eager whisper; "kill it, Jemadar; kill it, or tell some one to do so;" and he bent forward and touched his companion's feet.

"If thou wert not a coward," he replied, with a bitter sneer, and drawing away his feet as though they had been polluted—"thou wouldst take a sword and do it thyself; who would know? We should be busy, and the murder would be laid to the Dacoits; and then thou wouldst be sure of the inheritance."

"A good thought, a good thought," muttered the man to himself through his set teeth. "Surely I will come, for it is I who must open the gate for ye; it could not be forced. Listen! Our houses adjoin, and there is a door between. I go to him sometimes in the evening, and my wife goes to his. I can go that night and hide in the outer court till I hear the signal; then I can let all of ye in. There is another court and a door, but it is weak: after that, nothing; the house is open. Say, when can it be done?"

"For myself I like the evening best, about sundown; but some of my men are new and uncertain, and would rather have the darkness. To-morrow will be full moon, and the night before new moon may be the best, though it will be long to wait. Say the first night of the dark quarter, and we must get it done before the moon rises. I will come myself to see the place; meanwhile take two good men with thee, feed them well, and show them everything, but give them no liquor. Are there police in the village, or watchmen?"

"There are no police, and only two watchmen, Jemadar, who are harmless. There is no chance of disturbance or hindrance, and there is no one in the house after the workmen are gone. Come!"

"I will come, friend. Kalee calls me to do this, and I never falter when 'the Mother' leads. I dare not; I have vowed myself to her. Art thou as sure?"

"I am," returned the merchant. "I shall lose the jewels of my house, except thou hast pity and givest me a share; but it is better thou shouldst have all than that he should live and keep them."

"Be that as 'the Mother' wills," replied Azráel, gravely; "and now, friend, depart. What remains to be done rests between me and my people, and cannot be witnessed by the uninitiated. Ho! Govinda!" he shouted, "come hither." And, as the man appeared, he said to him, "Go with this good man, you and Jeyram, as ye came. Stay with him both of ye, and observe all he will show ye. The day after to-morrow I will come myself. Till then watch all carefully, and do your duty. Your shares will be safe with me, and if ye want money for a day or two, he will advance it. Embrace me, Maharaj," he continued, to the merchant; "and now depart, and be of good cheer."

The men who had concealed themselves, scrambled through the hole behind by which they had entered their place of concealment, and joined their associates unobserved; and in a few minutes all were summoned by their leader to the division of spoil, for he had already decided upon the shares in reference to the actions of each in the last affair. In this respect Azráel had the full confidence of his men; and now, except for an offering to Kalee, and a similar amount for himself, the rest was gradually divided till the bags were emptied. Then, rising to his feet, he cried, "Bring the axe, Munoher."

"Ah, master, that is joyful news," exclaimed the man, who, indeed, had been one of the listeners in the tree. "Not such another long tramp across the country, we hope; and yet all of us would go even to Dwarka or Raméshwur for the master. 'Jey Kalee!'"

No one answered: but instead, the invocation was repeated in a loud shout which rang through the glen, echoing again and again from the rocks, as though the spirits of the place had taken it up and were repeating it. It was a good preliminary omen. And now the sacred axe—a large, heavy blade, with a finely tempered edge—was produced by its keeper; and its various coverings being unfolded, it was held reverentially upon a piece of cloth of gold. As reverently was it deposited by him upon the pile of stones which served as an altar, anointed with liquid butter, turmeric, and vermilion—with a few flowers, hastily gathered, laid upon it.

The leader then approached it in a suppliant posture, and repeating a wild Sanscrit incantation, cried with a loud voice, "Behold, behold! I see her. Brothers, the holy Mother comes! Receive her, and pray her to vouchsafe us protection in what we have to do, and omens to guide us!"

As he ceased speaking and drew himself up to his full height, with the clear moonlight falling full upon him, glinting from the broad, bright blade of the formidable spear he carried, he might be well adored by his followers as an incarnation of power, and a fit executant of the will of the dread goddess he served; and another shout of "Jey Kalee!" burst from the men, to be carried on from rock to rock till it died away.

Just then, too, a huge vulture, sitting on one of the bare dead branches above, scared by the shout, awoke from his sleep, and with hoarse screams and heavily flapping wings flew across the pool to the right hand, and perched upon a pinnacle of the precipice beyond the fall; and for a moment the tree was filled with the indescribable twitterings of the birds which roosted there. But again there was silence, for no one spoke.

"Answer once more, holy Mother!" cried the leader, spreading out his arms to the sky; "answer, and bid us depart."

Almost as he spoke, one of a pack of jackals in the wood above the fall on the right hand, true to its habit of howling at the last watch of the night, broke into a short sharp bark, which was taken up by a score of others in his company, and swelled into a chorus of hideous clamour, which filled the glen and forest, and contrasted strangely with the monotonous roar of the waterfall.

"It is finished, brothers," cried their leader with an exultant smile; "the Mother accepts the service, and we will follow it up to her glory. 'Jey Kalee!'"

When there was again silence, he said: "Go not far away; be in the villages 'round about. I shall go to Shah Gunje to meet Buldeo and some others. My name will be the Brahmin 'Narrain Das,' and I shall be in the Temple of Krishna, without the town. Now depart. Ye have much money among ye; be careful; drink no spirit; boast not, and be cautious and discreet. Ere long I shall have need of ye, and all must come."

The orders were obeyed; and long ere morning broke, the glen was left to its usual condition of solitary beauty.

CHAPTER III.

THE GOLDSMITH'S HOUSE.

THE family affairs of Huree Das, goldsmith, putwary, and banker of Gokulpoor, were prosperous as his cousin and bitter enemy Ram Das had described them to the Dacoit leader, and as they have been recounted in the last chapter. His father, and his uncle the father of Ram Das, were both dead; and he and his cousin had inherited their several portions as left by the brothers. During the life of their grandfather, he, being old and infirm, had divided his property equally between his two sons, and there had been no further dispute. On the death of his uncle, however, Ram Das had taken counsel of one of the native pleaders in the district court, who advised him to lay an action against his cousin Huree Das, for half his property, on the ground that it had been the usufruct of the moneys received from the first division made by their grandfather.

Now the fathers of Huree Das and Ram Das had both followed the hereditary occupation of bankers and goldsmiths, being also putwaries, or hereditary accountants and registrars of Gokulpoor and other villages; but they had been unequal in their fortunes, and of the two the father of Huree Das had thriven and become wealthy, while his brother, an idle, thriftless character, had not only made nothing on his fortune, but had dissipated much of what had come to him in extravagant household and religious festivals and pilgrimages. The ancestral lands, however, had yielded him a comfortable income, and up to the death of the father of Ram Das there was no interruption to the harmony of the families.

It was not till his father's death that Ram Das knew how much the property had deteriorated; what heavy mortgages had to be paid off; and how entirely the moderate banking and trading business of his father had declined; and he had set himself earnestly to work to retrieve the neglect. He was an unscrupulous man in business, and frequently made desperate ventures in loans at usurious interest, to landholders of broken fortunes. He speculated deeply in the produce of the country, and had gradually been drawn into connection with Dacoits, and other professional robbers, who, bringing him ornaments and rich cloths from a distance, could sell them to him without fear of the detection of either party. Of such proceeds of crime had been his dealings with Azráel Pandé, and all were extremely profitable. His cousin, Huree Das, was, however, richer than he, and more respected; and prosperity seemed to attend him in every undertaking. Huree Das had married Seeta, the grand-daughter of Narendra, the goldsmith banker of Shah Gunje, a person of reputed great wealth, and high respectability and influence in the district. The cousins, in fact, had both been candidates, through their fathers, for the hand of the beautiful Seeta; but Huree Das had been preferred, and the marriage had been concluded, and in due time consummated.

Thus it will be seen that many elements of discord had arisen, if not of avowed enmity, between the cousins—which, on the part of Ram Das, had grown into bitter hate. He hated his cousin for his increasing wealth and prosperity; for the increasing respect he was obtaining from all classes; for his charity and hospitality; and for the possession of Seeta; and when the great suit failed, the cup of detestation overflowed. I will not trouble my readers with an explanation of the abstruse points in Hindoo law, on which the suit depended. Suffice it to say that Mr. Mostyn, the English judge of Noorpoor, who decided it, had come to a correct conclusion; but his award, carrying costs, was an additional subject of discontent to the disappointed litigant, and a deep, deadly desire of revenge had taken possession of him, and haunted him night and day. He had often thought of Azárel Pandé. whom he knew to be one of the most desperate and even dangerous characters of the country; but he came seldom, and years might clapse before he returned. Yet it was not so to be. Not many days before, he had received a message from him to come for what he had brought, and Ram Das had then gone to the glen privately. The ornaments brought by the gang had been delivered up. melted down, and, with the gold coins, given to Ram Das to sell.

Ram Das might have made his hideous proposal at their first meeting, and intended to have done so, for he had fully made up his mind to the issue; but there was no opportunity. The few days that had elapsed had produced no alteration in his determination, and the certainty of a terrible revenge had grown on him the more, while he knew that the present was his only chance. Azráel Pandé would not, he was sure, linger where he was, even in disguise; and there was no certainty of his return. The rich booty of his cousin's house was, he had felt, a bait that could not be refused by the Dacoit; and, for the rest, that his cousin would resist and be slain, he made no doubt; and even if he lived, he would at least have lost most of his detested wealth. What followed has been detailed; was there no misgiving, no remorse, no pity? None. Instead, only a feverish desire for consummation. A hideous and devilish plot, truly; but such an one as many an Indian judge has had to unravel in all its sickening details, while shuddering over the mental depravity which they disclosed. In this case were two separate phases. The one depending upon the bitter hate and envy of an otherwise apparently respectable and inoffensive individual; the other the calm, cool determination of a ruffian devoted to the hideous worship and profession he followed—looking to booty as his reward, utterly careless of life, whether his own or another's, and prepared to do murder, if needs be, as an ordinary occurrence in pursuit of his object.

The village of Gokulpoor was, as has been already stated, a small one. Two large stone houses occupied the centre, and round them clustered a number of more unpretending dwellings inhabited by farmers, and the artizans necessary to so small a community. A humble temple, built by an ancestor of th goldsmith's family, was the only religious edifice. The house of the goldsmiths were, however, of some pretension for such a place.. They were partly built of basalt-stone neatly squared, and partly of red brick; nor was there much difference between them. They were heavy blocks of buildings, with no openings to the outside; but open within to courtyards, round which were the dwelling-rooms of the family. At the base of the buildings were wide enclosures, which contained stacks of corn and straw, sheds for cattle and merchandise, and rooms for farm servants. In front of each was a narrow entrance-court, the high wall of which was joined to the house, and to this was a handsome gateway of carved stone, with an open guard-room behind it. The gate itself was made of massive wood, bound with heavy bars of iron, and could not have been forced if fastened behind. Above the gate. and round the upper coping of the house wall, the masonry parapets were pierced for musketry, showing that they had been designed in troublous times, when every man who possessed valuables used his best means to defend them. Two narrow courtyards lay between the houses, and a common door led from one to the other. In the old times it had been used daily; but since the estrangement began it had seldom opened.

It was the evening of the planned Dacoity, which nothing had occurred to hinder. The scouts had examined the house of Huree Das, and, on one pretence or other, had been sent into it on several occasions. The outer gate they saw would have defied the axe, but Ram Das had showed them how it could be opened from within, and where the openers might be concealed. The inner door which led into the body of the house was weak, and could be forced. Azráel Pandé, who had taken up his abode in a temple at Shah Gunje, four miles distant, had been giving recitations in the town, and was invited both by Huree Das and Ram Das to Gokulpoor. He had gone to the latter, had visited Huree Das, and noted the position of the household oratory, where, as Ram Das told him, the jewels of the family and all the ready money were buried under the floor, close to the altar, on which the household gods were placed. So far, then, all was prepared; and the gang was to assemble in the glen, which has been described, as evening fell.

At that time the household of the goldsmith Huree Das was in perfect quiet and peace. The business of the day was over, and by the light of a large lamp, Huree Das was checking the accounts of the day with his head assistant. This finished, the master rose, and went into an outer verandah, where several of his apprentices were still at work on some silver ornaments which had been commissioned. The execution did not appear to be satisfactory to the master, for he pushed one of the youths away from the pan of lighted charcoal, before which he had been employed, and seating himself in his place, took up the work which had been in progress, and began fashioning a stout silver wire into an intricate pattern, for an anklet, with great dexterity, while the apprentice looked on in amazement at the skill displayed.

"That is the way, you see, Govind," he said. "A slight blow here, a twist with the pincers there, then the two ends welded together thus, and the link is made. There, that will suffice thee for a pattern to-morrow; and if needs be, I will help thee further; but bad work will bring disgrace on us, boy, and ye need all of ye to be as careful of your master's honour and credit as your own."

"You are ever kind, master," replied the lad, "and I think I can do it now; but not if you look on."

"Well, try; I will return presently," and he left them and went into the inner part of the house. Ere he had gone a few steps, however, he was recalled; one of the workmen had been summoned to the court door, and returned saying that Ram Das desired to be admitted.

"He would have speech with thee, master," the man said, "but cannot stay long. May he come?"

"Surely," said the goldsmith; "though," he added to himself, "I wish he would stay away; his visits are painful and useless. What can I do in the matter? It has been his own seeking from the first. Yes," he continued aloud, "bring him hither."

The goldsmith sat down on the cushion near his account books and the lamp, and in a few moments his cousin entered. He rose to meet him, and they seated themselves together. There was a great contrast between them. Huree Das was a tall powerful man, and his habitual practice of athletic exercises, with which he began and ended the day throughout the year, had fully developed his fine figure, which, as he partly reclined against a large pillow, was fully displayed. His features were strongly moulded, and might become coarse; but their expression was manly, honest, and fearless, and his bright eyes were as soft and tender as a woman's. His cousin was spare and thin, and the thick quilted jacket he wore seemed hardly to increase his bulk. The hands were lean and bony, and the features harsh and forbidding, bearing the unmistakable expression of greed and deceit. His eyes were small, coal-black, and deep set in his head, overshadowed by thick bushy eyebrows, and were restless and furtive. As the man seated himself, he tried to smile; but his mouth seemed to forbid the effort, for the corners were drawn down, and the lips quivered as if with ill-suppressed hate, while he looked, as he was wont to do, in every direction, to see if any one were within hearing.

"There is no one near," said Huree Das, smiling. "You need not be afraid, brother. Have you aught to say to me to-night?"

"I fear I interrupted your work, for they told me that you were at the old trade; I ask pardon for it."

"They were blundering, and I set them right for a while, brother; but those lads need looking to, and I keep my hand in, as you know. I will not say you are welcome, Ram Das; and yet, why not? If your heart is as mine, why not? I bear no malice, and what has happened can be repaired."

"It can, brother, if you will listen to reason. Although I have lost my cause in one court, there are others, and the English are just in the end."

"Yes, they are just; and I will trust my case, even to Calcutta," was the reply.

"You have won the cause, and are confident; what if you lost it, after all?"

"Then I should be obliged to pay all you demand; and I would pay it, too, to the last penny, without a murmur."

"The honour of your house would be lost if you did not," replied Ram Das, with a sneer.

"It is in my own keeping, brother, and has never been suspected yet. You, least of all, have reason to question it."

"I least of all? then why these disputes, and why have I come to-night?"

"I know not; your thoughts are your own, not mine. I did not send for you, and would rather you had stayed away; or, if you have any proposal to make, that you should have sent your agent. As it is, speak out like a man, and I will reply as openly."

"Send them all away, and I will speak."

"All! who?"

"The workmen. I would not have a word of our conversation overheard. It may be the last between us."

"I hope not, brother; but as you will. They have worked hard to-day, and may go. I can take up what there is to do after you are gone;" and he rose up, went into the outer verandah, and dismissed the men, leaving one stove alight for his own work. When he returned he seated himself ~~as~~ before.

While he was away, Ram Das pondered deeply. It might be that a ray of compassion had entered his soul as the time he had fixed drew nigh, and impelled him to save his cousin; and yet it was hardly that, unless another point of his deliberation should confirm it. He would make another distinct offer of compromise to his cousin, and would lay before him all the arguments under which his wily pleader had extracted so much money from him. Should this succeed, the Dacoity could be averted. Some police could be summoned from a village about two miles distant, and posted in the house. The outer gate could be locked and barred. Huree Das might even be told of his danger, and thank him as his deliverer. Then came before him the dread of Azráel Pandé's vengeance, and of detection, and the certainty of his conviction should the police obtain information, and he shuddered as he sat, as if a cold wind had smitten him. So his thoughts surged hither and thither confusedly, finding no rest: but as his cousin again sat down and looked him full in the face, telling him that he should proceed, a child's cry came out of an inner room, and the man's worst passions leaped to it.

"I was a weak fool," he muttered; "a weak fool for a moment; let the matter go on as the dread Mother wills."

"I told you, brother, before," he continued, as Huree Das sat down, "that I would maintain the suit to the last. You have wronged me, and the English judge, who knows nothing of our law, has helped you. Nay, be patient and hear all;" for the gestures and half-spoken exclamations of his cousin were unmistakable. "My pleader has consulted an eminent adviser in Calcutta, who has laid the case before men even wiser than himself, and they all agree that the judgment of the Noorpoor Court must be reversed on appeal. Here are their letters, if you will read them."

"I tell you, Ram Das, once for all, I will have nothing to do with them, or with you, but in the open court; and you are wasting your words on the air," said Huree Das impatiently.

"Nay, but hear reason, brother. Besides the advice of my pleader, I now make you one more offer, and it is this. Let the expenses of the suit be shared between us amicably; and do you make over to me the lands in dispute, which your father bought out of the general stock, the jewels and——"

"And if I did, brother," said Huree Das, interrupting him haughtily, "should not I proclaim myself a cheat? Should I not become the laughing-stock of the country, to hush up a matter in which I had been proved right? Another might do it who was a coward; but I, though only a goldsmith, am no coward; and no shame shall fall on my father's memory from his son!"

"I have brought the agreement ready drawn up, if you will sign it," persisted the other. "There will be no disgrace in a friendly arrangement, and no one need know of it, for it is a matter between you and me. Read it; you will see that I make no further claim, and the shame of the defeat, if there be any, rests therefore with me; we can arrange the remainder ourselves. See, the deed is on stamped paper."

"It is thus I read it, brother," said Huree Das indignantly, "thus;" and he tore it in two pieces. As he held them in his hand, Ram Das tried to snatch them away, but his strength was as a child before his cousin's, who held him with the grasp of a vice with one hand, while with the other he pushed him violently back; and, setting fire to the paper, let it burn.

"So let our brotherhood burn," said Ram Das savagely, "and become ashes like that; the act well became thee, Huree Das."

"Thou hast a foul tongue, Ram Das, and beware how thou usest it," said Huree Das, releasing his cousin. "I am in no humour to bear with thy insolence."

"Nor I with thine," returned the other; "as thou doest now, Huree Das, so will the end be to thee and thy house. I have spoken," and he moved hastily away.

"Oh, husband," said a sweet low voice close to Huree Das, as he still sat moodily in his accustomed seat, "why didst thou provoke that fearful man? What did he want of thee? His last words—I heard them as I was passing the door—sounded like a threat. What could he mean?"

"So I thought, too, my life," he replied; "and I was thinking, also, what they could mean, when thy sweet voice drove his vile words pleasantly out of my thought. Let him threaten if he will; I am not afraid of him, or of his suit, and what can he do more than he has done? His last game was plausible enough; but I could not give him what belongs to our boy, Seeta. No! it is a fair fight in the courts of justice, and, if he likes, he can go on with it. I burnt a paper he brought me to sign, and he was angry, that is all."

"Nay, but I fear him, husband; are the gates fastened?"

"I think sometimes you are a little fool, Seeta, for all your learning; a fond little fool," he said, smiling. "Let it pass; there is no harm in him; cousins always quarrel, you know, and make it up again; and I, for one, bear no malice. When he has got all this litigation out of his head, I will set him up again; he has had losses lately, and they have soured his temper. Why, we have quarrelled, wife, since we were boys; and yet here we are, growing old."

"I pray the gods it may be so," she said; "and I may be foolish, husband, but I do fear him, and, most of all, to-night;" and she shuddered visibly.

"Get thee to thy bed, wife," he returned, laughingly, "and sleep away all these fancies. I will go and work a while, to get the sound of his bad words out of my ears, and his wicked face out of my sight. I will not be late, and will see that the gates are fastened when I have done. Go to the child; he cries for thee, and I will have the door of his court built up to-morrow; will that please my Seeta?"

Seeta went away; but her husband's words had not cheered her, and her thoughts had been heavy all the day. Since the strange Brahmin had come to recite, and had appeared to peer about everywhere with a restless curiosity, her mind had been filled with suspicion—with tales of robbers' disguises, and of fearful crimes in the country. Yet why should she suspect a Brahmin—a holy man who was so noble a reciter? She knew all he had so passionately poured forth, by heart. "Savitri" was her most loved poem, and he had recited it till many wept, for all the neighbours had come to hear. Still her mind was not at rest. She heard her husband for some time hammering the silver bars upon his anvil, then he went out and barred the gates, and came to her.

"Spread my bedding in the front verandah, Seeta," he said, "it is so hot;" and while she was doing so, she heard him in the oratory, reciting the evening worship. Then he went into his exercise room, and worked his clubs for some minutes. She was with her child, and heard him go to his bedding and lie down. It might be then about ten o'clock, and she could not sleep.

Without, Ram Das was busy. As he passed out of the house, the night was entirely dark, and, as he entered his own door, he found the two scouts standing behind it, where he had told them to await his coming. Then he shut the door, and barred it within, and the three men sat down in silence. After a while they heard Huree Das bar the outer gate; after which his steps crossed over to the private door, which he pushed and shook heavily, but finding it fastened, went away, and returned to the inner court, which he shut behind him. Presently Ram Das arose, and whispering to the men to follow, softly withdrew the bar, opened the door, and they passed into the enclosure. The large guard-room by the entrance, open to the court, was filled with bales of cotton and safflower, and behind these they hid themselves, close to the door, and waited. Two or three times the village watchmen on duty came to the gate, and finding it fast, went away. So they awaited the signal, the scouts with the indifference of practised robbers, and grim anticipations of an unusually rich booty; the other with a dull numbness of heart, though it throbbed fearfully, and with a passive anticipation of a life-long revenge. "What the goddess wills must be. Jey Kalee!" was all he could think, and he continued to say the words to himself mechanically, though no sound escaped his lips.

CHAPTER IV.

THE BANKER'S HOME.

About four miles—hardly so much, perhaps—from the village of Gokulpoor lay the town of Shah Gunje, a considerable place, and one of the principal mercantile marts of the province. About three centuries before, one of the Mahomedan kings—whether an Emperor of Dehly, or a King of Khandésh or Malwah, no one remembered, and the name had been forgotten—passing through the country with his army, had encamped near the spot, where forage and good water were abundant, and had established a depôt of grain and supplies there, which had assumed the title of "Shah Gunje," the "King's Mart," and in course of years had become a thriving town. It boasted of a chowke, or market-place, which was surrounded by the houses of rich bankers and tradesmen; and at the weekly markets held there every Friday in the year, all the produce of the country round—cattle and sheep, grain, condiments of all kinds, cotton and safflower in their seasons; bees-wax, honey and gums from the forests, brought in by the wild tribes who lived in them; cloths of all kinds, native and English; some English hardware, and copper and brass vessels made by workmen in the towns and villages about. These, with extensive stalls of sweetmeat and toy sellers, vendors of shoes and sandals, of parched rice and pulse, a few small goldsmiths and money exchangers, shoemakers, bangle-sellers, and women with hanks of cotton yarn, made up a motley but interesting assemblage of articles for sale, while the rich perfume of flowers, fruits, and vegetables, mingled pleasantly with all.

A busy scene, too; for there were throngs of people—a few spectators, perhaps; but for the most part buyers and sellers—dressed in their best. The men with clean, bright-coloured, or white turbans, and white cotton tunics; the women in sarees, or cloths of gay colours, white, red, blue, orange, or green; many with children on their hips, as they walked from stall to stall, or sat gravely behind the produce or merchandise they had to sell. The toy-sellers' booths were perhaps the most attractive places of the market, and many a stout lad went home that night proudly, with a wooden sword at his waist and a shield on his arm; while for the girls, were unlimited supplies of dolls, clay figures of tigers, cows, and goats, gaily painted, though rude in form; and for all, clay images of various gods and goddesses, as gaudy with red and yellow colours as the toys or the dolls.

Here and there were groups of Hindoo ballad-singers, quaintly clad, chanting the praises of Vishnoo, or Seeva, or Krishna, who appeared to be the favourite; Mahomedan fakeers, who sang couplets in praise of God and the Prophet, and seemed to receive as much as their Hindoo fellow-beggars from all classes; while in one quiet corner a burly Brahmin, naked to the waist, and with his long thick hair falling over his shoulders, was reciting an episode of the "Ramayan" to a crowd of listeners seated before him, and taking up from time to time the copper pice and cowries, with an occasional rupee, which were thrown on the sheet before him by the crowd. There were only two men with him, one of whom bawled his master's merits to the crowd; the other, a huge sullen fellow, who seemed to be a soldier, as he wore a sword, was chiefly engaged in twisting up his mustachios, and scowling at the people about him.

The Brahmin was Azráel Pandé, now ornamented with the most elaborate marks of caste in streaks made of wet sandal-wood paste, which had dried to a dull white. On his forehead was painted the broad trident of Vishnoo, filled up with the vermilion of the votary of Kalee; on his broad chest and muscular arms were other stripes and marks of the same substance, which enhanced the breadth and power of his form; and, as silent for a time he appeared to rest, he drew up his figure to its full height, and standing as he was on a heap of earth, was raised above the people, and had become an object as well of attraction as veneration.

The more active of the two men who attended him was Buldeo; the other, the bearer and guardian of the holy axe, which, except when it was used, was seldom absent from his person. It lay behind his waist, fitting into the hollow of his back, with all its coverings; and he held in his hands its helve, which could be instantly fitted to it, but which now seemed to be no more than a stout walking-staff.

"Come, my friends," bawled Buldeo stoutly, in his shrill voice, "come and hear my master. The loves of Krishna will be the next piece. Come all, men and women, and hear the merry story. Come and hear the learned Shastree, who has arrived from Benares and is going to Raméshwur, and help him with your charity. Give to the holy Brahmin! Give! give!"

"Cease thy bawling," said Azráel, in a low tone. "Hast thou watched the house?"

"I did, master, when you were too busy with the Shastree

to notice it. I saw Huree Das mount his pony, and a palankeen was carried out at the gate. They are gone home."

"Good!" replied the leader; "and they had no attendants?"

"None but two of the banker's guards, whom I know, and they will be back by sunset."

"Then it is complete, O Kalee!" he said to himself, "and the rest will be done. Dost thou see any of the men near?" he added, aloud.

"They are everywhere about, master, and none will fail thee at the tree. I will collect them, and bring them on;" and so saying, Buldeo resumed his cry, "Come and hear the Shastree, come and bestow charity! He who gives to a Brahmin delivers himself from hell. Give! give!" and the like, till the recitation began again, and, with a private signal to his leader, Buldeo departed.

Gradually, as the sun declined, the market broke up, stalls and booths began to be removed, and goods unsold to be packed Families and fellow-citizens trudged away to their homes, or mounted their low carts and were driven off; and ere the sun set, but few of the motley busy crowd were left. What remained of it were also preparing to depart; but, as they were chiefly townspeople, they seemed to be in no particular hurry. As the first lamps were lighted in the houses and shops, the space was clear; and beyond a few daily sellers of grass, firewood, and vegetables, would remain so till the next Friday came round.

Although there were several substantial houses in this market-place, that of the goldsmith and banker, Narendra, was the principal. Part of it, behind, was of two stories, neatly built of red brick and stone, and rose to a considerable height. This was the dwelling-place; and, except a few narrow windows in the upper story, was closed outwardly. Inwards, the rooms or galleries were open to a court-yard, and in the hottest weather a stout cloth awning could be stretched from side to side to keep the court cool. In front was another court, of larger dimensions, surrounded by a verandah, supported on richly carved teak-wood pillars, which, as well as the carvings on the frieze and architraves, showed a high amount of skill. In the central portion of these outer rooms was a deeper portion than the rest, elevated on a basement which was ascended by several steps; and over it, in the story above, was a spacious apartment which had a large oriel window, or covered balcony, of wood, also richly carved, and projecting from the wall, from which the female members of the family could observe not only all that passed in the market, but had a noble view of the country round for many miles. This room was now, however, seldom used. It had been the favourite resort of Seeta, the wife of Huree Das, before she left the house for her husband's, and she had sat in the balcony most part of the day with her great-aunt Ella, playing with her fine boy, of whom both were very proud. The old banker seldom came there. He sat always in his usual place of business at the head of the lower hall, on a well-stuffed mattress with a thick pillow behind him, both covered with muslin of spotless white; and he was in his accustomed place as the lamps were lighted. Towards the street, and opening into it, was a large gateway with double doors, in one of which was a small wicket; and above the gate, another small room with an oriel window, but not so large or so handsome as that above the hall. On each side of the archway were guard-rooms; and without, in the square, were verandahs or covered sheds on both sides of the gate, where the attendants of visitors could rest themselves. Within and without the house was scrupulously clean and pure, and without ornament, except the Sanscrit text, "Sree Govind Prussun," painted in bright yellow letters on the architrave of the outer gate, and in a neatly designed niche in gay colours and pretty patterns, which were traced upon the wall over the master's seat.

The owner of the house, Narendra, was, as has been before mentioned, a goldsmith by trade, and a banker of much reputation. He was now more than sixty years old, but was hearty and vigorous still, and his age sat very lightly upon him. His fine figure was as erect, his eyes as clear and soft as they had been twenty—aye, even thirty—years before, nor had his great prosperity left on his features any traces of care, or greed of money. No one could have said he was handsome; but even at first sight, the kindly cheerful benevolence and natural dignity of his countenance could not be overlooked, and knowledge of his disposition only enhanced admiration of his character and its solid virtues. If he had a grief, it was that he had no son to inherit his wealth and the business which he had created, now extending to many parts of India; but two sons had died in youth, and his first wife did not long survive them. He had married again, but the second wife died also; and all that remained to him was Seeta, the daughter of his eldest son, whose mother had lived some years after his death, but had in her turn passed away. Residing with him was "Aunt Ella," as she was usually called by every one—even by her brother himself—a widow, who will become known to us gradually; and by them both Seeta, the darling of the house, and the light of their eyes and hearts, was brought up. It was a sorrowful day for all when the fair girl had to leave them and join her husband, and Aunt Ella had pleaded hard that Huree Das, of whom she was very fond, should leave Gokulpoor, and come and live with them. Could he not go there when he pleased—it was so near—and see after his business? And Seeta, too, had pleaded as well as she could; but her husband was firm, and told her she must be mother of all who depended upon him, and do her duty, and so the matter had passed away. But Seeta was often allowed to go to Shah Gunje; and before her child was born Aunt Ella had come to stay with her, and see her safely through her trial. Then, when the child had been taken to Shah Gunje, there had been a great rejoicing. All the caste people had been invited to a feast; all Seeta's companions had joined in the festival, and sang hymns of praise over the child's cradle; and I am not ashamed to record, that all the dolls of the various houses were brought to the feast gaily dressed in silk clothes, and some of them with real gold ornaments and real pearls. Others perhaps were not so well off, and this caused their young possessors some envious feelings; but I am bound to say that all enjoyed the feast, all caressed and admired the baby, and went home very happy. Even now, the garlands of leaves and flowers, which had been hung over the outer gate, and round the pillars of the court, and over grandfather's seat, still remained there, though they had withered up long since.

Seeta had been there that day, and had sat in her old seat in the oriel window. She and Aunt Ella had looked over the bazaar, and she had held up her crowing baby to see it, and said to it in the joy of her heart: "Thou wilt sit here and be master one day, Laloo. Oh! may the gods grant I see that before I die."

It had been a busy day with Narendra. He had bought much and sold much; he had received payments from farmers to whom he had made advances for cattle, or seed, or produce, and he had lent money to others. He had received letters from correspondents in Mirzapoor, in Benares, in Calcutta, in Bombay, in Nagpoor, in Oomrawutee, and other places widely apart. He had received large remittances in bills, and some in treasure, and all had to be balanced and registered before the day's work ended. The day-book had, however, been made up, and he had just signed it; and the cashier, putting his pen behind his ear, and sticking his spectacles into a fold of his turban, was about to bring him the daily cash-book, which he would sign also.

As the old man came up he pointed with his finger to the balance, which was very considerable, and sat down awaiting his master's examination. Hastily casting up the totals, Narendra found the amount was correct, and rising and going into the treasure-room, the bags of a thousand rupees each were weighed one against another, the odd balance counted, and the place closed and barred for the night. By this time it was about eight o'clock. Some workmen, who had been busy with silver ornaments in the verandah below, were directed to cease work, and one by one they, with the clerks, departed. Narendra then went to bathe and eat his evening meal, and after a while returned and sat down in his old seat; and a prosperous day would be hardly complete without a game of chess with his friend the priest, whom he found waiting.

"Namascar, Maharaj!" said Narendra, with the usual salutation to a Brahmin—on perceiving the priest sitting by his cushion. "I worship you! Have I kept you long?"

"No, friend," replied the other. "As you went to bathe and eat I came in; but I told the servants not to disturb you. And how has the day gone with you? Prosperously, I hope?"

"Right well," replied the merchant gaily and happily, "as you said it would this morning. I have seen Huree Das and his wife; I held her child in my arms, and I saw the loveliest, happiest face bending over it and looking up to me, that ever existed."

"She might be a nymph of Indra's paradise," said the priest warmly; "no fairer woman ever lived: and the best of her is, that she still reads and studies. She bid me come to-morrow to Gokulpoor, and help her through a passage in a drama of Kalidas, which she cannot interpret. I will go, I think."

"If you go I will go with you," said the banker. "I want to see," he added, after a pause, "whether you and I cannot patch up that quarrel between the cousins, which appears to get worse instead of better."

"I thought it was at an end," replied the priest. "Huree Das told me he had won the suit."

"So he has, my friend; but Ram Das has served him with a notice of appeal, and the whole matter will begin again."

"He is a fool, then," said the priest. "I warned him that his pleader's advice was wrong, but he did not believe me. You see, it cannot hold in law that——"

"Well, I don't want to hear of the law, and I am sick of the whole affair," returned the banker. "All I want is that there should be an end of the matter, and I would gladly pay all Ram Das's expenses if he would take them."

"He will not take them, I think," said the priest. "He wants the lands, the office, and the jewels, and will be content with nothing less."

"Perhaps we could do something with Huree Das?" observed the banker, after a pause.

"He is just as obstinate as the other," replied the priest, "and I don't see that he should give up the smallest fraction. But let us see what the stars say. The suit is under Saturn"—and he took an almanac from his pocket—"now Saturn to-night comes into conjunction with the moon. Let me see: Aries, Taurus, Gemini, Cancer, then——" Here his voice grew lower, as he looked up and made calculations upon his fingers. "I can't well make it out," he resumed, "but the inference to be drawn from the calculation is, that the case will be settled at once, nay, perhaps to-night. It is the disturbing element which puzzles me, and till I am at home and consult my books, I cannot tell what it may be."

"I dare say," replied the old man. "As he talked the affair over with me to-day, I told Huree Das to be moderate, and indeed he seemed inclined to be reasonable; perhaps he sent for Ram Das, and they have made it up somehow. He is not a bad fellow."

"I say he is a very bad one, old friend," returned the priest. "I know him well, and never found good in him yet. Perhaps his new adviser is the Brahmin, who has been putting up in the temple yonder, and who was reciting in the bazaar to-day. Ah! he is a powerful Brahmin, Narendra. He knows the most awful mysteries of Kalee; he has all the sacred books on his tongue; give him but a cue anywhere, and away he goes like an arrow. But I never saw so villainous a face. Bah! it makes me creep to think of it; and some such ruffians for attendants, too. Well, thank Krishna, he is gone: he was mounting his pony as I left the temple, and may I never see his face again! Law? why, he had the whole Mitacshara by heart, and his tongue is as sweet as honey."

"Ah, yes," replied the old man indifferently. "Seeta told me that he had come to her house to recite, and had made her weep over the tale of Savitri; but that she dare not look at him, he was so ugly. But we are neglecting our chess, and I have been so lucky to-day that I must beat you to-night; and others may drop in. But you look tired; had you rather not play?"

"I will play one game with you, and you are sure to beat me, for my heart is with the stars," said the priest. "I wish I had not looked at them; but I will find it all out. I think I see that the Brahmin is the disturbing power; but I must say no ill of so great a Shastree, and I may be wrong." And they began to play.

Several friends dropped in gradually, and, as is customary, ranged themselves on either side, advising by turns; but the banker was the victor in the end, as he said he should be.

"Have you heard the news?" said Amba Das, a neighbour and banker. "Things go on strangely now-a-days."

"No," said Narendra, "I have been too busy to attend to any. What is it? No new war, I hope. The English have no one to beat now."

"No, no war, friend," returned the other; "but my firm at Benares writes, and I received the letter by express to-night, that the King of Oudh is to be deposed by the English, and the country taken by them. They expect the order daily, and men's minds are troubled."

"Is it so?" said the banker sadly. "They have taken Nagpoor and Jhansy; is not that enough? They are all-powerful, and in the main they are just; but why so greedy? Is no one to be left?"

"Now you mention it," said the priest, "the Brahmin told me that there were rumours of English interference in Oudh, and asked me if there was any news in the town. He said, too, that there would be trouble if they took the country, and was not over-complimentary to them, I think."

"They have their friends, and their enemies too," said Narendra, "and they might have more of the former than the latter, if they were wiser. But they know their own business, and we, least of all, who live and thrive under their protection, should say a word against them."

"There is to be a new land assessment, too, and they say that rents will be raised," said a Zemindar who sat near; "that would be tyranny."

"I have heard nothing of it," replied the priest. "The settlement has yet some time to run, and when the new one comes, as it must, we will talk about it. Now, farewell, friends; I have work to do, and must be gone."

"Remember to-morrow," said the banker.

"I will," returned the priest, "and will go with you."

I do not think the rest of the conversation need be described. The prices of exchange, of money, of produce, and the gossip of an Indian country town, would hardly interest my readers. The guests, however, sat far into the night, and as they left, the old banker went to his bed and slept soundly, while all his household, except the guards at his gate, were at rest too.

CHAPTER V.

THE FULFILMENT OF THE BARGAIN.

THE night passed. Seeta, after arranging her husband's carpet and pillows in the outer verandah, had lain down by her child's cradle, dozed for a while, then awoke, and could not sleep. She was nervous and restless, and could assign no reason for it. She had had a happy visit to Shah Gunje, and her grandfather and Aunt Ella had been as loving as ever, while the old man had taken the child in his arms and blessed him. Why should she fear? All was secure around her; two women servants in the room were asleep, the child, too, slept calmly, and the snores of some other servants in a distant chamber were the only sounds in the house. She did not now feel afraid of her husband's cousin, for had they not disputed again and again, and as her husband had said, what could he do more than he had done? Other enemies they had none, and her husband was honoured and beloved. Yes, he would be like her grandfather, and thought carried her on to a distant time when her son would be at the head of the guild, and would help his declining years.

A lamp was burning, and she took down one of her books from a shelf, and began to read "Savitri." How grand it was, where the young bride follows her husband's spirit, which Yáma, the God of Death, had taken, and how tenderly had the Brahmin recited the passage two days ago! Yet what a fearful man he was! He seemed almost to be near her now; and she shuddered and looked around her. The thought of this man had put further reading out of the question, for a dull, heavy feeling at her heart seemed to be caused by him. Could it be that he had cast an evil eye upon her? Then she arose and went to the altar without in the inner verandah where the sacred fire was smouldering, trimmed it, and rubbed some of the sacred ashes on her forehead and breast, and prayed that the evil spirit might pass away from her. She heard her husband moving, and went gently to the door and looked at him. He appeared only to have turned in his sleep, and night-lights were burning in the niche of the wall and in the oratory. "I will bring the child here and sit by him," she said to herself, and returning with her boy, sat down on the edge of the carpet. The night was far spent now; her husband, though he muttered sometimes in his sleep, as was usual with him, rested well, and she fanned him gently with her handkerchief to keep the mosquitoes from his face.

It seemed as if sleep would never come to her eyes. She was not tired, she was not drowsy; she suckled her child and laid it down by her, where it slept sweetly. Her whole faculties seemed to be strangely roused, and now she was near her husband, the indefinable dread which had possessed her had passed away. In the house there was not a sound audible; the very silence was almost painful. Without, in the village, the dogs barked sometimes, and the jackals bayed; but these were the ordinary sounds of the night, and she was used to them. Suddenly, however, she thought she heard a noise, far away in a small street, at the end of the village, as though of a challenge, which was followed by a groan, and she sat up erect, and listened with her heart throbbing; but the noise was not repeated, and there was again dead silence. She was glad she had not awakened her husband, as she had nearly done, and he still slept on profoundly. By this time, the wan moon had risen. She saw its light rest upon the wall of the inner court, and watched it as it spread, dimly lighting up the gate, and the familiar objects about it. The village dogs were still barking, and seemed to be excited; most likely they were quarrelling, or baying at the moon.

While she was thus thinking, she heard—there was no doubt about it now—the outer gate move as if it were shaken, but that sound ceased almost in an instant. It did not alarm her, for she knew it was the duty of the village watchmen to shake the gate in their rounds, and the noise she heard made her feel almost more secure; but the assurance was rudely dispelled, as the sound of shuffling feet, treading lightly, came from the outer court; and as she still listened, with her hand stretched out to wake her husband, a man's head appeared above the wall, on which the dim moonlight rested for a moment, and she saw the muffled face distinctly.

She could not speak; she could not cry out; she seemed to be fascinated and incapable of movement. She saw the figure rise rapidly, cross the wall, and drop to the roof of the guard-room, and then leap lightly to the ground, and with several sharp blows of an axe, break down the wooden bar fastening. Then the light of several torches suddenly blown into flame, dazzled her eyes, and a crowd of men armed with broad spears. rushed into the court.

She had almost in vain pulled desperately at her husband; but he awoke tardily, and it was only when the blows of the axe resounded through the court, that he seemed to realize the danger, and rising to his feet, snatched down a sword which hung from the wall, drew it, and crying to his wife to save the child, advanced to meet the Dacoits. He could see none of their faces, for they were muffled; but their eyes glanced savagely upon him, while none of them spoke. For an instant they seemed uncertain, as the goldsmith strode to the head of the steps, yet for an instant only. A tall, strong man, backed by several others, rushed upon him; a blow that the goldsmith aimed at him was parried adroitly, and by the lunges of several spears he felt himself desperately wounded; still Huree Das, closing with his antagonists, struggled bravely, as he retreated to the door of the oratory, into which he fell, powerless and dying.

Seeta had seen all, and yet preserved her senses through the horror of the scene. She had at first fled into the oratory with her child, and could not escape from it; and now, rallied by a desperation she could never afterwards account for, she stepped across her husband's body and came forth, with her boy resting upon her hip, and drawing the end of her saree from her head, and holding it in both her hands, she spread it out before the Dacoits. Her great beauty, the courage and devotion of the act, her sweet presence, clothed as she was in pure white muslin, stayed them for a moment, as she said in a low, musical voice, which hardly trembled: "Give him to me; O give my husband to me as my bridal gift! If you be men, do not refuse a wife and mother's petition, and ye will be blessed for it in years to come, ye and your children. Take all that is in the house, I will show it to ye; but O hear my supplication, and spare my husband!"

But there was no reply to her simple but impassioned appeal. The tall man and several others, with their spears raised, pressed forward, and a savage from behind made a desperate lunge at the girl with his spear, which she at once felt had wounded both herself and her child, for its warm blood gushed out over her arm, and she grew sick and fell. Then she heard a man with a squeaking voice say to another, who had raised his weapon to strike her again, "The child is dead, and the woman is dead, thou shalt not strike them again." Others had passed into the little room, and as she heard them pierce her husband again and again, she knew that all hope for him was gone. She felt that her wound was not fatal, and that her child still breathed: and she lay as if dead, listening to the screams of the servants, and to the noise of plunder of all that could be found. A man, pulling at her foot, had succeeded in unfastening one of her gold anklets, but he could not loosen the other. Another tore from her breast her gold necklace, and the bangles from her wrists; while, within the room, the dull thuds of a pickaxe near the altar, proved that the robbers knew where the jewels were, and were taking them.

Just then several shots were suddenly heard in the village, and a violent clamour arose; and several men rushed into the court crying out, "Away! away! the police are upon us; fly and save yourselves!" Azráel Pandé had been busy in the oratory. He had tried several places, and was just about pushing away the body of the goldsmith, which had indeed fallen over the spot where the valuables were buried, when he heard the clamour without, and listening for a moment as he let fall his pickaxe, and heard the cry of the men, and the shots that were fired: "They dare not close with us," he said, "the cowards; but we must go; come away!" As he passed out, he raised his spear over the body of Seeta; but she saw that his hand was held by a man near him, and the same squeaking voice said to him, "Do not strike a dead woman, master, I killed her myself," and they passed out.

The robbers had extinguished their torches, and without all was dark; but the lamp in the oratory still burned, and by its light as he passed over her, Seeta thought she recognized the bold features and fierce eyes of the Brahmin. Her quick ear, too, had caught the sound of the words he had spoken to his companions, for he had been alarmed, and had raised his voice above a whisper. Yes, it might be he, she thought; but her mind was stunned and confused, and her heart throbbing as if it would burst. Her husband lay beside her dead, yet she dared not move; they might still be there, lurking till the disturbance was past. Who would come to help them? Presently her child moved, and cried faintly, and she put it to her breast. He at least had been spared to her.

It seemed to her long ere any one appeared. She heard the sounds of musket shots and clamour; at first near, then dying away in the distance. She could see the court door, and people seemed to come and look in; but no one entered. Then one of the women servants with a scared face, and holding a lamp in her hand, came from within, and looking round the verandah, shrieked at the sight of the blood, and fled back into the body of the house. Seeta tried to rise, but was now weak from loss of blood; she even cried aloud to the woman, "Bheemee! Bheemee!" but no one answered. It was a fearful time. Should she die there with her husband? Yes, alone she would have died with him; but the child whom the gods had spared, for him she would live, she thought, if they spared her too.

But she was not long in suspense. There was a sudden clamour of cheery voices in the outer court, and by the light of several torches, the Darogah of police, some of his men, and a crowd of armed villagers, entered the inner court. Many kind hands of humble women helped her to rise, and carried her away from the scene of blood, and bathed her wound, and changed her clothes. It was in her side, and had bled profusely, and the same thrust had wounded her child also, in its thigh; but the barber who had been sent for said there was no fear for him, and her own hurt was skilfully bound up. She had lost every hope for her husband, and he had been found, literally pierced all over by terrible spear thrusts, any one of which, in his body, would have been fatal.

Presently Ram Das's wife came to Seeta, and shrieking wildly as she saw her, fell at her feet. "They have arrested him," she said. "Come away to our house, and save him."

"Who?" asked the girl, faintly.

"My husband! may he come?"

"No!" said Seeta. "I will not go. O keep him from me;" and amidst a torrent of adjurative denial of crime from the woman, the police Darogah entered the room.

"I would not enter, lady," he said, respectfully, "but I am a Rajpoot, and there will be no pollution. I have sent men for your grandfather and aunt, and they will be here presently. I have arrested Ram Das, whom I suspect, and my duty is to take your deposition, if you can give it. I have convened an inquest, and it is now sitting; and if you are strong enough to relate what happened, I have a scribe with me who will record it."

"And the robbers?" asked Seeta, "are they gone?" She was now very weak, and passed her hand over her eyes, dreamily.

"Yes, lady," said the Darogah. "I only regret that we were but three men, and one of them was wounded, and so they were too strong for us. They had slain one of the watchmen before they attacked your house; the other met us just as we neared the village on our nightly patrol. It is lucky we were in time. One of the men, however, is dying from a musket shot, and is past speech; the rest plunged into the tall jowaree fields, and we could not trace them. Now will you tell your story; are you strong enough?"

"I will," she said; "I will tell all I know, but do not let me be removed from hence. My child is with me, and they will soon come from Shah Gunje."

"You shall stay here, lady," replied the officer; "the members of the inquest can sit without, and hear what you say. No, no one shall remove you, lady. Be comforted, and all will be well with you. You have many friends, and the people love you."

Then he went out; and Seeta heard the shuffling feet of the members of the inquest come up the corridor, and as they sat down many were sobbing audibly. She gave her evidence calmly and distinctly—as will be detailed in another place—and signed the paper with a firm hand in the beautiful characters she had acquired. When this was finished, the members came in, and touched her feet in silence. They were mostly tenants of the house, and some of her husband's workmen who were householders. None of them could speak; but Seeta felt their kind homely sympathy, and was greatly comforted by it. Then they sat down outside, and gave their verdict as follows:—

"We [and their names were entered], being all householders of the village of Gokulpoor, were summoned by Ram Singh, Darogah of police, on the morning of the night of the fifteenth of August, 1855, about the third watch of the early morning, to the house of Huree Das, Zemindar, goldsmith and banker of the aforesaid village, to inquire into the cause of his death. We have taken the evidence attached, and examined the deceased's body; and we find that the said Huree Das was murdered by Dacoits, by twenty-three wounds of spears.

"Item. And we find that the house was robbed; but the property carried away is not yet ascertained.

"Item. And we have no evidence to prove who the Dacoits were who inflicted the wounds or who stole the property: but we unite in declaring that we suspect Ram Das, Zemindar of the aforesaid village, of knowledge of and participation in these crimes; and we have advised that he be confined by the police till the pleasure of Government be known.

"Signed by GUNGA RAM, Farmer, with his own hand, for the rest.

"Written by HURPAL, Scribe."

By the time these brief proceedings were finished, the dawn was breaking. The body of the unhappy goldsmith had been washed and laid out, and the stains of blood effaced as much as possible by the servants. Seeta had not been able to sleep, but she was quiet, and her neighbours watched her by turns. The police had charge of the house, and seals had been set upon all the rooms except the oratory, before which two men kept guard.

The wounded Dacoit had died without speaking. He was apparently a Boondéla, and thence it was supposed that the Dacoits had come from Bundelkhund, or the provinces bordering on it; and the inquest, having left the house of Huree Das, held a further inquiry upon the bodies of the Dacoit and the unfortunate watchman.

So, before morning broke, the Darogah had completed all his duty, and reported to his official superior as follows:—

"The petition of RAM SINGH, Acting Darogah of Soorpoor.

"Your servant was proceeding with two men from Soorpoor to Gokulpoor on the night of the 15th August. It was the bazaar day of Shah Gunje, and it was well to see that the roads were safe. We had nearly reached Gokulpoor, when Siddoo, one of the village watchmen, met us, and said another watchman, Rama, had been speared by Dacoits, and they were plundering the house of Huree Das, Zemindar. When we entered the village, the Dacoits opposed us in a large body, but by the good fortune of Government, one of them was shot, and one hundred and twenty-three rupees were found on him; the rest ran away. When we reached the house of Huree Das, we found he had been murdered, and his wife Seeta Bye, and his infant son Gopáldas, wounded. Some property had been taken from the house, but it is of no great value. One of my men, Shékh Emam, was slightly wounded, but that did not prevent him from doing his duty.

"Your servant, with some of the villagers, followed the Dacoits, but they escaped into the jowaree fields under the darkness; about this your servant is helpless.

"He endorses the verdict of this inquest and depositions, and requests orders.

"The signature of RAM SINGH, Acting Darogah."

The plans of Azráel Pandé had failed, though laid with his accustomed skill. As he left the bazaar at Shah Gunje, he had gone to the temple, and taken leave of the priest, saying he must make a stage towards Nagpoor that evening; and, attended by two men, departed. Then he proceeded to the glen, and found his men concealed in the temple. Resting there till nightfall, he had performed the necessary ceremonies to the sacred axe with due solemnity—a cock being sacrificed to it, and its blood sprinkled upon the weapon. What interest for him had the family quarrel of the goldsmith? None whatever; but there could be no doubt of the booty to be obtained. It might be ten, or even twenty thousand rupees, and with that what might not be done? At the last he disclosed to his men the place and the time, and by midnight all were to assemble in the mango grove close to Gokulpoor. He knew them too well to doubt that any one would be absent; and proceeding thither through the lonely fields, in parties of two and three, they had all assembled at the appointed time.

The rest we know. The bloody work was done; and as morning broke, the gang and their leader were again at the waterfall, bathing and washing the blood-stains from their persons and weapons. There had been little booty, and what had been found was divided on the spot; and when the division was over Azráel addressed them:—

"Where I go, brothers, ye need not know. When I can rejoin ye again, I will send word. This affair has been a failure: why, I know not; we must submit. Separate, all of ye, and take to the forests. For many weeks this district will be dangerous to all. I have divided what there was, and taken nothing for myself; but ye are all rich, and need only to be careful. Now begone."

Then the gang separated. Each man took the blade from his spear-staff and hid it in his waistband; and by paths through the deep jungles only known to themselves, were soon far beyond pursuit. As to their leader, he had protectors who afforded him refuge, and who will play their parts in this history.

CHAPTER VI.

WIDOW AND MOTHER.

Aunt Ella was always the soonest to awake in her brother's house, for she had many things to do. First, to trim the sacred fire, and prepare the oratory for her brother's morning sacrifice; then there were lazy women servants to be aroused and set to work, when all the rooms and the court had to be swept, and the floors washed with liquid mud, which dried soon, and kept them cool; there was water to be carried, and the kitchen to be attended to, and hot water prepared for her brother's bath; in short, the morning was perhaps the busiest time of the day. Aunt Ella was no Sybarite; her bed was a cool mat spread over a carpet on the bare floor, and her covering a sheet in the warm weather; all of the simplest materials, and when she arose, these were rolled up and put away. When Seeta was with her, they used to sleep in a room in the upper story; but on her departure with her husband, Aunt Ella had established herself in a chamber on the lower story, opening into the court. As she awoke, she called to the woman servant who slept near her, who rose and brought her water, and then the house was gradually aroused. It was now nearly daylight, and the cocks in houses around were crowing loudly to each other; the sacred fire had been trimmed, and the toolsōo leaves gathered for the morning worship from the altar in the centre of the court. Presently the gardener would bring his usual small basket of flowers, and then she would awake her brother, and the morning ceremony would follow.

But suddenly a great clamour arose at the gate, and she could hear the gruff voice of Bala Ram, the Rahtore Jemadar of the guard, asking hurried questions. Then the gate was suddenly opened, and as she hastened on to ascertain the cause of so unusual an uproar at so early an hour, she saw the head police officer of the town, Futéh Khan, who was intimate with her brother, dismounting from his horse, and several of his men with him. What could it be? what could have happened? It was barely dawn, but by the dim moonlight she saw him advance across the court with Bala Ram, and went to meet him at the head of the steps. Aunt Ella was not one who concealed herself, or shrank from seeing men who came and went, and her agitation was too great to stop her now.

"What is it, sir?" she asked hurriedly; "why have you come so early?"

"Where is your brother?" he asked, not replying to her question; "wake him and bring him here."

She had hardly turned, when the banker, hastily throwing a shawl over his bare head and shoulders, appeared at the door of the court.

"Why, Khan Sahib! what has happened?" he exclaimed. "Speak?"

"Send her away," he replied, pointing to Aunt Ella, "it is for your ears only."

"Go, sister," said the banker; "this is private."

"I will not go, brother," she said, gasping for breath; "I fear, oh! I fear for Seeta and the child. Let him speak. I will not go." And she sat down, covering her face.

"Proceed," said the banker: "good or evil, joy or sorrow, my sister shares all; and if the news concerns my children——" and the old man's voice broke down.

"It is bad news," returned the officer; "very bad. There was a Dacoity on the house of Huree Das this morning, and he was killed."

"And his wife, sir? O my child! my child!" cried Ella, in a voice of anguish. "She died too?"

"No, lady, she is safe. Somewhat wounded I hear, but safe. Come with me; she needs you and her grandfather. I have sent on a body of men already, and have come for you both. Be quick and get ready."

Aunt Ella did not lose her presence of mind. She arose and took her brother's hand, and led him away. She could not weep, she could hardly speak; but she knew what they must do, and do at once.

"Seeta lives," she said at last; "be thankful to the gods, brother, that she and the child are safe. I must order the palankeen and your pony. I can ride him, and you can go in the palkee; be quick and dress yourself. And here is the priest too: he will come with us; won't you, Maharaj?"

"O Wamun Bhut! O friend!" cried Narendra, now bursting into tears. "You are kind to come; what evil hath fallen on us? So young, so beautiful, and already a widow! O Seeta!"

"Nay, weep not, old friend; only thank God she and her child are spared to you," said the priest, earnestly. "Come, waste no time, there is much to do. We will bring her here, and you will have your old joy in the house; come. Ah! if I had only sought the stars sooner, this might have been prevented; but we, who know them best, are but blind fools. I tried when I went home, but the calculation was too abstruse, and I gave it up."

"Was it the Brahmin then after all?" asked the banker; "you seemed to suspect him."

"I will not say now, friend; there appeared many concerned, and I have my own thoughts about it. Come away, we lose time. She will be looking for us."

If a fresh, pleasant morning, as the day grew bright, with a heavy dew lying on the grass and fields of corn, could have made the morning ride agreeable, they were not wanting; but all were oppressed with grief and care, and went on in silence. Aunt Ella would not allow her brother to ride. Tucking up her garments, she mounted his ambling pony stoutly, and kept by his palankeen, while the priest and the police officer rode in front. Around them were the household guards with Bala Ram at their head, while two of the men ran beside the open doors of the palankeen, bidding their venerable master be of good cheer and trying to comfort him after their homely fashion. And so they reached Gokulpoor as the sun had just risen, and were met by the villagers with cries and tears. They shuddered as they entered the house of Huree Das, so lately the scene of violence. Everything appeared in disorder. Household articles, dropped by the robbers, were lying about the court. The body of the goldsmith had been removed after the inquest, and was being bathed for the last ceremony; but the blood-stains had hardly been obliterated, and, though women were washing the floor, a faint, sickly smell pervaded the house. It was a sad meeting between Seeta and her grandfather and aunt. She was very weak. She seemed scared and absent, as if she hardly knew them, and could say little; but as they knelt down by her bed and put their arms round her, she drew away her garment from the child, who nestled in her bosom, and showed him to them.

"He is safe," she said; "I thought he was dead, but he lives and is well. Do not disturb him; see, he sleeps peacefully."

"And thou, O my darling," said the old man; "surely the gods saved thee?"

"Yes," said Seeta, faintly; "but he—my husband—is dead. They have not told me, but I feel no hope."

"There is none, Seeta," said her aunt. "Think not of him, my darling, but of thyself and the boy."

"O take me hence!" cried the girl, throwing her arms round her aunt's neck; "take me away! My eyes are full of blood; I smell it everywhere; take me away!"

"Come to me, my darling," said the old lady, sobbing; "come to my heart, where thou hast lain many a day;" and she gathered the girl's yielding form to her bosom. "Fear not now, Seeta. It is a heavy fate for thee so young; but thou wilt bear it bravely, I know." Then she told Narendra to go away; he could do nothing there, and had better see to what was to be done; and he submitted, and left them.

The banker went to the front room and sat down. As he looked around, he saw that the stains of blood had been removed from the floor; but the lintels of the oratory were splashed with it, and within was a black pool, on which he dare not look. Ram Das was now sitting there, and was guarded by two police and some villagers. He appealed to the banker for protection.

"Why am I suspected, why am I confined?" he cried, passionately. "Because he who lies there dead"—and he pointed to the body, which had already been prepared for cremation—"and I had a family quarrel, am I to be thought his murderer? Is my honour to be dragged in the dirt? Did

I not come to him last night and make him a humble offer of settlement? His wife knows this; let her speak."

"Peace," said the police officer of Shah Gunje; "enough that this is a case of murder, and neither Ram Singh nor I can neglect our duty. I caution you, Ram Das, to say nothing to us; keep your defence for the magistrate, now you might commit yourself. Be careful and be silent."

"At least," he said, sullenly, "let me perform the usual ceremonies. I am his nearest relative, and there is none other to do them."

"Of course, we would not hinder that," said Ram Singh; "let it be so; they are making the preparations, and it will soon be done. You can bathe here and be ready."

"I cannot," he replied, surlily; "I cannot be pure in a house full of blood; I must go home."

"Impossible," said both the officers in a breath, "and whether you go or whether you stay, it matters little; there are Brahmins to do the work, and Wamun Bhut is directing them."

But Ram Das's thoughts were now set upon the inheritance and the family jewels, and he would not willingly forfeit one tittle of his claim by the non-performance of the ceremony.

"I will bathe anywhere," he said; "I will be ready."

So the ceremony went on. Near the stream which ran by Gokulpoor the funeral pyre had already been built up. Many Brahmins from villages around had assembled, and were repeating holy texts. There would be a large dole at the burning of the son-in-law of Narendra the great banker, and they sat in eager anticipation of it. What mattered to them the grief and misery inside—the widow and her infant son!

Presently the bearers for the body came in and said all was prepared, and they must take it away; and it was raised, dressed with flowers and the caste marks, and placed on the bier. Narendra got up and looked at it. The manly features were not distorted; but they wore the grim expression of the struggle in which Huree Das had died. Then the bier, which was made of pieces of green wood tied together, was raised, and those who had gathered around it moved on, and among them was Ram Das, who was guarded as before.

Then Wamun Bhut came to Narendra and said in a whisper, "We must take the child to light the pyre; where is he?"

"Seeta will never part with him," said the banker.

"She will if I ask her," returned the other, hastily; "where is she?"

Narendra pointed to the inner court, and the priest went in, and found the room in which Seeta was lying. She was awake, though she had been sleeping a little.

"We must take the child with his father," he said, briefly; "where is he?"

"It is impossible," said Aunt Ella; "the child is weak from loss of blood."

"He must come; O Seeta, be firm, my daughter, and send him," said the priest, anxiously; "else Ram Das will perform the ceremony, and your child will lose the inheritance."

"Canst thou not do it, master?" said Seeta, raising herself up.

"I could," he replied, "if the boy were not there, not else; be quick, give him to me."

"Take him, aunt," said Seeta, firmly; "it shall not be said of me that I lost my child's rights through foolish weakness. Take him, keep him from the sun and wind. You will not be long away?"

"It is but ten steps," said the priest; "when the child is a man he will bless his brave mother for this. Come, lady, they await us."

Aunt Ella had hardly been prepared for this result. She had always thought Seeta firm, but she had not known the strength of her niece's character: and how often is it that by desperate events alone some characters are developed! She said nothing, but she knew the priest was right; and she took up the child, and, throwing a saree over her head, covered the boy with it. He was fast asleep, and did not awake as he was carried out.

"O, but she is noble, my daughter, my beloved child," said the priest to Narendra, as they passed out; "could any one have given me thousands, they would be dirt before such a triumph as this. Now you will see!"

The bearers had carried on the bier, and the body—its many gaping wounds now visible to all—was laid on the pyre, with its face to the north. When Wamun Bhut and the banker arrived, the last ceremonies were being performed; and the sacred ball of rice and sugar, with other condiments, was offered to the corpse, and its name, Huree Das, the son of Ram Das, called aloud.

As the words were spoken, Ram Das advanced with a wisp of lighted straw in his hands to light the pyre as heir-at-law and nearest of kin, but Wamun Bhut drew him back.

"While his son is here thou hast no place in this matter," he said, sternly; and there was a shout of applause as Aunt Ella, bearing the child, uncovered it; and they took it as a good omen that the boy opened his eyes wide and crowed. Then Wamun Bhut took him in his arms, and walked round the pyre three times; and putting a wisp of straw into the boy's tiny hand, guided it to his father's face, and applied it to a corner of the pile; while others, watching for the signal, lighted it all round. Ram Das had slunk back as the pile blazed fiercely up, and his look of hate, as he watched what was done, was never forgotten by those who saw it. Then Wamun Bhut said the prayer to the Regent of Fire, and the ceremony was complete.

Aunt Ella did not stay; she bore off the child in triumph to his mother, and laid him in her arms, and he looked up smiling and crowed in his mother's face. Perhaps it was then, and then only, that Seeta had become thoroughly conscious. Her eyes had been staring and glazed, and glittered with a fearful lustre. Her mouth was parched, and her body burned with fever. Then, as she strained her boy to her heart and bent over him, a passionate flood of tears broke from her and relieved her. Aunt Ella was too wise to check them.

"Weep on, my child," she said; "the boy was a hero, a brave fellow indeed, and how all the people shouted for joy when they saw him! Be comforted, Seeta; this day thou hast saved his inheritance. Wamun Bhut was right; if he had not warned us, Ram Das would have lighted the pyre as heir-at-law."

Seeta did not reply, but her tears were now flowing silently. They did not remain long; Seeta would not eat in the house, but some milk had been given to her, and she was able to travel. Aunt Ella made the palankeen comfortable with soft pillows, and Seeta was carried out to the verandah, and placed in it, and attended by the household guards it proceeded to Shah Gunje, followed by Aunt Ella on her brother's pony.

But Narendra remained, for there was much to do. He was determined to leave nothing of value in the house; and in his presence, and that of the two police officers, the floor of the oratory was dug up, and everything that had been deposited there, with the treasure and partly finished ornaments, was recorded in a list drawn up by the village registrar, and signed by many who witnessed these proceedings. Ram Das alone refused to sign it.

"The property is mine," he said, "and for all the trickery of to-day I shall get it. Meanwhile, it is safe in thy keeping, Narendra."

After this, all that was moveable in the house was carried out, packed in carts, and sent off to Shah Gunje. Outside were bales of cotton and other merchandize, with a granary full of grain, and these were left in charge of the police. Then the rooms of the house were sealed up, a seal placed upon the gate of the inner court, and the house left to its own desolation. The last act of Narendra was the charitable dole which had been anticipated, and it was ample and liberal; while the widow of the watchman who had been slain by the Dacoits, received a generous donation.

The magistrate's decision came after a few days by express. All that had been done was approved of; but he did not see cause for detaining Ram Das as a prisoner, and he was to be released on bail, and his own recognizances in a heavy sum. He was a man of much substance, and had friends as well as Narendra; and when the bail was given, the police were withdrawn from his house.

The next night, as he was sitting alone, poring over his accounts, a servant said, "A man without would speak with you; he would rather not enter."

Ram Das's heart leaped within him.

"It is the Brahmin," he muttered; "I cannot avoid him. Yes," he said to the servant, "tell him I come."

As he passed out of his gate he saw a figure in the gloom, sitting on one of the steps.

"I must have five hundred rupees, Ram Das," said Azráel, in a hoarse whisper; "that matter did not succeed, and I have no money. Quick, I dare not come while the police were here, and now my life is nowhere safe. I have lurked about and have often come here by night, but had no chance of seeing thee. Quick, bring the money in gold."

"But give me my bond," said Ram Das,

"I will not," replied Azráel; "there is more due on it."

"But——"

"I tell thee I will waste no words on thee. Give me the money. I am desperate—and if thou wilt not, it will be an easy thing to enclose the note to the magistrate, and write that it was the price of the murder of Huree Das. Ha! dost thou understand?"

"I will give it," said Ram Das, humbly.

He could, he saw at once, make no terms. For good or for evil, he was in the hands of the Dacoit.

"If thou goest in, the door may be shut in my face," said the Brahmin. "I will go with thee. There is no one there?"

"No one, by your head and eyes; come!"

"You know," said the Dacoit, grimly, "I know where the

treasures are, but you need not be afraid. One affair like the last suffices for some time, and I would not harm thee."

They went in together, and receiving the sum he had asked for in gold pieces, Azráel Pandé departed. But the next night, the merchant dug another hole in a far-off court, and buried his treasure within it.

END OF PART THE FIRST.

PART THE SECOND.

CHAPTER VII.

SEETA'S ANKLET.

More than a year had elapsed; but no discovery had been made as to the Dacoity, and the crime remained as a blot upon the police administration. It had been preceded by several others, alike undiscovered, and one more had occurred subsequently, though not of so serious a character. Still, it was evident that Dacoity was a normal crime of this province—as indeed it was of but too many others. The Gokulpoor affair, with the murder of Huree Das, was, however, so remarkable an event that the utmost energy and circumspectness was enjoined upon the police authorities by a high official, who did not scruple to record a very low opinion of the district police in general, and of the English magistrates in particular; which, if it had an effect of extreme irritation, and was entirely undeserved, was not the less provocative of the most untiring efforts to trace the crime to its perpetrators.

The case of Ram Das, in particular, which promised to afford a clue, had undergone the most rigid scrutiny. He had, as has been already recorded, been suspected, and almost denounced, by the inquest; but though the fact of his having received two strange men and kept them up to the day on which the Dacoity occurred was proved—he had been able to show from his books that he had received a large remittance in coin from a correspondent in Berar, which had been brought by professional rokurreás, or treasure-carriers, strangers to the country, whom, after they had rested, he had sent away. On the body of the Dacoit who was shot a considerable sum of money had been found, which denoted a recent division of spoil; and among the coins were several rupees marked with the private die of the merchant. This, however, amounted to no proof of complicity or guilt, for his transactions in money were considerable, and the coin issued by him was always marked. These rupees, being in general circulation, might therefore have been obtained in any bazaar of the country. Nevertheless, they were separated from the others and kept.

Ram Das gave an unreserved account of his last interview with his cousin, and detailed what we already know. He produced also the letters of his legal adviser in Calcutta, and his notice of appeal against the late judgment against him was on record in the local court. Seeta, again examined by the head native authority of Shah Gunje, corroborated Ram Das's explanation; but owned she had been alarmed by his threat as he left her husband. She acknowledged, however, that her husband had used strong language; and, as this would naturally provoke a sharp rejoinder, Ram Das's words were attributed to the heat of passion, and he expressed his regret for them. Finally, a reward of five hundred rupees to any discoverer of the gang, and a free pardon to any two participators in the crime who had not actually committed the murder, was proclaimed in every town and village of the district. Narendra, on his part, offered a similar sum. A detachment of the Thuggee and Dacoity police, under an experienced detective officer, was sent into the province, and, so far as was possible, every means to discover the authors of the crime had been adopted.

So the months passed; and perhaps the first singular interest of the event began to grow more and more dim. Not only had the British portion of the province been ransacked for information, but the two chief native dignitaries, who held independent estates of large value, had been urged to assist; and they had professed their readiness to do so, with much zeal and cordiality. The Nawab Dil Khan Bahadoor had visited the Judge and the Commissioner, deplored the existence of Dacoity, and declared that if any of his subjects were found to have been connected with the Gokulpoor affair, he seriously hoped they might be blown away from guns, or hanged. He admitted that his soldiers were rude folks, and at times unruly, even to himself; and it must be confessed that the English civil officers had no high opinion of them in any sense. The Rajah Hurpál Singh was a boorish, rough person, believed to have been descended from the wild Gónds, and living on the borders of the Gónd forests; but he was somewhat popular with the young military officers, always ready to assist them in their hunting and shooting expeditions, and profuse in his hospitality; and he, in his turn, promised whatever assistance he could afford.

Seeta was now settled at Shah Gunje. She had never returned to Gokulpoor, and whatever related to her house, and to her husband's affairs, was managed by her grandfather and his agents. Narendra had the accounts of her husband's estate kept separately from his own; and it furnished a handsome income, which he held at her disposal. He had accepted the charge under trust, and associated with himself the priest Wamun Bhut, a respectable Zemindar, and two bankers of the town; and thus a punchayet, or board of five persons, was formed, who audited the monthly accounts. In outward appearance Seeta was not changed; nay, she had even become more lovely. Her growing beauty, indeed, almost distressed her aunt and grandfather. Why had it been given to her? Why should such charms be vouchsafed to a widow? They watched anxiously whether, when the anniversary of her husband's death came round, she would desire to perform the duties and ceremonies of a widow in full—have her beautiful hair shorn off, and break her ornaments on the place where his body had been burned—but there was no sign of this. Once, when Aunt Ella hinted at the propriety of such a ceremony, she drew herself up, and said, proudly—

"It is not a shaven head or a coarse garment that makes a virtuous widow, Aunt Ella! What I am, I will remain. Am I to disfigure myself to shock my boy when he grows up? No! if his father's death were avenged, this might—might—be thought of; but, till then, let it not be mentioned."

So her grandfather and aunt gave the matter up, and watched her. She was not the same simple girl in character that she had been before she left them, to be moulded and influenced as they would. There was now a strange aspect of determination in her eyes which was new to them, though with it, none of her sweetness had diminished. She was quicker in decision and more fluent in speech: more keen in her discussions, especially with the priest, whose pupil she had again become—than she had used to be; and even he was often astonished and perplexed by her ability, which put his own to sharp tests.

For her child, her love amounted to a passionate devotion, which affected all who saw it very deeply. She was almost his sole attendant, anticipating every want, and never allowing him out of her sight. By this time, too, the little fellow had begun to toddle about, and even to say a word or two; and he was very handsome, for the soft, regular features and lovely eyes of his mother seemed to be blended with the more manly form of his father's countenance. Seeta was—what Indian mother is not?—fearful of the evil eye, and she had hung round her son a necklace of charms set in silver and gold, which reached to his knees. When she took him to the temple for any ceremony, the doors of her palankeen were closed before she went out of her house, and never opened till she was within the sacred precincts of her teacher's temple. Between her books and the child, therefore, Seeta's time ought to have passed pleasantly; but was it so? I think not. If her grandfather had never allowed her to be educated, and if her education had not progressed to the point it had—which often caused Aunt Ella, who could not read a letter, great uneasiness—Seeta might have settled down into the dull, usual widowhood of Hindoo life; pious, absorbed in household cares, charitable, and patient, with no hope for the future, and praying that a dull mechanical life might pass away when her child grew up and entered upon his work in life.

But Seeta was not like this: the high spirit within her refused to be satisfied with what she saw in others, of whom her beloved Aunt Ella was a type. She indeed had no children; and she had no cares or aspirations. If her brother got his food regularly, if the servants were kept busy, if the poor were fed, if the household condiments, and the vermicelli in particular, were nicely prepared, if the buffaloes and cows were milked, and the butter boiled into ghee, if no ceremony, general or household, were neglected—she was satisfied; and if there were an error anywhere, she was miserable till it was corrected. Seeta could do all this as well as her aunt, and in some things she excelled her. Her grandfather would never eat vermicelli except it was prepared by her dainty fingers, and whenever he was ailing no one could please his palate but Seeta.

Not less devoted to her household duties than before she left them, Seeta was not else the same. Though she only read the sacred books and some poems and dramas, yet there were thoughts recorded in them which seemed to leap up to her own, to set her brain aching and her heart throbbing, not only at the Divine revelation, as she believed it to be, but at the language in which the strange metaphysical arguments were conveyed. Sometimes she failed to follow them; and, when she applied to her master, was often refused help! "They were mysteries which none but a Brahmin should know," he would tell her; "they were not fit for the tender minds of women," and so evaded her request; but Seeta was not satisfied. There were other passages, however, in which she revelled; the descriptions of natural scenery by Kalidas and Bawa Bhut, the rich episodes of the Mahabhárut and Ramayan, were like new senses to her. She could hear the rushing winds and waters of the poems, watch the glowing skies, and smell the perfume of the beauteous flowers. These were realities, not inventions; and often, as she sat in her oriel window while her boy played near her, she would lay down her book, and gaze on the wooded hills, the rich corn-fields, the stately groves, and the distant villages, glowing under the noontide sun, with a swelling heart and tearful eyes. And there was love too. The seers and warriors of old loved, and women loved; else who had written of love? What would it be to feel as those who so wrote and described it?—her heart gave back no echo.

Seeta had never loved. She had held her husband in respect; she was even proud of him, and he was fond of her—she was his darling! But that was not the love of the books. His life had not been her life, nor hers his. Yet such as that was not the poet's love—the pure ideal of a love which could be perfected only in Paradise! Ah! she had never known it; never would know it now; never could have known it with him! He would have gradually drawn her down to his own intellectual level, and her mind would have been stunted as it tried to grow. Now it was free! Yet who was there, among all she knew, to whom she could trace in her mind any real semblance of the divine passion? In truth, the quick, powerful intellect of her nature, so difficult to arouse, and so uncontrollable when once awakened, was leading her on by thoughts far beyond the scope of her ordinary life, and she could not stay them.

Amidst these dreams and unreal speculations, Seeta's life passed; and often as the good priest caught a glimpse of them, which he dared not follow, he would mutter to himself, "O that I had not taught her! and yet, who could restrain her ardent mind? Now she must follow what she gains, and I must lead her to the good. and put the evil of it far from her." But the course of her life, monotonous as it was, and promised to be, was suddenly changed by an event relating to her husband's fate, which was this:—

Noorpoor was a large provincial station, the head of all the administration of the province. There lived the Judge and the Civil Commissioner: and there were besides English troops and their officers, and a large town which had a great trade. It was an event in the life of any inhabitant of Shah Gunje to go there, and even her grandfather very seldom visited it; yet the news of Noorpoor reached Shah Gunje by letters and from visitors; and between the two towns were such relations, public and private, as belong to the ordinary affairs of life. Noorpoor had its weekly bazaar or market like Shah Gunje; and late in the month of August, 1856, an incident occurred which revived the story of the Dacoity at Gokulpoor, with an intense and fearful interest.

On one of the market days, a petty goldsmith, sitting behind a stall on which a few coarse ornaments of gold and silver were displayed, was accosted by a man bearing a sword and shield, who looked like a soldier, and asked whether he would buy some gold. Now Roopa, the man who was spoken to, was poor and old. He had made little that day, and the prospect of a transaction in gold, with one who could not know its market value, was not to be resisted. On the other hand, the soldier had selected the old man as the poorest goldsmith he could find; because while he might obtain from him a fair portion of the value, he would be less likely than another to disclose the nature of the transaction.

"Of course, valiant sir," said Roopa, "it is my business, and I will give as fair a price as any goldsmith in the market. What have you to sell?"

"It would be well if we were more private," said the man. "I don't like exhibiting my family ornaments in public. If you would leave your stall and come with me, I would show them to you in a more quiet place than this."

Roopa looked here and there to see if there were any of his friends disengaged; but his stall was, in truth, by itself, and there was no one very near it. "I cannot leave my things here," he replied; "and I have no one upon whom I can depend. Do not be ashamed: 'The goldsmith and the washerman, you know, must be trusted in the house,'" and he quoted a familiar proverb.

"Well," said the man, "I want the money, for my rent is due, and I must pay it; so look." And unloosing some folds in his turban, he produced a gold anklet of much beauty, and held it out.

The goldsmith took it and examined it carefully. "If you have more such jewels at home," he said, "happy is the woman who wears them."

"Ah, yes," returned the man carelessly; "they made good things in the olden days, and if luck had remained with my house, I had no need to sell this. Say, what wilt thou give for it?"

"The gold is good," said Roopa, "and the anklet is heavy," he continued, tossing it in his hand; "but there is the alloy. Let me look at it with my spectacles."

As he did so, Roopa almost started and gasped for breath. Below the rim at the back, were the private marks of Narendra of Shah Gunje, and Huree Das of Gokulpoor, and both were quite distinct; but he had seen enough, and hastily turned over the anklet to look elsewhere.

"What ails thee?" said the man; "why didst thou shake? Is the gold bad?"

"Noble sir," replied Roopa, "I have ague in this damp weather, and a cough, that was all. Do you know of any medicine for it, you soldiers?"

"We kill sometimes, but seldom cure," he cried, laughing; "but let us settle this business first."

"Well, of course," said the goldsmith, "I mean to do so. Will you keep the anklet, and remain by my poor stall while I fetch scales and a touchstone? I will be back in a moment; Gunput Das yonder has them, I know."

"Don't be long, then," replied the man; "if you are, I may help myself."

"Ah, sir! they would not be worth the taking; I will return in the twinkling of an eye."

So the soldier remained at the stall; while Roopa, under the vision of five hundred rupees' reward, which would be wealth to him, hurried to his fellow craftsman's stall, that lay beyond. Passing two of the policemen, however, in a crowd of people, he whispered to one whom he knew: "There is one of the Dacoits in the Gokulpoor case now at my stall. Get near it gradually, and while I am weighing his gold, seize and bind him. He is armed." Then he went and borrowed the scales and the touchstone, and went back to his stall.

"Well, you see, I was not long, sir," he said, "and I have run fast. Let me first try the gold with the stone, and I will weigh it when my hand is steadier; no doubt the gold is very pure," he continued. "Good, good! Look!" And he held up the touchstone to the man's face. "Its mark is better than that or that: but there is a good deal of alloy and sawder to be deducted. What do you say to fifteen rupees a tola?"

"Say sixteen," said the man; "you goldsmiths are all cheats. If I had to buy it you would charge me twenty or more."

"Of course, of course, my friend," returned the goldsmith, laughing, "else how could we live, sir? how could we live? But sixteen is a long price nevertheless."

"Weigh it, I say," cried the man, impatiently, "and be quick: you talk too much."

Roopa had talked on purpose, and was rubbing the stone with the gold to gain time. Now he saw the police were approaching, and that his customer evidently grew uneasy.

"I don't like those fellows; do they ever interfere with you?" asked the man, looking round.

"Never," replied the goldsmith. "I have a good character with them, and they never look into my doings. See, sir, the gold is exactly fifteen tolas and a half;" and he held up the scales between his finger and thumb. "Fifteen and a half tolas: you can see for yourself. My hand is steady, and a hair would turn the scale. Are you satisfied?"

The man's attention was completely absorbed by the process of weighing. The goldsmith had put a red seed into the scale, taken it out, put in two, taken them out, and so had protracted the operation as long as possible.

"Yes," said the man, "it seems right; now for the money."

As he spoke the words, he was roughly seized from behind; and as one of the policemen held his arms, the other slipped a pair of handcuffs over his hands, and took away his sword. He looked from one to the other savagely, but made no disturbance.

"If I had ye both in a clear field, I would give an account of ye," he said, grinding his teeth; "now I am helpless!"

"And here is the anklet of Seeta Bye, the wife of Huree Das," said the goldsmith, triumphantly. "See, here is his mark and Narendra's; I know them. Ask him about it. Take it, sirs, and register my claim for the reward."

"You must come with us to the station," said one of the men, "and swear to this matter;" and drawing their bayonets they moved on. The mere fact of a prisoner escorted by two policemen was little heeded in the bazaar, as it was an act of very ordinary occurrence; but others joined them as they passed through the crowd safely.

The examination proceeded rapidly, but was strangely interrupted by the prisoner's confession. "It is all true," he cried out suddenly, "and there is no use asking questions or writing. I will tell all. I was in the Gokulpoor business, but I did no murder; the man who did it is in the bazaar, if you have courage to take him."

"Who and what is he?" asked the police officer who was taking the depositions.

"Never mind who he is, or what his name is," replied the ruffian; "for the matter of that he has a hundred. Go ye to the Mutt of the Gosayn Bheem Geer, and you will see a tall Brahmin of Oudh, teaching: that is the man, bring him to me."

A plan was arranged at once, and two parties set out. The Mutt, a small temple in the centre of a street, would intervene between one party and the other; and only one of them might be seen by any person at the steps of the Mutt. Some of the men had observed the Brahmin already, and had even listened to him. They knew exactly what to do.

Azráel Pandé was sitting on the steps of the Mutt, painted to the waist, as we have seen him at Shah Gunje, and teaching. He saw four policemen approaching him, and for an instant felt uncertain what to do; but similar parties, patrolling the bazaar, had passed him several times in the course of the afternoon, and this no doubt would do the same. But as the men neared him, two of them rushed upon him assisted by the others, the patrol from the other side followed; he was thrown down, and the handcuffs forced on his wrists.

He had struggled violently, and was out of breath. As he panted, he cried, "Lo! the tyranny of the Feringees. Who see this insult to a poor Brahmin and will not avenge it?" and again he writhed fearfully, but was held down.

"Be quiet," said the corporal in command of the party, "take it easy; the armlets will hurt you if you don't. Come quietly."

"For what am I arrested?" he asked.

"For the murder of Huree Das, goldsmith, of Gokulpoor," was the reply.

Azráel Pandé made no answer. He at once rose to his feet, and as the party closed around him, he was marched on, guarded carefully.

The police Darogah was waiting the result anxiously; and the prisoner once said sharply, "He will kill some of them, if he has time to fix his spear."

But Azráel had not had time. The shaft of the spear was lying beside him like an ordinary walking staff, and the spear-head was found in his girdle; but the policeman who had first reached him, as powerful a man as himself, had pinioned his arms at once, and he was helpless.

"Salaam, Jemadar!" said the prisoner, as Azráel was brought in, "I am here before you, and I shall tell all. Dohai Feringee ka!" he cried with a loud voice, "Justice from the English! I, Beerbul, demand my life according to the proclamation, and I will tell all. Dohai! Dohai! But first take his spear from him," he continued; "if he gets a hand loose, some of ye will be killed. It is in his girdle."

A policeman felt for it, and produced the blade. Broad, and with a long, fine point, the edges were as sharp as a razor, and there were two rings, with dots between them, of inlaid gold on the lower end.

"Now fit it on the staff," continued the prisoner, "and you

will see, what killed Huree Das, the goldsmith, and many another."

It was in truth a fearful weapon, and was put aside.

Then silence fell on all, as the prisoner, in a clear voice, begun his tale.

CHAPTER VIII.

SEETA'S TESTIMONY.

THE evidence of the Dacoit tallied in all respects with the facts already recorded. The police officer had cautioned him that what he said would be used against him, and that he himself had no power to confirm the proclamation in his case; but the man was excited, and only cried the more, "Dohai! Dohai! let me speak! let me speak!"

These arrests, and their consequences, spread at once over the bazaar. Several of the best goldsmiths were called upon to examine the anklet, and one and all not only recognized the marks of Narendra and Huree Das, but one man deposed that the links of it were the work of Narendra's own hands, and that no one could make such but him. After hearing the proceedings, Narendra's correspondent at Noorpoor wrote a full account of the whole to him, and promised further news as it should transpire.

Narendra had been much affected by the news. It was, as it were, beginning the miserable affair over again, and he dreaded its effect on Seeta. The letter had come by private express, and very rapidly; and it was next to impossible that any one in the town could have heard of the event but himself. He would not have Seeta learn it at second hand; and though his clerks sitting round the room, the cashier and the book-keeper, were most curious to hear the news, Narendra would tell them nothing, and at once went upstairs to his grand-daughter. He had the letter in his hand as he entered her room, and Seeta, who was playing with her boy, looked up in some amazement.

"Thou shouldst not see me thus," she said, hastily gathering up her beautiful hair, and drawing her saree over her head. "O grandfather, what is it? And thou didst not send word? Would I not have come to thee?" and she rose and touched his feet.

"I would have no one know it before thee, my child," he

said, sitting down beside her; "this letter is from Noorpoor, and it tells me the fellow to thy anklet has been found."

"Found!" she cried, "and the men who took it?"

"Not all," he replied, "only two of them as yet; one had the anklet, and he has confessed. The other is——"

"The Brahmin!" exclaimed Seeta; "I know it, I already know it," she continued, clapping her hands in her excitement; "I have thought it, I have seen him in my dreams. Ah! the gods are just, and the brave English will not fear him as our people would. Justice will be done! Dohai! Dohai!"

"Calm thyself, child," said the old man, gently; "it is a serious matter. I love the English, but they are no respecters of persons; and thou wilt have to go before the magistrate if I cannot get him here to take thy evidence."

"No! not here, not here," said Seeta, now much excited; "let me go to the court. What will the magistrate do to me, a widow? Do not all men praise him and love him? I was not afraid of the Brahmin, when I stepped over *his* body to meet him and——"

The flood of recollection had been too powerful, and Seeta burst into a torrent of passionate tears and sobs which brought Aunt Ella to the room hastily. At the sight of her Seeta rallied. "I will go," she said, more calmly; "no one shall stay me!"

"Where?" said the old lady, looking with bewildered eyes from one to the other; "where? What is all this? Seeta, what has happened?"

A few words explained all; and Aunt Ella, whose courage nothing could daunt, said at once, "Yes, she is right; she shall go, brother, and ought to go. It is no disgrace to one like her, who has never hid her face, to show it for the sake of justice—justice to her child!"

"Well," said Narendra, "you are both against me, and I have done; but think how many will look at her; and if she's afraid, and breaks down, what will become of our house?"

"I fear nothing, grandfather," replied Seeta, firmly, "nothing. In such a time, and to speak out my heart to one who would believe what I say, I would go even to Calcutta!"

"Oh! there is no fear of that," said Narendra; "the matter will be decided either at Noorpoor or here; we shall know soon. So if I get a summons, shall I agree that you will appear?"

"Send it to me if it is in my name," replied Seeta, "I am not afraid to sign it."

And when it came, the day after, she signed it, "Seeta, the widow of Huree Das." The summons cited her to appear as a witness in the Court of the Hon. Cyril Brandon, Acting Deputy Commissioner of Noorpoor, at Shah Gunje, on the tenth day of September. It was now the twenty-sixth of August.

At Noorpoor, the examinations went on rapidly. The full confession of Beerbul Singh, the approver, had been recorded; and for the apprehension of some of the Dacoits concerned, who lived in the territories of the Nawab and the Rajah, parties of the Dacoity police had been despatched, who brought in ten of them in the course of a day or two. They seemed to be desperate ruffians; and were heavily ironed and strongly guarded, and kept apart from each other. Mr. Noble, the Assistant Commissioner in charge of the station, was a young man who had recently joined the service. He had already distinguished himself in his examinations, and had been appointed to Noorpoor; but he did not see his way clearly in so important a case as this, and sought counsel from Mr. Mostyn, the Judge, who advised him to send the case for preliminary investigation on the spot by the Acting Deputy Commissioner, now absent on a distant tour, and to prepare him to meet the prisoners at Shah Gunje as soon as possible.

All these matters of official detail were soon arranged; and the prisoners were despatched on two carts, under the charge of a detachment of police, and a party of the irregular cavalry at Noorpoor. Among them was Azráel Pandé, who, in all the examinations, had conducted himself with haughty defiance, and seemed to be indifferent to his fate. He had denied participation in the Dacoity distinctly, and with some violence. He was a stranger, he said, from Oudh—a Brahmin, going on a pilgrimage to Raméshwur in pursuance of a vow, and taught and expounded the Shastres as he went. But this explanation had no effect upon the authorities, and no relaxation of his confinement had given him a chance of escape. At the end of the first march, however, an old comrade, now one of the police, was on guard over him; and was easily persuaded to contrive his flight if it were possible. They could traverse the jungles, Azrael said, with safety, and he had many friends who would shelter them both; but the opportunity did not occur, the guards were too vigilant, and in the course of a few days the escort reached Shah Gunje, and delivered up their prisoners safely, and were detained for their return.

Early on the morning of the tenth of September, as Seeta was looking from the oriel window over the town, she saw in the grove near the priests' temple beyond it, a white tent rising slowly under the trees, and knew that the time of her examination drew near. How often had she seen the tents of the English magistrate pitched there before, without a thought of him or of his business? He came and went at stated periods, transacted his public affairs, received visits, and departed as he came; now, however, it was very different. She seemed to have a direct concern with him. Would he be kind and considerate with her, or would he be rough and haughty, as she heard many English were?

But she thought kindly of him. Every one spoke and thought well of him, she knew, and many were warm in his praises. He was courteous and just, she had often heard, and harmed no one. Surely he would do justice and help a widow and her child! If she were excited at the thought of appearing in an open court, she concealed it; and when her aunt came to her presently, and told her to prepare herself, she arose and obeyed her cheerfully. "I shall take my child with me," she said quietly. "I must show his wound to the magistrate." It was in vain that Aunt Ella tried to dissuade her. What evil eye might not be cast upon him? The dreaded Brahmin might curse him, curse them both; but Seeta was very firm. "We are in God's hands," she said gently. "O Aunt Ella, help me; but do not try to alarm me or turn me from this my duty and my solemn vow, and I will not fail."

Eleven o'clock had been fixed as the time, and Seeta was dressed and ready. Never had her aunt and her grandfather seen her look more radiantly beautiful, as she descended the stairs, with her child on her hip, and reached the basement floor. Aunt Ella was deeply moved, and put her hands on her head to bless her.

"Put your hands on my head," she said humbly to her grandfather, who was also ready. "Bless me and the boy, and no evil can come nigh us." Narendra could not well speak, but he did as she wished, and his prayer for her was earnest and fervent. "The priest is here," he continued, "and will bless thee too, Seeta, and we will all go together." And then Wamun Bhut came forward and laid his hands upon her head and the child's, and blessed them both. "Be fearless, daughter," he said; "no one will harm you or distress you, and least of all Mr. Brandon."

It was not far to the tents. The prisoners had not arrived yet, but were on their way, and the palankeen was put down in the shade, where the party seated themselves under a large mango tree at a little distance and waited patiently. Seeta's child was in the wildest delight, for the camp was a new sight to him. The fresh green grass was covered with tiny wild flowers; the white tents, the people moving about them; the horses and camels, and a great elephant, almost bewildered the boy; but he looked brave and fearless, and his mother caught him to her breast with a glow of pride.

Presently they heard the clanking sounds of heavy irons, and the prisoners and their guards moved up the slope of the knoll on which the tents stood, at a slow pace. Seeta's eye at once recognized the tall figure of the Brahmin; but she could not see his features. She shuddered as the scene of blood appeared once more before her eyes; but her spirit seemed to rise within her as the time passed. At home, and since the summons, she had often felt anxious and nervous; but as her hour of trial came near, all feeling of apprehension had passed away. She might be ashamed before the magistrate; but she had a solemn duty to do, and was fearless. Then they saw the magistrate, a tall, fair young man, with a quick, strong step, pass from his private tent into the public Kucherry; and after an interval of almost breathless silence among them, a messenger came forward and cried in a loud voice, "Seeta, widow of Huree Das, appear in court and give your testimony!" And the party arose and followed him.

There had been some previous depositions and other papers read, such as the verdict of the inquest, the police reports from Gokulpoor, the depositions of the goldsmiths of Noorpoor, and others; and the magistrate was examining the signature of Seeta's summons with a curious interest. The characters, "Seeta, widow of Huree Das," were very delicate and beautiful; he had never seen such before, and he marvelled that a woman could have written them. "Surely they are not her own," he said to his Serishtadar, or head officer. "No woman could write like this."

"She is a strange girl," he replied, "and people say she is very learned. Yes, the signature is her own doubtless; no man could write like that." And hearing this, Cyril Brandon only wondered the more. "What would she be like?" In his own mind he had concluded that Seeta would be in no wise different from other women of her class; quiet, modest, and timid, yet in no degree interesting; and having directed her to be called in, he looked round.

The tent was a large one. At one side of it were the prisoners, now sitting on the ground, guarded by police Sepoys;

on the other, the scribes and officers of the court were seated writing. Near Mr. Brandon were his Serishtadar, a quick-handed scribe to write depositions, and a pleader from Noorpoor, who attended on behalf of the prisoners in general, and of the Brahmin in particular. Cyril Brandon was seated before a small table, on which were writing materials and a book for reference.

As Seeta and her aunt entered with the priest and her grandfather, the tent door was somewhat darkened; but as she took the place assigned to her, the light from without fell full upon her, and the young magistrate thought he had never seen any woman more lovely. He could, indeed, scarcely suppress an exclamation of surprise; but he checked himself, and holding up the summons, said gently, "Seeta, the widow of Huree Das, is this your signature?"

"It is mine," she said modestly, raising her eyes to his. "With my own hand I wrote it, and I come of my own free will."

The large dewy eyes were soft and pleading, but not irresolute, and the girl was quite calm. Seeta had dressed herself in a rich silk saree of a green colour, shot with crimson, which had heavy borders and ends of gold thread, and the end, which she had passed over her head, fell on her right arm and contrasted vividly with its fair colour and rounded outline. If her features were not exactly regular, they were very sweet and full of expression; her eyes were large and soft, of that clear dark brown which, like a dog's, is always so loving and true. If the mouth were a shade too full for exact symmetry, it was mobile and expressive, and the curves of the upper lip constantly varied. For a native woman, Cyril Brandon had never seen any one so fair or of so tender a tone of colour. Such, he remembered, were many of the lovely women of Titian's pictures—a rich golden olive, with a bright carnation tint rising under the skin—and Seeta's was like them. One in particular came to his memory like a flash—the wife of the Duc d'Avalos, in the Louvre picture; or Titian's Daughter, carrying fruits and flowers, at Berlin. He could not see much of Seeta's figure; but the small, graceful head, the rounded arm, the tiny foot, the graceful movement of the neck, and her springy lithe step as she had entered the tent, assured him that it could not be less beautiful than the face. It was curious, too, that all present in the court had been excited, and a sound as if of a long-drawn breath had gone out even from some of the prisoners, who still sat on the floor.

"You are called, lady," said Cyril Brandon, "to speak to painful circumstances; but fear not, you are under the protection of the law, and no one can harm you. You must affirm in God's presence that you will speak the truth, without fear and without prejudice. What is your age, and where do you live?"

"I will speak the truth," she said calmly, "before the gods and you. I have no fear. What I saw I will tell. I am seventeen years old, and I live now with my grandfather, who is present."

"Will you be seated?" he asked, when this was recorded.

"No," she said, "I am not tired, and would rather stand," and so was told to proceed.

We know so much already of what she had to say, that there is little occasion to repeat it. Seeta narrated how she had spent the day at Shah Gunje, how her grandfather had sent her home in his palankeen, and how she had employed herself till the evening, when Ram Das came in. She had not heard all that he had said; but she had seen her husband tear up a paper, and set fire to it; and that Ram Das had tried to snatch it from him, but had been held back, and there was a slight struggle, after which Ram Das rose up in anger, and went away. She was vexed, she said, and anxious, because there had been already so many altercations between them; but her husband made light of it, told her to go to rest, and went to work at some ornaments that were needed; and it was, perhaps, midnight when he ceased. By his desire she had laid his bedding in the outer verandah, where he sat by day; but she did not go to him for some time, as she was tending her child.

"I could not account for it," she continued; and we may now follow her deposition. "I was sad and could not sleep; and I took the boy and sat down beside my husband, and kept the musquitoes from him. I don't know how the night passed; but I was wide awake, and was waiting till sleep should come to me. After some time I heard a cry and a groan a long way off, and I had nearly awakened my husband, but nothing followed, and I was tranquil again. By this time the moon had risen, yet there was not much light. Then I heard a noise as if the outer gate were shaken; but I said to myself, it is only the watchmen, Rama and Boodoo, and I felt no fear. And there was silence again, perhaps for five minutes. Then came the sound of treading feet. I thought it might be our people coming in from watching in the fields; but no one spoke.

"Then the sound came nearer—nearer, nearer!" said the girl, with strange action and emphasis; "I pulled at my husband, but he only turned over and said, 'Let me sleep, Seeta,' and he would not awake. Then I saw a man's head appear suddenly over the wall, about as high as that!"—and she stretched forth her arm—"above me and before me. I tried to cry out, but my tongue was parched, my mouth was dry. I could not speak or scream, I could not pray. I was as one stricken with dumbness. I only pulled at my husband the more, and he pushed my hand away. Then the man, who I am sure saw me, leaped down on the roof of the guard shed, then to the ground, and cut the wooden bar of the door in two with his axe; and then, and then only, did my husband awake and rise. 'Away, Seeta!' he cried, as he snatched down his sword, 'save the child;' and as he spoke, four men with blazing torches rushed in, followed by others, all with muffled faces. I do not know how many. My husband met them at the head of the steps, with his sword in his hand, and made a blow at the leading man, who was very tall, and stout like him; the men with the torches were on each side of the steps. I had run into the oratory, the door of which was not closed, and I could see everything as if it were day. I had my boy in my arms, and he was fast asleep; he rested, as he does now, on my hip. It was but a moment, when I saw my husband struck by the tall man in the chest with a spear, and others struck him also. He staggered back covered with blood, and fell towards me. I tried to catch him, but he was too heavy, and I fell with him, I believe. I think, sir, now, that he was then dead, for he never moved that I remember."

She appeared to pause, and Cyril Brandon asked her kindly whether she would not have water.

"No, sir," she said; "I have not much more to tell, and the scribe does not confuse me. He writes exactly what I say, does he not?"

"Exactly," he replied: "word for word as you speak. Go on."

Then she continued: "I thought he was not dead, and had only fainted, and I know not what put it into my mind, but I took my saree thus"—and she let down the end from her head, and held it out in her hands—"and stepped over my husband, and entreated the men to give him to me as a bridal gift, for the sake of their mothers and their children. O, I implored them to hear me for my child's sake! You know, sir, I could not make a more solemn appeal, and our fathers have told us that it is never refused. Ah, sir! they did refuse it—they did refuse my cry!" and for the first time, Brandon saw the tears rolling down her cheeks.

"The tall man sprang forward with a muttered curse, and he and two others struck their spears into my husband's body many times; while a Dacoit, ere I had ceased speaking—another man—made a lunge at me with his spear, which wounded me in the side, and my boy in the leg. Look, sir, here is the scar of my wound," and she raised her saree from her arm for Brandon to see it; "and here is my boy's wound too; look at it, sir. I am only speaking the truth before you and God.

"Then I lay as if dead, though I saw all that happened. One of the men came and tore my necklace from my breast; another tried to loosen my anklets, and took one. I see it on the table now, and this is the fellow-one;" and she stooped down and loosened one from her ankle. "Compare them, sir. My grandfather gave them to me, and he and my husband made them with their own hands, and put marks on them. Then, as the man was pulling at the other anklet, I heard a shot without, and a great clamour; and the tall man inside came out: and as he moved, he lifted his bloody spear to strike me again. I was quite conscious, and saw a gold rim round it glancing in the light, and there were gold dots on it."

"Would you recognize it if you saw it again?" asked Brandon.

"I think so; nay, I am sure I should," she said, firmly; "there were two gold rings and some dots between; and I had seen them while the man was digging the floor with a pickaxe and had put down his spear; the blade was close to me."

"Is this it, lady?" asked Brandon. "Show it to her, one of ye."

Seeta shuddered visibly; but, looking at Asráel Pandé's spear, the weapon found on him at Noorpoor, she said, in a firm clear voice, "That is the spear; here are the gold rims round the shaft, and the gold dots between. Yes, it was that by which my husband was killed."

"And were you wounded by it?"

"No, sir, that was a long narrow blade; but I should know it, I am sure, if I saw it."

"Let this weapon be sent for," said Brandon; "they ought all to have been here. Have you more to tell?" he enquired of Seeta; "if so, proceed."

"I have said that the tall man lifted his spear upon me," she continued; "but as he did so, a man next him said in a cracked, squeaking voice, 'Do not strike a dead woman, master; I killed her myself;' and so they passed on. I owe my life, sir, to that man, and should know his voice among a thousand." As she spoke, one of the prisoners, who had stood in the centre of the row of twelve, by a desperate effort and in spite of his irons, rushed across the tent floor and threw himself at Seeta's feet, with his arms spread out, sobbing and crying in almost a child's squeaking treble, "It was I, lady, it was I; O save me! for I saved you and the child. O, I will tell all! I will tell all! whether I live or die, I will tell all!"

"Sir," exclaimed Seeta, again sobbing, "that is his voice—that is the man. O spare him for my sake, and the child's whom he savêd!" and she held out her saree as she had done before.

If there was one time more than another in the course of her deposition in which Brandon had been struck with the wondrous beauty and spirit of the girl, it was now. With her eyes sparkling with excitement, her cheeks wet with tears, her head bare, her bosom heaving, her arms stretched out to him, her figure poised on her advanced foot, pleading to him—entreating him to spare the man who had spared her! Such a scene might be told in a romance, he thought, but here was very grave reality.

"I will make him an approver, and his life is safe if he is true and faithful," returned Brandon; "and now look round, lady," he continued, "look on the prisoners, and see if you recognize any of them. Put them one by one in the broad light, sepoy, that she may see them plainly."

Seeta looked at them, one by one, but shook her head. Azráel Pandé was the last but two in the row, and she paused before him. "This is the Oudh Brahmin," she said, "who recited in our house the day before the Dacoity, and in that of Ram Das the day before that. I remember him perfectly; he has jagged teeth. If he, indeed, was the owner of the spear, let it be decided whether he killed my husband, or another. And O, sir!" she continued to Brandon, "when the tall man spoke to that man in the oratory"—and she pointed to the prisoner who had cried out to her—"he said these words, 'They dare not close with us, the cowards; but we must go—come away.' If you will get him to repeat these words, I shall know the voice; but I was almost certain then, that it was that of the Brahmin who recited 'Savitri' to me the day before."

Azráel did not speak. His adviser told him to be silent; but the prisoner, Buldeo Singh, was irrepressible: "He said them to me—he said them to me," he cried, "just as he raised his spear to strike her. How true she is!"

"Silence in the court!" cried Brandon; for a murmur of wonder and admiration had arisen. "There must be no speaking or demonstration. Let the witness's deposition be read over, and let her sign it and depart; that is," he added to the pleader, "if you have no questions."

"I have none to this witness," he replied; "I shall cross-examine her on the trial."

Then Seeta's evidence was read over to her, and she said it was correct; and sitting down, she took the paper, and in the same handwriting as before wrote, "Seeta, the widow of Hureo Das. This is the truth."

"You may take her home, Narendra," said Mr. Brandon, "and be proud of her all your life. Never before, in the course of my experience, have I heard evidence given so clearly, so firmly, or so minutely. I honour her, sir, and every one in this court sympathizes with her, and with you."

The old man broke down fairly; but he said at last, "To say we are grateful for your courtesy, sir, is little. I would we knew how to show it. I thank you, sir, on the part of my granddaughter, most humbly." And as the old man spoke, Brandon thought he saw a soft expression of gratitude on the girl's face and in her eyes, which he had not seen before, as she passed out. Should he ever see her again? Most likely never; for the trial would be held at Noorpoor, and he would perhaps be far away.

He had yet much to do, and many other witnesses had to be examined. Of these, perhaps, Wamun Bhut, who swore distinctly to the prisoner Azráel, to his having lived in the temple close by till the afternoon of the Dacoity, and to Buldeo and three other men, who were in attendance on him then—was the most important.

So next day the case was completed, and eleven of the gang committed for trial at the Noorpoor court. One, Buldeo, was held back as Queen's evidence, and the case at Shah Gunje closed; but to the last day of his life, Seeta's testimony was not forgotten by Mr. Brandon.

"I told you, grandfather, and you, Aunt Ella, that I should not fail," said Seeta, with flashing eyes, as she went out; "and now it is done, and he was kind to me. And was not the boy a hero? Did he blench from the trial?" But they were too much moved to reply.

CHAPTER IX.

SOCIETY AT NOORPOOR.

THE Honourable Cyril Brandon was at present Acting Deputy Commissioner of the Noorpoor District. He was in reality the first assistant; but his superior officer, Major Grant, broken down by long-continued illness, had gone to Calcutta on leave of absence, and had written to say he should proceed to England, if permitted to do so, on sick leave. Mr. Brandon had, therefore, the prospect of a long incumbency. He was descended from an ancient family which was possessed of considerable estates in ——shire; and Hylton Hall, the family seat, a noble specimen of the Tudor style of domestic architecture, was one of the show places of the county. In the reign of Queen Anne, George Hylton, conspicuous for his loyalty and important local services, was raised to the peerage under the title of Baron Hylton, of Hylton. Many thought, in consideration of the antiquity and proud local position of the family, that the acceptance of a peerage was unnecessary and derogatory, and might have been avoided or declined; but the person on whom it was conferred was an ardent loyalist, and held that compliance with the wish of his Sovereign was his true test of duty. Cyril Brandon's father, Cyril, was the youngest of two brothers; the eldest, John, held the title and estates, which, having been encumbered by heavy mortgages in the lives of his father and grandfather, were considerably reduced in income, and afforded only a comparatively small allowance to Cyril, the youngest, who, being educated for the Bar, had succeeded fairly, and with his allowance from the estate and his wife's fortune, lived comfortably in London and on the Continent by turns.

John, Lord Hylton, had married; but his wife was delicate, and she eventually died childless. About four years before the date of this history, Lord Hylton had also died, and his brother Cyril had succeeded him. If this event could have been foreseen, it is most probable that he would have provided otherwise for his second son than by sending him to Haileybury College, and allowing him to enter the Civil Service of India; but the young Cyril had chosen this profession deliberately. India, and its history and people, had always fascinated him: and he studied the great characters who had gained fame there, and burned to emulate them. In England there appeared to be no chance of distinction except by a lifelong strife. He might accept an annuity from his father, and take his chance at the Bar, in the army, or even in the church. He was offered help in any of these professions; but he chose the Indian Civil Service in preference to all, and after some opposition on the part of his mother, was allowed to do as he wished.

About two years ago, his father, who had been always somewhat delicate, suddenly drooped and died; and he was succeeded by his eldest son, John, the present Lord Hylton, who, with his mother and sisters, Florence and Augusta, made up the number of the family. Florence was older than Cyril, and had married early, indeed before he went to India. Augusta, several years younger than himself, was still unmarried. There had been two children between Cyril and her, one of whom, a boy, had died as a child; the other, Julia, after giving great promise of beauty and talent, fell into a consumption, and had died shortly before her father, and many thought that this event had hastened his end.

So it was, that Cyril Brandon had come to India; at first as plain Mr. Brandon, but assuming, on his father's succession to the title, the distinction of Honourable, according to custom. It is not necessary for me to follow his progress in India. If even he had been unconnected with the peerage, his strong talent would have soon won him a good position. He had studied hard at Haileybury; carried off repeated prizes in Sanscrit, of which he was very fond, and in Persian, law, and other branches of the college course; and his perfect acquaintance with French and Italian, gained as a boy in the frequent residence of his father at Paris, Florence, and Rome, gave him a great advantage over his fellow-students in regard to modern languages. He was deficient, no doubt, in Greek and Latin: but had gained enough of both to preserve him from actual failure. He was an excellent draughtsman and artist: and his mother, herself an admirable musician, had had him well taught at Florence, both to play and to sing.

Under the effects of successful examination at Calcutta, therefore, the influence of many, and perhaps unusual, accomplishments, and a pleasant cheerful manner and presence, combined with the strong interest of his family connection, young Brandon was offered his choice of the department he would serve in; and under the advice of a friend, who held a high official position, he chose the Non-Regulation Provinces, as affording the best field for exertion. "Think for yourself, act for yourself," wrote his friend; "never fear responsibility, and when you can see your way to an improvement, state it boldly, and you may be sure that the present head of the Government will not fail to support you, and will notice you when you least expect it."

Cyril Brandon had now been six years in India. He had landed a thin, spare youth, with, as his mother thought, a delicate constitution. Indeed, she had feared for him if he remained in England: and the greatest reason for her compliance with Cyril's ardent desire to serve in India was, that he would grow up in a warm climate. He had now passed over the crisis, and from the first his health had been perfect. He was tall, extremely well made, and graceful in his movements. His features were not perhaps strictly regular, yet he was, no doubt, very handsome. What you saw at once were a broad, white forehead, over which his glossy brown hair clustered in heavy waves, strong eyebrows, with very clear, earnest blue eyes, shaded by long dark eyelashes, a pleasant mouth, a bright complexion, very white teeth, with a full chin, in which, and in the face generally, there was much character and determination. He wore both moustache and beard, of a rich brown, soft and curly; and his complexion, always pale in England, was now ruddy and healthy. The climate of the high plateau on which his district was situated, was, for India, bracing and genial, and had suited him exactly. From the first he had followed field sports with ardour, and there was no better shot, either with gun or rifle, and no bolder rider in the country.

Among the native people of his district, he had already become even more than popular. His never-failing affability and good temper, his cheerful patience, his ready accessibility, even to the most humble, his evident desire for the improvement and advancement of all classes, and his efforts, as much as lay in his power, to soften down the hard mechanical actions and rules of official life—had won him, as I have said, more than ordinary popularity; and as he became better known, year by year, the fine qualities of his character had become more and more appreciated. He did not know it, but many a dame, humble as she might be, repeated his name with that of her household gods each night, as she lighted the lamp before the simple shrine of her faith, and taught her children to say it. Many a rude village poet had written ballads, and the minstrels had sung them to his praise, at village festivals. He had perfectly acquired the common vernacular dialect of his province, and spoke it almost as one of the people; and he was able to read and answer his ordinary letters without difficulty or error.

Cyril Brandon had many native friends of all classes. He

had studied their manners and customs very deeply, and the people were therefore perfectly at ease with him; but he was so strict and so impartial in his duties, that no one ever dreamed of taking a liberty. He never permitted flattery, which few dared attempt. Perhaps Cyril's high birth and family, which were known to all soon after he arrived in the district, helped him considerably; for there is indeed no point on which natives of India are more curious, and none which, when joined with other qualities, so soon or so completely influences popular estimation, as gentle descent; and Cyril's justice and generosity, and the sweet charm of his manner, blending the real with their ideal, won all hearts. He had enemies no doubt, as who has not? for he had put down crime with a strong unswerving hand, as far as he could trace it; and he was equally stern in the suppression of all petty exaction, oppression, and peculation. While he admired the simple habits, the charity, the devotion, and faith one to another, in many relations of life among the people, yet their faults were equally prominent to him; and while his official duties necessarily brought out the strongest points of deceit and crime, he would turn, with never-failing appreciation, to the higher qualities by which he was surrounded.

I wish, I wish heartily, that there were more men like Cyril Brandon, though there are still many. Such as he had won the highest honours of Indian administration, had been rulers of millions of the people, had led armies and conquered, and still lived as household words in the thoughts and memories of all creeds and classes. Not such, however, are the men who declare India to be "an infernal hole;" who speak and think contemptuously of its people, who deny them their sympathy and help, who hold them as "niggers" and "black fellows," as if they were negro savages, who override them haughtily, who despise and refuse their society, and never even attempt their friendship, and consider themselves demeaned by any concession to their manners or long-existing customs. Are not these men understood? Surely they are, and despised also! and alas! that only too many such have sprung up in these latter days, who, in their arrogance, deem themselves wiser than those good and great men, who set a mark upon their times which will ever live in the annals of India's history.

If the sketch I have given of Cyril Brandon be appreciated by the reader—and it is no ideal portrait—he will understand, perhaps, how Narendra and his granddaughter had been affected by his simple courtesy and kindness, and how, as they returned home, they had reviewed every incident of the day. How proud were Narendra and Aunt Ella of their child! how proud was Seeta of her boy! Every now and then Aunt Ella had taken him from his mother, and had tried to amuse him; but the little fellow seemed to think that his place was by his mother, and he was restless until he got to her again. Never had Narendra seen so much of the magistrate before. Occasionally, with other members of his guild, he had paid an official visit, but little passed then. Now he could converse freely with Wamun Bhut about him; and I think the evening game of chess, as Seeta sat by listening to all they said, was badly played by both. The priest had lived more among the people at large than Narendra, and had heard more than he. Now, he told many a pleasant tale of Cyril's justice, and many, many an incident of daring in the pursuit and capture of robber gangs, and the slaughter of tigers by the brave young magistrate. Many a proof too of the respect and love in which he was held by all classes. And Seeta listened wonderingly. Then he was a scholar, as well; and Baba Sahib, the Serishtadar, had told him how he had found his master reading the "Bhugwut Geeta" and other Sanskrit books far into the night, and had often to help him, or send for a Pundit to do so. And all this sank into Seeta's heart.

The day after, they had to go again to the Kucherry, and Seeta had selected a narrow spear with a long double-edged blade, as the weapon by which she had been wounded, from among a heap of arms shown to her, which was declared to be the property of one of the prisoners, and had been found in his house. Narendra and the priest had to be cross-examined by the pleader, who tried to browbeat them, but in vain; and the presence of Azráel Pandé in Shah Gunje on the day of the Dacoity, and before that, was sworn to by many witnesses. In short, the preliminary evidence was complete. Several other members of the gang had since been arrested, and were in the Noorpoor jail: Seeta and others, as a matter of form, had been bound over to appear, and the case was formally committed for trial at Noorpoor. But Ram Das had escaped, at least for the present.

The society at Noorpoor was much like what exists in other English stations of the same class where the civil and military are combined; and we may see something of it by-and-by. A good deal of excitement had been caused by the recent arrival of a young lady from England, Miss Home, who had joined her parents, Dr. Home being the chief surgeon of the station. The mess of the —— native infantry had arranged to welcome her by a ball; and an invitation had come to Cyril, whose camp was now not far from the station—at least within easy riding distance. Writing therefore to his friend Mostyn that he should come to stay a day or two with him, Cyril rode into Noorpoor on the morning of the ball, called on some of his friends after breakfast, and took his "tiffin" or lunch at the mess; but he saw few of the ladies, who, it may well be supposed, were deep in the mysteries of their several toilettes. Not that there were many ladies either, and of them only a small proportion danced; but there were two unmarried ones present, and to them the certainty of the appearance of Cyril Brandon at the ball was put forth by those to whom they belonged with much emphasis.

"My darling," said Mrs. Home, rushing into her fair daughter's room as Cyril had just left the house, "he *is* coming to the ball, for I heard him tell your father so; now, mind you are careful."

"Of what, mamma?" asked Lucy, looking round—she was helping the domestic tailor to take the creases out of a rumpled grenadine dress, which had not been improved by its journey from England.

"Why, of Mr. Brandon, my pet," she replied; "you know he is an Honourable, and the brother of Lord Hylton, and his mother is Lady Hylton."

"Well, I suppose she is," said the girl, laughing; "what in the world does it matter to me? I wish you would explain to this stupid man that I don't want the dress pawed, and I can't make him understand."

"Never mind the dress, Lucy; it will be the best there, and you will be the prettiest girl. If—if Mr. Brandon now should notice you, Lucy, don't check him, don't snub him—you are very fond, I think, of snubbing young men, even when——"

"When they are staff officers, mamma!" she said, demurely, and with a low curtsey, "as you told me the other day. Oh no! I could not think of doing such a thing to the 'Honourable Cyril;' but I dare say he is as great a bore as any of them, talking of nothing but what the men of 'Ours' do, and their horses, and the mess, and tigers, and pigs; but if he *is* nice, may I dance two or three times with him?"

"You may dance twice, but not more the first time, my dear," replied her mother; "so be careful."

But Lucy Home did find Cyril Brandon very different to the rest of her male acquaintances: and she interested him, too, considerably. She was very pretty, had a very interesting, soft, expressive face, and a good figure. She looked like a lady, and was by far the best-dressed person in the room; indeed, I should hardly like to describe the faded and tumbled condition of many of the ladies' garments, for fear of being called ill-natured. Cyril Brandon had not felt himself obliged to dance the first quadrille, which consisted of twelve couples—the twelfth being made up by two youngsters of one of the regiments—so he stood looking on, chatting to Mostyn. I am afraid they were both somewhat free in their remarks in regard to some of the ladies. However, when the quadrille was ended, Cyril went up to Mrs. Home and begged to be introduced to her daughter—a ceremony which afforded her sincere pleasure. He had been attracted by Lucy's good style, and asked her for the first waltz. Lucy bowed her acceptance, and they went away together. Mrs. Home watched them as they flew round the room to one of Gungl's best waltzes; and certainly they were a remarkably handsome couple. Even Mostyn, who looked on, said to himself, "He might do worse than take her, and if they don't try to fling her at his head, he may."

They did not converse much while they were dancing; but when the waltz ceased, Cyril took Lucy to a seat, a long way from her mother, and sat down by her. Then they began to talk of common things, of ordinary books, of pictures, and of music. I should have written he, instead of they, for Cyril had gone over all the subjects he could think of, in the hope of interesting or exciting her; but she had replied very little, so little that he attributed it to natural shyness; and when she had finished another quadrille with a captain of Irregular Cavalry, Cyril asked her for the ensuing galop, and danced it with her. Certainly, for the time, he was interested, and the girl's sweet pleading face told him he had interested her; but he felt there was no echo of what he had spoken of—none. She had not read much, she said, only school-books. She did not draw. She had never seen pictures except when Uncle John had once taken her to the Exhibition in London, but she remembered none of them. She was very fond of hearing music, she said, but she played a very little, and could never learn difficult pieces or sing in parts. Yes, she had learned some ballads of Claribel's and others, which were very sweet; but they did not teach her more, and perhaps she did not care enough about music to teach herself any. Novels? Oh no; her aunt would never let her read novels at home; but the girls at school had some, which were delicious, and she had read some in the station library. Perhaps we need not further dilate upon Lucy Home's accomplishments, which were indeed but too few. French? She only knew it from her exercises, she said, but could not speak it. Italian? Oh, not at all! I believe Cyril would have gone on with his quiet cross-questioning, which did not appear to disturb his partner in the least; but he became ashamed of it, and rattled on to her of matters of station life, told her he lived like a wild Indian, which perhaps she partly believed, and proposed another war-dance, as he called it, which was a polka mazurka, and which he danced after a wild German fashion. Then he took her in to supper.

Mamma did not interfere; she was, indeed, in the highest condition of delight; but other matrons thought Lucy a terrible flirt, and the captain of Irregular Cavalry had stood beside one of the doors gnawing his moustachios in cruel vexation. Why, he thought he had made some impression, but that fellow Brandon with his airs——

"Well, mamma," asked Lucy, when they got home, and she was undressing, "did I snub him?"

"No, indeed, my darling, you behaved beautifully, but you shouldn't have danced the last mazurka with him; there was that poor Captain Hobson looking quite miserable."

"But oh, mamma, he dances so beautifully and lightly! Hobson can't dance a bit. I couldn't refuse Mr. Brandon."

"What were you talking about, Lucy, so long?"

"Oh, nothing," she said; "only books, and music, and pictures, and all that sort of thing; but he is too clever for me, mamma; I was afraid of him; I could not say a word."

"Nonsense, child," replied her mother; "all I know is that there was no one there to compare with you, and I am sure he thought so too."

"Cyril," said Mostyn, as they walked home, "you have been flirting desperately, young man. What will the matrons say? Is it to be?"

"Don't be a goose, Philip," replied the other, laughing—they always called each other by their Christian names—"I was only picking her brains."

"And did you find anything in them?"

"Much chaff, but no grain," said Cyril; "and yet she is very pleasant, for all that—a relief, you know, after the jungles' monotony."

"Then get you back to them as soon as may be, my dear boy," he replied more gravely, "else you may do her harm and yourself too."

"I will only wait for the mail, which will come in to-morrow, and answer my letters, and then farewell to the fair Lucy. I assure you I talked no nonsense to her; not a bit, upon my honour."

"So much the better," said his friend drily; and they separated for the night.

CHAPTER X.

LETTERS FROM HOME.

The friends were sitting at an early breakfast next morning, when an attendant brought in the letters for both. The English mail had arrived; and setting aside a heap of newspapers and official despatches, Cyril hastily opened "the family budget," as he cheerily called it, and took from it several letters. The first was from his mother. As he read it, Philip Mostyn, who was reading his wife's despatch, thought he saw Cyril's brow contract and his features grow grave as he refolded the letter and put it down.

"No bad news, I hope, Cyril?" he said. "You looked grave as you read."

"Well, I couldn't help it," he returned. "You see, my lady mother has lost so many of us, and my father too, that she is getting all sorts of fancies into her dear old head about Hylton, and thinks he is delicate; and then she writes me a sermon about speculative young ladies, and implores me to avoid them—just as if——"

"You hadn't been flirting with Lucy Home all last night. Eh, Cyril? Oh, not at all. You needn't blush."

"Don't talk nonsense," was the reply. "What did I tell you last night? I did not talk nonsense; and upon my word, Philip," continued Cyril, "now that I think of it, I am quite ashamed of my 'Mangnall's Questions' sort of examination; but when she said she knew nothing I could not believe her, and went on trying to find out whether she did not know something. It was too bad, wasn't it?"

"Ah!" said Mostyn, "that is the sad fate of too many of the bright children we Indians send home. We think, and are told, that they are being taught everything, and too many of them return to us knowing nothing. But what does it matter after all?"

"Not matter?" cried Cyril. "Why?"

"Well, there is an example in point in poor Lucy. She is

very pretty, very; so lady-like too, and dances like a fairy. She can sing a song or two tolerably, and play a waltz or a quadrille, but is no musician; and upon my word I believe that's all. She has evidently no æsthetic tastes, but she is a capital hand at worsted-work and crochet, for I saw some of it myself. She appears very good-natured, too, and bears with that dreadful old mother of hers sweetly. Perhaps she won't object to sew buttons on her husband's shirts when she gets one, and so she need be in no fear of a long spinsterhood."

"You are horribly satirical, Philip."

"I am only speaking the truth," he replied. "If all men in India were as æsthetic—that's the word, isn't it?—as you, girls would have to be specially educated for them in England, and we should have flights of blue-stockings coming out by every mail. But they are not, you know; and so girls like Lucy Home do very well, and settle down into capital wives. What do you want more?"

"Well, I want something more, certainly. But let us see what my lord has to say. I hope he's not as croaky as my mother. There," he continued, after a time, "that does not read like a sick man's letter." And he threw it across the table. "You may read it all, Philip."

It was a record of good sport, and hearty enjoyment of it. Lord Hylten had done well on the Moors in August, and was then anticipating good sport with the partridges at Hylton. There would be plenty of pheasants too, and they would have a pleasant party. Because he had caught cold last winter, and had a bad cough, his mother chose to be anxious, and wanted him to go to Nice! But the whole thing was absurd, and he looked forward to the hunting with a determination to enjoy it. "As to your coming home, which my lady is always thinking of," ran one sentence, "don't think of it on my account; and unless you like, or need, to come, stay where you are. I think you would get tired of England in a month, and long to be back among your own people. What would I not give to be with you one cold season and shoot tigers!"

"A very good letter," said Mostyn, as he handed it back, "and there is no sign of failing health in it. But I hope, Cyril, you are not thinking of going to England; it would be madness to give up your chance here. I had a letter from Calcutta yesterday, and my friend —— mentions that he had seen Grant put on board the steamer with no hope of life, only the barest chance, and you are sure to succeed him."

"I trust he may recover with all my heart," said Cyril:

"but when he comes out again it will be quite time for me to think of a change home. Till then, nothing will induce me to go; and if anything happened to poor Grant, and I am appointed, there is really so much to do. No, I shall write to my mother to-day and tell her I cannot come."

"That will be better than going to call on Miss Lucy," returned Mostyn; "but I must be off to Kucherry, and I leave you to your chat with my lady. Of course you will tell her that you danced six dances last night with the prettiest girl——"

"Will you be quiet?" cried Cyril. But Mostyn had fled, after discharging this parting shot.

Cyril thought for awhile before going to his room to write. He had lighted a cigar, and went out into the verandah to one of the luxurious chairs which were always there, and smoked in peace and quiet. He felt no anxiety for his brother, whose strong, manly writing and its cheerful tone he read again, and put the letter into his pocket with a sigh of thankfulness. "I will tell him to get a wife and settle down," he said, "for we all desire to see him happy; and he might do so, now that the estate is lightened of its load." Then there was Augusta's letter to read; and that sprightly young lady, after a detail of some balls and parties, had taken up her mother's injunctions against marriage in India and wrote thus:—

"*I* don't urge you to come home, Cyril; you are very happy and very useful where you are; and though we should be *delighted* to have you, I for one—and John is quite of my opinion—should be miserable if you came home and gave up your work while your heart is in it. Still we have our fears, mamma and I; and I quite share her dread of your marrying and settling there. We feel how lonely you must often be, with nobody but natives about you; and we fear lest some bright damsel, who might come to Noorpoor, should captivate you and take you from us. Don't be angry with me for writing this, for mamma is *really* anxious about it, and frets herself, darling old thing. No, dearest brother! by-and-by you shall come home and take your choice. I have fully determined on being one of your wife's bridesmaids, and I will wait patiently till the time comes. If you were to marry out there, what should we know of *her* people? They might be *horrors*, you know. But enough of this. I would, I declare, rather you married an Indian princess than *any* of the young ladies who go out—the lovely Ranee Gowreepoolee, if you like, who no doubt is first cousin to the great Panjandrum."

So Cyril, having finished his cigar, went into his room to write, and we, who are privileged, may look over his letters and see part of what he wrote to his mother:—

"I cannot come home," he said, "and you would not wish to see me if you knew all I had to do, and how unfavourably such a step might influence my future prospects. Grant, poor fellow, owing to his weak state of health, has left the affairs here in much arrear. The authorities are urgent with me to set them to rights, and I will, I must do it. There are a thousand things wanted: roads, bridges, schools, dispensaries, police reform, and revenue reform; but I may spare you the detail, which you could not follow. If poor Grant were to die—and I have heard the worst accounts of him—I think I should succeed him, for my friends would not forget me, and I know Lord Dalhousie has put a good mark against my name. In any case I am safe, God willing, as acting for Grant for two years, and I can do much in that time—not all, perhaps, that I wish, but a good deal; and should he return, and there is then nothing else to do, we can discuss the subject again—not before. For myself I should prefer not returning till my first ten years are over, and I can demand my furlough. And altogether, when you think the matter over, I am sure you will agree with me. As to John, he has written me the heartiest letter I ever got from him, and there is not a trace or a sign of failing in it; so I pray that he may be spared to us many, many years, and that he may soon marry and be happy.

"As to myself, dear mother, do not be anxious on that score. In a station like Noorpoor, girls come and go, of course—many have come and gone; but I want none of them. My work is wife and children to me. I live in it, I love it, and there is no room for a wife in my mind—none in my occupations, none in my designs. What could I do with a wife in my constant travels about in this rough country? She would either have to stay alone at Noorpoor, or be sent to the Hills. I have seen enough of such miserable separations not to attempt them myself, or expose one I loved to them. I shall write the same to Augusta, who has delivered a homily to me after her own fashion, and says I may marry a Ranee if I like—not one of your dreaded young ladies; and I am quite of her opinion, only I don't see where the Ranee is to come from, or know where her cousin, the great Panjandrum, lives; else I might leave a card on him. Don't be angry with this foolishness, dearest mother, but content yourself with my assurance that I am as much afraid of speculative young ladies as you are!

"I wish you could see how beautiful my dominions are at present. The weather is like an English spring, and I can ride or shoot at all hours. But I have not been shooting lately. I was obliged to go to a distant part of my district, to investigate a horrible case of murder and Dacoity, which has created an unusual sensation, as the person murdered was a very respectable and even wealthy person. I had never been there before, as that portion of the country was under poor Grant; but I enjoyed it greatly, and the scenery is quite indescribably beautiful. There are deep glens breaking down from the table-land, covered with wood, and giving the loveliest views of the low country far away. There are waterfalls and precipices, forests which seem to have no limit; and where the country is open, such fertile plains and undulating ground, studded with thriving towns and villages! O that I could show them to you! and indeed for a while my wild life would be pleasant to you, though you would soon tire of it. I have to go there again soon, for I want to lay out a road, and to have a dispensary and hospital built at Shah Gunje; and you know I have to be my own surveyor, and civil engineer, and architect, and all sorts of things. I shall have plenty of shooting too, for nobody has interfered with the tigers there as yet, and there are abundance of them, with bears and panthers, and deer; and if I have time I can perhaps, get to where the bison are. I should like to send you a skin and a head of one for the hall. Don't be anxious about my health. I assure you I am a great, big, stout fellow, with rosy cheeks, a thick beard, and a noble appetite; and the more I am out after game of all kinds, the better for me. Some day or other I will take notes of one day's work of all sorts, and when I have time write them out for you. I think they will amuse you immensely. Now, I can't write more, for I have to answer John's and Augusta's letters, and have a heap of officials to reply to besides. I am not in the station for good, only for the day, and shall ride out to my camp in the morning, which is thirty miles off. I only came in for a ball, and was dancing—with a very pretty partner too—till two o'clock this morning! What will you say to such gay doings at Noorpoor?"

"Well, have you finished your despatches?" asked Mostyn, as he returned from his Kucherry in the afternoon. "You have had a quiet day, I hope, and no one to disturb you. Now I shall sit down and have a smoke, to soothe my nerves. Come and talk; you have written enough."

"I have written to them all, and even told the mother that

I had been dancing with a very pretty girl till two o'clock in the morning. Was not that valiant?"

"Very," said Mostyn. "And you didn't go and see her—on the sly, you know? *pour faire les adieux?*"

"No," replied Cyril, laughing, "I leave that to you, on my behalf, to morrow. Go, my dear fellow, and tell her all sorts of stories of work, work, work; and that I am departed out of sight for many a day—gone to the wild Indian life I told her of. And I hope Captain Hobson and she will have settled everything before I return."

"I hope so too," said Mostyn. "Hobson is a very good, kind fellow, and she could not do better than take him. If my wife now were here, she would have it all over in a fortnight. Yes, I will go to-morrow and make your excuses. I am not afraid of Lucy; but I know mamma will hate me for ever and a day. 'For ever and a day I wears a green will-il-low,'" he sang dolefully. "Oh dear! Oh dear! And you really go to-morrow, Cyril?"

"Yes, I have ordered my horse to be ready at four o'clock," he replied. "And please tell your Khansaman to get a cup of coffee ready for me."

"Of course, of course, and some hot toast. They shall be ready. But I had hoped you would stay for that Gokulpoor trial. I have been reading over the papers to-day. By Jove, what a case it is! and what evidence that girl Seeta gave! I never read anything like it. She will come to the trial, I hope."

"I think so," said Cyril; "nay, I am sure of it; and if she gives the same evidence before you as she did to me, you will be as much surprised as I was. I shall never forget that morning of her first examination. Even old I'·bá Sahib was moved to tears, and I can't say much for my own eyes."

"Indeed! Well, I wish you would come in to see how the case goes. I have fixed the trial for this day week; and Noble tells me there may be one or two more apprehended of that desperate gang."

"All that I hope, Philip, is that this trial may break up the Dacoity system in the district. Ordinary crime one can prevent, perhaps; but these systematic combinations, like Thuggee, are hard to break. Here is Noble coming," he continued; "he may tell us something."

"I have got four more of them!" exclaimed that young man, as he ascended the steps. "Hurrah!"

"Where?"

"Oh," said he, "lurking about; one in the town, another in

a village close by, and two more of the Nawab's precious ruffians. They had bolted, it seems, on the first alarm; but the approver said they would come back, and some of those Dacoity police laid hands on them last night very cleverly."

Then they fell to talking of the case, and the district affairs generally, and with these we have no concern; but my readers may like to hear something of Mr. Mostyn, and I will tell what I know.

Philip Mostyn was the judge of the province—judge civil and criminal, and judge of appeal in certain cases. He, too, was of a good English family, but not a noble one. His eldest brother, Edward, held the Mostyn estates, and resided at the family seat, Morton Hall, which was in the same county as that of the Hyltons, but they were some distance asunder. There were two other brothers; one a Chancery barrister in fine practice; the other, the rector of the quiet parish of Morton, the living of which belonged to the family. Mr. Mostyn was at least ten years senior to Cyril Brandon in the service, if not more; but the fact of being fellow-county-men had first drawn them together, and a certain congeniality of mind completed an intimacy which now was like brotherhood. Mostyn had no accomplishments; he was not very æsthetic in his tastes or his pursuits. He could neither play nor draw, though he could sing a little; nor had he the refinement which much of a continental education had imparted to Cyril. He was not a sportsman in a very great sense of the word. His principal amusements and means of taking exercise were in an early game of racquets in the station court, and as many games of billiards on his own beautiful table as he could get any of the youngsters of the force at Noorpoor to play with him, after he came from Kucherry.

But in all that pertained to his official work, Mostyn was a valuable and excellent officer. A good linguist, and deeply read in Hindoo and Mahomedan law, as well as in that of England, his eminently judicial mind led him to clear and practically correct judgments, and there were fewer appeals against them than was the case with most others. His business was never in arrear, and from his high independent character, ability, and profound legal acquirements, it was supposed, with truth, that he would be removed to the highest court when there should be a vacancy. Mostyn possessed the entire respect and confidence of the people of his province; but he was not, so to speak, popular. He might have been so, perhaps, had he served in the miscellaneous department to which Cyril belonged; but he had adopted the judicial line from the first, and this had kept him more apart from the people than others; yet he was courteous to all, and very patient, and these are qualities deeply appreciated by every class in India. There was not a man in the whole province who did not feel that in the Judges' Court all were equal in his estimation; that the chicanery of native pleaders was transparent to him; that exercise of undue influence was impossible; and that every case was safe to be tried on its merits.

Philip Mostyn was married. Before Cyril was ready to come to India, Mostyn had taken his furlough, and had married in England a lady, the daughter of a neighbour of his brother's, and they had gone at once to India. They were at Noorpoor when Cyril arrived there, and was received by them with a warm welcome, which grew into affection.

Mr. Mostyn had heard from his wife by that mail; but beyond telling Cyril, when he asked how she was, and when she was coming out, that she was well, and sent her love to him, he had said nothing. The fact was, that an arrangement, long canvassed, had been made, by which his wife was to bring out with her his half-sister Grace, who was the only offspring of his father's second marriage, and was now nearly eighteen. Mostyn did not mention this in consequence of his *badinage* regarding Miss Home. He thought perhaps it might be misunderstood; but Mrs. Mostyn had written that she was coming out by the next mail, and her husband wished to get over the Dacoity trial before he should be obliged to proceed to Calcutta to meet her.

CHAPTER XI.

A DISCUSSION AND A THEORY.

THE day of the Dacoity trial had arrived, and the case had excited so much public interest on account of the parties concerned, that long ere the hour of assembly the Court House had been crowded, while hundreds of people had assembled without to gather information. The Nawab Dil Khan Bahadoor, of Futtehpoor, had already seated himself near the judge's chair, and his swashbuckler retinue were swaggering about outside. A strong guard of Sepoys was drawn up before the entrance, and inside was a body of police to preserve order. Cyril Brandon had ridden in from his camp early in the morning, and after breakfast the two friends, with Mr. Noble, had proceeded to the court together. There had been some struggle in Cyril's mind as to whether he should attend at the trial or not; but, on reflection, he thought that his presence might give support and encouragement to the girl who had so deeply interested him, and he was very anxious she should not fail. On the conviction and punishment of this desperate gang and its notorious leader—for many particulars of his former life had come to light—the suppression of Dacoity in the province mainly depended, and this was a question he had much at heart. He had therefore come, as he had promised Mostyn he would do, and took a seat apart from him, so as to avoid the appearance of influencing the proceedings in any way. In a short time the clanking of the irons of the prisoners was heard without, and sixteen men were placed in the dock, strongly guarded by police with drawn swords. An Englishman who did not know the customs of Indian procedure would have missed a jury, for Mr. Mostyn tried the case entirely himself.

After the usual preliminaries, which need not be detailed, the first approver who had claimed the protection of the proclamation, Beerbul Singh, was brought into court. His irons had been removed, but he was still guarded. He was called upon to affirm the truth before God, the act of accusation was read to him, and he gave clear, bold evidence against his former comrades, specifying the duties which had been assigned to each in the Gokulpoor Dacoity. He himself had carried one of the torches, and one other torch-bearer was now present, whom he pointed out; two more were not yet apprehended, but he had told where they might be found. He declared Azráel, the leader, to be the first man to spear Huree Das, by several thrusts; that he himself had taken the anklet from Seeta, and had not given it up. He pointed out the leader's spear, and said that he had washed it when the gang bathed at the waterfall, before they separated. The approver was slightly cross-examined by the pleader on the defence, as also by Azráel at great length; but his evidence was far more confirmed than shaken.

Buldeo, the man with the shrill voice, who had thrown himself on the mercy of Seeta and Brandon at Shah Gunje, was the next witness. He too had received a free pardon, and had given much and most valuable information, through which a good deal of the property carried off in the Dacoity had been recovered in various places, and was now spread out in court. He produced the sacred axe with its coverings, which he had buried in his house, and declared the number of Dacoities in which it had been used; that preceding the Gokulpoor affair having been done in Western India. No attempt was made to cross-examine him; and every word he had spoken had the impress of exact truth. From first to last of the murder of Huree Das, from the meeting in the glen to the attack upon his house, he never failed in a single particular; and his statement in regard to Seeta caused a thrill of agitation in the court, which had to be suppressed.

Next followed the evidence of the old goldsmith, Roopa, which need not be repeated; he swore to the transaction between himself and Beerbul Singh, and again recognized the anklet.

The next witness was Seeta, who was led into court by her venerable grandfather, carrying her boy. A chair was offered to her, but she simply declined it; she was not used to sit in one, she said, and would rather stand. It was impossible for the judge not to be struck by her exceeding beauty and grace. He, like Cyril, had never seen such an Indian woman before, and he could fully understand Cyril's warm description of her in the letter he had written after the enquiries at Shah Gunje. Seeta saw Cyril, for she was not far from him, look at her earnestly and encouragingly; but his presence gave her much assurance, and her examination proceeded.

She was far less excited than when she had given her first evidence, and she told all that had happened at Gokulpoor, with a gentle firmness and clearness, which deeply impressed Mr. Mostyn and all that heard her; and there was breathless silence in the court when she pointed out the leader of the gang as her husband's murderer, and to other men, whom she saw for the first time, as having also speared him. She pointed out the anklet and portions of her necklace as her own property, and the leader's spear as the weapon by which her husband had been killed; and she showed her wound and her child's. The attempt to cross-examine her by the prisoner's counsel broke down after a few trivial questions, and finally she was told by Mr. Mostyn that she might retire.

"You have done a painful duty, lady," he said, much moved; "but you have done it to your own honour. If I could now express to you the respect I feel for your character I would: but this is not the place. You may go. You will not have to attend again."

If the excitement in the court had been hitherto kept down, it was now irrepressible. The address of the judge had broken down Seeta's firmness, and she was sobbing passionately; and the cries of the spectators, both of pity and admiration, rang in her ears as she was led away by her grandfather. She thought Cyril Brandon had looked at her kindly, as indeed he had; but though he had longed to say a word of congratulation to her, as she passed out, he was silent. Then all the other evidence was gone through, which occupied the judge till the evening, and as the sun was near setting, the pleader was called upon to make the defence of the prisoners; but he broke down. "I have nothing to say or to urge," he said; "let my lord the judge do justice, according to the evidence;" and Mr. Mostyn was brief and stern in his judgment.

"Azráel Pandé," he said, "you were formerly a private in the old 34th Native Infantry, and were discharged for insubordination. The marks on your person, and your description, which I have obtained from your old regimental register, agree perfectly. Afterwards, you were a notorious leader, under the name of Gungah Singh, in the insurrection in Bundelkhund, where you escaped. Since then you have been a Dacoit, and might be tried on many charges of murder, and robbery with violence; but the present is sufficient. You have led a merciless career of the worst crime, and for the last, the sentence of this court is, that you be hanged by the neck in the gáol of Noorpoor till you are dead."

The prisoner did not reply. He was heard to mutter something indistinctly. Then two were sentenced to death; and the rest, some to penal servitude for life, others to various terms of imprisonment. The court then rose, and the famous trial was finished. It was strange, perhaps, that the originator of the crime had escaped detection; but there were reasons for that, which will be known in their proper place.

Mostyn had invited a small party of the officers of the station to dinner, but I fancy he was too much engrossed by the trial to entertain his guests as he was wont to do; indeed, he looked exhausted, and the party broke up early. Mr. Noble had, however, excited much interest at his end of the table as to the bearing and evidence of Seeta: and was several times obliged to appeal to Cyril and Mostyn to confirm what he said; and thus it arose that the incidents of the trial came to be discussed by all parties in the station, and in particular by most of the English ladies, whose subsequent applications to Mostyn to be allowed to see Seeta, became amusingly importunate. Seeta, however, with her grandfather—for Aunt Ella had been left in charge of the house—had quitted Noorpoor the morning after the trial, and were on their way home.

When the guests had departed, Mostyn said he could not sleep, and proposed to Cyril that they should "take a weed." It was a balmy, moonlight night, and the flowers of the garden, and creepers about the porch and pillars of the verandah, sent forth an exquisite fragrance. "I am keeping you up, Cyril," said his friend, "which is a shame, considering your long ride to-morrow; but it's yet early, and I for one can't sleep. I can't get that girl out of my head. What a lovely creature she is, and so modest, yet so firm and dignified! Did you ever hear such evidence?"

"Never," replied Cyril, "as I told you in my letter. But the first time she was excited; to-day she was calm, and, if it could be, more beautiful. Yes, you are right, there was true and real dignity about her. She knew where she was. She knew what to do; and if ever there was self-possession in the world, she displayed it firmly, not only in her bearing, but in her speech. Didn't you remark that?"

"I did, Cyril; but it seems so strange."

"No," he replied; "it only proves how little we know of native women, and how impossible it is to know anything more except in a case like this, which breaks the ice. Here is a girl who, I hear, is well educated; she is a good Sanscrit scholar, and you see at once that her intellect is expanded. How many there may be like her we shall never know. We could not ask her grandfather to dinner," he continued, laughing; "nor could Seeta go to a ball, exactly. Yet, were she at one, I can imagine the sensation."

"And really," added Mostyn, "upon my word, if Rose were here, I would have asked her to go to Seeta, and——"

"You would not, Philip. What! After trying her husband's murderer, and sentencing him to death, ask Seeta to your house? Would not that be thought odd by the people?"

"Perhaps," he said; "and I can well wait till I can interest Rose about her. She is sure not to leave Shah Gunje."

"It is not likely, Philip; and yet such imaginative girls among Hindoo widows often take up religious penances, and go pilgrimages, or devote themselves to charitable acts. I should not be surprised in the least if Seeta did something of the kind; for she must have some vent for the feelings of her passionate nature."

"Oh yes," returned Mostyn. "You see she can't marry again; and yet she might, for she is only a Soodra. But I doubt whether such a girl, with her intellectual perceptions awakening, would willingly marry any dull, ignorant fellow of her caste.

Indeed, I often think that if there were not our horrible social prejudices against it, many of us would be happier with such a wife than with some of our own people. I think such a one as that girl would be more interesting, more useful, more easily satisfied, and——"

"But they could not be married," interrupted Cyril; "and such a girl as that could not be a mistress. It would be simply shameful!"

"No, certainly not; but I am not so sure about marriage," he replied. "*I* think if any Englishman married a Hindoo or a Mahomedan girl, after the customs and belief of her sect, and in the good faith that such a marriage would be binding on him—— why! have not many of our old dignitaries done this, and lived happily all their lives?—and—and—and many others. What a grand effect had the marriage of Akbar to a Rajpoot princess upon the people at large! How it harmonized with all the jarring interests of those days! what a hold it gave him of the country and its affections!"

"And do you think, Philip, that any Rajpoot prince, or Mussulman nabob, would give his daughter to a 'Feringee'?"

"Faith, I do," replied Mostyn, "if the marriage were fully recognized by the customs of our society and by the legislature. As to family considerations, none of us, proud strangers as we may be, need be ashamed of theirs, which are as old, as noble, and as great as our own."

"You would be a bold innovator," cried Cyril, laughing; "but all the spinsters would be up in arms against you."

"Ay! and their mothers too," returned Mostyn; "but you know I am only putting the case hypothetically. I don't suppose it will ever be; but for all that there is many a Hindoo girl, like Seeta, who would be an ornament and a blessing to any man, and to his family also; though, perhaps, it is best, after all, that it is not attainable."

"Why, Philip?"

"Because of our social prejudices, which you and I can't overcome. Because of old Mrs. Grundy, who is as powerful here as elsewhere in the world—more so, perhaps. Because our perceptions are narrowed with our isolated positions, and become incapable of extension; and because, if a man, one of us, married a native lady—married, I say—he must exclude himself from society, which would require a strong mind; and must undergo temptation if he entered it, which would require even a stronger to resist."

"Then the thing is impossible, Philip?"

"I did not say it was," he replied, laughing. "I have stated the arguments for and against, as well as I could, and leave them to you. Any way, you and I can have no concern with them. If the question ever arises, it will only be after many, many years. Now you had better go to bed, and I too. By the way, did I tell you that Rose was coming out, and that my little sister Grace is to accompany her?"

"No, you did not," said Cyril; "but I am very glad to hear it, and I hope she will bring a new piano and a lot of new music with her. Can you write to tell her to do so?"

"No; she will be in Calcutta by the mail after next, I hope, and I have applied for three months' leave to meet her; and she is bringing out the piano, and, no doubt, heaps of music."

"I don't suppose I shall see you then till they come," said Cyril, "and don't get up in the morning. So good-bye. I wish you all a happy meeting, and will come in and see you when you are settled. Good-bye, and God bless you."

CHAPTER XII.

NO ENGLISH.

FROM the court Azrael Pandé was removed to a solitary condemned cell in the gaol, and guarded more closely than before. At last justice had overtaken him, and his execution must follow when the confirmation of his sentence should arrive. He had no hope of its commutation, none; and indeed he would rather meet death than undergo transportation over the black water—the sea—to a strange land. He knew that when the sentence arrived he should be visited by the magistrate and warned for execution in two days, or at most three; then, when the time came, he would feel the hands of the outcast hangman about his neck, and he should die, die polluted, and be buried like a dog. There would be no fellow-caste man to perform those needful ceremonies for his soul, which must perish in Nurruk, the worst hell of his faith, or live there for ever and ever; and she, that witch Seeta, had been the cause of all. But for her, who would have seen him strike down the goldsmith? who could have brought the crime home to him? O for revenge on her, for revenge on the faithless comrades who had betrayed him! O for freedom once more, and a better band of followers to strike down the traitors; and men should yet tremble at his name, while the proud Seeta should be his slave—far away in the Eastern lands, she should be his slave till she died. As his mind revelled in her beauty, he raved in the night; and his fearful dreams and shrieks of vengeance were listened to by the sentinels and gaolers who gathered round the cell with shuddering awe, till they were stopped by his being awakened.

Again he thought whether the confession of all his crimes, the denunciation of all his old associates, the recovery of all the property he had robbed, might save his life; and, more than all, whether the first mover in the Gokulpoor transaction might be denounced! Would that save him? Not now; he could have no share in the pardon of the proclamation. No, he would die; and perhaps in the evil nature of this ruffian, a rude sense of honour, the remembrance of his first vows and oaths to the fearful profession he had followed—still lingered.

And so the days passed, till one morning he heard Mr. Noble, the assistant-magistrate, with the Darogah of the gaol, approaching his cell, attended by an escort, and he knew his time had come. His name was called, and he came forward, and was told that the sentence passed on him had been confirmed, and that on the fourth day he would be hanged at six o'clock in the morning. Had he any last wishes? None, he said, with an air of bravado, as he twisted up his moustachios; "I will leave my curses on the English. If they will give me some hot Julaybees (sweetmeats) to eat before I die, it is the last favour I shall ask of them."

But Azráel was not even then without hope. Among the guards present was his old comrade, Gokul Tewary, who looked at him significantly; and all that day Azráel watched for his coming in a fever of impatience. As night fell he heard the sentinel relieved: and a few moments afterwards he saw a hand raised to the bars of his cell, which dropped something through them. Nervously opening the rag in which they were wrapped, he found two small files and a lump of butter in a leaf, and understood that his friend was faithful. It was an easy matter to file through the rivets of his irons without noise, and when he had completed this, he tied the rag, which he had before asked for as a cover for the iron which hurt his leg, over the rivets again, and was ready to obey any signal which might be given him; but, as the third morning dawned, he had almost given up hope. On that day, however, Gokul Tewary was on guard over him early, and had told him what could be done. Some work was going on in the gaol, and the workmen would be paid in the evening. If he dared to attempt escape, he must go out with them then. They would fly together to one of the old unknown haunts, and be soon safe from pursuit. "If you are detected and taken," he continued, "you must die to-morrow morning, for the scaffold is put up over the gate, and the executioner is here—I have just seen him."

Azráel Pandé had few misgivings as to the course he would take. If he refused his old comrade's offer he must die, and die in pollution of, to him, a Brahmin, the most horrible character. If he escaped, there were his old wild freedom, the surest anticipation of revenge on the hated English, on Seeta, on his faithless betrayers—on all who had been concerned in his detection and sentence. In another matter, too, there was much to be done and little time to do it in; and he knew he was expected in quarters and by men of whom as yet we know nothing. If he were detected, then death would follow; but for that he was prepared. These thoughts had hardly passed through his mind, when Gokul Tewary came again to the door, and asked him what he had determined to do. "I have the duplicate key of your cell," he said, "and I am on duty over you in the evening again. When the time comes, I will open it and lead you out; be ready soon after the sun has set."

"You should not speak with the prisoner," said the Darogah, who passed on his rounds.

"He was restless and making a noise," replied the man, "and I was telling him to be quiet, that is all;" and the Darogah, after shaking the door of the cell, went on his way.

By the evening, Azráel Pandé had removed his irons, and was ready for flight; and as dusk was falling, he heard the key of his cell turned gently in the lock. A moment after he was in the courtyard of the gaol, and the door of the cell was locked after him. Throwing a coarse black blanket, which his comrade gave him, over his head so as to conceal his face, he passed on, and joined a throng of workmen who were leaving the gate of the gaol. He saw, too, that his comrade was close behind. In the gateway was a guard of police, which he must pass; but they did not interfere with the workmen, and without a challenge, and unnoticed, he passed out, and was free once more. For a moment Gokul Tewary had been detained by the corporal of the guard, to ask where he was going; but he had satisfied that functionary, and now followed Azráel; and, as he joined him, the two men made off towards the open country in the fast-falling darkness, and were soon beyond chance of pursuit. They spoke little; once Gokul Tewary asked where they should go, and Azráel had answered to Futtehpoor, and they were again silent.

Now running, now walking fast, and avoiding all habitations, they had reached their destination, some seven miles from Noorpoor, ere their flight was discovered.

Futtehpoor was the capital of the Nawab Dil Khan's small dominions, where he always resided, and kept up a retinue of disorderly retainers, who, in many respects, and for excellent reasons, were the terror of the country. The judge and magistrates of Noorpoor were unanimously of opinion that the whole of them were Dacoits and common thieves; and the fact of the majority of Azráel Pandé's gang having been apprehended there, and in the villages about, had materially strengthened former suspicions. The Nawab had expressed the highest indignation, and had given up the men at once—indeed, he dared not refuse—and, as we know, had asked permission to attend the Dacoit's trial, and had heard—perhaps with some satisfaction—the sentence of death upon their leader. Upon the principle that dead men tell no tales, he would be relieved from all chance of detection in having shared the Dacoit's plunder, and urged him on to the commission of several notorious affairs; and after congratulating Mr. Mostyn on the purity and dignity of his justice in the case, he had taken his leave. Till, however, the news of the confirmation of the Dacoit's sentence had reached him, the Nawab's mind was not at ease; but as he heard that the day of his execution had been fixed, he had resumed his usual serenity.

Much astonished and perplexed was the Nawab, therefore, when, early in the morning, after the escape of Azráel and his accomplice, an attendant awoke him, saying that the magistrate of Noorpoor was at the gate of the citadel, and demanded instant speech of him. There was no denying an official visit, which was evidently of importance, because of so unusual a time and character; and the Nawab, hastily rising, and desiring Mr. Noble to be admitted, threw a shawl over his shoulders, tied a muslin scarf about his head after a rough fashion, and went out and seated himself in the verandah which opened into a small courtyard. The Nawab was hardly pleasant to look on now; his bloated features, deeply pitted by the small-pox, had an expression of alarm and weariness combined; his eyes were heavy and red, for he had not slept off his nightly dose of opium; he was unshaven and unwashed, and his large sensual mouth was marked with the red stains of the pán he had eaten overnight. His thick bull neck looked flabby and dirty, and the fat, hairy arms and hands, which protruded from under the shawl, completed an appearance which was, in truth, most forbidding.

In a few moments Mr. Noble entered, booted and spurred,

with an unmistakeable revolver in his leather waistbelt, which the Nawab regarded with some alarm; but he rose to meet his visitor, and advanced a step or two with his arms outstretched, as if to embrace him. This was, however, declined; Mr. Noble had evidently no idea of near contact with so unwholesome a looking person, and he bowed and stepped back. He was a slight, fair young man, with a pale face, and somewhat red eyes; and, being very shortsighted, usually wore blue spectacles. His appearance was not, therefore, very formidable, in spite of his revolver, and the Nawab, looking at him from head to foot, backed into his own seat, and asked his visitor civilly to be seated.

"I cannot sit, Nawab Sahib," he replied, "and I cannot wait," and the Nawab rose again. "I demand of you the Dacoit Azráel Pandé, whom we know is in Futtehpoor."

"Azráel Pandé? Puna-i-khoda! protection of God!" cried the Nawab; "why, I thought you had hanged him this morning!"

"He escaped from the gaol last night," replied the magistrate, "and one of the police, an old comrade of his, we suspect, with him. The trackers have brought us here, and the tracks do not go farther; you must either produce him or be responsible for him."

The Nawab was really alarmed. A great wave of disagreeable thoughts came up in his mind. He had made sure that Azráel would be hanged as the sun rose, and now he had escaped, and was tracked to his old lair. What was to be done?

"Escaped!" he exclaimed. "What were the guards about? what was the Darogah doing? Escaped! and from the condemned cell! Ajaib! Wonderful, I can hardly believe it! yet you are here, Mr. Noble."

"Yes," said Noble, calmly, "I am here, and shall not go away till the man is given up. Remember, Nawab Sahib, how many of his gang were found among your people; you would do well to free yourself of suspicion by Government, in giving him up to me."

Dil Khan would have blustered if he had dared; but he was not brave, and he feared to provoke the quiet determination of the young Englishman, backed as he was by a native officer of the Irregular Cavalry who stood by him, and by twenty troopers outside, the tramping of whose horses was heard distinctly.

"I am a poor servant of the English Government," he said, "and my life and my estate are at their disposal. I have not seen Azráel Pandé, but at his trial. He has not dared to come to me. Sir, let your trackers come into the town, and let every house be searched, including this poor palace of mine. If Azráel Pandé is found, take him away and hang him at once, and the world will be rid of a villain and a murderer. Shall I come with you?"

"Yes," said Mr. Noble, "come. You need to do all you can to free yourself from any doubt of your good faith." And the Nawab, calling for his shoes, put them on, and followed his visitor out of the castle.

They searched everywhere, but to no purpose; and what place is there like a native town for eluding pursuit? "If he has only taken to the old place," thought the Nawab, "no tracker that ever lived could find him; but I would the English had hanged him." So till late in the afternoon Mr. Noble and his men remained. After all, the trackers might have been mistaken. With what wonderful instinct they had taken up and followed the impressions of two men's feet, over fields, over grass, and through copses of jungle—now losing, now gaining them again—excited Noble's admiration; but near a garden of the Nawab's, under the hill on which his castle stood, they had finally lost them and did not recover them. The Nawab had hindered nothing; on the contrary, had appeared to assist to the utmost of his power: and when a slight breakfast was sent to him from the castle, he had washed his hands, and inviting Noble to eat some of it, had helped him. "It is but a hunting expedition," he said, laughing, "and you must not fast."

"I shall leave some of the Dacoity police here," said Mr. Noble, as he was about to depart, "and I am sure you will help them."

"That will I, sir; I have already offered a reward of a hundred rupees, and if the man is caught, I will bring him to Noorpoor myself, and wait there till I see him hanged. To think only that he should have caused you so much trouble!"

"He will cause more before he dies if he is not caught," said Noble.

"And you will not forget my compliments to the Judge Sahib, and the Colonel Sahib, and to bear witness to what I have done. Mashalla! if I can only catch the fellow, it will make a good name for me. A safe journey to you, sir," and they separated. Nor was the Nawab sorry, as he sat at his favourite oriel window in the castle, when he saw the arms and spear-heads of the troopers glinting brightly as they passed up the slope of the Futtehpoor valley, and disappeared over its ridge. "Now they are gone, I must see if Azráel is there," he said to himself, "and get rid of him as best I can."

To the garden already mentioned, a flight of steps, cut partly through the rock, descended from the interior of the palace. They were intended for, and used by, the ladies of the Zenana, when they wished to take the air; and by them the *détour* of the fortification, and part of the town, was avoided. In the garden was a large well with which these steps were connected; for they opened into two underground chambers, always neatly kept, which were used by the ladies in the hottest weather, and which were connected with the gallery of the well by a passage now filled up with brushwood. These chambers had often been the retreat of the Dacoit before, and Azráel Pandé had made directly for them after his escape. He had forced his way through the dry sticks as he reached the place in the night, and they had been carefully replaced by him and his companion before daylight. Even should the passage be discovered from without, a way of secure retreat up the steps into the Nawab's citadel, would enable them to escape. As Azráel Pandé lay there with his companion, they had heard the voices of the searching party, and even distinguished that of the Nawab; but they had passed away, and all was still. Dil Khan had at least been true, and Azráel waited impatiently for his coming, for he knew he would come.

In the evening the Nawab went down the steps and entered the first of the rooms. He had some time ago purchased a revolver, had learned its use, and had placed it in his waist carefully covered, yet so disposed that he could use it in a moment. He found the men seated before the embers of a fire, and a small lamp, in a niche above, threw a flickering light on their faces. Azráel had heard the Nawab's step, but he did not rise as he entered the place.

"And you escaped and are here, my friend," said the Nawab.

"Yes, I have escaped, and I am here," was the only reply.

"And I saved you to-day, Azráel. Else they had found out even this hole in the earth," continued the Nawab.

"For your own sake, Dil Khan, not mine. It would have pleased you had they hanged me as they have the two poor fellows who died to-day."

"And why for my own sake?"

"Because I know more than they do. I have paid you often, Nawab, for protection, and now you must pay for mine. Do you understand that?"

Dil Khan trembled; and he thought for a moment whether it would not be better to shoot the Dacoit as he sat, and take his chance with his companion; but he feared the man too much. If the shot failed, his life would not exist for a moment.

"Don't be surly, good friend," he said, after a pause; "we have served each other, and are so far even. If you have given me money, I have saved your life; and now I think I have the best of it. What would you have?"

"I want money to travel," replied Azráel; "and you must not refuse it. I have to go into far lands—to go to my people; and to do much which you may know of hereafter. Ay! and share in too, if you are faithful."

"Money!" cried the Nawab. "You know I have none. Every morsel of land I have, is mortgaged to the bankers of Noorpoor; every rupee of rent is forestalled, and the jewels of my house are pledged too. How I and my people live from day to day I hardly know, and the arrears of my servants are frightful. How can I keep up my poor dignity on what I have?"

"You had once larger lands, and the English took them from you."

"Yes," he replied; "and my curse, and the curse of my house, be on them for taking nearly all, and leaving me a beggar."

"We can revenge ourselves, Dil Khan, presently," said Azráel, "if we are patient. For me, who have escaped them, there is but one thought; first to destroy those who brought me to this pass, and then the rest. Yes, the days will soon come for that, and the men, too, in thousands; but I must have money now. Give me a thousand rupees, and I will leave this place before daylight."

"I have not a hundred rupees in my treasury, and it is useless to ask me, Azráel. Can nothing be done—no business?"

"In my old way?" he asked, as a fierce grin distorted his countenance. "Yes, if I had the men. The best of those I had are gone, poor fellows."

"The banker, Narendra, and the fair Seeta, gave evidence against you, and hers would have hanged you. O man, art thou grown dull?" replied the Nawab.

"No," replied Azráel, "but it is a fearful risk; and yet—revenge on them would be sweet indeed:" and for a moment he writhed under the remembrance of Seeta's beauty and his own visions in the gaol cell! "But the men," he cried; "the men!"

"Well," said the Nawab, coolly; "you know as many as I do, and more. There are some here among my people who must do something or starve, and there are some at —— and ——. You don't want many."

"No, not many; but all these are untrained, and Narendra's house is not a walnut to be cracked by the blow of a fist. And the axe is wanting; the Feringees have it."

"What axe? why, my smith would make you twenty if you want them."

"You would not comprehend me if I were to tell you," replied Azráel. "Let it pass, the others may have one."

"Yours did not do much for you in the Gokulpoor matter, my friend," said the Nawab, with a sneer; "but you know your own business best. Remember that Narendra's house will afford you ten thousand rupees, at least, if you are clever. Nay more: why, the man is worth lakhs. Now listen; I can give you fifty rupees, and will bring them. With that sum you can go to Ryna or Janpoor, and be safe with your people there, till you arrange everything. I have no more to give, and you must depart as night falls."

"Go then," said Azráel, "and bring it."

"Is he to be trusted? O brother," said Gokul Tewary, in an earnest tone, "let us be gone and join our people for the other work. It is time, and why should we risk the danger of staying here?"

"Not till I have brought away Seeta and made her my slave," said Azráel, gloomily. "That girl is my fate. She crossed me at Gokulpoor, she crossed me in the trial, and she will cross me again;" and he became silent.

"Have you thought it over, my friend?" said the Nawab, as he re-entered the chamber; "here is your money."

Azráel counted it silently. "Yes," he said, "I will do it, if only for my revenge on that girl; and you shall have your share as before. It may help you to pay the bankers."

"Good," returned the Nawab. "I thank you, as you trust me; but I want no money; only bring the girl Seeta to me, and you may keep what you get to help your other work, whatever it may be. Will you do this?"

"If it can be done, I will bring her here," replied Azráel; "here—and you may do what you like afterwards. Does that content you?"

"I have already told you that I trust you, and that is enough. Do not stay here, the place may not be safe against another search. And the two men?"

"Keep them," replied Azráel. "Keep them safe till there are no English."

"No English? Are you mad, friend?"

"I am not mad, Nawab Sahib," was the reply. "I say again, when there are no English, I will release them."

"No English," muttered the Nawab to himself as he ascended the steps. "No English! would there were none! But what does he mean? No English! he is mad!"

CHAPTER XIII.

WARNING AND RESCUE.

About a fortnight after the event related in the last chapter, Cyril Brandon was sitting one evening, after the work of the day was over, in his easy-chair before his tent door, enjoying the cool air, and resting in his quiet fashion, till his servants should bring his dinner; after which he would go on with translation work as long as he could. The escape of Azráel Pandé had annoyed him very much. Certainly two of the worst of the prisoners had been hanged, several were to be transported, and others imprisoned, and so far, the desperate gang had been broken up; but the leader was once more at large. All his antecedents had transpired at the trial, and proved him to be one of those merciless monsters who, under the cloak of devotion to Kalee, habitually committed murder; and whom no vigilance could check, and no laws terrify. Where would he strike the next blow? That he would abandon his fearful pursuits, even under a sense of the danger he had escaped, Cyril thought most improbable, nay, impossible; for the votary of Kalee, in her most horrible form, was, he knew, ever driven on by thoughts of her vengeance to attempt the most desperate enterprises. He must be very careful, and the police must be very vigilant. In his own jurisdiction all this was possible; but in regard to the independent states near him, he was, in truth, almost helpless. But the crime of Thuggee had been suppressed with a strong hand, and Dacoity had been systematically attacked, and might be overcome in like manner, though that would take a longer time. Well, in any case, he would do his best. The Nawab, and Rajah Hurpal Singh, must be more closely watched; for that both harboured Dacoits, and shared in their plunder, he had but little doubt; and of the two, though outwardly most complaisant, he believed the Nawab to be the worst. At the trial, how he had glared upon Seeta! how he had appeared to gloat on her beauty! "Well," said Cyril to himself, "if we English do nothing more, we at least keep such people in check. In the old times, or were the Nawab ruler here, would that poor girl be safe? No, hardly for a day."

So thinking, and revolving many such subjects in his mind, Cyril saw a man with a rough blanket on his shoulders, and a stick in his hand, approaching rapidly, who prostrated himself on the ground, and then rising, held out the stick, in the cleft end of which was a paper tied securely, and a feather attached to it. This was a rude fashion of sending an express, often practised in the country. The stick passed from village to village; generally very rapidly, and the letter being tied in the cleft, was quite safe. The man cried out for reward, and Cyril, ordering some copper coins to be given to him, went into his tent, where his dinner was now ready. He had often received such rude despatches before, and this excited no particular interest, as the bearer of it had said he did not know whence it had come; but as the stick lay beside him, he took it up from time to time, and examined the envelope more strictly. The letter was sealed with sealing wax as well as gummed down, which was unusual. It was directed to him, and on the back was written, "Emergent, to be delivered with speed! speed speed!" and when he had finished his dinner, and putting his legs on the table (who that has so luxuriated in India can ever forget it?), lighted a manilla, he took up the stick again. The thread, that had tied it, was carefully cut with his penknife, and the letter as carefully opened. The characters were large and roughly shapen, but they were perfectly legible. The contents ran thus:—

"To the noble Mr. Brandon, the salutation of his slave, and the peace of God.

"Further. I am well by the grace of God, and your slave hopes you are the same.

"Further. There is to be a Duróra on the house of the banker Narendra of Shah Gunje, on the third night of the dark quarter of the moon. Be this known to you.

"Further. The man that escaped from the gaol at Noorpoor has arranged this, and will do it himself, and many with him.

"Further. The banker will be killed and all his treasure plundered, and the lady Seeta will be carried away. So it is determined.

"Further. Be careful of yourself. He that writes this is a

friend, and writes truly. You have a good name, and should be warned of danger.

"Further. Make strong arrangements to save the banker and Seeta, for which you are all-powerful. Do not rely on the police. Send troops—they are not cowards before Dacoits. Save Seeta; she was once saved.

"Written by your slave and well-wisher. May your prosperity increase. I have written *truly*."

There was no signature to this strange document, only a rude drawing of a dagger.

Cyril read it again and again, with growing interest. Who could have written the warning? There would be no clue to this, but there was no doubt it was one, and a very earnest one too. The third night of the dark quarter of the moon? He was well acquainted with the forms of Hindoo dates, and this was the first night, and there was ample time. "Ah! so you are soon at your old work again, Azráel Pandé," he said to himself, "and I will meet you. This matter must not be trusted to others." Then he revolved in his mind whom he could best rely upon; and there were four men, two of them Sikhs, in the police detachment which formed his camp guard, who had behaved well on many occasions, and were his constant attendants in expeditions against tigers and bears. It was twenty-five miles to Shah Gunje; but if he left camp early next morning he would be in good time. Then he sent an attendant for his trusty assistant, Baba Sahib, the Serishtadar, on whom he could thoroughly depend; and after a while he arrived.

"Read that," said Cyril, handing him the paper; and the old man read it and sighed.

"So soon!" he said. "No one can help them but the gods and you. What will you do?"

"I will go," replied Cyril. "On that I am quite determined; and that villain shall not escape me. Get me a turban, and a very common native dress that will fit me. My own would attract attention."

"My old padded tunic might do, sir," he replied; "it is too large for me; and here is my turban. I will send for the dress."

It came quickly, and Cyril put it on. Baba Sahib was a tall, stout old man, and the garment fitted Cyril exactly. So far, therefore, one arrangement was made. "Take my ambling pony too," he said; "it will carry you well, and your own horse and saddle would be recognized. Will you have an escort?"

"I will take the four orderlies," he said; "have them warned for a hunting party early to-morrow; and they are not to put on their uniforms. I shall leave all servants here, and I think the banker will give me food."

"Ay, and all his treasures too, if you save Seeta from that ruffian," said the old man in a cheery voice. Baba Sahib was proud of his master, and this new proof of his energy and determination was very grateful to him. "If all were like him!" he said, as he walked home. "May the gods bless and protect him!"

The translations had been put aside, and Cyril had gone to bed. He did not sleep at once; the excitement was too great; but presently he slept soundly, nor did he awake till his servant aroused him in the morning, and told him that Baba Sahib's horse was come, and the men were ready. "Shall I give them the guns?" he asked.

"Only the small-shot guns, Kassim, and some balls. Get breakfast ready while I bathe and dress." And when his master emerged from his sleeping-tent dressed in Baba Sahib's tunic and turban, the servants wondered exceedingly.

Cyril was not long in preparing. He loaded his revolver carefully, and hid it in a voluminous waistcloth. His long, thin riding-boots covered his legs; and when he mounted the Baba Sahib's spirited palfrey, he might have passed, at a little distance, for an ordinary traveller. His four orderlies had dressed as if for a hunting expediton, and wore no uniform.

"Where are we to go, sir?" asked Golab Singh, one of the Sikhs.

"I will tell you presently," replied Cyril; and they pressed on in the direction he pointed. They travelled leisurely, resting occasionally by the side of a stream, and attracted little notice. A guide was taken from every village on the road to Shah Gunje; and as the party reached Gokulpoor, Cyril told them of his destination. Then, as night was falling, they entered the town, and went direct to the banker's house. There was some demur in admitting the party at so strange an hour; and while Ram Singh, the old Rahtore, and his men, were bidding them begone, Narendra himself came forth to ascertain the cause of the altercation.

Cyril bent down from his saddle and whispered hurriedly in the banker's ear, "I am Mr. Brandon. Let me in before I am seen. I will tell you all pre ently." Then the great gate was opened, and they were admitted.

Narendra was much puzzled, as indeed he might well be.

What could have brought the Commissioner Sahib there, and in such a dress? But he was not long in suspense; and when Cyril told him why he had come, the old man bowed his head, and burst into tears.

"I do not deserve this," he said. "What am I to you, sir, that you should risk your life for me and mine? Go, let the police come; they will be enough."

"Not so," replied Cecil; "I do not quite trust them since the Brahmin escaped. This is a matter for myself. Can you depend on your own men? How many have you?"

"Six," said the banker; "all Rajpoots, and true to the death."

"Then we must arrange them about," said Cyril. "I fear we may inconvenience the house, and perhaps make it unclean; but there is no help for that. I have four men of my own, and ten are enough; but my fellows have fasted all day. Can you feed them?"

"Yes," said the banker. "My household food is being prepared, and they will not object to it."

The preparations, the conference with Ram Singh and his men, and the positions to be taken up by each, occupied some time; and Aunt Ella and Seeta, who had been in the upper room, had become curious about the unusual commotion.

"What can it be?" said Seeta. "Do not let them wake the boy. Go and see."

Aunt Ella went down, but was put back somewhat rudely by her brother. "This is no place for women," he said. "A guest has come, and his men are all about. Go up to Seeta and stay with her."

But Aunt Ella was by no means satisfied; and she watched quietly. She saw a tall figure, in a brown quilted tunic and big boots, arranging men here and there, and these men were armed. They all spoke nearly in whispers, and she could not hear what was said; but she saw her brother speaking with them too, so there was no fear of him. Then her brother came and called to her—she had hidden behind the door—and bid her get food quickly, for the guest was hungry and needed refreshment. Ella now wondered more than ever; and having given the necessary direction to a servant, went up to Seeta, whom she found listening anxiously.

"I can't make it out at all," said Aunt Ella, nearly crying; "your grandfather is cross, he will have the food before it is ready; and there are strange men below all armed, and a big, fair man giving orders. He is as fair as an Englishman; but I must go to the kitchen, and do you keep quiet."

Seeta's heart gave a great bound within her, and she sat down almost unable to breathe. "It must be he," she thought, "he who was so kind, and I shall see him once more;" and she rose and went downstairs. There were no men about, and looking into the front hall, she saw unmistakeably that the stranger sitting in her uncle's seat was indeed Cyril Brandon: that was enough. Why he had come she knew not; but a sense of blessed security stole into her heart, which moved her to tears. "I will go and sing the evening hymns," she said to herself, "and pray for him;" and presently Cyril heard a rich, sweet voice chanting the evening Hindoo litany in an inner room.

"Who is that singing?" he asked.

"It is Seeta," said the banker; "I ought to do the 'Bhujun' myself, but I am old and she always sings it; I love to hear her."

It was a delicious voice truly, and the slight accompaniment of a tumboora increased its effect. Cyril listened while the hymn lasted without speaking; as it finished he said, "They ought to be told, Narendra, and prepared for what may happen; will you do this, and get them into a safe place?"

"I think," said Narendra, "if they knew you were here it would comfort them; yes, they ought to know;" and he went for them, and Aunt Ella and Seeta entered with him. Neither was changed in the least; and the curiosity both expressed, increased, if it were possible, the beautiful expression of Seeta's face. As Cyril arose and saluted them both, the women bowed down and touched his feet, then went and sat apart, while Cyril explained why he had come. Both were brave women; and, though deeply agitated, were comparatively calm. There might be resistance, Cyril said, there might be bloodshed; but there was no fear, and if they would keep quiet in the upper rooms, all would be well. But Seeta would not have it so; and she rose and said humbly, with her hands joined before her—

"I did not blench from peril once, when the Brahmin came and I will not now. O my lord! let me remain, I could not stay alone"—and she came, and again touched his feet—"Aunt Ella will take care of my son."

Cyril saw that she was quite calm; her soft brown eyes were suffused with tears, but there was no failing in them; Aunt Ella was sobbing and beating her breast, and she at last arose and went away; and Cyril said, "Be it as you will, but keep inside the court, for there may be rough work." Then Seeta went up to her child; and gradually, as night advanced, silence fell upon the house, and the men had taken up their several positions. The outer gate had been left ajar as if it had been carelessly fastened; some blankets had been thrown over logs of wood in the guard-room to represent sleeping guards, and all was prepared; Cyril heard Seeta come down the stairs from above, and in the dusk saw her seat herself in the verandah of the court, but not far from him.

Midnight passed, and the town watch went their usual rounds, beating their drums and blowing their horn, and crying out, "The second watch is past, sleep in peace!" Then all in the town was still, except the occasional bark of dogs, and again there was silence; but the time was surely nigh. In about two hours more, while all were watching, Seeta rose suddenly and said to Brandon, "I hear them, for they are near; be ready!" and as he was warning the men to be silent, they heard the outer gate broken in by the blow of an axe, and a rushing of men's feet through the inner court, and saw the light of blazing torches. Cyril was standing in front near the steps, and as the light fell upon him, Seeta saw his fine figure proudly drawn up and ready. Strange that the Dacoits did not at once see him, but he had been concealed by one of the thick wooden pillars. Cyril let them rush in confusedly, and up the steps. He recognized the tall figure of the leader, though his face was muffled, and covering him with his pistol, fired; a man dropped, but it was not Azráel. Again and again Brandon fired rapidly, and in the confusion, which had become general—for the concealed men had rushed from their hiding-places, leaped into the court, and attacked the Dacoits—a man drove a spear through his right arm, and it fell powerless to his side. The whole had been the work of hardly more than a minute. Five of the Dacoits were lying wounded or dead; several had been captured, and the rest having extinguished their torches, escaped in the darkness, as they had come.

Seeta had seen two men fall before Cyril's weapon; then she had seen him beset; and the reeling, surging figures prevented her from approaching him, but only for a moment. She saw him struck, and the gush of blood which followed, and ran to him. "Come away! come away!" she cried, and tried to draw him to the inner court, but he put her aside gently.

"Bring me some water," he said. "Do not mind the wound, it is but a scratch, and I must see to my people."

While she went to fetch it, Cyril looked round. Some one had relighted one of the Dacoit's torches, and everything could be seen distinctly; and one of his Sikh orderlies came up and said, pointing to the court, "Three of them are dead, one is dying, and none will live; none of us are hurt. Shall we run to the station for the police?"

"Yes," he said; "keep the men we have taken safely." And he sat down, for he felt sick and faint.

"Drink this, sir," said Seeta, who had now returned with a silver cup full of cold water, and Cyril drank eagerly. No more delicious draught had ever passed his lips, he thought, as he looked gratefully at the girl; but still he was faint, for the wound was bleeding much, and Seeta saw his head drop on his shoulder.

"Quick!" she cried to the Sikh, who was giving some directions; "come to your master, he is wounded! Quick, carry him after me."

Several of the men ran to Cyril, and taking him up gently, carried him into the verandah of the inner court, and laid him upon a low bed; he felt faint and weak, but he was quite conscious. Narendra was standing by him, and Seeta was kneeling by the bed. One of his men was unfastening the knots of the tunic, and it was quickly removed. "We must get to the wound," he said, "and stop the bleeding, else he will faint again;" and it was soon exposed. It was above the elbow, and the spear had gone through the fleshy part of the arm. "We must have a good barber for this," continued the Sikh; "it is no slight scratch, sir; but never mind, it will soon be well."

"I will wash it, sir," said Seeta humbly to the Sikh; "let me do what I can."

"Well," replied the man, "your hands are lighter than mine; wash it well, while I look after the affairs out yonder," and he went away.

Aunt Ella, who had now come, brought warm water, and between them the wound was soon washed and bound up; and a fomentation of herbs, well known to the old lady, was concocted and set to boil in the kitchen. As it was, however, Cyril already felt refreshed, but the wound was very painful. He heard the voice of the police Darogah without, giving directions, and after a few minutes he came in, much concerned at what had taken place.

"Have you got any more of them?" asked Cyril. "Do not trouble me now; I will see to everything in the morning."

"No, not yet," replied the officer: "none of the Dacoits. They must have separated at once, but men are in pursuit; and we have got a palankeen, and eighteen bearers beside it, which was in a bye street. What could that have been intended for? I have confined them all."

Cyril knew well, but said nothing. As he looked at Seeta, who sat at the foot of the bed with her face concealed, he felt grateful that he had saved her; and then he thought how daringly had the Dacoity been planned. The police station was at a considerable distance, and before any alarm could have been given, the whole of the robber's scheme might have been executed. Then Aunt Ella came with her fomentation, which relieved the pain, and stopped the bleeding; and an old barber very cleverly put a stitch into the wound, and bound it up tenderly; and, much soothed by this, Cyril fell asleep, while the women watched by him, and fanned him by turns, and his men sat without, talking together in low tones.

CHAPTER XIV.

STRICKEN TENTS.

Cyril Brandon felt weak as he awoke soon after daylight, for he had slept little. He could hardly realize, at first, where he was; but the events of the past night rushed into his mind with great vividness. There was no one by him but two of his orderlies, both asleep; and there were no sounds in the house but a low, soft singing, like what he remembered to have heard the night before. It was Seeta singing the morning hymn, while Narendra and her aunt were engaged in their worship, and, indeed, also in a prayer of thankfulness for having been preserved from great dangers.

After this was finished, all three, I think, were troubled what to do about Cyril. What would he like to do? Did he bathe, and what would he eat? At last Aunt Ella said decidedly that a light "kicheree," and some tamarind water, would be best for him; and Seeta declared she would make them, and departed to get them ready. Meanwhile Brandon had awakened his men, and Golab Singh, the Sikh, a great, bearded fellow, raised him gently, as he inquired after his wound; and as Brandon sat up, brought him the ewer and basin, which had been set ready by a woman servant, and poured water over his hands. Then Cyril felt refreshed, and with his attendant's help went out and sat down in the outer hall. The court had been cleansed, the floor of the hall newly plastered, and a fresh white cloth spread over the banker's cushions, on which Cyril seated himself. All looked neat and pleasant, and the morning air was brisk and reviving. Narendra found his guest sitting there, and bowed down before him. He could not speak at first; the old man's heart was too full for words. "All we have is yours," he said at length; "you have saved our house and our lives at the risk of your own, and you have shed your blood for us. O that we could prove what we feel, till we die!"

"Let it pass," said Cyril; "it was but my duty. I came for one purpose, and in that I failed; but perhaps the police would have done no better. Azráel Pandé escaped me."

"Yes," said the banker, "and we shall hear no more of him now for a long time; but he is a wicked Brahmin, and when Brahmins are bad, they are worse than others. He would have taken Seeta, sir, and you have saved her."

"Ha! then you know that?" cried Brandon.

"Yes," replied the old man, gravely; "I know it. Else why was the palankeen there? And one of the Dacoits confessed all last night, after you lay down, before he died."

"Since you know so much," returned Cyril, "you shall know all. In the pocket of the tunic I had on yesterday you will find a letter; bring it to me. Can you guess who wrote this?" he asked.

"Yes," returned Narendra, after reading it. "I think it must be Buldeo, the man whom Seeta saved in your court. I can think of no one else."

"Perhaps," said Cyril; "and we will see what the Darogah says about it. Ah! he is here. You are welcome, Abbas Ally; what news have you?"

The old officer came up the steps, took his sword out of his belt, and, with a sorrowful face and a low obeisance, laid it at Cyril's feet. "I will not take it up again unless you tell me," he said respectfully, but with tears in his eyes; "I should have been with you last night, and my lord is wounded; but I feel as if I were a coward, for being absent."

"Do not think so for a moment," replied Cyril, anxiously; "and I blame myself now that I did not send for you. I think you would have managed the matter better than I, and that Azráel Pandé would not have escaped. Take up your sword, and wear it as you always will, honourably; and as the decorations you bear vouch for your having done."

"I thank you humbly and gratefully, sir," he said, replacing his sword; "but no, Azráel's scouts must have been in the town, and would have known that I had come here. You were disguised, I hear, and they did not know you. One of them, who was taken, has indeed confessed as much. You were seen, but not recognized, and they thought you a visitor to Narendra."

"And where did the Dacoity come from?" asked Cyril.

"From Janpoor," replied the Darogah; "in the estate of Nawab Dil Khan Bahadoor; but the men have been near this for some days, lurking in the jungles, waiting for their leader."

"Ah! I, too, have had my suspicions about the Nawab. We must see to him, my friend."

"When you are able to hear the depositions, sir," continued the Darogah, "I will bring them to you; but not to-day. You need rest. Is there no quiet room you could arrange for him here," he asked of Narendra, "till his tents and servants come up? I have sent for them."

"My whole house is his," replied the banker, "and he well knows it. Yes, there is the room above—my child's room. I will see to it directly."

Then the priest Wamun Bhut came in, bringing a native physician of the town, who felt Cyril's pulse gravely, declared he was very feverish, and that he must dress the wound again, and give him a soothing draught. "I will be back directly," he said; "meanwhile let him be removed from hence. It is too much exposed here."

When Narendra returned, he said all was ready; and with the aid of the priest, Cyril was conducted up the stairs to the spacious room above. Seeta and Aunt Ella had been busy there for some time, and had spread a carpet, and arranged a low bed for him, which, with its snow-white sheets and pillows, looked very inviting, and he lay down and felt at rest. How kind and considerate they all were! he thought gratefully. Seeta was not there; but Aunt Ella came presently with a covered dish, and a silver cup full of tamarind water. "You must forgive our ignorance," she said; "we do not know what you eat; but this is plain food, and will do you good, and Seeta has made it for you; and here is an English spoon we had, for you to eat with; we know you English do not use your fingers."

Cyril was amused and gratified: and the simple "kicheree" seemed to him delicious, and the tamarind water also. He ate to the old lady's satisfaction, though he could not finish all. "Will Seeta come to see me?" he asked; "she might perhaps dress my wound when the doctor comes."

"If he will let us," she replied, "we will do it together; but he might object to a woman's hand. In any case she will come to you to thank you. O sir!" she continued, bursting into tears, "what can we not do for you, who have saved her, our child?"

Then presently the doctor came and opened the bandages. He would not let the women touch the wound; they were not always pure, he said, and knew nothing about such matters. But he was a skilful man; and when the operation was over, and the arm bound up again with a cool poultice of herbs, Cyril felt easier, and the soothing draught given to him allayed his fever and thirst, and he slept quietly for many hours. Once he thought Seeta had come in, with her boy in her arms, and had bent over him weeping; but she had gone away without speaking. Perhaps he had dreamed this; and yet the impression was too strong to be put away, and she might come again.

And she did come. Towards evening he was dozing, and saw her enter; and thinking him asleep, she came and looked on him and sighed.

"I am not asleep," he said. "Do not be afraid, but sit down and speak to me."

"I am not afraid; but you are not to speak," she replied; "the doctor said so. Perhaps to-morrow I may come. I want you to look at my boy, and I will bring him. He is all I have left, and he will not be afraid of you."

"Why not bring him now?"

"No," she said, "you are to be very quiet, and must not speak any more;" and she left the room.

"What a strange girl!" thought Cyril, "and so beautiful!" And he dozed again, and fell into confused dreams about her, which he could not follow. Then in the evening kind Aunt Ella came again with food, but he could not eat much, and Narendra and the priest came too, and sat awhile, and two or three others; and the doctor followed, who gave him another draught; so he was not lonely, and that night he slept well.

When he awoke Cyril felt better and stronger, though still weak. He had, indeed, lost much blood. His orderlies had kept watch over him by turns during the night, and now Golab Singh, the Sikh, was sitting quietly at the window looking out.

"You are to have a bath," he said, as Cyril called him; "the doctor said so; and it is ready. I will bathe you, and the water is in the room there. Get up, sir. I have borrowed some clean clothes from the banker, and you will be comfortable." And he assisted Cyril to rise. Was there ever anything more delicious than that warm bath and the scrubbings of the rough Sikh? Cyril was passive under his hands, and let him do as he wished. All the pain and unrest seemed to pass out of him, as water, hotter and hotter, was poured over his body, and he was at last enveloped in a hot dry sheet. Then a muslin tunic of the banker's and a fine waistcloth were put on him, the sleeve of his wounded arm being cut open; and he was led again to his bed, and fell into the most refreshing sleep he had yet enjoyed.

When he awoke and had eaten, it was past noon. "Seeta will come to you by-and-by," Aunt Ella had said. "The doctor says you may speak a little, but you are not to do business with any one. She will read to you if you like, or sing to you." And so he waited.

Presently Seeta entered the room, with her child on her hip. Cyril saw at a glance that it was much changed. The eyes of the little fellow seemed to have grown larger, and he was pale and sallow; his neck and limbs appeared to have shrunk, and he breathed heavily. The dilated pupils and heaviness showed some affection of the head.

"I have brought him to you," she said. "Look at him. The English know everything, and you may be able to help him; no one else can."

Cyril stretched out his left arm, and the boy at once bent forwards and went to him, looking wistfully into his face as he sat on the bed.

"He is not afraid of you, you see, sir," said his mother, "nor am I. It is so strange——"

"Why?" asked Cyril. "All children come to me without fear."

"Yes, I understand now," she said, dreamily. "It is because you are good. Children know who are good to them; and I am but a child, for I feel no fear of you—I never felt any; and this is so strange to me. You are English, and people fear you; but I do not."

"I would rather they loved me," said Cyril gently, "than that they feared me."

"Yes, many love you too," she returned gravely, "but it is a love with fear, and we have no fear. Nor grandfather, nor Aunt Ella, nor my boy, nor I. We only love you and worship you, as we do our gods."

"Nay, lady, do not say that," said Cyril. "To worship man as a god, we English think sinful; but there is love for all, and for God also, and in that we are not apart. He saved my life last night. Am I not grateful? Buldeo saved your life once; yet you would not worship him!"

"No," she replied, "not him, though I am grateful. But you are very different. He did not risk his life for us, and you did freely, and without a thought save to protect us. You are an incarnation of God's power, and so we would love you and worship you. See, even the child submits to you!"

And indeed it was true, for the little fellow had nestled close to Cyril, and still looked up at him with his great wondering eyes, as he occasionally stroked his face and beard with a loving touch, which Cyril did not repel. But he changed the subject. "You have a book there," he said; "they tell me you can read. Will you read to me?"

"It is Sanscrit," she replied modestly, "and you will not understand it; but I can explain it as I read."

"I understand it somewhat," he said. "I learned it in England, and I read it often. What book is that?"

"'Savitri,'" she replied; "it is a part of the 'Mahabhárut.' Do you know it?"

"Yes, lady," he returned. "Read on, and I will listen."

She read slowly; but in her sweet, musical voice the beautiful couplets of the old Hindoo poet sounded as he had never heard them before. Cyril had only heard them read in the nasal sing-song tone that Pundits generally use; but this was very different. Seeta grew more and more excited with her subject, and the intonations of her voice followed the variations of the exquisite story. It has been foretold that Savitri's husband is to die; and while they are in the forest his death-trance comes upon him, and he cries, "Dearest, I can stand no longer!" Then

> Down upon the ground she sate her, laid his head upon her breast,
> And the loving, gracious lady, lull'd her Satyavan to rest.

"Go on," said Cyril; "a fine passage follows. Or let me read it. I will try; but do not laugh at me."

She handed the book to him, wonderingly. "O! I will listen," she said.

Brandon read carefully. The passage had been a favourite college exercise and he knew it by heart: and in India he had acquired much of the proper cadence and pronunciation of the poem. Yáma, the Lord of Death, comes, a dread presence, and takes away the spirit of Savitri's husband; but she fears nothing:—

> Wheresoe'er my husband goeth, in the way where he is led,
> There Savitri, faithful ever, still unfalteringly will tread.

"Yes," cried Seeta, interrupting him, with the tears glistening in her large, soft eyes, "she went, the wife with her husband —into death. She had no fear of death. So I would have gone once, for my duty, as he died; but that was denied me, and the child lives."

"For your duty," said Cyril, "not for your love?"

"It is the same," returned the girl. "There can be no duty without love. But you must not read. See, you are already flushed, and that is bad for you. I will finish the book, for they are happy in the end. I should not leave you with a gloomy thought. Enough that I have my own." And she read on.

"Will you not sing something to me?" he said, when she had finished. "I would rather your voice lingered in my ear than the Sanscrit couplets, grand as they are!"

"I will," she replied. "I do not know many songs, I only sing the hymns; but I remember one a minstrel sung once, and I got Wamun Bhut to teach it to me. Will you hear it?" And she rose and took up her tumboora, which rested in a corner of the room; and after tuning it to a chord, sung an old Hindee ballad, which may be thus rendered:—

I could not speak with him
Those fondest words that I had treasured up to tell.
My streaming eyes were dim
With tears which then, alas! from me unheeded fell.
Rude blows the bitter wind,
Cold is the driving rain, nor place I have to dwell;
Ah me! from them unkind,
No pitying word, no sheltering love I find.

"I cannot sing more," she said, breaking down. "I will finish it another time, perhaps, if you like it. Now, come, Laloo, we must go."

The child put out his arms to her, but still looked at Cyril, who bent down and kissed him. "Go," he said, "to your mother. Don't be afraid of him," he added to her; "he seems very quiet."

"Ah!" returned Seeta, "that is what I fear; he used to be so noisy, till we went to the trial; I think I ought not to have taken him there."

"Why?"

"Because of the Brahmin and his evil eye, sir; but I should not fear, God is so good to me."

So passed three more days, and as they had become better known to each other, Seeta had laid aside much of her reserve. Day after day she brought her books, and they read passages of the "Mégha Dutta," or Cloud Messenger, by turns, and scenes from the dramas, and had many a pleasant dispute over them, which Wamun Bhut had to settle, wondering, as Seeta did, that Cyril knew so much. Aunt Ella told Cyril he must be a son whom God had sent her in her old age, and he must be obedient like one; and he had been obedient at once, and ate what she gave him, and he enjoyed the quaint, affectionate simplicity of the good old lady as much as he did the sterling kindness and instructive conversation of the banker and the priest. He played games of chess with them both, and held his own fairly, and he was visited by many of the banker's friends; thus he was never alone, except when he wished. His tents and servants had arrived, but he did not need the servants, and as they were Mahomedans, hesitated to employ them in the house; as to the tents, the worthy doctor would not hear of them. The fever of the wound was not gone, and Cyril felt it had not; he could not use his right hand to write much, and though he admitted Baba Sahib, and gave orders on any important cases, I do not think that much real business was transacted; and as Mostyn had left Noorpoor, Cyril only wrote a few lines to Noble, to say he had been slightly wounded, and would get to work again in a few days.

But before a week was gone, the pleasant sojourn in the banker's house came to an end. In spite of Narendra's remonstrances, good Aunt Ella's scolding, and Seeta's evident anxiety and reluctance, he must go to his work; and when the doctor said the wound was now healthy, and would soon heal, he went. It was not a parting for good, for there was much to do at Shah Gunje, and the farmers had already assembled for their yearly settlement of revenue. Cyril had said they should all come some day to see his tents; but to Seeta it was very sad, and she stood sobbing at the door as he passed her and said some cheery words. "He will forget me," she said to herself, as he descended the stairs; "and I? ah me, I cannot forget now."

But Cyril did not find his tents pleasant, and his wound had not improved by the change. The cold at night affected it, and the doctor said he ought to return; yet that was impossible. How he missed all the loving attention he had received! How he longed to hear Seeta read once more, or sing to him, in that sweet low voice of hers, the old Indian ballads of which he had grown so fond! But it was all at an end, he thought; it was a pleasant dream which the realities of his life had broken, but which would never be forgotten.

Narendra had been sorely puzzled how to give something to Cyril in memory of that night, but he knew that he would, and could, accept nothing of value; and he had consulted Baba

Sahib on the subject, who had suggested that a small silver salver with an inscription of the day and the year of the Dacoity, and the names of himself, Aunt Ella, and Seeta, would be enough and would be gladly received; and Narendra at once had it put in hand, and finished all the rich chasing himself; Seeta wrote the letters on it, and her grandfather engraved them. So when it was ready, Narendra took it one evening to the camp when business was finished, and praying to be pardoned for the liberty, presented it respectfully.

I think Cyril was deeply affected by this simple act of kind thoughtfulness. He could speak little; indeed, as he took the salver from the banker, and held out his hand to receive the wreath of flowers which Seeta had strung for the occasion, there arose a lump in his throat which he could hardly repress; but he said, "I will keep it safely, Narendra, and the flowers too, in memory of you all, and I will tell them in England of my kind friends here, when I go there: my mother will value this gift as much as I do."

That day Seeta had arranged a visit to the temple with Aunt Ella to make offerings for the child, and her grandfather had accompanied them. It was impossible not to see that the child grew weaker, and took less nourishment day by day; but the simple faith of the household could only find one vent, except their prayers, in an offering at Wamun Bhut's temple, and they had taken the child there to be blessed solemnly, and laid before God. It was after this ceremony that Narendra had taken the salver to Cyril; and as he returned, he told them what he had done, and what Cyril had said. "No, he will not forget us now," he continued, "and being alone he will remember us the more. Look! it is very sad to see such a man alone."

They looked to where he pointed, and though it was growing dusk they could see Cyril sitting in his chair before his tent alone, except his little dog Muff, which lay at his feet; and the tears were streaming from Seeta's eyes, as she prayed silently, "O God! keep him safe, keep him safe, for the sake of his mother and all who love him." Next day they got a message to say he was obliged to leave on business; and when Seeta looked from her oriel window, the morning after that, she saw that the white tents were gone.

CHAPTER XV.

UNCERTAINTY.

Cyril Brandon's absence from Shah Gunje did not lessen the trouble of mind which had beset him. It was accountable to him that the Hindoo girl should be perpetually in his thoughts; that he should dream of her at nights; and that through the day her pleading, wistful face, and dewy eyes, should come between him and his work so constantly—"What was she to him, or he to her?" Thrown together, as it were, by strange circumstances, it had been impossible for him not to feel a keen interest in one so beautiful, so interesting, and so entirely different from any one he had ever seen. He knew now, what he had never known before, that such women as Seeta might, and did, exist among the people. He had often felt the intellectual power of the strange girl to be equal with, or, indeed, superior to, his own, in their discussions upon the books she had read to him; and those pleasant interviews—when her first reserve had given way before the mutual appreciation of beauties or difficulties in the texts of the old Hindoo poets—now returned on his mind with irresistible force. Seeta seemed again to be seated before him with her book on her lap, her finger pointing to a favourite passage, and her face upturned to him as he lay, full of interest and excitement: her eyes flashing, her sweet mouth partly opened, showing her little pearly teeth, her cheek glowing with the lovely Titianesque colour by which he had been so much struck on first seeing her, and her dark wavy hair (it was not black) escaping from the knot in which it was loosely tied, and falling in soft curls over her neck and shoulder, tinged, where the light caught it, with threads of gold. Such a picture was but too often present, I think, for Cyril's peace of mind and former content with his loneliness: "If I had only been able to make a drawing of her," he often said, "how I should have prized it!"

Then one heavy temptation would follow; and I should be sorry if my readers thought I wished to exhibit to them any ideal perfection in Cyril Brandon. He was, as all men are, subject to temptation; and though a fine, manly fellow, kind, considerate, and clever, was not exempt from liability to error. These struggles he well knew himself, and being habitually of a devout mind, prayed for right direction in all things; but the present was the sharpest trial which had yet come upon him?

What if the girl loved him? and that might be, or might come to be—could she not live with him? She was a widow, and of no value to her family; she would probably never marry again, but live out a useless, lonely life till she died; or she might become a devotee—that beautiful hair cut off—disfigured—and pass her days in wandering from shrine to shrine all over India, dressed in the coarsest garments, and undergoing the severest privations. With him she would be happy in her own way: she would have a new object in life, and what tie had she now to her own home? Her child was dead. Baba Sahib had told him, a few days after they had left Shah Gunje, that it had fallen back suddenly in her arms, and breathed its last quietly, and she was in terrible grief. Well, indeed, he knew how her life was bound up in that child, and that there was now no other vent or object for her love. But he would make her happy again if she would come to him: and how many as good as he had formed such connections, some for life and others till they married? The more Cyril thought on this plan, the more feasible it appeared; and he determined to write to Seeta and ask her to live with him. I think he felt certain that she would come; and, perhaps, with the common estimate of Hindoo character which too generally prevails, he did not give the girl credit for higher motives of honour and self-respect which might influence her.

And one night, when he was alone, and his tempter was busy with his soul, he sat down and wrote—wrote such words as he was sure Seeta would read with secret joy and exultation, and would not reprove him. But—and I may say it not irreverently—his mind, as he read it over, presently rejected what he had written; rejected it as dishonourable and insulting, and he prayed to be delivered from his temptation; and as he cried, "Lord, I am sinking; save me ere I perish!" he tore up the letter into small fragments and burned them. In Seeta's intercourse with him he remembered that he had never detected any trace of levity, and he felt that she believed him, as she had told him once, pure and good. Her place in life, melancholy as her future seemed to be, her grandfather's wealth and respectable position, must have raised her above any thought of such dishonour as he had nearly proposed. Any disgrace to them would involve his own, with his superiors, and with all the people of the country; and to forfeit these would be madness. Above all, it would be sin—deliberate sin before God, and must be put away. So thinking, long into the night, Cyril went to his rest, and slept more calmly than he had done for many a night past; and when he woke in the morning he was refreshed, and did his work through the day to the admiration of Baba Sahib, who congratulated him on his complete recovery.

"Now that you are quite well, sir," he said, "I think you should go to Shah Gunje and finish what there is to do there. I kept most of it from you then, for you were really unable to work; and it must be done, as you know as well as I. There is nothing of importance remaining here."

"Be it so," returned Cyril; "my arm is well now, and I can go whenever you please. Yes, I know there are several cases to try, and the revenue affairs have been already too long deferred. All must be looked to speedily."

"Then I will warn the people, and to-morrow we can finish all there is here. It is only twenty miles to Shah Gunje, and we can halt a day between. Will the day after to-morrow suit you?"

"Certainly," replied Cyril; "I am quite ready; and we shall see Narendra again. I wish we could tell him that we had caught Azrúel Pandé; but the police are still at fault. I think he must have left the country. We need not stay long at Shah Gunje."

"Not long, sir; only a few days."

Perhaps Cyril thought that there was danger in moving his camp to Shah Gunje, but the work must be done; and though he might see the banker and enquire after Seeta's health, he felt, and thankfully felt, that the temptation which had beset him and distressed him, had been graciously removed from his mind.

At Shah Gunje, however, Seeta was in sore strait. Her existence, as we know, had been bound up in her child. He was the only barrier between her and the now dreary widowhood of her life. With him, too, had died the hope that he would succeed to his father's estate and business, for all the hereditary property must now pass to Ram Das, who had, indeed, lost no time in putting in his claim to it, and to the funds held by Narendra; and he would have all, except the small portion which she would inherit as a widow. Possibly she might adopt an heir; but that was a distant contingency, and might not be allowable. But if she did, what could he be to her in comparison of her boy—her child, who had been once saved, and on whose existence her own life seemed to depend?

I need not dilate upon her inconsolable grief. Those who read these lines may be able to estimate what it was, better than I can attempt to describe it, and understand how the loving heart of the girl was broken down by her great sorrow.

Day after day she sat in the balcony we know of, silent, rarely weeping, looking out to the temple where she had laid her boy before the Lord of Life, who had not heard her, and near which they had buried him. Nor were the white tents there, nor did she hear of their coming.

Good Aunt Ella was at her very wits' end. She had tried to arouse Seeta, and to interest her in common household matters. She had invited many of her old companions to come to her, and they had come, and in their homely way wept with her and tried to console her, in vain. She had asked Wamun Bhut to remonstrate, and the good priest had done his best; had read to Seeta passages out of the holy books which enjoined resignation and faith, and had told her how all worldly things were but illusion, and that she must now devote herself to attaining the reality. And he read to her parts of her old studies; but when one day he began "Savitri," thinking it would interest her and strengthen her faith, she looked at him sadly and put her hand on the book to prevent him. "Twice I would have gone to death," she said; "once for my duty with him, and once for my love with Lalco; but the Lord of Death would not permit me. O may he come to me soon, that I may follow them? Why should I live now? No one would miss me, and you would all remember me."

By-and-by, as the days passed, they thought she was calmer, and she often wept, which Aunt Ella thought to be a good sign. "It will ease her heart," she said to herself, "and it is very heavy still. When I became a widow I wept and wept for a year, and then peace came to me; but I had no child—none but her, and if she were taken then I too must die! Night after night the dear old lady watched by Seeta's bed, fanned her gently to sleep, and then lay down beside her on the carpet. She often heard Seeta mutter in her sleep, and heard her call upon her child; and rising, patted her gently to soothe her. But one night the dream seemed to be changed; instead of the child's, the name of the English gentleman who had saved them was sweetly murmured, and as Aunt Ella looked she saw a gentle smile spread over the girl's face, the rigid expression relax, the pale face flush with colour, the lips become red and humid, instead of white and dry, and a tear trickle from the closed eyes; while the girl's bosom heaved, and she sighed, but not in pain. At first Aunt Ella thought this only a dream of what had been, and of Seeta's gratitude; but again and again, night after night, it came, and distressed her. She dare not mention it to her child; but she noticed more and more that

Seeta rarely left the window during the day, and that a wistful, dreamy gaze was fixed upon the grove where the white tents had been. What if they should come again?

And one day, as we know, as Seeta rose and looked out as usual, the tents were rising under the trees. Aunt Ella was near her, and was at once startled by the cry, "Look, aunt, look! the tents are being pitched, and he will come!" And there was a bright expression in her eyes and an earnest look in her flushed face that the good lady had not seen for months. Was she glad to see it? Not for that cause, which revealed to her the secret of the nightly dreams. Not that the man they all respected and loved, should now be nearest to her child's heart. Ah, yes! the grief for the child had been terrible; the crisis of it had been anxiously looked for; Seeta's death or life had seemed to hang in a balance; but this newly born excitement was a worse grief to Aunt Ella than even the child's death. Still she would watch.

Narendra went, the day after his arrival, to see Cyril, and they had a long conversation. The banker detailed the circumstances of the child's death, and their hopeless attempts to comfort his mother. "I think," he said, "if you had written to say you were well, and that the wound was healed, it would have diverted her thoughts; for even since yesterday, knowing you are well, she has been more herself. Will you not come to see her? I cannot send her and her aunt here, you know; and I am sure a word from you would do her more good than all our preaching."

"Perhaps," replied Cyril, "once before I go; but I shall stay many days for my work, and she will hear that I am able to do it. I wish her well, Narendra, and I grieved to hear of the loss of poor little Laloo. How fond he grew of me there! Tell her I have not forgotten him or her, nor the time I was with you; she and Aunt Ella must send me some sweetmeats and some pickles—they were so good."

Narendra delivered his message, and perhaps—for it was only natural—enlarged in a simple fashion on all the Commissioner Sahib had graciously said. Seeta's heart leaped to the words she heard, and she and Aunt Ella set themselves to work to prepare all that they thought Cyril had liked best when he was with them; and Seeta strung some garlands of flowers and bid Aunt Ella put them round his neck with her own hands. Then one evening, when all was ready, and Aunt Ella knew Cyril would be alone, she took them to him.

Now, good Aunt Ella had insisted on going alone; first,

because it would be indecorous to allow Seeta to go with her; secondly, she did not want the priest, who had offered his company. She was not afraid of Cyril, and needed not her brother's or the priest's countenance. And thirdly, because, for reasons only known to herself, she was uneasy about Seeta, and would "have it out" with Cyril about her. So Aunt Ella went to the camp and delivered her baskets full of good things, and gave instructions to Cyril's servant how he was to prepare them for his master; and when he had gone away she said, "Is there no one near, sir? What I have to say to you no one must hear; it is between ourselves."

Much wondering, Cyril rose and looked about; but there was no one. His usual belted attendants were sitting in front of his tent a long way off, talking to the banker's men, who had come up with Aunt Ella, and as the story of the Dacoity was being told over again, all were interested.

"No," said Cyril, as he returned; "there is no one—what have you to say? speak freely."

Aunt Ella came from the place where she had stood hitherto, and sat down close beside his chair; and she put her hand gently on his arm to give more earnestness to her words. Aunt Ella was habitually quaint and blunt in her speech, and she did not feel disposed to indulge in many words, or in compliments, on this occasion.

"You came to us in our need, sir," she said, "in your great kindness, and you saved our lives, our property, and our honour. You shed your blood for us, and if you had been of our own kindred you could not have done more. For that we pray that God may reward you, and He will do so. We are simple folks, sir, and when you were wounded and lay ill, you were as a son of the house, and no one hid their face from you. We would have given our lives for you; and had no reservation. Seeta and I sat with you, and she read to you—and——" but here Aunt Ella's voice, which had been quavering, now broke down, and she burst into tears.

"Yes," said Cyril, "I admit all, Aunt Ella, and you know I shall never forget what happened, and all your kindness; but you must not cry."

"Ah no!" replied the old lady, wiping her eyes; "it is no use crying! You will never forget it, but I wish Seeta had forgotten it—I wish she had never seen you."

"Why?" asked Cyril, though his heart smote him, as he asked the question.

"Why? because she loves you, sir; because in the night she

dreams of you, and murmurs your name, and says love words that I dare not repeat. She does not know this, and by day she is calm; but I know the words are lying at her heart. Since you came she has been restless and excited; she seems to have forgotten the child; she asks me twenty times a day whether you are well—what you are doing—whether your wound is healed—till I get quite provoked with her. What are you to her? It is bold—it is immodest that she should ask. Have you—have you, sir," she continued, grasping his arm suddenly "corrupted her? have you seduced my child?—If you have—nay, do not speak—take her, and do what you will with her. She will be dead to us, and the dishonour will rest with you, not with us. O sir! we loved you so, we loved you so.—You should not have brought this upon us; it is more than I, than Narendra can bear, and we were better dead."

Cyril was deeply moved by what he heard. "I am innocent," he said, "and she is innocent—as a child she is innocent before God, of what you think."

"Then swear to me by your God, and your mother, that what you say is true," cried Aunt Ella, kneeling before him, with tears streaming down her cheeks. "O swear this to me, and I will depart in peace with you."

"Before God, and by my dear mother," he replied earnestly, "I swear to you that this is true."

"I am content," she replied; "and thankful, sir. Forgive me that I doubted—yes, doubted, and feared, too, for she is so beautiful, and you are both so young. Now, sir, one boon I beg, for all our sakes, and Seeta's most of all. Go away. Go as soon as you can finish your work; do not delay. Go far from hence. Let it be between us as though we had never met, as it was before the death of Huree Das. If that had not been, we should never have known you. Do not return this year, or for as long as you can possibly be absent; or let some one come in your place. Do not ask after us, or seek to communicate with us; we shall go on in our old way, and Seeta will get accustomed to that in time, as I have done; if not, she will die. Will you do this?"

"I will," replied Cyril. "You have done well to tell me, and I would not for my life that a breath of dishonour fell on your house. Go, you may trust my honour."

"I do trust it, sir, I do trust it; and forgive me if I have spoken beyond the bounds of respect. I am grown old and foolish now, and could not help what I said. I will tell Seeta that you have taken her sweetmeats, and that will content her.

And now, sir," she continued solemnly, as she rose, lifted up her hands, and placed them on his head; "take an old woman's blessing, who loves you as a son. It will not harm you; take it as you would your mother's, and I will go home happy. You will not forget us!"

Cyril could not speak, for the old lady's sudden action and words had affected him to tears! "May God keep you all safely!" he said at length, as he took her hands from his head and kissed them. "Now leave me," and she went away.

Yes, Seeta seemed content when she heard that Cyril had accepted her little gift, and day by day she sat alone, looking, as was her wont, at the busy camp where her thoughts were; but on the fourth day after Aunt Ella's visit, as she went to the altar on the housetop to gather toolsee leaves for the morning worship, she looked again to the camp grove, but the white tents were there no longer.

CHAPTER XVI.

AUNT ELLA'S COUNSEL.

If Cyril Brandon's mind had been in a condition of unrest when he left Shah Gunje on a former occasion, it was hardly probable, considering the cause, that it would be in any degree more settled after Aunt Ella's revelation. If it had been possible, he would have removed next morning to the other end of his district and remained there, but that was not possible; and he remained three days, when he told Baba Sahib, who was really anxious about him, that he was not well, that the place did not agree with him, and that he must move about for change. Baba Sahib strongly recommended him to go at once to Noorpoor and consult the doctors there; but he would not hear of this. In a few days he would be better, and would return; if not, he would go to Noorpoor and get advice. It was clear to Cyril's mind that he could not bear the strain on him much longer. That the Hindoo girl loved him there could be no doubt, and that she was very miserable was equally certain. Again and again had the temptation been near him, suggesting specious arguments as to his possession of Seeta, and his enjoyment of life with her; and again and again, in nights of agitated thought, had he nearly yielded. But his strong mind had not yet been thrown off its balance, and he had been supported, he well knew how. Should he even resign his appointment and go home? That indeed was a last resource; but should he be any better there than here? He thought not; and for many reasons which we know of, his resignation now was impolitic and impossible. Some days' absence would remove the load from his heart, he thought: and he went.

But his old Serishtadar was not by any means satisfied. His master had moved his camp almost without warning, and for once had not taken him into his confidence. Many of the Zemindars were still at Shah Gunje, waiting their term of settlement; and Mr. Brandon knew this as well as he did: and there was much work to be done elsewhere. If he were really ill, why not go to Noorpoor to recover? No, there was something more than he knew; there must be, else why this vacillation?—a phase of his master's character which the old man had never seen before. Why this erratic avoidance of Shah Gunje? Had any distressing news arrived from England? for Baba Sahib knew almost as much of his master's affairs there as he did himself; but he had mentioned nothing about them, though letters had reached him by every mail regularly for some time past. What then could it be?

Baba Sahib had sat thus pondering for some time, when a sudden thought struck him; and as it rose in his mind, the old man's cheeks seemed to burn with a flush of pain and concern. As Aunt Ella was returning home after her interview with Cyril, Baba Sahib had met her, and had observed that she was much agitated, and her eyes swollen with weeping; and he had passed her with a few words of kindly greeting. What could have been the purport of her visit? Could his master have done evil to Seeta? Perhaps Baba Sahib had but a feeble conviction of the virtue of Hindoo Soodra widows, especially of any so beautiful as Seeta, and so learned; and I also doubt whether he considered that such persons should be educated, and taught to read the holy books as well as Brahmins. But no. His master, the soul of honour as he knew him to be, could not have yielded to temptation or seduction. He had been Narendra's guest, had eaten of his salt, and had been nursed, lovingly and tenderly; he could not have betrayed them! So Baba Sahib put away the thought at once, vexed with himself that he had ever allowed it to rise. Still, however, it remained there, and he thought he would watch carefully over his master's honour as his own.

At Shah Gunje the time passed away drearily. Aunt Ella, though she had not spoken to Seeta on the subject of her interview with Brandon, was yet watching the girl very narrowly, and was dismayed at the condition in which she remained. Now that the camp was gone, Seeta seemed hopelessly dull and melancholy, and nothing would arouse her. What household duties she had to do were performed mechanically and without interest. Her once cheerful voice was almost silent, and she was often found by her aunt in tears. Even the books were laid aside, and all her little amusements were neglected. Nor could Narendra arouse her to any exertion; nor in the daily games at chess, in which the old man had always delighted, was there any satisfaction, for Seeta was absent and careless, hardly knowing what she played, and making perpetual mistakes, which almost provoked him.

Nor could he arouse her to the necessity of his making an adoption, a subject often anxiously discussed between him and his sister. For Narendra had formerly adopted Seeta's child, and now he was dead, another heir was necessary. There were none available for the purpose but the children of distant relatives, and which to choose was the difficult point. He had hoped that Seeta would decide; but she had said he might do as he pleased, and that she was quite indifferent as to his choice. She could not love another child, she said; and since her own was gone, it would be better to leave the matter undecided, or allow time to elapse before it was considered. In vain had the good priest striven to arouse the girl to a sense of duty on this point; she was hopelessly listless and indifferent, and many an anxious conversation had passed between him and Narendra on the subject. All they could think was, that it was her child's death that had so deeply affected her: and they agreed that the wisest course would be to give her more time to recover. The priest even hinted that he thought a visit to Benares, and the performance of certain ceremonies that he could direct, would be the surest method to arouse Seeta; and that the change of scene and air would revive her. If Aunt Ella had told what she knew, it would probably have brought matters to a crisis sooner; but she was content in knowing that Brandon was gone, and from all she could hear it was not likely that he would return that season.

In this, however, she was disappointed. It was impossible for Brandon to neglect his duty, or to postpone what he had to do at Shah Gunje. Nearly a month had elapsed since he was there before. Baba Sahib had watched very carefully, but there had been no renewal of intercourse, either by letter or by message, with the banker's house, and he had come to the conclusion that his master was perfectly safe. When, therefore, he had proposed to return to their work, Brandon had assented cheerfully.

Again, one morning, as Seeta had gone to the altar on the terrace to gather toolsee leaves, she saw that the camp was being pitched. She had had no hope that it would return. No one had told her of such a possibility. All whom she had dared to ask on the subject, had told her the Commisioner Sahib had gone away for the year, was in a distant part of the province, and would not return; and her grandfather had even spoken to her of his intention to go to Mr. Brandon and lay the matter of adoption before him, and ask his advice in regard to it. The joy which she felt when she was now assured of his return was too vivid not to be noticed by Aunt Ella; and as Seeta flew down the steps, crying to her, "Come and look—come and look; the tents are there again!" and her glowing face betrayed her emotion—the worthy old lady received, to her mind, the most decided confirmation of all her suspicions. But there was no help for it now. She could not tell Mr. Brandon to go away; she could only rely on the pledge he had given to her, and in which she fondly believed. Thus several days passed; and beyond a kind message from Cyril to inquire after their health, no communication had occurred between the camp and the banker's house. So far Aunt Ella was quite satisfied; and as one of the usual annual ceremonies at the temple had to be performed, she saw no objection to taking Seeta with her, as she had indeed always done before.

The temple was, as I have said before, close to the grove in which Cyril's camp was pitched. Some one, in former days, had chosen this rising ground for its beauty, had built the temple there, and planted a large grove of mango and tamarind trees, which had flourished in great luxuriance, and under their grateful shade the camps of the English civil officers were always pitched. From the knoll there was a glorious prospect over an undulating country, richly cultivated and wooded; and far away were some of the bolder mountains of the province, bounding the view with their ever-varying colour as the sun rested on them. Even without any formal religious ceremony to perform, the terrace of the temple, and the small room which belonged to its officiating priest, Wamun Bhut—often the scene of Seeta's studies with him—had a charm for her which she delighted to enjoy. The fresh, fine air, the sense of freedom, the exquisite view over the country, formed a welcome change from the town-house and its unavoidable confinement; and on this occasion were more than ever enjoyable. Seeta and Aunt Ella had gone there early, and they had determined to stay till the evening. They had performed their devotions, and laid their simple offerings before the image, and had watched the crowds of town and country folks who passed through the courts, or sat in groups on the terrace, enjoying the scene as much as they did themselves, and eating the sweetmeats or other food they had brought with them. On the other side was the camp of Cyril Brandon, and the busy scene of people passing to and fro—petitioners, red-belted messengers, groups of villagers sitting under the trees, while their scribes were writing their petitions or making up their accounts. Beyond, Mr. Brandon's horses, the horses of his escort of police, camels, and his single elephant, all made up a scene of curious interest to Seeta, who had seldom been so near it before.

Of Brandon himself they knew nothing; but Seeta knew where he was, and well remembered the large white tent in which she had seen him first, now more than a year ago, and the whole scene was as fresh in her memory as if it had occurred yesterday. Then, as the sun declined, and a large tree behind the tents threw a broad shadow over the grass, they saw the servants spread a large carpet and place a chair, while people from all sides gathered round, and some sat down, while others stood in groups, and conversed together. Presently they saw Cyril, and Baba Sahib, with their scribes, come out of the tent, and as Cyril received the salutations of the crowd and returned them, he sat down and the business of the evening began.

Sometimes Seeta could see him, sometimes the people shut him out from her view; but she saw enough to assure her that he was well, that the paleness which had followed his wound had given place to his wonted ruddy colour, and that he could use the wounded arm freely. Should she ever speak with him again? O but for one word, even to hear him ask her if she were well—that would be enough, and all that she could hope for now. In the house, in her own room, they had not seemed far apart; but in his camp and busy life, how should he remember her? I think, if Seeta had gone home under these impressions, that she would have grown more contented with her lot, and would, in time, have ceased to grieve as she had done: and that it would have come to her more and more assuredly, that there was a gulf between Cyril and herself, which could not be passed. But it was not to be so.

Cyril's Petitioners' Court, as it was called, was a curious and interesting scene. There had been some instances, on his first arrival in the province, of the attendants and messengers intercepting petitions, or requiring petitioners to pay gratuities ere their cases could be attended to: and Cyril, to prevent this, had instituted a petition box, which was set up at some distance before his tent, and near which no official servant was allowed to remain. The box was locked, and there was a wide slit in the lid through which petitions could be deposited. In the evening the box was placed before Cyril when he took his seat outside, and unlocked; and one of the scribes, taking out the papers as they came, had the name of the petitioner called out, and the document was read in his presence, and disposed of at once by endorsement or otherwise.

It is hard to say, whether mere curiosity to hear what was going on—and Aunt Ella was fond of excitement in her own way, fond of caste meetings, of recitations by Brahmins, plays, and other public gatherings—or a desire to see Brandon once more, perhaps to speak a word with him, led her to say to Seeta —they were sitting on the terrace of the temple—"I will leave you here, and go and see what is doing yonder. An old woman will never be noticed, and I should like to know what orders are given on Ram Das's petition for the lands at Gokulpoor, for I know he is going to present one. I will not be long, and then we can go home. Your grandfather will like to hear what Mr. Brandon orders in the case;" and so Aunt Ella departed, and Seeta, longing to be in her place, watched her enter the crowd of petitioners and their friends, and then lost sight of her.

Aunt Ella's curiosity was gratified. She heard Brandon order Ram Das's petition to be referred to the native district office for report, and would have come away; but it was pleasant to listen to all that was going on, to hear what every one wanted, and to see how patiently her son—for she always in her heart called Cyril so—did his work, and how graciously he spoke to all. At last she turned to go, and had got but a few steps towards the temple, when one of the scarlet-coated messengers, whom she knew, overtook her, and said respectfully that she was to wait till the court rose, for that his master wished to speak with her.

"How could Cyril have seen her?" Aunt Ella thought; what could he have possibly to say to her? what would Seeta think of her absence? She was much puzzled, and vexed that she had gone at all; but she waited patiently, saw the crowd disperse, saw the ministerial officer take leave, and Mr. Brandon proceed into his private tent; and then the man, who had not left her, said it was time to go, and she went, with her heart beating.

There was no one in the tent but Cyril, who was seated on the side of his low bed, and who rose, took her hand kindly, and placed her on the carpet by his side. She could not see his face very well, for the tent was dark; but she thought he spoke in an agitated tone, and she would have given worlds to escape. What could he have to say? But she was not a moment in suspense.

"Aunt Ella," he said, "I have sent for you to bear a message from me to your brother, Narendra. I might have waited a day or two perhaps, but I saw you in the crowd, and I then determined I would not delay. I have tried to forget Seeta—no, not forget, for that could not be; but to think she could never be more to me than she has been—but it has been impossible, for I love her more than I can tell you, and my life is sad without her. I want you to tell your brother, that if the rules of your caste will allow of it, I will marry her; marry her as my lawful wife in all honour, if she will accept me. If this cannot be, he must tell me so without reserve; and I will go away, and never, while I live, return here. I would cast no dishonour on you, and the highest return I can make for Seeta's love is to make her my wife. Do you hear all this?"

It was hard to say whether Aunt Ella had heard it or not. She had heard him say something about Seeta and marriage, and she had looked at him wonderingly with her mouth open and her great eyes staring: and as he asked the last question, she had fallen forward on his hands as he had stretched them out—gasping, but without speaking; but she had not fainted, and she revived presently, and looked up dreamily as she passed her hand before her eyes.

"You did not hear me, Aunt Ella, you did not hear what I told you," said Cyril, as he chafed her withered hands. "It is little to say, and I tell you now again, that I will marry Seeta if you and Narendra will give her to me."

"I do not know, I cannot say," she replied; "and I dare not tell my brother; send for him, tell him yourself, tell him now. Or stay," she continued, rising; "you know Wamun Bhut, he is our priest—he knows all that can be done—you may speak to him as you would to Narendra. Come at once!" and she pulled him towards the tent door; she had forgotten Seeta in her agitation.

It was but a few steps to the temple gate, and there was no one in the court, all the worshippers had gone. Aunt Ella, motioning Cyril to stay where he was, went into the temple, and a moment afterwards reappeared with Wamun Bhut.

"Tell him," she said eagerly, "what you told me, and he will decide rightly, for he loves us, and we trust in him in all things."

The priest looked from one to the other wonderingly, but his heart misgave him as he thought of Seeta. At last Brandon spoke—

"It need not be repeated, for what had been said to Aunt Ella has already been recorded. They all trust you," he continued to the priest, "and my honour as well as theirs is in your hands. If this can be, let it be done at once; if not, let me know, and I will depart, and return no more."

Seeta had been sitting within the little room which the priest used, looking over the fair landscape—she had watched the sun set in a glory of golden and crimson clouds, and now the purple-grey shadows of evening were stealing over the scene before her,—wondering why Aunt Ella did not come, yet hoping that Cyril might have detained her, and was sending some kind message by her. She had heard her aunt call to the priest, had heard them talking with some one, and had moved to the door to meet her aunt to go home, when she saw the three figures close by her—so close that she could have touched them—and heard Brandon's last words, "I will depart and return no more." Perhaps she hardly knew what she did; but as the sad tone of the words fell on her ears, she believed them true, and unable to control her emotion, stepped hurriedly forward, and throwing herself at Cyril's feet, clasped his knees, and wept passionately. "You will leave me, you will leave me!" was all she could utter.

He raised her up gently, and drew her to his heart: "Never, Seeta; if they will give you to me," he said: "where I go you will go, if you will be my wife. Speak before them, or else let me go, and I will depart for ever."

Seeta had shuddered at the strong caress, and had wellnigh been overwhelmed by her emotion. She could not utter a word in reply, and her tongue seemed to cleave to the roof of her mouth; but the dream of her latter days was fulfilled, and she knew she was loved. If she had died as she felt his arm close round her and her head sunk on his breast, she would have died happy.

"Speak!" cried Aunt Ella and the priest almost in a breath. "What wouldst thou, Seeta?"

"I will go with him, if ye give me to him," she said with difficulty; "yes, I will go!" and she withdrew herself gently from Cyril, and throwing her arms round Aunt Ella's neck, wept sorely as she led her away.

"You had better retire, sir," said the priest; "we are none of us calm enough to talk more; I will see Narendra to-night, and consult with him as to the future—and—and—" he added with hesitation, "if you get a letter from me, depart at once; you will see that it is necessary for their honour and your own."

CHAPTER XVII.

"I WILL KEEP HER VERY SAFELY."

BEFORE office hours on the following day, Baba Sahib had sent word so Cyril that he had some business of importance to communicate, and had been desired to come as soon as possible. His own anxieties had been renewed, as he had seen Aunt Ella conducted to Cyril's tent the evening before, and he resolved to remonstrate. On the other hand, Cyril was equally desirous to tell what he had determined, and to ask his faithful friend's advice; and as Baba Sahib seated himself, Brandon at once opened the subject.

"I did not ask your advice, Baba Sahib," he said, "because in a matter like this no man can ask counsel of another; he must do as his heart directs him, under God's will. I thought I could put Seeta out of my thoughts, but I found that impossible, and I have asked them to give her to me in marriage."

"When?" cried the old man, eagerly.

"Last evening," returned Brandon, "I saw Aunt Ella among the crowd, and told her to remain; and I then asked her for Seeta. She took me to the temple to see the priest. I found Seeta there, and told her."

"Thank God, sir! I thank God humbly that your honour is safe, for men's tongues were wagging freely in regard to your comings and goings. Have you had any reply?" asked Baba Sahib.

"None as yet," said Cyril. "The priest said he would write as soon as he could; indeed, that man coming yonder may be his messenger."

It was so, and they read the letter together. A few lines in Sanscrit, to this effect; "Narendra will come with me to the temple to-night; meet us there, and bring Baba Sahib with you."

"I will not fail you, sir," he said, "in this or in anything.

At least," he thought, "it will end the matter one way or other."

In the evening they met in the priest's room, in the temple court. It was quite dark, but a small lamp was burning in a niche. A small carpet and a pillow had been arranged for Cyril; and as he entered he took off his shoes as he saluted the Brahmins, and sat down. The priest was the first to speak.

"I told Narendra," he said, "and Ella also related what you had asked. I told him what you had said to Seeta, and his desire is to hear all from your own lips."

And Brandon did not hesitate. From first to last he told all—his surprise, admiration, respect; then how love for Seeta grew on him day by day, though he had been silent; what his struggles had been, and his final and firm determination, before he left Shah Gunje, to propose the only honourable course within possibility. "It is for you to give a reply," he said. "You are her elders and guardians; and if it cannot be, I must submit and go away; and I think—I hope—that Seeta will submit too."

"And you tell me this, sir! of your own free will, duly considering the result, and will not fail?" said Narendra, nervously.

"No one has influenced me," replied Cyril, "and I am free to do as I please, and as my honour needs. I will not fail. Many men among us have done the same, and I am no better than they. Trust me, if you can, for your child's sake."

"I will trust you," replied the banker, earnestly. "I need no further proof of your high principle. It is only what all men say of you. Now listen, friends," he added to the others, "and if, after hearing me, you think that I can give Seeta to him with honour, you will decide. You are Brahmins, and know far more than I do. Many years ago—centuries—when the Hindoo princes of Beejanugger ruled over Southern India, and the Moslems held Goolburgah, there was a great war, on account of a daughter of our craft, who was very beautiful and learned, like Seeta. The Rajah of Beejanugger desired to carry her away from Moodgul, where she lived, and sent his horsemen to seize her; but the Moslems prevented this, and a bitter war followed, in which the Moslems were victorious. Then the Moslem king sent for the goldsmith's daughter, whom his son had seen and loved in secret, and married her to him; and she bore him children, who sat on the royal throne of Beeder. We, sirs, are descendants of that family, and no spot or blemish fell on our caste for what was done. Now one of the kings of this land again seeks a daughter of our house, and we can give Seeta to him, because, being Soodras, our women can marry a second time; but should I be wrong, ye, who know the law, will tell me so, and check the error in time."

Long and anxiously did the two Brahmins argue the question, and both were learned men. That a Soodra woman could marry a second time there was no question: but that she could marry a Christian was doubtful, because it was a contingency nowhere provided for. Still, so long as the woman preserved her caste, the marriage was binding on her; and if she joined her husband's faith, then the question lapsed out of Hindooism altogether, into a law of which neither could speak.

On his part, Brandon explained his position. He could not be married by his own ceremonies unless his wife was a Christian. If she joined his faith of her free will at any time, he would then marry her again by his own rites; but if she remained in her faith, he would not seek to influence her, or to disturb her caste in any way. If they had children, they would become Christians, as they could not be Hindoos. As to Seeta herself, if English people desired to know her and honour her, it would be well; but if not, she would not miss them, and would be happy with him.

Narendra and the priest were happier that night, I think, than they had been for some months past, and, I may add, Baba Sahib also. His only misgiving was, as to Brandon's noble family. What effect would the news have on them? But his master had undertaken to satisfy them, and that was sufficient. It had been agreed among all that the sooner the ceremony was concluded the better; and Wamun Bhut, having consulted his tables, found that in about a week an excellent day for the marriages of Soodra widows would happen; and they might be married at the temple if the preliminary ceremonies were concluded at the banker's house. Brandon pleaded much to be allowed to see Seeta once before the day fixed, but this Narendra gently forbade.

"Take your wife to you in all honour and all men's respect," he said. "After that, she is yours, not ours, and her happiness lies with you. We give her freely, and we can trust you to provide for her every comfort you see that she needs."

Then Cyril once more broke up his camp, and went away for a few days; but, as Seeta now knew, only to return. The time must come when she would have a personal interest in those changes; meanwhile, her whole trust was in the man who had chosen her, and asked her to come out from among her people and be his wife. She was very happy—too happy to speak much. If she saw her grandfather's venerable face wear a look of care, and tears often tremble in his eyes, there were cheering hopes poured out to sustain and comfort him; and the assurance given, that she should never be long away.

As to dear Aunt Ella, she was sorely bewildered indeed. To think that Seeta should marry her son—the son she had adopted in her heart; that she should be one of the English ladies—the very Queen of all the province—she, that little Seeta who had grown up in her arms—and that she should not be afraid! She had been afraid of Huree Das, she knew, but he was rough; and she was not afraid of Cyril. No; Seeta was not afraid. There was indeed that thirsting to be his, which had pursued her for many a day and night, and in its fiery spirit had wellnigh withered up her being. Of Cyril's kindness and love for her she had no doubt. She would be his own "Savitri" now, not of duty only, but of love, too—a faithful wife till she died. No more terrors of dreary widowhood; no solitary objectless days, and nights of sleepless unrest and doubt. I will not say that her thought was not crossed by uncertainties; but, for the most part, the future seemed bright, very bright, before her; though her old companions could not understand her at all, nor why the English Commissioner Sahib was to carry off the richest and most beautiful girl in the country.

So at last the day came, and good Aunt Ella's hospitable preparations were at an end. I need not recount how many Brahmins were fed, nor what *largesse* was given; how ample a *trousseau* was provided for Seeta, far more than she could carry away; nor how her new anklets and ornaments were far more beautiful than her old. I am afraid, too, that the tedious ceremonials of a Hindoo marriage would hardly interest my readers, and I therefore omit them. Everything had been done that could be done. True, Ram Das and some others of the guild were absent; but still many friends had rallied round Narendra, and no one had attempted to prevent the marriage which the Brahmins had sanctioned. Cyril had gone through all for Seeta's sake. He had suffered a red bridal dress and a turban to be put on him, and had followed all that Baba Sahib told him to do. When the procession of flambeaux and Brahmins went up to the temple at dusk, and fireworks were let off by the way, he had attended in his own palankeen, followed by Seeta. At the temple he had seen her, followed by Aunt Ella, walk thrice round the shrine, and the ceremony was finished; and when the spectators and friends departed, he went to the palankeen by which Narendra and his sister were sitting.

"It is finished," said the old man. "Now no one can part you but God. Take her, Mr. Brandon, take her, and be kind to her."

"I will, Narendra," he replied; "and she shall come herself after a while, and tell you she is happy. Now put her hand into mine, you and Aunt Ella, and I shall feel as if you had really given her to me.—Ah, yes, that is enough, and I thank you both. I will keep her very safely, do not fear. Are you ready, Seeta?"

She could not answer. So Cyril shut the doors of the palankeen, and, calling to the bearers to take it up, turned and walked away by its side.

CHAPTER XVIII.

THE NAWAB'S COMPLAINT.

PERHAPS it was under some sense of embarrassment that Cyril Brandon wrote the following letter to his friend Mostyn. On most momentous changes in life it is far easier to satisfy one's self than one's friends, more especially when any uncommon act, in the world's estimation, has been the result even of good faith and ample consideration. The world at large, of which friends form a portion, is not inclined to give credit either for one or other of these material points, without the certainty that they existed; and as it is impossible to come to a knowledge of this, and conclusions, in ignorance of their causes, are inevitably drawn from events themselves, so in the ease of Cyril Brandon, the world, he thought, and thought truly, would be busy enough. Perhaps, therefore, it was with the hope of anticipating the public verdict that he wrote to his friend, and in this respect my readers must judge for themselves:—

"Camp, November 10, 1851.

"MY DEAR PHILIP,—

"You are entitled to hear from me of what may be misrepresented or exaggerated by common rumour, which I will try to anticipate. You will not have forgotten Seeta, the granddaughter of Narendra, the goldsmith banker of Shah Gunje, nor our conversation in the evening after the trial. I am not going to plead your opinion as any excuse or justification of what I have done—far from it; but of my own convictions, and sincere love and respect, I was married to her yesterday by a ceremony of her own faith, which may be termed 'Gandharba,' and declare her to you as my true and lawful wife. If at any future period she should wish, of her own accord, to join our faith, I will marry her according to Christian rites; for the present, though they were pagan, she is mine under the *lex loci* and the custom of her caste, which does not forbid the marriage of widows.

"I hope you will tell your good wife of this, and that I shall in time hope to receive her congratulations. I ask them because I know her to be superior to ordinary scandal, and to the opinions of some of the women—I won't write ladies—who will discuss the matter at Noorpoor. You will both have to know my wife before you can in the least understand what she really is. I am not going to describe her, for much as I know of her mind now, it is nothing to what time will unfold to me gradually; and as to her beauty, you, who have seen it under trying circumstances, know how great it is.

"I will come into Noorpoor as soon as I possibly can after I hear of your arrival with Mrs. Mostyn and your sister; but poor Grant's arrears are really too heavy to be neglected even for a day, and I must set them right before I think of a holiday. I should like to be with you at Christmas if I can, and I hope Seeta's cottage will be ready before then. I am presuming that you will not delay at Calcutta, so please send me a line to let me know your movements.

"With my kindest regards to Mrs. Mostyn, and my compliments to your sister, if I may present them, believe me ever

"Your affectionate friend,

"CYRIL BRANDON."

While this letter was on its way to Calcutta, it may be anticipated that the news it contained was very freely discussed in Noorpoor. The Nawab of Futtehpoor was the first to receive the intelligence, for he employed one of the junior scribes of Cyril Brandon's establishment, on a small gratuity, to chronicle the daily events of the Commissioner Sahib's camp and life. These precious records were of the usual description of native court news-letters, or "Akhbars," and contained the intelligence "that the Commissioner Sahib had risen at daylight, and had gone out shooting. That he had returned and eaten his breakfast, after which 'the exalted gentleman' had received Baba Sahib Serishtadar and transacted private business with him. That the Kucherry had opened at ten o'clock, and had continued till five, when the Commissioner Sahib held a court outside, to receive the petitions of the poor. Afterwards he had gone to dinner," etc. These details differed little day by day, and the Nawab was often weary of them; but his news-letter reader and writer held his position in too great esteem to omit a word, and every despatch was read carefully to the end. On the day of Cyril's marriage, however, the camp news-writer had a glorious subject for comment, and he wrote the following, not as an "Akhbar," but as a petition to the Nawab himself, marked "To be read in private by the Moonshee Sahib, the learned Syed Ally," and he had despatched the paper by express:—

"To the exalted in rank, of high dignity, the protector of the poor, Nawab Dil Khan Bahadoor, the salutation of his slave, in the name of the Most High.

"A great tyranny has been inflicted, a grievous wrong done, of which my pen is ashamed to write. The honour of the English, which used to be so vaunted, is now besmirched, and has become foul dirt. Praise be to God, and a thousand thanks, that no such crime has ever stained the purity of the true believer! The eyes of the exalted Nawab will open wide, his ears will be filled with the groans of the oppressed, his liver will burn with indignation, when he reads what I have to write. Amen, and Amen!

"The banker Narendra, of Shah Gunje, is well known to my lord as a man of high credit and respectability. He had a granddaughter, Seeta, wise and learned. Her beauty could only be described by the rarest of poets, and your slave dare not dilate upon it, lest the arrogance of attempt should be crowned with the mortification of failure. What had been their previous relations is only known to the All-Seer and to themselves. Last night there was a service at the temple near the camp, and Brandon Sahib went there and carried away the beautiful Seeta by force. The banker and his sister followed them, crying wildly and beating their breasts, but to no purpose: the foul deed had been accomplished. There is much excitement in Shah Gunje, and much pity for the banker. The goldsmiths are all excited, and are crying for justice; but who will listen?

> The dog who was guarding the sheep,
> Has became a wolf, and is devouring them.

"What more can I write?"

"Horrible! detestable!" cried the Nawab, putting his fingers into his ears, as his Moonshee read the letter. "Read no more, Meer Sahib; enough and too much. Behold the villainous hypocrisy of these English! Every one believed that Brandon Sahib was as chaste and virtuous as Joseph. Even Hindoos called him an incarnation of their gods. Now you know, my friend, what he really is. There is always a straw in a thief's beard, and now we see it. Touba! Touba! for shame! for shame! Inshalla! I will obtain justice for these poor people; and let them come to me—to me!" he continued, patting himself on the breast. "I will get them justice, if I have to go to—to—Calcutta for it. I hate that Brandon. Is he not always threatening to enforce the decrees of courts against me, to attach my estates, to make a beggar of me? Inshalla! it is my turn now, and justice will be done. First let me tell his people and unmask this hypocrisy. Yes, my friend, I will go to the Brigadier. Order out my retinue, my state palkee. He shall see, Inshalla! that I am somebody in these times."

"Khodawund, my lord," replied the secretary, who was sitting on his heels in a respectful attitude, at the edge of the Nawab's divan. "I—I fear——"

"Fear what?" cried Dil Khan, twisting up his mustachios. "Fear! don't talk to me of fear."

"God forbid!" said the secretary meekly; "but your Highness can't go in the palankeen, for there are no bearers; they went to their villages yesterday, and declared they would not return till they got their arrears of pay."

"Ah, that's true!" said the Nawab, with a sigh; "but order the elephant."

"Pardon," replied the secretary; "but I heard the driver say yesterday that he would not put the howdah on the poor beast, he was so thin. Moreover, he would not be seen driving him through Noorpoor, for all the boys to laugh at."

"Did he? did he say that, the ——" cried the Nawab, in a fury; but we must spare the reader the volley of expletives which were hurled forth. "Let him get the beast ready directly, or he shall be flogged till there is no skin on his back. Do you hear? Begone and give the orders. I am not to be trifled with to-day. Am I not going for the sake of justice, Inshalla?"

"Forgive your slave his presumption in speaking at all," said the secretary humbly, and rising with his hands joined; "but your Highness's well-wisher thinks——"

"What do you think?" exclaimed the Nawab, impatiently; "what does it matter to me what you think?"

"If I may say it, my lord, it is this, that the Brigadier will hardly thank you for this news. Why not let the accursed

English manage their own affairs, and eat as much dirt as they please?"

"I will cram it down their throats, the Kafirs," vociferated the Nawab furiously. "Go! quickly, Meer Sahib. Get the men ready. I will leave this at once."

"But the men said yesterday that none of them would stir a foot, unless they got some pay," whimpered the secretary.

"Ah, is it so? Well, tell them they shall have a bellyful of sweetmeats at Noorpoor—that may tempt them," said the Nawab, as his secretary turned to depart. "Poor fellows! poor fellows! if it were not for those decrees, I could borrow more; and Azráel Pandé is not here to help me. What can have become of him, I wonder? he ought to have returned by this time. No English, no English," he said; "what could he have meant? Ah! were there no English, I would soon settle with the bankers."

So, in spite of all hindrances, the Nawab dressed himself in his yellow satin tunic, threw a shawl over his shoulders, and was prepared to go forth by the time the retinue was ready. As he mounted his elephant, he saw that his mace-bearers had no maces, and the Nawab Dil Khan without his two silver sticks would lose dignity. "Where are your maces?" he cried to the men; "go fetch them."

"We pledged them for food, Nawab Sahib," said one of the men impudently; "you have food enough, while we and our children starve!"

"Go on before, both of ye," he replied, without noticing the taunt. "Give my compliments to the Colonel Sahib, and say I am coming to visit him on business of importance."

It was not far, as we know, to Noorpoor, and before noon it was announced to the Brigadier that the Nawab's "Suwarree" was approaching.

"Confound the fellow!" he exclaimed to his staff officer, Captain Hill, who had been transacting the usual daily routine business with his chief. "What can he want? I hate his cringing speeches, and I suspect he hates me too; but I need not be uncivil. You had better stop, Hill, and hear his news;" and presently the Nawab arrived, his attendants noisily shouting his titles before him, and was received civilly.

"You had something to say, something to tell me of importance," said the Brigadier, breaking rather an awkward silence; and as the Nawab fidgeted visibly in his chair—"what is it; can I assist you in anything?"

Dil Khan looked at Captain Hill nervously, and then to the

Brigadier, who understood the movement, and said, somewhat haughtily, "I have no secrets from my friend Captain Hill, and you need have none, Nawab Sahib; speak freely."

"Let them both eat dirt; why not?" thought the Nawab; "I will not spare it to them."

"Oh, it was nothing, nothing very particular, sir," he said aloud. "Have you any news about Mr. Brandon?"

"Mr. Brandon? No. Have you heard anything, Hill? He has not been wounded again by the Dacoits, has he, Nawab Sahib?"

"No, Colonel Sahib, no, not by Dacoits, but he is wounded—he—he—he!—this time by love, as most of us have been in our day, sir, and he is young and handsome; but he need not have done wrong—he need not, with the character of a just Englishman, have committed this tyranny! Ya, Alla!" cried the Nawab, lifting up his eyes and hands, and raising his voice, "that I should have heard what I have of an Englishman, of one of that great, just people to whom our wives and daughters are sacred."

"What do you mean, Nawab?" hissed out the Colonel viciously. "What do you mean by alluding to Mr. Brandon as you have? Beware! You may say more than English gentlemen can listen to, and transgress the bounds of respect."

"God forbid!" said Dil Khan piously. "What I have to say grieves me, as it will grieve you, sir. Mr. Brandon has seduced and carried away the granddaughter of Narendra, the banker of Shah Gunje, a man held in universal esteem and respect. He tried to recover her, but was beaten out of the Commissioner's Camp, and the whole country is wailing for him."

"It is quite impossible!" exclaimed Captain Hill; "I know Cyril Brandon as well as if he were my own brother, and what you have heard is a malicious lie. It is strange, Nawab Sahib, that you, who profess to be his friend, should credit such a thing for a moment."

"It is no lie!" returned the Nawab humbly. "Inshalla! I can distinguish between lies and falsehood; and you will hear a confirmation of this ere long. If you will ask the bankers of the bazaar to-morrow, I dare say they will tell you of it. Abominable!" he continued, "treacherous! Is there no justice for such tyranny among you English? There used to be in the old times, but now——"

"Silence!" cried the Brigadier, interrupting him, "you are forgetting whom you are speaking to: this is beyond the limit of respect, and you had better go, sir, before I forget who you are, and turn you out of my house. You have permission to depart," he continued, rising, "and begone!"

Dil Khan rose, and glared savagely at the two officers. "When there are no English!" he muttered between his teeth, "when there are no English! this insult will be avenged.—Do not be angry, Colonel Sahib," he continued aloud, "and forgive your humble friend for his free speech; I only thought I was doing well to tell you of this before you heard it exaggerated, by common rumours, and I came on purpose."

"No matter what you thought," returned the Brigadier brusquely, "you had no business to come with such scandal to me; you have your dismissal:" and Dil Khan retired, and the clashing bells of his elephant were heard in the direction of the town.

"By Jove!" said the Brigadier to his friend, "what if this should be true? Only think of that quiet fellow, Brandon, doing such a thing, and by force too!"

"I can't and won't believe it," replied Captain Hill. "I dare say Brandon is no better than most of us; but to do anything rough or dishonourable, I can't and won't believe. I have heard of the girl, though. She gave evidence here on the Dacoity trial, and Mostyn, now I remember, raved about her beauty more than his good wife would have liked to hear perhaps; and when Brandon was wounded, I believe that girl helped to nurse him."

"Whew!" whistled the Brigadier, "is it so? By George! that beast of a Nawab may be right, after all, and Brandon may have carried her off! Well, well! we can't help the follies of young men. I only hope he may not suffer for his prank, for I have always liked him; he had never any of that d——d civilian conceit about him, though he is the Honourable Cyril."

"Honourable to the last drop of his blood," exclaimed the other warmly; "and, for my part, I don't believe a word of the matter. But you will see, the *ladies* of the station will get hold of the report which the Nawab has evidently gone to disseminate, and a precious bit of scandal it will be to them."

"Well! we must get through these papers, Hill. There's the Adjutant-General's letter by you, just hand it to me," said the Brigadier, and the usual business proceeded.

Captain Hill, however, was right; the matter, whatever it was, had got abroad, and Mrs. Smith's ayah, who had been to the bazaar to buy pán, told her mistress of it when she got home. The pán seller, the bangle women, the tailor's wife, the goldsmith's wife, her particular gossips, had all agreed in the same story; and the goldsmith's wife was crying, because so great a man as Narendra had been disgraced. Yes, it was all quite true; and as every one had added what they pleased to the Nawab's story, the affair had soon assumed gigantic, and even bloody proportions.

Mrs. Smith was an industrious woman. Captain Smith had borrowed money from the Agra bank, to send home three children; and as there was a temporary lull in the succession, Mrs. Smith was alone. Could she live on herself, or on Smith, who was a quiet plodding sort of man, always buried in big Persian and Hindee dictionaries, or talking to a snuffy Pundit, who spoke through his nose, about the Vitul Pucheesee or the Prém Ságur? Smith intended to go up soon for a first-rate examination, and hoped to get a civil or political appointment; and he never interfered with his wife's pursuits, nor she with his. I have said she was industrious, but it was after a peculiar fashion. She was never known to sew, she did not read much, and the novels in the station library were very old. She had no accomplishments, and had neglected and forgotten the little music she ever knew; for as she said, "The children, you know, prevented me from practising." So, wanting in these sources of occupation, Mrs. Smith set herself to work, steadily and perseveringly, to study her neighbours' affairs, and succeeded quite to her heart's content. It is true there was no scandal at Noorpoor, or materials for any among its quiet, dull people. "Nothing like 'the Hills,' you know, my dear; there one used to hear *such* things;" but it was pleasant at least to find out who got the best joints from the butcher; who had a new bonnet, or pattern—muster, she called it—of a dress body, or Garibaldi, sent her from England; why Captain Jones had quarrelled with his wife yesterday, and had not made it up; why the Browns had discharged their khansaman—they were always changing their servants; who had a plum-cake specially baked for them; or who had received a tray of fruit from the Nawab, and why? Perhaps I need not follow the peculiar investigations of this lady any further, for they extended into nastier places than my readers would like to visit. Nowhere, however, was her industry at fault; and in her ayah and sweeper woman she had indefatigable assistants, who were stimulated to exertion by occasional small presents of one kind or another, and no doubt invented a good deal, at least we may hope so, of the nastiest details.

How delightful, then, was this new scandal! how true and

how circumstantial it appeared! Mrs. Home lived in the next compound or enclosure, and there was a private way through the gardens of both houses. Mrs. Smith at once took her parasol and ran over to her friend. Miss Lucy had gone to spend the day with the Hills, and there would be an evening party, so she was happily out of the way. The doctor was at his office, and she found Mrs. Home alone.

"O, my dear," she said, as she entered the bedroom, where Mrs. Home was reclining peacefully within her mosquito curtains, "I have such a *delicious* story to tell you, and all *quite* true. Do send the tonjon for Maria"—that was Mrs. Jones. "I really won't say a word till she comes." She did tell it all, however, to the matron's wondering ears, and had the delight of repeating it soon after to Mrs. Jones. We could not listen to, or record, what these friends said to each other without a blush, and had better draw the curtain; but the last words Mrs. Home was heard to utter, as she sobbed, and was wiping her eyes, were: "Shameful—shameful! and I had—I had—so thought—he liked Lucy. Don't you remember the night of the ball——;" and as the curtain prevents my hearing more, I had as well close this chapter.

But the result of the Nawab's mission to Noorpoor was, that a general combination among the matrons of the station ensued against Mr. Cyril Brandon, with a determination to exclude him from their society. I do not think the men, except Hill and the chaplain, cared very much; and both of them took the news—as it became known that Seeta was actually with Mr. Brandon, and a considerable addition was being made to his house—very much to heart. The issue seemed to depend, however, on the view the Mostyns might take of the matter—how Cyril Brandon should be received by all parties; and till their arrival, people commented on "the connection," as Mrs. Smith termed it, with a profuse expenditure of the most candid and virtuous indignation.

"How *can* he show his face among us again, my dear?" said Mrs. Home to Mrs. Smith; and Mrs. Smith and Mrs. Jones—the three friends representing the Mrs. Grundy of Noorpoor—echoed, "How can he?"

CHAPTER XIX.

A RETROSPECT.

After the close of the Afghan war, much discontent was manifested in the Bengal native army. The massacre of the Kyber Pass was bitterly remembered, and the English Government was held, by the men of Oudh and Bahar, to be responsible for the loss and desolation which had fallen upon the thousands of families of those who had perished in the miserable retreat from Kabool. If this did not affect the majority of the men in actual service, so as to form a ground for complaint or mutiny, there was another subject which every day became, in their minds, one of paramount importance; one which grew with the times, and the increasing dominion of the British power. The Bengal Sepoys had hitherto been employed, with a few trifling exceptions, in India only, and chiefly in those provinces wherein their homes lay. True, they had marched as cheerfully into Affghanistan as the Rajpoots had in the times of the Moghul Emperor, Akhbar, and that tradition was not dead; but it had been as a temporary and exceptional service, it was well paid while it lasted, and. it was believed, would not recur again. Sinde, however, had become British in 1843, and, it was at first determined, should be garrisoned by native troops from Bengal. So, therefore, regiments were told off for the duty from among those which lay on the frontier of the Punjab; and one, the Sixty-fourth, when on its march southwards, mutinied for war-pay. It seemed to the men that it was no part of their contract to serve in, to them, a foreign land, without the substantial reward of increased pay; and under the sympathy of the whole of their comrades throughout the army, the Sixty-fourth refused to proceed. Eventually, and relying on a unwarrantable promise made to them by their colonel, they did march, and arrived in Sinde, where the truth was made known to them. Then they mutinied again; but subsequently became penitent at Lucknow, and only the leading men of the mutiny were punished.

Similar in spirit and design was the mutiny, in the same year, of the Thirty-fourth Regiment, then stationed on the Punjab frontier. Disaffected to the core, it presented no feature or chance of redemption to loyalty: and it was marched to Meerut, where native officers and men, guilty and innocent alike, were, at a public parade, stripped of their uniforms and cast adrift, with every accompaniment of disgrace, to become the leaven of much further mischief than that which had prevailed. The wisdom of the act was questioned by many then, as it came to be in subsequent years; but the authorities had decided that an overwhelming necessity existed for the enforcement of discipline in the native army, and for a time the fate of the Thirty-fourth seemed to have effected the desired end. What became of the regiment no one knew, or perhaps cared to know very much; the men were neither watched nor traced, and seemed to have disappeared among the vast population to which they belonged.*

Of one, however, we know; a restless, vindictive spirit, who for twelve years, had roamed through the country, disseminating the leaven of his own regiment, wherever he went, with a skill and pertinacity which were worthy of a better cause. Immediately after the scene at Meerut, Azráel Pandé had betaken himself to the jungles of Bundelkhund. He had become a leader in the local insurrection that followed; had narrowly escaped capture; and though ever welcomed by Sepoys, and supported by his rare talent of recitation, became, under a vow to Kalee, the Dacoit leader of whom this tale has had experience. This man had traversed the Punjab, where, in 1849 and 1850, a spirit of mutiny prevailed, which was suppressed with difficulty, and was similar to that of 1844. He had passed then from station to station, from regiment to regiment, carrying messages and letters, urging, instigating, and exhorting all. He went too to Dehly, and Umballa, and Meerut, finding everywhere existence of the same spirit; but, while many were like-minded, the majority hesitated and hung back. There was no general combination, and no settled purpose anywhere.

The question among all was merely mercenary; whether, in fact, they should serve in the Punjab on ordinary pay, or demand and exact the war allowances. If he urged a combined movement of mutiny, the elders wagged their heads, told him that the salt of the Koompanee Bahadoor was still sweet, and till it became bitter in their mouths they would bide their time. Most of the petty intrigues of the Dehly Court were known to him; but they excited no interest or sympathy among his comrades, and so the Punjab excitement gradually appeared to die out. Regiments in their turn came and went in ordinary course; and, after the example of the disbandment of the Sixty-sixth, the idea of further mutiny seemed to have passed away.

When Azráel Pandé escaped from Noorpoor, he betook himself to his old courses; for he was practically safer among Sepoys than in the country at large. Again he made his way to Meerut, Dehly, and other large stations, and heard from his friends, with exultation, that the discontent, which had seemed to slumber for awhile, existed in deeper force than ever; and he soon learned also that the smouldering fire needed but a breath to be blown into a fierce conflagration which should cover the land.

Was he singular in this? Indeed, no. Wherever he went he found others as active and earnest as himself; working, if not exactly to the same end, at least in the same direction. He found that the ordinary Brahmin priesthood were rapidly becoming aroused to the dangers that threatened their faith, and had become active missionaries of sedition. He heard of Mahomedans who, with bolder views, were organizing means for the overthrow of English power, the restitution of Mahomedan sovereignty, and a pure profession of their faith; but there could be no real help from such sources. Brahmins might preach sedition, but they could not arouse the people; Mahomedans might aim at the re-establishment of the throne of Dehly, but that would bring no relief to Hindoos; indeed, perhaps the reverse. Even if both combined, of which there was no possibility, and succeeded in exciting rebellion, what could be effected by rude mobs, bent on the plunder of their own countrymen? So long as his old comrades were faithful to the salt they had hitherto eaten, he knew that any rising would be crushed out before it could attain a head. Any destruction of the English, therefore, must depend on the united efforts of the men to whom he belonged, who now, as he believed, were everywhere coming to the resolution which should place the result beyond doubt. Everywhere, too, agents of the new movement seemed to be swarming. Hundreds—nay, there might have been thousands—busy like himself. Some, his old comrades of the Thirty-fourth, others men of the Sixty-sixth, the last disbanded; again, discontented spirits who had taken their discharge from the army and public service, and agents of traitorous Rajahs and Nawabs, Jogees, Bairagees, pedlars—all such forming a vast host. Was it possible that the seed they sowed broadcast should not bear fruit? Old grievances had, indeed, died out, and their interest had passed away; but others, far more powerful and exciting, now existed in their stead.

As he travelled eastwards, he met a wave of more than discontent, for it amounted to absolute terror, surging up from Bengal, and spreading far and wide over the land. He heard but one cry, "Pollution!" not only among Hindoos but Mahomedans. True, nothing was definite as yet, but the dread existed, and was increasing at every step of his progress. Priests, merchants, artisans, farmers, and soldiers—were alike affected. It was a terrible engine; but none could be more effective for his purpose. The terror of pollution came home with fearful force alike to every Hindoo, of every caste, and to all Mahomedans. Pollution could not be escaped; it could not be remedied. It concerned both the bold and the timid; and even the most timid grew bold under the influence of the new and possible danger. The excitement which now prevailed was different from any that had ever preceded it, and more intense. Had the time, then, come when the English, the authors and contrivers of this new tyranny, were to perish—to be destroyed in one huge popular commotion, from which none could escape? Not come exactly, and yet perhaps was very near; and the now venerable prediction of the terrible Sumbut 1914, to which all alike looked, and in which all believed, might be fulfilled.

I think, as I hope, that this seeming digression, in a slight retrospect of some events of preceding years, will be forgiven; for it is necessary to my readers to show them, in some sort, the spirit and temper of the time which concerns this tale, and the designs of many who were actors in those events which have already found a memorable place in history, and will be followed up by every historian of India who may write in the future. But it is no part of my design to record history in this book. I have already placed some characters before the reader who are playing their parts, and others must follow as the plot thickens.

CHAPTER XX.

AZRÁEL PANDÉ.

On the night of the 10th November, 1856, there was a meeting in the "lines" of the Thirty-fourth Native Infantry, then stationed at Barrackpoor, near Calcutta. The old Thirty-fourth had, as I have mentioned in the last chapter, been disbanded at Meerut in 1844; and the present regiment, which had been raised a few years afterwards, retained, in no small degree, the traditions of its predecessor. Azráel Pandé knew most of the men; he had met their delegates in many stations of the army. He had visited them on several previous occasions, and he knew that they were faithful to the new cause in which so many had embarked. He had reached Calcutta after a rapid journey, and had brought with him letters and messages from many regiments, which had already been read with interest. That night he was to leave Calcutta again; and a final meeting had been arranged to bid him farewell, and to hear his last injunctions and counsel.

The "lines" of Sepoy regiments in India form, as it were, villages, with broad streets between the houses, or cabins, which are all of one pattern. They contain a well-sized room, which can be divided by a partition, when necessary; the walls are built of clay, or sun-dried brick, and the roofs thatched. Each company has its separate row or street; and each man a house to himself, except when two of the same caste may desire to live together. These "lines" are generally planted with trees, and have a pretty and comfortable appearance. The houses of the native commissioned and non-commissioned officers are superior to those of the privates, and in some instances have separate enclosures or gardens.

One of these separate houses in the —— company of the Thirty-fourth, now the scene of the meeting, belonged to a jemadar, or native lieutenant of the regiment, with whom Mungul Pandé, his cousin and Azráel's nephew, a private in the regiment, lived. He had applied for leave to hold a recitation of religious books at night, and to be allowed "lights and singing," which was not unusual, and had attracted no particular attention.

Azráel Pandé was the reciter, and the reading had continued late into the night. One by one the listeners had departed, and those who had come for a special purpose alone remained. The jemadar looked closely round the room to see if any one not in the secret were present, and went out to ascertain that all was safe; and on entering again, he carefully put out the lights, except one small lamp which burned in a niche, and even were it noticed from without, would attract no particular attention. Then he barred the door, and said, "We may speak freely now, brothers; let Azráel Pandé tell us what he has heard, and what he would have us do. Gather close to him, that he may not need to raise his voice."

There were about twenty men, tall and strong, as men of Oudh and Bahar always are; men with handsome, regular features and fair skins, descendants of the Aryan warriors of past ages. They were not all of the Thirty-fourth, for there were other regiments at the station who had sent delegates to hear counsel, and make arrangements. These men now huddled together on the earthen floor; and Azráel Pandé, their teacher, naked to the waist, his head bare, his long, soft, wavy hair thrown back over his shoulders, and his forehead, breast, and arms painted with the sacred marks of their faith, sat in a raised seat above them, on which his host generally slept. The light from the lamp flickered, and cast weird, varying shadows about the room, and now and again rested brightly upon him, showing his broad, muscular frame, and lighting up his stern, savage features; but the faces of the men before him were in deep shadow: and all that could be seen of them, closely muffled as they were, was their gleaming eyes, as one turned to another in the most exciting portions of their teacher's address.

"Brothers!" he said, when all were silent and still, "I am not one unknown to ye. What part I played in the old Thirty-fourth ye know well, and I need not remind you of it. What I have done since, ye do not know; but for twelve years, wherever I could strike a blow against the Feringee power, I have not failed to do so. Wherever I saw hesitation, doubt, or cupidity among our people, I have preached, I have urged, I have entreated them not to forget the past, but to cling together for their honour and their caste, in a time which the holy mother, Kalee, told me was to come. I have borne hunger and thirst, poverty and weariness, in my wanderings from place to place. I have been tried and sentenced to die: and I should have been hanged in pollution, but for that poor fellow who sits among ye, who saved my life at the risk of his own. As a Gosain, as a Bairagee, as a Jogee, as a pilgrim carrying Ganges water on his shoulders for hundreds of miles—as a Brahmin expounding these holy books before me, I have travelled throughout the length and breadth of the country. I have attended fairs, and markets, and holy shrines. I have been the honoured guest of great Rajahs, and even of Nawabs; and—O listen, brothers!—I have heard but one cry—a cry that came from the very souls of the people—deliverance from the English!

"Why is this? Listen, and I will tell you. Which of us, on the march, as he stepped into any one of the holy rivers, has not cried out, 'Jey Gunga Mata!' and then, 'Jey Koompanee Bahadoor!' With such cries our fathers went to battle, and won a thousand victories. But that is past. The 'Koompanee' is not as it used to be; it is no longer an incarnation of our gods. It has changed into a mean, cheating robber, who farms this great Hind of ours from the Government of England, and robs it of all it can carry away. Where do those great ships yonder take the cotton, and the indigo, and the silk which the poor ryots have produced, but to England? Do they bring us anything in return? No! nothing but what we have to buy, and very dearly; and even the old Moghuls did not tax our salt and our opium. When the 'Koompanee' was as a prince, we served them; and shed our blood for them, in faith and honour. They were our fathers and our mothers. But now?—listen to what they have done.

"Three years ago I was at Noorpoor. The Rajah, who had been kind to me, died. No adoption to perform his obsequies was allowed, and his soul now wanders in hell. Then the Feringees seized his kingdom, confiscated his wealth, and even the clothes and jewels of his wives; and these, and their horses and elephants, their bullocks, were sold by auction, and the 'Koompanee' took the money. Listen further. In the same year the Rajah of Jhansy died, a man who flew the English flag over his fort with his own. He left his little kingdom to be taken care of by the English for his descendants; but they seized it themselves, and kept it fast. In the west they took Sattara, and the family of Sivajee are beggars. Well, all these were State acts, and concern distant people. You have not heard their groans and cries as I have; and let them pass.

"But the greed of dominion has come nearer to you. It has come at last to our homesteads in Oudh, where our people have lived free for thousands of years; and Oudh has become Feringee, like Nagpoor and Jhansy. Is not all this true, and need it not be avenged?

"Do not murmur," he continued, stretching out his hands over the now excited men. "The time comes—nay, it is near,—when you may shout 'Jey Kalee' with me, and bathe your hands in the hot English blood. Do not murmur, my sons, but listen. Have I told you all? Nay, if it were so, the loss of these kingdoms need not concern you. Those that lost them might cry and wail, but that would not affect one rupee of your pay, or one yard of the land ye possess. The English are too wise to interfere with them. But is there no more? What did I hear the people in the meeting of the Dhurma Subha say, only two days ago? What did I hear the Brahmins in the temple of Kalee, when I worshipped there to-day, say among themselves, and to us strangers? 'Come here no more!' they cried. 'The order is gone out from the new Lord Sahib, that all Hindoos must become Christians, for the Queen of England has so determined. Come no more!' they cried, beating their mouths and their breasts; 'this day—any day—the holy temple of the Mother whom we serve, may be defiled with cow's blood!' Ah, yes; they believed this, those wise old priests, and why should not we, my sons?"

Then there was a low, hoarse murmur of, "We have heard it: we believe it!"

"Yes," he continued, "you believe that, because the wrong comes home to yourselves. But listen further. We soldiers used to feel that we were safe against going over the sea. Now I hear on every hand, a groan of despair that you are no longer safe; that when the order comes, you must go over the black water, which washes out all trace of caste. You, every one of you that hear me now—every Brahmin and Rajpoot who heard me to-night—every one of the tens of thousands who serve in the army—must go—go to-morrow, if the Lord Sahib wills it—over the sea. If you by chance escape this fate, your sons cannot. Every man who enlists now, must swear on the Ganges water, and holy toolsee, to ensure the destruction of his own caste! What horrible mockery is this! Yet they will require you all, young and old, to go, or they will blow you away from their guns.

"Why are you quiet? Why have you borne this? This order is nearly half a year old, yet you have done nothing! Where is your honour, where is your caste? Do I speak to Brahmins and Rajpoots, or to outcast Mléchas and leather-dressers? Does not this come home to your hearts? When you return from the sea, will your wives embrace you? will they put your children into your arms? will your stalwart sons admit you into your homes? I tell you they will not, they dare not! They will say to you, 'Begone! ye are polluted.' They will not give you a cup of water were you even dying of thirst at your door. They cannot look upon you; they will shout to you, 'Ye were cowards to lose your caste, and had better died!'

"Ah, yes!" he cried, as he wiped the foam from his lips; "you may writhe there, and murmur, and weep; but you, who are Brahmins, know that this is true, as well as I, a Brahmin, who tells it to you. But listen, I have yet more to say. Am I inventing tales to frighten you with? Not I. What the English do, they spread abroad that all may know it; and look you, my sons, how hellish are their contrivances to sap the very foundations of Hindoo faith and purity. Now the law is gone forth, that Hindoo widows may marry again—Brahmins, Kshettrees, Soodras alike!—Think, any one of you, where your honour would be, if your widow married another man? Where would be the old respect and love which sealed the devotion of its life by holy suttee? Now, every woman who pleases, may, like a prostitute, take a new husband. Think of the pity of this: think of the sin of it! Brothers!" he cried, with his hands outstretched and quivering, and his eyes flashing, "such are your own wives now, such are your mothers or sisters, for such have the English made them. I thank God that this misery is saved me, that mine died years ago, and that I have no child to endure pollution. There were times when Brahmins and Rajpoots plunged their swords and spears into their wives' hearts when there was even a suspicion or a dread of dishonour. As I traversed Rajpootana, I heard many an old ballad which told of such things—for these memories never die—and I could say them to you; but no! you could not feel them: you are dead—dead to honour—dead to shame—dead to your faith! You have no caste, how should you understand the thoughts or the honour of those who still hold it? Are you silent?"

They were silent, for most were sobbing, some gnashed their teeth. and drew their breath in hard gasps and sighs.

"Another few words would I speak, my sons," he continued; "and you know this last ignominy better than I do. What are these new muskets which have been sent among you? Did not the old win all Hind for the English? win it with your fathers' blood, freely poured out. Did not thousands of our people perish in the Khyber amidst the snow and ice—whose blood cries for vengeance? Did not these men die with the old guns in their frozen hands? We, in the former times, did not want cows' and pigs' fat for them: our arms were strong enough to ram down the cartridges that we used, and our bullets then were as deadly as these; who ever withstood them? Now, the Feringees must have new cartridges and new guns, which require the fat of cows and pigs. I tell you there is no sense in this, no reason for this. Who is there in Hind left to fight? We, the men of Oudh and Bahar, have conquered all, even from the Sikhs. Ah, yes! see, brothers! the Sikhs and the Goorkhas don't mind fat, and they will be brought down on you in thousands and tens of thousands, to blow you away from guns, or to send you home to cover your faces and weep like women. So there is no need of this change of arms; but this is certain, that when you have once handled and bitten these fat-besmeared cartridges, you had better go to the Padré Sahib, and take the Baptisma at once. Poor fellows! you will have no caste left, and all the waters of Gunga Mata will not wash out your impurity. What will it then signify if you are all made to eat together in messes, as the white soldiers do? and then you will have cows' fat and pigs' fat in plenty, and Christians and Mléchas to cook your food. There is an order gone out about that in gaols already, and what are you better than convicts? They have put chains on the land, these English. There are iron roads and iron wires stretching up to Dehly, and now going on to Pesháwur, upon the land and its people. When they reach the Indus, yours will follow. You with your caste who would have protected Hindoos, will no longer be Hindoos, but Christian slaves—unable to protect them!

"Do not weep, brothers, do not groan! This is no time for weeping. Arise! be resolute! Strike! for the sake of your honour, your faith, and your caste. When there are no English, you will be free. Be like me, who have vowed this day before Kalee Mata, that every Feringee man, woman, or child must die, and that she shall lick their blood. O! I will feed her with much of it, and it will be sweet—sweet!—for they are her direst enemies. Do not speak!" he continued, in the same hissing and mocking tone in which he had addressed the men. "I know your hearts, I know what ye would say. But one thing I ask. If you are men, if you have still faith and caste, reach forward your hands one over another, and touch these books!" and the men rose to their feet and did as he had desired.

"Now swear," said Azráel solemnly, "by this holy Geeta, by the five products of the cow, and by my feet, that when the time comes, ye, and those ye represent, will strike in for the faith! That ye will refuse, even to the extremity of death, to take the cartridges, and to go beyond sea!".

"We swear!" replied the men, in a hoarse whisper, "Jey Kalee Mata, we will be true to thee, even to death!"

"Good, my sons!" continued Azráel; "she, the Mother, will help us all in our oaths. Now listen to her last words: 'Be cautious! wait for the signal! Do not anticipate it by any foolish haste which will bring destruction on us all. It is but for a little time; the English are in sore strait, their country is small, and they have few soldiers. They have now war in Europe with the Russians, and war in Persia, and they will soon have war in China. They have to send more of their troops from India, and already they have not half their usual number, and still they trust us. Ha! ha! ha! Well! they might have done so safely, had they kept their old faith!' Now depart: I go to Cawnpore, to Agra, to Dehly, to Amballa; Gokul will go to Dinapore with your letters. Write what has happened here to every camp in the army, but cautiously; and when Sumbut 1914 begins, the signal will not be long deferred. Now go! I leave my brother's son, Mungal Pandé, with you; be careful of him as one of your own."

Then the men passed him silently one by one, touching his feet reverently with their hands, and then their own foreheads and breasts, and so glided out of the door into the darkness of the night. Before morning had dawned, Azráel Pandé rose and took leave of his host and his nephew, conjuring them to be faithful, and went to take his place in the northern train, on one of the iron chain roads that were to bind India and enslave its people!

"O Mother! wait, wait but a little," he murmured, stretching forth his hands towards Calcutta, "and thou shalt have the blood."

CHAPTER XXI.

ELYSIUM.

WHAT a new and blessed life was that which gradually opened upon Seeta! To love, and be loved, to have a stake in life shared by one who was all-powerful to protect her, to be admitted to her husband's confidence, and to feel that she assisted his endeavours to increase the prosperity and the happiness of the people he governed! To feel, too, the dawning conviction that his high position had immeasurably increased her own, and that in time—for the thought was yet only dim in her mind—the people who now paid her reverence, might hereafter bless her memory! It was like a new birth, and she was grateful, very grateful. If, in the midst of her wildest joy, thoughts would sometimes arise at which she shuddered—that her husband's caresses were pollution, that she was not of his people; that strangers far away might claim him and rend him from her—they were but for a moment, and a bright smile from him, a cheering word, a certainty that he was true to her, came as a loving balm to her spirit, and she was content and happy. If she had been beautiful before, this new life had made her far more so; the flush in her cheek, the joyous sparkle of her soft, expressive eyes, the entire devotion of her manner, which could not find vent in words, satisfied Cyril Brandon that he not only possessed her love, but that there was no reserve between them; nothing to prevent her growing intellect from expanding to the full, and satisfying the passionate longings of his own nature.

It was a happy life they led in camp. Seeta had brought with her only one servant, her old Bheemee, who had nursed her from infancy, and had never left her. Now she was somewhat infirm and deaf, but she was able to perform the simple services she had to render; and though the woman had had her misgivings as to her darling's marriage with a stranger, yet she had become accustomed to Cyril, who had ever a kind word for her, and she was satisfied that he loved Seeta very tenderly. By day, Seeta did not remain in camp; a lodging was always found for her in the house of the village goldsmith, wherever they might be, where she might join the family worship, and eat the simple food prepared by her own caste people. All day she remained secluded, reading her books, listening to the dames' gossip who came in from time to time, playing with their children, hearing many a tale of poverty and distress, and distributing the ample means which Cyril placed at her disposal, in gifts which cheered sad hearts and made her own happy. In the first days, after they left Shah Gunje, Cyril had warned her against admitting petitioners on any pretence, or listening to specious tales of wrong, which could only be settled in his own courts. This, indeed, had been at once attempted; but the haughty scorn with which it was repelled prevented its repetition. Even the old Serishtadar grew proud of Seeta, and told Cyril how faithful and discreet she was, and how loved and respected wherever she went. "She will be more popular than you, sir," he said, "one of these days, and she has knit the people's hearts to you more than I can tell. It is no flattery, sir; it is the truth."

How anxiously Seeta looked every afternoon for Cyril's palankeen, which was to take her to him! It used to be set down in the court of whatever house she might be in, and she would enter it and shut the doors, and then it would be taken out and carried swiftly to the camp; and, the day's work done, she found her husband waiting for her; or, meeting her at a little distance from his tent, they would stroll on together, with Muff, the Skye terrier, for their companion. Cyril often told her playfully that she would soon become secluded altogether, like a Mahomedan, and she would own that she was not now the wife of a humble village goldsmith, but of the Commissioner Sahib, whom all revered, and would not look on her if they could.

Of a village goldsmith! and would have been so still but for her husband's fate. As such, what perceptions would even her books have opened to her, what change could have taken place till her death? A life of simple house duties and cares, and no knowledge of the world beyond Gokulpoor. She might have had children, but the life would not have varied; she would not have desired it to change. Any alteration would have been impossible. Now, what a contrast there was! How all her perceptions were awakening! how keenly she felt that, with all her book knowledge, how little she really knew; how little even her old teacher, whom she had thought all-wise, knew in comparison with her husband! For Cyril was leading her mind gently, and almost imperceptibly, to his own sources of knowledge. He told her of his own country, described his home and the foreign lands where he had been, and where she might go with him some day, if she would—some day, when they were grown old. How she wondered at his accomplishments, at his sketches of herself, which he seemed never weary of making; and indeed there was always something new and beautiful to strike him in her graceful and artless attitudes. Then there were drawings of the people, of carts and bullocks, of villages and temples; rough pen-and-ink sketches of characters in his court, and one of herself, when she had first given evidence, with her hands outstretched, holding her saree—which she could not look on without tears; and there were the temple, and the camp, and Shah Gunje lying below the little hill, and her house, and the oriel window looking towards the camp. Perhaps she did not quite understand these drawings at first; but she soon came to do so, and to wonder whether she should ever do like them. Perhaps she might, for her grandfather had often employed her to draw patterns for his chased work; and the design for Cyril's salver had been her own.

Gradually, too, his knowledge of music came upon her as another wonder. When he was at Noorpoor, Cyril never neglected it, and kept up his piano studies, as he did his Italian and French; but in camp he had only a guitar, and he would have been surprised, perhaps, when he took it up in the evenings as the door-screens were let down, to have seen his servants gather about the tent outside, and listen wondrously to his sweet, rich voice. And so Seeta too had come to hear it in her turn. Her own knowledge, small as it was, led her to feel and appreciate most the low sweet melodies he sang, which affected her to tears very often—pleasant, soft tears, welling out of the love in her heart, which would not be denied. I know, too, that Seeta was often a steady helpmate to Cyril in his evening work. She could read the current vernacular papers with as great ease as most of the office scribes, and many a translation was made, she reading and he writing in English, which seemed to him not half so laborious as when a sleepy clerk droned out what he had to read, and very often missed whole passages.

They were never idle, these two strangely united beings: never passed a heavy hour; and though he might often be weary with the day's work, his evening companion gave Cyril new energy and life, refreshed him, and amused him more than he could almost realize. If he had not been patient, perhaps her keen and active thought might have wearied him; but his effort was to direct and restrain, rather than stimulate the passion for knowledge which he saw was awakening in the girl's mind. "She is mine for her life," he used to think, "and there is time enough to bring out all these strange graces and mould them into form and exercise. I must be careful not to excite her too much." It was a change, too, from the old Sanscrit, to read to her passages from Italian and English poets, and translate them to her as best he could, well knowing how impossible it was to render the force and beauty of the originals, yet observing how keenly she appreciated every tender thought, every simile which accorded with her own loving perceptions, and every description of natural beauties.

"Yes," she said, one evening, "I know now, when there is love, it is all the same there and here; at least it used to be when our poets wrote. Now, here such love is dead, except with you."

"Tell me, Seeta," he answered, "when you felt it first. Had you no love before you knew me?"

"None," she said decidedly, "none! He who died did not win me by love; he did not ask it, and I did not feel it. He said once, a harlot could be loved, not a wife. His love was with his trade and his money: those were his life, as they are of all like him. I never heard of love; I read of it in my books, but no thought within me stirred to answer it. Do you remember the play of 'Málati and Máhdava'? That is all love, you know; and it is so beautiful! I can understand it now. Yet I used to read passages like this without emotion:—

> Love spreads through every vein like subtle poison,
> And like the fire that brightens in the breeze,
> Consumes this feeble frame,—resistless fever
> Preys on each fibre. Fatal is its fury!

Now, I could not understand that then. Ah, me! perhaps you will think me foolish, husband: but afterwards I came to be like poor Málati:—

One thought alone possesses her, and still
She dwells upon her love. Her garb is loose—
Her soft lip quivers—starting drops suffuse
Her gentle lips—her bosom palpitates,
And her dark eye in soft abandonment
Most languid floats. Each look and gesture speaks
The fond desires that agitate her youth.*

"I could not help it, Cyril, even while Laloo lived; and when he died, ah! it was terrible then, and to whom could I tell my grief? Aunt Ella? Oh no! she never knew love, not even a child's love; and her husband, she has told me, often struck her. So I tried to bear it till you came."

"And suppose I had gone away, far away, and never spoken, Seeta?"

"I should have died, and no one would have known of my pain. I often dreamed of death then; and as I sat in the window looking for your tents, my soul would seem to go away into dim, far places, and then would return to me. I used to think that some day it would not return to my body, and that would be carried away and burned; and they would remember their little Seeta for a time, and all my pets would miss me, and then they would die too—Aunt Ella, and the old man, and all would be at rest for ever. And you, Cyril, when did you love me?"

"Nay, Seeta," he returned, "I could answer you out of your own books; but I hardly think you would be much the wiser. I made my choice, for I thought I understood more of you than your own people did. I came and went, and came again: and I even tried to go away for good; but I could not, and so—and so I am here with you, my darling, and you grow dearer and dearer to me every day. And you trust me, Seeta? Why do you weep?"

"Yes, I trust you," she replied gravely. "These tears are but of joy, and when my heart swells I cannot help them. Trust you? Do you not remember the sweet tale I read to you of Savitri, who followed her husband into death? You are as dear to me as Satyavan was to her; and were it to be to me as to Savitri, I would not fail. Do you think I would?" she continued, laying her hand upon his arm, and raising her pleading eyes to his. "Perhaps I may be tried some day, and then you will believe Seeta."

"Hush!" he said, putting his hand over her mouth. "I believe you, wife, else I had not asked them to give you to me;

* H. H. Wilson's translation.

but we are young, and may hope to grow old together—may we not?"

"I do not know," she said dreamily. "Sometimes still, my spirit seems to go away from me and leave you; and it would be better so than that I should stay if you were gone, even for a little. I think—I think, Cyril, that I am too happy, and you are too good to me. Why are you not angry sometimes at my foolishness? Yes, you are near me now, and I am happy—oh, so happy!"

I need not dwell on scenes like these. They are only of that old, old story, which has so many a change in the telling, and which goes on from heart to heart, and lip to lip, through all lives where people love, till hearts are cold and lips are dumb! I have other things to speak of, and must not linger on this, to them, sweet, pleasant time of their lives. It was growing near Christmas, and Cyril was beginning to look forward to the arrival of the Mostyns, which he knew was soon expected at Noorpoor. He had had only one letter from his friend in answer to his own, already recorded, and it ran thus:—

"Benares, November 25, 1856.

"MY DEAR CYRIL,—

"I could not manage to write to you from Calcutta. There was so much to do one way or other, that I had not a moment to myself; and the contents of your letter required much deliberation. I have considered what you wrote over and over again; and indeed you are seldom absent from my thoughts. I cannot sufficiently admire your resolution in doing what you have, so honourably and avowedly. Any other connection would have been unworthy of you, and I should have mourned over it very grievously. And yet, dear friend, I cannot help wishing it had not been, and that you and Seeta had never met. This marriage is so strange, so unusual, that a thousand evil things will be said by some of our people of whom you know. You will not care for them, I am sure; but they will exist, and will require all your strength of mind and patience to overcome. I am certain your wife is all that you write she is; but I cannot help wishing, for all our sakes, that she were a good English girl, fit to take her place by you in the world's doings, and in the joy and sorrow of your lives. That, however, cannot be now; and as for myself, so long as you are honoured and happy I am well content. I may even—which will give you sincere pleasure, I know—assure you of my wife's sympathy and good wishes. I did not tell her at once, for I did not know how she would take the news; but since we left Calcutta I have told her all, from beginning to end; and I showed your letter to her, which assured her greatly. Shall I tell you that at first she resented the whole thing, and was huffed about it? Even so; but she returned to it again and again, and ended by humming to herself, 'C'est l'amour, l'amour, l'amour!' and saying that if you were satisfied she must be. As to my sister Grace, who is one of the sweetest and most innocent little mortals that ever breathed, she made no objection. 'Why shouldn't he marry a Hindoo lady, if he loved her?' she said naïvely. 'And I don't see why you two should make a fuss about it.' And with this simple verdict she dismissed the case out of her court; and I dare say it will content you more than mine.

"I hope to be at Noorpoor by the 15th December, and you must manage so as to be able to get there by Christmas Day, *at latest.* Don't come sooner, for my wife wants to have everything arranged for you. The new piano is an Erard, quite lovely; and there are heaps of new music. My wife and Grace have been studying under Garcia and Campana, and, to my thinking, sing divinely. They created quite a *furore* in Calcutta, and had all the world at their feet. You, however, must judge for yourself. And now farewell for a time. Remember that you eat your Christmas dinner with us; and you may take all the kind wishes you please from my wife.

"Ever your affectionate friend,

"PHILIP MOSTYN."

Nor did Cyril go to Noorpoor before the day appointed—Christmas, 1856. If it had not been for the Mostyns, he would far rather not have gone at all: for at this season of the year his camp life was at its very pleasantest, his work going on swimmingly, and all his predecessor's arrears were being cleared off. Everything seemed to him to look brighter than it used to do, and Seeta was growing more and more dear to him daily. Brandon had no intention of becoming the subject of comment by some parties he knew of; had no desire to see ladies' Ayahs prying about his house. If Seeta were to know any one, Mrs. Mostyn was the only lady who should know her; and her sister Grace too, if she pleased. It would be very pleasant to see his shy little wife coming to know good Englishwomen, whom—or one at least—he had respected and loved. And he heard, too, that Seeta's cottage was ready. Baba Sahib had even gone into the station and had looked after it, and had the little oratory consecrated by Brahmins; and a priest had been appointed to tend the sacred fire while Seeta was absent, and to perform daily service in the little sanctuary. Seeta knew nothing of all this; Cyril had not even told her of the new cottage; and as the time came near for them to go to Noorpoor, she had expressed some anxiety as to how she was to be disposed of there, which had been easily dissipated; and she knew that her grandfather had many friends, bankers, in Noorpoor, who would receive her. So, on the morning of Christmas Day, Cyril rode early into the station, met no one, and went direct to his own house, where his servants had preceded him overnight, and awaited Seeta's arrival, who was to follow in the palankeen. She had never been out of her quiet country town and village, until she began to travel with her husband; and as she neared the station she opened a little of the palankeen door, and looked out timidly, to see what she had heard so much of all her life. Passing through the native town—which she did not like as well as her own Shah Gunje—she soon saw the great lake, and the old fort by it; then came wide roads and bungalows, as the bearer running beside the door called them; houses lying among shady gardens. "And the Commissioner's house is near now, lady," he said; and soon afterwards she saw they entered a gate, passed up a neatly gravelled walk, with flowers on each side of it; then round the end of a house, and into another part of the garden, more beautiful than the first. Then the door was opened, and her husband was there to greet her; and as the palankeen was put down she heard him tell every one to go away, and helped her to rise from it.

How beautiful all seemed about her as she stood up and looked around! Stretching into dim, shady walks, with the lake glittering beyond, were trim paths, which divided beds of bright roses and flowers which she had never seen before. "They must be English," she thought; and indeed many of them were so. Before her was a neatly clipped privet-hedge, and beyond it, on a gravelled space, stood a cottage, one end of which joined the house itself, and thither Cyril led her. Garlands were hung over the door, and as it opened she saw Brahmin women within, who broke cocoa-nuts at her feet and Cyril's, and waved lighted lamps over them from head to foot, singing a hymn of welcome and a prayer of increase and happiness. Then dear old Aunt Ella, whom she had not at first seen, advanced with her arms outstretched, and tears welling from her eyes, and caught her to her breast, put her hands on her head, and blessed her. It was all just as if she were being welcomed home again, and only one grand figure was wanting. Then inside were two rooms leading into each other, cool and pure; and beyond them a Brahmin, in a small chamber, was chanting the morning litany.

"So far I can come, Seeta," said Cyril; "the rest belongs to you alone. Take her," he continued, to Aunt Ella and the Brahmin women, "and show her what there is. I will wait here."

Seeta could not speak; her heart was too full. Who could have anticipated such thoughtful kindness, such protection of her caste! Where Brahmins had worshipped, where Aunt Ella was, she might surely live. She passed on into the oratory, made her obeisance to the altar and to the two Brahmins near it, and chaunted some verses of the morning hymn from the "Vedas." Then old Bheemee called her, and she went out into a court, where was a bath-room and a kitchen, and—could she believe her eyes?—her own pet antelope Gunga, which knew her, and now tugged at the rope to get at her; and the two parroquets and the old black myna, in their cages, who all screamed together and fluttered their wings to escape to her. When she had kissed them all she went back; and as Cyril stood waiting for her she fell at his feet, and clung sobbing to his knees; and when he raised her up and folded her in his strong arms, and told her, with a smile, that it was all hers, and she must not be foolish, she clung the more to him, as she looked up with brimming eyes and said she could not help herself, and he must forgive her. Then he left her to make her own arrangements with Aunt Ella and Bheemee, and went into his garden. Cyril was very happy, because he knew he had gratified his little wife, and anticipated all thoughts of impurity of caste. So, as he was walking about and his gardener was showing him all the new flowers and the luxuriant vegetables, he heard Mostyn's whistle as he came through the gate in the boundary hedge from his own garden, and went to meet him. Their hands met in a loving grasp as each wished the other a happy Christmas, and many of them, to all they loved; and Mostyn put into Cyril's hands a packet of letters which had come the day before. "As you were coming in," he said, "I would not let them send them out to you."

Cyril opened a demi-official letter marked "Private," which in some respects had an unusual appearance, and read the following:—

"DEAR SIR,—

"I am directed by the —— to inform you that you have been this day appointed Deputy Commissioner of the Noorpoor District, *vice* Grant died at sea. His —— hopes that you will continue to apply your eminent talents to a province which has already much improved under your direction, and will, he is assured, continue to do so.

"I remain," etc.

"That's civil, Mostyn, read. Seeta! Seeta! come out, and hear good news. I am now real Commissioner," said Cyril, stepping towards her door. "Come out, child. You mustn't mind Mostyn. Why, you will have to see him every day."

Seeta was naturally shy. The timidity of an Indian woman was natural to her, and her awkwardness was perfectly understood by Mr. Mostyn.

"No, don't mind me," he said. "I too welcome you to your home. I hope it pleases you. We have been doing all we could with it."

Seeta looked her gratit[illegible] she dare not reply; but Mr. Mostyn saw in her rich, brig[illegible] colour, in the flush on her cheek, and in her graceful movements, that her beauty was even increased, and that Cyril had not exaggerated it.

"Come and have a talk," said Cyril. "My little breakfast is just ready." And he led Mostyn away.

CHAPTER XXII.

BUSINESS AND PLEASURE.

"WELL, Philip, that was good news, wasn't it? pleasant too, coming on Christmas Day. Poor Grant! I'm very sorry for him though," said Cyril, as they sat down.

"Ah!" replied Mostyn, "I don't know that there is much to grieve about: he was one of those people in the world who have no kith and kin to signify, and whom no one misses. He was incurably ill too. I think death must have been a great relief to him."

"You say that, Philip, to smooth over my stepping into a dead man's shoes; but really I am glad to be my own master at last, and beat my own drum. And how is Mrs. Mostyn? and I may add, your sister?"

"Both flourishing, thank you, and neither have lost their English roses; and such a display of finery is laid out for to-day, that I tell them they ought to be ashamed to go to church in it—I'm sure the parson won't be obliged to them. Why not come over to breakfast and see them?"

"Not this morning, Philip. I must answer this and a lot of other letters, and there is the home despatch to get through."

"But you will dine with us; it is an old invitation?"

"O, of course; I am longing to hear the new piano, and to hear them sing. They know about Seeta?"

"Yes, they know too she is here; but you must not be annoyed if Rose does not come to see her just yet, though, faith, she is dying to know her, and so, indeed, is Grace."

"O, no," returned Cyril, "I would far rather they did not come while I am here now; it will only be for a week or so. When I return for good; it will gratify me much if they are kind to her."

"And she—Seeta I mean—what am I to call her, Cyril? she won't think it unkind!"

"On the contrary, Philip, it will relieve her very much to be taken no notice of at present. What she has been most beseeching me for the last week is, to keep the English people away from her, especially the ladies; she is afraid of them."

"And me too?"—

"No, not you; she has seen you before, remember, and re spects you like a father."

"Well, I will do just as you please, Cyril," he returned; "I will come and have a chat with her now and then, if she will let me. I dare say my wife will say nothing to you about her, and you can break the subject to her or not, as you like; but I am really longing to know Seeta. How very lovely she is grown, to be sure! one would hardly recognize in her the pale, thin girl who gave evidence in that trial."

"As you know her better, you will admire her more, as I do, Philip; she is a rare creature indeed."

Then they fell to talking of Calcutta and public affairs there, with which Mostyn was by no means satisfied.

"You have no idea what a stir that order about enlistment has made," he said; "we, who live out of the world, know nothing about what is really going on, and the papers are too timid to speak out on any subject, and perhaps they have got a hint not to do so. Then, again, Hidoo widows' marriages; and there are the new drill, and the Enfields, and the cartridges; and the Sepoys at Barrackpoor and elsewhere grumbling, and between you and me, they don't ever grumble for nothing. I tell you, Cyril, I don't like this, and hope no evil may come of it all. I hate these new-fangled laws; can't they let the people alone? And what do you think? When I was at Benares, my old Pundit came to see me, and asked me in a timid, stuttering kind of way, whether an order had not come from the Queen, to have all the people in India made Christians? Of course I laughed at the thing, and told him he was a fool for listening to such rubbish: and he said he wouldn't, though he could not prevent people in the bazaars from talking. Now, I don't like that either; but there appears, at any rate, to be no excitement up here as yet; mind, I don't like to enquire, or if it should exist, to issue a proclamation as they did in Bengal, and got a very clever snub in reply for their pains. He, or those who wrote that letter, did it very neatly, and proved from the proclamation itself, that Government had showed its hand in the game, and *did* mean evil; but we had best keep our eyes and ears open. I have spoken to the Brigadier, who, like myself, is not easy about the cartridges, or, indeed, any of the new-fangled military orders, and holds his own opinions, which are of the old school; we will get him to dinner on New Year's Day, and pick his brains. Meanwhile, we need not croak to ourselves, and there may be nothing in it, after all, to frighten anybody. We always live over barrels of gunpowder, some one said long ago, but they haven't blown up yet."

"It is very sad," replied Cyril, "very; but I have heard nothing, though I have been living literally among the people; and if my little wife had heard such rumours, I know she would have told me of them. Do the ladies know anything of this?"

"Well, perhaps, something," replied his friend, "but not very much. Not enough to cause them uneasiness as yet, and Rose is not one easily frightened; she only heard what people were talking about, and, to say the truth, laughed at it. Well, as you won't come to breakfast, we shall see you at church, I know, and I will introduce you to my sister."

"No, I can't come now," said Cyril; "I have to stop and look over all these letters, and the family budget to read, and some other things to see to; but I will come to church, and you shall introduce me afterwards to your sister."

"Good-bye then for the present, Cyril, and mind you make yourself smart," and Mostyn went away.

Cyril sat down to his letters, and found them very pleasant ones. There were several about his new appointment from men whom he respected and esteemed, not only congratulating him upon his promotion, which indeed he had fairly earned, but intimating that the confidence in him was so great that he might look comparatively soon to higher office. There was a cheery letter from his brother, who had been hunting all the season with great enjoyment, saying he felt as "strong as a horse;" and in spite of dear mother's croaking about the winter, had passed a much pleasanter one than he would have done at Nice, or Mentone; the dullest, to him, places in the world, and that he should attend "the House" after Easter.

A happy letter from his mother followed, and one from Augusta. There were no anxieties now, and they seemed to have entered fully into his views of the chances of promotion; but all expressed their earnest wishes that if he attained it, he would come home and see them as soon as practicable. So all was well, and Cyril was very thankful. Nothing but the direst necessity could separate him from Seeta now; and it would, he knew, be a sore trial to her to let him go, and once more live for a season with her grandfather. "She would do it," he said to himself, "but I am thankful my poor girl is not to be so tried."

Then he dressed himself carefully. None of the rough camp garments, but proper English clothes, very neat and *distingué* of their kind, befitting the season, now cool enough, indeed often cold. The hat, long disused, was nicely brushed, a pair of light-yellow gloves put on, and so equipped, he went to show himself to Seeta.

"Here I am in real English clothes," he said merrily; "do you know me, little woman?"

"O, I know you," she cried laughing; "or do I know you? Let me see." And she got up and looked him all over, and felt the soft gloss of his black surtout. "You have a very pretty scarf round your neck, and beautiful gloves, but I don't half like you for all that. So long as you have these fine clothes on, I feel as if I dare not touch you, and you belong to your people, and are a very great man; but I don't know them, and I like the old ones much better, for they are mine. Am I not right, Aunt Ella?"

"Well," he returned, "I can't help it, and it is only for a few days, so you must make the best of me. Now I am going to church, and you may not see me for ever so long, for I have some visits to pay afterwards."

"I am quite happy with Aunt Ella and the pets," she said, "and, do you know, the old black myna has never ceased talking since he saw me. How can I thank you enough, Cyril, for all this surprise and delight? It is a happy day to us all, and you are Commissioner at last. Do you know, sir?" she continued, making him a saucy reverence, "do you know that one of your subjects is not afraid of you? Now go, and be happy among your people."

And he went, riding his beautiful Arab, Sultan, joining friends who were also riding to church like himself. About half-way the Mostyns' carriage whirled past him, and he took off his hat. When he entered the church he saw them all in their pew near the pulpit, but his own was in the opposite aisle, and the reading-desk intervened between them.

But what a sensation had the new arrivals created! I will not attempt to describe Mrs. Mostyn's and Grace's dresses; I only know that one wore light lavender, and the other the lightest of pale blue silks: that they had the most bewitching of Paris bonnets of the newest fashion, that they wore hoops, then only in their infancy, and that altogether their costumes were remarkable for their good taste and elegance. I am afraid the beautiful service of the day, the burst of joy that Christ the Redeemer was born, and the gracious message that Angel choirs had sung, "Peace on earth, good will toward men," with the short, tender sermon of the chaplain that followed, fell upon some inattentive ears, and upon minds too much absorbed in the contemplation, perhaps envy, of new Paris millinery, and the two sweet faces that could be seen by many over the edge of the pew where they sat—to attend to heavenly things. This was the first appearance of the ladies in public, so to speak. They had arrived only a few days before, and were too tired by their long journey, and too long unpacking and settling everything in the house (for Mr. Mostyn had been living bachelor-fashion while his wife was in England), and they had seen nobody. Of all in church, Mrs. Mostyn only knew a very few; the Brigadier and the Hills, Dr. Home and his wife, and the commandant of the artillery, who was unmarried; all the rest were new, had come with new regiments, and, as Mrs. Mostyn whispered to Grace, "did not look very promising."

The service came to an end; the artillerymen, fine, stout fellows with ruddy faces, marched out clanking their spurs and sabres, and were followed by the infantry and congregation, of whom Cyril and the Morlands were nearly the last. He had preceded them, and was now standing near the porch of the church awaiting them; and as they came out, Mrs. Mostyn, with the cheeriest of smiles, put out her hand, which he grasped warmly, and declared she was charmed to see him again. "And you are looking so well too, Mr. Brandon," she said, "as well as if you were in England; and now let me introduce you to my sister. I hope you will soon come to know each other better." For a moment Cyril was almost confused by the frank manner of the young girl, who stood before him with heightened colour, and put out her hand kindly. "I seem to know you already, Mr. Brandon," she said, "I have been hearing so much of you."

"I am really flattered," he returned. "I hope your brother has given me a decent character, for he is a very old friend, you know."

"That's as it may be, and you will find out more if you will come to tiffin; will you?" said Mrs. Mostyn, as she stepped into the carriage.

"It is really churlish to refuse," replied Cyril, "and yet you must kindly excuse me to-day. I have duty visits to pay, and letters to write, for work won't stay; so you must kindly let me off till the evening."

"Very well," she replied, "I suppose there is no help for it; mind you come early, and bring some music;" and then the carriage, which Mostyn now drove himself, whirled away.

And while Cyril is paying his visits, and leaving his cards, we, being privileged, may hear a little of what other people thought of all they had seen at church.

"My dear Maria! how can you think so?" says Mrs. Smith to Mrs. Jones, who had been praising the dresses and style of the new-comers; "for my part, *I* thought them distressingly over-dressed, not to say vulgar. That girl's light blue silk might do for a ball-room perhaps; but the idea of wearing such a thing by day! Then look at those hoops, how monstrous! I tell Smith, I shall never—never—never—wear anything so outrageous. I am quite content as I am; *I* don't want gaudy finery."

Indeed, the poor lady was obliged to be content; for what with bank demands, and the rather recent march to Noorpoor, Smith's monthly balances were of very minute proportions, and the green silk dress Mrs. Smith had put on, which was her best, showed unmistakeable signs of frays, splits, and stains.

"I should like to get the 'musters' of Mrs. Mostyn's dress, and the lovely peaks before and behind, and of Miss Mostyn's bonnet. Could not you get them for me, dear Mrs. Home? you know her so well," said Mrs. Jones, "and Lucy could share them with me."

"I can do nothing of the kind, my dear," said Mrs. Home, sharply; "you can go and ask for yourselves; Mrs. Mostyn and I were ***never*** intimate. She is so very English, and so very exclusive, not a bit like any of *us*, and she seems ten times more stuck up now, than she was before she went home. But did you see what she did? I was really quite ashamed of her; if it had happened before I went into church, I'm sure I couldn't have gone there at all."

"No!" cried both in a breath, "what was it, dear?"

"I dare say you had gone away," continued Mrs. Home; "but I and Lucy were waiting for the carriage; and what does my lady do? Why, step up to young Brandon, as bold as you like, and shake hands with him ever so long, and then she introduces him to her sister. Fancy any *lady*, knowing a man who had put himself into a position like Mr. Brandon, and introducing him to her sister! and they shook hands too. It was positive pollution. I'm sure I would no more think of doing that myself, or allowing Lucy to do so, than—than——!" but as no simile came to her help, she continued, "and that's what people bring from England with them, where we know society is growing most immoral. It's quite shocking, isn't it?"

"But she is the Judge's wife," said Mrs. Jones, timidly, "and we can't quarrel with her; I hear they are going to be very gay too."

"Yes," observed Mrs. Smith, sharply; "I see what it is, Maria: you are hankering after these people; but she's a civilian, you know, and you're only a poor sub's wife. If I were you, I wouldn't be a toady. I suppose we shall hear of your calling on the bride next."

"The bride! whom do you mean?" cried Maria.

"Oh, don't you know? Haven't you heard of the other new arrival to-day?" continued Mrs. Smith; "a most interesting person, truly. Can't you guess? O, how stupid you both are! Why, the black bride, to be sure! The Honourable Mrs. Cyril Brandon, if I *must* speak plainer. My Ayah saw her come in this morning in a beautiful palankeen, and Chuprassees running before and behind, as grand as you like, and her black face now looking out of one door and now of another, and the people salaaming to her all along the bazaar. Quite a triumphal entry, my dears! Now, Maria, there's a chance for you; perhaps Mrs. Cyril may lead the fashions, and cut out Mrs. Mostyn, and you can get 'musters' of her nose-rings, and toe-rings, and jingling anklets like nauch girls. 'Rings on her fingers and bells on her toes,' you know; all, no doubt, of the newest Shah Gunje fashion."

"You don't mean to say so!" cried the listeners in a breath.

"I do: the woman is here, actually here among us! and it is

given out that she is married, too, by some 'Mumbo Jumbo' rite; and so she is the Honourable Mrs. Cyril," replied Mrs. Smith.

"It is horrible, positively a shocking public indecency; and we must get our husbands to send a memorial to the Governor-General, don't you think so?" said Mrs. Home.

"I don't think they care a button," continued Mrs. Smith. "When I told Smith about it this morning, he said to me, 'Jane, don't be a goose; what's the woman to you or you to the woman? Go to church, my dear, and pray to be delivered from evil speaking,—' and he finished the sentence, my dears; every word of it, too, and I was so angry, I could have thrown anything at him. No! we must act for ourselves, and I for one won't rest till we get her out of the station, the horrid wretch; living close to the Mostyns, and in that lovely cottage, too! I will set my Ayah to find out all about her at once."

"O, do tell us, dear, when you have," said her companions, as they separated.

Meanwhile, the innocent author of all this virtuous indignation was supremely happy in her new home; everything was so perfect, so bright, and so beautiful. The garden was full of luscious perfume from beds of mignonette, and roses, and orange and lime blossoms. Bunches of all sorts of flowers had used to come into camp daily, with vegetables; but they were too often faded. Here they grew in all their luxuriance. Cyril had told Seeta that all the garden was hers, down to the water of the lake; and after their morning meal, Aunt Ella and she had wandered about in thankful wonderment. The myna and the parrots had screamed themselves hoarse, and the former was solacing himself by repeating, in a solemn manner, some Mahomedan prayers in Arabic, which he had learned in his youth, and which Seeta had tried to drive from his memory, by teaching him Sanscrit verses. Thus all were jumbled together in a strange fashion, and the old bird was evidently very happy. Seeta, too, had heard everything about her grandfather; how Cyril had asked him to send Aunt Ella and the pets, and had written often "in his own hand, too," to say that his wife was well and happy. So it was a pleasant, cheerful morning; and when Cyril came home, he took his wife into the great bungalow, which seemed to her dreary enough; for there was only a bachelor's furniture in it; but in the drawing-room were many pictures, some of Cyril's, some Italian copies from old masters, and among them a Cenci, whose sad eyes seemed to follow Seeta's everywhere. Portraits of his mother, brother, and sister in water colours, and many others. Then there was the piano, now shut, which Seeta took for a cabinet; and as Cyril opened it, and ran his fingers over the keys, the girl, who was looking at a picture, started, and ran to him. "What is this?" she exclaimed.

"What I told you of in camp," he said. "Now, listen. I shall have to play something to-night at Mostyn's, and may as well run over it. Sit down beside me and listen."

She watched him as he opened a book, and selecting one of Mozart's sonatas, played it through. It would be wrong to say that she understood it all, but at portions of the varying melody he saw her fingers involuntarily beating time, and her lips quivering with excitement.

"Well," he asked, as he finished, "do you like it, little one?"

"Ah! it is too beautiful," she said, with a sigh, "too beautiful! Do not make me weep to-day, now I am so happy."

"I will sing to you, then," he replied. "By-and-by you will get accustomed to this music. Yes, it is very beautiful, and affects me as I play, sometimes almost to tears. I could play you some that would make you cry, darling, but not to-day."

So practising songs, running over accompaniments which he used to play for Mrs. Mostyn, the afternoon wore on, and, I am afraid, all letters were forgotten or put aside. As evening fell they walked down the garden to the lake and the little boat-house, and Cyril showed his wife the pretty boat, in which he promised her many a sail by-and-by. There standing, the sun went down in its glory, and the pink and crimson clouds and golden glow were reflected in the calm lake as in a mirror, and the frowning towers and battlements of the grim old fort near them stood out sharply against the sky. How beautiful it was! How Seeta's spirit was steeped in happiness! and, after her old fashion, the tears came brimming to her eyes. "You did not tell me of all this," she said gently. "I am so grateful to you, Cyril?"

"Yes," he said, "it is very lovely, and I often looked at it long ago, and wished for some one to share it with me; and now I have all I wished for."

"All?" she asked. "Only a poor little Hindoo girl."

"And she is enough," he answered gaily, and drawing her to him; "but I must go and dress. I have other new clothes to show you."

And in time he appeared in his evening suit, with a white waistcoat and faultless shiny boots, and looked, she thought, handsomer than ever. "It is beautiful," she said. "Go and be happy with your friends. It is your festival day. I shall go to sleep, for I am tired, and you will come and wake me."

If Cyril had been struck with Grace Mostyn when he was introduced to her at church, as he entered the Mostyns' drawing-room, she now appeared radiantly beautiful. She was dressed simply in white silk, like Mrs. Mostyn, and the dress was beautifully made, and showed her exquisite figure to perfection. Perhaps Grace Mostyn knew that she was very lovely, as her brother had told her as she entered the room. It is not easy to describe this girl, whose fresh, innocent features beamed with sensibility and grace. She was very fair, and the pure English colour was as fresh as ever; that gentle mingling of the most delicate carnations with white which no women's complexions but those of England can boast of. She had large blue-grey eyes; shaded with long, dark eyelashes, very soft and gentle in expression, but often contracting and sparkling with merriment, a small straight nose, with pink, transparent nostrils; and a mouth formed in soft curves, with fresh, moist, rosy lips, which were slightly open, and showed a little of the small, white, pearly teeth. Her light-brown hair, so wavy and soft, fell in natural curls from the back of her head, and was plainly braided in front over the white, broad forehead. Grace Mostyn was somewhat under the middle size of English women, and Cyril hardly knew which was most attractive, the beauty of her face, or of her figure, lithe and rounded as it was. A fair Saxon face, with not a shade of guile about it: as tender as it was full of grace; but varying with every thought and emotion. "A face Sir Joshua would have loved to paint, and to which he alone could have done justice," thought Cyril as the light played about it while he sat opposite to her at dinner. She had not evinced the slightest embarrassment with him from the first, and all she said impressed Cyril with the delicate and highly toned culture of her mind.

How much they had to say to each other, these three old friends!—what spirits was Mrs. Mostyn in as she described her English visit, and how thankful she was that they were all safely reunited, even for awhile!—and how sincerely she congratulated Cyril, as did Grace, on his new dignity!

The two gentlemen, for there were no guests that night, did not linger over their wine. Mostyn said, "You must hear them sing;" and they got up and joined the ladies.

"You ought to begin, Mr. Brandon," said his hostess, "for the sake of old times."

"Indeed I shall do no such thing," replied Cyril. "I am grown rusty, quite rusty in the jungles, while you are fresh from your great masters."

"Well, then," said the lady, "come, Grace, and sing. What shall it be? 'Sull' aria?'" And they sang the exquisite duett charmingly.

Cyril had heard Grisi and Persiani sing the same, but, he thought, never more delightfully. Then "Giorno d' orrore" followed, and many others, some new to Cyril; and one of Campana's "Dimmi che m' ami."

"I ought to be a tenor, you know," said Mrs. Mostyn. "You must learn this—to sing with Grace, and I shall abdicate."

Then Cyril played the Mozart sonata, and sang "Vivi tu" and some others of his old songs; and, as a finale, they chose the lovely trio in "Norma," "O di qual sei," in which Cyril used to take a part before Mrs. Mostyn went home. But voices must tire, and pleasant evenings come to an end. Indeed, it had grown late; and when they had discussed the trio, Cyril bid them good-night and went home.

Seeta did not wake as he approached her, but he saw a sweet smile on her lips as he bent over her. Aunt Ella, who had been lying on a carpet beside the low bed, woke up and stretched herself, and Cyril motioned to her to be silent. "How softly she sleeps, my pet," he said to himself. "How lovely she looks, and yet how they contrast with each other, Grace and she! Will they ever meet?" Then Seeta woke, and said, "O, I was so happy in my dreams, Cyril—I was so happy! And now you are come at last, and I waited for you till my eyes were heavy. And they were kind to you?"

"Very, very kind," he replied; "they are like my brother and sisters. Yes, it was all delightful."

And thus Christmas Day, 1856, had closed in peace.

CHAPTER XXIII.

THE GOOROO'S SENTENCE.

In spite of all her happiness at meeting with Seeta, Aunt Ella had a sore grief at her heart, which she dared not tell her of: and which, it appeared to her, concerned not only her brother, but all of them very deeply; and it was this. Not long after Cyril had taken Seeta away from Shah-Gunje, the Gooroo, or spiritual director of the goldsmith caste, arrived at the town, and commenced his usual inquiry into caste disputes and irregularities, which it was his privilege to make and to settle. It may not be generally known to my English readers, that the Hindoo castes of India, Brahmins and Rajpoots the highest, as well as the many lower grades, are all under the direction, and indeed government, of directors or priests, who from time to time visit their several jurisdictions, and regulate the religious as well as the social affairs of their people. The Brahmin "Swamees," or lords, are in fact spiritual princes, or popes, and can alone confer the highest sacraments on their own and lower castes. In their several degrees, the Gooroos of inferior castes follow up the more learned injunctions and directions of the Swamees, and in many instances are responsible to them. No act of caste neglect, or social irregularity, fails to become known to these authorities; and any defiance, or wilful breach of caste rules, is severely punished by them. It is thus that every caste is preserved in its purity, and becomes a source of pride, whatever its rank in the social scale may be, to those who belong to it.

It may be conceived that an event like the marriage of Seeta, was not one likely to remain unknown: and was considered by the Gooroo to be of such importance, that when he heard of it he determined to proceed without delay to Shah Gunje. He had received many letters on the subject from members of the goldsmiths' guild in different towns and villages, who, knowing nothing of the circumstances, were in much alarm; but the most urgent were from Shah Gunje itself. Many of the members of the caste there had attended the ceremony of marriage, and had eaten of the marriage feast; but Brahmins had eaten too, and Brahmins had performed the ceremony, so there could be no danger. There was this difference, however, that the food for Brahmins had been cooked by people of their own class; whereas that for the goldsmiths had been prepared in Narendra's own house.

It is probable, perhaps, that but for one member of the caste, Ram Das, of Gokulpoor, the rest would not—backed as they were by the Brahmin priest of the temple and his party—have taken any steps in the matter, and would have allowed it to pass unchallenged; for Narendra was a man universally respected and beloved, and his knowledge of caste proceedings and requirements was so profound, that the adjustment of ordinary local disputes had been left in his hands by the Gooroo himself. Ram Das was, however, vindictive. He had proposed marriage with Seeta, which I did not care to record particularly when it occurred, and had been contemptuously rejected both by Narendra and Seeta. He vowed revenge at the time, and Seeta's marriage afforded him an opportunity for it too precious to be lost. It was he who had written to the Gooroo, imlporing him to come and save the caste from a disgrace and humiliation, which was the greater because of the rank of the person who had infringed its rules. "If Narendra is not punished," he wrote, "who will give us their sons or daughters in marriage? I have not eaten with him as others did, who now lament doing so; but there are many who will have no peace till they receive the saerament of purification from your hands."

Narendra and Wamun Bhut heard that the Gooroo had been invited to come to Shah Gunje, and the reason was beeoming daily more obvious. Many of his neighbours, who used to come in constantly for an evening chat, or game at chess, now came no longer. Persons who visited him on business even, gathered up their garments with a gesture of pollution as they entered or departed. Several of his best workmen and clerks absented themselves on one pretence or other, eausing great inconvenience and some loss. It was clear to Narendra that the erisis must eome; that it was one in which his friend, Wamun Bhut, might defend, but eould not materially help him; that there was no use appealing to English law, and when the sacraments of his faith would be denied him, no authority but his Gooroo and his caste could restore them.

If Cyril had been at, or near Shah Gunje, at this time, his presence might have made a diversion in Narendra's favour; but he was nearly a hundred miles away, and there was no chance of his returning. I question, too, even if he had been there, whether Narendra would have asked Cyril's aid, or accepted it; equally, also, whether Cyril would or could have interfered at all, in any capaeity. If the question had to be tried, it were better disposed of without delay; and if he had erred on the score of caste, he must pay the penalty and submit to the discipline which he himself, in hundreds of instances, had assisted to enforce before. Just then, too, Cyril had written to him to ask that Aunt Ella might be sent to Noorpoor to meet Seeta, whom he should take into the station for Christmas, and might bring with her all the old pets which Seeta often missed; and he wished that Aunt Ella should eome several days before they could arrive, and satisfy herself that the purification of the new cottage was complete.

I need not, perhaps, detail the partieulars of a caste dispute. If such a subject ever comes before an English judge in India, he finds himself perplexed by the application of laws whieh no statute has ever attempted to define—the laws and preeedents of popular custom—which, in point of fact, are in some respects stronger than the written law, whether Hindoo or Mahomedan. In certain cases, the written law, in its mighty power, puts aside the other, and justly; but in a caste dispute, the written law does not provide for the solution of questions of eating and drinking among castes, the performance of religious ceremonies, or the regulations of social polity. It is the province of popular caste custom to do this. Narendra knew this perfectly; and when he sent his sister to Noorpoor, had made up his mind to await the inevitable issue.

The case went against him in the Caste Punchayet. It was in vain that he pleaded the existence of the old Mahomedan alliance; in vain that he had acted under the advice of Brahmins learned in the law, and that second marriages were customary among their people. The Gooroo, a well-meaning man in his way, told him that he himself ought to have been applied to, and that he only ought to have directed so unusual a ceremony. That the general law, when interpreted by Brahmins, might sanction such a marriage, yet it was a breach of caste custom. Narendra must, then, proceed at once to Benares, wash out the fault in the Ganges, and bring back a certificate of purification. He must pay a fine to the caste, to be employed in a feast when he returned, and in donations to the poor; and Aunt Ella must be purged also.

Aunt Ella knew that trouble was coming on the house, and she prayed hard to be allowed to remain and share it with her brother; but he would not hear of this. "I know what it will be, if they condemn me," he had said. "I shall have to go to Benares, and take you too. But O! the disgrace of it, and the humiliation before Ram Das, and the rest of them, are hard to bear."

"And it was all her fault," his sister replied; "but for Seeta, we should have still been honoured."

"Peace! be silent, woman," he had replied sternly. "Only for him who saved us I should have been dead, and she dishonoured by a ruffian; now she is Mr. Brandon's beloved wife, honoured by all the country, and will be so when this petty spite is passed away. Be patient and watch, and the issue will be as God pleases. She has gone out from among us, but need we love her the less, sister?"

Aunt Ella well remembered this stern rebuke, and had carried out her brother's orders implicitly; and under the certainty of Seeta's happiness, and Cyril's care of her, of which she had now ocular proof, Aunt Ella doubted no longer. "If even we have to go to Benares," she said to herself, "what does it signify? Have I not been saying I would go there every year, and now if the time is come, good; if not, I can stay with Seeta." For all that, Aunt Ella's anxiety and grief did not depart from her.

It was indeed come; for Narendra had not delayed at Shah Gunje after the sentence was pronounced against him. He had arranged his affairs in a few days, written to all his correspondents, given instructions to his head agent and manager, and inviting Wamun Bhut, with several other Brahmins, to accompany him at his own cost, the party left Shah Gunje, the popular feeling being decidedly in the banker's favour; and the sinister desires of Ram Das, who had persuaded himself that Narendra would appeal to Mr. Brandon or the judge, and thus involve himself in further caste disgrace, were, for the time, ungratified.

They arrived at Nourpoor the last day of the year, and Narendra did not fail to have the news conveyed to Aunt Ella and Seeta. Seeta was wild with delight as she rushed into Aunt Ella's kitchen, and fell on her neck sobbing and crying out, "He is come, he is come! O Aunt Ella, go! take the palankeen, and bring him here; I have a house for him now; and I shall be so glad."

But when Aunt Ella burst into violent tears, and beat her breast, and Seeta looked wildly at her, wondering at her sudden grief, the sad tale could be no longer delayed, and, choking with sobs, Aunt Ella told all she knew. It was not all, but enough to account for her brother's sudden arrival.

Seeta was too indignant to weep; her spirit rose, as it always did with emergency, and she cried out against the tyranny which had been exercised by the Gooroo. "It is all the doing of one bad man who had Huree Das killed," she said, "and the English will do justice in the end. We impure! Well, the time will come—yes, it will come, I know—when Ram Das will be sent by them over the black water." If Cyril had been at home she would have flown to him at once; but he was absent at his Kucherry, and despatching Aunt Ella in the palankeen when she had become calmer, Seeta awaited the arrival of both.

After the first excitement had passed away, Seeta began to reflect. Had they then really become impure, and forfeited their social position? She called to mind what it had been in former days, when her grandfather, respected by all, was the head of the caste, not only in Shah Gunje, but through the country on all sides. How people brought their troubles to him, and he did justice to all with a firm but merciful hand. How their daily worship and the ceremonies and festivals of their faith were all performed. How large and bountiful was his charity! and now the brand of disgrace had been put on him, which could only be obliterated by penance, public and costly. As she thought of all this, for an hour or more alone, the feeling, nay, the certainty that her own wilfulness, her own passion, had caused this misfortune, pressed hard upon her, and the hot blood surged from her heart to her brow and cheeks and neck in a flame, scorching her, till she hid her face in her hands and gasped for breath. Sometimes before, a similar feeling had caused a shuddering terror that her husband's caresses were poison; that she was polluted by them; and these thoughts returned to her with redoubled force. Then she had put them away from her, trusting in his love, trusting in her own faith; but now they would not yield. Her spirit seemed to call aloud to her to rise, and fly from further temptation and sin, to depart at once to Benares, and wash out her offence in penance there! Surely her grandfather would take her, and they could all return to Shah Gunje and live in the old simple fashion. What mattered if she suffered, what if she died, she would at least die pure, "and there would be no reproach on them any longer. Let him but come," she cried aloud, "and I will tell him all; Cyril will release me, and I may go away and all shall be but a dream of the past."

Almost as she spoke, Cyril stood before her smiling and bright. "To whom are you speaking, Seeta? what is a dream of the past? where did you find that in your books? What is the matter?" he continued anxiously, as he now observed her white, scared face and bloodless lips. "What has come to you, little one? you are not ill? Aunt Ella, come here—quick," he cried.

"Do not call her," said Seeta mechanically, "she is gone to fetch my grandfather; I am alone."

"Your grandfather! Why, he is at Shah Gunje; you must be ill or dreaming, Seeta. What has frightened my pet? Come and tell me." And he sat down on the low divan, and drew her to him.

For a time she resisted, and turned away from him trembling; but her love was too strong to bear the strain, and she dropped into his outstretched arms and lay on his breast, still trembling and shuddering; but clinging the more closely to him as he bent over her, parted her hair from her forehead, and kissed her. That true, fond heart could not break away from him, and as she clung to her husband the more, the terror that had possessed her began gradually to pass away. Yet she could not speak; her throat was choked, and her mouth parched with the intensity of her mental struggle. It was in vain that Cyril implored her to speak to him, to tell him what ailed her, what had frightened her, or if any one had spoken rudely to her; and his face flushed as he thought of one terrible man who might have been prowling about and threatened her. Then he took her up in his arms and carried her to the inner room and laid her on her low bed, and went out to the court to call Bheemee. "Has any one been here?" he asked; "has your lady been walking in the garden?"

"No," she said, "no one, and my lady did not go out to-day in the garden; she was alone after Aunt Ella went away in the palankeen. I have been cooking here, for they said more food would be wanted for Narendra."

"It is most mysterious," thought Cyril; "what can have happened? Bring your lady some cool water," he continued, "she is not well;" and the woman followed him with Seeta's silver drinking-cup in her hand. "Seeta," he cried, "look up, little one, drink some water, and tell me what has alarmed you. He has not been here—that villain who escaped?"

Seeta rose and looked wildly about her; it seemed to Cyril, as she drew her hands slowly across her eyes, that she hardly knew where she was; but Bheemee handed her the cup, and she took a few sips, which seemed to choke her. Then she saw Cyril, and stretched out her arms to him and cried: "Oh, I will not go, I will not go; do not let them take me away from you, Cyril, else I shall die!"

"No one shall take you away, my pet," he said gently. "Do not be afraid." "If she could only cry!" thought Cyril. "Her face has that hard, set look which I remember when first she told me her sad tale; and tears can alone relieve her. She is quite hysterical." So he laid her head again on his breast, and patted her as he would have done a child when it is weary and fractious. Presently he saw tears dropping silently from her closed eyes and falling upon his hands—those silent tears which cause no pain; and again she said, almost in a whisper, as to herself, "I will not go away. If I am impure, I am with him, to live and to die." And her face grew calmer, the hard lines faded softly out of it, a rosy flush spread itself over her cheeks and forehead, and he heard her say faintly, "Cyril, Cyril, come to me!" She had evidently no idea of where she was.

"I am here, Seeta," he said. "Look up, my darling." And he kissed her.

She opened her eyes widely, and for a moment; their unmeaning stare struck him with sudden pain, but only for an instant. As they closed again she spoke. "I have had a horrid dream," she said, again clinging to him, and hiding her face in his breast "What did I say, Cyril? did I speak?"

"You said you would not leave me; they must not take you away. Who has frightened you, Seeta?" he continued gravely. "Come, you are better now. Sit up, and tell me all about it."

"No," she replied, "only here, only here, on your breast. I have no refuge but this now." And she told him all she had heard from her aunt. "They will be back presently," she continued, "and grandfather will tell you the rest. I thought—I thought, Cyril, that I ought to go away to Benares with them, and never return to you. And I was quite alone, and some horrid fancies beset me, till I felt mad, I think. I saw you come; and I remember no more, but that I thought they wanted to take me away; and that was foolish, Cyril, for did they not give me to you?"

Then he soothed her, and told her to go and bathe her face, and be ready to show her grandfather the house and the oratory, and the garden. "And I will take him into the bungalow and talk to him afterwards," he said.

Nor was it long before Narendra arrived. He and the priest had walked leisurely from the town, and Aunt Ella was following in the palankeen. It was a loving meeting between Seeta and her grandfather. They had not seen each other since he had put her hand into her husband's at the temple, and bid them depart. Seeta bent low at his feet and touched them reverently, as he entered the cottage and looked about. Perhaps it was too English for him, for he sighed as she led him into the oratory, where he bowed before the altar, and took some ashes from the sacred fire and rubbed them on his forehead, after his own custom at home. Then she led him into the court and showed him Bheemee busy in her kitchen, and the beautiful bath of white marble, and the old pets, who all knew him and saluted him; the myna crying, in a hoarse croak, "Namusear Maharaj!" "Ramchundra!" exactly like his old book-keeper, as he entered the office daily and sat down.

"Is it not like home, grandfather?" she said.

But Narendra shook his head. "Your home, child, not mine now," he said sadly. "Aunt Ella says she has told you what has happened; but it only concerns us, not you, so be comforted.

Show all this place to Wamun Bhut, and he will be able to speak to it if necessary hereafter. Now let us go to Mr. Brandon. I have much to say to him, and I will return presently."

"And you will come back for your evening meal, grandfather?" she said, gaily.

"No," he said, "that must not be now, Seeta. Till I am purified, I can neither eat with you, nor drink, nor sit down in your house. You would not bring further trouble upon me, my darling! Why, I should even pollute you."

Poor Seeta! all her trouble seemed to be opening afresh, and she could not restrain her tears. She only said meekly, "You know best, grandfather. When you and Aunt Ella come back we shall be happy, and I will come to Shah Gunje to see you."

Then, leaving Seeta with the priest, and whispering to him to comfort her, Narendra sought Cyril.

They talked together long and earnestly. Narendra, after congratulating him on his appointment, the news of which had delighted the people, told Cyril that he had submitted to the Gooroo, to avoid contention and great strife; and as to his pilgrimage to Benares, he was glad of it for many reasons, both religious and as concerned his business at Mirzapore, now so largely increasing. He must see the railroad, too, of which every one was speaking as a wonder; and Aunt Ella had long had a vow which must be fulfilled—she must perform the ceremonies suited to her age and her widowhood. "But," continued the old man, "be under no concern for Seeta, and do not let her vex herself by thoughts of impurity. Her caste is as good as ever it was, and she is too proud and pure herself not to maintain it. The Punchayet never mentioned her, never prohibited me from associating with her; and they dare not, sir, vex your wife. I have just vexed the child myself," he said smiling, "as I would not sit down, nor eat the dinner she has made for me; but there is no use in running fresh risks. She sees that herself, I think; and I will go to her again before I depart from your house."

"Now you are really going to Benares," said Cyril. "I want you to do me a great favour, and I speak to you, not officially, but as one friend to another. Mr. Mostyn has mentioned to me some strange rumours he heard at Benares from his old Pundit in regard to the very subject you are going upon—caste."

"Yes, sir, I know them already," said Narendra, interrupting him; "my correspondent at Mirzapore wrote them to me a few days ago."

"And do they believe them?" asked Cyril.

"No more than I do," cried the old banker indignantly. "We, who have grown rich and are growing richer under the British Government, are at ease about our caste."

"I am sure you are, my friend," replied Cyril, "and will ever continue to be so; but I should like you very much to ascertain whether what Mr. Mostyn heard—is—is—believed; or, at any rate, whether such rumours exist anywhere. In short, Narendra, find out all you can; it may be of use to us here, and to the Government; and write to me yourself—you know I and Seeta between us can make out all your letter."

"I will," he said, with a sigh; "I only deplore that there should be need. I leave early to-morrow, and now bid you farewell. Take an old man's blessing again, sir," he continued, "and forgive this liberty." And he put his hands on Cyril's head. "May God keep you and Seeta! You have been very kind to her, Mr. Brandon, very kind; and I can say no more now. Let me go to her, and tell her what I feel, but cannot express to you."

CHAPTER XXIV.

MICHING MALECHO.

"My dears," said Mrs. Smith to her two friends on the first of January, 1857, after the greetings and kisses of the new year had been exchanged, "there is really no getting at that woman; my Ayah has been to the house several times, but my lady is guarded as close as if she were a Mussulman's wife, and the people there actually told my Ayah, if she came prowling about again, they would put her into the guard. There is an old aunt, I hear, with madam, who is as sharp as a needle; but I am not to be done," she continued, "no, my dears, she will be *very* sharp if she escapes *me*. But do you know they are all in a horrible mess? it is really quite delightful."

"Mess?" cried the friends, "then the Mostyns have ordered her away, I'm sure," said Mrs. Home; "of course they couldn't have a creature like *that* living near them."

"Not a bit of it, my dear," continued Mrs. Smith; "they've lost their caste. Ha! ha! ha! Isn't that grand?"

"And serve them right," said Mrs. Home; "but how do you know that, Jane?"

"Ah, my Ayah, you know, is great friends with a goldsmith's wife in the town; and she told her yesterday, that madam's grandfather, who is really a great banker, belonged to her caste, and had been put out of it, and is obliged to go and do penance at Benares, and wash away the sin this girl has brought on them. Really it is very sad to see so respectable a man brought to such a condition, and by our 'Commissioner' too. What will the natives say! Smith tells me, that even the Sepoys, when they hear of it, will be very savage, and there will be no holding them; in short, he quite frightened me yesterday by all he said."

"What about?" asked her friends apprehensively.

"O, about the new Enfields, and the cartridges, and the 'temper'—that's the word he used—of the Sepoys at Barrackpore and Dinapore, and half-a-dozen other places. I'm sure I don't care a button about it, you know; but Smith said so, and so I put that and the banker together, and if *we* do such things, my dears, what wonder if the poor natives take offence, and do worse! Well, I was thinking of this last night, till Smith came to bed; you know he is reading hard now, and sits up too late; and I hit upon a plan to get rid of that horrid creature, and here's what it is. But can I trust you both?"

"Do tell it!" said Mrs. Home. "O Jane! to think you could not trust me."

"Or me!" added Mrs. Jones, who wiped away a tear; she was a very sensitive little woman.

"Very well, now you promise, I will tell you both what I thought of; and that is, to separate those two. Mr. Brandon may be as mad as he pleases about the girl (and men do get so mad. O dear!), and she is fooling him on to any extent; but if they fell out, you know, he would go one way and she another, and there would be an end of the scandal, and I am sure Lady Hylton would be very—very much obliged by me, a poor little mouse, cutting the lion's net!"

"It seems very nasty to interfere at all," said little Mrs. Jones, who at heart had perhaps some sympathy with the strange love affair, which seemed to her to be quite romantic.

"Oh, bless you, not a bit of it; do you think, dear Maria, *I* would do a nasty thing?" cried Mrs. Smith, with a sneer: "if you think such rubbish, I'd better hold my tongue at once."

"Be quiet, Jane," said Mrs. Home soothingly; "you know I quite approve of all you do, Jane, and if that wretch were gone, we should have that nice Mr. Brandon among us once more as he used to be; we've asked him to dinner and the Hills have (Hilleses, Mrs. Home said), and the Messes, and he won't go anywhere."

"Except to the Mostyns, my dear," remarked Mrs. Smith, rather maliciously perhaps; "he is always there, except when he is sailing about with that girl in the indecent way he does. If men will have black 'companions,' you know, they ought to keep them to themselves, and not stuff them under our noses. I hate the thought of it. I feel quite sick as I look at them through the glass, and see that fine young fellow with his arm round her, and both of them laughing like children."

"But I thought she was his wife," put in Mrs. Jones timidly. "You said he was married, Jane, and Jones tells me he is, and it's all right."

"She is as much his wife as you are, Maria!" replied Mrs. Smith; "is she, Susan? That marriage is all to be washed out in the Ganges, and that's why the banker is going there. And listen, she—that woman—is ever so rich, I hear, and if she goes back to her grandfather, he will get her money, and if she has—has—children, you know, he can't touch it. Don't you see?"

"Is there then——?" asked Mrs. Home. "O Maria, how dreadful it would be! Can't you find out, Jane?"

"If you will only be patient both of you, I will do my best; but why should we delay when there may be a chance of that danger? My plan is, that *she* should be told that *he* is going to be married."

"Married! and to whom?" cried Mrs. Home. "I'm sure I would not have my poor child mixed up with a report like that for all the world, and the Doctor would be very angry if she were."

"Do you think I am such a goose, Susan," replied her friend, "as to mention names? Take two facts: there are two very nice spinsters here, dear Lucy and Grace Mostyn; as to poor Harriet Clay, I put her out of the question; and there is one very nice, very handsome, very eligible young man, a capital catch, who has a good appointment, and a title, and may be a Lord perhaps one day—who, we'll suppose, wants a wife. Well, *we* needn't believe it until we know for certain; but suppose a report arose in the bazaar that he was going to be married, no names need be mentioned, and of course *she* would hear it!"

"And if she did, why should she care?" said Mrs. Jones. "I'm sure there were fifty reports about Jones when we were at the Hills, but I didn't care, I knew I had got him—safe, safe—*I* didn't believe the lies, and *she* won't if she loves him!"

"But she will, you'll see she will, my dears! it's very different between us and natives," returned Mrs. Smith con-

fidently. "That girl is a proud, jealous, little thing, I am sure, and when she hears about him, she would just flounce away, and he might whistle for her."

"Yes, I quite agree with you, Jane," said Mrs. Home; "we should do *any*thing to save that fine young fellow from the scheming natives that *she* will get about him."

"I don't see that," remarked Mrs. Jones; "but of course *you* two can do as you like. I won't have any hand in it."

"Then I *shall* do as I like, my dears; and when the black bride is gone, you may thank *me* that there will be room for a white one," said Mrs. Smith.

"But she is not black, is she, Jane?" asked Mrs. Jones, who was a great reader of Byron, and was certain that Seeta must be as beautiful as Haidée or Gulnare.

"No, she is as fair as any of us, and very pretty too," said Mrs. Smith; "at least, she looked so through the glass; but she's a native, and they are all niggers, and—and—I hate them—that's all. Who's going to the Mostyns' this evening?"

"We dine there," said Mrs. Home, "and Lucy comes in the evening. I think all the station people are asked."

"And there will be a dance, I'm sure," said Mrs. Jones, "for I heard Jones telling the bandmaster what music to take."

So I think we may leave these friends to their devices, and look after some of our other people. It was a pleasant day at Noorpoor; carriages and buggies were being driven about the station all day by callers; young men went "peacocking," as they called it, in their best and neatest trim; officials like the Brigadier, Mr. Mostyn, and Cyril Brandon, received complimentary visits from their subordinate officers and clerks; and trays of almonds and sugar-candy, with garlands of flowers, were presented by the two Serishtadars, the bankers of the bazaar, and the traders of the cantonment; and neat little speeches were made by the donors and recipients. Even the Nawab Dil Khan Bahadoor was busy paying visits, and offering his congratulations; and the jangling bells of his elephants were heard all over the town and cantonment during the day. The Brigadier had not told Cyril of the visits we know of, nor of the Nawab's malevolence, and Cyril received him with what civility he could muster, and perhaps thought the Nawab a little more blustering and consequential than usual, and was glad when he went away. Then Cyril strolled through Mostyn's garden to the house, to see whether the evergreens he had helped to arrange in the morning were properly put up; and Mrs. Mostyn insisted that he should practise one or two things with them. "We won't ask you to tiffin," she said, "for we are all in a mess, and the Khansaman won't let us have the dining-table. We are going to be *so* grand! but I don't know what all the frumps will say to a *dîner à la Russe*. Adieu! Au revoir."

How sweet Grace had looked! how deliciously she sang!—a pure, round soprano, not very high, but most tender and flexible; and though thoroughly instructed, by no means showy. But Grace could sing the most florid of *bravuras* if she pleased; and any one who had ever heard her sing Mozart's "Al Desio," or "Ah non giunge," or "Qui la voce," never forgot them. As to the simple "Dove Sono," or "Batti, Batti," they were even more delightful and perfect; and it would cause quite a sensation at Noorpoor to hear such performances.

Cyril went back to Seeta, and told her he would not leave her again till evening. "Give me something to eat," he said, laughing; "I am very hungry. I can eat here, though you won't eat there," and he pointed to the bungalow; "and I enjoy your simple food better than all the cook's good things. They have all gone to help at Mostyn's big dinner, and I have brought a spoon and a fork and a plate to you, to beg."

Seeta, though alone, was very happy that day. Her grandfather had come to her the evening before, after he left Cyril alone, and explained everything to her, and told her not to fear. Wamun Bhut, he said, was perfectly satisfied with her arrangements, and had suggested she should look out for some poor Brahmin, who would see after the house when she was gone. Then Narendra had blessed her; so had the priest and Aunt Ella, who, with many tears, left her child. "We shall be back by the Busunta," Narendra had said, "but I will write." In the early morning she had helped Cyril to cut flowers for the Mostyns' table, and had arranged several bouquets herself with that rare faculty of combination of colour which belongs to most natives of India. "I will show Mrs. Mostyn that these are yours," Cyril had said, "and I am sure she and Grace will think them the prettiest of all." She knew the meaning of their names now—"Rose" and "Grace"—and thought them so pretty! Seeta was now learning English very fast. With her talent for the acquisition of language it came easily to her; and through the medium of a Hindee grammar and dictionary, and a translation of the "Prém Sagur" and some school-books, she made progress every day. It was a new occupation entirely, and she longed for the time when, like Cyril, she could read the poetry of England. She had begun to write too; and altogether, I am sure Cyril was proud of his pupil.

When Cyril had eaten the plateful that Seeta brought to him, she fetched her books and wanted her lesson, but he would not have them. "This is the New Year's Day," he said, "and every one has a holiday, so we will be idle. It is not often I get a whole afternoon with my pet. By-and-by we will go out for a sail, and you shall steer. I want Rose and Grace to come some day; but they are afraid of me, though they have come over the great sea. I wonder what they are doing there, at the old house—the mother and Augusta and Hylton?"

"Thinking of you, Cyril," she said, "I dare say; but they don't know of me, I suppose?"

"Not yet," he replied; "but they will know by-and-by."

"I shall never see them, Cyril. Perhaps it is best, for they would not love me," she said, timidly.

"I think if they saw and knew you they would love you dearly, darling; but you must go over the great sea, and leave all your caste behind, to see them."

"Do you think I would not do that for you, if it were necessary?" she said, with her eyes flashing.

"I do," he replied, "and more than that."

So they chatted on till the sun grew lower; then they went out on the lake, and Seeta steered the boat, while Cyril managed the sails. How lovely it was!—the clear, deep water, the pretty gardens of the cantonment, the town and the fine old fort, the great bastion of which was washed by the lake. Perhaps Mrs. Smith's telescope was fixed upon them. If it were they cared not.

When he was dressed for the evening party he went to her again and kissed her, and told her not to be afraid, for that she was well guarded, and he would come back as soon as he could.

There were twenty-four people to dinner altogether, as many as Mr. Mostyn's table could hold. Certainly, as Mrs. Mostyn had told Cyril, they were not a little smart. All the new dinner service, purple and gold; the new glass, the silver centre-piece and vases, and glass dishes, filled with flowers and fruits, the glossy Irish damask tablecloths and napkins, formed a rare and beautiful picture never before seen in Noorpoor. Then there were new lamps, "warranted to burn under punkahs," on the side-tables, and two candelabra on the dinner-table, of six lights each; and everything looked brilliant and sparkling.

"I wonder whether they will like it, Grace?" said Mrs. Mostyn to her sister, as she gave a few finishing touches to the flowers. "It is such a contrast to the old style of 'Saddley

Peero—Burra Khanas;' that means saddle and turkey—big dinners, you know. Then you had a big saddle of mutton at the top and a turkey at the bottom, and a ham, and all the *entreés* ranged as thick as they could stand down the sides; and we poor women were knocked about and splashed with gravy. Dear me! I remember a gentleman once told me that when he and his wife gave their first dinner they ordered their Khansaman to do everything 'proper;' and what did he do, my dear, but put two of everything on the table! So there was a turkey and saddle at top, and the same at the bottom, a boiled leg of mutton in the middle, and one opposite to it, and so on, fowls and all. Wasn't it funny? But the funniest thing I ever remember was the ram. Now do listen. When we were at ——, not long after we came out married, a grim old colonel promised me a party, and I teazed him till he issued the invitations. He had a big bungalow, and room for a 'Burra Khana.' Three days before the dinner I was riding past the house with Philip and Captain Jackson, and Philip pointed out to me a huge ram—a regular fighting ram, my dear, such as the natives keep to knock their heads against each other—and it was crying out 'Baa! baa!' continually, and tugging at a cord by which it was tied to a bush, and walking round and round defiantly. 'We shall have to eat that ram,' said Philip, gravely, 'see if we haven't. "Baa! baa!" Poor beast! better you had had your brains knocked out.' Well, to shorten my story, the morning of the party, as we went to look, we saw no ram; he had become mutton; and in the evening, as the colonel handed me to my seat, there, sure enough, was the back of the poor beast made into a saddle; and when I looked up the table I saw his legs and shoulders here and there. But the worst of it was, that Captain Jackson, who sat next to me, and who was very short-sighted, put up his eyeglass, and, first looking at the saddle, ran his eye up and down the table, and then turned to me and said, in a whisper, 'Baa!' so like the old ram that I was in fits, and did not know what to say; and when the colonel, who was a little deaf, said, quite innocently, 'What did you say, Jackson? Saddle? Yes, it's a fine one, isn't it? Gram-fed, upon my honour! I wouldn't give Mrs. Mostyn bazaar mutton, you know,' I fairly laughed out."

"And did you eat ram?" asked Grace, who was laughing heartily.

"Not a bit of him," cried her sister, "and my old friend was rather huffed that I didn't. O! the smell of the beast it is in my nostrils still! but come away and dress, like

darling! Inshalla! as the Nawab says, we shall be something to-night."

And so they were; it was a hearty merry party, and even Mrs. Home had forgotten poor Seeta for the time, and shook hands graciously with the handsome Deputy Commissioner, and wished him a happy new year, and the *dîner à la Russe* went off to perfection. The dishes were well served; a Portuguese butler carved the ham, and the courses went on regularly. Then the wines were almost iced by the mess "abdar," or water cooler; there was plenty of champagne, and the guests were happy. Cyril had been obliged to take Mrs. Hills to dinner; but he sat between her and Grace, and both were pleasant and chatty all the time. When all was finished, and the servants had retired, Mr. Mostyn proposed the Queen: the Brigadier, the ladies very gallantly: and Cyril, the health of their host and hostess, making a neat speech, said, how glad all were at Mrs. Mostyn's return among them. Perhaps a little of the drawing-room door had been left open, for they heard the ladies laughing at the cheers which followed. "And now, gentlemen, as you are not drinking wine," said the host, "shall we go to the ladies and hear some music?" It was clearly not a time to pick the Brigadier's brains about the Sepoys.

The drawing-room was now full. I will not attempt to describe the ladies' dresses, but they all looked very nice, notwithstanding the new "musters" had not been got at. Pretty Lucy Home looked her best, and was civil to Brandon, but not very; she seemed to fancy Captain Hobson, who commanded the Irregular Cavalry, much more; and some of the ladies only bowed to him, while Mrs. Smith looked the other way. Then the music commenced, and all were charmed, as well they might be, to hear such sweet strains and such accomplished performers. It was too bad of Mrs. Mostyn to say to Lucy Home that she heard she played *beautifully*, and to lead her to the piano, where she scrambled through a school piece; but as Mrs. Mostyn said afterwards to Grace, "I couldn't neglect her, my dear, all the Scotch blood of the Homes would have been up." And some one told Mrs. Mostyn that Hobson had a capital bass voice, and she went to him and insisted that he should sing, which he did very good-naturedly, and joined Grace in "Crudel, perchè finora." After thanking him, Mrs. Mostyn said laughingly, "I shall enlist you in the Noorpoor Opera Company, and you must come and practise with us, won't you?" And he agreed to do so very willingly, for he was an excellent musician, and devoted to his violoncello.

When the music was over, the dining-room door was flung open, and the band in the verandah struck up a quadrille. All the tables had been removed, and there was ample space for dancing. And they did dance with good will. Brandon was careful this time; but as her mother had told Lucy that she might dance one dance, she accepted Cyril for a waltz, and enjoyed it heartily. She, poor child, had happily as yet no knowledge of Seeta, and of her mother's confidences with Mrs. Smith. And then Brandon danced two round dances with Grace Mostyn, and found her perfect, as he knew she would be, and "did his duty" to all the rest in quadrilles.

About three in the morning, when the stars were shining brightly, and the air was now keen and almost frosty, the various guests took their departure, thanking their fair hostess for the most charming evening they had ever passed at Noorpoor.

"And it did go, Philip, didn't it, capitally—*dîner à la Russe* and all, didn't it, Mr. Brandon?" cried Mrs. Mostyn. "Delightfully indeed," both responded; and Cyril, after receiving a pleasant commendation of his usefulness and good behaviour, wished them all good-night, and went home.

Seeta was still up; "I have been listening to that sweet music," she said, "it came so soft and sweet through the trees; but I could not hear you sing, only a little once, when you sung by yourself. And you have been happy, Cyril? and you didn't eat beef? for if you did you mustn't touch me."

"I have been happy, and I didn't eat beef, so I may kiss you, little one," he said, gaily. "There was not one there like my Seeta."

Not one? Was Grace Mostyn forgotten? I think not.

In like manner, in many a station of Northern India, passed the evening of New Year's Day, 1857. No cloud was seen to cause alarm or mistrust among their gay and thoughtless circles, but it was rising nevertheless.

CHAPTER XXV.

THREATENINGS.

ALTHOUGH ten days had passed, Cyril Brandon had not moved into camp. Baba Sahib, Serishtadar, was uneasy on two points: first, the district work, most important at this season; and secondly, a suspicion, which he tried to put away, but could not

entirely succeed in doing, that Cyril did not, after all, mean fairly towards Seeta, and that the Judge's beautiful sister would prove too great a temptation to be resisted. He knew of Cyril's social rank, and of the possibility that he might attain his brother's place and title. He knew, for Cyril had confided it to him, that there had been anxieties in regard to Lord Hylton's health; and he thought he saw a beautiful and accomplished girl being purposely, as it seemed to him, now thrown in his chief's way. "Of course," Baba Sahib argued to himself, "the English, like ourselves, look, as far as possible, for good connections for their children, and it is only natural they should do so. Mr. Mostyn would rather see his sister married to a man of high family belonging to his own service, with good prospects, than he would give her to a military man; and who is there at Noorpoor that can be compared in any way with my dear master?"

So far there was no doubt; but Baba Sahib resented any desertion of Seeta. She was not one who could be put away, as he had heard of in the case of others many a time, with a gift of money and a pension for life. Cyril had declared Seeta to be his wife; he himself was witness to the marriage, which could not, by Hindoo law, be broken. Yet, after all, what he had heard might only be idle rumour. A bangle-seller, a woman who served his wife, had told her of this rumour, which had distressed the old lady, and Baba Sahib had desired her to contradict it, as an idle tale, and she did so. But the town and cantonment barbers had got hold of it also, and told it to those whose heads or faces they shaved. Thus the probable marriage of the Commissioner Sahib to Miss Mostyn became a rare subject for discussion and gossip in the bazaars; and, in spite of Baba Sahib's precaution, was, he saw—when even some of the establishment asked him if it were not true—very freely canvassed. "I must get him away from this," the old man said to himself. "There is no smoke without fire, if it be only a spark. What do the gossips care? And many would not pity Seeta or her grandfather if she were sent away; but there are more that would do so in the country, and who would resent such a breach of faith. Yes, I must get him away."

But it was not easy to move Cyril, and that week it was impossible, he said: he could not refuse to dine at the brigadier's on Monday, at the mess of the —— on Tuesday, at Mr. Mostyn's on Wednesday, nor to be absent from the Nawab's party on Thursday, at Futtéhpoor; but he would "think of it" the week after. That would involve nearly another fortnight, and Baba

Sahib sighed and held his peace, as he said to himself sententiously, "What is to be is to be."

If Seeta sadly missed her husband, as she truly did, it was no more than he had told her to expect at this "festival time," when he should be from home perhaps every evening; and she tried to make the best of it bravely enough. But the girl was not used to be alone, and had never been lonely in her life. Even at Gokulpoor people were constantly dropping in to see her; and at Noorpoor she had had companions of her own age, with whom she shared dolls' feasts, garden parties, ceremonies at the temple, and all sorts of varied though humble pleasures. Now she had not a friend or a soul to speak to, except old Bheemee, who seemed to be growing deafer and more crabbed every day; for she too, poor old soul, was sighing for village gossip, and the pleasant company of fellow-servants and old acquaintances.

Cyril always paid Seeta a visit after he had dressed for the day; and before he left her for his Kucherry set her her English tasks, and kissed her, and said he would get back as soon as he could and take her out for a sail on the lake. But I am sadly afraid he did not get back as soon as he could on all occasions Somehow or another there was always new music to be practised at the Mostyns', which he could not refuse, and where his welcome seemed to grow warmer and warmer every day; and that sweet, fresh face of Grace's to beam with greater pleasure and intelligence as she selected her favourite pieces and sung to him, now without reserve, and with all the skill and *abandon* of her great musical talents. I am afraid, too, that even Seeta's English lessons were but slightly attended to, and the sail on the lake often altogether missed. He must go and dress, and so went away, leaving her alone. She did not know what kept him so long away, but accepted the plea of business—business, without a doubt or suspicion.

I am sure my readers would not thank me for a detail of "Saddley Peeroo" station parties. One was like another—saddles of mutton, turkeys and all—with little variation. The same people and the same round of gossip and discussion, were but the passing events of the hour, leaving no impression, and were, in truth, weary enough. But at his own dinner, and that of Mr. Mostyn's which followed it, the Brigadier was gradually led to talk of old times and scenes, and of the present discussions in the papers about the Enfields, the new Enlistment Act, and other matters of military significance. At Mostyn's, indeed, he was more than usually communicative. He went at length into the causes of Sepoy disaffection and mutiny—traced them up to the Afghan war, the Sikh war, and the siege of Mooltan, when the Bengal troops had to work with Bombay troops. "And we all saw the difference, to our shame, Mr. Mostyn," he said, "those little Mahratta fellows would work in the trenches like Englishmen, and never took off their accoutrements on guard, as our petted men who jeered them, did. Do you think we dared to ask our high caste people to do the same? Not we; there would have been a mutiny on the spot. Yes, Jacobs' clever letter went to the root of that matter and many another! but who would or *dare* attend to its wise and practical considerations?"

Sir Charles Napier had formed his own conclusions when he acted decisively in the case of the Sixty-sixth; but, as the Brigadier said tersely, had lost his head and temper in the discussion with Lord Dalhousie which followed, and had been defeated by superior skill in debate. Who was to tell the truth? For his own part he believed the Sepoys to be rotten to the core, as a majority, though some were no doubt faithful and true; and now their malady must run its course. Who could stop it? What English force they had now in India was barely enough to hold the stations they were at, and a few regiments even could hardly be united; and yet there was a talk already of decreasing it still further for the China war, while that in Persia was not yet over! All this seemed to him madness, absolute madness. What was a new Governor-General to know about the real temper of men in whom his predecessor had so implicitly trusted? Who was to break to him particulars such as he himself had observed all his life, and now believed to be swelling into some uncontrollable torrent? "I don't think I am betraying confidence, gentlemen," he continued, "but when I was with Henry Lawrence, one day in 1843, he showed me an article he had written and was going to send for publication somewhere, and part of it struck me so like a prophecy that I asked him to let me copy it. Now, I found this copy to-day, and thought I would read it to you, if it would not bore you;" and when all protested it would not, he read as follows:—

"'We forget that our native army is composed of men like ourselves, quick-sighted and inquisitive on all matters bearing on their personal interests, and who can appreciate our points of superiority. . . . At Cabool we lost an army, and we lost character with surrounding states; but I hold that our worst loss was the confidence of the native soldiery. Better had it been for our fame if our harassed troops had rushed on the enemy and perished to a man, than that surviving Sepoys should be able to tell the tales they can of what they saw at Cabool.'

"And then, gentlemen, he goes on to say what would be the effect at any large station if the native infantry suddenly rose and seized the depôt just as the rains sets in; and he mentions Meerut, Dehly, etc., in reference to other contingencies, and continues thus:—

"'Let all this happen in Hindostan on the 2nd June, instead of among the Afghan mountains in November, and does any sane man doubt that twenty-four hours would swell the hundreds of rebels into thousands; and if such conduct on our parts lasted for a week, every ploughshare in the Dehly States would be turned into a sword?'

"I don't know, gentlemen, whether this was ever published; I only hope it was, for it is so true a warning. But these were his thoughts in '43, and here is '57, and yet we are far more unprepared now than we were then. The date—2nd of June—which he specifics, is strange: for already we are hearing mutterings of thunder. What may there not be on the 2nd of June at Meerut and Dehly? I have already determined what I shall do, gentlemen, if trouble comes," he continued; "but this is neither the time nor the place to disclose it; nor could I evince mistrust or alarm when there is happily no need of the latter yet, though the former increases day by day. I know, too, you will all assist me, if the time for action should unhappily come. But it may pass away, as danger has on many a previous occasion, and as I trust, in God's mercy, that it may do now."

Perhaps that evening the music did not go as merrily as usual, for it was impossible for all who heard the fine old soldier speak, not to ponder deeply upon what he had told them out of his great experience.

But the station gaiety did not stop, and the Nawab's annual party was an event to which all looked forward with pleasure. Futtĕhpoor was such a pretty place, the Nawab so kind and hospitable to all, and it was such a pleasant ride on horseback or in palankeens, or on the elephants he sent, in the cold early morning and in the cool evening. The Nawab had no good tents of his own; but the mess tents of the regiments, and the private tents of his particular friends, were all at his disposal. The messman of one of the regiments was caterer, its mess supplied wine; and whatever he did with other debts, the Nawab always contrived that this bill should be paid at once, Hence, on every consideration, the party was always popular, and on this occasion not less so than usual. In one large mess-tent was laid out a sumptuous breakfast, to which the Nawab's kitchen had made large contributions of excellent dishes. There was a drawing-room, and there were some separate tents to which the ladies and gentlemen could retire in the heat of the day, or lie down and rest themselves. Mrs. Mostyn had been at similar entertainments before, and did not, indeed, care to go to this; but she could not well stay away; and as it was Grace's first experience of a native entertainment, she was in high spirits at the thought of it. Cyril was to join them in the morning early, and they would all ride home together; and he told Seeta of this, and she bid him go as usual, though her heart seemed strangely heavy. "I will work at my English," she said, trying to smile as he said, "Good-bye; take care of yourself, my darling."

It was a delightful ride; now and then with a brisk canter through the cold air—now and then walking their horses, they reached the spur of elevation which bounded the valley of Futtuhpoor, and looked down upon the town: and it was truly a fair scene. Futtehpoor stood against a low rocky hill, which there broke into the valley below. It was not a large town; but its picturesque position showed the white-terraced houses and red-tiled roofs to the best advantage, and as the sun shone on them, they looked bright and comfortable. Above them, crowning the point, and occupying a good deal of the slope, stood the Nawab's castle or fort, a fine mass of buildings, with towers at the corners—from one of the tallest of which floated the English flag in honour of the day—and outworks strengthened with bastions and curtains stretched into the town in several tiers, having spacious courts between. The colour of the fort was a fine rich brown, harmonizing with the tone of the hills, and contrasting vividly with the bright green of the sugar-cane, young wheat, and other crops, with which the fertile valley was covered. Beyond stretched undulations, which increased in height till they mingled with a high range of rocky hills, covered with wood, some miles distant. Below the fort and town, was the Nawab's garden, full of palms, cocoa-nut and aréca, and a fine grove of mango trees, in which the white tents seemed to lie snugly, and increased the effect of the landscape.

Our party involuntarily stopped on the ridge to look at the scene, and Grace's admiration was most genuine. The fore-ground broken by rocks and bushes, and low wild date bushes, was full of rich reds, browns, and greens; and the eye was carried by the continuance of the ridge, to the fort and town in exquisite gradations of colour. By the early sun, the shadows of the ridge were thrown broad and clear over the slope of the hill, and over the lower part of the town, the upper portion of which, and the castle, were bathed in light. Then the distances, more and more tender in greys, purples, and blues, with faint indications of local colour, stretched away to the purple hills which met the sky.

"O what a sketch—what a picture it would make!" cried Grace to Brandon, as she clasped her hands in delight. "The castle is like a German baron's, only far grander; and but for those minarets, and that dome in the town, it might be a German scene altogether. Have you never sketched it, Mr. Brandon?"

"I have," he said, "many times; and I will make a drawing for you, if you will have it."

"Thanks," she replied, moving on. "You are always very good to me; only that it would give you so much trouble, I should prize a sketch so much," and she looked her thanks gratefully.

Gradually, all that could come from Noorpoor dropped in, party by party, as they had before arranged: and, as the Mostyns had been, were met at the door of the tents by the Nawab, dressed in gorgeous cloth of gold, and welcomed in courtly terms. What politeness can excel that of a Mahomedan gentleman's, whether it be sincere or otherwise? He did not eat with his guests, but sat near Mr. Mostyn, recommending the good things to him, and chatting pleasantly; and now and then venturing a remark to Mrs. Mostyn, whose Hindostance, though terribly ungrammatical at times, was fluent enough. Grace he had hardly seen before, and, had he dared, would have sat gloating on her beauty; but Cyril Brandon was watching him narrowly, and the Nawab felt himself checked, and went away.

I need not describe the amusements which people under these circumstances betake themselves to. Young men had brought quoits; there were some bows and arrows, and a target, and Aunt Sally, lent by Mrs. Mostyn, for those who chose to use them. In the tents there were chess and cards; but most seemed to like strolling about, or sitting under the fine trees.

In the afternoon the Begum Sahib was to be visited; and the ladies walked up to a pavilion on a bastion of a fort, not far off, where the members of the Nawab's zenana were assembled, and returned without much edification. "If these plain, hard-featured women were specimens of the beauty of the country, what could Mr. Brandon's wife be like!" speculated Grace.

"And what could have induced him to marry one of them?" True, their dresses were very magnificent, and the groups and costumes would make splendid pictures; but the women! Pah! they had blackened their teeth, disfigured their mouths with eating pán, and, to Grace's and Lucy Home's apprehension, looked simply disgusting.

Then, after an early dinner, the guests were each presented with bottles of utr of roses, and garlands of flowers were thrown round their necks; and they departed, as they had come, for Noorpoor. I do not think the evening ride home was as pleasant as that of the morning. The freshness of the day was past, and the ladies were hot and tired. Riding-habits, however light, are not pleasant costumes for a whole day.

"I won't apologize to you for not asking you to dinner," said Mrs. Mostyn to Cyril, as they reached the gate. "The fact is, I did not order any. Grace and I will get some tea, and go to bed."

"And I will come and smoke a cigar with you, Cyril," said Mostyn, "if you will let me."

"I shall be delighted," he replied. "Come as soon as you like." And he cantered on to his own house. He was glad to get home; glad for a time to be out of sight of those pleading soft eyes which had so often met his that day, and had listened, if I may say it, to his tales of local mediæval history and the legends of the bold Barons of Futtehpoor who had won their territory from the Hindoos in the time of Akbar, and held it through all changes and revolutions. He had answered all her simple questions about the people and the new scene in which she was that day: told her how they lived, what they believed, how they had joys and sorrows like themselves; and he had interested her more than she could have thought possible. Even Mrs. Mostyn declared she had never heard so much from him. Then they had been at the same places on the Continent, in Italy, Germany, and France, and they recalled scenes and pictures to each other's memory. Cyril had never seen so much of Grace Mostyn before; never had been able to "draw her out," as it were; and it was almost with a feeling of pain that he kissed Seeta, who sprang to meet him, and thanked him for coming so early. "I thought you would have stayed at the Judge's," she said.

"No, they were very tired," he replied, "and did not want me, and Mr. Mostyn is coming presently. I wish him to know you better, and then he will understand——"

"Understand what?" cried Seeta.

"What you are, little one, for it is only I who know it yet. And what have you been doing all day?"

"O, I went into the garden, and I came back, and fed the pets, and then I sat down and read my English. Then I sent Bheemoo to the bazaar, to find out a bangle-seller, and she brought one; but she had nothing that would fit me, and will come to-morrow; and—that's all, I think, Cyril. And you?"

"Only the usual things which I detest always; but we had a pleasant ride to Futtehpoor; and the Nawab was civil enough. What more can I tell you? Now, you are to make our tea to-night, so send Bheemoo for the things while I hear you your lessons."

When Philip Mostyn came, Cyril showed him Seeta's exercises, and made her read to him, which she did slowly, but with a faultless accent; yet she would not trust herself to speak. "By-and-by," she said modestly; "not now." And Seeta was very happy that night: Mr. Mostyn's kind manner and his perfect knowledge of her language put her at ease at once. She made tea for them with a naïve grace; and, in her soft white muslin saree, looked indeed very beautiful and charming altogether. Then Cyril asked her to read some of her old Sanscrit studies, and she read part of "Savitri" to Mr. Mostyn, which he remembered as an old college study, and was glad to hear again; and thus the evening passed very pleasantly.

"I don't wonder at it all," said Mostyn, as he went home through the garden; "but O! that he had waited for Grace! They would have suited each other exactly—and Rose says so too. But dear me! dear me! how stupid we are, for how could we have anticipated what has happened, and they could not have come out any sooner? But Cyril, poor fellow, will get tired of the monotony of that girl, brilliant and wonderful as she is. He will miss the freshness of an English intellect. That pleasant talk under the trees to-day; could that girl have followed what they said? Impossible! And how Cyril was excited, and how well Grace spoke up to all he said.—No! this won't do; it can't last. There must be unity of thought, or no thought at all, to provide married happiness. But that girl has too much thought by half. How she dashed into the mysticism of the old Hindoo fathers as she commented on that passage in 'Savitri,' and grew eloquent upon 'Spirit' and 'Matter,' and how pious and humble she is at heart, though her eyes flashed and the colour flushed over her sweet face! But those thoughts are not his, I fear; and Rose may be right, that it won't do. Well, we shall see."

"Did they ever ask after me?" Seeta asked Cyril, when Mostyn was gone. "He is so kind to me, and I am sure his wife would be so too."

"Not once," he replied; "I have left it to themselves to do as they please. They know all about you, and I suppose it will come right in time. I am sure he will tell his wife what he saw of you to-night, and her too!"

"Grace!"

"Yes, Grace; I should like to see you together, and like her to love you, my pet; you could learn far more from them than I can teach you."

CHAPTER XXVI.

LEPROUS DISTILMENT.

THAT night Mr. Mostyn had a long talk with his wife. He told her of the evening he had passed; of Seeta's charming manner, and, for a Hindoo girl, great learning; and how rapidly she was acquiring English. "She read to me," he said, "in one of the sweetest voices you ever heard, and not a bit like a native; and she *is* charming, there's no doubt about it, Rose; and she made tea for us too, with all the grace you can imagine; but, nevertheless, I was thinking as I walked home——"

"It won't do," she said, laughing; "I knew your thougths, Philip, and so finished your sentence."

"You are a witch, Rose," he returned, "for indeed that was really what I was thinking; and this is the reason," and he detailed to her the tenor of the soliloquy I have recorded.

Mrs. Mostyn sighed. "It is a pity, a sad pity," she said, "as much for his sake as the girl's. Of course she is madly in love with him, how could she help that, poor thing? and then it is such a romantic story altogether. But I could really cry when I think what poor Grace has lost; I am sure she likes him."

"I hope not," said Philip gravely.

"Well," returned his wife, "I didn't think about the matter much till to-day; but I couldn't help it as they talked together under the trees at Futtehpoor, there was such harmony in what they said to each other, and thought of; and then she followed him about with her eyes. Do you know, sir, that people who have gone through the fever, are quick to see it in others? and

I heard a little sigh too, now and then. I think it quite impossible that two creatures, like Grace and he, with exactly the same tastes and accomplishments, and the same sweet tempers, can be indifferent to each other; and that's what I fear for her sake."

"I wish——" said her husband.

"Nonsense! Philip," cried Mrs. Mostyn, "there's no use wishing—the question is what can be done?"

"Well," he said, "you wouldn't let me finish my sentence; my wish was about you. Look here; you know he must be absent in his districts till the hot weather, and I don't want you and Grace to pass the first hot weather here: why not go to the Hills, you two? and save her pain, if it is to be pain."

"O Philip!" cried his wife, "do not talk so, darling—no more of this horrible separation could I—could either of us bear. Let Grace alone, do not mention him to her; or if you do, praise his wife. She is so earnest, so right-minded, and so thoroughly English, in the best sense of the word, that she will soon come right, even if she may have been touched. No, the solution rests with Mr. Brandon himself; and I think, for his mother's sake, for his family's sake, that he ought—really ought to get free, and then we may well leave the rest, to be or not to be, as God wills. Couldn't you ask him about Seeta?"

"That is quite impossible, my love," said Mr. Mostyn decidedly; "I would as soon ask Cyril Brandon to commit forgery, as I would that he should think of dishonour to that child. There have been, and are, men that would do it, to get a lovely English girl like Grace, but not Cyril Brandon. I may tell him not to come here so often, if you like; but anything more put out of your little head, my pet, and go to sleep."

Next day, when Cyril Brandon had gone to his Kucherry work, and left only one of his Chuprasses on guard at the house, with directions, at Seeta's request, to admit the bangle-woman when she came—that person was accompanied by another woman, carrying a basket, and they were duly ushered into Seeta's presence. She was sitting in the outer room, studying her English as usual; but she laid aside her books for a time, and sat down on the floor to submit to the necessary operation. Bangles, worn by Indian ladies, are usually slender rings of glass, plain or ornamental; and it requires great skill and practice on the part of the women who put them on to do so without breaking them or hurting the wearer.

"And why have two of you come," asked Seeta, "so far from the town?"

"Hers might suit you better than mine," answered the woman, "but I will try to fit you. Hers too are more expensive; and a rich lady like you might take a set or two from her, to keep by you; you can't get such in country villages."

"How do you know I am rich?" asked Seeta, laughing.

"O! every one knows that, lady. Are you not the granddaughter of Narendra the banker? we have heard of you often; and do I not serve all your caste in Noorpoor?"

"And what do my people say of me?" returned Seeta.

"That you are very beautiful, very learned, very good, and very charitable," said the other woman who now spoke, and who, as may be surmised, was Mrs. Smith's Ayah, playing a new part; "and they say all the English ladies are jealous of you, because you have taken away the Commissioner Sahib from them."

"That is untrue," said Seeta, flushing; "no one can grudge me what God sent me."

"They are very spiteful, those English ladies, and very unkind to we black people, lady, and should be feared," continued the Ayah. "If I were you, though I am only a humble slave, I should hate them. We who live among them are very different to you, and those who come and go from country places. We know them well."

"And why should I hate them?" asked Seeta, "they have done me no harm, and I shall do them none."

"Ah! you are an innocent dove," replied the woman; "too innocent to know the English as we do. Have we not seen many like her come and go, sister?" she said to her companion. who was trying set after set of bangles upon Seeta's fair round arm, all of which were too large—"come and go, and slink away, and perhaps die—when their English lords married."

Seeta started, as if she were stung. "Do not pull away your hand, lady dear," said the operator, "you might cut yourself;" but the sad tone, the pity of the other woman's voice, seemed to have a terrible fascination for Seeta.

"Married?" she asked.

"Yes, married, lady; and more's the pity. The English must marry some time; it is their caste to do so, and they can only be married to their own people, and by the Padré Sahib, that every one can tell you."

"I know that," said Seeta, quickly; "my husband told me so when he married me by our rites."

"It may be that you are married as a Hindoo," replied the

Ayah, "but not as a Christian; when you are one, the Padré will marry you. But I am only a poor ignorant slave, lady: I only tell you what the goldsmith's wife told me; ask her; and you must forgive me if I cause you pain. You asked what the caste said, and I have told you; why don't you go among your people, and hear for yourself? I think the English ladies do not consider you married, else they would come and visit you; they would be kind to you in their way—some of them—if you were——"

Seeta's cheeks were in a flame. That then was the reason why Mrs. Mostyn had not come to her, and they lived so close to each other, with only the garden and shrubbery between; yet she had never even seen Mrs. Mostyn or Grace. Had they purposely avoided her? "Tell me, tell me truly, woman," she cried, "did the English ladies ever come to the others you know, and who went away?"

"Never, I swear by your neck, never! Ah, they are too proud, lady. The pride of the English men is great, but that of their women is greater to us;—and they even beat their Ayahs, poor things!—who serve them. But you will be angry with me for saying this, when your lord is English."

"He is beloved everywhere; women bring their children to him to bless, and light lamps in his name,—before I ever saw him, I have done that myself in my house," cried Seeta, passionately. "And Mr. Mostyn is the same; I want to know no more of their people, they are enough for me. Now go, both of ye, and you may tell the goldsmith's wife that when my grandfather returns, I will come to see her;" and she gave them a liberal present, and dismissed them.

When they had gone a few paces from the cottage door, the Ayah looked back and returned; "I would have told you one thing," she said, "but for her, and she is gone on. Buy this set of bangles from me, and I will tell it. I am only a poor humble woman, but I would save you distress and shame if I could. Thank you, and my blessing be on you for helping a poor widow," she continued, as she took the money she had asked for the ornaments. "Listen—though it pain you. He, your lord, is going to be married to the Judge's sister: every one says so, even the English ladies. Is he not always with her, and they sing together? Was he not with her all day yesterday at Futtehpoor, and the news is stronger than ever this morning? Go, my poor bird; go back with your honour to your home, before it is too late. Go!"

Seeta's eyes seemed to swim, and her knees trembled. She

sat down on the threshold, covering her face, and her very heart seemed to stand still, as she heard the horrible tale; then for a moment she rallied and looked up, but the woman was gone. What she did afterwards, for she moved about mechanically, she never knew; but she, at last, went and sat at the door till the shadows were lengthening over the garden, waiting for Cyril. And he came, radiant as usual, and cried to her, as she ran up the grand walk—

"Come, Seeta, there is a glorious breeze, and I could get away early, come and have a sail. Why—what ails you? again that scared face?"

"I heard—I heard, Cyril," she said, falteringly and hoarsely, for her breath was parched, "that you are going to be married. Is it true? O husband, is it true? Tell me at once; and let me go; you would not have shame come upon your Seeta. O my lord, is it come to this—so soon, so soon!"

"My wife, my darling," he replied, though a pang smote him, "you have believed in me, trusted me, and now must trust me more. Who has told you this infamous story? Ah, I see, you have new bangles on; it must be that woman whom you sent for, and I was a fool to let her come to you. Seeta, Seeta, look up, my pet," and he drew her head on his heart. "Let this pass from you; I declared once, before God and your people, that I would be true to you, and I am true. If I have gone among my own people, and if I know the Mostyns as I do, it is only because they are as my brother and my sisters."

Now she was weeping passionately; she could not but believe him. "I trust you; I do trust you, Cyril, even to death," she murmured, "but those horrible words are like a hideous dream."

"Come then," he said, "and forget them. I would punish that old devil; but I must be as careful of your honour as my own. Let her go, and promise me not to send for her again. Come, put a good shawl about you, and the fresh air will drive out the dream." And she went with him, and was calmed and soothed, as he said she would be.

"I ought to go to the Judge's to-night, for I have promised them," he said, as they returned; "but I will not go unless you are well, Seeta."

"Stay with me, Cyril," she murmured, imploringly; "I do not often ask you, but I am afraid to be alone to-night." And he stayed with her, and knew that her pain had abated, though it had not passed away; and perhaps his own thoughts were oppressive too.

He would not, indeed, have left her the next evening, but a note had come from Mrs. Mostyn, insisting upon his presence: they had some people to dinner, and he need not come to that, if he pleased, but he *must* come afterwards and help them; and Captain Hobson would be there, etc. Cyril showed this note to Seeta, when he received it at his early breakfast, which he liked to take in her cottage. She wished him to go to dinner; but he would only accept the compromise, and asked her to prepare some of her own good things, which she sometimes did to her great delight. Then he came home from Kucherry early, and they went out for a sail; and Seeta seemed quite in high spirits, as she brought in her little dishes afterwards, and helped him to what he would have: and at the proper time he went away to the Judge's, and was the first of the evening party. Mr. Mostyn called to him to come and join the gentlemen; but he said he was very happy where he was, and stayed in the drawing-room.

"So you wouldn't come to dinner, Mr. Brandon," said Mrs. Mostyn; "and you didn't come to practise after Kucherry. How I should hate dining alone; I'm sure I couldn't eat a morsel."

"I was not alone," said Cyril, boldly, for he had never felt truer to Seeta than he did then. "My wife made a little dinner for me, and a very nice one it was, and saw me eat it, too, which I did very heartily." It was the first time he had ever mentioned her, and Mrs. Mostyn blushed up to the roots of her hair. If Grace had heard him she made no sign, and went on assorting music for the evening. Mrs. Mostyn had looked at her, but saw no change in her countenance.

"You are very good, Mr. Brandon," returned Mrs. Mostyn, in a low tone, "and I quite forgive you. I seem to blame myself for not having been to see her, but Philip told me she would rather not this time. When you come back, I must make friends with her; Philip tells me how delightful she is."

"You are very kind to say so," he replied, "very kind. Philip was quite right in what he told you. The fact is, that Seeta is studying English very hard, and hopes some day to be able to talk with you easily; and I will tell her what you say. It will be a great incentive to her progress, which, so far, is really surprising, even to me."

"Very well, then, I leave it all to you both," she said.

"What are you two whispering about there?" cried Grace from the piano.

"I was only scolding him for not coming to practise to-day; but he is very penitent," said Rose.

"He may well be so," she returned, saucily. "Had we not that 'Lucia' duett to practise? and I'm sure I don't know how it will go to-night."

"Make your mind quite easy, Miss Mostyn," replied Cyril. "I really could not come, or should not have denied myself the pleasure. It is sure to go."

The announcement of some ladies prevented further conversation on the subject; and the evening proceeded as was usual with them.

Seeta sat for awhile, trying to read; but the words seemed to fade out of her eyes, and instead came the figure of the bangle-seller, and to her ears the horrible words she had heard: "Go, before it is too late! Go!" As yet, no jealousy had possessed the girl; and since she had told her husband what had distressed her, his kindness had reassured her, though not entirely, and a leaven had remained which was now working. "If I could only see them together," she thought to herself, "I should know all, and then—if it is true—I would go away quietly, though my heart should break. If he is to be happy, let me die." Then a sudden idea struck her. She knew where the Judge's drawing-room was, for she had seen it often from her garden. Could she not listen and see? Bheemee had gone to sleep, and some of her sarees were hanging up in the bath-room. Hastily divesting herself of her own dress, she put on one of the coarse garments of her servant, took off her gold anklets, and went out at the cottage-door into the garden. There was no sound but the steps of the sentry pacing on his beat, and a faint strain of music from Mr. Mostyn's house.

Again and again her steps faltered, and once she had wellnigh returned; but the spirit that possessed her hurried her on. She must see, she must hear, else there could be no peace; and so she went blindly on up the path which led to the house, crouching like a hare behind shrubs at times, till she was near the place she sought. The drawing-room had been built out from the house by Mr. Mostyn, when he came to Noorpoor, into the flower-garden. It had a solid terrace roof, very pleasant to sit upon in the hot, close evenings; and the basement of the room and its verandah was about four feet from the ground, concealed by thick flowering shrubs. Now the light streamed from the glass doors over the flower-beds, from which the sweet odours of tuberoses and mignonette rose into the still air. Silently and cautiously she gained the place she wished. Music was coming from within in the rich harmonies of concerted pieces; but she dare not stay to listen, and creeping under the thick bushes, sat as in a dream, vainly striving to compose her thoughts. Yet to no purpose—the one dread that possessed her shut out all other considerations. Several times Cyril's strong, clear voice reached her alone; again it mingled with others, and with one sweet woman's voice most of all, and she felt it must be that of Grace Mostyn. She looked up, raising herself, and could see the room filled with English ladies and gentlemen, sitting or standing, and she watched them with a dull, dreamy interest hardly definable.

Presently she saw a lady seat herself at the piano, and Cyril and a young girl take places on each side of her. How lovely the girl seemed! How exquisite her soft, wavy hair; her bright, delicate colour, like a rose-leaf; her small pink ear, and her lily neck, and arms and shoulders! "That must be Grace," she thought. "Yes, he is right; she is more fitting for him than I. No nymph of Indra's heaven could be purer or more lovely." At that moment her almost delirium prompted Seeta to fly at once, no matter where or to whom—some of her people in the town would give her shelter; but the music began again, and she listened in a kind of rapture. "Dimmi ehe m'ami ancor." Cyril had translated that to her, and played it to her, wishing her to try and learn it by ear. "T'ami, t'amo." Ah! that sweet love, it did not seem feigned now; it was to her real, but not hers—not hers any more. They could not sing it so, and not feel what they sang so deliciously.

Then the song ceased; and Cyril, stepping to the glass door, threw it open, and Grace Mostyn and he came out together into the verandah. Seeta again crouched down into her hiding-place. She was so near that she could have touched them, but she dare not move, and sat with her hot, burning eyes looking up to them both.

It was careless talk between them. "A breath of fresh air is pleasant after that hot room, isn't it, Miss Mostyn?" he said.

"Very," she replied; "it quite revives one. How beautiful the garden looks in the light! That great palm-tree is really lovely, Mr. Brandon."

"You are in exquisite voice to-night," he observed. "By-and-by I shall ask you to sing 'Dove sono' for me, unless you prefer anything else."

"I will make a bargain with you," she returned, laughing. "I will sing 'Dove sono' or 'Vedrai carino,' or both, if you will sing 'Il mio tesoro' for me, or 'Vivi tu.'"

"That I will," he said, cheerily. "Now come in, for the air is cold, and you have no covering."

"What is that?" said Grace, pointing to the bush below them. "I thought I heard a sigh, and saw the leaves move."

"Nonsense!" cried Cyril, laughing. "If you did, it was only some pariah dog; those brutes are always prowling about. Get in, and I will shut the door."

Grace was right; she had heard a sigh—a soft, grateful sigh, from the girl who crouched there. Seeta had expected a demonstration of love. She had listened to the intonation of Cyril's voice with apprehension which was choking her; she thought it might change to the tones she knew, which lived in her heart. She thought the girl's tones might change too. She did not quite understand what they said, but there was no mistaking the careless, easy manner, the pleasant laugh of friends—but not lovers. She had not called him "Cyril," but "Mr. Brandon." I think that never—never in all her most intense happiness had the relief of that moment, the sense of peace and security in Cyril's love, been exceeded in Seeta's mind. She did not wait; she hurried home as she had come, changed her dress, and sat up waiting for her husband; and when he came, she flew to meet him, and threw her arms about him. "My own, my very own!" she cried, "why did you come away so soon?"

"Well, they all broke up, and so I came away, little one. Ah! you are yourself now again, my pet; I see it in your eyes. I thought that horrible woman's tale would get out of your foolish head. And is it all gone, Seeta, never to come back?"

"Never," she said, "never!" and her heart smote her that she had, even in thought, mistrusted one she knew to be true.

"And now I have good news for you," he continued gaily. "I shall move into the district on Tuesday morning. The Mostyns have never seen the Gáo Mookh, and we will all go there. They will sleep there, and return next morning; and we will go on in our old fashion."

"O, I shall be so happy again!" cried Seeta, clapping her hands; "and I have a vow at the Temple there, which I will pay."

I do not think I need to return to Mrs. Smith's conclave, where she told her friend, Mrs. Home, what the Ayah had done and said, and how it had all been managed so cleverly. As to little Mrs. Jones, I think she was beginning to be ashamed of the plot; and perhaps it did not very much interest Mrs. Home. It was very plain to her that Cyril had no care for her fair daughter, and the Nawab's party had quite cured her of that idea. On the other hand, it was pleasant to observe the increasing attention and interest of Captain Hobson, who, though he might not ever be a lord, was heir to a good property at home, and, to her mind, was far handsomer than Cyril Brandon.

But I have done with Noorpoor for the present, and the station must be left to its normal condition of dulness.

CHAPTER XXVII.

THE GÁO MOOKH.

It was about seven or eight miles to the place where Cyril had proposed to spend the day, and Baba Sahib was overjoyed by the order to move, and obeyed it with genuine and undisguised alacrity. "So there was no truth in the rumour after all," he thought, "and his honoured master was true." Mr. Noble had only ridden into Noorpoor for Christmas Day and the Mostyns' dance, and the station work was left to the native assistant and the treasurer, who could ask advice, if they needed any, from the Judge. Never, therefore, in his life had Baba Sahib left the dull station Kucherry with greater satisfaction than now. The Revenue returns were everywhere nearly ready; and though a fortnight had been lost, the time could be easily made up, and he could depend on Mr. Brandon. So the whole establishment was taken on to a large town beyond the "Gáo Mookh." Cyril's and Mr. Mostyn's tents were ordered out, and pitched under the great mohwa trees near the waterfall. Seeta had sent word to the Brahmins to prepare what was needed for her little ceremonial, and left earlier than Cyril, to be, as she said, out of the way.

Before sunrise, then, the four friends had mounted their horses, and, with the two troopers of the Irregular Cavalry who always attended "the Judge" in his rides, set out on their pleasant little journey. How fresh and pure the dewy air felt everywhere! while in some of the low valleys there was even a suspicion of hoar-frost. Over the villages they passed, hung the blue smoke of the night and early morning, like thin wreaths of mist, unable to ascend into the higher and heavier air, but which the sun would soon disperse. People came out of village gates with humble offerings, jars of milk, and flowers; and village girls poured libations of water before the horses of the party, with many a merry laugh and Godspeed. They rode through one prosperous, comfortable village where Cyril pointed out improvements he had suggested; and he and Mr. Mostyn spoke kindly to the head men and farmers who crowded about them. Cyril was often at Grace's side, telling her, in his pleasant and thoughtful manner, of the husbandry, as they rode through luxuriant fields of wheat, barley, and pulse; of castes and trades, of superstitions and religious observances and habits of the people, among whom she could now realize that she was dwelling. Here and there shady lanes, with high hedges and trees, reminded her of England; and again date trees, foreign shrubs and flowers, and an occasional Hindoo temple, or humble mosque or tomb, brought her back to India.

After passing a valley, the ridge they ascended had a level summit, though the ground rose before them. There was no cultivation; but the surface was covered with short crisp grass, now growing brown, with a fine mellow tint. Large mohwa trees like English oaks, and wild mangoes like sweet chestnuts, dotted the plain, which stretched upwards to a crown of rocky hills, to the right; while to the left, on the summit of the plateau, they had glimpses of blue tender distances and many ridges of rugged hills. The ground was firm and springy, and they cantered on through the park-like trees with a sense of enjoyment to Grace that she had not felt in India before, all was so fresh, so new, so enjoyable. "If this is a specimen of your district, Mr. Brandon," she cried to him, as they pulled up after a half-mile gallop, "no wonder you are always pining to be in it, and glad to escape from our dull station. If I were you, I should never go there at all."

"I must go sometimes," said Cyril; "I can't help myself. But you are right; I would rather be out among my people, than see them only in their worse aspect in my station Kucherry. This bit of country is very pretty, and you would hardly expect the like so near Noorpoor; but I prefer Shah Gunje by far. It is nearer the edge of the plateau, and the views there are truly exquisite; so lovely, indeed, that they quite foil my poor efforts at landscape. You would do them much better. But see, there are the tents; and I hope you are hungry, both of you, with your ride."

Slightly below them, in a hollow, the mohwa and mango trees stood closer together than on the upland; and the slope down which they rode was part of a valley which stretched upwards and round the end of the rocky hills to the right for a considerable distance. A pool of blue water gleamed here and there; and again a white spot of foam marked a rapid or a small cascade in the course of a river which was becoming evident at the foot of the slope on which they were. Beyond it the ground rose again, and seemed to be similar to that over which they had come, dotted with grand old trees.

"But where is the waterfall, Mr. Brandon?" cried Mrs. Mostyn. "You must not cheat us of that."

"Follow me," he said, "and I will show you what I think one of the prettiest views of it; but I'm afraid there isn't water enough to give it its full beauty:" and he turned his horse up a round knoll which was close by, and they followed him along its crest till they reached a point where it seemed suddenly to fall into a chasm. The ladies uttered a cry of delight.

Before them lay a deep valley, the sides of which were sheer precipices of basalt, some four hundred feet in height, which showed the richest colours, from black to brown, yellow and red. Here and there the rock was smooth; but, at the upper end, it was broken into huge prisms, which, fretted away by ages of exposure, in some instances stood apart from the rock in fantastic forms, and were garnished by tufts of waving grass and creepers covered with flowers. At the upper end of this amphitheatre, which was of no very great width, a portion of it narrowed sharply, and out of it spouted a jet of water of considerable volume, which fell clear of the precipice in a cloud of fine spray, wafted here and there by the wind, and showing portions of brilliant rainbows as the bright sun caught its changes. At the foot of the fall was a deep, dark pool, fringed with graceful bamboos and reeds which continued down the glen and up the sides where there was no rock. A dull roar from the fall came up to them now and then, mingling with the murmur of the river above and below as it chafed in its rocky bed.

"I never heard of this before," cried Philip Mostyn. "Why, Cyril, it's glorious! Glorious!"

"I didn't like to say much about it," he replied, "for people often think one makes swans of one's geese. I only found it out one day last year, when I had followed some 'sambur" from below, and I determined then that I would bring Mrs. Mostyn here when she came out. It's a strange place, and I think most lovely. The river is the Incherna—a pretty name, isn't it, Miss Mostyn?—which rises in the hills about thirty miles off. You see there is comparatively very little water in it now, but it must be a magnificent fall in the monsoon. You can make out the white mark, high up, on both sides of the head of the water."

"I don't think it could ever be more beautiful," said Grace;

"a great body of water would fall straight down, whereas, look at those beautiful swayings to and fro which it has now. One might fancy it like the filmy garments of a nymph, a sort of Indian Lurline."

"And that, indeed, is the tradition," replied Cyril; "some celestial nymph of Indra's heaven, who fell in love with a mortal —which was wrong—was changed into a river, and, in despair, precipitated herself over this precipice, to which she still clings."

"Are there many such legends?" she asked.

"Yes," he replied, "enough to fill a volume, if any one would collect them. These people are not dull and insensible, as you may have thought, Miss Mostyn; and there is hardly a rocky knoll, a quiet lake, a giant tree, a broad river, or a secluded glen like this, which is not, in their belief, peopled by spirits, nymphs and fauns, or the scene of some event in their traditions. At night, they say, this is an eerie place, and the wails of the poor nymph are terrible to hear; but there is a temple on the edge of the precipice, quite safe, and people go there to make offerings and cast garlands into the stream, as omens of their hopes; and it is often, I hear, a gay place during the day. Its priests live at the last village we passed. From the tower of the Temple, there is a sublime view of the precipice and the glen, and I will take you to it by-and-by; but you should sketch this, Miss Mostyn, you could do it justice."

She did not reply, for the beauty and grandeur of the place, so little expected, had brought tears into her eyes, and she turned her horse. "I will try," she said timidly; and they rode on to the tents.

At breakfast, one of the mounted police, who had been left behind to bring on the day's letters, delivered them; and Cyril, begging to be excused for a time to look over his official correspondence, went to his tent. Seeta was not there—she had gone to the Temple—and he read over all the documents, and drafted some replies to be written next day; and Mr. Mostyn was occupied in a similar manner.

"Well, Grace," said Mrs. Mostyn, "what shall we do while they are busy? I vote we take chairs down yonder, and sit under those noble trees; you can bring your drawing things, and make a sketch of the Temple."

"The very thing I was going to propose," she replied, "it will be delicious. Come along."

And chairs were brought after them by a servant, and placed where they wished.

From the spot they had chosen, the little Temple, a very

humble edifice, with a high conical top, was not far off; and they could see persons moving about its terrace. There were several female figures pacing round and round the building, and several Brahmins, with bare heads, attending on them.

"I should so like to see these people nearer," said Grace, after a time, "and put in their figures; I can't well catch them from hence, they move so often. There wouldn't be any harm in that, would there, Rose?"

"Not a bit," she replied. "Let us go by all means; I want to look into that gulf. How wonderfully the spray and mist swirl up, yet there is no wind!"

And they went on. Seeta was busy with her little ceremony, and some Brahmins and their wives were helping her. Mrs. Mostyn did not know she was there; she thought that she had gone on to Cyril's camp, and that the figures they had seen were those of country folks; but as the ladies ascended the steps which led to the terrace, they met Seeta and her old servant on their circuit round the building, and the Brahmins following, chanting a hymn with her. How sweet and rich her voice rose, even above the dull roar of the fall. Grace drew back, but Mrs. Mostyn could not restrain the generous impulse that rose within her.

"You must be Seeta," she said, smiling, and holding out her hand, "but I see I must not touch you now, I will wait here."

"I thank you humbly, lady," she replied, "I am Seeta. I will come to you directly;" and the hymn rose again as she moved on, while the ladies listened and watched with curious interest.

"I have finished now, lady," said Seeta, after some further circuits of the Temple. "Will you come and look at the fall? it is quite safe, for there is a parapet for people to look over;" and they rose and followed her.

The Temple was built almost on the verge of the precipice, but a little, as it were, in advance of the mouth of the fall, so that the upper part of it, and the wall of the precipice beyond, could be well seen. As they looked over, into the gulf, both involuntarily stepped back, for the bottom could not be distinguished, and looked fathomless. The whirling cloud of spray which glittered in the sunlight, like diamonds, and in which rainbows appeared and disappeared in continuous change, filled the air, and the huge spout of water, blue as a sapphire, seemed to shoot out from the verge and plunging into the cloud to disappear. Beyond, the precipice, jagged and broken at the top, went sheer down for several hundred feet, resting among trees and graceful bamboos, which concealed its base; all the rocks were vivid with colour, while flocks of wild blue pigeons and green parroquets wheeled hither and thither in the air.

"Do not be afraid," cried Seeta, taking Mrs. Mostyn by the hand, "it is quite safe here;" and thus assured, they stood with the girl and looked down, wonderingly, into the abyss.

"It is no use thinking of sketching this," said Grace to her sister, who thought she might try; "it is far beyond me. I may try an outline just as a remembrance, and I will put you in the foreground, so stand as you are."

Grace's was a true and rapid hand, and she had soon completed what she wished. As she showed the sketch to her sister, Seeta saw that she, too, had a place in it.

"I wish I could speak to her," said Grace to her sister; "she understands you very well."

"I wish you could, Grace. Seeta," she said, slowly, "can you speak a little English to my sister?"

"I will try," she returned, timidly, in English. "I am very glad to see you, Miss Mostyn; will you shake hands with me?"

"That I will," replied Grace, and put out her hand with a kind gesture.

"And I must kiss you, Seeta," exclaimed Mrs. Mostyn; "you are, indeed, a darling—what a shame it is that your husband would not let me come to you before!"

"It is better thus, dear lady," she replied, in her own speech; "when he gives me into your hands, I may love you and serve you."

"Very well, then, we shall meet at the tents by-and-by;" and at tiffin, when Cyril joined them, they told him all. "She is so lovely, Mr. Brandon," said Mrs. Mostyn, "the fresh air had given her quite a colour; why, she is as fair as any of us, and so graceful, too."

"Not quite so fair," replied Cyril, laughing; "but I am so glad you like her, and so thankful that the ice has been so pleasantly broken. I hope you will know more of her; and I am quite sure the more she knows of you both, the better."

"But she said you must give her to us, Mr. Brandon; what did she mean?"

"Only a little ceremony which I will perform by-and-by," he replied, smiling; "she has not come from the Temple yet. Are you tired, or will you go again? Come, Philip, you at least have not seen the fall;" and when they were ready, the ladies put on their hats and went with them.

Seeta had been watching her friends, the Brahmins, enjoy a good meal; and she was standing on the steps, her face glowing with pleasure, as the party ascended them, and she saw Cyril, and Mr. Mostyn, who saluted her courteously. "Seeta," he cried, "come and know my wife and sister. I rejoice that the curtain has been happily drawn, and that you have already spoken to each other."

Seeta looked imploringly at Cyril, who said, "That is my business, Philip, this time. I must give her to them in her own fashion. Come, Seeta." And he took both her hands and put them into Mrs. Mostyn's and Grace's. "Be kind to her, dear friends," he continued; "she is worthy of your love, else I would not have done this."

Poor Seeta's sensitive eyes were brimming with tears, but they were very happy ones, and she seemed to nestle to Grace, whose hand she held.

Then they went and looked over the wall again, and watched the whirling mist and the ever-varying shoot of the water, and the grim cliffs glowing in the sun, and the wheeling birds and ever-changing rainbows, till the shadows were lengthening. Grace finished her sketch, and Cyril added touches to the two figures and corrected the likenesses, till no one could have mistaken them. At last Mr. Mostyn said, "Come, good people; the wind is blowing the spray over us, and Seeta is thinly clad. Come away; and we will return another time, God willing, and stay a week. It would be glorious!"

"There is a little ceremony here, dear lady," said Seeta, "which many perform from the rock yonder at the Gáo Mookh; and there is no danger, for there is a wall. People who wish for anything—for health, for riches, for children, for happiness—throw a garland into the water. If it swims out on the stream and goes over the fall, the wish will come true; and if the rocks catch it, the gods will not listen—so they believe who pay their vows here. After all," she added, smiling, "it is very foolish to think so; but the Brahmins declare they believe in it, and they are wise people. I must try, for I have made my vow and done my worship. Will you too cast in with me? Men," she added, looking at Cyril, "are not allowed a part in this matter. The nymphs' water is for women only."

"O, by all means! What fun!" exclaimed Mrs. Mostyn. "Come, Grace, and try your luck."

Perhaps Grace thought it was a heathenish proceeding, which she need not perform; but there was a kind of fascination in the little ceremony, and she agreed at once.

So they descended to the rock, which stood out a few feet above the stream in the narrowest part of the gorge. At its foot was the "Gáo Mookh," or Cow's Mouth, a rude carving, now strewn with votive garlands. A jet of sparkling water poured from the orifice and mingled with the river. It was most probably a strong spring; but the popular belief was that it came from the Ganges. "Jey Gunga Matá!" cried Seeta, who led the way, and threw a garland on the sculptured effigy, and the rest followed her.

They looked upon the most rapid portion of the stream a few yards only from its plunge over the precipice—a deep blue mass, unbroken, smooth as glass, and rushing on with a faint, rustling murmur. They almost felt giddy as they gazed.

"Now, lady," said Seeta to Mrs. Mostyn, "choose your garland from the basket, and throw it into the middle of the water, and wish what you please. I have made mine long ago." And Mrs. Mostyn took up a garland of white flowers and did as Seeta bid her. They all watched it sail steadily down and disappear. It was now Grace's turn. "She need not tell us what she wishes," said Seeta to Mrs. Mostyn, with a sly smile; "that she can keep in her own heart. Ah! she is lucky too. See how hers floats away safely. Now it is my turn. Look! O, I am so happy!" she cried, clasping her hands. "God hears me. Look!"—and she suddenly turned to Grace—"it is gone too!" But Cyril, who had been watching with an amused interest, and from his position could see the farthest outwards, observed the garland, whirled by an eddy to a rock at the side, caught by the rushing water, and, broken, disappear. He said nothing, for Seeta would have been distressed; but the little incident was never forgotten.

Then they walked up to the knoll where they had first seen the fall, and Grace sketched in the outline and put in some light washes of colour; while Cyril made a separate sketch of this group for her foreground: but it was growing late; and after watching the sun sinking into the west behind distant ranges of dim mountains, and the gorgeous changes of the sky, orange and sea-green, and crimson-purple and gold, they returned to the tents.

And the evening was very pleasant. With closed tent-doors and the curtains let down, the friends chatted on, after dinner and tea, and sang to Cyril's guitar, and Seeta drank in their sweet voices greedily. How quickly reserve had passed away; and how happy she was now! Then they asked her to sing, and Cyril bid her sing what she had first sung to him; "when

"I was wounded," he added, to Grace, "and she nursed me." And Seeta shyly consented; and, tuning Cyril's guitar to a simple chord, sang the sweet plaintive melody, "I could not speak with him," which Cyril translated, at Grace's request. Perhaps my readers will not object to the song entire, and I wish I could write them the plaintive melody also; but unless Mr. Arthur Sullivan will arrange the music, who will ever know it?—

> I could not speak with him,
> Those fondest words that I had treasured up to tell;
> My streaming eyes were dim
> With weary tears, which then, alas! unheeded fell.
> Rude blows the bitter wind,
> Cold is the driving rain, nor place I have to dwell,
> Ah, me! from them unkind,
> No pitying word, no sheltering love I find.
>
> Ah, now, I vainly cry,
> Hadst thou but liv'd, dear lord, dear heart, so fondly loved,
> Thou wouldst not see me die
> So desolate, nor fail that love so long, so truly, proved—
> Rest, rest, O breaking heart!
> Peace cometh soon to thee that nought hath ever moved.
> Ah, why delay thy dart?
> Kind death, take me to him that never more we part.

"It is a sad song; but I am very fond of it," said Cyril. "She can speak to me fast enough now, though," he continued, laughing; "and that is growing quite an old story now."

I do not think Grace Mostyn slept very soundly that night. Perhaps she was too tired and too excited; perhaps the girl's sad song haunted her; but I think there was another much more painful reason—in a dream, one of the sweetest of her young life, being broken. Ah! she must not think of him now—never again, as she had thought, happily for a brief time only.

Next morning, when it was daylight, they met again, and the friends took their cups of hot coffee together before they separated; and Seeta came in comfortably muffled up in a shawl, and the ladies kissed her and bid her good-bye. She must come back soon, and then they should know each other better. So they went on their several ways. They might not meet again, they thought, for months.

PART THE THIRD.

CHAPTER XXVIII.

SOCIETY AT NOORPOOR.

THE middle of February had arrived, and the Thirty-fourth and other regiments at Barrackpoor had neither been idle nor grown indifferent to the matters they had at heart; and their private meetings were more frequent, and the tone of the men had become more savage and resolute. The news they had spread to stations in Upper India had done its work; and their friends everywhere assured them of sympathy and help, as concerned the cartridges and every other insidious attempt of the English against their caste and religion. In what form this feeling should be demonstrated had not, perhaps, then been decided; but their stern resolutions had not been shaken, and as the combination proceeded the hopes of all rose in proportion. Sumbut 1914 was near—that terrible year of pestilence, famine, tumults, wars, and destruction, which was to overwhelm their old masters, the "Koompani," in a destruction as wide and awful as it would be complete; and every one believed alike. Hindoos of all classes who heard or read the yearly almanacs, knew the dire prophecy to have been calculated exactly a hundred years before, after Clive's victory of Plassey; and, as fixed by planetary influences and injunctions, believed it was irrevocable. The Sepoys had completed their contract of a hundred years of faithful service, and yet their masters were now seeking, as they believed, in a bitter proselytizing spirit, to defile them and pollute their sacred caste, which was more precious than life, for without it life with honour would be dead. What cause had they given for this outrage on their faith—a faith which they had maintained unsullied for thousands of years? Had they not marched devotedly through the bitter snows and frosts of Afghanistan and the burning plains of India, everywhere shedding their best blood, while their achievements were splendid victories? Yet now, all seemed to be forgotten and rudely flung aside. The greased cartridges was the first attempt of their infatuated masters in the direction which was but too surely manifest, and must be resisted to the death. Nothing had ever been done before like this; but Sumbut 1914 had already thrown its dark shadow on the dial of time, and its behests must be obeyed. There might, there would be, a struggle to amaze the world; but it must come, and the Koompani Bahadoor must expire in blood.

Still no outward demonstration was made by the men of any of the regiments at Barrackpoor, and parades and ordinary duties went on as usual. There were mysterious fires in the cantonment; the telegraph office, and occasionally an officer's bungalow, were burned down; and thus a condition of unrest arose among the English residents and officers, which was very painful to all—for there was a conviction, fast spreading, that these fires were not accidental. Nothing, however, could be discovered; and by a strange coincidence, as it seemed, news of similar occurrences arrived from Ranee Gunje; but there was no outbreak anywhere. That event was now, however, very near. The delegates sent by Azráel Pandé and the meeting we know of, carried letters to the Nineteenth, at Berhampoor, and found that regiment excited in many respects by the prevailing rumours; but they had heard nothing for certain till about the middle of February, when a detachment of the Thirty-fourth arrived on escort duty, and was followed by another of the same corps a week after. The wild stories told by the first, of the prevalent apprehension by the Brahmins of the Temple of Kalee, and others, were confirmed with exaggerated particularity by the second; and the tale of the low-caste Lascar who had taunted a Brahmin Sepoy with loss of caste because of the greased cartridges, was repeated, and flew from mouth to mouth, exciting terror and amazement. The Nineteenth drank in the poison greedily, and with childish credulity had, the morning after, mutinied on parade, and refused to take the blank ammunition served out to them. It is true the men afterwards submitted and did their duty; but, in connection with other current events of the month, this outbreak augmented the universal feeling of disquiet and suspicion at every station of the army where the news was read. Everywhere had the question of the cartridges been discussed. New means of greasing them had been invented and practised, to which the men had made no objections; but nevertheless the mistrust on both sides did not diminish, it increased; and the case of the Nineteenth, though the men had committed no overt act of violence, showed what might occur anywhere and at any time.

A sentence of disbandment had been at once recorded against that regiment by the Supreme Council; and it was ordered down to Barrackpoor. The men knew nothing, and suspected nothing; on the contrary, indeed, it may be easily believed, looked forward with high pleasure to meeting their friends of the Thirty-fourth, and other regiments there. Meanwhile Calcutta was strengthened by the arrival of Her Majesty's Eighty-fourth in the steamer which had been sent for it to Rangoon; there were many anxious consultations with the General then in command of Barrackpoor, who assembled his troops and told them of the fate of the Nineteenth as a warning, and spoke to them in his well-known, kindly, popular, and persuasive manner. Nevertheless, an undercurrent of treason discovered itself now and then; and an attempt was made one day to tamper with the native officer who commanded the guard over the mint of Calcutta.

On Sunday, the 29th of March, a new incident occurred, which excited fresh alarm. My readers will not, perhaps, have forgotten Mungul Pandé, Azráel's nephew, a Sepoy in the Thirty-fourth, who, having heard his uncle's address, had brooded over it, perhaps, more than others of his comrades—had burned with impatience for the day of rising, and had with difficulty been restrained from violence. That day the jemadar, at whose house the former meeting had been held, was on duty in command of the regimental quarter-guard; and, possibly, the event had been arranged between them. Be that as it may, as Mungul Pandé heard of the landing of a party of European soldiers on the river-bank that afternoon, he took up his sword and musket, and calling through the lines of his regiment for all to follow him, rushed on the parade-ground.

It was said he was intoxicated with bhang; but I think his religious ardour and thirst for blood supply ample motives for the frenzy that possessed him. No one interfered with him or checked him; but no one supported him. He fired at the sergeant-major and at the adjutant, and wounded them both badly with his sword. Meanwhile the parade-ground was crowded by Sepoys; but no one attempted to capture or shoot down the furious mutineer, who was shouting to his comrades to join him and fight for the faith, with every term of persuasion and adjuration. After a time, the noble old General, his three sons, and other officers arrived, and rode at once upon Mungul Pandé. He did not flinch, or make an attempt at escape; but, after a moment's hesitation as to whether he should kill his commander, lost heart, and turning his piece against himself, fired, and fell to the ground. He was not, however, dead, and was carried away into confinement.

If the Thirty-fourth had then risen, it is far from improbable that the other regiments would have joined them; but, in fear of the Eighty-fourth, they all hesitated, and sent out emissaries to the Nineteenth, then only ten miles distant, from whom, however, there was no response; and on the morning of the 31st, that regiment—now penitent, and praying to be pardoned, declaring they would serve over the sea, and beseeching their old General to let them punish the Thirty-fourth, who had seduced them—marched upon the parade-ground at Barrackpoor, piled arms, and ceased to be soldiers. But further ignominy or dishonour was spared them. "My sons," said the General as he addressed the native regiments drawn up, "yonder go four hundred Brahmins, and a hundred and fifty Rajpoots, safe in their caste and religion, free to worship where they please; would it have been so if their pollution had been desired by the English?' So, for a time, all was again tranquil, and local anxiety, in some sort, subsided; but the first blood had been shed on both sides, which was to swell into a torrent ere it quenched the fire that smouldered. Mungul Pandé, and the jemadar known to us, were tried as soon as possible, found guilty by their brother officers, and hanged; but even that stern example did not neutralize the evil leaven of the Thirty-fourth, or that of any regiment which witnessed the executions; and as the news of them spread rapidly through the native army, the thirst for revenge became stronger. There had been two martyrs to their faith already, and their fate was accepted as a new proof of what would befal others. Of all present, the Thirty-fourth was perhaps most deeply and most justly suspected, and its partial disbandment was a question which remained for future solution.

Meanwhile Noorpoor continued in its usual dulness. As the hot weather approached, the English residents saw less and less of each other, and although the hospitable mansion of the Judge was ever open, and Mrs. Mostyn led the society as well as she could, I think she almost wearied of the heavy task. Grace tried very hard to bring out pretty Lucy Home's talents, if she had any, played easy duetts with her patiently, and attempted to teach her to draw; but it was all very uphill work—the girl was forgetting the little she had ever learned, and, perhaps, she had never learned enough to induce herself to take more trouble. "It was so hot," she said, and therewith all her energy departed. It was hot, certainly; but Grace and her sister, when the house was shut up early, found the days still very bearable, and the evenings and mornings were cool and pleasant; and, a brisk canter in the fresh morning air, and a drive in the evenings, kept them strong and well, and the roses did not desert their fair cheeks.

I will not say that Captain Hobson was as useful in their music as Cyril Brandon had been, but he was useful nevertheless; and his fine rich baritone voice blended with Mrs. Mostyn's and Grace's in many a duett and trio very charmingly, and his violoncello almost lived now in a corner of the drawing-room, and much was done with it. Hobson was a fine stalwart fellow, of great stature and strength, with a grand, curly, dark-brown beard falling over his chest, moustachios of a lighter tint, and strong, wavy brown hair—very handsome, too, with keen, steel-blue eyes, a laughing mouth, a short, strong, resolute nose, and a rich, ruddy brown colour, full of health and vigour. Hobson had highly distinguished himself in the Sikh war, and was a dashing *sabreur*, before whose sword many a brawny Sikh champion had gone down, not, however, without leaving mementoes in the shape of sharp sabre cuts about his person. Every one knew that Hobson's father had offered him a handsome allowance if he would come home and settle, and that in the course of nature he would inherit a good property; but Hobson was essentially a soldier, devoted to his profession, fond and proud of the regiment he now commanded; and the regard of the men for him equalled, or seemed to equal, his for them. Not very learned, perhaps, was he, or studious, though he had passed creditable examinations; nor did he read much of anything; his only accomplishment was music, of which he was passionately fond.

Could such a man, continually in our sweet Grace Mostyn's company, fail to be touched by her beauty, her grace, her rare accomplishments, and her charming good-nature? It was quite impossible that it should be so; and yet he saw no chance of exciting more than a friendly—very friendly, if you will—interest in him. He was no vain fool to risk that which he knew he must risk and lose in any precipitate attempt to win her; but, with all his heart, he would have given her his strong, manly love if he had thought there was a chance of its being accepted. I am sure the Judge and Mrs. Mostyn had many a private talk together on the subject, and had Grace evinced any hopeful feeling, would have given her to him very cheerfully; but there was no such demonstration—not the slightest—and they respected her feelings in careful abstinence from the subject. I am afraid, too, that Mrs. Home and poor Lucy were in despair at seeing the evident defection of the dashing Captain, who, though kind as ever, did not seek Lucy nor come to the house more than he could help.

"I'm not equal to Grace Mostyn, mamma," she said one day, with a sigh, and some genuine tears, "and I never shall be; and Captain Hobson doesn't care a bit for me now"—in which conclusion, indeed, she was quite correct.

There were others at the station, however, to whom the maternal solicitude gradually extended itself. "There are as good fish in the sea, my darling," she observed, "as ever came out of it; and you needn't despair of catching one of them, sooner perhaps than you think;" and Lucy, who knew she was to be married some day, because she was very nice, and very pretty, grew content to wait.

As to the rest of the Noorpoor society at that period I have nothing to record. Elders read the papers and discussed the cartridge question, with other topics of the day, at early breakfast, and at the messes. Youngsters went out shooting and hog-hunting, or made parties to the Gáo Mookh, on the beauties of which Mr. Mostyn never ceased to descant—played at billiards, attended the band, studied Hindostanee, and killed time as best they could. As for the ladies, there is little to record of them. Mrs. Hill might have proved a pleasant companion for Mrs. Mostyn and Grace, but there were cogent reasons for not going out at present, and she obeyed them; and, perhaps, to Mrs. Jones and Mrs. Smith the excitement of Seeta's presence in the station was wanting, for the Ayah assured them she would never return, and her mistress's investigations were directed into other local subjects as before. But the Brigadier, watchful over all, grew more and more uneasy.

"What do you think of the news this morning?" said Mr. Mostyn to the Brigadier, who paid him an early visit one day, but would not go into the drawing-room where the ladies were sitting, and requested to see him alone. Mr. Mostyn had not yet gone to his court; he was engaged in reading over the papers of a new suit—Ram Das *v.* Seeta Bye, widow, and Narendra, banker—in regard to the property at Gokulpoor, which had lately been instituted, and had disturbed him not a little.

"I don't like it at all," he replied, "not at all. I don't know where the mistake is, but there is one somewhere. Why should this cartridge question have arisen? Surely we have wise men enough at the head of affairs to know the extreme danger of any attempt to introduce these new-fangled arms. Let the English regiments have them by all means, and the more the better—they will be all the stronger; but why on earth we should seek to make Jack Sepoy as strong as ourselves, passes my comprehension. *Quem Deus*, etc., you know."

"I hope it's not come to that," replied the Judge, smiling.

"I really don't know that it is not, Mostyn," returned the Brigadier. "I cannot assure myself at all. I have letters from Umballa, from Meerut, from the Punjab, Dinapoor, and other places, and they are mostly to the same purport: mistrust everywhere—every one uneasy—and yet perseverance in this most absurd and dangerous project. Now, you see, the first blood has been shed—I pray God it may be the last! But I fear not; there is too much mischief in the air, and combination has gone too far, as is evident from the case of the Nineteenth, and the news we receive by the papers. I knew that regiment, though I never belonged to it, and a nicer one, or easier to command, I never met with; the men mostly Brahmins and Rajpoots—grand, high-caste fellows every one of them; and I don't think they could have been properly managed, or they would not have been the first to commit themselves. But they are gone now; and in spite of their cheer to Hearsey, will spread their poison everywhere; and if Government disbands the Thirty-fourth, as it is said they will do, they will follow their friends, and set every station in a blaze. They are as bad a lot as the old Thirty-fourth were, and that's saying a good deal."

"And how are we here?" asked the Judge. "I don't hear of anything unusual."

"Nor have I, nor are we likely to hear," replied the Brigadier; "and we are safe so far, that we are not likely to have the cartridges sent to us. We are happily out of the way: and I think and hope that till the Sepoys are actually trodden on, they will not turn on us; but there is no harm in taking precautions, I think, and that's what I have come to speak with you about; and I can do so here without danger of being heard."

"By all means speak freely, and let me know your plans," said the Judge; "no one can hear us, and the ladies are in the drawing-room."

"Well, then," continued the Brigadier, "we should contrive some place of security, and the old fort appears to me very well adapted for the purpose. I went over it yesterday, and though some of the buildings are ruinous, no doubt, yet there are others which, at a pinch, might be made very serviceable and weather-proof. Now, can you help me to clean it all out? You might, for instance, employ all the prisoners you can spare; by-and-by I shall be able to help you with Lascars and Coolies. My beginning the work might excite surprise; but your doing so would not be noticed. What do you say? Mind, no one is to know of this but you and me."

"You anticipate an outbreak, then?" said Mr. Mostyn quietly.

"To say the truth, I fear one, and for the reasons I have given. I only hope I may be wrong, and then I will give you leave to laugh at me as much as you please. I wish Brandon were here, that we might have the advantage of his clear head; but I suppose he will not return for some time."

"I don't think he will," replied the Judge; "this is his busiest time; but he can be sent for—a word from me would bring him in at once. And now I think over your project, I like it, and I will order the prisoners in to-morrow. I will go into the fort this evening and see what there is to do, and I will write confidentially to Brandon to-day. I dare say he will come as soon as he can; but he could do nothing, at present, more than ourselves."

"Nor can any one, Mostyn, except take precautions. We have enough of Europeans and guns to defend the place against all comers, except they had regular artillery; and it is on the 'pale faces' that our security, humanly speaking, depends. Enough, then, for the present." And the Brigadier shook hands and departed, while Mr. Mostyn wrote to Cyril explaining what had been determined upon. "I wish Rose and Grace were at the Hills safely," he said, with a sigh; "but Rose won't hear of that, and if there is the remotest chance of trouble, would be more determined to stay than ever; so, perhaps, it is best as it is."

CHAPTER XXIX.

A WIDOW INDEED.

NARENDRA had returned from Benares, and had fulfilled the injunctions of the Noorpoor Punchayet and his Gooroo; performed all the necessary ceremonies and purifications, and brought letters from the chief Brahmins and heads of his own caste guilds, certifying, not only that he was pure, but that he had bestowed large sums in charity, and had entertained his caste at a sumptuous feast where he had eaten with all. For these reasons, and his great wisdom and respectability, he was commended to the friendship and protection of the Gooroo, and the goldsmiths' caste everywhere.

On his arrival at Noorpoor, Narendra had not, as may be surmised, found Mr. Brandon and his grand-daughter; but he entertained his caste people, who received him joyfully, and wrote to Cyril, requesting him, if possible, to come to Shah Gunje, for he had much to tell which he dared not write by the ordinary post from Benares. In addition to the certificates regarding himself, he had requested one in respect of his grand-daughter, for whose offence, if there had been one, he maintained he had atoned as much as for his own; but this was not so readily procured. Wamun Bhut pleaded for her to the Brahmins, and obtained from them confirmation of his own views on the subject of the marriage, which was all he desired; but the goldsmiths' guild was more difficult to manage. The members of it resented the marriage, which they declared united the caste to an unbeliever, defiled by eating cows' flesh. He could never be purified, nor his wife, so long as she lived with him; but she might nevertheless visit her grandfather and aunt, and might live in the house; but she must eat apart from them, and the household utensils must not be used in common. This was all Narendra could obtain, and he thought, though he did not show it to the guild, it might satisfy Seeta. In any case, there was no appeal now. Some of the Benares guild had even blustered, and declared that Seeta must separate from Mr. Brandon; come to Benares, bathe in the Ganges, have her head shaved, and her bangles broken off, wear coarse clothes, and comport herself as a widow. But there were others who looked upon her with more pity when they heard her history, comprehended the high honour of the English gentleman, and thought hopefully of the connection; and they were happily the most numerous.

Thus Narendra was ready to receive his grand-daughter; and, in consultation with Wamun Bhut, a proper day was ascertained, by certain conjunctions of the planets, on which she should enter the house again after her long absence. How earnestly and anxiously did Aunt Ella yearn to see her child once more, from whom she had never been separated so long before in her life! What stories she had to tell her of the journey, of Benares, of holy temples and shrines, of the crowd of pilgrims, the fearful Jogees and Bairagees, who filled the streets, and the stately processions and ceremonies!

Dear Aunt Ella was much altered, and by no means improved, by the results of her journey and her vows. The soft grey hair, always so neatly braided over her temples before, and made up in an ample knot behind, was now gone; her head was clean-shaved, and an unsightly stubble often covered her skull, which the barber only could remove. Her plain, homely features seem to have grown larger and coarser under this process, though their kindly, loving expression still remained, and would never alter. Formerly her clothing was handsome, if not costly; she had dressed herself as became the widow of a man who, though she had borne him no children, had yet been able to leave her a comfortable portion, which her brother employed well and profitably for her. It provided for all her wants; and her brother, too, was fond of seeing her wear good clothes, and gave her handsome silk and muslin sarees, as he did to Seeta—on festival days—sarees with rich borders of gold thread or silk, costing much money.

Now all these were gone: and instead, a greyish white garment of scanty dimensions, which reached only a little below her knees, made of a thin woollen serge, very mean-looking and uncomfortable, was all that she was allowed. Bodice she had none: and her right arm appeared naked to the shoulder, the skin being fair to the point at her elbow where the former sleeve had reached, and the rest brown, which gave her a patched appearance very disagreeable to see. She wore no golden anklets over her instep, pleasant to hear, as their tiny bells chinked as she moved about, warnings to lazy wenches in the kitchen to stop gossip and do their work. No golden bangles or bracelets were now on her arms or wrists, no earrings, and no massive gold zone round her trim waist;—all that she was allowed was a plain silver bangle on each arm above the elbow, and a silver ring round her neck. She had often laughed at herself—ay, and cried too—as she looked in a glass; but now Seeta was coming, and Mr. Brandon, what would they think of her? "And they would have made her like me," said the old lady to herself, "some of them; but she is safe now with the English."

I think Aunt Ella was afraid at first to venture through the town to Wamun Bhut's temple, for fear rude boys should laugh at her in her changed condition; but she was not naturally timorous. Daily ceremonies had to be performed, and no one could do them but herself; so one day she tucked up her short garment, till her sturdy legs could be seen above her knees, threw a sheet over her shoulders, took a long staff to keep off the dogs, and marched boldly out; and much surprised and gratified was the old lady to find that most people seemed to respect her more than before! Men and women joined their hands and put them up to their noses and foreheads, and many of the women touched their feet and breast, and made their children do so too, and asked her for her blessing—all of which was very new and pleasant. They had not done this when she wore fine clothes, and on festival days sailed majestically through the streets up to the temple, her rich saree of thick purple silk glistening and rustling as she walked, with the heavy gold zone clasped in front over it; and the popular demeanour now, was, I am sure, a great consolation to the pious worthy woman.

Besides, she had learned some new holy texts and charms at Benares, which were most acceptable to all her household gods, and to Krishna, whom in particular she worshipped at the temple. She was the only woman in Shah Gunje who had seen the holy mother Gunga and the Sacred City; and in these respects she had an immense and most enviable superiority over all her old cronies and gossips, who came to visit her by scores, and to ask her to relate her adventures. Seeta, perhaps, was seldom enquired after. She had voluntarily gone out from among them to the English, of whom they knew nothing; and most of her friends considered that Aunt Ella's transformation was intended as an expiation of her own sin in allowing Seeta to depart, and they accepted it as such with devout thankfulness.

When Seeta heard of her grandfather's and Aunt Ella's return from Benares safe and pure, she was very thankful, and made her offerings at the temples of the town near which Cyril's camp was: fed some Brahmins, and comported herself as a Hindoo woman ought to do when those dear to her, who have been absent on long and difficult journeys, return safely. Cyril wished her to go at once to Shah Gunje, where she would arrive on the third or fourth day, perhaps, and the police should escort her all the way; but she said truly, that she wished them to get settled: that she should be in their way if she went too soon, and that he might depend her grandfather would write when it was fitting for her to come, and a proper day had been fixed by Wamun Bhut. So about a fortnight had passed when the long-expected letter came from Narendra, addressed to them both, and sprinkled over with red colour and gold-leaf dust, as it were for a marriage.

Narendra, in truth, was very happy except for one care, which must be told to Mr. Brandon only. His business had been very prosperous during his absence, and his manager had done his duty well. He had himself brought large orders for local produce from Mirzapoor—others would follow, and his agency accounts would show large balances at the close of the mercantile year. What was he to do with his growing wealth? Whom had he to leave it to? Should Seeta have children, he might bestow much upon them; but there must be an adoption. He had taken the solemn sacraments at Benares, the brand of which on his broad chest was still white where the skin had peeled off, and he had been admonished, both by the Punchayet and the Brahmins, that he must not be neglectful while yet strong and well, in regard to a provision for the ceremonies for the repose of his soul after death, which only a male heir could perform. There was no hurry, however, about this, and he had already fixed his mind upon a youth, the son of a distant relative who resided at Nagpoor, of whom he heard a good account. Yes, he would invite him to Shah Gunje, and if he proved worthy, he should reside with him and be his son.

Mr. Brandon was punctual to his time, and Seeta went direct to her old home. How pleasant it was to look again on the familiar scenes of her childhood, and how vividly the dread event of her husband's murder flashed on her memory as she passed Gokulpoor in her palankeen when the sun was rising! She could not look on the old house, and shut the doors of her palkee; but women of the village were assembled to welcome her, and they put their hands over her, and cracked their fingers as they had done many a time before. Thence, every tree, every field, every hamlet, was familiar to her; and as she reached the last rising ground and looked over the pretty town, she saw her grandfather's house overtopping those around it, and the dear oriel window where she used to sit and watch—then without hope.

Nothing had changed outwardly; but in herself she could

already trace much change. New thoughts, new aspirations, new incentives to exertion, had taken the place of those old dreamy studies of hers, which perhaps in some degree had lost their savour. Though as yet she knew but little English, her husband's mind was a book which unfolded itself to her more and more every day. What countless stores of knowledge did he not seem to her to have treasured up! While to him, to train and satisfy her intelligence was always a pleasant and grateful task. There was no dulness or apathy to encounter; on the contrary, a bright, keen, deep-thinking mind, full of the truest enthusiasm and perseverance, never tiring him, but indeed watching him with an earnest reverence and love which deeply affected him, and in which he found rest when he was wearied by his day's work.

One great trouble which possessed Cyril at first was, how he should amuse Seeta: whether her thoughts, after the first excitement had passed away, would not revert to her old life and its humble pleasures and occupations, and she would pine for them. But they had not; and thus the mutual esteem had increased. Their life had not changed from what it had been from the beginning. His own work never altered from day to day. The routine of official papers, references, suits, and hearing petitions read, went on like so much clockwork, and varied only in the subjects for consideration and decision, some investigations into matters which required alteration and reform, promising valuable results. What was possible in regard to new roads, school-houses, bridges, police-stations, and other public works, had too a full share of his attention. Cyril had taught himself simple surveying and plotting, which proved useful to him in settling many a boundary dispute which had cost blood in old times, and which perhaps, in some cases, the parties concerned would have preferred being left an open question. Thus every new proposal or report that he submitted, carried with it proof of having been well considered by himself, and the authorities to whom they were forwarded, felt a conviction that an earnest, right-thinking man was doing his work with conscientious labour and ability.

Is this a digression? I hope not; for it is well for my readers to know how one man, with perhaps one English and a few native assistants, governs a province in India as large as one of the divisions of Ireland—as populous, perhaps more so—accepts the responsibility of such a task, and fulfils its duties, multifarious as they may be. Such men as Cyril Brandon exist in scores; earnest, laborious, and striving for the prosperity and comfort of the people committed to their charge, conscious, doubtless, of many shortcomings, but still striving, and, as I think, not in vain.

But while we have been thinking of such matters, Seeta has passed the town gate, sees everywhere through the chink of the palankeen doors, which she had not opened, familiar faces, hears familiar street cries, sees old friends at their doors and shops, and none altered. It is as though she had been there only yesterday, and yet she had been absent some months, and had travelled all over the broad district. Then came the chowke, and the early sellers of firewood and vegetables and eggs, and the flower-woman with her garlands for morning worship. And when the bearers turned into the old archway, and jars of water were broken before her, and the guard of Rahtores, with Dévee Singh at their head, salaamed to her, she knew she was once more at home. When the palankeen was put down on the ground in the inner court, she stepped out quickly, and in a moment Aunt Ella's arms were around her as of old, while the wife of Wamun Bhut waved over her, from head to foot, a tray with lighted lamps and grain, pulse, and flowers upon it, and some of the sacred powders and ashes, with which her forehead was marked. A row of women sang one of the welcome hymns, as to a bride, and on the top of the steps was the noble figure of her grandfather, his arms stretched out to her with a glad cry of joy. Then Seeta touched his feet reverently as he put his hands on her head—nor do I think either could have spoken—and she was led by Aunt Ella, the women singing the hymn before her and carrying lighted lamps, to the altar she had always tended, and she took some cool ashes from it and passed them over her forehead and eyes, as she had used to do. Truly her welcome had been complete and happy!

It is not thought lucky among the people of India to notice that friends look well; on the contrary, a curious custom prevails of bewailing altered appearances after absence, of regretting how thin they have become, and the like; and as they stood there, good Aunt Ella, whose tears had flowed plenteously as Seeta stepped out of her palankeen, now wiped her eyes, and condoled with her child on her miserable condition of body; but at the same time she was passing her hands over her, and felt an inward satisfaction at finding her child very round, and firm, and plump, with her cheeks glowing with health—very different indeed from what she was when she left. And this truly was the case. Constant change of air, and exercise, a light, happy heart, pleasant occupations, and Cyril Brandon's love, had converted the pale, morbid girl that she remembered, into a new creature, full of life and health.

Dear Aunt Ella at the same moment was undergoing a similar scrutiny from her child, who now had time to notice the utter and painful change. Aunt Ella's garment had fallen from her head, and showed the shining knobby skull which had been newly shaved, and gave so painfully grotesque an appearance to her features. Seeta's eye ran over the scanty, homely dress, and her heart was pained. "Such would they have made me," she thought, as she turned away almost with a shudder.

We may leave her, however, to Aunt Ella's care, and to receive visitors after her old fashion, who crowded to see the "English lady," believing they should find her altered. But Seeta received all in her own old simple fashion, as she sat at the oriel window, and looked out with a blessed sense of peace on the dear white tents. And we may now follow Narendra, who went up to Cyril's camp before his daily work should begin. How thankful the old man was to see him again, and how grateful for his care of Seeta, I need not relate; and when the first enquiries were over, Brandon led him to the subject nearest his own heart, and nearest perhaps to Narendra's.

"I will not speak here," said the old banker, "of what I know; come to the temple with me—the priests' room is empty, and it is but a step. We have to be very cautious;" and Cyril put on his hat and followed him.

"It is all worse than I thought to the eastward—much worse. It was so bad at Benares that I dare not write," said Narendra excitedly, as they sat down.

"What is worse?" asked Cyril, somewhat amazed.

"Have you not heard them—the reports about the destruction of caste? Ah! I am glad you have not, for they are very awful and terrible, and men's minds are most unsettled. Whence they came I know not; but there were rumours at Benares and Mirzapoor, that the very salt and flour we eat, the grain we grind, was being, and would be, polluted; that caste was to perish, and we were all to become sweepers. These rumours, sir, were spreading fast. Every one talked of them; and many, I am sorry to say, believed them. There were reports, too, of the advance of the Russians and the Persians, who had beaten the English, and of the Dehly family rising under them to power; and, alas! there were to be no English; the Sepoys were to destroy them, because of the greased cartridges."

"So you heard that too, Narendra?"

"I could not fail to do so, Mr. Brandon. The people said

the Sepoys were to be defiled first, then they would not hesitate to coerce all other Hindoos. It was all part of the same plan. The very priests in the temples said there would be no worship there till after Sumbut 1914, and then it would be Christian, if the English did not die."

"And was all this openly talked about?" asked Cyril.

"Not openly, perhaps, but the very air seemed full of it; the water one drank, and the food one ate, seemed to taste of it. Every one seemed craving for blood—the blood of the Feringees—to wash out the stain on their faith. It was madness, sheer madness, Mr. Brandon; and O, sir, when a whole people become mad, who or what can stay them? and who can avert the prophecies of the coming year, which all have watched for with intense interest for a hundred years past? True, many an evil prophecy has passed by happily, but this already heralds its own fulfilment. Sepoy regiments have already mutinied; many have bound themselves, they say, to resist caste pollution, and more will follow those examples. O, Mr. Brandon! go from us; save yourself for the sake of your mother; leave Seeta with me, and if we live through 1914, I will keep her for you safely; but save yourself, even for her sake!"

Cyril was much touched and troubled; he had no doubt whatever of the old banker's honour or veracity. "Both are above suspicion," he said to himself; "but if there is mischief in the air or in the minds of the people, who can stay it?" He had sat without speaking, and Narendra again implored him to take measures for his own safety.

"I don't think you know me yet, Narendra," he said, smiling. "I shall not go, whatever happens. We English can die at our posts, but we never leave them. I am grateful that you have given me your confidence, and I will watch; but do not break a word of this to Seeta. Does Aunt Ella know of it?"

"No, I think not. What I heard was among men; they had not told the women," replied Narendra.

"And have you heard anything here?"

"Nothing, sir; though I and Wamun Bhut have been on the watch. But the bad wind will not be long before we feel the blast of its poison, and my last private despatches from Mirzapoor were full of alarm. I will show them to you if you wish."

That night Cyril was alone, for they had detained Seeta, as he wished they should; so he wrote a long letter to Mostyn in answer to the one he had received, and as he knelt down, prayed that tumult and bloodshed might not arise in that fair land, in whose government he felt, more strongly than ever, that he had a part—a very trifling one perhaps, but still a part.

Before the week had expired, Cyril had received a more anxious letter from Mr. Mostyn than the first, begging him to come into Noorpoor even for a day, and that he should send a palankeen for him and station bearers halfway. This could not be evaded, and sending on only his servant, and bidding Seeta make herself happy during his absence, he went into Noorpoor, leaving his tents standing.

CHAPTER XXX.

STRUGGLE AND VICTORY.

"Mem Sahib now know Kishnee not tell lie," said Mrs. Smith's Ayah to her mistress, early in the morning after Mr. Brandon's arrival at Noorpoor. "Mr. Brandon, he come; but Seeta, she not come—no, not any more come, you see. Mr. Brandon, he tired of caste—caste, caste, always caste; plenty trouble come, and more comin'—I know—goldsmith wife tell me; she say no one eat with Seeta now, then Seeta very angry, give bad words to all. Then Gooroo say, will shave him head, make him widow. So Mr. Brandon—ah! he dear good gentleman—he leave his black woman with old banker, and he come here, away, to Missy Mostyn."

Mrs. Smith's Ayah was a Madras Christian woman, or called or believed herself one, and spoke a curious dialect of English, which, rude as it was, her mistress perfectly understood. I need hardly tell my readers that the ingenious fiction she had just related to her mistress had no foundation in fact. The goldsmith's wife had certainly speculated on the possibility of another caste fracas, and on what might happen if one arose; and this, by a simple mental process, had been converted into a reality, which was very racy, and exciting to her mistress.

"And serve her right," cried Mrs. Smith, "if her head *was* shaved! Such wretches," she soliloquized, "ought to be set on donkeys and carried through the bazaar, for seducing fine young fellows like Cyril Brandon. I wonder, too, what Mrs. Mostyn will say now to her *dear* friend whom she kissed at the waterfall—pah! the nasty thing, I wouldn't have touched her with the tongs."

And afterwards the affairs of poor little Seeta and Mr.

Brandon were very freely discussed by the trio of whom I have recorded particulars already, and the immediate marriage of Miss Mostyn to Cyril was accepted as a fact.

Little thinking that his arrival had caused the sensation I have recorded, or could be attributed to any other motive than duty, Cyril gave himself up to the pleasant society of his friends with unmixed pleasure. Seeta was happy with her people; he with the Mostyns again; what could be more delightful? It was true he could not stay long, but his presence evidently so cheered them all, and they seemed to rely so implicitly on his calm, clear judgment, that before the day was past he had dispelled much of the gloom by which they had been overcast.

But that gloom had not been without cause, and Mr. Mostyn had had no secrets from his wife. Again and again he had implored her to take Grace to the Hills and be safe; but both had protested earnestly against any separation whatever. Both were strong and well, and on the score of health needed no change; and should there be danger, they would be no safer there than with him—not so safe indeed—and tormented by anxieties for each other. Letters had been received from all quarters by the residents at the station, and others were daily arriving. Mr. Mostyn had received several anonymous warnings, evidently from native sources, telling him that, because he was honoured and respected, his safety, and that of his wife and sister, were to be accomplished only by his immediate departure from the station for England. "Go to Bombay," was written in one of these letters; "you will be safe, for the bad wind of Sumbut 1914 comes from the East. Another had been shot, tied to an arrow without a head, into the garden. Mrs. Mostyn and Grace had found it only the day before, and Mr. Mostyn and Cyril deciphered it between them. To Cyril's perception, the style and the writing were like those of the letter he had received before the Dacoity in Narendra's house; but that was in his desk at Shah Gunje, and all they could discover from the letter before them was, warning to be ready, to watch the native troops, to send their valuables into the fort, and to move into it on the least sign of alarm. The writer was watching too, and would do good service, he wrote, because he loved the English.

By these alarms, the reports from English stations were confirmed in their significance. No matter whence the letters came, the extreme west of the Punjab, or the extremest east of Bengal, the purport never varied. Youngsters made light of it in their letters to each other; but more thoughtful elders grew graver and more stern. Everywhere now—for April had begun, and

Sumbut 1914 had been written in bankers' ledgers and letters from March 25—the same cry of destruction of caste was flying with fearful speed. It had reached Cawnpoor, Meerut, Agra, Dehly, Umballa, and was flying on to the Punjab. The result of the cartridge question at Umballa had been futile, though the Commander-in-Chief had addressed the Sepoys himself, and his kind speech had been faithfully translated to them. For one that believed the truth, there were tens of thousands who gave full credence to the lie; and the conviction seemed to be verified by the breaking out of fires in that cantonment, similar to those at Barrackpoor.

Then followed the strange, mysterious incident of the chupatees, or unleavened cakes, which passed through the country like a fiery cross, with very unaccountable rapidity. No message came with them: whence they came and where they were to go, nobody knew. They were carried by runners from village to village all over the North-west, and as far south as Berar; not one escaped them, not one refused to make ten others and send them on. They were one of the many portents of the time, and have never since been accounted for. They passed Noorpoor, as they had other stations, and both Mr. Mostyn and Cyril endeavoured—as who in authority did not?—to trace them, or account for them—but to no purpose.

As to the reports in the bazaars at Noorpoor, I might fill more than this chapter with them. The childish credulity of the ordinary Hindoo native of India has no equal in the world. Trained in his youth to believe the astonishing, and to him beneficent, miracles of his gods, his mind is prepared, as it were, to receive any human exaggeration and invention without question, and for any cause. Perhaps, therefore, it is not strange that when the purport of the weird Sumbut 1914 was disseminated, any rumour whatever that might arise, any portent that was visible or imagined, was accepted as a divine revelation, and believed in faith; and the air they breathed, as all felt and acknowledged, was filled with dire rumour and dread anticipation. It seemed as if a mighty volcano were heaving, and only needed some fiery breath of air to explode, destroying all.

Now, some one was coming with an army twenty miles broad and twenty miles long, which was to sweep every living Englishman from the face of the land. Again, fakeers had been seen on flying horses riding through the air by night, and crying, "Woe to the English, woe!—the poisoners of our food!" Letters were received from Cawnpoor and other stations on the Ganges, bidding grain merchants beware of poisoned flour—of flour with which cows' bones had been ground in the English mills, and was to come from Meerut; and that the salt and ghee were alike polluted. The native troops at Noorpoor seemed, however, to be quiet and faithful; no cartridges troubled them, and they could afford, for the time, to laugh at other stories. It was clear that delegates had not as yet reached them, and one regiment at least had promised voluntarily to give up any that might arrive. The cavalry were a different class altogether, and for the most part Mahomedans; all heard the prevailing rumours, but they did not seem to care about them, and Captain Hobson was easy.

The Brigadier had, however, made his determination, as we know, at the very first indication of alarm, and with Mr. Mostyn had carried out the arrangement of the fort very perseveringly and well. At first it was given out that a new gaol was to be built, and the fort was required for the prisoners. Then, that other gaols were too full, and it was to receive those for whom there was no accommodation; and no suspicion was excited. Gradually, however, the large granaries were filled with wheat and other provisions, ample stacks of fodder were set up, the powder and shot were quietly removed and placed in the magazines: all the buildings and rooms in an old palace were whitewashed, sheds were constructed, and it was clear there would be accommodation for all the Christians there were at Noorpoor—rough and humble perhaps, but yet safe, while there was plenty of room for Mr. Mostyn and others to pitch their tents. Cyril chose for himself a small octagon room in the bastion which was washed by the lake, It belonged properly to the outwork or faussebraye of the citadel; but there was a pleasant look-out from the arches which formed the windows, and it would be ample for his purpose. It was evident to him that Seeta must remain with her grandfather at Shah Gunje till the present trouble was past; and he had no apprehensions in regard to her safety.

Did any of them realize, at that period of the gathering of the storm, what it would be when it broke, or whether it would break at all? Perhaps a very few thoughtful minds in India did realize it to the full, and grew anxious and careworn, though not a man flinched from the result. There were occasional panics, certainly; but there was no exodus of the English, and men kept their wives and their children, if they had any, to defend them, and to share with them whatever might befal. In times like these such men look to the future more than ordinarily, and make their last arrangements with the world;

and in this respect Mr. Mostyn and Cyril Brandon were not wanting. They committed the interests of those dearest to them in brotherly confidence to each other in case one might be called away; and I need not detail them. Cyril had already insured his life for a considerable sum at Calcutta in favour of Seeta, and, with her own property, the whole would maintain her respectably. Mr. Mostyn was, however, doubtful about her property, and told Cyril of the suit which had lately been instituted against her by Ram Das, her first husband's cousin.

"It is a difficult case," he said, "and ingeniously drawn up; but it cannot be tried for a long time, and these troubles may be over before then. It is very strange that you have heard nothing about it."

"Nothing, Philip; nothing was known at Shah Gunje when I left. But, indeed, it scarcely signifies, on Seeta's account, how it goes, for her grandfather has, I know, made a large investment in Government paper on her behalf, and in her name. He did this at Benares unknown to me."

"He is a grand old fellow that," said Mostyn; "he at least will be true to us, when we may need friends. And how about your two feudatories?"

"I don't like them," replied Cyril. "The Nawab writes me civil reports, and says he has been obliged, on account of dangerous rumours, and as he is well known to be a friend to the English, to increase his levies; but they are only ragamuffins of the country, who need not be feared. As to Rajah Hurpál Singh, I hear he has become very warlike, and talks about recovering all his ancestral domains. A great many bad characters have collected about him, and I should not wonder if our friend Azráel Pandé were one of them. His is just the evil spirit for these times. But I can take no notice of either at present; we have enough to do to think of ourselves."

And Cyril was right, for now came the news of the mutiny of the Seventh Cavalry at Meerut, who had refused to take the cartridges, and a large number of the men had been confined; but the Brigadier found comfort in the presence of enough English soldiers there "to eat up every Sepoy," as he said, little dreaming then of what the crisis would be. There seemed also a wilful blindness as to the designs and movements of the Royal family at Dehly, and of the Nana Sahib of Bithoor, who, never having left his estate before, was now travelling between Cawnpoor and Dehly, and also visiting Lucknow; and others, who, like the Nawab and Rajah Hurpál Singh, were openly increasing their levies. Outwardly, therefore, by the close of

April, a great gloom had fallen over the land. Wellwishers to the English—and they were many—trembled, as the mutterings of distant thunder began to be heard, and the oppression of the coming tempest to be felt. Nowhere was there rest, or freedom from apprehension, in any class, English or native; and the portents of Sumbut 1914 could no longer be doubted.

In spite, however, of evil rumours, and preparations to meet the shock if it should come, the time passed pleasantly with the friends. I need not repeat old scenes, or record operations, but as Cyril was living in Mr. Mostyn's house, except to sleep, he was naturally thrown more into Grace's society than had been possible before. Seeta, then unmentioned, had now become a household word among them; and her quaint Hindee letters, of which Cyril read portions, and her little attempts at English, like a child's, amused and interested them. She bid Cyril stay and make himself happy with his friends, and not think of her; they were taking good care of her. This was at first; but gradually a cloud came over her letters. She, too, had heard of the evil rumours, and had troubles of her own, too, which deeply distressed her, and which I shall mention, by-and-by, in their turn.

Captain Hobson was a continual guest, stepping in in the evenings, or to the early breakfast after his parade, when letters were opened and current topics discussed. It was plain to Cyril how deeply he admired Grace Mostyn; how his eyes followed her, and how tender, and yet how manly, was his demeanour to her; but he saw, too, that Grace made no response. "He may win her in time," he thought, "when this trouble is past; and he feels that this is no season for his suit; but she will be safe and happy with him, if she will accept him." So he reasoned with himself, or tried to reason; but truly this period was more dangerous to Seeta than the first at Christmas and New Year; and, in spite of mental resolutions, both were thinking of each other more than was warrantable under the circumstances. They were often alone together in the house, for Mrs. Mostyn could not always be watching, nor did she desire to watch them, for she had now abandoned her first hopes; and Mr. Mostyn's work went on as usual. The view of the Gáo Mookh Fall was in process of becoming a fine picture, and Grace and Cyril worked at it in turn with pleasant talk, ranging over the subjects both most loved; and so, with occasional practices and sails on the lake, which were cooler than carriage drives, the days passed, and the horrible realities without were, for the time, unheeded.

One day, the post brought the mails from England, and the usual amount of letters from all parts; and it had become a custom for those assembled at the Chota Hazree, or light early breakfast, to read out portions of their news, from all parts, which indeed now differed little one from another. Mr. Mostyn saw that as Cyril looked over one of his English letters, his face became anxious and distressed; and as he read another which had a large official seal in red wax, he appeared even more troubled; but he put them into his pocket, and joined in the general conversation for a time, and then, saying he had letters to write, got up to leave them.

"You will be back to breakfast, Mr. Brandon," said Mrs. Mostyn; "don't be late;" and he replied that he would come, and went across the garden to his house. But time passed, and he did not return; and when breakfast was finished, Mr. Mostyn said "he was sure there was something wrong in those letters, and must go and look after Cyril, and would send for breakfast if he wanted any."

Indeed, there was very much wrong with Cyril Brandon that day, for his friend found him sitting at his writing-table, with his head lying between his outstretched arms, and the two letters open before him. Mr. Mostyn had come in quietly, without being announced, and Brandon did not notice his approach till his friend touched him on the shoulder, and said kindly, "Why, what ails you, Cyril? No bad news from England, or, indeed, from anywhere, I hope? What distresses you, my dear fellow? Can I help you? There is nothing so certain to drive away trouble as to let another share it."

Cyril looked round at him as he partly raised his head, and groaned aloud. "I am cut to the heart, Philip," he said, "by what lie there. I did not think Hylton would be so cold, so unkind to me; and O! I love him so. And the other is even worse than his; but read what Hylton writes—it is so short, so unsympathetic."

Mr. Mostyn did not reply; the thought flashed on him what Lord Hylton might have written if his brother had told him of Seeta; and, taking the letter from Cyril, he read it through twice. After some preamble about ordinary home affairs and his own health, Lord Hylton had written thus:—

"Your account of what you have done in the way of marriage, Cyril, surprised and distressed me beyond expression. I have tried to put it away from my thoughts, and have allowed several mails to pass without alluding to the subject, so perhaps you may have concluded that I don't care about it, or approve of it.

But I do care, and I can *not* approve; and I beg you to understand this perfectly. The person who lives with you under the form of marriage you have patched up may be as beautiful and accomplished as Nourmahal; but I only see in her a designing native of India, who has lured you on till you have committed yourself, and cannot draw back; and from my heart I wish that you had never seen her. She could *never* take her place as your wife here, and the idea of recognizing such a person as Seeta, as a member of our old family, is, as you must see yourself on reflection, perfectly absurd and impossible. O Cyril! my dear, dear brother, I write in sorrow, not in anger; but your eyes *must* be opened, and I am the only one to do this. You left it to me to tell our mother and Augusta, and for that I am grateful. If you had written to either, the subject would have broken our dear mother's heart. Were I to tell either of them, I should be an accessory to your folly, and I have therefore burnt your letter, and no word on the subject shall ever escape me. One thing only will I add, and that is, if any amount of money will satisfy the girl, or her people, you have only to draw on me. No matter what the amount may be, your freedom will be the cheapest and most valued purchase of my life."

Mr. Mostyn laid down the letter with a sigh, and Cyril did not know how much his friend then sympathized with the writer, or perhaps he had never shown it.

"That's the other," said Cyril, handing one to him which was headed "Demi-official. Private and Confidential."

Mostyn looked at the signature, and saw it was from the official by whose advocacy Cyril's confirmation as Deputy Commissioner had been effected. It was very short and precise, and ran thus:—

"April 15, 1857.

"Dear Mr. Brandon,

"I have been inexpressibly shocked and grieved to hear, from unquestionable authority, that you have formed a native connection, which has become the scandal of your whole district and the station of Noorpoor. In the present excited condition of the native mind, unusual caution is required from us all; but in the deliberate seduction of the granddaughter of a respectable banker you have not only set our own laws of morality at defiance, but violated those of the natives who have been entrusted to your care.

"I, therefore, as the person who, believing you worthy in all respects, recommended your appointment in permanence, and rejoiced that I had succeeded, consider it to be my duty to the

State to recommend, on public grounds, your removal from all active duty, unless, indeed, you can assure me, very shortly, that there is no longer cause for my displeasure."

"That's enough to distress a fellow, Philip, isn't it?—to come the same day, too. God help me, what shall I do?" said Cyril, as Mostyn laid down the letter upon the other. "What shall I do?"

The tears were falling from Philip Mostyn's eyes as from a woman's, as he looked at Cyril earnestly, and with a love and compassion in them which could not be mistaken; nor could he speak at once. At last he said—

"It will, indeed, cut you to the heart, dear Cyril, and you will think me hard too; but I am another brother, and my heart goes with your brother's. As to the other, it is simply pragmatical impertinence; but there is power in the man to do mischief if he chooses, and the dullest must understand that he has the will, if you——"

"Why if, Philip?" cried Cyril, starting to his feet and his eyes blazing. "You—you of all men alive to say 'if!' Do you know what you mean?"

"I know perfectly, Cyril, but I will not say a word—no, not a word—if you stand there glaring at me. I will leave you with the letters till you are calm, and you can send for me again if you want me."

"I am a fool, I dare say, Philip," returned Cyril, sitting down and dashing his hand across his eyes. "I thought you were going to say I should give up that poor girl; but don't say that—by your love for me, don't say that!"

"If I had not that love, dear Cyril, I should be silent," he replied, sadly, "and watch you go on to ruin—no, not to ruin, perhaps, but to disgrace; and I cannot be silent! Your brother you may satisfy, your mother has no suspicion; but we all know what that inexorable man is; how narrow his mind, how deep his prejudices, and what power he has. He has resented the connection, and will never change his opinion; and there are enough about us here, perhaps, to back him up. Can't you send for Narendra, and let me talk to him? To my idea, Seeta loves you so truly, so devotedly, that she would go willingly to death rather than evil or trouble should come nigh you, and we all believe in her. I have said only the truth, Cyril, and can say no more. It is a question which admits of no argument, and must be Yes or No, and no more!"

"I cannot answer you now, Philip," said Cyril, gloomily. "Let me fight out my own battle in my own heart. If I don't come to dinner, you will understand the reason; but at present I must be alone. Don't mention this to Mrs. Mostyn and your sister, it would only distress them to no purpose."

"I will not," said Mostyn, and went away to his work.

Cyril Brandon, though he had been sorely tempted before, had never faced so fiery an ordeal as this. "It is to be Yes or No," Philip had said, "and no more." On the one hand, love to his mother, his brother, his sister—the very honour, as Hylton had written, of the family seemed at stake. His own high official position was at stake, too; and deprived of his office, he might be sent to rusticate for two or three years on a pittance, and have to begin to climb the ladder again. These thoughts, however, passed away from him; he could rely on his mother's and sister's love for him; and Hylton, who had looked to his marrying in England, was, perhaps, vexed and disappointed for a time and would come right. For the official threat he came to care very little, as he paced up and down his room rapidly. "I can give scores of instances of native connections in far higher places than mine," he thought, "and few have dared, as I have, to avow marriage." But one temptation would not leave him, and that was the thought of freedom for the sake of Grace Mostyn. Ah! that had sat before at his very heart, and was busy there now—very busy—shutting out for the time poor little Seeta and her claims on his love and protection; for there arose a thousand delicious, rapturous sensations of a love which his mother and sister would hail with delight and share with him; which he could show in England and among his countrymen here with pride, and without a moment's apprehension; a love of which he had no doubt—none—that it would be given if he asked.

If he should now sit down and write a line to Seeta—"I cannot maintain my honour, my people object to you"—it would be enough, he knew, to separate them for ever. No need of Mostyn or Narendra. She would take it, as many a Rajpoot woman had taken the fatal stab from her husband and died in his arms, conscious that his honour was safe—and die like one. Could he so kill her? As that pleading face he had so often caressed came up before his mental vision, he shuddered—shuddered to remember how he had sworn to himself before God to be true to her, to love and cherish her; how, too, what her people had risked so unselfishly in giving her to him; and should he now hesitate to maintain his faith?

He took no count of time that day, and the shadows lengthened. His servant had come to ask him to eat, but was frightened at what he saw, and retreated at once before the impatient gesture of refusal; but his strong mind could not bear the tension, and Cyril threw himself beside his bed and prayed, as he had done once before, "Lord, I sink! Lead me not into temptation!" And after awhile there seemed to glide gently into his heart the gracious assurance, "It is I, be not afraid." Many, perhaps, may blame Cyril Brandon that the world's course was put aside by him; but the man's faith, though it had bent before the storm of passion, was not broken, and as it passed away, left his mind serene and steady. That evening he went to the Judge's to dinner, and was perhaps more grave and thoughtful than usual; and when he bid them good-night, Philip Mostyn followed him into the garden, and said, "I have been reading your face, Cyril, to-night, and I am ashamed of what I said this morning. Will you forgive me?"

"I have nothing to forgive, dear Philip," he returned, putting his hand on his friend's shoulder, and looking into his eyes. "Only rejoice with me that, tempted as I was, I did not lose the faith I had plighted to my little girl, and shall never lose now."

"I am thankful," said Philip, "to hear it. My thoughts have been with you all day. Many would perhaps differ from, and even blame you; but I respect you more than ever, Cyril. Good-night!"

"Good-night, Philip." And I think Cyril's sleep was sweet and dreamless. In the morning, when he woke calm and fresh, he wrote to his official superior as follows:—

"My dear Sir,

I have had the honour to receive your demi-official letter of the — instant.

"I know not from whence you have received your information, and regret only that it should have been so gross and vile a misrepresentation. The lady you allude to is my wife: married to me by the Hindoo rites of her faith, which cannot be broken, and which I respect.

"In regard to my official duties, I have hitherto, under your confidence, striven to discharge them with all the zeal and ability of which I am capable; and I hope that I shall not be found remiss in any of them, or in my solicitude for the welfare of the people committed to my charge.

"I remain, your faithful servant,

"Cyril Brandon."

CHAPTER XXXI.

THE CLOUD SETTLES OVER THE GOLDSMITH'S HOUSE.

So long as Mr. Brandon remained at Shah Gunje, matters in the banker's family had gone on smoothly and pleasantly. It had certainly been a shock and a trial to Seeta, when she was told by Aunt Ella, with many tears, that she could not eat with her, because she was now "Bhugut," and had devoted herself to a religious life; nor that she should cook for her grandfather as she had used to do; because, since he had taken the "Moodra" sacrament, he was "Bhugut" also. As to his eating with the women, that had been impossible before; for, like all Hindoos, his meals were served entirely apart from them in the kitchen, which was also the eating-room of the family. Nor was it pleasant to Seeta to find certain drinking vessels and plates set apart for her sole use; and when by chance, or in forgetfulness, she touched another, that Aunt Ella passed it through a flame of the sacred fire, and said a prayer of expiation over it. This, however, was also set down to the effect of the sacraments and holy pilgrimage, and was acquiesced in as a necessity; and notwithstanding, the time passed away pleasantly. The worthy priest came, and insisted on Seeta's reading the Sanscrit exercises, and they had their usual friendly wrangles over hard passages, and over stout games of chess; and in the evenings, when the day's work was done, she would sit in her old corner by her grandfather's great cushion, and watch his chess battles with the priest, or with the Moolla of the mosque, or the head native officials of the town, who often dropped in to hear the news, and gossip of the place and district. One day Seeta took out all her old dolls from a chest, where Aunt Ella had put them away very carefully, and dressed some of them in new clothes. Ah! that strange love of dolls in many an Indian woman is often a part of their character, never leaving them even in old age. I remember to have once found an old Hindoo princess, whose years had reached far beyond the term of man, engaged in a true dolls' feast; and as she introduced them to me one by one, and presented me with sweetmeats in their names, told me their histories, and who had played with them besides herself, but had one by one been called away before her. Perhaps this was second childhood, but I think not; her faculties were all bright and sound, and if her dolls took her memory back to early days of a happy girlhood, who could doubt her pleasure in them? And Seeta was yet a girl. Her early blossom had faded, as we know, and had been laid to rest, poor little fellow! All his playthings were there, and the sight of them cost her many a tear; but the dolls were not changed—they were as bright, as stolid looking, and, I might add, as ugly as ever, though their clothing was so rich.

It was strange, Seeta thought, that some of her old companions, though all had been to see her, and had stared at her in a curious fashion, had not asked her for a dolls' feast at the garden beyond the town. "Perhaps," she said to herself, "they are shy of me because I am the Commissioner's wife, and dare not ask; but I will show them that I'm not a bit proud or stuck-up, though I am proud in my heart." So she sounded Aunt Ella on the subject, who had her doubts at first, whether it were fitting that she, a "Bhugut," could enter into such foolish amusements: but as Aunt Ella was as enthusiastic on the subject of dolls as she had ever been, and had helped Seeta in new dressing the old ones with great satisfaction, she joined heartily in the idea; as to the cost, it was but a trifle, and her brother would never miss it. So the preparations began; nor will I say how much and how many kinds of sweetmeats were prepared, what quantities of Aunt Ella's renowned vermicelli were made, what bags of the finest rice were picked, or how the gardener was told to reserve all the ripe fruit and vegetables in the garden.

When all was ready within doors, Seeta went out to the garden to have it cleared, and the dry weeds and grass under the great mango trees removed. Then swings were put up, and screens arranged for the cooking places, and some light sheds to sit under. The garden, to be sure, was not like that at Noorpoor, but there were beds of sweet-scented roses, grown for Aunt Ella's famous rose-water and utr, and beds of gay poppies, like tulips, for opium, and purple amaranths, and lime and orange-blossoms, and tuberoses which perfumed the warm air. And all this being settled, Wamun Bhut was asked to look for a proper day, and he fixed one; and Seeta sent out her invitations, written on red paper in her own beautiful characters, to her old friends of all castes, from Brahmins downwards, even to some Mahomedans; and as Brahmins would dress the food, all alike could eat. Everything promised well outwardly; but inwardly it was not so serene.

For the evil wind was now blowing at Shah Gunje. All had not felt it, but some had, and warmed under its influences. Ram Das's correspondents at Cawnpoor, Mirzapoor, and Benares, as well as in Calcutta, had written to him in cipher, that before the end of May, not a single Englishman, woman, or child, would be living in the land; they would all be killed by the Sepoys, and the Mussulmans, and the millions of Hindoos who would rise with them; and if he had any transactions with the English he must close them. These letters, and many others, he showed to bankers at Shah Gunje in secresy, and in return they showed theirs, and found all agree in general terms. Some even already declared that the old King of Dehly would be emperor once more; others from Cawnpoor had reported that Dhóndo Punt, Nana Sahib, would be Péshwah; but one and all had already come to a conclusion that there would be no English any longer, and that caste would be avenged.

What an opportunity it was to pay off old scores! The Commissioner Sahib had gone to Noorpoor, evidently to save his life, and to marry the Judge's sister, and take her at once to England, reports of the probability of which had been sent by the goldsmiths of the town to their friends at Shah Gunje, with the news also, that the Judge Sahib was removing his property, and they would all go together. Even if Mr. Brandon were present, who cared! He dare not interfere with caste proceedings; he had not done so before when he was at his full power, and he had given Narendra no protection. "Let Narendra be cited again before the Punchayet," cried Ram Das to a party of his caste who had been assembled to meet him; "let us refuse all social intercourse and privileges to him, because he has kept a vile defiled woman in his house, and has wilfully broken the orders of the holy priests at Benares. If you don't do this, my friends," he continued, "I will do it myself. I have no fear of the old man, nor of the Commissioner; I will proclaim you all to be polluted, and our Gooroo is prepared to do the same; we cannot bear with this indignity. And, listen, the goldsmiths at Noorpoor are ready to come forward; they know more than we do of what happened when Seeta went to the Gáo Mookh, and ate, and drank wine with the Judge Sahib and his wife and sister. They will speak to that, brothers, and tell you particulars. Fools! do Narendra and his women, sheltered by the English, think they escape the scrutiny of the caste? Ah! they must be taught better things. A man I know, a holy Jogee from Benares, told me only yesterday, that there were to be no English. Their gods had forsaken them, their country was ashamed of them, and would not help them, and they are doomed to a man."

"That is because they took the Raj of Nagpoor," observed a

Nagpoor goldsmith who had come on a visit to Shah Gunje. "Did they not loot the poor Ranees' Palace, and sell all their jewels by auction? Ah! no good will come of that, be sure."

"Have they not looted Oudh and Jhansy, and a thousand other places? let them go! Even the Mussulmans would be better," said another.

"Yes," added the eldest of the party, "and here one of them has defiled our caste and thrown dirt on it. Which of us dares to go abroad now, to have it thrown in his face that a goldsmith woman is the mistress of a cow-eating Englishman? O friends, O brothers, have you no honour, no self-respect left? I say that I have lived seventy-two years, and the like of this has never happened anywhere before. Nor can we be safe from pollution till that wanton's head is shaved at Benares, and till she becomes 'Bhugut' like her aunt, and wears a woollen garment of serge. What is she that she should escape punishment?" And then it was determined by the assembly that Narendra should be summoned for having allowed Seeta to live in his house, and to eat there; and it must be purged from her presence.

I do not think that Seeta fared much better at the hands of her old companions, the daughters of the goldsmiths who lived at Shah Gunje. Perhaps she had never been very popular with them. Her strange learning, her beauty, her innate modesty, and perhaps a degree of natural exclusiveness that led her apart from others—raised her above them; for as she grew older, her mind had expanded and was expanding, even while Huree Das was alive: while theirs had narrowed and grown duller. All these old companions were now wives, some with children about their knees, and they had resented Seeta's second marriage as, at the least, unseemly; for they esteemed themselves as high as Brahmins in this respect, who kept their husbands' honour safe, and never married again. Yet they had gone to see Seeta notwithstanding, and, as we know, stared at her after a strange manner.

One day afterwards, several of them had met together to discuss gossip, and it was now as plentiful on Seeta's account in Shah Gunje as it had been at Noorpoor.

"She is just as proud and conceited as ever," said Radha, who was always considered a beauty, and was a fine plump girl about Seeta's age, with a baby at her breast. "I don't think her good-looking now at all. Why, she does not put 'soorma' on her eyelids, nor 'missee' on her teeth; they are as white as a maid's, and she a widow and has had two husbands. Isn't it shameful affectation; and she wears a satin petticoat like a dancing girl. Ah! she is much changed; for shame! for shame!"

"And she doesn't eat pán," cried Gungee, another old companion. "I asked for a few leaves when I was with her, as my bag was empty, and she told me she had given it up, because her man did not like it; and Aunt Ella had none because she is 'Bhugut,' and I was the whole day without a leaf, hot as it was."

"And did you see," exclaimed Chimma, a third girl, "that she wears an English ring on her finger, with sparkling diamonds in it, and nothing on her toes; and she has not dyed her hands, or her feet, or her nails with méndhee, and they look so raw and ugly; and as to her skin, it is white and red now like Feringee women who drink wine; and her conceit, it is worse than ever; she looked at you all sometimes, as you were playing with her dolls, as if you were dirt in the street! I'm sure I for one, am glad that I could never learn to read, if it was to make me like her, wooden face as she is."

I durst not, perhaps, record more of this conversation, which is not edifying, and grew more and more coarse and spiteful, and not very decent, as the speakers heated with their talk; at last, Radha asked whether they were all going to Seeta's garden party, a question which was answered by a chorus of scornful and derisive laughter.

"It is well you are not," continued Radha, "because I know more than you; and it's much if we are not all out of caste already. My husband told me that—but you must all touch my neck, and my child's head, and swear not to mention what I say, or he will beat me. There, enough. Now that you have done what I asked you, listen, sisters. She, that vile harlot, went to the Gáo Mookh with the Feringees, and was obliged to be taken away in a palankeen—she had drank so much wine; and she ate with them too."

"Her head should be shaved!" cried all in chorus, interrupting the speaker.

"They are going to do that," continued Radha, with her eyes flashing; "and we girls shall yet see that fine Seeta hobbling up to the temple with a shaven head and nothing to cover her legs, and a big stick in her hand, like Aunt Ella. Now will you go to the dolls' feast? Thank Krishna, we goldsmiths can be pure. Let the rest be defiled, Brahmins and all, what care we!"

It was a lovely day; and some clouds, and a little rain that had fallen during the night, had cooled the air, now fresh and elastic. Seeta dressed herself simply in a white saree, and, as she bent down to touch her grandfather's feet, he could not help noticing her beauty and grace. "She whom the King of Goolburgah married, and became the mother of princes, was no fairer than thee, child," he said; "go and be happy with your friends," and truly Seeta expected to be so. Aunt Ella would not come with her in the palankeen. "It was 'English,'" she said, "and she was 'Bhugut;'" and she tucked up her scanty dress between her legs, took her long stick, and marched off, though the bearers protested they could carry them both.

Seeta found all her preparations for the feast in full progress. The Brahmin cooks were rushing about carrying jars of water from the garden-well, and there was a savoury steam of various good dishes and frying pancakes rising from the kitchen among the leafy trees overhead, and many guests were arriving. Brahmin women with their children, and all other good Hindoo castes, and some veiled Mahomedan women, who went into the private enclosure and removed their coverings, and with their children made themselves happy; and all the children present ran about the garden, pulled the flowers, plagued the old gardener, mounted the swings, and swang with many a happy shout, till their feet touched the branches. All the dolls, too, were set out on a carpet covered with white muslin, with small cushions for their backs, looking, as was their wont, very solemn and stolid, but admired and petted by young and old, nevertheless. Then, as the evening came on, they asked Seeta to sing to them, for she had brought her tumboora, and she sang "I could not speak with him," till some of the young girls wept at the sweet plaintive melody and words. But Seeta had nearly broke down, for she was sad at heart when she saw that not one of her old friends, or their mothers—her own caste people—had come to her feast, and what would she not have given to tell Cyril that, and hear him soothe her; but he was far away. When she reached home, she knelt down at her grandfather's feet, and clasped his knees, bursting into a flood of tears; she could not tell him what had happened—he knew it already.

"My child," he said, kindly and solemnly, "I know what grieves you; but have no fear, I am summoned to the Punchayet to-morrow, and I will not fail to set all in order. They cannot refuse the decision of the Benares Punchayet about you. So be comforted; this petty spite cannot injure you." And Seeta was solaced by his assuring manner and confidence; but still a dread remained, and Aunt Ella moped and grumbled all the evening.

In the morning, Narendra attended the Punchayet, and took Wamun Bhut with him. As he had expected, he was accused of violating the decision at Benares, in having received Seeta; but when he produced the formal declaration in her favour, many of the assembly put it to their foreheads, and acknowledged its power humbly. Ram Das, however, who had been silent, seeing the departure of several members of the guild, broke forth in a passionate appeal to all.

"When that was written," he cried, in his shrill voice, "those, who kindly wrote it, had faith in Seeta Bye, and in the purity of Narendra. They had not heard, as I have, that she had already eaten and drank with the English at the Gáo Mookh, or that she had done sorcery there to kill me. Let that pass, for I am not afraid of a wanton like her; but I am afraid of our sacred caste, and of her devilish arts of yesterday, to draw your mothers, wives, and daughters into her own evil plight, and I thank the gods I was able to send them warning. Listen to the goldsmith from Noorpoor, Nunda, whom you all know; he will tell you what happened at the Gáo Mookh." And the man named rose, and said that his wife had heard from a lady's Ayah who was present, that Seeta had eaten with the English, drank wine, and been carried away in a palankeen.

Then arose a hoarse murmur among the people, which no one could stay. "Cast her out! Kill her for her witchcraft! Shave her head! Let her be sent to wash in Gunga Mata, at Benares."

"Look!" continued Ram Das, "look at Narendra; he has nothing to say for his child! His head is bowed down with the shame that has befallen him. Let him seek his friends, the English—his relations, now! and see if they can save him! I tell you, friends, they are doomed—the Sepoys will kill them all. A cry has gone forth over the land, 'Let there be no English!' and there will be none. The gods pity us at last, and will cause the scourge of the English tyranny to pass away."

"Thou foul mouth!" cried Wamun Bhut. "Peace! they are traitors who listen to thee."

"Peace! I will have no peace," screamed the infuriated speaker, "till that harlot passes before me with her shaven head to thy temple, and the English are dead."

"Come away!" said the Brahmin to Narendra; "the bad wind of 1914 has blown upon them all, and they are mad—come away!"

Seeta had been miserable while her grandfather was absent.

What new phase of indignity he had to encounter, and for her sake, she knew not; but she dreaded the Punchayet, and above all Ram Das, the instigator and leader of the new movement. Aunt Ella, too, was dull and miserable, and had sat wringing her hands and sobbing all the morning, and much inclined, I fear, to lay blame on Seeta, as the author of the mischief. And when Seeta saw her grandfather return, leaning on his staff, supported by the Brahmin, and almost tottering as he walked, she flew to the head of the steps to meet him, and held out her arms; but the old man put his face aside, and refused them. Then he walked to his seat, and threw himself down, burying his face in his hands, and putting away hers as often as she touched him. What could have happened? At last he spoke, in a voice so hollow, so changed, that she shuddered as she listened.

"Were you at the Gáo Mookh with your husband and the Judge?" he asked.

"I was," she replied; "what of that?"

"Were you in their tents, and did you go away in a palankeen?"

"I was with the Judge's wife and sister, and they were very kind to me," she answered, her eyes filling with tears. "Yes, in the morning I went to camp in the palankeen; I always travel in that—he will not let me ride."

"Enough," said the old man, faintly; "take her away, Wamun Bhut; I would be alone."

"I will not go, grandfather," she cried, passionately, "till I hear what they have said of me. Tell me, Wamun Bhut, if he will not speak. I would rather face the danger than shrink from it. Speak!" and the Brahmin told her what had been said, and by whom.

"It is a vile lie, a blow aimed at my honour and his," she said firmly and resolutely; "but there will be justice done in the end, as will be done for Huree Das. Be comforted, grandfather," she added, kneeling and kissing his feet. "Seeta did not eat and did not drink with her friends. If you believe that, I am comforted, as you will be. Never by thought, or word, or deed, since you gave me to him, has Cyril ever hurt my caste, or ever will. Here, holding your feet, I say this before the gods and to your heart; O, do not reject your child."

For a time, a long time it seemed to the girl, the old man struggled almost convulsively with the oppression at his heart, and put her away as she clung to him weeping; but nature and his love could not be resisted, and at last he held out his arms to his child. "Wert thou polluted I would share even that with thee, Seeta; but my soul tells me thou art pure—purer than I. Let me sleep now, for I am weary, child, very weary."

Next morning came the written decree of the Punchayet that Narendra should purify his house from Seeta's presence, and that she must proceed to Benares and put on widow's clothing ere she could be received into her caste; till then she was outcast and accursed.

Nor had noon passed ere Ram Das had been arrested and confined by the native officer of the town for uttering seditious words in a public assembly, which many had heard and reported. Bail for him was offered to a large amount by his friends; but the officer was resolute and faithful, and had determined to stop the evil rumours now coming so thickly, if he could.

"Mr. Brandon must know of this," said Narendra, when the priest came; "as Seeta's name has been mentioned in the notice to me, and a sentence recorded against her, it is an insult to him as much as to me; I must write at once."

"Do not write," said Wamun Bhut; "lend me your palfrey, and I will go myself; he will take me there by the third morning. When I return, the purification of the house can be done: till then keep a good heart. I will tell Seeta what I am going to do, which will comfort her; and meanwhile, the arrest of that foul-mouthed traitor will keep the rest in check."

CHAPTER XXXII.

THE MISSION OF AZRÁEL PANDÉ.

While the events I have recorded were passing, Azráel Pandé had been busy with his evil mission, and had nearly fulfilled it. From station to station after he reached Cawnpoor, he had laboured mightily in the cause of his religion and his caste; and with exultation which he could not conceal, he saw success to be imminent. Not all the wrongs of the Afghan War, not all the refusal of extra pay, not even their lax discipline, had ever moved the Sepoys of the whole army like their present belief that caste was threatened—the caste which had defied the efforts of the grim old Mussulman emperors and their mail-clad Tartar warriors from beyond the Oxus, for hundreds of years, to break or throw down. Azráel was a man who, as he told his fellow-castemen of every regiment he visited, had but one thought, one passion of his existence—the destruction of the English in fulfilment of the holy prophecies of Sumbut.

And these feelings were intensified to agony when news of the mutiny of his beloved nephew, and his execution, and that of his cousin the jemadar, reached him at Umballa and Meerut, the one following the other at a short interval.

If he had had any feelings of compunction hitherto, he thenceforward threw them to the winds. At Umballa, at Meerut, and Dehly, he urged the Sepoys, in early April, to an immediate rising; but they were not ready yet, so he went on into the Punjab, travelling by long and weary stages; but his mind, ablaze with thirst for vengeance, rendered his body, for the time, proof against fatigue. At last, at a remote station, he broke down, but only for a while, and a fanatic Zemindar gave him an elephant on which he could travel as a holy Brahmin might do. Then he returned to Meerut after the Seventh Cavalry had mutinied, and, for the sedition he preached, was turned out of the town and station by the English authorities, he and the rabble who followed him. Thence he went to Jhansy, where he found new and good material to work on, and bid the Twelfth Regiment and the Artillery be ready for the signal when it should come, and spare none of the accursed race. Not only did he find that Hindoos were ready to act, but Mussulmans also; for the dread of loss of caste had reached them also, and with it the exciting news that the monarchy of Dehly would be re-established, when the power of the true faith would prevail over that of the hated Nazarenes and rise to its ancient splendour. Perhaps Azráel little thought of this; all he could see and pray for was the English destruction, and so, like an evil spirit of the time, he passed on, raving, and preaching his fearful mission as he went.

What tie had he now to life? Should he be apprehended by the English, and recognized, his execution by the hands of the outcast hangman was certain. So polluted, had Mungul Pandé and his cousin died at Barrackpoor. He himself had done his work; and when the insatiable "Mother" was gorged with blood, he might not fear to meet her, whether he flung himself from the beetling rock of Oonkar Mandutta, on the Nerbudda, or plunged into the meeting of the holy waters at Allahabad, or died in some battle with his foes. But there was one thing to be accomplished first—his revenge against Cyril Brandon and Seeta, which he had never foregone. When there were no English, she at least would have no protector. Her grandfather's hoards might be his, and with the girl as his slave, his revenge would be full. No tender feeling, even such as might be engendered by a wild passion, had place in his heart; he only burned to possess her; to degrade the proud, beautiful creature he had seen—who had been able as yet to escape him, and who had brought his life into peril—to the condition of a slave, and to watch her die, if she could die, of the indignity.

After Jhansy, then, Azráel Pandé passed on to Futtehpoor, and he reached the town on a day the events of which, as they concern this history, I must not fail to make mention; and leaving his elephant and attendants in the yard of a temple, he betook himself, when evening closed in, to the old place of concealment in the Nawab's garden, and put the usual signal, a small orange flag on a pole, in the tree above the well, as he had used to do, and where, sooner or later, the Nawab would not fail to see it. There were stores of flour and oil, pulse and ghee, in the apartment, with his old cooking vessels; and he surveyed these with a grim satisfaction that he was not forgotten.

Nor, indeed, was he. Nawab Dil Khan Bahadoor was beginning to understand the meaning of "no English," for rumours had come thickly to Futtehpoor. He had gone into Noorpoor, and had visited the Brigadier and Mr. Mostyn, and had ascertained that the reports of the fort having been put in order were quite true. He had found those gentlemen grim, though civil, and prepared for the worst whenever it might come. He had offered to the Brigadier to take charge of the military stores and guns in his fort, which was strong, whereas that of Noorpoor was weak; but he had said nothing about the English soldiers, except that they could encamp outside; and he had warned the Brigadier against the Sepoys, who, he knew, were only biding their time. But the Brigadier would not listen. "Noorpoor was," he said, "quite strong enough, as those would find out who might try to take it; but he was thankful for the Nawab's offer, and hoped they would remain good friends."

Then Dil Khan had called upon Mr. Mostyn and told him all he had said to the Colonel Sahib. I am sure, however, that Mr. Mostyn was as intractable as the Brigadier. The treasure was already safe in a magazine in the old fort, where English soldiers guarded it; and as to the ladies, though they could not help laughing heartily at the idea of living in the Nawab's zenana in charge of the persons they had seen, yet I am afraid the very offer of protection on his part, gave them a more vivid conviction of coming danger than they had had before. Still they were resolute and cheerful, as indeed were most others at the station.

At that time, to say the truth, the Nawab was very undecided as to what course he should pursue. If there were to be "no English," there must be some one in their place, and his neighbour, Rajah Hurpál Singh, was stronger than he. In old times his own ancestors had wrested his present estate from the ancestors of Hurpál Singh, and the feud had gone on between them, but the Nawab's father had held his own bravely. Dil Khan was, however, no soldier—only a braggart reared in a zenana, and so become sensual and indolent; very unlike his predecessors, whose swords were on their thighs, and their shields on their backs, for the greater portion of their lives. Of the two, Hurpál Singh, with his wild forest men and his own clan retainers, was now far more warlike and formidable: but so long as the Nawab should be protected by the English, he was safe.

The Nawab understood his position perfectly, and it now came to this, whether he should cast his lot with the English, or whether he should join the Rajah when the time came. In spite of the refusal of his offers by the Brigadier and the Judge, he knew both to be friendly to him, and that any attempt against him by Hurpál Singh was impossible. His own head wife, Kureem Khanum, as she was named, with the title of "Nujm-ool-Nissa," the "star of women," was thoroughly English in her opinions. She respected and loved them; she would have been true to any English ladies who might have put themselves under her husband's protection; and she it was who had urged the Nawab to go to Noorpoor and offer his services at once, when the bad wind began to blow. There was, however, another wife, named Zeenut-bee, who came of a proud and haughty Pathán family of Dehly, which had a suspicion of royal blood in it. She was on bitter terms of jealousy with the other, and when the bad wind arose, filled the Nawab's mind with ambitious thoughts of Moghul monarchy, and of the increase of his own dignity and dominions; and the result proved that the Nawab's fluctuations of opinion were adroitly taken advantage of.

On the day preceding that on which Azráel Pandé reached Futtehpoor, the arrival of a learned Moulvee from Dehly had been announced to the Nawab in the early morning, and he had gone out on horseback to the town-gate to meet him. He saw a stout, well-dressed man, riding a strong Kabool pony, and attended only by a servant, who rode another, on which were the saddle-bags, filled with clothes and other necessary matters. The Nawab was, perhaps, somewhat disappointed. His wife Zeenut had told him, as she had heard by post from her brother at Dehly, that the Moulvee who was coming was a great man, deep in the king's confidence, and was sent on an important mission to various places; among others to Futtehpoor. Thus the Nawab had expected he would travel on a royal elephant, or in a palankeen perhaps, attended by a large retinue; and the appearance of a single person, and a servant, did not satisfy the Nawab's idea of a royal ambassador. They exchanged civil salutations, however, and rode up the courts together; the Nawab's mace-bearers (the silver maces had been redeemed, as harvest dues had come in) crying out his titles as usual. As they rode into the inner court, and dismounted at the entrance to the interior, the guest, begging first that his palfrey might be well rubbed down, and get some coarse sugar, said, as they ascended the steps together, and the mace-bearers were still crying out in the court, "Ah, Nawab Sahib! such poor titles are unworthy of so exalted a personage as yourself! Perhaps what I have brought will please you better, but you must wait, good friend, a little; I have ridden all night, for three nights, and am weary. Order my saddle-bags to my apartment, let me have a bath and some rest, and I will join you in the evening."

All this was done, and the Nawab was on the tiptoe of expectation to hear what the gracious royal message might be. His wife Zeenut clapped her hands, and declared the star of his good fortune was rising at last; but Kureem Khanum was fearful, and dreaded the evil wind from Dehly, of which this person was a messenger.

Before the guest had risen, the Nawab, after his afternoon prayer, was sitting at the oriel window alone, meditating on what might be going to befal him. It was not quite dusk yet, and he thought, as he looked into his garden, that he saw a thin wreath of blue smoke rise from the well. He rubbed his eyes as his heart bounded within him, looked again, and a slight flutter of the orange pennon assured him that Azráel Pandé was there. He dare not evade the signal, and was too curious and anxious to delay; so, putting his revolver into his waistband, he went down the stairs in the rock, and making the usual signal, entered the underground apartment.

Azráel Pandé could not rise or step forward to meet him; he had drawn the sacred circle around him, and was cooking some food. There was no lamp, but the fire gave enough light, as it blazed from under the iron plate on which cake after cake of unleavened bread was being baked.

"You saw the signal, then, Nawab Sahib," said Azráel, as the Nawab, with some ceremony, asked after his health, and continued, "Look at me; am I fat? am I what I was when I left you? Look what long travel and misery have brought upon me;" and he drew up his tall figure, now lean, gaunt, and shrunken in appearance, as the glare fell on it from below; "I am well, well enough for the Mother's work that is coming; are you ready?"

"Ready!" said the Nawab; "for what?"

"Did I not once tell you there should be no English, and you did not know what I meant? Do you understand now? Has none of the wind of 1914 reached you, or are you a fool, to be deaf and blind? What have you done at Noorpoor?

"I? Nothing; what could I do, Bawa Sahib? I only——"

"Call me not 'Bawa Sahib,' Nawab; my name is Azráel Pandé. Have you forgotten me?"

"No," was the reply; "I have the two men safe still; but what should I be if the English knew of them? I suppose you can understand. When are they to be released? They are a danger and a burthen to me, and they eat——"

"When there are no English, not before," replied the ruffian. "What have I been doing? Listen," and he gave a rapid sketch of what he had done, and of the fate of his nephew. To the Nawab his eyes had appeared hollow and glassy, and his cheeks wan and withered; but as he spoke his eyes glittered and flashed, his lips were specked with foam, the hot blood rushed to his face, and swelled the veins of his forehead as he almost shrieked his cry for vengeance. "When there are no English," he continued; "when that witch and sorceress, Seeta, is brought here, to be my slave, and I can crush her beautiful neck under my feet; when this arm and hand have been wetted in the Commissioner's blood, I shall be satisfied, not before. Now, wilt thou help me?"

"What can I do," said the Nawab distractedly. "What can I do? Could my poor levies take Noorpoor? Why, they are all in the fort now, soldiers and guns, and powder and shot, and the English ladies, and the Christians, and the treasure; and the Sepoys are yet true. O Azráel! you talk like a child, not like yourself."

"If you cannot help me, I think Hurpál Singh will," said Azráel, with a sneer. "He would be glad to have his chance where there are no English. Listen; I hear Brandon is at Doodpoor. Give me a hundred men, and let me loot his camp. You can do that. I don't want you."

"I dare not," said the Nawab, "nor would the men go, I tell you, till the Sepoys at Noorpoor mutiny; not a man here will move against the English. I can't trust my people."

"Then I must go to Hurpál Singh," returned Azráel. "What I have to do must be done now, and I must be back at Meerut by the sixteenth day of May, to see the end."

"And why do you not go to Noorpoor?" asked the Nawab, with a sneer in turn.

"Because I dare not risk myself there, Nawab; every one knows me, and I have too ugly a face to be forgotten."

"Ha, ha, ha! capital!" laughed the Nawab, interrupting him; "so you are still afraid of the English? When there are none, you know, you and I will be alike. Is it not so?"

"And whom have you got in the castle, Nawab? I heard you had an arrival," said Azráel, suddenly changing the topic.

"He is a Moulvee from Dehly, and his name is Zea Oolla; that is all I know about him at present."

"Zea Oolla!" cried Azráel. "I have seen him, and he may remember me. His business and mine are pretty much the same, and I should like to hear what he has to say; I can come and listen at the door of the staircase."

"But you must not come in, my friend," said Dil Khan; "the Moulvee is a holy man, and might not like the presence of—of—one not of his own faith."

"You were going to say 'Kafir,' Nawab," muttered Azráel between his teeth; "I will be even with you when Hurpál Singh loots your palace;" and he added aloud, "I will come. Go now, for my bread is burning, and see that my elephant gets food, and my people also."

The Nawab found his guest seated at the window smoking a hookah which had been served to him, and apologized for his absence. "I always take a stroll in my garden in the cool of the evening," he said carelessly; "you shall see it to-morrow."

"Ul-humd-ul-Illa," replied the Moulvee, casting up his eyes, "that I have reached a civilized place, and have so noble and so hospitable a host as Nawab Dil Khan Bahadoor, after all my wanderings and sufferings for the faith and his Majesty the Emperor. Praise be to God and the holy Prophet, that their poor servant has found favour in their eyes, and that I am with you. Thanks, a thousand thanks, for these mercies. A goodly house, a strong castle, and many retainers to defend it against the enemies of the faith, who are as many and strong as the legions of Satan. May they burn with him in hell! An excellent cook, too; and the pilao, and kabobs, and koorma were delicious!"

"Ameen!" said the Nawab, piously, "may they burn in hell! But who are they, Moulvee Sahib? We hear of the

Russians, who are accursed Nazarenes like the English, and the Persians, who are accursed Sheeahs, and——"

"The Russians!" exclaimed the Moulvee; "who has been misleading you, my friend? Have I not travelled from Kabool, where the Refuge of the World, his Majesty, sent me on a mission? and do I not know that they and the Persians are our friends, and are coming to drive the English from our country? That was all settled long ago, and they have now beaten the English in their own country, and are coming fast."

"And will they be any better than the English?" asked the Nawab.

"Better! I should think so," was the confident reply; "for they will be our servants. These English call themselves our masters, but, thanks be to the Lord, there will soon, very soon, be none of them. In a very few days, all will have perished and gone to hell."

"Ah, is it so, really? I have heard the same from others, but as yet there is no sign of that hereabouts."

"Nor will there be till the time comes," replied the Moulvee; "and that is now very near. The Sepoys will kill them all, and we need only to look on and strike in when the time comes."

The Moulvee thought he detected a tone of considerable indecision in the Nawab's speech, and that his best chance of success lay in going at once to the point.

"Listen," he continued; "while we are alone, listen to the gracious message I bring you from the Refuge of the World, our lord the King. I have no fear to tell it to you, whose ancestors served the Throne, and won honours and rank from it. He said to me, his poor servant, not many days ago: 'Ride to Futtehpoor; take the patent of nobility I have had executed to Dil Khan Bahadoor; tell him from me to be bold and valiant as his fathers were; place on him the robe of honour I send him, and greet him as a champion of the faith. On him and his heirs for ever, as long as the sun and moon endure, do I bestow the province of Noorpoor, with all its revenues; and I raise him to the dignity of a Commander of Five Thousand, with the title;'—but no, hear me read the gracious patent I have brought here with me—and let me rejoice with you, my friend, on its purport. Behold the Imperial seal, and those of the chancellor, and all the officers of the court. In old times this would have cost a lakh of rupees, now you have it free;" and he waved out a long scroll—beautifully written on paper sprinkled with gold-dust and mounted on crimson satin—before the astonished eyes of the Nawab, who took it up, put the seal to his eyes and heart, and rising, made the tusleemát or three obeisances, as to the royal presence itself.

"Ah! then you feel the honour," said the Moulvee, "as I thought you would; now, listen to the gracious words."

They were indeed, as had been described, very gracious. With all their valour, the Nawab's ancestors had never gained such honours before, and the title of Bahadoor was all they could show of Imperial favour. Now the Nawab was created "Moomtaz-ool-Oomra," "Mooneer-ool-Moolk," "Aftab-ood-Doulah," "Nawab Mahomed Dil Khan Bahadoor, Futteh jung." How grand and sonorous was all that to hear, how grateful to his ambition! and then followed the enumeration of all details of the Noorpoor province, in Pergunnas, or counties, and their villages, according to the ancient records of Todur Mul. Not one was left out, not even Hurpál Singh's estate, which however was assigned to him, if he proved faithful. The Nawab could hardly believe it true. "Is it true, O is it true?" he cried, with his face quivering.

"Wait," said the Moulvee, who retired to his chamber for a moment, and returned, "look! if my friend is not satisfied, then I am dirt in his estimation; let me put it on now, to-morrow all shall see it in Durbar."

It was a loose garment of honour, of yellow silk with small red flowers printed on it. Dil Khan knew the Imperial colour and pattern; and as the Moulvee flung it over his shoulders, with a gaudy tinsel necklace, he took the hem of the robe and kissed it fervently; "I am not worthy of the honour," he said, "I am but a very humble slave of the Refuge of the World."

"Mobarak bád, I congratulate you, Nawab Sahib," cried Azráel in his strong deep voice. He had been sitting behind the staircase door, and looking at the scene, while he had heard the conversation with a secret joy; "receive the blessings of the poor Jogee, and may your honours and prosperity increase," and he advanced with his arms outstretched. Azráel wore nothing on his person but the scanty waist cloth of woollen serge, clothed in which he had cooked and eaten his meal, and his head was bare; his body was covered with caste marks, and a large spot of red colour was painted in the centre of his forehead. His lean, tall, gaunt figure was now fully displayed, in the light of the large cresset with many wicks, and his fierce countenance looked even more hideous and repellant than it had done to the Nawab, when he had been with him.

"La-houl-illa!" exclaimed the Moulvee, starting back in amazement, "us tagh-fur-oolla." Who art thou, son of the

Devil, to intrude here in the presence of pious Moslems? Kafir, begone!"

"If thou dost not speak civilly," said Azráel, grinding his teeth, "I will strangle thee; and fling thee out to the jackals and the vultures. Who am I? ask him there, he knows me well."

"Peace!" cried the Nawab. "O friend," he continued to the Envoy, "he is Azráel Pandé, and when hunted by the English, I shelter him."

"Azráel Pandé! Ah! I have heard of thee," said the Moulvee, edging away from the horrible figure. "If thou art the man, wert thou at Dehly once, and at Meerut a few days since?"

"I was at Meerut, and passed you on the road, on my elephant."

"Ah, I remember now, the 'mad Jogee,' as the people said, who cried, 'There will be no English! woe to the English!'"

"As I cry now, Woe to the English, woe! let them die, as they will die, speedily," cried Azráel. "But what is this mummery?" and he pulled the Nawab's robe. "Art thou a child, Dil Khan, to be caught with a bauble?"

"It is no bauble, friend," the Nawab replied, stiffly. "I am 'Moomtáz-ool-Oomra;' I know Dil Khan no longer. Look at the patent!"

"Poor vain child," said Azráel; "and what came with this sugar?" and he took up the deed. "What plaything have they sent thee?"

"Do not touch it, do not touch the robe—the gift of the king of kings!" cried the Moulvee, stretching out his hands. "Touba, Touba! for shame, it is pollution!"

"I had better strangle him, Nawab. He is too pious to live;" and taking a small thin handkerchief from his waist, Azráel began to handle it in an ominous manner.

"Let me say my prayer of faith, and I can die," said the Moulvee, calmly. He was at least no coward; and, indeed, Azráel looked as if he meant what he had said.

"Tut! let us be friends, Moulvee Sahib; only be civil, for I am a Brahmin of Brahmins," he said quickly, "and holier than thou, O mean priest! one who has seen the Refuge of the World, poor decrepid old man. Hast thou forgotten the Jogee at Dehly, who came at night, and told ye all to be ready, for the hour was nigh? Now we are here together, and two men working in the same quarrel need not insult each other. Listen; even to-day, he, your friend there, was lukewarm in the great cause; if you have gained him by these trifles, they have been well bestowed. How, Dil Khan, is it so?"

"Friends," replied the Nawab, stretching out his hands to each in succession, while the tears streamed from his eyes, "do not quarrel; bestow me as you please. Let the English die as they are doomed, and may the Emperor and the Faith flourish. Deen! Deen! If I died now, I should be happy."

We need not follow the council that ensued; but they were agreed on many points: first, that they should watch the rising of the sixteenth of May, when, as the Moulvee said, all the English at Meerut and Dehly and other stations would be dead; after that, the proclamation, which had been brought by the Moulvee, should be issued. If the garrison of Noorpoor moved, well; if not, Azráel Pandé promised he would visit the Sepoys in disguise and excite them, when the Nawab should raise his standard and assemble his five thousand. So the plans, which required much consideration, were discussed till the night was far spent, and as Azráel descended the steps down which the Nawab lighted him, he said, "I shall go on before daylight to Hurpál Singh! what I have to do cannot wait, and if I can kill Brandon, you will have one enemy the less. I leave you in good hands, and am content." Then the Nawab carried the patent and the robe of honour to Zeenut-bee and hung the bauble necklace about her neck; but he dared not visit the "Star of Women," who had been greatly troubled and grieved by the news which was now spread among the household.

CHAPTER XXXIII.

REUNITED.

BABA SAHIB, Serishtadar, was transacting business with Mr. Brandon when Wamun Bhut reached Noorpoor late on the third day after he had left Shah Gunjè, for the banker's palfrey had carried him nobly. He was hot and weary; but before seeking rest he had ridden at once to Mr. Brandon's house, delivered the message he had brought, and described the scene he had witnessed at the Punchayet. The details were unexpected by both, and vexed and annoyed them very considerably. After they had heard all, they agreed that there was only one course to pursue—to return to Shah Gunje immediately; and as a day would be required for some necessary preparations, and to send on Mr. Brandon's horses and a set of bearers to stages on the road, Wamun Bhut could take rest, and be prepared to follow with the Serishtadar, who would travel more slowly.

Before he left Noorpoor, however, Brandon was anxious to ascertain the source of the vile allegation which had been made against Seeta. The goldsmith, Nunda, was well known to Baba Sahib, as well as his wife, whom he believed to be an arrant gossip, and he undertook to sift the matter to the bottom that night and to report the result in the morning. At dinner in the evening Cyril informed the ladies that his presence at Shah Gunje was unavoidable, and he must leave them, at least for awhile, for his district work was nearly completed, and he trusted he should be able to return soon. They were much moved and grieved; for troubled as the times were, they felt in Cyril a true support, and his confident, cheerful demeanour often chased away sad forebodings, though no actual danger was yet apparent. They did not bid him good-bye, for he would be with them till the evening of the next day.

Over their cigars, however, after the ladies had retired early, for there was no music that night, Cyril told his friend what had happened, and asked his advice as to what he should do. Cyril, at the first hearing of the scandal, had been inclined to punish Ram Das severely; but, on consideration, had come to think he had better take no notice of the caste decision against Seeta, and leave Narendra to do his part as might be necessary; and Mr. Mostyn was quite of the same opinion.

"We have no power, judicially, over caste matters," he said, "except they become subjects of appeal; and, even then, any interference is of very questionable worth. It is very possible that Narendra may have transgressed its rules in admitting his granddaughter, and he will be a far better judge of what he has to do than either I or you. As to Ram Das, he is clearly indictable for seditious expressions, and it was a plucky thing of the Tehsildar and his Darogah to confine him. The only pity is that poor Seeta is mixed up with all this, and so your hands are tied; but you can afford to be magnanimous and to let him off with a nominal fine for once, and take security for his good behaviour in future. I dare say even that will not stop his vile tongue; yet there are plenty as bad as he of whom we are taking no notice, and we must bide our time. But are you right, Cyril, in going into the district alone in these fearful times? On whom can you depend if there is any outbreak here? You might be cut off, my poor fellow, before any succour could reach you, even if we were able to send any. I think you had far better send your Serishtadar to clear up things at Shah Gunje. Write to

Seeta to come in with your establishment, and yourself stay with us."

No doubt the advice was good, and given in true affection: while staying where he was would have been very pleasant. But Cyril was not satisfied. "I shall be the last man out," he said, "and, so long as I can, I will travel among the people, and keep them loyal. Were I to shut myself up here, the field would be open to any and every traitor or adventurer, who might mislead all. No, Philip, my duty is there for awhile, and must be done. You know you have all my papers, in case of anything happening to me."

"Well, I should do the same myself," he replied, "if I were in your place. But please, Cyril, take every precaution, and tell that dear little wife of yours to keep her ears open; they may hear more than yours."

"I will, Philip, be most careful, for all our sakes. What I am most uneasy about is the attitude of Hurpál Singh. If he raises the forest tribes, they can give much trouble and do much mischief. I think, however, I have some influence among my old hunting companions."

Then they separated for the night, and early next morning Baba Sahib arrived, with the wife of Nunda, the goldsmith, who hid her face in her saree, and wept plenteously. "I have found it all out," said the Serishtadar triumphantly, "and the story is an invention from first to last; but is it not strange, Mr. Brandon, that it should have originated among your own people—among the ladies here, or some of them?" he added, more carefully. Then he related what we know already, how Mrs. Smith's Ayah, a Christian woman, had beguiled the goldsmith's wife, how she had got access to Seeta and had terrified her, how the news of Cyril's approaching marriage to Miss Mostyn had been promulgated, and how, at last, the goldsmith's wife had been drawn on incautiously to speak of the possibility of another caste fracas, under the assurance from the Ayah that Seeta now ate and drank with Mr. Brandon and the Mostyns, as a matter of course. "Ask her yourself, sir," continued Baba Sahib; "she may tell you more than she has told me, if she is not frightened."

But the woman was not frightened after Cyril gave her his assurance, and enjoined her to speak the truth. She was only too glad to shift the responsibility to another. She repeated circumstantially all that she had said before, and wound up her tale by declaring that the Ayah had followed the party to the Gáo Mookh on a pony that had been hired for her in the bazaar; and that, pretending to perform ceremonies herself, she had watched what Seeta did, and how Mrs. Mostyn had kissed her and taken her to the tents. And in the evening she had prowled about them and heard singing inside, till the owner of the pony would stay no longer, and brought her back to Noorpoor.

Here was a revelation indeed, which he had not dreamed of! He now remembered to have seen a woman at the shrine of the fall by herself; but he had taken her for a villager, as she had mixed among the Brahmins and others who were worshipping there. Should he then take official notice of this, and demand that the author of the calumny should be given up? That, however, he saw would lead to many complications: he had no actual jurisdiction over the cantonment, which had a police of its own; nor was the woman acting for herself. He knew Mrs. Smith's talent for making inquiries into all sorts of subjects was in constant exercise; but why his poor Seeta should have provoked her malice, he could not divine. In future her peculiar interest in Seeta might be prevented, but the past was irremediable; and, after breakfast, when Cyril told his friend all he had discovered, he found him to be of the same opinion as himself.

"Why is it," said Philip, "that at every station we find women of that stamp, who live in the free exercise of their vile imaginations?"

"I suppose it is much the same everywhere in the world," returned Cyril, "and you may add men, too, sometimes."

"No, I won't," said Mostyn, "and if there should be any such rascal, he can be silenced; but none of us can stop such women's lies and mischief."

"I am going to try, Philip, at any rate, in this case. I can't have poor Seeta made the victim of such persons as Mrs. Smith. I shall write to her now, telling her what I know, and I shall thank her not to be meddlesome in future; I don't think she will show the note to her husband; and if she does, he will be sharp enough on her, for he is really a kind good fellow."

And Cyril did write, and Mrs. Smith did not show his note to her husband; she was now perhaps more spiteful than ever, and what she did will be related in its proper place.

Meanwhile Seeta had been in sore straits and very miserable on many accounts. Her grandfather did not believe the vile story of the events at the Gáo Mookh, and she was so far comforted; but he was now more strict in her separation from them in household matters; he gave her a different cooking place, and her water vessels were separately filled. Her clothes also, when the washerwomen brought them, were kept apart from his own, and he objected to her touching him as he sat or moved about, all of which gave Seeta deep pain and uneasiness of mind. Narendra did not dispute the caste decree for purification of the house; he would, he thought, have ordered the same in the case of another, and he was preparing for it by the time Wamun Bhut should return. He had even speculated on the possibility of sending Seeta to the priest's house, in case the Punchayet should become importunate; but the confinement of Ram Das had checked the threatening of some of the members, and he was not further molested.

Of all, however, the conduct of Aunt Ella cut Seeta to the heart most keenly. No longer was she taken to the arms of the dear old lady, and fondled like a child, as she used and loved to be, and to feel her aunt stroke down her soft wavy hair and pass it through her fingers; not once did her aunt ask her to wear this, or wear that, or did she now come into the oratory when she was singing the morning and evening liturgy, and join in it here and there as before, with her harsh gruff voice. If Seeta went near her, Aunt Ella edged away if she were sitting, or avoided contact with her if she were standing or moving about. She even gave her the rice and materials for her food, as if to an alien or one of low caste, on a platter, and not with her hands. As to the silver and copper vessels, Aunt Ella would no longer touch them at all before she had satisfied herself by passing them through the fire; but that did not suffice now, and a servant had to do it. To all appearance, Aunt Ella had given herself up to her "Bhugut" with an ascetic fervour, that to her might be vastly edifying, but which to poor Seeta was most distressing. She got up at unheard-of hours, bathed in the coldest water, performed her morning sacrifice, and then went into a corner of a dark room, and baring her head, sat like a Jogee or a grim Bairagee, telling her beads, and ejaculating "Ram" at every bead as fast as she could; sometimes she said Seeta also, that is, she said Ram, Ram, Seeta-Ram, which came glibly to her tongue; but the name seemed to trouble her, and she forsook it for the monotonous "Ram! Ram! Ram!" which, by the time she finished a thousand or so, began to sound like the croak of a bull frog. Aunt Ella was no accountant; but she knew that a certain number of reversals of her rosary made a thousand, and when she had got to the end of her beads, she turned the rosary round and went back as she had come. All day long and till late in the night, except when she was at the temple or employed in the household duties, which she could not neglect, the same "Ram! Ram!

Ram!" went on in its monotony of weary repetition; and the good woman was actually coming to believe that she could see the end of her nose, which indeed was an ascetic feat worthy of a Jogee, but which the natural stubbiness of that organ seemed to render impossible.

I must, however, do dear Aunt Ella justice. She was not so hard as she seemed to be, nor was her rigid asceticism crushing out entirely the tender humanity of her nature. The temple was the place where she had given her darling to Mr. Brandon, and blessed her; and the white tents were pitched close to it as they had been on that never-to-be-forgotten day. Now, as she looked on them, as she remembered how Seeta had come from the priest's room and fallen at Mr. Brandon's feet, her heart swelled and the tears rained from her old eyes, and her heart yearned to Seeta, wilful as she might be, but as she fondly trusted, not polluted. Of these outbursts of love, Seeta, however, never knew; and to preserve her own caste inviolate, and continue her severe religious exercises, the dull call of "Ram! Ram! Ram!" never ceased. How often, as the girl passed that dark chamber and saw the grim figure sitting in a corner, did Aunt Ella yearn for her child to come to her; and perhaps if Seeta had gone and thrown herself at the dear feet, Aunt Ella's old affection would have found vent; but Seeta was afraid. Once or twice she had unwittingly, by a word or laugh, spoilt her aunt's account, who forgot where she was on her rosary, and had been rebuked so sharply, that she had gone away to weep.

What was to be done? Shunned, avoided by her own most loved and most honoured people, as well as by her caste-folk, Seeta found no rest. Sometimes she sat dreamily in her old window, with her English books on her knees and her dictionary by her, and looked at the white tents, still standing, but, alas! now empty. Sometimes she took her grandfather's palankeen to the garden and sat reading there under the deep shade of the mango trees, now loaded with ripening fruit, watching the screaming flocks of paroquets which flew restlessly from branch to branch, or listening to the soft cooing wail of the turtle-doves, and the monotonous song of the gardener to the bullocks which drew water from the well, and to the pleasant rush of the water as it passed into the trough whence it ran over the garden. I think this was the only true respite that Seeta found then: for, once she re-entered her home, the dreary, gurgling "Ram! Ram!" fell on her ear, and the grim figure sitting in the dark room could not be passed without a silent reverence, which received no notice. O, how the girl longed for her husband's return! It could not, she knew, be much delayed, and with what joy did she again anticipate the daily change of scene and place, and his sweet, sweet company. Yet she had not yet been spoiled for home. Had her grandfather and her aunt treated her as before, she had been happy as a bird with them; but, since the visit to Benares, the growing asceticism of their lives seemed to be hardening their very hearts against her, and the dear old times to have passed away for ever.

Cyril did not delay on his journey, and Shah Gunje was reached in the appointed time. The Darogah of police had called at the banker's to say that Mr. Brandon would arrive on the following morning; and Seeta's heart bounded with joy, as she watched the camp from her window, to see the well-known English flag rise on the flagstaff and flutter from its summit in the morning breeze. Straightway she despatched Bheemee with the two dishes that she had been preparing herself since before daylight for Cyril's breakfast, and a loving little note, asking when she might come, for she had much to say.

Cyril, who had felt stiff as he dismounted from his horse, had walked about a little and gone into the temple court, and was standing on the terrace, hoping that Seeta might make him out from her window, when Aunt Ella came from behind the temple in one of her circuits, crying "Ram! Ram!" as usual. She was bareheaded, and her skull was shining in the bright sun; her garment was tucked between her legs far above her knees, and she carried a brass lota in one hand full of water and béyl leaves, and her bamboo staff in the other. She did not notice Cyril, but he felt sure the strange figure that passed him must be Aunt Ella, and as she returned he called to her, "Aunt Ella, come here and speak to me. How is Seeta?"

Poor Aunt Ella! her heart was in her mouth. What would she not have given to go to "her son," to pass her hands over him, and crack her knuckles, as she had always done before? He was soon holding out both his hands to her, and smiling in his old pleasant way. She would have given all she possessed to have put down her lota and thrown herself upon his neck and told him all her grief. Poor soul! It had been a sore, sore struggle to hide it from Seeta: but this was even worse, for her love and honour for Cyril were very great. Still the dread "Bhugut" came between them. She had forgotten her count, and how many times she had been round the temple, and all must be done over again! So, with a cold glassy stare from her great eyes, Aunt Ella passed on, and "Ram! Ram! Ram!" began again.

"Not a word about Seeta! what has come to the old lady?" Cyril said to himself. "Well, I shall see her in the evening, and hear all about them." Then, at office time, all the people gathered together as usual, and he had a busy day; and after he had dined, he was sitting outside his tent with her own chair placed for Seeta, when he saw her palankeen coming up the slope, and went to meet her. I need not tell of a happy evening; but Seeta would not enter upon the particulars of the last few days. "She would tell him of them some other time," she said, "when Wamun Bhut came; but not now. Why should they vex themselves with what had passed? Her people had been as kind as they could be," and that was all she would say. "Had she been happy?" "I am happy now, Cyril," she murmured, as she buried her face in his breast, "but I have not been happy, and O! I longed for you to return, even more than in the old time, when the 'white tents' used to go away."

On the third day afterwards, when Baba Sahib and Wamun Bhut, and the goldsmith's wife had arrived, the case of Ram Das was opened, in which Wamun Bhut was a chief witness. There was, however, no lack of other witnesses against the man; many had heard his seditious cry, "There will be no English,' and all seemed anxious to purge themselves of connection with it. Truth to say, the loyalty or seeming loyalty of Shah Gunje appeared to have increased mightily under the imputation of disloyalty which Ram Das had brought upon it; and trays of sweetmeats, almonds, raisins, and sugar-candy, with garlands of flowers, were presented to the Commissioner Sahib in unusually profuse quantities. Finally, Ram Das was found guilty, and Mr. Brandon, as it was a first offence, sentenced him to a nominal fine, adding an admonition to him and to all who were present, against believing the evil rumours of the time. But Ram Das was also sentenced to enter into recognizances to find two securities in heavy sums for future good conduct, and presence if called for; and as the man left the court to make arrangements for his bail, Cyril thought that, except Azráel Pandé's, he had never seen a face with a more hateful and malignant expression.

As to the Punchayet, Wamun Bhut was delighted to find them ashamed of their proceedings and sentence against Seeta. When the Noorpoor goldmith's wife and Wamun Bhut explained how the report about Seeta had arisen, which many had actually believed or professed to believe, they would even have withdrawn the injunction to Narendra to purify his house; but this the banker would not hear of, and as a preliminary move in the matter, the Brahmin asked Seeta whether she could stay by day at his house or in his apartments at the temple, where she could bathe and cook, and would be close to Mr. Brandon, and Aunt Ella would be with her; and, of course, Seeta had no objection to the temple or to Aunt Ella either. What a blessed change was all this to the dear old lady! I will not say that she was unchanged, for her asceticism, now growing on her, had already left indelible marks on her mind; but she was much mollified and comforted by the certainty of Seeta's innocence, the withdrawal of the sentence against her, and the recognition of her by the Brahmins of the town. True, the women of the goldsmiths' caste were obdurate as to not eating with her; but Radha and the others had gone to Seeta at the temple, taken their children, and explained why they could not come to the dolls' feast, and they had all laughed and cried over old times. At least, there was no doubt that their husbands made no objection to their coming, or that Seeta lived in the priest's apartment, humble though it was: and she could not have done that if she had eaten cow's flesh and drank wine at the Gáo Mookh.

For a time, too, the evil wind of 1914 had been stilled at Shah Gunje: but it was rising in other quarters, and Cyril hastened to meet and stop it as he had done where he was. The ceremony of purification had been performed by the banker; all appeared satisfied, and the goldsmiths' caste of Shah Gunje, men, women, and children, with all the Brahmins, had eaten at the house, while other castes and poor folks feasted in the garden. Cyril was satisfied that he could leave the good old man in peace, and he fixed the day after the ceremony for quitting Shah Gunje for the season. Every one came to bid him farewell kindly, and in many instances with demonstrations of affection which he could not refuse, and had no reason to doubt.

But it was a sad parting between the old people and their child. Aunt Ella, forgetting her invocations, sat all day in the priest's room declining food, hardly speaking, but praying in her heart for her child's protection. She could no longer doubt Mr. Brandon's love for Seeta; of that there was proof both in words and deeds, far beyond question: but she would have to share his trials, perhaps his danger, and what that might be the gods only knew. Seeta tried to cheer her; and as she lay once more on her aunt's faithful loving heart, bid her not to be afraid, for she was a faithful wife like Savitri, and for all her trials that gracious lady had been rewarded by the gods at last. In the evening, too, came Narendra to Mr. Brandon, and they talked long and earnestly as to future events: and Cyril gave him a memorandum he had drawn up in English and Hindee as to his provision for Seeta in case of evil accident to himself. Then they went to the temple to take away Seeta, for the tents, except one, had gone on to a village some miles off. Ah! it was a sad scene. The old man holding his child once more to his heart and sobbing like a woman, while dear Aunt Ella put her face to the wall and was convulsed with grief, refusing all Seeta's and Cyril's consolation. "I shall never see her again, never," was all the old lady could say, "but she is yours, sir, not ours now, yours only; they will not let us keep her." Nor did Cyril's assurance of bright days in store for them all, give her any comfort. It was too painful to be endured: and the banker at last putting Seeta into her husband's arms, said in his old firm voice, "Take her, Mr. Brandon, take her now as you did once before; we know you better than we did then, and trust her with you to death. When the evil wind has ceased to blow, and 1914 passes away, if the Lord will, we may meet happily again: till then may He protect you both. Once before you took my blessing with you, now again receive it," and he solemnly blessed them, and calling his sister to follow him, went out.

Cyril and Seeta went to the verge of the terrace and watched them as they descended the slope towards the town. Once they saw Aunt Ella sit down to rest, and even the sound of her bitter sobs came up to them in the still hot air; but her brother raised her up, and so they gradually passed away out of sight.

"Mine more than ever thou art, my lord and my life," said Seeta, as they turned towards the tent, "mine now, till I die."

CHAPTER XXXIV.

A LULL BEFORE A STORM.

After leaving Shah Gunje, Cyril Brandon had moved from place to place, wherever he thought his presence would be most useful, encouraging the timid, warning those who appeared to be growing disaffected, and striving, with all his energy of mind and body, to prevent the outbreak, which, on many accounts, appeared more imminent than before. Some of the most powerful landholders were resolute to maintain order, and willingly and cheerfully gave their aid. Others, however, were sullen and intractable, not crediting the power of the English Government, and desirous, if tumult should begin, of prosecuting those old hereditary feuds with their neighbours, which had hitherto been happily restrained. Everywhere there was abundance of alarm; but Mr. Brandon saw with satisfaction that the majority of the forest tribes were as yet faithful, and dreaded the local ascendency from which they had once suffered.

Rajah Hurpál Singh was, however, an object of alarm to all well-affected persons. He was a sullen, vindictive man; harsh and often cruel to his dependants, and with difficulty restrained at any time. Now, very many of the worst characters of the district had gathered round him; he had repaired his strong fort, and was evidently on the watch to begin offensive operations, if he should have the chance of them. He had excused himself from visiting Mr. Brandon, and wrote that the evil times rendered it impossible for him to leave his position, even for a day; but that he was watching the course of events, and should give what aid he could, if circumstances enabled him to do so. Azráel Pandé had not visited him in vain. He had heard from the Rajah his tale of long existing wrongs for which the English had given him no redress. They had not restored lands he had claimed as ancestral rights; they had prevented his wresting from Nawab Dil Khan the property his ancestors had acquired by force in the days of the Mahomedan kings, and had thus abetted the Nawab's usurpation. In the districts, too, his rights of black-mail, in levies of grain and money from villages, had been abolished; and his petitions, even to the highest English authorities on these matters, had been coldly answered and refused.

All this was good ground for receiving the evil seed; and it had come up, and was flourishing to Azráel's satisfaction, who had explained to the Rajah how, and how only, his wrongs could be righted when the hated English were dead. Though Azráel had not given up the Nawab, yet Hurpál Singh's company and associates were much more to his liking. He had no sympathy with the bigoted, intolerant, Moulvee from Dehly: he did not as yet see what course the native army would take: and for his own part desired, and preached where he could, the revival of a glorious Hindoo Empire and the destruction of all polluted unbelievers. The burly giant smoked Gánja as well as himself; and but that they would defile these pages, I might record some of their proceedings. I repeat therefore, confidently, that the evil seed was flourishing.

What could Mr. Brandon do more than he was doing? To have marched a force to Joynugger and brought the Rajah to submission, was the only measure that would prove effective:

but he had no hope of doing that; no troops from Noorpoor could move out now, for mutiny there might be imminent, and other stations, for many hundred miles around, were in the same condition: so he must wait and watch. And Baba Sahib was becoming very seriously uneasy: he heard, most likely, more than his commissioner. and could see no way out of the troubles that now appeared so threatening. Those who had wealth were burying their treasures or sending them to more powerful persons to keep. Petty landholders were repairing their forts and collecting men to man them, and the sense of security and peace that had pervaded the people only a few months before, was fast disappearing before the evil wind that blew. No persuasion, no activity, could stop the rumours which came from the East and from the North, or drive them from the minds of the most faithful: and while they dreaded, there were many—too many—that rejoiced. Baba Sahib now implored Mr. Brandon to go back to Noorpoor. "Why," he said, "should you stay out in the country exposed to daily peril, and living with your life in your hand? Who could protect you? Already among the police there have been some desertions to Hurpál's Singh's levies, and in these times none are to be depended on. What can you gain by more striving? the people must take their course; no one can check an evil which is like the cholera or the small-pox, and seizes whom it will. At least, if you will not go, let me despatch all the clerks and scribes, who are living in a state of terror, to Noorpoor. Let them take the heavy tents and records, and we can remain together to watch, if you will;" and when Cyril pressed him to go too, for he thought the old man's advice was good, Baba Sahib said, with tears in his eyes, "No, sir, my place is with you: but send your wife with the people."

Cyril told Seeta of this, but she would not listen; she resisted, even to some petulance, all that he said, and he did not press her. He felt more than ever that separation from her at such a time was impossible; and had not Mrs. Mostyn shown the same spirit when, before him, Philip had pleaded, even to tears, that she and Grace should go to the Hills! Indeed, Seeta seemed to throw herself into the excitement of the time, with a spirit and ardour her husband had little expected to see. Mrs. Mostyn and Grace had been passive, as they were obliged to be; but Seeta's blood was up. Her soul revolted at the idea of treason to the English and of danger to her Lord. Her own guards, who had known her from childhood, and who reverenced her as if she were an incarnation of divinity, were true, she felt, to the death. There were but six, to be sure, Rahtore Rajpoots, whom her grandfather had persisted in sending with his child: grey, stalwart fellows, who had guarded many a remittance of treasure by the banker, and defended them against many an attack in wild places; and with their commander Luchmun Singh, a giant in stature, watched their beloved charge day and night, sleeping about the tents, and ever ready to meet strife should it come. Seeta herself was fearless and resolute. She would not have Cyril go to Noorpoor a moment before it was absolutely necessary: and enjoyed, after a strange manner as it appeared to him, the excitement of their situation, and the wandering from place to place, making light of the constant and frightful rumours, and anonymous letters of warning which now arrived frequently. In such a mood was it at all necessary to send her away, or likely she would be content if she were absent from him? Her husband felt it was not; and I think in his heart rejoiced that he had a companion whom no danger could appal.

Their little camp was now at Doodpoor, a favourite resort of Cyril's when the season was at the hottest. The tents were pitched in a huge mango grove, where the trees had attained a size beyond that of English oaks, and their interlacing branches formed an almost impenetrable shade. The village was upon the edge of this grove, and was large enough to afford them the supplies the now reduced camp needed. The head authority of the place, who owned much of the land and farmed it himself, was Bulram Singh, partly Rajpoot and partly Gónd, a keen sportsman and constant companion of Mr. Brandon's in his hunting excursions: a man devotedly faithful and true. His village, too, was very strong, with a stout mud wall with towers at intervals all round, and a tall square castle in the centre with bastions at the corners, and outworks beyond. Doodpoor was therefore a safe place of refuge, and Bulram's clansmen sent information from all quarters.

How serene and beautiful the grove was, the giant trees reaching into the distance, with vistas of the dim blue horizon! How soothing the absolute silence, except from the busy tree birds, the occasional twitter of the little grey owls who peered from behind branches and out of holes with their bright round yellow eyes, and the chirrup of the squirrels who chased each other from place to place! How lazily the lizards crawled out and sat basking in the sun, inflating their scarlet or blue throats, and enjoying the fervid heat: and when night fell, the men of the escort and the servants would gather together round one with a hand drum and sing by turns, trolling out some ballad with a merry chorus, while the camels' bells tinkled faintly as they ate their fodder. Never perhaps before had Cyril and Seeta been more perfectly happy than in that outwardly unquiet time; never had they come to learn so much of each other, or been more united, than with imminent danger staring them in the face. There was comparatively very little to do, and the few native reports and references that Baba Sahib brought every morning, were soon dismissed. There was ample time therefore for Seeta's lessons: and she seemed to have gained so much at Shah Gunje, that Cyril marvelled at her aptness, and persisted in speaking to her in English, and correcting her when she was at fault. "I do not fear you now with Mrs. Mostyn and Grace," he said, "they will be surprised as much as I am," and truly the desire to speak with them had been one great incentive to her progress.

One evening, as they sat outside their tent enjoying the fresh breeze that had succeeded the heat of the day, Seeta, who had been some time silent, was rallied by her husband on the apparent gloom that possessed her. "What are you thinking of, little one?" he said, "no bad news has come to-day."

"Not of that," she replied, looking up, "but I was thinking—— Well, I am almost afraid to tell you: but when I was very sad at Shah Gunje, and thought they would send me away from them and discard me for ever, I met with this passage in one of the books you gave me to read, 'Come unto me, all ye that are weary and heavy laden, and I will give you rest.' They are God's words," she continued simply, "I know, and they comforted me more than the 'Bhugwut Geeta.' So I used to take the book to the garden and read it, and I used to say, 'I am weary, Lord, very weary, give me rest.' I do not know to whom I prayed, but rest came with you, and He had heard me. O! I was sorely grieved then, Cyril; you will never, never, know how sad I was, and I could not tell them. Was it wrong to pray to your God? Would He care for me?"

Cyril's heart leaped to the girl's words. Had then a dawning of true light come into her mind? How often he had prayed that such should be vouchsafed to her! Now it might be so, indeed. "My darling," he said tenderly, "God is your God as well as mine; He never turns from those who cry to Him in their need, and in humble faith."

"Yes," she returned quickly, "there is the same in the Geeta; but your book is so tender, so simple, that a child could understand it, and who but Brahmins can understand the mysteries of the Geeta. They will not even teach them to Soodras like me; and He who spoke the words which are in your book, told all to come to Him, like little children, without fear. But the Geeta does not say so. May any one go—any one like me, and pray at His feet as if they were a father's?"

"Any one," he replied; "any one who with a simple heart goes to Him asking for help, will be directed what to do. 'Fear not,' He said very often: and those who believe in Him do not fear—they love and trust. When did you think of this, Seeta?"

"I cannot say," she murmured. "When I have seen you read your book and kneel down and pray, I have longed to know what you said, and to whom you prayed, for I have often heard that the English had no religion; but that is false, for you went to your church at Noorpoor, and say prayers night and morning; and on Sundays you read to the English writers. Then as I learned more English, I used to read in your book; but I could only understand a very little till I went to Shah Gunje, and Wamun Bhut one day gave me one in Hindee which a padré had given him at Benares and he had never looked at; then I could follow the English quite well here and there, and I am never tired of reading now, though much of it makes me weep, and be angry too: but I cannot understand many portions yet. No, you must not teach me," she continued, interrupting him as he was going to speak; "I have understood much, and God will teach me more, if He will."

"Who goes there? speak, or I shall fire," cried one of the Sikh orderlies who was pacing up and down a short distance in front of the tents.

"It is I, Buldeo," replied the person addressed in a high cracked voice which Cyril and Seeta instantly recognized; "where are the Sahib and the lady? Take me to them, I come on an errand of need."

"Bring him hither," cried Cyril.

"You need not be afraid," said Buldeo to the Sikh, "I have no arms, and I will leave my staff here."

The challenge and call had now aroused the guard, and Luchmun Singh took a few men and went for a circuit round the trees, while Buldeo was led on to the tents by two others, and as he reached Cyril, who was standing with his revolver in his hand, he fell at his feet and besought him to hear what he had come to tell. "Leave me with the master," he said to the orderly, "if I am false he can shoot me; what I have to tell him no one must hear but himself."

"And must I go away, Cyril?" asked Seeta.

"No, no," cried the man, "stay! you were not afraid once, lady, nor will you fear now. Sit down, and let your slave sit, for I am weary of long travel."

"From whence?" asked Seeta.

"From Jeynugger, lady; it is more than twenty cóss (forty miles), and the road is bad; but I am here, listen. I was in Hurpál Singh's camp yesterday, and he has now about two thousand men, and more assemble every day. He gives them rations, but they are willing to wait for pay, and he will have ten thousand they say in all, and Sepoys, when they come; but never mind that, Azráel Pandé is there, and that is why I am here. I have seen him, and know what he is going to do, so I have come to warn you."

"What is it," asked Cyril, "and how come you to know? you dare not speak to him, he would murder you."

"Yes, he would murder me if he could, but he can't, for Kalee protects me. My only brother Foorsut is with him," Buldeo replied, "and I know Foorsut would strangle him for me at any moment if there were need, for he is one of the old Bhutotes of Feringea's gang, whom Sleeman Sahib wanted to catch; but I would rather see Azráel Pandé hanged by a leather-dresser, because he is a Brahmin. Listen; I have followed that man everywhere, even to Calcutta, where he stirred up the Thirty-fourth to mutiny, and his nephew Muugul was hanged by the shoemaker. Thence he travelled faster than I could, for the Sepoys gave him money; but as I followed I heard of the Jogee Brahmin who was preaching the loss of caste, and the pollution of flour and ghee, and saw the effect everywhere. Nor was he alone; there were hundreds such as he, Jogees, Bairagees, and even Mahommedan priests, preaching death to the English for pollution of caste.

"At Meerut I met Azráel again; some one had given him an elephant, and he wanted some of our old men to help him, so Foorsut and two others joined him. I went to the magistrate to give information, but he did not believe me. I had lost the certificate the Judge gave me, and I was as though I was not. Azráel was noisy and beside himself, and the English gentlemen turned him out of the town; but I knew all the Sepoys had agreed to murder the English on the fifteenth of May, and told this to the Sahib; still the magistrate would not believe me, and said they had two thousand English soldiers and did not fear ten thousand Sepoys. What more could I do? But now listen to more.

"I followed Azráel to Futtehpoor, and when the Moulvee arrived from Dehly I heard there was great rejoicing in the fort; but the Nawab would not move against Noorpoor—he dare not. So Azráel asked him to give him two hundred men to attack you and carry away the lady, but Dil Khan would not do that either; then Azráel went on to Jeynugger, and Hurpál Singh welcomed him, and gave him the command of five hundred men. The day before yesterday, at night, my brother came to me and said, 'Buldeo, the Sahib and the lady are in peril, go to them at Doodpoor, and tell them Azráel will be upon them with two hundred of his men whom he has selected. He will slay Mr. Brandon and carry off the lady, of whom he is always raving, and declaring her to be a witch. Go then at dawn and bid them depart to Noorpoor, for they cannot else be saved.' Then I asked, Why are they firing cannon from the fort and guns everywhere? and he replied, 'The English at Meerut are dead, and the Sepoys have gone to Dehly to the King. An express came to the Rajah and one to the banker at Jeynugger,' and it is true, true as I live."

"Impossible!" cried Cyril. "There were nearly two thousand soldiers at Meerut and not many more Sepoys. This news must be false. Are you sure you are not mistaken?"

"I am not mistaken. They have been looking for this news; but did not expect any for a week yet, or more. It was after Azráel heard it from Meerut and the banker, that he determined to attack you. He will have reached Bysona by noon; it is only a hamlet in the jungle, for he knows all the by-paths as well as I, and he will rest there till evening; then he will come on here and will arrive about the third watch of the night as he proposed, for he said you and the lady would be asleep. What is that?" he said, starting to his feet and listening. "I thought I heard bells. Hush! yes! they are bells, but they are on the Noorpoor road, and English news comes for you."

It was true, though neither Cyril or Seeta had heard them at first, and their jangling clash at each rapid step of the foot runners who carried them, was soon distinct, as also the lighted brands they carried. Those who were in similar positions as Cyril in India at that time, may, as they read this, remember similar events and estimate the flush of dread and apprehension that possessed them; and to how many did such messages and expresses carry tidings of murder and massacre, or warning against danger? The packet the men delivered was an express from Mr. Mostyn, and the men who had brought it flung themselves down on the grass panting. There was "emergent," both in English and Hindee, written on the packet, and a feather attached to it.

Cyril broke the seal anxiously, and read as follows:—

"Noorpoor, May 13, 9 A.M.

"MY DEAR CYRIL,

"I have only time to write a very few lines, for this must reach you as soon as possible. All the native troops at Meerut mutinied on Friday, the 10th, and went to Dehly. Many of our people were murdered by them, but the number and names are not known. I send you the 'Mofussilite Extra,' which has reached us to-day. The Sepoys here have evidently heard some news, but what it is I don't know, and they are much excited. I do not know what may happen before the day is out, but I am going to send the ladies into the fort. For God's sake come in on receipt of this. Every one is most anxious about you, and my wife and Grace are fretting for you and Seeta. COME AT ONCE; but if you find you can't get into cantonment, linger about anywhere near, and send us word where you are.

"Ever yours,
"PHIL MOSTYN."

And the "Extra" of the "Mofussilite" ran thus:—

"Agra, Monday, May 11, 1857.

"A telegraphic message from Meerut states that the troopers of the Third Cavalry have mutinied, setting fire to their own lines and several officers' bungalows: killing and wounding all European officers and soldiers they could find near their lines.

"In a station like Meerut, with the Sixth Dragoons, Sixtieth Rifles, and European artillery, it may be presumed that the mutineers had a very short race of it. Further particulars have been sent for.

"The Calcutta Government Gazette announces the disbanding of seven companies of the Thirty-fourth Native Infantry.

"Letters from Meerut state that the eighty-five troopers Third Cavalry have been tried. Those most to blame have been sentenced to ten years' imprisonment, others to five years."

Such was the announcement that passed through India of the first outbreak of the tumult and massacre that followed.

"We must go, darling," he said, "and go at once to Noorpoor. It is true that the Sepoys have mutinied at Meerut, as

Buldeo had heard at Jeynugger, and what else he has had to tell us must be true also. Mr. Mostyn writes that the Sepoys are much excited, and that we may not be able to get into the station——"

"If not, my lord," interrupted Buldeo, joining his hands, "I can take you where no one will ever find you, not even Azráel Pandé. Ah! lady, was I not true? I have not forgotten that you saved my life once and he gave it to me—and mine is of no value, so long as you and your lord are safe. Give me a pony, sir, anything to ride," he continued to Cyril, "for my feet are blistered, and I can walk no further."

It was now about ten o'clock, and they would have ample time. The small tents were at once struck and loaded, and mustering all that were in camp, Cyril and Seeta led the way into the village beyond. For some days past they had used themselves to be ready at a moment's notice, and Seeta had had a male dress made up for her, with a pair of long riding-boots of soft red leather. Cyril had tried her, and she had proved an excellent horsewoman and a bold rider; and as she now caracoled along on her spirited little mare, he felt assured that nothing could overtake them.

Their friend Bulram Singh was soon aroused; and, with Baba Sahib, came with torches to ask the reason of the sudden movement, and was told all: and while Baba Sahib went to prepare himself for the journey, Cyril awaited his return chatting with Bulram, around whom his clansmen had gathered. A striking scene it was, the torch-light flashing upon the rough strong features of the men, and glittering from sword hilt and spear, matchlock and shield. "I would not leave you, my friend," said Cyril, "but I do not like to bring Hurpál Singh upon you and your people!"

"Do not fear for me, sir," he replied, "so long as I have two hundred of my own clan to defend me. I am stronger than you, and Hurpál Singh dare not attack me, nor you, if you stay in my castle; but you are better with your own people perhaps. Who is to be your guide?"

"I," said Buldeo. "Perhaps you have forgotten me, Maharaj?"

"Ah!" said the chieftain. "No, I have not forgotten you; but take two of my men also, in case you forget the road by night. Go by —— and ——; the road is quite safe and secret. And the moon will soon rise, sir," he added to Cyril. "Do not delay, and may the gods keep you and the lady safely.—Jey Koompani Bahadoor! Brandon Sahib Bahadoor ke Jey!" he shouted to his people, who returned the invocation heartily as the party moved on.

So they travelled on through the night, avoiding every village, and by secluded paths that Cyril could hardly have conceived. When the sun grew hot next morning they rested under some wide-spreading môhwa trees, by the side of a small brook; and as the shadows lengthened they pursued their journey, not a little anxious as to what they should hear as they neared the station: but there all was quiet, the usual sentries challenged and allowed them to pass, and before midnight they had reached their home, wearied perhaps, but safe and thankful.

A messenger from Bulram Singh had followed them at daylight, bearing this note to Mr. Brandon:—

"Buldeo was quite true; they came at the third watch of the night and searched the grove for your tents, then some men came to the gate and tried to force it with an axe; but I was there, and we fired on them and killed two; there were others wounded, who were carried off. When I followed I could find no one, and the people had gone as they came.

"Be this known to you and the lady. Send me news of your welfare by my people."

So Buldeo had been right, and they had had a narrow escape.

CHAPTER XXXV.

"WHERE THOU GOEST I WILL GO."

It was a happy meeting between the friends, when Mr. Mostyn came early in the morning and called briskly to Cyril to "get up and come out and have a talk." All then is well, he thought, as he dressed himself rapidly, or Philip's voice would not be so cheery. And all was well so far; everything was quiet at the station, and as far as could be ascertained, the Sepoys and their native officers were as yet uncorrupted and faithful. "There was a good deal of excitement," Philip said, "when the Meerut post came in the day I wrote to you, but the native officers of the regiments went to their commanders and asked the truth, which was told them as much as was known; and the day after, the Brigadier assembled all and spoke kindly to them: told them they had had no temptation, and no trials from the cartridges; that they must see on reflection how false the rumours about pollutions of flour and caste must be, and how shameful it was for soldiers to mutiny and to murder officers who had been like fathers to them. 'You all know, or have heard of Colonel Figgis,' he said, 'who was truly a father to his men, and stood by the Sepoys on every occasion.' And he said what he could say, Cyril, but it is a bad business. We have not heard all, for posts are missing; but we have heard that Dehly is gone, that many of our people there have perished miserably, and the fears are, that the mutiny will spread to every station, and involve all in ruin."

"And the Europeans at Meerut did nothing?" asked Cyril.

"Nothing; when they might have nipped the rising in the bud; absolutely nothing," replied Philip, "till night, when they tried to follow the rebels, but did them no damage to speak of, and they got clear away. Yet, just think, they were three times as many as those whom Clive led at Plassey, or Munro at Buxar, when they defeated armies more than fifty times their own strength. It is very sad, but there was panic from the beginning, and no one seems to have kept his head. Wasn't it a curious fulfilment of Henry Lawrence's prophecy that the Brigadier read to us? and so near the time, too! And what news do you bring? How is Hurpál Singh?"

"As bad as he can be, Philip. Last night Azráel Pandé, who is with him, would have cut me off, to a certainty, but for a true and timely warning that I received about nine o'clock as Seeta and I were sitting outside our tent. That faithful creature, Buldeo, brought it from Jeynugger in time to put ourselves in motion, else we had perished without doubt; and I had felt so secure with Bulram Singh!"

"Ah!" said Philip, "that's just what I was fearing; but, thank God you are here, both of you."

Then Cyril told his friend all he had heard from Buldeo of Azráel Pandé's treason, and his travels from station to station early in the year; and how Buldeo had warned the authorities at Meerut, yet they would not listen, and how Azráel had been received by the Nawab and Hurpál Singh. "I think," he continued, "Hurpál will overrun all that part of the district and do much evil, but we are helpless just now. And the Nawab?"

"Ah!" said Philip, "he is just the same as he was; writing me civil letters, and pressing me to come more than ever—on account of the 'delicacy' of the times—to Futtehpoor with the ladies; but *timeo Danaos*, you know, and we are quite snug in the fort. You have no idea how comfortable the old place looks."

"And the ladies, are they there?"

"No," he replied, "though they slept there the first alarm night; but it seemed so absurd to remain when all was quiet, that they came back in the morning and have been here ever since. They will be so glad to see you at breakfast, and Seeta, too, when she can come. How is she?"

"Bravely, Philip. She rode with me all the way here on her mare; and from first to last has never blenched or caused me a moment's trouble. I look at her and marvel at her genuine calmness and trust in God. Yes, she will come to Mrs. Mostyn by-and-by, when she has slept off her weariness."

After Seeta arrived she had gone to her little oratory and found the sacred fire alight, and that the old Brahmin and his wife had kept everything pure and clean in the cottage; then she fell down before the altar and prayed her humble thanks for safety. When she first awoke she heard Cyril and Mr. Mostyn talking in the verandah; and when he had gone, she joined her husband, and they walked round the garden in the cool morning air. Nothing was changed, and though the heat had dried up the grass, there were still roses and flowers in abundance. From the water's edge they looked up at the grim old Pathán fort, where people were moving about on the ramparts and bastions, and he showed her the room he had chosen in the great tower with its oriel window looking out on the water, and told her what he had done to make it comfortable when she was at Shah Gunje. The wind was rippling the surface of the lake in little wavelets, and all looked quiet and beautiful. "And now go and get your breakfast," he said, "for you have to come to see Mrs. Mostyn and Grace afterwards; they are longing to see you."

"I think," said Mrs. Mostyn after breakfast, and after she and Grace had reiterated their thanks and congratulations upon Cyril's providential deliverance from danger—"I think I ought to go and bring Seeta. Don't you remember, Mr. Brandon, how she would hardly know me unless you put her hands into mine? I ought to go, I am sure. Will you take me?"

"It is a kind thought, Mrs. Mostyn, very kind and considerate," he answered, "and she will love you more than ever, I know. I thought she hesitated a very little when I told her I would come for her; and if I read her heart aright, I saw there just what you have proposed."

"Then we will both go, Mr. Brandon," she returned cheerily. "Just put on your straw hat, Grace, and come along. There is shade the whole way; and we shall see the pretty cottage, too."

So they went, those two bright fair women, in their pure white muslin dresses, on their kindly mission. Cyril preceded them by a few steps, and called to Seeta to come out. "You should be at your threshold to receive your visitors," he said. And at that moment the two ladies emerged from the shrubbery, and advanced towards her, holding out their hands.

Seeta had not expected this simple act of kindness, and the tears rushed to her eyes as, after her fashion, she touched their feet and passed her hands over their faces; nor could she speak; but Mrs. Mostyn was not so reticent, and kissed her heartily, as did also Grace, and all reserve was past. Then they looked over the pretty cottage, and saw the simple oratory and the sacred fire burning, and Seeta's books and English exercises, and wondered at the beautiful hand she wrote. In this respect, indeed, she had improved vastly: for one of the English scribes in camp, a young Brahmin who wrote like copper plate, had given her lessons. So when they had seen everything, they were taken to Seeta's pets, and the old black myna said his Mahomedan prayers, and coughed so naturally that the ladies laughed till they were tired. Then Mrs. Mostyn and Grace took Seeta by the hand and led her through the garden to their house.

How well Seeta remembered the night when she had well-nigh wrecked her peace as she cowered below the shrubs under the drawing-room! How different was all now! "And you must sing to me, both of you," she said as they entered the drawing-room, which, to Seeta, appeared a paradise of beauty.

"I will," said Mrs. Mostyn, "if you will speak English, not else, so you had better begin at once."

"I will try," replied Seeta timidly, and in small easy words. —"When he is not here I shall do better, and you will teach me, will you not?" she added to Grace. "You are not older than I, and yet you know so much; and I, too, want to know. You must both love Seeta and be kind to her, for she has no friends now, only you."

There had been many letters awaiting Cyril's arrival; and when Seeta went home in the afternoon she found him busy over them: but he did not look happy, and she put her arm round his neck and asked him what had troubled him.

"This first," he replied; "but it only made me angry for a moment, and it is as well you should know. Here is a man who has no business to address me on the subject, writing that he requests I will send you away and live alone. What do you say to that?"

"Ah!" she returned, "then you have caste, too, and may be put out of it like me; but I did not leave you when they told me I must. I don't think they know us, Cyril! Rose and Grace would not send me away from you!"

"No, indeed," said Cyril. "As to this man, if the bad times don't quiet him, I must find out some other way. But that is not what troubled me; it is my brother's health, which, my mother writes, is failing again."

"And she wants you to go to her, I know she does," said Seeta anxiously. "Tell me the truth, must you go, Cyril?"

"I could not now, if I would," he replied. "I could not leave my post, even if allowed to do so. But don't be anxious, my pet, there is no real illness and no alarm, and I hope by the next mail there may be better news."

"I—I would send you to them, Cyril; O, I *would* send you, indeed, if they want you. I should be quite safe here with Rose and Grace. I could not go to Shah Gunje, unless the Punchayet sent for me and bid me live with my people as before; and I should be very happy with Grace, and she would teach me, and you would write——"

"Now don't be getting impossibilities into your little silly head, Seeta, or fancying what may or may not be. Quite enough to do that when we have to act, in any case," he returned, interrupting her. "Come, we will go and have a sail."

"But you must tell me truly when you hear again," she said, pleadingly. "I would let you go to them, indeed I would. I would send you, Cyril, if there were need."

"I know you would, my darling," he said, "but it must be a great need that would take me from you, even for a day. That dear old mother of mine fancies Hylton is ill if he only sneezes or coughs; and this is one of her miserable letters; so we will wait, and hope that he may be better!"

Perhaps the ladies we know of hardly relished the return of Seeta to the station, and the obvious good place she had gained in the affections and regards of Mrs. Mostyn and Grace; but there was no use taking active measures against her now; and Mrs. Smith awaited the results of her pen, since she found even her Ayah somewhat shy of bringing information. For the goldsmith's wife and the goldsmith had little relished their long journey to Shah Gunje, or the facing of the Punchayet, or the slander against the Commissioner Sahib's wife, which was attributed to them; and the goldsmith told the Ayah, if she troubled his wife any more he would complain of her to the police; and the bangle-woman was intractable too; so the Ayah, like her mistress, had been thrown on her own resources.

If I had thought it worth while to admit them into this history, I might record Mrs. Smith's first gushing effusion to the high personage, lamenting the scandal at Noorpoor, and commenting freely on Mr. Brandon's shockingly "immoral" proceedings; and how, after Seeta's re-arrival, she had written again, declaring she was sure the same high personage would regret to hear that his excellent admonition (which she presumed had been forwarded) had been pointedly disregarded, and that the scandal was greater than ever, and she had signed herself "Vigilant." Indeed, she had sent an anonymous paragraph to the —— Independent: but this the Editor was too wary to print. The most triumphant stroke, however, she considered, was a letter to Lady Hylton, which she had sent under cover to a friend in Calcutta to be posted, "because the country posts were so untrustworthy." She had written it in March, and she expected a reply in June or July, when the whole matter of Seeta would, she had no doubt, be blown up. At present, therefore, Mrs. Smith was not openly aggressive, and occupied herself in other enquiries.

So the days passed after the old fashion; and Seeta had even come to know other ladies, who visited Mrs. Mostyn as friends. Mrs. Hill brought her fine baby to show to Mrs. Mostyn, and was kind to Seeta, with whose exceeding grace and beauty she was greatly struck, and Seeta's English was improving every day. Good old Mrs. Pratt, too, the kind chaplain's wife, after a colloquy with her husband, went to Mrs. Mostyn and asked her to send for Seeta, and Rose was glad to do so. "I was a missionary before I married Mr. Pratt, you know, my dear," said the old lady, "and have been used to talk with native ladies; so I shall put Seeta quite at her ease." And, indeed, in this respect, Mrs. Pratt had a great advantage over the others, for she had studied Hindee deeply, and was an excellent linguist. She might, the dear woman thought, be brought to a knowledge of the Truth; but she knew she must be careful.

Altogether the station was very quiet and even pleasant, though the weather was hot; but it was not to remain so long. Azráel Pandé was chafing at the inaction of the Sepoys at Noorpoor, when all elsewhere were in arms and many English had already perished, while the standard of the Royal house was flying triumphant over the palaces and towers of Dehly.

More than a fortnight had passed since Mr. Brandon and Seeta had arrived at Noorpoor; and one evening Buldeo, who had been absent for some days, returned suddenly and found them sitting outside the cottage in the garden: and the news he delivered did not fail to excite their anxiety.

"Azráel," he said, "has come back to Futtehpoor, and is angry at the delay here. Some Sepoys have visited him, and they are planning a mutiny; but my brother tells me that all here are not unanimous; and they dare not risk anything; but they have asked Azráel to come to-night and speak to the delegates from the regiments. Will you come, sir, and listen? I know the place well; it is an old temple which lies at the back of the Infantry lines not far from hence; and there is much jungle about it: a lonely place, and dreaded at night on account of ghosts and goblins; but perhaps," he added with a merry twinkle of his eye, "I know something of them, for it was one of our old places of assembly; and there is a hole in the wall where you can look through safely. There will be no danger, and if there were, why, we are enough for the cowards if you take the Rahtores."

Cyril had made up his mind while Buldeo was speaking, and as he answered, "I will go," Seeta sprung up and said, "And I too: I could not stay here, Cyril, I should die of fear, but I should have none with you. O! I will come and be beside you; let me come!"

"Yes," said Buldeo significantly, "let her come; she is no more afraid than any of us, and she must never be left alone now, or without her Rahtores."

"I don't like it, little one," Cyril said in English, "but you have no fear. What if there were trouble?"

"I should be as I am now," she replied, proudly. "I can share all with you, or I am not fit to be your wife. Let me go. I will put on my man's dress, and no one will notice me."

"When are they to assemble, Buldeo?" asked Cyril.

"At midnight, sir," he said; "but we should be there before that to make our place safe. Ah!" continued the poor fellow, "you are one of the noble blood, and have no fear. I would go to death with you. You will not be able to see, but you can hear."

The place Buldeo had mentioned was perfectly well known to Cyril. An old ruined Boodhist temple which had now no worshippers. It was hardly half a mile distant, in a solitary waste spot behind some gardens. He had often sketched the place, and knew the ground near it perfectly. About ten o'clock Buldeo came in and found both equipped and ready. Cyril had a brace of revolvers in his girdle, which he had carefully reloaded, and a stout heavy stick in his hand, which he preferred to a sword. Seeta was standing by him in her simple boy's dress, with her face muffled, and carried her own toy revolver in her girdle. The six Rahtores and the Sikh orderlies were also ready; and Buldeo carried a short heavy spear, his old weapon. Then, after a few words of caution from Cyril, they moved on, led by the old Dacoit, warily and swiftly.

When they were close to the temple, whose black ruined mass stood out against the sky, Buldeo motioned them to sit down silently, and went himself to reconnoitre. "No one has come yet," he said as he returned, "but we must take our places;" and he led them on through a wilderness of custard apple bushes and other thick shrubs up to the court wall, there high and entire, except a large hole through which the interior could be seen perfectly: and they all took their seats and waited. The cover was perfect; it was quite impossible they could be seen, and the hot night wind which moaned through some large tamarind trees above deadened every other sound.

Presently they saw one or two dark figures arrive by the front entrance and sit down silently on the steps of the temple, and gradually the space became filled. No one spoke; it seemed as if an assembly of the dead had gathered there, so still and ghostlike were all who came in one by one and took a place. Midnight was striking from the gongs in the lines, when there appeared some stir among the people, and three dark figures advanced from the entrance: of these two sat down on the steps and one remained standing, though the gloom of the night and the trees above prevented his figure being seen at all distinctly.

"Are you all here?" said the man in a low deep voice, which Cyril and Seeta well remembered.

"We are here," some replied; "sit down and speak!" And the figure sat down.

I need not, I think, repeat Azráel's former address, which my readers have, perhaps, still in their memory. There was nothing new in his now passionate appeal against loss of caste, against existing wrongs, or against the tyranny and cupidity of the English; but as the speaker warmed with his subject, he dilated bitterly on the murders, at Calcutta, of his cousin and nephew, martyrs to the cause, and he urged their revenge, for which the men of Meerut and Dehly had already done their part and would do more.

"On the palace of Dehly," he continued, "now flies the standard of the King, and thousands of our people have joined it already, while the coward English hide themselves like women.

There were two thousand white soldiers at Meerut—were our people afraid? And when they marched out of the station with their drums beating and colours flying, did any one dare to follow them? Why are ye laggards, my sons? Why do ye put up with loss of caste and loss of honour? Have ye no shame left? If ye leave them to fight for the faith, will they receive you when there are no English? Ah! it will then be too late to cry, Hai! Hai! would we had struck in! Do you think that they, our brothers, would have thrown aside rank, pay, pensions, and honours, without they had cause? They would be but dirt, I think, in comparison with caste and faith; and so in their wisdom and valour they thought too, and decided that the English should perish. Now, while there is time, you can join them with your honour saved. Rise as one man; let not one white man or woman escape: give the harlot who lives with the Commissioner to me, to be sent to Benares and shaved, and humbled. Will ye bear even with that humiliation and scandal which to every true Hindoo in the country around us is degradation? Listen! I have come from Rajah Hurpál Singh, who has already twenty thousand good soldiers; from the Nawab Dil Khan, who has ten thousand and many guns. When you have destroyed all here, come to them and be welcomed by me!"

"Let us go now," cried a young Sepoy, raising his tall figure among the crowd. "Let us begin at once. Why delay?"

"Not yet, my son," said Azráel. "Not yet; be not mad like Mungul Pandé: wait for my signal, and be ready, all of ye. I shall not delay many days now. Let the English remain unsuspicious. Do your duty and attend your parades, but be ready. Keep your money about your persons, and when the time comes, rise, burn the station, and slay! There are no English soldiers to prevent you; none to fear. Those there are have hidden their faces in the fort, and dare not come out. And if they did, do you fear them? If you do, you are cowards and leather-dressers, and I, Azráel Pandé, will proclaim your infamy through every regiment, and through every village of Oudh and Bahar; and they, your brothers now, will blow you away from their guns. Have you heard me?"

"We have heard," was the response.

"And you will be ready?"

"We will be ready. We are ready now!"

"Enough," said the speaker; "I trust in you. And now bid me depart, for I have far to go ere morning. Remember my words and wait, wait patiently, praying to Kalee Mata. Let none of you, not even the brave fellow that spoke to me, err as my poor Mungul Pandé did from over-zeal. Ah! yes, you will avenge his death, and give English blood, for his blood, to the Mother."

"We will! we will! Fear not and go!" was their low hoarse cry. Then the speaker rose and was surrounded by an excited crowd, some sobbing, others weeping like children as they touched his breast and feet.

Cyril Brandon could no longer restrain himself. He had several times tried to distinguish the figure of Azráel Pandé as he sat on the step of the temple, but he could not, and the gloom was so profound, that in the mass before him no individual could be recognized. Now as the traitor rose, and his tall figure stood for a moment against the sky, Cyril could not be mistaken, and covering him with his pistol, fired; while, as confusion arose, he discharged other barrels in succession among the crowd. He saw three men drop, for Seeta had fired also, and raised a shout in English: "Come on, men, come on! let not one escape!" and the crowd, without turning, rushed forward pell-mell into the darkness beyond. At the same moment, Luchmun Singh and the Rahtores with Buldeo, ran round the wall to the entrance; and meeting the fugitives, began to lay about them indiscriminately with their heavy swords, shouting their war-cry of "Hurree Ból!" with "Jey Koompani Bahadoor!" which rang out high above the whistling of the hot wind and the rustling of the trees above.

None attempted to resist but one man, who, after slightly wounding a Rahtore, was instantly speared by Buldeo: the rest disappeared as they fled into the darkness. Where they had gone the party neither knew nor cared, and in a few moments they were alone.

"We must not delay, master," said Buldeo, who was laughing heartily; "and who shall say our 'Duróra' was not a good one? But I will just see who are dead. I should be sorry to find Azráel, for I wanted him for the shoemaker."

Cyril followed him and looked at three men lying inside the court, of whom one was breathing and asked faintly for water. Outside were four others, of whom none could speak, and some wounded had got away. Azráel Pandé had again escaped.

"Come away!" cried Buldeo; "we have done enough for one night. Come quickly; and we must run, Mr. Brandon, lest they should rally and follow us. Let the dead lie there till the morning, and we shall know who they are. Take care of the lady, sir, or shall we carry her?"

"I think she can run as fast as any of us," replied Mr.

Brandon smiling; "but we both, and all of us English, owe you much for your fidelity and courage, more than we can ever repay."

"No money, no money, sir," cried the man, bursting into tears; "only put both your hands on my head, that is enough for a slave like me;" and Cyril and Seeta did so. "Now run."

"My darling," said Cyril to Seeta as they slackened their speed—round whose waist his arm had rested while Azráel Pandé was speaking—"and you never trembled once. O brave heart! I shall be indeed proud of you when I tell to your friends what has happened."

"No! I did not fear him," she said, looking up in his face; "but I do fear the rebels for you, my lord, and for them, my darlings."

"You need not fear now," he said; "we know what the Sepoys may do, and will be prepared. Let us go to the Judge's if they are still up; perhaps they have been looking for us." And they now stepped on again with speed. When they reached home the gongs in the lines were striking one.

"The Judge Sahib and the ladies have been so alarmed about you, sir," said Kasim, the butler, "and we could not tell them where you had gone. It is only a moment since Mr. Mostyn was here."

"Then we will go to them as we are," said Cyril. And in a few moments he had tapped at the drawing-room window, and cried out, "Philip, we are here, all safe. Let us in."

Mrs. Mostyn and Grace were sitting at the table as her husband admitted Cyril and Seeta. The ladies had evidently been crying, for their eyes were red and swollen.

"Thank God, you are safe, both of you!" cried all in a breath; "and Seeta, too, with you. O my darling! you should not so expose yourself," continued Mrs. Mostyn. "But how well she looks in her boy's dress, Mr. Brandon. Where have you been? There were shots heard, and the servants came running in, crying the Sepoys had broken out; and we were so alarmed for you, for no one knew where you had gone."

"I was with my lord," said Seeta meekly; "he will tell you all. We women of India are used to rougher scenes than you; and if he had died, I should not have returned." And the ladies, who could not speak, covered her with kisses.

"If there is a cup of tea to be had, let me have one," said Cyril to Mrs. Mostyn; "it will loose my tongue, which at present is dried up. As to Seeta, she is never thirsty. I do believe she enjoyed what we did!"

Indeed, the girl's cheeks were glowing, and her eyes sparkling with excitement. She had never looked more lovely. "Tell them all," she said. And then Cyril related what they had seen and heard, till the hot night was far advanced.

CHAPTER XXXVI.

"PREPARATION."

As the morning broke, there was necessarily much excitement at Noorpoor. The whole station was full of rumour and anxiety. The Sepoys of the regiments collected on their parade grounds in groups, but were without arms; enquiring from their officers what had taken place in the night, as several men had been found with severe sabre-cuts, lying near the lines, who had been carried to the hospital, but refused to tell what had happened to them. Many, no doubt, knew well enough, for the assembly which heard Azráel Pandé's address contained both Sepoys and non-commissioned officers: and there was much speculation among the loyal, whether there had not been a fight among the Sepoys themselves. For the present, however, the groups dispersed quietly; but with the conviction that whatever had occurred, would eventually transpire.

Very early too, Mr. Noble, to whom the police had reported the fact of a conflict having taken place at the ruined temple in the night, took a body of them, and proceeded to the spot. A few people had collected there, and among them some Sepoys in undress; but the dead had not been disturbed, and were easily recognized. Inside the broken wall were three, killed by gun-shots; outside four, with fearful sabre-cuts and spear-wounds. Three were Sepoys, whose names were given by those present; and one of the dead was a noble young fellow of the Grenadier Company of the —— Regiment, by name Isree Tewáree. "Ah!" said one of the Sepoys, "he was always threatening, and saying he would kill the English, but he used to smoke so much 'Gánja' that we thought him mad. He has only got what he deserved." There were also two of the district police without uniform, one Mahomedan scribe in the Commissioner's department, on whose body a number of Persian letters were found, with "Akhbars" of the Nawab's proceedings; and there was a man whom no one knew, armed whom sword and shield, who was pronounced to be one of the Noble retainers, or a villager from without. Mr. Noble assembled an inquest on the spot, which recorded a verdict, "That the seven persons deceased had come to their death by violence, the cause of which was unknown." Mr. Noble then went to the homes of the policemen and the scribe, and searched them for papers; and in the latter was found a goodly bundle of the Nawab's letters and Akhbars, and drafts of communications to him, the latter proving, when afterwards read, of a very treasonable character. The writer of them had, however, gone to his account.

With all these documents, and what little information he had picked up, Mr. Noble came to Mr. Brandon and made his report, hearing in his turn what I have already recorded. Then Baba Sahib arrived, and heard the same; and another Persian scribe was sent for to examine the news writer's papers, and a sad disclosure of treachery and falsehood they proved to be. The draft of the celebrated letter about Seeta, too, was there, much interlined and altered, as if the writer had taken special pains with its composition, which indeed he had.

Soon after, Mr. Mostyn walked in from his garden to take his early tea, and the party was joined by the Brigadier and Captain Hill, who had been to the temple to see the dead: so all the chief authorities of the place were assembled to discuss the events of the night. Of course Mr. Noble grumbled good-humouredly at not having been allowed the chance Cyril had had; and more especially as he was in charge of the civil duty at the station: but Mr. Brandon satisfied him by saying, as was only the truth, "that he had had no time to make arrangements, and that if the police had been employed, most likely no discovery of the latent treason would have been made." As an emergent case, therefore, he had managed it after his own fashion.

"And right well, too," said the Brigadier; "I never heard of a thing of the kind better done. But you are an old hand now, Brandon, after your adventure at Shah Gunje. And that ruffian escaped you again, after all?"

"He did," said Cyril, "as far as I know; but if ever I covered anything dead in my life it was his head; and he was not much more than ten paces from me, I think. Perhaps the people with him carried him away; but we shall hear of him, I dare say. I shall write to the Nawab to give him up to justice, but I have not the slightest idea that he will be sent in."

"Nor have I," remarked the Brigadier; "and there is

nothing I should like better than to march the brigade to Futtehpoor, and ask for him; but in the present doubtful condition of the Sepoys, I dare not trust the men."

"Have you, then, had any greater suspicions than usual?" asked Mr. Mostyn.

"I have, and I have not, Judge," he replied; "I have no fault to find with the men hitherto; but yesterday we heard some unpleasant reports of nightly meetings, though neither I nor the commanding officers could trace them. One thing, however, I am determined upon, Brandon, as I have said all along: to run no risk. I shall move all the Europeans into the fort this evening, for there is only a sergeant's guard there at present; and I shall not bring them out again till all this storm of mutiny is over, and I think you had better send all the treasure you have in also. I have some already; but much of your revenue has come in lately, I know, and you must have a good deal more now. Think what a temptation it must be for the Sepoys, if they are untrue, with only themselves to guard it!"

"Certainly," said Cyril. "Baba Sahib will see to it directly."

"And the Colonel Sahib can perhaps send the European soldiers to take it away as they go to the fort," added the Serishtadar; "it can go in the tumbrils."

"Not a bad idea, Baba Sahib; and Captain Hill will come and see it all done," said the Brigadier to him. "And now, gentlemen," he continued, "shall we take up the affair of last night? I must have courts of inquiry upon the dead and wounded men; but the rest, as the temple is out of the cantonment boundary, remains with the civil power. Your evidence, Brandon, will, however, be wanted. Will you come to the mess-house at eleven o'clock? I shall be there myself." And Cyril said he would go with pleasure.

"As to the ladies," continued the Brigadier, "I cannot take upon myself to speak: but if we are all prepared, as we shall be, and a patrol of officers goes round the station every night, I think they need not fear, and I know how disagreeable it would be for them to leave their comfortable houses in this weather. But I shall make known to all, that whoever may come shall receive the quarters that have already been allotted. I don't wish, indeed, that any may have to go into them, but it is as well to leave the point open."

So it was all settled: and Captain Hill rode with a company of English soldiers in the evening to the treasury, where the bags of rupees were loaded upon tumbrils, and carried off, leaving only enough for daily use. It was in vain that the native officer and Sepoys of the treasury guard protested that their honour was at stake in the removal. Captain Hill could only say it was the Commissioner Sahib's order, and must be obeyed, and at sunset the English bugles rang out cheerily from the high cavalier of the old Pathân fort.

Several ladies followed the English detachment; among them Mrs. Smith and Mrs. Jones, but by far the majority remained at their houses. They were not yet afraid, and pretty Lucy Home was becoming quite a heroine. As to the Mostyns and Cyril Brandon, their houses were quite close to the fort, and were covered by its guns, and the road to the postern on the lake passed the end of their gardens; they could escape easily, therefore, at any time, in case there should be alarm in the lines or the town, and they remained as they were.

It was really surprising to see what had been done in the fort by the Brigadier and the officers. Some of the old guns which had lain on the ramparts and bastions since the last Mahratta struggle, were cleaned and examined, and found worthy of carriages. The parapets and loopholed curtains of the fort were repaired; the rough road up to the gate levelled; the ditch and the interior cleansed out, and the counterscarp mended. Every building was nicely whitewashed, and new earthen floors laid down. In short, the interior, which could have accommodated a thousand men, looked, as it really was, secure and comfortable.

The fort had been built on a natural elevation, which sloped steeply towards the lake. On each side was a broad dry ditch, with a counterscarp and short glacis, beyond which the natural ground had been scarped to a height of from ten to twenty feet. There was a fausse-braie all round, which at the entrance gate was double, with large bastions and traverses, and a double dry ditch. The whole formed a height, especially where the citadel stood, which overlooked everything for miles around, and the air was therefore cooler and fresher than in the cantonments, and the men liked it extremely. A church even had been arranged in one of the large empty palaces, and a hospital also; so all was complete.

As to Cyril and Seeta, if they pleased they could go to the postern, or water-gate, in their boat, or they could walk; and once there, a path led to the tower which Cyril had selected as the most private. Close to it were a series of chambers formed by arches in the curtain, and these Cyril had had partly closed up. One was made into a new oratory, one into a kitchen, one into a bath-room, and in another the old Brahmin and his wife, who had refused to leave Seeta, were to take up their abode. A store of flour and other provisions was laid in, and some simple articles of furniture were put into the octagon pavilion room—a low camp bed, two or three easy and other chairs, a table, and some bookshelves—and when arranged and Cyril's pictures hung up, the place looked really pretty.

As has been said, it was an octagon, corsesponding with the shape of the bastion. In front, the centre division had a small oriel window and balcony, and on each side were two open niches, into which rough window panes and glass had been fitted. The style of the room was Pathán Gothic, very elegantly conceived, for the groins and mouldings of the arches were led up into the centre of the ceiling, where they met in a carved top or crown, and the ceiling was in the same curve as the pointed arches. From the windows the view was really lovely. At foot, the lake, bounded by its dam at the further end, nearly a mile distant. On one side the native city, and several ghâts, or bathing-places, with flights of steps which entered the water, and were constantly occupied by bathers and water-carriers. Opposite to it were some English bungalows and their pretty gardens; the Brigadier's occupying the highest point, where the flagstaff stood, and the red ensign of England fluttered and waved against the far blue distance. From the roof of the tower, on which was a gun, the Sepoy lines and parade ground could be seen, as well as much of the distant rolling country; but the mass of the citadel, of which the tower formed an outwork, obstructed the view in other directions. For himself, Cyril had contrived a kitchen and bath-room out of similar arches to Seeta's; but the mass of the bastion lay between them, and they did not interfere with each other. It may be supposed, therefore, that these quarters were both secluded and comfortable, and Seeta and her husband often visited them, speculating whether they would ever be needed, and looking out on the gorgeous sunset when the glory of the evening clouds was reflected in the lake, and the distance was filled with glowing golden haze.

And they were very happy; Grace and Seeta had become fast friends, and Seeta could now speak with her on ordinary matters with apparent fluency, which seemed daily increasing. Grace often heard Seeta her English lessons, and made her read; and the evening music was always a delicious treat to her, especially when Captain Hobson came, and their voices blended in the fine trios and quartetts of well-known Italian operas. "Guai, se te sfugge un moto," from "Lucrezia Borgia," was almost her especial favourite, when the rich bass of Captain Hobson, and Cyril's fine tenor, mingled with the plaintive wail of Grace Mostyn; and indeed there were many others. Very often, too, good Mrs. Pratt came and sat with them, cheering all by her resignation, and truly pious trust in God's great mercy, and engaging Seeta sometimes, though not often, in religious discussion, for she felt how deeply the girl venerated the words of Him, which even children can understand and believe. But, nevertheless, she found Seeta so strong in her own conviction of the purity of the old Hindoo Vedic belief, in which Wamun Bhut had instructed her, and so opposed in her faith to the practice of popular or ordinary Hindoo idolatry, that the good lady well knew it would be no easy task to sap the foundation of Seeta's religious citadel, or to break up her metaphysical convictions: and, very advisedly, she did not press the subject. "There is good seed sown, my dear," she said to Grace, one day, "and it must germinate and grow: and I shall be much mistaken if it does not. I am no match for her in metaphysics."

In ordinary matters of business at Noorpoor there was no change. The Judge attended his court, and Cyril Brandon his Kucherry. The Sepoys were steady, duties went on as usual, and the excitement of the affair at the temple had apparently passed away. If there had been, or were still, treasonable characters at work, they were more reticent and careful than they had been. There was only an occasional post, or letter, from the scene of tumult at Dehly; but the news that came was in all respects most fearful, and by the end of May there was no longer doubt that the treason was as widespread, as it was for the time becoming successful.

Mr. Brandon had written civilly, but strongly to the Nawab, in regard to the immediate delivery of Azráel Pandé, a convicted felon, against whom sentence of death was recorded, who had escaped, and assisted to stir up the army to mutiny, and whom he himself had heard deliver an exciting and treasonable address at the temple near the station. He was warned that his own character was in the last degree suspicious, and that if he persevered in it his eventual ruin must follow.

The Nawab did not immediately reply to this letter. He sent a profusely complimentary message by his Moonshee, to the effect that he was devoted to the English, and that his own life depended upon their favour and protection, and that he would write as soon as possible. The fact was, that his counsellor the Moulvee was absent on a mission from the Nawab to Hurpal Singh, the object of which was to induce the Rajah to forget old grievances, and unite with him in the common cause against the English: and when the Moulvee returned, not at all well pleased at his reception by the burly Rajah, the Nawab showed him the letter he had received, and asked his advice. "We must temporize, my friend," said the Moulvee; "we are not ready to act, and the Sepoys at Noorpoor are not with us yet. I will draft a reply which will satisfy the Feringee for the present;" and he wrote as follows, in Persian, which I translate:—

"To the exalted in rank, the illustrious in station, the kind to his friends, the just of the world, the refuge of the poor, Cyril Brandon, Sahib Bahadoor, Commissioner of Noorpoor, salutation and the peace of the Almighty!

"Praise be to the Lord, and thanks a thousand, that my lord has condescended to write to his humble friend a kind, monitory letter.

"The forefathers of this suppliant were men of war, and faithfully served the Koompani Bahadoor in many wars and troubled times: therefore this suppliant, who is no warrior, and desires peace and good-will, enjoys what they gained, and is grateful. Hitherto, his face has shone with the brilliancy of truth: and please the Lord, it will not now be blackened by the malevolence of evil speakers and slanderers.

"Your friend observes with sorrow, that he is accused of sheltering Azráel Pandé, the Dacoit, and devilish misleader of men: and that his sincerity is also doubted. Well, so it is the lot of many virtuous in life to be misunderstood, and this suppliant cannot avoid his fate; he is helpless before its decree!

> "The decrees of the All-wise are wonderful and mysterious.
> By whom can they be resisted? True suffering is silent.

"Certain it is, that some days after the disturbance at the temple, your suppliant heard that a Jogee had been killed by a gun-shot, and that he was carried away and burned directly; so there is no trace of him. If he should have been Azráel Pandé, your friend will rejoice that that evil man is dead.

"What more can I write? May the Lord keep you in safety, and may your honour and prosperity increase daily for a hundred years?"

"There, I think that will do for the hog," said the Moulvee. "It will throw him off the scent; and may his grave be defiled by dogs when he dies."

"Ul-humd-ul-Illa!" cried the Nawab, "it is a wonderful and learned letter: by all means let it go;" and it was written by the Moonshee on gilt paper, and duly transmitted by a horseman.

"I wonder if Azráel Pandé *is* dead," asked Philip Mostyn, as the friends read the letter between them, for the Judge was the better Persian scholar of the two; "you covered him, you said, when you fired at him."

"No more dead than I am," said Cyril, "or Buldeo would have found out. Perhaps he is wounded, however; but my spy has been gone some days, and until he returns we shall not know. I think I hit him, Philip. I think I did, and hard, too."

CHAPTER XXXVII.

SCOTCHED, BUT NOT KILLED.

In a small obscure village of the Nawab's estate, named Ryna, Azráel Pandé, wounded terribly in the face, was, as it seemed, nigh unto death. His gaunt figure was stretched on a rude pallet, and a coarse dirty sheet, stained with black patches of dried blood, was thrown over him, through which the hard outlines of his naked body could be traced. The place he lay in was the only room of a small house belonging to a retainer of the Nawab's, who had been one of Azráel's gang in former times, and to whom the Dacoit leader had been sent, for concealment and security, on his arrival from the scene at the temple. Cyril Brandon had not been mistaken in his supposition that he had covered Azráel with his pistol, when he fired: for the ball had struck him in the right jaw, shattering it, and fearfully mutilating his cheek; a few inches lower, indeed, and the ruffian would have been laid dead with the others we know of: but he had escaped. Supported by some of the Nawab's retainers, who had accompanied him, they had avoided the attack of the Rahtores, and hastily placing the wounded man in a rough black blanket, which one of them carried, had borne him off rapidly in the direction of Futtehpoor. What to do with him when they arrived there, they knew not, for his former place of concealment was unknown to them; but one of the men went privily to the Nawab, who at once decided that it would be impossible to receive him, and forthwith despatched him to the village where he now was, and directed his servant, for so he supposed Foorsut to be, to follow.

Azráel Pandé had arrived in miserable plight indeed; and it was wonderful how he had survived the journey. As a Brahmin, he could not take water from the people who carried him; here and there a village Brahmin was found, who held water to his lips, but the wound had swelled fearfully, and at his shocking appearance several of those who had endeavoured to help him fled, when the handkerchief that had been thrown over it was removed. He had, however, reached the village alive, and Foorsut had summoned the local barber to dress the wound; but he, too, had refused on looking at it, declaring the man must die. Towards afternoon, a Mahomedan surgeon, in the Nawab's employ, arrived, who extracted the ball, or what remained of it, removed some pieces of bone and teeth, and bound up the wound, feeling assured that when inflammation set in the man must die; and as he reported this to the Nawab, on his return, I think it would have better pleased that nobleman if the worthy doctor had brought news that his patient was dead.

But Azráel lived. His spare, muscular frame, his abstemious habits of food, and his grim tenacity of life, had so far preserved him; but he was in sore plight indeed, and in agony from the pain of the wound, which even his iron endurance could not bear. In the outset he had been insensible. Soon after he had been taken up he had fainted from the shock of the wound and loss of blood, and throughout the day he was only aware that he continued to be carried onwards, though whither he knew not, and could not ask. At Futtehpoor he had revived a little, and had made gestures to be deposited there; but the Nawab's orders were positive, new bearers and a new escort had been provided, and thus he went on from village to village—helpless, and only occasionally conscious.

Some days had elapsed, and the barber, taking courage and assisted by a friend from the next village, had opened the bandages, and had cleansed the wound and applied simples to it with good effect. Still their patient was often delirious, and raved till it was fearful to listen to him; and once he had torn off all the dressings, when the bleeding had burst out again, and they thought he must die, but death did not terminate his sufferings.

After some days' search, Buldoo, who had gone round all the old places of concealment in hope of finding his brother, but in vain, discovered him at last in the village where Azárel lay, and heard, not without surprise, of his condition. "He is quite insensible," said Foorsut; "now and then he opens his eyes, and a Brahmin woman comes and feeds him like a child; yet he can speak sometimes, though I am frightened at night at what he says, and when the devils that he calls come about him he screams, and is convulsed, till I can hardly hold him. Come and watch with me to-night, and you will see."

"He would know me," said Buldeo.

"If he did, he could not hurt you,' replied his brother, "and he is too mad to know anybody but me; all he wants is 'Gánja,' 'Gánja,' perpetually, and somehow or other he contrives to smoke, but it is as if a dead man held the hookah, and I get frightened by myself."

"Well, I am not frightened of him, brother," returned Buldeo, "and you and I have seen too many dead folk in our time to be terrified by a live man who looks like one of them. Yes, I will come. But are there none of our old people near?"

"No," said Foorsut. "Bussunt, in whose house he lies, has gone to Futtehpoor for to-day; his women departed at once to another village, and, except for the Brahmins who come, I am alone. Do not fail me for once."

Buldeo did not fail his brother; and, at night fell, he entered the room and sat down in a dark corner. In a niche of the wall, near the head of the pallet, a small lamp with two wicks was burning, and a brass cruse of oil stood by it; the light therefore fell from one side upon Azráel's face, which was terrible to see. The bandages about his jaw and cheek were blood-stained and dirty, and where the wound was, the side of his face seemed to have fallen in. The heavy, rugged, grey eyebrows hung over eyes that were deep sunk in their sockets, causing the high cheek-bone of the left side, and the aquiline nose, to be more prominent than before. His colour was a deep ashy grey—livid and ghastly. The bony throat and grizzled chest were bare, and one long sinewy arm was thrown across it over the sheet, with the wasted hand clutching the other in the paroxysms of pain when his features were convulsed.

They watched long, but Azráel did not speak. Occasionally a muttering sound escaped his lips, and deep moans, when he was in pain; but he was apparently asleep, or at least unconscious, and Buldeo watched him with an intense fascination, which he could not repress.

"It would be good to strangle him," he whispered coolly to his brother; "we could take his head to Mr. Brandon!"

"I have often thought of that," returned Foorsut, "but I have no certificate from the Judge like you; and if the English didn't hang me, they would send me over the black water, or make a weaver of me at Jubbulpoor. No, if he does live, it is his fate. And there is another thing, too: he has been reading the 'Gurúra Poorán,' and performing those Shaktee ceremonies, the most secret and terrible, which it almost kills one to think of. So he belongs to 'Kalee Mata' now, and we dare not touch him. She will take him when she chooses; and that is why he has lived. Any one else must have died, but he won't die this time."

"Yes, that quite alters the matter, brother, so we must wait the 'Mother's' pleasure," said Buldeo, resignedly. "But look! Is he waking?"

Foorsut rose and went to the door, looking up to the sky, which was heavy with electric clouds. "Yes, he will wake soon now," he said; "it is near midnight, and Azráel is growing restless and convulsed. Don't be frightened if he sits up. But help me if he is violent."

Almost as he spoke the frightful figure arose in the bed to a sitting posture, and opened its great eyes with a glassy, vacant stare, looking around slowly. They evidently saw nothing; but the lips were moving rapidly, and the features were working with passion or with pain. Azráel appeared as if in some hideous dream, and for some moments he did not speak. Suddenly the features seemed to relax, and the hard staring eyes to fill with tears, while the lids closed over them, and the gaunt, sinewy arms were stretched out. "Seeta! Seeta!" he murmured. Buldeo could hear the name perfectly. "Seeta! Seeta! O beloved, come to me! O beloved, give me thy love, as thou hast mine! O lotos feet; I hear the sound of thy softly tinkling anklets! O lithe and swaying form advancing with dainty steps, I would embrace thee! O sweet Chumpa blossom, thy luscious perfume reaches me! I live, I drink it in! Seeta, I die! Come, touch me and this agony will cease. Seeta, listen; a Brahmin calls thee. Come! come! . . . No heaven of Indra's is more blissful to the nymphs than mine will be for thee!"

"Ah, witch, sorceress!" he now shrieked, "polluted as thou art, come to me! Seeta, dost thou not hear? Whither wouldst thou fly? Harlot! I will defile thee! I will crush thee! Thou shalt be my slave; and thy paramour Brandon shall not save thee from Azráel Pandé!

"Seeta, come, I will forget all. Ha! wilt thou fly from me? Nay, then I will pursue thee. Stay! . . ."

"Now seize him, brother," said Foorsut, "and hold him

down. Once he got out to run after 'Seeta,' and had wellnigh strangled me. He is always worst when he dreams of her."

Buldeo had heard the raving, and shuddered as he heard it. Then this ruffian loved his young mistress, for whom he would die; and she must be protected. Only from dread of Kalee, Azráel Pandé had been strangled that night. Now Buldeo flew to his brother's aid, and between them they held down the struggling convulsed figure. Presently it was still; and Azráel woke and said, "Foorsut!"

"There is your hookah, Maharaj," was the reply. "Take a few pulls at it, and you will sleep again; the Gánja will do you good."

While Buldeo supported him, Azráel inhaled the fierce intoxication of the hemp leaves in rapid whiffs, swallowing the smoke, or passing it through his nose. At last he dropped the hookah and fell back on his bed, snoring heavily.

"Now the devils will soon come to him, brother," said Foorsut. "Don't be frightened; they never do me any harm, but they plague him, I think, asking for blood. This is what happens every night and mostly all day; and those who have to watch for me run out frightened. Listen! it is beginning; that's how he calls them."

"Om! Om! Om!
Praise to thee,
O Bhugwati!
Divine Chamanda,
Dwelling among graves.
Bearing a skull,
Borne on a car,
Drawn by Spirits,
O Kala-rátri!
Mother of black night;
Large-mouthed,
Many-armed,
Sounding thy bell,
Sounding thy drum,
Loudly gnashing
Thy bloody teeth;
Clothed in skins,
And thy body
Full of blood.
Lapping it,
Lapping it,
With thy tongue.
Praise to thee,
Divine Kalee,
O praise to thee!"

He seemed to pause for awhile, and was much convulsed;

but the incantation, for so it seemed to be, was resumed in the same low muttering sound as before.

"O thou that delightest
In flesh and blood,
Be propitious!
Be propitious!
Quickly accomplish
Our desires.
Enter here.
Enter, enter!
Tread, tread!
Dance, dance!
Why delayest
Thou to enter!
By thy necklace of beads,
Dripping blood,
By thy necklace of skulls
And its serpent brood,
Enter, enter!
Tear, tear!
Slay, slay!
O victory to thee,
Mother of life!
Hrrám! Hrrám! Hrrám!
Pierce, pierce,
With thy trident
Reeking with blood!
Kill, kill,
With thy thunder!
Strike, strike,
With thine axe! . . ."*

Then the words became indistinct and blurred, and seemed to mingle strangely with the low muttering of distant thunder in the sky. For the night had been hot and still; sheet-lightning was playing among the clouds, and now and again flashed with a blue glare into the room.

"I don't like him," said Buldeo; "he is a devil, and was never a man. I have heard him say all that before when he used to be at his worship. That 'Hrrám! Hrrám! Hrrám!' it is terrible. 'Hrrám! Hrrám! Hrrám!' it rings in my ears as if it were the tramp of a legion of devils with iron feet. Ugh! I have a mind, brother, to go out and leave thee. The thunder and the rain are better than that fearful 'Hrrám! Hrrám! Hrrám!'"

"By our mother's head, do not leave me," implored Foorsut, joining his hands. "Leave me not till this is past! To-morrow Bussunt will be back, and I don't care then. Listen! he is speaking again. I will give him what he wants;" and he held

* From Sir W. Jones's translation of the "Gurúra Poorán."

the Gánja pipe to Azráel's lips, and after a few rapid inhalations his voice seemed to come clear and full, though the words were sometimes indistinct. A scene from the drama of "Málati and Máhdáva" had come to his dreams, which, when they could follow it, ran thus. "He speaks for Kalee Mata," said Foorsut, shivering with fear. "Listen, she is here!"

> "Upon my flight,
> Horrific honours wait. The hollow skulls
> That low descending on my neck depend,
> Emit fierce music, as they clash together,
> Or strike the trembling plates that gird my loins.
> Loose stream on every side my woven locks
> In lengthening braids. Upon my ponderous staff
> The string of bells light waving to and fro,
> Jangles incessantly. My banner floats
> Upborne upon the swelling breeze, whose tone
> Is deepened by the echoes it awakes
> Amidst the caverns of each fleshless skull,
> That hangs in dread array about my person."

Then there was a pause of stillest silence, save for the low muttering of the thunder without, and the heavy pattering of large raindrops.

After awhile the scene was resumed:—

> "Now wake the terrors of the place, beset
> With crowding and malignant fiends; the flames
> From funeral pyres scarce lend their sullen light,
> Clogged with their fleshly prey, to dissipate
> The fearful gloom that hems them round. Pale ghosts
> Sport with foul goblins; and their dissonant mirth,
> In shrill respondent shrieks, is echoed round.
> Demons of ill, and disembodied spirits
> Who haunt this spot, I bring you flesh! . . .
> Strange forms like foxes flit along the sky . . .
> And now I see the goblin host." *

"Mother! Mother!" he shrieked, with his arms outstretched and quivering, and his eyes staring into vacancy. "Thou art present! I see thee! I worship thee. I adore thee! Listen to thy slave. Take them; kill, slay thine enemies; drink, drink their blood—the blood of the English. Ah! it is sweet for thee, Mother divine. Spare not one. Let them die, women, and children at the breast! Azráel sends them, hundreds—ay, thousands, to thee—as he swore he would. And, O Mother! slay, slay. Be drunk with blood! let it redden Gunga Mata's white breast, and thou wilt rejoice! Take the witch, plunge

* From H. H. Wilson's translation.

her into hell! Seeta! O Seeta!" he cried more fiercely, "would I could kill thee for the Mother. Seeta! O Seeta!" he continued, resuming the old tender voice, "if thou wouldst love me and come to me, thou shouldst live a queen!" Then his hands dropped, and he threw himself back exhausted.

"He will be quiet now, and shall have no more Gánja," said Foorsut. "Yet stay; he has risen again and is pointing at you. He sees you; go!"

"False-hearted villain and traitor," cried Azráel, "hast thou come to mock me?"

But Buldeo heard no more. He slunk out of the room and crouched outside beside the door. Then he heard his brother protesting that it was a dream, and that Buldeo was far away with the English. And Azráel spoke no more. He had sunk into his old lethargy, from which even the rising storm, the fierce blaze of incessant lightning, and the crashes of thunder, did not arouse him.

CHAPTER XXXVIII.

AN OMINOUS VISIT.

WHILE the rain was yet falling heavily, for the monsoon had almost commenced, and the dawning light of morning enabled him to see the path, Buldeo left his brother, and made the best of his way to Noorpoor. "Azráel will be more savage than ever, when he recovers," he thought; "and we must watch him more narrowly; but it would be well, I think, if Mr. Brandon tried to capture him as he is, and that they hanged him at once; that would prevent mischief." And full of this scheme Buldeo hastened on, and on his arrival at Noorpoor presented himself to that gentleman after his usual fashion, and accounted for his absence by relating what he had seen, and the fearful night he had passed with the raving man.

"'Hrrám! Hrrám! Hrrám!' I shall never forget the shouts and the screams of that devil when the other devils came to him," said Buldeo; "we didn't see them, but Foorsut said they often came; and when the lightning played about the room, and there was a smell of sulphur in the air, I could have sworn they were present; and the 'Hrrám! Hrrám! Hrrám!' went on, till I ran outside. And then, sir," he continued in a whisper, "he raved of the lady, and that was worse. I would have strangled him then, but that he is a votary of the Devee

Mother's, and such we dare not touch; but you can, you must hang him! Come yourself, with some horsemen, to-morrow night, we can easily surround the little village, and carry him off lying in his bed, as he is. There are plenty of people there to carry it."

There was nothing Cyril Brandon would have liked better than the adventure, but he had promised in the next affair, whatever it might prove to be, to employ his assistant, Mr. Noble, and was loth to deprive him of a chance of distinguishing himself, even in so apparently trifling a service as the apprehension of a fugitive Dacoit. But in reality the importance of the capture of Azráel Pandé had become more and more pressing. The effect of his treason upon the Sepoys at Noorpoor might cause them to rise at any moment; and though the force of English soldiers in the fort assured protection to all Christians, yet any rising was to be deprecated, as well for the loss it would cause, as for the bad effect it would produce in the country around. Cyril had also thorough dependence upon Mr. Noble's intelligence and activity, and felt assured he would do all that was possible.

Mr. Noble was delighted at the enterprise; and on hearing of it, Captain Hobson had volunteered, if he could be permitted by the Brigadier, to accompany Mr. Noble and the police with a party of his own troopers; and the Brigadier having no objection to aid the civil power, all those concerned prepared without delay for a night march to the village of Ryna, not more than twenty-four miles distant. Buldeo was provided with a stout active pony, and was told by Mr. Mostyn that he need be under no apprehension about his brother, to whom, in consideration of his fidelity and valuable services as a spy, a certificate had been granted temporarily, which he would have confirmed by the highest authorities at a future time; and Buldeo, putting the precious document to his eyes and breast, deposited it in a safe fold of his turban. Then the gentlemen concerned dined at Mr. Mostyn's, and discussed the probable issue of the adventure till it was time to leave. And the detachment of cavalry and some picked horsemen, under their native officers, having drawn up in the road opposite to the Judge's house, all took their leave, with earnest wishes for their success—which indeed appeared inevitable—from their friends, including the ladies.

"I think we shall get him this time, little one," said Cyril to his wife, joyfully, as he returned home. "Lying wounded as he is, and with Buldeo to guide them, they cannot fail to succeed; and I hope they may, for Azráel has escaped me twice, and one might almost believe that he bears a charmed life!"

"I do not know," she replied, sadly; "my soul is ever heavy when I think of that man, and the evil he is permitted to do; and he has powerful friends now."

"They cannot protect him in this case," replied Cyril, decidedly, "and he is too weak to escape; we here shall know the day after to-morrow. So cheer up, my darling! and do not fear one who would have done you evil once, if he could, but is now helpless."

"And from whom you saved me, Cyril. Ah, that once! may it be for ever!" she said, turning away her eyes, which were full of tears at the vivid recollection of Azráel's attack at Shah Gunje. "I almost wish you had gone, and that I were with you."

"What! in the mud and the rain? No, Seeta, you are better here; and Mr. Noble and the Captain can do as much as I."

But for all their hopes, the expedition returned baffled and disappointed on the third evening; and, mud-bespattered as they were the officers told their adventures.

"We went on during the night, which was clear and cool," said Mr. Noble, "admirably guided by Buldeo, who led the way on his pony. He was never at fault for a moment, and avoided every village we came near, striking across fields and waste lands, and again finding the road in a marvellously expert manner; and we reached Ryna just before daylight. Then Hobson surrounded the place, which is little more than a hamlet, and I dismounted and went with two or three men, led by Buldeo, to the house where, no doubt, Azráel Pandé had been, but we found it empty. There was the bed on which he had been lying, and a sheet stained with blood, and some dirty foul bandages scattered about—ample proof of what had been there—but Azráel was gone. Then we searched every house, every corn-stack, every conceivable place where he might be concealed, but to no purpose, for half the day. The people of the village were at first alarmed, and had bolted into the fields; but they soon returned, and told us that the day before yesterday a party of strange men, who appeared to be Dacoits, had come with a litter, and carried away the wounded Brahmin in the evening. None of them were known, and where they had gone, except to the eastward, none could tell; it was no business of the villagers, and no one had followed them. Then Hobson and I took some of his men, after they had eaten, and beat up several villages. Here and there the people were civil enough, and sometimes surly too; but no one knew of the litter or the Dacoits—if they were Dacoits—who came; and we returned—done! I am very sorry," he added; "but really we did all we could do, and all I can say is, 'better luck next time.' I have got the sheet and the bandages, filthy and offensive as they are, and Buldeo swears to them. I paid for all our supplies, and brought away the receipts."

There is nothing more provoking and misleading, perhaps, in any police experience, than the absolute, calm, impenetrable stolidity of Indian villagers, when they desire to conceal a fugitive or crime of any kind. In a purely native state, perhaps, half a dozen of the chief men would have been laid on their backs in the blazing sun, each with a heavy stone upon his chest, or some ground chilies, mixed with ashes, would have been put in a bag and tied over their mouths; as, indeed, some of the horsemen had suggested might be done at Ryna, when the tokens of Azráel's presence had been shown to them. But Mr. Noble and Captain Hobson could resort to no such rough practical devices; and thus they did not hear, what they might otherwise have extorted—that, during the day following Buldeo's visit, an empty palankeen of the Nawab's, well escorted by twenty mounted men, and attended by the Mussulman doctor, had arrived; that Azráel Pandé, after the bearers had rested, had been carefully put into it; that the village had furnished a pony for Foorsut, and all had gone off in the afternoon to Futtehpoor, where they had arrived safely, and the wounded man had been placed in the underground room, and was now assiduously and indeed skilfully attended.

"Well, we can't help ourselves this time," said Cyril. "I don't believe in the Dacoits myself, and I think we shall find out that the Nawab has taken his friend into good keeping. And how did you find the country?"

"As we went," replied Captain Hobson, "we knew little about it; but as we came back, matters looked queer. Every village had shut its gates, and we could see armed men on the walls and bastions. At one place, a crowd on a hill had a flag, and beat drums violently, and blew horns. Then a body of the Nawab's horse, about fifty men, with a large number of matchlock men—two or three hundred, perhaps—with flags and drums, had taken up a position and fired shots into the air. I think if we had been weaker they would soon have attacked us; but as I edged towards them they moved away, and at last the whole took to their heels and bolted. My men and the police were mad to get at them; and, indeed, if they had fired at us, I should have made very short work of them."

"I think my friend the Nawab Sahib is running up a long bill," said Mr. Noble, laughing; "perhaps he will send you a cartel of war, some of these days!"

"I wish to goodness he would, Brandon," said Captain Hobson; "I am sure it would be far better for all our native troops to be doing something, than to be for ever brooding over the reports that come. I should like to have that rascally Nawab brought to his senses, and Hurpál Singh too, before they do mischief."

"I am afraid there is hardly a *casus belli* yet, Hobson, against either. Azráel's case falls short of one; and we can't prove, whatever I may suspect, that he is now at Futtehpoor," said Mr. Brandon. "But if there is to be a declaration of war, I shall not be sorry."

There was no declaration of war, certainly; but the Nawab, next day, sent an aggrieved letter, in his usual style, which I need not repeat. He complained that a party of cavalry had gone, without his permission, to his village of Ryna, done violence to the villagers, extorted a considerable sum of money, and taken and carried off large quantities of grain and forage, on pretence of searching for Azráel Pandé. They had invaded the privacy of families, and insulted the women, and deprived them of honour.

"God forbid that I should think, my friend," continued the letter, "that justice will not be rendered for these insults, and restoration made of the property which has been carried off; but I must state explicitly, that my honour—the honour of a nobleman, which has never been impugned—suffers from your unfounded suspicions in regard to the Dacoit, Azráel Pandé; and that any repetition of this suspicion, or any search of my villages without my authority, will cause a diminution of my friendship, and unpleasant results to you in my complaint to high authorities. You are a young man, and inexperienced, and in this I find an excuse for your conduct."

"Whew!" whistled the Judge, when he had read the letter, "this is not the declaration of war which Hobson wanted, but it is uncommonly like gross impudence. You are quite justified in what you did, Cyril, under the Dacoity Act, sec. 18, of 1843."

This remark, and much other conversation, which I need not record, occurred when Cyril had visited the Judge's house on his way to Kucherry, but he had yet to learn the more offensive form in which the Nawab exhibited his present disposition to insult.

The Nawab had occasion to despatch one of his favourite Mámas, or confidential women-servants of his zenana, to Noorpoor on a particular errand, but her chief mission was to Seeta herself. The Máma had delivered the letter to Mr. Brandon early, and left word with the attendants at his house that she should call again for the reply, should there be any, as she returned; and when Mr. Brandon had gone to his work, and she had ascertained that he would not return till the afternoon, she had gone to the house and asked to be allowed to wait in the garden till the answer should come. Seeta, to whom the message was brought, thinking no evil of the woman, allowed her to come: and saw the Máma, a tall, portly dame, well dressed, and, like others of her class, with no pretensions to seclusion, walk about the garden, holding a small silver hookah in her hand, smoking as she walked, and talking in a loud voice to another woman-attendant with her, when the gardener very civilly offered her a bouquet of flowers. As the sun was hot, Seeta good-naturedly went to the door of her cottage as she passed, and asked her to come in and rest herself.

"That I will, my beauty," said the dame; "you live here secluded; but every one has heard the fame of your charms, and I see now that they are not exaggerated. You do not remember me; but I was once sent by the Nawab Sahib to buy pearls from your grandfather at Shah Gunje. You were then a widow, and had a child. Is he here?"

"No," replied Seeta, "he is dead." She did not now like the woman's appearance at all, nor the free manner in which she had been accosted. Máma Jumeela was not an agreeable person to look at. She was tall and fat—unwieldly indeed. Her features were coarse and bold; the flesh of her cheeks and double chin hung in folds to her short neck, and on each cheek were moles, from which long bristly hairs extended, and on her upper lip was almost a strong moustache. The thick lips and teeth were blackened by the use of missee and pán, and her eyes were painted with antimony after a fashion which increased their bold, licentious appearance in a most disagreeable manner. For the rest, the Máma Sahiba wore a profusion of rich gold ornaments on her neck and her arms, and her heavy earrings had pulled down the lobes of her ears till they rested upon her huge round shoulders. Her dress was a vivid scarlet petticoat, made very full, of rich heavy mushroo, or Indian satin, and a bodice of striped yellow silk, over which was a short shirt of transparent muslin, buttoned at the throat, and falling over the band of the petticoat. Above all she wore a "doputta," or scarf, of thin Benares muslin, of a brilliant light green, covered with flowers of silver tissue, and with ends and border of gold thread brocade. This was somewhat frayed, perhaps, but still remained gorgeous. All day had the dame displayed her magnificence through the bazaar at Noorpoor, sitting cross-legged in her palankeen, with the doors wide open, smoking her silver hookah, which was filled from time to time by her attendant, and receiving the salutations of all beholders. This splendour was, however, lost upon Seeta, who, with her slight, graceful figure, and her simple dress of pure white muslin, afforded as great a contrast to the Máma Sahiba as can well be imagined.

The woman seated herself on the low divan with a heavy flop and grunt, and looked round her with much contempt, feeling the cover of the seat as if to estimate its value.

"Nothing but cheap, coarse chintz," she remarked, with a sneer. "It should be satin, for a dainty one like thee to lie on. And the place is poor and mean, after all. Touba! fie! They told me he kept you in a palace. Ul-humd-ul-Illa, the Feringees have no palaces, only the Nawabs. And what is inside there?" she continued, rising from her seat.

"You cannot go in there—it is private," said Seeta, rising also, and standing resolutely before the door of the inner bedroom.

"Private!" returned the woman, with a scornful toss of her head. "Private! It is a new thing to hear that goldsmiths' women are private, or Feringee women either! Touba! No, my pretty bird, thou shouldst be in a better cage than this—private and honoured, with jewels to wear, and fine clothes like mine, and money to spend, and a score of women to wait on thee! And," she whispered, with a horrid leer in her flashing eyes, "a Nawab to love thee, one who burns at the mention of thy name. Ah, what wouldst thou not be with him, my dove? Has he not sent thee this?" and she drew a necklace of fine pearls from her bosom.

Seeta's soft eyes now dilated and flashed defiance, and she pushed the woman's face from her with all her force. She almost gasped for breath, and could not cry out.

"Ah, that's the way with all of you, at first," said the woman, in a wheedling tone, "but you will come right in time. Take it, my darling, my heart; take what a kind lover sent you, and by-and-by he will send an army for you, which shall be the retinue of their queen."

Seeta broke away from the woman and rushed to the door, calling for help; and several of her Rahtores and the servants came running to the spot.

"Take her away! take her away!" cried the girl, pointing to the Máma. "If Mr. Brandon comes, he will kill her. Take her away!"

"What's the matter, Seeta?" said Cyril, anxiously, as he suddenly stepped from behind the shrubbery which led to the Judge's garden. "I heard your voice ever so far off, and I ran on. Who has frightened my pet?"

"Look! she is there, Cyril," said Seeta, trembling, and pointing to the woman, who was now advancing. "I cannot tell you what she said, but O, the insult and the shame of it!" and she burst into tears.

Cyril knew the woman by sight as well as by reputation. He had seen her in attendance at the tents when the Nawab gave his last party; and he immediately suspected, from Seeta's agitation, what had happened.

"Come out!" he cried, "come out! You are a woman, else I had beaten thee. What dost thou here? Who sent thee?"

"The Nawab Sahib sent me, whose slave you and all Feringees are or will be soon," replied the woman, defiantly. "'Beat me!' he will beat thee with his shoes when he comes with his army to take her away. Would she stay with a cowardly Englishman, a Kafir, when she might be mistress of Futtehpoor? Never mind, my pretty one! Fear not, my dove, what he says to you. His days are numbered now, and thou shalt be free. I, Máma Jumeela, will come for thee, I——"

But Seeta had turned and fled into her oratory, where she lay prostrate before the altar, sobbing as if her heart would break. "O that I had not been born, that he should be insulted for me!"

"Begone, devil!" cried Cyril, from between his set teeth, and lifting his hand. "No, I will not strike thee nor touch thee. But listen. If ever thou art seen in Noorpoor again, the police will take thee, and I will have thy head shaved, thy face blackened, and send thee on an ass to thy master. Begone, lest evil happen to thee!"

"Ha! ha! ha!" laughed the dame. "I am not afraid, Brandon Sahib. If you live you may shave my head; but you will die, like the Feringees at Jhansy, and be sent to burn in hell. Salaam, Sahib; your slave departs!" and Máma Jumeela stalked away to her palankeen.

"My lord, my lord," said the Rahtores and servants and Chuprassies who had assembled, "only let us blacken Máma Jumeela's face, that she may show herself to the Nawab."

"Let her go. Do not touch her. I order you not to meddle

with her. Her own shame goes with her; but if she comes again," Mr. Brandon continued, "I will do as I said. Let her depart," and he turned in to seek Seeta.

Máma Jumeela did not, however, get away as easily as she thought. The servants pelted her palankeen with mud, and followed her till a crowd of urchins took up the sport, and hunted her to the place where her escort had remained without the bounds of the station, hooting and abusing her in the rich free style common to Indian gamins.

Máma Jumeela was furious, for her grand new satin petticoat was splashed with mud. As she tore her hair, she cried that her honour was gone—she would walk barefoot to Futtehpoor—she would have the life-blood of Mr. Brandon—and his wife should become a slave. And her ravings became unfit to record as she took dust from the road and threw it upon her head. But she was finally coaxed into entering the palankeen, and was carried on to Futtehpoor, to tell her own version of the tale to willing ears. "A thin, pale-faced chit, after all, like a Feringee, not worth the trouble I took for you," she said to the Nawab. "If you will have one, why not take Missy Mostyn, or both, if you like, when their men are killed, like them at Jhansy?"

"Ah, yes," echoed the Nawab, "like them at Jhansy, and that will be soon now, Jumeela, very soon. I will give thee Brandon to spit upon; will that soothe thee? But thou shouldst not have gone to his house."

"Before he dies—before he dies. Dil Khan! Remember thou hast promised," cried the woman, "while there is life in him to see me."

Cyril found it no easy task to soothe Seeta. She had been grieved before, but never insulted, and her high spirit had thoroughly revolted at the indignity put on her husband. "You don't know how much it means," she said to him; "how deep, how flagrant the insult is, my darling; but we are helpless at present to avenge it."

"Let it pass, Seeta," he replied. "The Nawab is a fool, and we don't know whether that horrible woman was ordered to come to you or not. Do not mention what she said to you to Rose and Grace; it would only distress them, but you can say that the woman was insolent and threatening, and I turned her out."

Yet it was a hard blow; and it was not till she had gone to Grace, and tears relieved her, that Seeta was herself again.

Jhansy! That dreadful women had discharged a parting

shot, which rankled in Cyril's mind. What could have happened there? He had heard nothing of late of that place. No one had mentioned it; no one had had letters, that he knew of, from Jhansy. But he had work to do, and he sat at the table in Seeta's drawing-room, as he called it, drafting official reports, while Seeta was with Grace, when an attendant announced that Baba Sahib was in the bungalow, wishing to speak with him, and he went there.

"I hear distressing news from Jhansy, sir," said the old man, evidently much affected. "The Twelfth, the Cavalry, and Artillery all mutinied on the 4th and joined the Rance, and every Christian, except two or three who escaped, were put to death on the 7th or 8th. Not one survives; not one man, woman, or child! I would strongly advise you and Mr. Mostyn to go to the fort with the ladies to-night."

"But are you certain about this? It is very terrible," said Cyril.

"There is no doubt at all of the event," replied Baba Sahib. "Malchund, the banker, who has an agency there, read the letter he had received by express, and others have the same news. Every one has heard it by this time, even the Sepoys. The Nawab's salute the day before yesterday, was for news of the 'victory' at Jhansy, which he, too, received by express. No, sir, there is no doubt whatever of the news," continued the old man, wiping his eyes. "None; and it is said that one poor gentleman shot his wife and then himself, rather than surrender."

And who that was in India at the time, has forgotten the thrill of horror with which a letter that gave an account of the scene was read all over India, or could restrain his tears at the narrative of the sufferings of those who escaped from Nougong? The first letter was, long afterwards, proved to be false; but the miseries endured in the flight from Nougong were not exaggerated.

"And Nougong is gone, too," continued Baba Sahib; "but the English officers got away, escorted by some of their men. May God keep them safely!"

"God help them, indeed! We all pray for them, Baba Sahib. But till there is a movement here we will not stir. We must do our duty at all risks."

And so around them the trouble thickened, for the evil storm of 1914 was raging fearfully everywhere.

CHAPTER XXXIX.

PEACEFUL DAYS INTERRUPTED.

It was strange, notwithstanding the news of mutiny and massacre everywhere around, that the native troops at Noorpoor remained as yet steady. Those who need to do so, can learn the events of the month of June, 1857, from the several histories and narratives that have already been written, and there are few, perhaps, of the readers of these pages that have not already borne them in mind. The fiercest portion of the fanatical storm of Sumbut, 1914, broke in that month on every station in the wide valley of the Ganges and Jumna; and in most of them, precious English blood had been shed in pitiless massacre. I need not call to remembrance the noble and patient, though unavailing, defence of the entrenchments at Cawnpoor, and the inhuman slaughter of those who surrendered, when defence was no longer possible; nor that of other captives there which followed, under, if possible, still more miserable and terrible circumstances, and when their rescue, under Havelock's heroic exertions, was apparently close at hand. I need not record events at Lucknow, where a few devoted men were defending themselves against tens of thousands of infuriated Sepoys and people of Oudh, with a devotion and valour which has rarely been equalled, and never surpassed. Nor how, at Dehly, that fierce strife had commenced which was to continue yet for months, while the fate of British dominion seemed to be suspended, and while, though Sepoys, regiment after regiment, in the Punjab had mutinied, one strong, resolute mind rallied loyal Sikhs about him, and despatched men, money, and munitions of war to the scene of strife. These events, and the succours of English regiments, many of whom were now fighting their way to the upper provinces in the fierce heat and pouring rain, belong to the domain of history, not to this tale, and will be read with untiring wonder and interest for generations to come.

Now and then, stragglers from distant stations, who had escaped or survived local tumult and massacre, reached Noorpoor, and were tenderly cared for. Men who had lost wives and children, delicate women who had never in their lives known hardships, and who too, had lost husbands and children, by musket-shot, or by exposure to the pitiless heat and exhausting fatigue—who had tramped, almost barefoot and in rags, for a hundred miles and more over stony roads, with feet blistered and bleeding—suffered extremes of hunger and thirst, and with faces scorched and swollen out of all recognition—dropped in one by one, or in small groups, telling their miserable adventures to hearty sympathizers, and thanking God that they had reached a haven of peace and security.

How many a tale of misery, such as it is hardly conceivable could be endured, we know of, or have read of: but how many more are there which will never be known, save to those who suffered them! Native feeling towards the unfortunates seemed to vary. Sometimes it was fierce and brutal, and helpless refugees were slain; again it was pitiful; and children, men, and women were sheltered in town and villages, clothed and fed, and helped on their way: else who had escaped? The English were not all dead, nor were like to die, though men like Azráel Pandé had done their evil work, and were still doing it perseveringly. Many a native Prince and Baron was weighing the probability of English or Native ascendency, and some cast their fortunes and swords into the scale of one, and some into that of the other. We know the English cause preponderated in the end; but then it was not clear to all that it would preponderate. The men who thought it would not, deluded with false powers and hopes, had their own ends to gain, like Dil Khan; many had old feuds to renew, and territory and power to recover, like Hurpál Singh, who are but types of others situated as they were; with much at stake truly, but much to gain too, if there were no English.

Perhaps the same feeling pervaded other and lower classes, though for very different causes. Landowners, who had suffered from what they deemed oppressive settlements, and local cesses, who remembered old times, when they paid pretty much as they chose, and had the means of escaping and defying the imposts of local native officials, rejoiced at the prospect of emancipation from strict control. Suitors who had been defeated in English courts threw English decisions to the winds, and took the law into their own hands. Bankers whose usurious dealing with the people had been checked, looked eagerly for opportunity to renew old practices of exaction, and make money in heaps. Thieves, Dacoits, and the lawless swash-buckler soldiery, who had ill-succeeded in turning their swords into ploughshares, rose in thousands, plundering the peaceful and industrious. And yet, at the very worst, there was a strong, deep-lying attachment to English rule, to English faith and honour, and to that ample protection of property to the meanest as well as to the richest, which a powerful English Government had afforded, that pervaded all the most valuable portions of the population, and bore good fruit in time.

I need not, perhaps, record how anxious the good old banker of Shah Gunje was at this period, or how each recurring report from his agencies at Benares, Mirzapoor, and other great commercial cities in the disturbed provinces, "that the English rule was doomed," "that the English were perishing in every successive outbreak of mutiny," sat grievously at his heart, and admitted of no comfort. Nor were his advices from Noorpoor more consolatory. His friends there wrote, that though no outbreak had occurred, yet one must inevitably take place: that many treasonable agents were at work, and that the evil storm must burst there, as elsewhere, sooner or later. He knew it was no use, yet he wrote to Mr. Brandon and to Seeta imploring them to come to him. He did not dread the caste guild for her or for himself now, in comparison with their safety; and he thought if Mr. Brandon came, that the loyal in that portion of the district—and there were yet many—would rally round him, and defy Rajah Hurpál Singh, who was far more dreaded than the Nawab. Aunt Ella, too, wrote to Seeta, bidding her to come and be safe with her; but as to the rest, I think her increasing asceticism had narrowed her mind and blunted her old loving perceptions. The incessant "Ram! Ram! Ram!" was, if possible, more absorbing than ever, and the marks on the wall of her private room showed now some hundreds of thousands, and might soon reach to millions, and so help to effect the eternal repose of her soul after her death. It was little less than impious, she thought, that her brother was still engaged in his business, at a time, too, when great terror and confusion existed in the world; and she often besought him even, with tears, to wind up all, retire to Benares, and lead a holy life till he died. But the old man was resolved to stand by his order, and to help the English if he could; and he threw all his weight into the loyal portion of the population of Shah Gunje. Should it fall from the English, it must belong to the Nawab or to the Rajah; and in either event there was nothing to be apprehended but violence and exaction.

Mr. Brandon and Seeta duly received these letters, which had been despatched to them by two of the banker's treasure carriers, who also bore a considerable sum of money in gold, and bills on Noorpoor, for Seeta's use, and to help their flight if they should determine to go to him. If it had been possible to make a diversion in the Shah Gunje district, Mr. Brandon would willingly have undertaken the responsibility of it at any personal risk; but as he and Seeta anxiously discussed the subject, her intimate knowledge of her old neighbourhood left no hope that there would be any chance of present success. The persons mentioned by Narendra were certainly influential and respectable landholders and merchants; but they had neither the means nor the men to effect the desired purpose. Besides, local war had not yet broken out, and might not break out; nor did Mr. Brandon, or Mr. Mostyn, or Mr. Noble believe that it would not, for both the Nawab and the Rajah were increasing their turbulent levies with very small means of supporting them, and when these came to an end they would be obliged to let them loose upon the country.

If it had been possible to make a tour of the district with a strong military force, and to have thus overawed disaffection, Mr. Brandon, in his civil capacity, would willingly have led it; but who could venture to say what the real temper of the native soldiers was, or what their ultimate purpose might be? No such expedition could be complete in effect without English soldiers, and if they were withdrawn, the risk of the fort of Noorpoor, where all were safe, would follow. Besides, the monsoon had opened, and promised to be a heavy one: the fair-weather roads were now deep in mud, and to pass heavy guns over them, where the lightest carts could not travel, would be impossible. On all accounts, therefore, the Noorpoor council agreed that it was most advisable to undertake nothing but measures for local safety, and these were now as complete as possible.

The officers, and such of the Christian clerks and other subordinates as were able men, took night duty as patrols; well armed, and for the most part well mounted. Arrangements were made for their reception in the fort, and for their prompt assistance in case of attack. The guns on the fort bastions covered the Sepoy lines, on which a fire of shells could be poured at any time: and they also dominated the city, in case of any treachery there. So far, therefore, as cautious foresight could provide, every possible arrangement against surprise or treachery was complete. No natives were admitted into the fort, except the servants of the soldiers and officers, and two howitzers, loaded with grape, commanded the outer gate and the glacis beyond.

With the military officers, the civilians and their clerks took their regular turns of duty, and never was Seeta absent from her husband's side. Dressed in her boy's clothes, she rode her spirited mare gracefully and boldly, and to the admiration of all; and many marvelled to see the girl, apparently so jealously guarded before, throw off the restraint habitual to her countrywomen, and follow her husband in a duty which was never perhaps without danger. Of danger such as this, danger, even in open fight, perhaps, so long as she was near Cyril, Seeta had no fear. In the latter she had not certainly been tried, but in the night patrol she took a strange delight. No matter what the weather was, calm or storm, fair or drenching rain, the active hardy girl never failed, never hesitated when Cyril's turn came round, to ride with him, and to share whatever might befal..

Seeta indeed thought this a positive escape from danger; for she now dreaded the Nawab equally with her first implacable enemy, against whose dangerous designs Buldeo's warnings were constant and emphatic. Buldeo and her giant Luchmun Singh had especially warned her against ever being alone by night. What might not a resolute, experienced Dacoit like Azráel Pandé contrive and execute? they said. True, he could not be discovered, but it was this very fact that gave Buldeo most uneasiness. "He could not have travelled far in the condition I saw him," he said to Mr. Brandon, "and he must be at Futtehpoor, if I could only find him; but Foorsut is not to be seen, and perhaps Azráel has discovered that he is my brother, and has destroyed him. But I have not given up my search yet, and often, when you miss me, I am there watching." Cyril Brandon had not under-estimated either danger to Seeta; and he shared her apprehensions. At first he had proposed that she should go to Shah Gunje; but the absolute terror with which she heard the proposal, prevented any renewal of the subject. "How could Narendra protect me?" she said; "once he would have died, but for you; and I—— If they knew that I were gone there, is it possible that they would not carry out their designs? Ah, darling, I should never see you again if I once left you, never! And here I am safe, safe as you are. If you die, I can at least go with you into death. I could not live now without you."

"Philip, and Rose, and Grace would take care of my pet," he said, half in earnest, "while trouble lasted; and then there would be Narendra and Aunt Ella afterwards."

"They might care for my body, if it lived," she answered, "but my soul would be with you, Cyril. No—my body could not live if you were gone."

"Then you shall stay, little one," he answered, "and I will

never teaze you again about Shah Gunje. What we have to endure shall be shared together now, come what may."

In truth, Seeta was growing out of old ways and perceptions very rapidly. Grace Mostyn had taken this strange girl to her heart, and was making her more and more like herself. Simple-minded, Seeta always was, with all her strange lore: unselfish, and deeply pious after her fashion. She was persevering and studious, with a quick, retentive memory, and ready perception. Grace found no difficulty in teaching her, and it was a strange pleasure to her to find the new thoughts awakened in Seeta, stirring her soul to its depths with a vivid enthusiasm. She was beginning to read and understand portions of Milton and Shakespeare: and in the latter, because the action of his dramas accorded most with her old Sanscrit studies, she took a passionate delight; an almost feverish interest indeed, at times, in some of them, which Cyril was obliged to check, and which gave him more insight into the unaccountable passages of her old life than he had ever obtained before. If he had allowed her, she would have denied herself proper food and rest in the pursuance of her exciting studies; and often Cyril had yielded to her entreaties when she could not sleep, and allowed her one of her favourite plays, or Jeremy Taylor's "Holy Living and Dying," which Mrs. Pratt had given her, and which had fascinated her from the first, and out of which she was fond of learning simple sentences by heart: while the "Pilgrim's Progress" she could read in her own tongue.

"How can we keep her back, Mr. Brandon?" asked Grace one day, almost with a look of despair; "she puts us all to shame. No sooner have I shown her any favourite passage of my own, in any book, than she hides herself somewhere, and gets it by heart. 'How little do we know of you English,' she said to me yesterday, 'how little of your faith, or your books, teeming with glorious thoughts, and the fresh stores of knowledge that are ever opening to you. While for us—no one writes now; no one thinks; we are as the dead, with those whose very language is dead too.' What could I say to her, Mr. Brandon? Will you tell me how to teach her better, or how to check her?"

But Cyril could not. "You are very, very kind, to teach her at all," he said; "or to take the trouble you do with her. I don't think you can restrain her now. She knows enough to incite her to know more, and she will persevere till she falls back on herself, and is as content with her English as she is with her Hindee and Sanscrit. But it must be dull work giving my wife such lessons?"

"No," she replied quickly, "I delight in it. I look to Seeta's share in my day's occupation with as great pleasure as my own. If you ask why, I will tell you."

"I do ask why, Miss Mostyn."

"Then it is because I come to know her heart: to see all the love, all the devotion, all the intense yearning to fit herself for your society. Much as you believe in Seeta, I do not think you know how she loves you. Now she cannot find words to express what she feels; for she says, her own tongue is too gross and too dull. 'I could talk to him in it like Juliet,' she said once to me, 'but he would laugh at me, and I should be ashamed now, though I feel I was like Juliet once. But I should rather, far rather, be like Imogen. She, you know, went to meet death when her husband sent Pisanio to kill her, and she would have died in her truth. Ah! dear Grace, I can never read that scene without tears. She was so true, so tender, so loving, so faithful. There is but one like her, in all our dramas—Savitri, of whom you know. She went into death for her lord, and I—I should not fear death for him.' Perhaps," continued Grace, and then broke off, smiling through her tears—"is there anything at her heart that makes her think so, Mr, Brandon, anything that I can reason or soothe her out of? Indeed I would try, for I love her now so dearly."

Cyril's heart smote him, for he knew of the dread and the danger; but he would not tell them to Grace. "It is only her excitable nature," he said, "marvellous in its intensity, and needing all our care and guidance; and I may say 'ours' now, since you have a part with me. Will she not take to music? that would help to turn her thoughts from other subjects."

"Not much," replied Grace: "she finds the mechanical part of learning the notes difficult: but she has a quick and correct ear, and a most delicious voice; not so high as mine, but far more full and rich—I quite envy it. She knows more than you think of by ear, and the notes guide her; but I only teach her simple melodies like 'Home, sweet Home,' and 'Vedrai Carino.' She was singing them like a bird to-day, and entreating me not to tell you, when Rose came in and kissed her, and she began to cry, and ran away home. I could not have believed that any Hindoo girl could ever be like her."

"There can be no doubt that there are many such who do not know their own powers," returned Cyril, "and have no means, like Seeta, of discovering them; and it will take years, perhaps generations, for our education to reach them! Yet, cold as it is, how earnestly the girls in our schools strive whenever they have opportunity. They quite equal the boys."

In all this progress and discussion Mrs. Mostyn had taken but little part, for she knew that Seeta was in better, because more patient, hands than hers, and she would not interfere with what had become almost a necessity of Grace's otherwise monotonous life; and if, Rose thought, her sister could bring Seeta, in any degree, up to her own standard, it was the nearest thing to being Mr. Brandon's wife herself; all she herself had ventured upon was instruction in needlework, in which she excelled, and in which Seeta was sadly deficient. So, after the English lessons of the day were over, and the ladies took up their work, Seeta had gradually joined them and proved an apt and diligent pupil, especially in embroidery, for which she evinced decided talent, and had worked collars and cuffs for her friends, and even some trimmings for their dresses with great delicacy.

Thus the time passed; and pleasantly now, for the first alarms had subsided, or the society at Noorpoor had become more used to look danger in the face, and so to fear it less; but before many days of July had passed, all Cyril's and Seeta's apprehensions had been re-excited.

One evening, it was Cyril's turn for patrol duty, and he had asked some friends who were to accompany him to dinner, leaving Seeta to read as usual close to one of the windows of her cottage. By day this was Seeta's favourite seat. The China roses, trained on one side, with an ever-blooming jessamine on the other, gave out a pleasant perfume and encircled the window frame like a bower; and the garden, with the sparkling waters of the lake beyond it, and the grim old fort above, where the English flag floated from the high cavalier, made up a picture she loved to look upon. Some showers had fallen during the day; but the night was clear, and the stars shone with almost unusual lustre. She had looked at them for awhile, leaning on the low window sill, and then shut the casement and betaken herself to her favourite "Imogen," whose words she was teaching herself line by line, shutting her eyes as she repeated what she read.

Once she heard a rustle, as she thought, and looked up, but there was nothing; it might be the birds, who had nests in the thatch and in the creepers. Across the lawn, not far from the stables, was the guard-room, and she saw forms moving there, and the police sentinel walking up and down. From the dining-room there came the sound of cheerful voices and an almost chorus of merry laughter, in which she could distinguish her husband's voice distinctly. She smiled at her own fear and again sat down to read.

Presently she heard the rustle repeated, and, as she looked up, beheld a sight which seemed to curdle her blood. Right against the pane was the horrible countenance of the Dacoit, fearfully changed and partly bandaged up, yet never to be forgotten. The fierce eyes glared at her from their deep sockets, the grim face, ashy grey and wan, was within a foot of her own, with the light of her candles flaring upon it, and the features working savagely and threateningly as if trying to speak. Once before she had seen a face as brutal look over the wall, and often seemed to see it still: but this was far more horrible in the intensity and malignancy of its expression. If her revolver had been within reach, she had shot at what she saw, but she had left it in the inner room with her boy's dress. She did not lose her presence of mind, but ran to the door crying for help. At that moment too the Dacoit had been seen by one of the guard, and there was a rush across the lawn, and shouts of, "Seize him!" "Stop him!" Buldeo was absent.

Cyril heard his wife's cry, and the rush of the men, and with his friends started up and leaped into the garden. Many ran hither and thither confusedly. The Judge's guard was alarmed, and joined in the search, for one of the Rahtores declared he had seen a figure near the window of the cottage, and one of the police was sure it passed a shrubbery at the foot of the garden; but though the gentlemen mounted their horses and examined every road to the place, no one was to be seen. Azráel, however, had again had a narrow escape. As he heard Seeta's cry he had traversed the garden rapidly, and, under screen of the hedge and trees, had plunged into the lake, dived among some high reeds, and sat there till the confusion was over.

Cyril at first tried to persuade Seeta that she was mistaken She was trembling and sobbing now with her head lying on his shoulder, but she persisted in declaring she was right.

"It is cowardly," she said at last, "to be afraid! What could he have done to me with you so near? And we have the rounds to go, Cyril; the ride will do me good, and you would not leave me here alone? Come and see if any marks were left, for the earth is soft below the window."

True enough, there were several marks of two long bony feet, and traces of them through the garden to a hole in the hedge in which were freshly broken twigs. Beyond, there was nothing. Azráel had been alone.

Cyril did not attempt to dissuade Seeta from her project. He would not have left her alone then for worlds, and he then determined to take her to the fort next day, where no Dacoit could enter. It was evident to him that Azráel's design was to examine the cottage; and it was impossible to say when it might not be attacked in force. Before long, therefore, the party, joined by others, was proceeding leisurely through the broad roads of the cantonment. But the night did not pass without incidents, or so securely as its predecessors. As the patrol passed onwards, suddenly a lurid light shot up into the sky, and on turning into another road, they saw one of the officers' bungalows, not far from the lines, in flames, which increased in volume every moment. Two young men lived there together, and were now outside in their night dresses, with their revolvers in their hands, and crowds of Sepoys running to the spot with water-pots. Many were helping to remove furniture and boxes, or endeavouring to pull the blazing thatch from the roof, while two or three active young fellows had climbed up the thatch to the ridge, and were pouring water on what remained entire, which, however, nothing could save. There appeared no want of sincere goodwill in most of the men, who, when the Brigadier and their several commanders arrived, cheered them lustily with loud shouts, and Brandon also as he rode forward to meet them; and Seeta's heart bounded as she heard the ardent welcome cry of "Brandon Sahib Bahadoor ke Jey." But from the dusky outskirts of the crowd, which surrounded the blazing building, rose some ominous shouts of "Deen! Deen!" and jeers at those who were assisting. Some thought the fire accidental, but to Brandon it was clear that here, as elsewhere, active mischief had begun with Azráel Pandé's appearance, and had left its mark behind.

No Christians slept in Noorpoor that night; all were ready dressed, men and women, waiting the signal from the fort—the first gun. But the night passed quietly, and there were drills and guard mountings as usual in the morning. No further risk, however, was to be run; and in the afternoon Mrs. Mostyn and Grace walked up to the fort, joining other ladies there, and watched Cyril and Seeta sailing on the lake till they ran their boat under the tower, and ascended by the water-gate to their quarters.

CHAPTER XL.

DIL KHAN'S TROUBLES.

"And so you saw her there, Maharaj?" asked the Nawab of Azráel Pandé, as they sat together in the room we know of, by the well. "Yet it was a mad expedition, my friend. Suppose they had caught you?"

"They would have hanged me by the hands of the leather-dresser, and you would not have seen your friend again—that's all," he replied gloomily, and fell into silence.

"But Seeta," persisted the Nawab—"how was it that she escaped you?"

"Because your people were cowards—cowards!" he hissed from between his teeth, "and hung back when we reached the boundary marks. Had they done as they swore to do on the axe, she would have been here now; and she is there—the witch—the sorceress! It was her devilish spells that checked the men, and filled their hearts with fear. Do I not know that? Did I not hear her reading them out of an English book, and see her? O Seeta, I saw thee! I thought I could feel thy breath on my cheek as I listened and watched. Seeta, Seeta, thou didst not hear as I spoke, as I whispered to thee to come and be my queen."

"You rave, my friend," remarked the Nawab, drily; "and raving about a puling, wooden-faced girl like her is unseemly in an old man. While you were sick and in fear, you said what you did not know of. But now that you are well, thanks be to the Lord, all those follies, and your devils, should pass away."

"Ah! we do not know who come, Nawab, or you would not be here; you would be afraid to hear their 'Hrrám! Hrrám! Hrrám!' Do you not hear their iron feet? Listen!"

"If you are going to call your devils, and Huree Das, the goldsmith, about you, I shall go, Azráel Pandé, and leave them with you;" and he rose to depart.

"Stay," cried his companion; "they are gone—you need not fear now. Yes," he continued, with a shudder, passing his hands over his eyes, "I see many now who never came before; and there is the old man at Gudduk with his spear-wounds gaping, and all the women dead lying about him, and—— Yes, it is all blood now—blood in my eyes, blood in my heart, blood of the English who are gone to hell at Dehly and Cawnpoor and

Jhansy, flowing in a great stream, and more following. O Mother divine! more, more, till thou art full!"

"Nay, this is worse and worse," said Dil Khan to himself. "I must turn him from his blood. And what of the Sepoys, Maharaj? Did you see them, as you said you would? Do you hear what I say? Never mind the devils; they will come another time, when you want them."

"Reach me that hookah. I feel too weak to live," returned Azráel; and as the Nawab handed it to him, he took two or three pieces of lighted charcoal from the live embers near him, put them upon the hemp leaves in the bowl, and inhaled several long breaths of smoke. "Now I will talk to you, Nawab Sahib," he said, more collectedly, "but not much, for this wound hurts me still. What did you ask me? Perhaps my mind was wandering—it often wanders now."

"About the Sepoys," said Dil Khan. "I am beginning to think you are wrong about them, my friend; and if the Brigadier and Brandon—may they burn in fire!—brought them and the 'sojers' down on me with their big guns, I don't think you or I could hold this place."

"Peace!" cried Azráel, waving his hand. "You speak as a child. Was there not a Sahib's bungalow burnt in the lines last night; and did you not see the blaze from hence?"

"Yes, of one poor house," replied the Nawab, with a sneer. "I expected a blaze which would have lighted up all the country round."

"Ah, you don't know, you don't understand yet; that was only the beginning," said Azráel. "Was I not there, and dried my clothes over the hot ashes of the house? Did I not see Brandon, and the witch Seeta on her horse with him, and the Brigadier, and all the officers? And we cried, 'Deen! Deen!' and jeered the men who were bringing water and trying to put out the fire."

"Well, well, I know that," returned the Nawab impatiently; "and the issue of it was, that all the officers and the Mem Sahibs have gone into the fort, and I should like to know who is to get them out of it. Touba! Touba! There will not be a Nazarene to send to the Shaitan who waits for them. Thou hast delayed too long, my friend, and had better try elsewhere."

"Not too long, Dil Khan; though, had I not been as I am, it would have been different. Could I help this?" and he pointed to the wound. "Let it pass. The men are ready now, if thou art ready. Speak!"

"Ahem! the Moulvee is not returned yet," said the Nawab,

hesitatingly, "and till he comes I dare not act; and thou art not strong enough yet, my friend, to lead thy five hundred warriors."

"Five hundred cowards, you mean," exclaimed the Dacoit, scornfully. "Fifty of them that I took with me last night slunk away among the bushes, and ran away when the Feringee patrol was half a mile off. Are these soldiers? We must wait for true soldiers, Dil Khan."

The Nawab rose and went away. He was not easy in mind. Not to mince the matter, he was now full of apprehension and doubt. True, wonderful news reached him from Dehly; and by the royal Akhbars he was informed that thousands of Nazarene Kafirs were being daily sent to the infernal regions, that the victories of the imperial armies were perpetual, that thousands upon thousands of true believers had already made their obeisance to the Asylum of the World, and that, when all the English had perished, the Emperor would take the field in person and receive the congratulations of his loyal and devoted subjects. But with some of these news-letters had come a letter from his second wife's brother, which set that ambitious dame a-crying, and did not quite corroborate the news of the Akhbars. The English army was lying behind the ridge above the city, and blazing shells were being fired from their batteries which wounded many, and turned men's livers into water. There were Sepoys in thousands, and more arriving by regiments; but there was no head to them, and they often quarrelled and sometimes fought among themselves. Where was her husband, of whom such great expectations had been formed? Why did he not appear with his warriors and defend the King of Kings? Why did he dally with necessity, and shelter himself in the fort of Noorpoor, which of course he had taken long ago?

It was very well for her brother to ask such questions, yet how was she to answer them? Dil Khan could not only not give her comfort, but found himself railed at by the fierce woman for cowardice, for inaction, for ingratitude to his benefactor the Emperor, who had bestowed the highest honours upon him. He could not persuade his wife that the tinsel necklace which was hardly worth ten rupees, or the robe of honour which proved on examination to be soiled and frayed, would not move an army or supply his pressing necessities; and, failing to establish this point, he left the furious woman to her passionate weeping, and went to the "Star of Women," who was not often, perhaps, favoured with a visit.

But here more vexation awaited him. The good lady had

no patience to hear tales of imperial victims, or catalogues of infidel Feringees, sent to keep the "Shaitan" company. She was, at heart, a true friend to the English. The Mem Sahibs of Noorpoor had always been gracious and kind to her, and she loved them; as to the sweet Missy Mostyn, she would rather go to her and protect her herself than she should come to any harm. The "Star of Women" had been a local beauty, and had many local connections of some weight, as landholders, all around Futtehpoor. With them she had constant intercourse, and she knew that to a man, though they might be helplessly neutral for a time, yet if opportunity offered, they would strike in for the English.

Under these circumstances, the Nawab found himself reproached, not bitterly perhaps, but very sadly; reminded of the long friendship which had existed with the English from the days of Lord Lake to the present. Was all this to be thrown away, and his very life and estates risked?

I wish, indeed, that the course of this history admitted of my showing my readers more of this excellent woman; kind, charitable, benevolent to her dependents, content and thankful for her lot—in spite of the younger sister wife—pious after the tenets of her faith, simple and gracious in her manners, and beloved and honoured by all—there was no more popular or respected lady in the country, or one who had more deeply gained the affections both of Mahomedans and Hindoos, than Nujm-ool-Nissa Khanum.

"What should you do?" she said, in answer to her lord's question as he sat before her with his turban awry and his fore-finger between his teeth; "what should you do? Why, go to the Brigadier, and the Judge Sahib, at once. Say you have been misled, ask them to forgive you, and proclaim by beat of drum that you will stand by the English to the end; for, in the end, my lord, they will conquer all. Did they not conquer before? If the Almighty has sent a scourge upon them, they will bow to it, and rise again. If you will not go, send me to the Judge's lady. I would go to the Queen of England for you, if there were need. O, my lord! let not men speak evil of you, but rely upon the faithful English to reward you, as they will, for loyalty."

"They took Jhansy and Nagpoor," he said, bitterly; "since then I have not trusted them. Let them die, as they are dying everywhere, and will die. Had their fathers been like this generation, my ancestors had fought them to the death, as I will do! Inshalla! as I will do! Be silent, if you value my favour and your own honour! else——"

"I have but spoken the truth," she replied, meekly; "the rest is in God's hands. May He protect you, and lead you aright."

All this, and much more that I need not record, afforded no comfort to the Nawab Dil Khan. There were divisions in his house, and wherever he went he had found himself opposed; and more than once, for several days, he debated in his mind whether it would not be the safest and the wisest plan, after all, to go to Mr. Mostyn and the Brigadier, and cast his lot with them frankly and truly. There was nothing to cheer him and support him, as he was. If he went to the secret chamber, he found his guest either raving from the effects of the drug he smoked, or the opium he swallowed; or sunk into a maudlin condition, crying to the devils he worshipped, or defying or entreating "Seeta." On all points, therefore, the Nawab Sahib was troubled, and miserable enough; finding his only consolation in submission to his fate—his "Kismut"—to lead him as it would.

It had needed, indeed, the influence of the Moulvee, to arouse Dil Khan from his lethargy and perplexed helplessness of mind; and in due time that worthy appeared: full of confidence, radiant with news of victories in Oudh, at Cawnpoor, at Futtehgurh, at Banda, besides those of Jhansy and many other places. The Nana Sahib of Bithoor had collected the mutineers of the provinces around him, who, with all their guns and munitions of war, were preparing to march to Dehly on the one hand and Calcutta on the other, where all the English "Kafirs" were to be driven into their ships or into the sea. There had been risings in the Rajpoot States, and the native troops of Sindia and Holkar, impatient at the inaction of their masters, had in part mutinied; and were preparing to take the field when the rains should cease and their artillery could travel.

"The whole of the Mahratta 'Cumpoo,' the old battalions of the French heroes, an army in themselves, will join the Nana Sahib, who is to be Péshwah. At Poona, the Mahratta Princes are ready, and their people to a man. Arcot, Vellore, Seringapatam, and the Moslems of the South, are waiting the last signal, and at Hyderabad and Nagpoor all is ready. Will you linger in the race for glory to the Faith?" cried the Moulvee with excitement. "I have been long absent, I know, but I have travelled far and fast, and have gathered the news I now give you from English sources, not our own. Even the English newspapers are full of alarm and apprehension."

"And Dehly?" asked the Nawab.

"Events never looked brighter or better," he replied. "The

English army there breaks its strength against the old fortress, like waves against a rock, and falls back in flakes of powerless foam. They get no nearer to the walls: their guns are worn out, and they have no new ones. Ha! ha! ha! let them rage there. When we all move against them, they will be swept from the face of the earth and sent to hell. Now I have news for you: I have been to Jhansy, and have seen Lukshmee Bye, the Ranee. She would have you join her after Noorpoor is taken. She has twenty thousand men. Though the English took her kingdom once, she has already recovered it. She has opened up all the treasures that were hidden, and she is generous and open-handed; the Nana supports her with a hundred thousand men; the Talookdars of Oudh, with fifty thousand. I tell you they have more than two lakhs (200,000) of soldiers now under my knowledge. Join those to the armies at Dehly, at Gualior, at Indoor, everywhere, and what have you? Five hundred thousand warriors for the Faith at least! while, if there are ten thousand English troops now in all Hind, widely scattered and unable to help each other, it is all. Is he with you; he, the Brahmin—the Jogee—what you will—who seemed to hold the men of Noorpoor in his hand? What has he been doing?"

"He was badly wounded in the face, and I thought he would have died. So he has done nothing," replied the Nawab; "and I am tired of him; for, whether from weakness, or from smoking Gánja, he has become a dreaming enthusiast, seeing visions of the devils he worships, and altogether very unpleasant company; but he is stronger now, and his wound is nearly healed."

"Good!" returned the Moulvee, rubbing his hands. "I have brought him a few old friends, who did good work at Jhansy. They will cheer him up, I dare say. You need not look alarmed, Nawab Sahib, they will do you no harm."

"It was not that," said the Nawab, "only—suppose they should hear it at Noorpoor, they might——"

"Of course, I mean that they should hear. What else were you thinking about? I say leave these Oudh men to themselves; they know what to do and how to do it too. When you have all the Noorpoor Sepoys about you, you will feel strong, and can march to Jhansy. Now you are weak, you think, eh? Was that what you thought of, my friend?"

Nawab Dil Khan sighed; what could he do before his "Kismut," and he sighed again. That must decide for him now, for he had no energy of mind to resist the Moulvee, and the men had arrived too. There was a stir in the courtyard without, and an attendant announced that the Sepoys demanded instant admittance. The Nawab nodded assent, and the Moulvee said for him, "Let them come in and make their salaams," and a moment afterwards about twenty men, entering with their right hands upheld, raised a shout of "Jey Kalee Mata!" "Nawab Dil Khan Bahadoor ke Jey!"

"Ye are welcome, my friends," said the Nawab, rising; "welcome to a poor house; will ye not be seated?"

The men made military salutes, and sat down on their heels in two rows. They were in undress, but they wore their belts over their clothes, and held their muskets in their hands, ready for use if it might be necessary. Grand stout fellows all of them, like their brethren everywhere; twisting up their moustachios, and looking round them with a curious interest, at the high arched hall, and at the Nawab, by turns. Not one of them spoke.

"This brave soldier," said the Moulvee, joining his hands to the Nawab, "is Colonel Goor Bux Tewaree, once a Havaldar of Artillery, and now commander of all the Artillery at Jhansy, with the rank of 'Colonel.' Be pleased to let your favour rest upon him. Colonel Sahib," he added to the man, "rise, and sit among us, as a friend. I think your people may be dismissed to rest, for they have had a long march;" and, at a signal from their leader, all rose, and repeating their military salute, filed out of the hall.

Then the three entered upon the condition of the country, the disposition of Hurpál Singh, and the chances of carrying Noorpoor; and the result was not pleasing to the ex-Havaldar, nor did it tally with the florid picture which the Moulvee Sahib had drawn at Jhansy. The quick military eye of Goor Bux had detected at once the utter weakness and uselessness of the Nawab's levies, and he half regretted he had come so far on such an errand. He heard that Hurpál Singh was a ruffian, bent only on local plunder, and of no use as an ally. There remained, therefore, only the garrison of Noorpoor. "Where is Azráel Pandé, my Gooroo?" asked Goor Bux. "Why is he not here to meet me? Before we decide on anything I must see him."

"If you are not afraid of a madman, I will take you to him myself," said the Nawab. "For my own part I always take this in case of trouble," and he pointed to his pistol; "but he will not fear you, who were once his pupil. You will remain here, Moulvee Sahib, and we will return presently." Then he rose and opened tho staircase door, and, motioning to Goor Bux to follow, began to descend the steps, telling his companion, as he did so, of Azráel Pandé's wound, and his raving, and his terrible cry of "Hrrám, Hrrám, Hrrám!"

"Ah," said the man, "I see he has been reading the 'Gurúra Poorán.' That is what comes to most of thom. No, I am not afraid; lead on."

CHAPTER XLI.

"CONSPIRACY."

We have seen the place, and the man who lived there; and his weird worship, and his alternate fits of gloom and excitement. Perhaps, knowing the fearful nature of the course to which Azráel had committed himself, and the unhallowed arts and rites he practised, even his former pupil and friend shuddered as he approached the room; and Foorsut, who was sitting in the outer chamber, whispered to tho Nawab, "You had better wait; they are all with him now, and his shrieks have been worse than ever. He has drawn his sword and has been worshipping it. I had to kill a cock for his sacrifice this morning, to smear it with blood; look!"

"Let me go to him," said Goor Bux, "I know a spell that will quiet him, be he never so violent, if indeed he be not gone beyond that. Stay here till I call; you must not shoot him; nor must he kill you," and he stepped on lightly into tho gloom. Goor Bux had a strong iron-bound quarter-staff in his hand, and feared no sword; but what he saw arrested his steps at once.

The light was dim, and the room was so full of the smoke of burning incense, that the cresset in a niche of the wall barely burned. Far off, as it seemed, two smaller lamps glimmered before a rude low shrine or altar, in front of which Azráel Pandé was sitting bare-headed, and with only a narrow silk cloth about his loins, in an attitude of devotion or meditation, reading from a narrow oblong book which lay on the ground before him. By his side, and ready to his hand, a naked sabre, spotted and stained with gouts of blood and spots of red powder, glistened in the light, and he was muttering, in low tones, the weird Sanscrit incantation which has been quoted, in part, before.

Goor Bux at a glance knew it was the man he sought; but

O! how fearfully altered! The long gaunt body and neck were now little better than skin and bone; the very skin was withered and wrinkled. The powerful muscles of the arms were, perhaps, less wasted, and rose sharp and iron-like in their outlines. The hands, spread out on the thighs, were long and lean, their dark purple veins, as also the veins of the forehead, standing out like knotted cords. But the face was hardly to be recognized as Goor Bux saw it. The right side seemed almost gone, and a wide cicatrix, hardly yet healed, covered the jaw and most part of the neck and cheek, and had drawn down the lower eyelid and the corner of the mouth, in a ghastly manner, which gave a frightful expression to the countenance.

"Hrrám! Hrrám! Hrrám!" shrieked the Dacoit, starting to his feet, seizing his sword, and cutting into the air with a force which caused every stroke to whistle.

"Destroy, destroy!
Pierce, pierce!
With thy trident,
Reeking with blood!
Come, come,
O! Mahéswara,
O! Kapalini,
O! Kamarini,
O! Máha Káli!
Enter, enter,
Hear and come,
Hear and come!
Hear and come!"

Then he stood erect, with his sword stretched out, panting for breath, and his eyes staring into vacancy. "She does not come," he said moodily, as the point of his sword dropped with a helpless action, and he almost fell into his former position. "She will not come till there is more blood. She is hungry, she thirsts! Will that poor sacrifice satisfy her? Nay, but see! see! there!"

Before he could rise, Goor Bux had divested himself of his upper clothing, stepped behind him, and muttered a Sanscrit spell, which had a strange effect. Azráel sat, as it were stiffened. No feature moved, and his glassy eyes looked out with no speculation in them into the gloom. Then the other took incense from a brass plate near, and some of the red powder beside it, with which he smeared his forehead; and entering within the magic circle which Azráel had marked around himself, first made obeisance to the altar, and, kneeling down before him, drew several long inspirations in succession.

"Enough," he muttered, "enough, Mother divine! else I should be like him," and he sat down and watched; but not for long. Azráel seemed to sigh, the tension of his neck relaxed, and as his chin fell on his breast, tears dropped silently from his eyes upon his hands.

"Rise, Azráel Pandé!" cried his companion; "I, Goor Bux Tewaree, am nigh thee, and greet thee in the name of the Mother. Jey Dévee! Kalee Mata ke Jey! Máha kalee ke Jey! Arise, and embrace your pupil. Ah! if thou hadst not taught me that spell, Gooroojee, the Mother had taken thee."

"Thou, Goor Bux? How, art thou here?"

"He brought me," returned the man, pointing to the Nawab, "else who could have found thee here under the earth?"

"What hast thou done?" asked Azráel eagerly. "My terrible dream is gone from me now; speak! are they dead? The English!"

"All that were at Jhansy," said Goor Bux; "we kept them all safe; then I made a great sacrifice to the Mother, and had them all killed for her as you bid me. There were nearly a hundred.'

"And you spared none?"

"Not one; nor child, nor mother, nor maid; but they have killed more at Cawnpoor, hundreds! The Nana Sahib left none alive? Ah! the Mother has drunk much blood! but thou, her priest and votary—how it is thou hast sent none? Beware lest she take thee; thou art perilously near her when she comes on thy calling!"

"I know it, I know it," returned Azráel, gloomily; "she comes and returns empty; and I must follow when she beckons, for I have sent her no blood from Noorpoor."

"Will you come with me to the men, Gooroojee, and rouse them?"

"I am weak," answered Azráel; "but the sight of thee has given me new life, and there is something, perhaps, in this wasted body still;" and he rose up, and struck the hollow of his thighs and his breasts in succession with the palms of his hands, like an athlete.

"Shabash! well done, friend; that was done like a wrestler. Now thou wilt be thyself again," cried the Nawab.

"Let him stay here with me, and let his people put up in the garden," said Azráel to the Nawab. "One day with them, seeing their familiar faces, and hearing the speech and songs of my country, will give new life to me. We can pull down the wall there, and let in air and light, and they can come and go as they please."

"Be it so, friend," said the Nawab, "and truth to say, I know not where to put them. But if they are content with the garden pavilion, they are welcome to it; only do not let them light fires there."

"Let me go and tell them, then," said Goor Bux. "I will bring them hither, and the Nawab Sahib can send our provisions here. I will not be long away."

But several days still passed, and no move was made on either side. Strange, Foorsut thought, that he had not seen Buldeo since he had come to Ryna. Where could he be? Nor was he at Noorpoor with Mr. Brandon, for Foorsut, on some pretence, had gone away for a few hours, to look for him. "But I must go now," he said to himself, "for the new men have come, and there will be evil; and Azráel will not miss me among his friends." Nor indeed did he. The wall in the arch was pulled down, the room opened to the well, and Azráel could sit looking at the brawny youths who swam and splashed and dived in the water, and passed the day with song, and tale, and laughter, as in the old times of the Thirty-fourth. It was strange to see how the Dacoit's energy grew again powerful; and how his strength had improved by the time a week was past. Much of the old force had returned to him; and when his friend was sure of this, there could be no longer delay.

Goor Bux had already sent spies into the cantonment, who had seen men of both regiments; but there did not appear among them that unanimity which was essential to success. It is not to be supposed that such a condition of affairs could restrain two such men as the ex-Havaldar and Azráel Paudé. It was evident they must go themselves; and they went one night to a village near Noorpoor, whence they proceeded on foot to another deserted temple, on the outskirts of the town, situated on the bare upland, where there was no possibility of surprise.

This old building occupied the summit of a low round hill, now covered with short green grass; and from its porch could be seen the lake, the town, the fort now twinkling with lights, and the camp. There was no moon, and the sky was overcast; nor was there any light in the temple. Those assembled sat in darkness, and scouts had been placed at distances around. There was silence among the group huddled together before the steps of the porch; but the night wind, heavy with moisture, sighed through the pillars of the low hall, while the unearthly cries of hyenas and jackals came up from the outskirts of the town, as they fought over the garbage and carrion which had been thrown there. I need not, I think, record what passed, for there was little new to be told. What there was to say, was left by Azráel Pandé to his more experienced colleague, who took up a new line of persuasion, and could at least assure his listeners, that all ranks who joined the Ranee of Jhansy, or the Nana Sahib of Bithoor, drew double pay; that he, a Havaldar, a sergeant, was now a full colonel, with five thousand rupees a year, an elephant and retinue; that the Ranee and the Nana Sahib required all the men they could get; and all this seemed, to those who heard it, a far more rational ground for action than the ravings of Azráel Pandé. Goor Bux could also tell them of the armies in Oudh, of the work doing in the siege of the Residency of Lucknow, and that the Talookdars were up, and their old Rajahs were fighting for the Faith. How Dehly held out, and how Gualior and Indoor were coming in turn; for on all these points he was as well informed as the Moulvee.

"Come, some of you," continued Goor Bux, "to Futtehpoor. You can get away after roll-call, and be back before gun-fire in the morning, and I will ask the Nawab to have a nauch, when we can discuss these matters more comfortably than in this dark hole, and see each others' faces."

This was a new and pleasant phase of the matter, far pleasanter than Azráel's fierce denunciations and appeals to religion and loss of caste. None of them had lost their caste, none had eaten flour mixed with bone-dust, none had handled the greased cartridges; but double pay and a share in the glories their brethren were winning everywhere, were inducements which could hardly be refused, and to ratify these there would be a nauch too, for which any of them would have gone farther than to Futtehpoor; and thus the invitation was cordially acceded to by the delegates. On the fourth day they were to visit Futtehpoor and come to the Nawab's garden, where they would be welcomed.

Meanwhile, Foorsut had betaken himself to the neighbourhood of Mr. Brandon's house, and the hooting of a horned owl, which Buldeo knew perfectly, arose from the trees in the garden, now soft, now loud, and changing its place constantly. How well Buldeo recognized the old signal! His brother was alive, then; no other could hoot like that. So he arose silently, and went out from Seeta's cottage, where he now slept, and betook himself to the garden, answering the cry, but in a shriller tone; and while the police sentinel was throwing stones into the trees, Buldeo found his brother, and by the cessation of the hooting the sentinel was no doubt satisfied that he had driven the ill-omened night-birds away.

"There was not much time for talking, for Foorsut was anxious to return; but he told his brother where Azráel was, and of the terrible time he had passed with him. "Now," he continued, "Goor Bux, the Artillery Havaldar, from Jhansy, and twenty-five of his men have arrived, and Azráel is become a new man. They are at the temple to-night to meet men from the regiments here; shall we go and listen in the old place?" The idea was delightful to Buldeo, and, returning for his spear, the brothers set off together, Buldeo giving by the way a relation of his own adventures and his unavailing search for his brother.

At the old temple, however, there was no one. Both pried curiously about and listened for an hour or more, but all was silent as the grave. It was evident there was some other place of meeting, and, as they parted, Foorsut said, "The time is near now. Goor Bux Tewaree is not one to be idle, and our Maharaj has become young again. The Havaldar said a spell over him which drove away the devils and 'Seeta,' and he does not smoke half the Gánja he used to do. All this is bad—and they must be careful up yonder," and he pointed to the fort, "and stir not till the peril is past. I will come with further news when I can. Now I must go, brother," and they embraced and parted.

To Cyril Brandon this news was not, perhaps, unexpected; but what could be done more than was done? In the fort, all was secure and vigilant, and without? Well, a few days more, perhaps, would determine; and by the Brigadier all officers were enjoined to gather what information they could, and to watch the tempers of the men very narrowly.

When the new "Colonel Sahib" proposed a nauch to the Nawab, Dil Khan appeared to enter into the idea with great satisfaction. Of course the Sepoys should have a nauch; nay, he would even write to the Brigadier to allow Sepoys to come to the party, so as the more to throw him off his guard; but to this both Goor Bux and the Moulvee objected. "His heart is only half with us, my friend," said the Moulvee, "and he might—you know I don't say he would—let the Brigadier know that you and Azráel Pandé are here, and bring down the white people upon us, and there are nearly three hundred and fifty of them at Noorpoor, if the officers are counted." So the Sepoys were not invited, and Máma Jumeela was privately despatched to Noorpoor to negotiate with the famous Peri Buksh and some other dancers and singers to come and perform. Not in gorgeous attire, as she had gone to visit Seeta, did the dame proceed to

Noorpoor this time, but in plain if not mean attire, and in a closed litter of humble pretensions and appearance, which excited no attention; and thus she was set down in the courtyard of the Peri's house, outside a very substantial, even respectable-looking mansion, though perhaps the least that is said of its interior, the better.

As Máma Jumeela withdrew her bulky figure from the confined litter, she stretched herself, and, seeing the Peri come into the verandah of the basement to inquire who had arrived, held out her arms to her, and waddling up the steps, embraced her young friend, and cracked her fingers and even elbow-joints over her after her most peculiarly loving fashion. I do not need to mention the terms of the bargain that had to be driven; but the issue was that, for a handsome present from the Nawab, and what she might gather from the spectators, Peri Buksh was to come early the next Thursday, and stay as long as she pleased in the castle, and Máma Jumeela, having achieved so much of her purpose, betook herself to the minor stars of Noorpoor.

Peri Buksh was the type of many of her sisterhood at Noorpoor and elsewhere. She had come of a "good family" of dancers and singers, the oldest in the province, and most renowned. Centuries ago, her progenitors had sung and danced before kings of Malwah and Khandésh, who had invested the family with priveleges and endowed them with lands: and before Akbur and Aurungzebe, who had confirmed these grants. Very often had the Peri to perform long journeys and to sing and dance at saints' tombs or at village temples, to fulfil hereditary obligations and obtain her dues; and if she could not go herself, she sent one of her subordinates, of whom there were several, who had been adopted or purchased, and educated for their profession in life. The family of the Peri were therefore esteemed "highly respectable," and she, by hereditary right, was the head of the district guild of "Tuwaifs," or dancers, and thus possessed considerable influence and authority. Of course she, as every one else, had heard of the bad wind of Sumbut, 1914, but it had not affected her. If her politics were considered, I think she would have been found on the side of the English, who, she said, were "good people, and helped her very often." And, like most others, she had a special reverence for Mr. Brandon, whom she esteemed a popular hero. I will not say either, that she had not tried to fascinate him sometimes; but she found him, though always accessible and civil, cold as ice, and perhaps respected him the more. When he married the goldsmith's granddaughter she was charmed by the act;

and also by the kindness he showed to his wife. "He is a good fellow," she said to her people, "and if all the Feringees were like him, we should hear no more of this bad wind." Such being her sentiments, she would rather the Nawab had not asked her to come and dance for him; but she could not well refuse, for many of her rights and lands lay among his villages; and if, as was said might happen, he became master of the country, he would punish her for contumacy.

The Peri was a fine full-grown woman of about twenty; not very fair, perhaps, in complexion, nor yet dark, nor very tall either, but with a round supple figure of exquisite proportions, which she well knew how to use in her dances. She had, moreover, a very pretty face, with a well-shaped mouth and fine eyes, with the use—or misuse—of which she was perfectly acquainted. She had been educated too, to some extent, in Persian and Hindee, in the latter of which she kept her accounts; and, indeed, she was a very keen lover of money. When the Peri at the proper time, therefore, appeared in the Nawab's hall of audience, the many chandeliers of which had been specially lighted, a general murmur of applause ran round the guests, who sat on both sides of the fine room, leaving the centre free for the performance. She was dressed in a close-fitting garment, with long sleeves and a very full skirt, much plaited in at the waist, made of the finest transparent muslin of a light violet colour, trimmed nearly to her waist, with rows of broad gold brocade lace, as also about her shoulders and bust with the same. This dress was confined slightly at her waist by a scarf of bright green muslin spotted with gold, whose ends of gold brocade fell on her left side, and had the effect of raising the skirt a little so as to show her trousers of the richest cloth of gold. With one end tucked into her waistband, a splendid Benares scarf, of filmy amber muslin gauze, profusely flowered with gold, having borders and ends of the same, passed over her left arm and head, and fell over her right shoulder. The gold ornaments on her head and arms were all handsome and in great profusion; and her gold anklets, whose tiny bells chinked as she walked, had a row of large diamonds on their bands, which flashed as she moved, and gave a charming effect to the tiny graceful feet on which they rested.

The girl, with two companions, also nearly as richly attired as herself, and her band of musicians, advanced slowly up the hall, and having made a profound obeisance to the Nawab, and slighter salutations to the Moulvee and the "Colonel Sahib," who sat on each side of him, with a general sweep of her hand to all that were sitting around, the party sat down, forming one of the principal and most beautiful groups present. There were many other spectators; officers of the Nawab's own levies and household; and the Sepoys who had come from Jhansy and Noorpoor, all mingled together now, sat in rows upon their heels, in almost a kneeling posture, as the most respectful; their faces tied up with gay scarfs over their jaunty bright turbans, and their general expression grim and stolid.

There was nothing particular in the dance, for Indian women dancers only move in short tinkling steps to their simple music; but in the lithe supple sway of her figure, and of her small graceful head and neck, the Peri, always remarkable, now exceeded herself. She appeared, in a spirit of mischief, to address herself particularly to the Moulvee; who sat blinking on his seat, stroking his long thin beard, and telling his beads. His round bullet head and sanctimonious expression, apparently defiant of the girl's charms, provoked her to use them freely. If the Moulvee were proof against the dancing, or had been able to restrain himself, he was far otherwise when the Peri began to sing, for her voice was indeed very rich and beautiful, and her shake perfect. For one song she was especially celebrated; and the Nawab, calling her to him, whispered to her to sing it. "Sing it to him," he said, pointing to the Moulvee, "and do not spare him."

I dare say many of my readers have heard "Soobuh dumeed, Shub goozusht," with its refrain "Soono, zera-i-gooftogoo," and will follow this version of the original, though its force and spirit can hardly be rendered.

The morn has broke
The night is past,
From sleep awoke,
I rise at last.
O, damsel dear!
Wert thou a dream!
Thine eyes so clear
In witching gleam!

Listen, to all I have to tell!
Last night, beside the river's brink,
The ruby wine, by sips, I drink,
A charmer near me blushing sits,
Brightly the torch-light past us flits.
Around her form I cast my arms,
Fearing no ill but love's alarms;
Yet, when I wake, I'm all alone!
My Fairy, and her love, are gone!
Ah, yes! perchance it was a dream!

II.

No! not a dream! I see her yet!
With wine I drank, my lips are wet;
The fierce delight still through me thrills,
The passion which all reason kills!
As heart to heart, and lip to lip,
I, from my charmer, nectar sip,
O! rapture that I dare not tell!
Nor longer on its torture dwell.
    Alas! 'twas sweet, and yet a dream!

III.

I rested in the garden's shade,
Around me fountains softly play'd;
Their falling, murm'ring, waters' sound
Lulled me to rest in sleep profound.
But now, again, that vision's near!
Scares away sleep with trembling fear!
I linger on those rosy lips,
Once more, my soul their nectar sips!
    Away! 'twas but an idle dream!

The moon has broke,
The night is past, etc., etc.

Some of my readers, too, may be able to follow the singer in the expressive action which the words demanded; and who could exceed the accomplished Peri Buksh in pantomine? The graceful swaying of her body, the now repelling now inviting action of her beautiful arms, the glances she shot from her sparkling eyes, and the rapid evolutions of her tinkling feet, were simply enthralling and bewitching to an extent the Moulvee had never before encountered; and his *sotto voce* expressions of wonder and admiration, which his sacred calling forbade him to express aloud, could hardly be restrained from bursting forth with the loud cries of "Shabash!" "Bravo!" "Success to you, my darling!" and the like, which arose from the guests and Sepoys all round the room. This, however, though gracefully acknowledged by the Peri with smiles and waves of the hand, did not satisfy the girl. Suddenly she sat down close to the Moulvee alone, but followed by her musicians: and winding and waving her arms to and fro, while her jewelled hands almost touched his face, sang—

"As heart to heart, and lip to lip,
I, from my charmer, nectar sip,
O! rapture that I dare not tell!"

Again and again were the words repeated, until the Moulvee

fidgeted upon his seat, looked this way and that, spluttering out exclamations partly of admiration and partly repellant of the witching damsel.

"Ya Alla! Begone, shameless one! Where am I? Wonderful—enchanting—tormenting slut! Bravo!—Alla defend me! Witch, sorceress, begone! Nay, stay! La houl illa! Punna, punna! protect me, protect me! Ya Kubeer, Ya Kureem O!" he cried, with increasing fervour at every ejaculation.

"You had better give her a couple of gold mohurs, Moulvee Sahib, and let her go," said the Nawab, laughing heartily, as indeed were most of the company.

"Touba, Touba! Begone, witch!" cried the priest, fumbling in his pocket for the coin, and taking out several. "Thy spell is on me! begone!" and he dropped the gold coins into her hand.

"I should like to dance before the throne of the King of Kings," said the girl, joining her hands demurely as she rose. "Thou wilt not forget me, Moulvee Sahib, when I come to Dehly to witness the rejoicings on his victory."

"No! I will not forget!" he replied. "Go! Shookr, Shookr! thanks, thanks! a thousand!" he continued to the Nawab, and taking a long breath; "anything to get rid of her." And he resettled himself in his seat and shut his eyes, telling his beads with increasing rapidity and saintly fervour.

"She will come again, Moulvee Sahib. The Peri is seldom content with one visit; she will have some more of your gold pieces," said the Nawab, in a whisper.

"Nay! God forbid!" returned the priest, piously. "Keep her away! keep her away, for the love of the Prophet! she hath cast a spell on me already. Ya Michaeel! Ya Jibbraeel!" he cried, invoking the angels; "deliver me from her magic and sorcery. Ameen! Ameen! Touba! Touba! Only to think of it—that I, Zea Oolla—should feel the power of a witch!"

But the Peri did not return. She wandered hither and thither about the hall, sitting down wherever she found a likely group; and the Sepoys, altogether charmed, gave bountifully. I think that night the girl reaped a plenteous harvest. But she had done more. At first, a few apparently careless words had reached her ear which caused her to listen more attentively, as she saw the ex-Havaldar go from group to group, and give his orders; and changing her place more frequently after her performance was finished, she heard the men conversing in low tones of what was to be done to-morrow, at the evening roll-call, when the Noorpoor troops should rise. And after she had received her dismissal, and was quitting the Nawab's palace, Máina Jumoola met her with an excited manner, and took her aside.

"It will all be done to-morrow," she said, in a whisper, "and I will go on an elephant with a thousand men and bring away the girls myself."

"What girls?" asked the Peri.

"Missy Mostyn and the goldsmith girl," she replied; "both are wanted. But don't tell, 'for your life.'"

CHAPTER XLII.

A WARNING BEFORE OUTBREAK.

GRACE MOSTYN and Seeta were sitting in the octagon room next morning, for it was always quiet and safe from intrusion. Cyril would not have his wife fear the ladies of Noorpoor, now that she was among them in the fort, on common ground: and once Seeta had been sitting in what was called the ladies' drawing-room, in the old Patlián palace, which was common to all, with Mrs. Mostyn and Grace, when several had come in, and she thought had stared rudely at her, walking round her, and eyeing her from head to foot with suspicious wonder. Mrs. Smith had been one of these, with Mrs. Home and one or two others of their "set:" and after, as Mrs. Smith said, "they'd had a good look at her," they went away to discuss poor Seeta's appearance, not certainly in a flattering manner.

"I wouldn't sit in the room with a 'nigger' woman," said Mrs. Smith, afterwards, indignantly sniffing the air, "no, not for worlds; and you may say what you like about her being pretty and fair, and all that. She is none the less a 'nigger,' my dears, one of the horrible black people we live among, who would murder us, as they murdered the poor dear things at Dehly and Jhansy, if they could. I'm not going to have her come and sit there just as if she was one of us. I shall make Smith complain to the Brigadier, if she attempts it, I can tell you. Mrs. Mostyn may have black people in her own room if she likes, that's her husband's affair: but the idea of her bringing one here! Just think of it, my dears!"

"I quite agree with you, Maria dear," said Mrs. Home, "and I shall not allow Lucy to go to Grace Mostyn for lessons, if that black girl is to be there. Only just think of my darling girl being exposed to such contamination! I hear these black women are *horrible* in their conversation among themselves. My Ayah tells me *such* stories. Things, you know, that I should be ashamed to mention, even to you, my dears; and how Grace Mostyn can teach *that* girl, passes my comprehension entirely. Certainly, she appears to like teaching, just like a governess, you know; at least, Lucy says so."

"And I have no doubt she was one," said Mrs. Smith, exultingly, and as if a new light had entered her mind. "Now I think of it, the way she plays and sings is *quite* professional, and she knows ever so much Italian and German. Yes, depend upon it, she was taught how to teach. No one knows, my dears, what girls have been before they are brought out to be married. One ought to be most careful whom one knows, really one ought. Why, that dreadful prosy old 'Mother Pratt,' as the boys in the regiment call her, was only a missionary, and was never in *good* society; and Mrs. Mostyn, for all she is the Judge's wife, need not be so stuck up about that 'governess' sister of her husband's. Bah! I wonder any of you can endure any of them, the nasty conceited things."

I think we may conclude from the foregoing that Mrs. Mostyn, Grace, and poor Seeta had little in common with this "set" of the Noorpoor ladies, and that Grace preferred quiet mornings in the octagon room in the tower, where Cyril seldom came to disturb them. For although they had removed to the fort, he and Mr. Noble still attended the Kucherry regularly, and though there was comparatively little to do, in local matters, the reports of the district native officers required close attention and immediate replies. Baba Sahib was busy with the revenue and statistical returns, and, in short, as far as ordinary current business was concerned, there was ample employment for all.

There was now a break in the monsoon, which had, as yet, been exceptionally heavy. The weather was much like English summer, fresh, soft, and warm, with light clouds flying before the regular south-western breeze, and their shadows chasing each other over the lake and fair landscape, spread out beneath the friends as they looked from the oriel window, sometimes joined by Mrs. Mostyn, but more frequently alone, reading or working, or Grace drawing as usual. The lake, now full, and sparkling in the bright sun, or changing when a cloud passed over it, as Seeta said, "like Grace's sweet blue eyes," was ever new to them; while the distance beyond was even more variable in the soft purple tints of the rugged mountains. As to the old fort, its towers and walls, with views from its ramparts, the quaint old buildings, and the many elegant portions of Pathán Gothic architecture with which they abounded—had already afforded Grace quite a small portfolio of sketches and drawings: and Cyril, when he returned from his work, was always ready to put in groups of figures, with his accustomed spirit and skill.

So, on the morning after the Nawab's nauch, and as I have already recorded, Seeta and Grace were sitting together, Grace drawing, and Seeta reading her morning lesson, when old Bheemee came to the door and said, "Come out, lady; Buldeo and Luchmun Singh want you." For an instant Seeta's calmness forsook her, as she thought something might have happened to her husband: but she rallied herself at once, and went out to them.

"There is a woman, a dancing girl of the town, Peri Buksh by name; I know her well," said Buldeo, "who is below there," and he pointed to the water-gate, "and wishes to see you directly. I wanted to bring her up, but the English soldiers won't let her pass, and I can't speak to them."

"What does she want?" asked Seeta, "I know no dancing girl here; why has she come?"

"I think it is about the Nawab," said Luchmun Singh; "she did not know you were here, and came to the house, looking for you, and said she had come from Futtehpoor. She was so glad when I told her that you and the ladies had been here for some days, so I brought her up. You had better come to her;" and Seeta, calling to Grace that she would be back directly, went down the slope to the gate, and found the Peri alone, sitting unconcernedly among the English soldiers of the guard, trying to speak to them in the few words of camp English she had picked up, and laughing heartily at her own attempts. But "Good morning, colonel," "How do you do," "Very well," and the like, were not suited to further her purpose. As Seeta now turned into the archway, the Peri leaped lightly from her seat to the ground, and touching her feet, put her own hands to her forehead, and eyes, and heart. "What do you want?" asked Seeta, timidly, for she did not know but that the girl was a second emissary from the Nawab.

"I cannot speak here," said the Peri respectfully, and even humbly; "we must be alone; you need not fear a woman, and I will tell you all."

"I am not afraid," replied Seeta—the girl's earnest, wistful look had at once dispelled suspicion—"come with me to my house; there is an English lady there, but she will not understand you."

"Missy Mostyn?"

"Yes," continued Seeta, "she is my friend. Let her pass up with me, if you please," she added in English to the corporal of the guard, who, as also his men, had saluted her; "she has business with me."

"Certainly, mum," answered the corporal. "We have orders to mind you. By Jove, lads," he added as the girls passed on, "that last's a stunner, isn't she? Such a leg and foot, as she dangled them from her seat there, I never seed afore. Why, she leaped up to the basement like a circus girl. Maybe she's a player; and such queer English as she has!"

"Ah! corporal," said a grim old veteran, "them d——d Pandies has some fine girls among 'em for certain; and that's one if I ever seed one. Look how she walks; a fine stopper. And as to Mrs. Brandon, why, men, if she'd only English clothes on, bless her sweet face, she'd be the prettiest girl in the station; and how sweet she speaks, just like an English lady, to be sure."

When Seeta had reached the octagon tower she bid her companion follow, and Grace looked up as they entered, and rose on seeing the Peri. "Who is that?" she asked.

"She has something to tell," said Seeta, "and appears anxious. You don't mind her: she is a dancing girl?"

"Not at all," said Grace. "Indeed; I should like to make a sketch of her, she is really such a lovely figure; but your husband would do her more justice. Do you think she would sit to me after she has spoken to you?"

"I will ask her, Grace. Yes, she says, you may make a picture of her; but I think she is half ready to cry," and Seeta pressed the girl to speak freely.

The Peri's first answer was a burst of tears, in a passionate sobbing flood, and while Seeta soothed her, "Do not touch me; do not touch me," she cried, putting away Seeta's hands; "I am vile and unclean. I am not worthy to come near either of you, to be in your house or be in your presence, for you know what I am. Every one knows Peri Busksh Tuwaif. Forgive my presumption: but there was danger, there is danger, and I came to warn you, Seeta Bye, and your friend. You are both in danger."

"What does she say, Seeta?" asked Grace; "she looks at me."

"Wait, and I will tell you presently; she has not told me yet," returned Seeta; "she is strangely agitated."

Yes, the hardened dancer and singer, the mocker of the

saintly Moulvee, abandoned to many evil courses, was yet a softened woman as she threw herself at Seeta's feet, and clasping her knees, cried through her bitter sobs, "They would have taken you, Seeta Byo, and you, Missy Mostyn, to Futtehpoor, and made you both their slaves. O! thank God! thank God! that you are safe, and beyond their power. Yet Máma Jumeela and a thousand men will come for you to-night. She thinks you are yonder, below, in your houses; but O! I vow thank-offerings to all the saints, that you are here, and that you have not refused to see me and hear my warning."

Then the girl told Seeta of the rising that was intended that night, and the plans of the "Colonel" from Jhansy, either to lead the Sepoys there, or besiege Noorpoor and take it with the Nawab's guns.

"I wish my husband were here," said Seeta anxiously to Grace. "He must know what this girl says. See, though she is only a dancing girl she can be loyal and true. There has been evil intended to us, my darling, but we are safe; thank God! O! thank God! I must send Buldoo to Cyril. Can you wait to speak to my lord?" she asked of the Peri, as she wrote a line to Cyril. "You are not afraid of him," she added as she returned from the door.

"I afraid?" replied the girl, now smiling. "No one, not even a child, is afraid of Mr. Brandon. We repeat his name when we light our lamps, and I know many a ballad about him, and you, Seeta Byo, that I could sing to you; and I know the love songs that Báz Bahadoor, the king of Mándoo, wrote for the girl who died for him, though she was but a dancing girl. She was an ancestress of mine, and she proved, as I will do to you, that we too can love and be faithful. Now, while your husband is coming I will wait, and she can make a picture of me if she will."

I do not know that it was a very successful sketch, for Grace was too agitated by what Seeta gradually revealed to her, to draw with her usual boldness and skill; but the face was very like, and a few light washes of colour gave the girl's draperies a reality of effect. It was a reminiscence of a day, and of an incident, which could never be forgotten.

When Cyril came, the Peri told him all her story, more calmly now, and more definitely, for she had been put at ease by Seeta and Grace, and had behaved modestly and with discretion. She was quite positive on every point, and very clear in her explanations. As she left Futtehpoor, the Nawab's "army," as she called it, was already under preparation. They were to march to the Nawab's boundary, and meet the Sepoys as they came away. Then all were to unite, and storm the fort.

"Keep a watchful guard on the water-gate by which I came up," said the Peri; "they may attack it when they find the ladies are here. At present Máma Jumeela believes they are in their houses. Now let me go, sir, and may God keep you; but I have no fear; I should have none here, were I you. If I may, lady," she said to Seeta, "I will bless you both. God even hears the prayers of the dancers; and do you put your hands on my head, both of you, and I shall be grateful. Though we may never meet again, do not forget Peri Buksh;" and when she had removed their hands, and kissed them, she went away with Cyril Brandon, to be passed through the gate by which she had entered. "Do not let a man stay below," she said as they parted; "better that your houses should be burnt, than that a life should be lost. Now I have warned you."

"I will look to it directly," replied Cyril; "and while I thank you in the name of all here for your good faith in coming to me, you may rely upon me that it will not be unrewarded when better times come."

Cyril Brandon, as he rode up from his Kucherry, had noticed the men of the — Regiment standing in groups upon their parade ground, and talking in low tones. One fellow, who appeared excited by Gánja or spirits, had cried "Deen, Deen!" and some jeering laughter had followed. "Had I known what the girl has told us, I would have brought away what remains of the treasure," he thought; "but there is not very much left there." Then he went to the Brigadier, who had a tower like his own at the other end of the fort, above the gate, and found him, Captain Hill, and other officers assembled, looking with their glasses to the parade grounds, and evidently thinking that there was mischief going on. Both the commanders of the regiments were there, and Captain Hobson also, who did not seem at ease about his men; and of the others, one was uneasy also, and had been warned not to go near the men by the native adjutant. As to the other, he was cheerful; his faith in the attachment of his men, and his confidence in the Soobadar Major of his regiment, Drigpál Singh, could not be shaken.

Perhaps it had been a harder struggle for that fine old Soobadar Major, than his commanding officer knew. Most part of the previous night he had sat upon the parade ground, reasoning patiently with the men of all ranks, telling them of the delusions which had been sown broadcast among them, and reminding them of the victories their forefathers had won.

"Look at these scars," he cried as he bared his chest; "look at the honours I wear. I am a Sirdar Bahadoor, and could I be faithless? If ye rise against those who are as fathers and mothers to ye, shoot me first here, as I stand, or swear to me to be loyal. It is better to die than to see you faithless." And he had prevailed; and their commander, who had come on the parade with several officers, hearing the men were assembled, was welcomed with tears and sobs, and cries of loyalty and truth; yet they could hardly believe them! How many elsewhere had received like assurances, and yet had been shot down?

It was clear to the old Soobadar Major that a rising would take place; but he did not expect it for some days. Strange Sepoys, Oudh men, had been seen about, who pretended to be on their way home from the Dekhan; and since they had been seen, there had been agitation; but, nevertheless, Drigpál Singh did not expect mutiny for some days. The Peri's information proved, however, quite correct in the sequel; and prepared at all points, the Brigadier and some of the officers, with Cyril Brandon, and Mr. Mostyn, sat on the terraced roof of the Brigadier's tower, watching what might take place, while the officers, English soldiers, and artillerymen had all taken up their posts on the towers and gates. Men do not speak much at such times, and the anxiety of all was far more intense in its pain than the actual presence of danger. Hobson and other officers had gone to their men, and few were now present.

The evening was closing in, and some lamps had even been lit in the native town. The moon was yet young, and shed a dim uncertain light; but there was no mistaking a signal which rose high in the air from the direction of Futtehpoor. Three rockets shot up in succession, and the last broke into a shower of blood-red balls.

"Look," cried the Brigadier, as the first rocket rose; "we shall soon see who are true and who are faithless; for my part, I suspect all, and it is a reckless waste of life for any officer to go among the Sepoys. Those who go must do so on their own responsibility."

Almost as he spoke, a vast discordant clamour arose from the lines furthest from the fort, and many shots were fired in rapid succession. As a dark mass assembled on the parade ground of the ——, it swayed about for awhile, then at length seemed to consolidate itself, and marched on. "Shall I fire, Brigadier?" cried an artillery officer on the cavalier. "I see they are the —— as yet. They are firing on the ——. I can see them through my night glass quite distinctly. None of their officers are with them."

"Fire!" cried the Brigadier; and they saw two shells, hurtling through the air, fall among the mass, which instantly broke away and fled. And now many bright lights showed among the lines of the regiment that had mutinied, which grew into a conflagration of the Sepoys' houses, and from the roofs of several thatched bungalows flames arose high into the air. There was only a gentle breeze even at the fort; but it was enough to fan the flames, the glare of which spread all over the parade ground. The guns were now silent, for there was nothing which afforded a mark, only small parties running across the plain escaping from the burning lines, to join the main body, which, under shelter of some gardens and trees beyond, could not now be seen; but the sound of the tumult was appalling.

Suddenly, there broke from the further end of the infantry parade, two officers, one bareheaded, pursued by a body of cavalry at their utmost speed, brandishing their sabres which flashed in the bright light, while their shouts of "Deen!" "Deen!" came up on the wind clear above the roar of the flames, and the tumult everywhere. They were Captain Hobson, and young Temple, his second in command; and it was now, indeed, a race for life. Both were well mounted; but the cavalry horses were fresh and speedy, too, and it appeared as though they must be overtaken and slain before their eyes. Captain Hobson's charger seemed almost growing feeble, and he lagged behind, when Temple reined in his own, and they were again together spurring madly. Once Hobson turned in his saddle and fired at a horseman who led the rest, and was close behind him, but who fell directly from his horse, which, after dragging his body for a time, careered riderless over the parade ground. The scene was watched with breathless and speechless interest by those who beheld it, and hope was almost dead; when again the cool, watchful officer of artillery shouted "Fire!" and shrapnel shells from both the howitzers rose slightly in the air, and burst over the mass of the pursuers, who turned and fled, leaving a ghastly, writhing heap of horses and their riders on the ground.

Then a sight ensued which gladdened many a heart. The other regiment, well formed in columns of companies, rushed out of the shelter of their lines, and with shouts of "Jey Koompani Bahadoor!" dashed at the double up the parade, bayoneting, as they passed, the wounded troopers and Sepoys they found there. At their head rode their commander and the adjutant, with their officers along the flanks, waving their swords as the steady compact mass passed onwards, their bayonets flashing, and their scarlet uniforms glowing under the light of the fires around. Onwards! still onwards, towards the mutineers, from whose mass under cover, dropping shots now proceeded. Cyril Brandon could no longer control himself; he must strike in with the faithful, loyal men, and he might save the treasure. No one saw him go, but he was well armed with sword and revolver; he had always liked the regiment, and he was sure he could be of use. As he ran through the gates, he met Hobson and Temple just entering them, and saw Hobson was bleeding from a sabre-cut in his breast, and his horse's neck and chest were dropping blood; but English soldiers were supporting him, and in the darkness and confusion, Cyril passed out of the gate.

During all the tumult, some of which, but not all, they could see from their place by the gun on the octagon bastion, Mrs. Mostyn, Grace, and Seeta stood breathless and watching. Mrs. Mostyn was almost hysterical; but Grace and Seeta were calm, and both were praying silently. They did not know what had happened; but it was evident that the Peri's warning was true as regarded the Sepoys, and it remained to be seen whether it would be as correct in regard to the attempt upon themselves. By the side of the gun stood the Irish sergeant who commanded it, and the men, peering hither and thither through the gloom of the fast closing night, but seeing little.

"Look out, sir," cried the sergeant to the officer who now commanded the guard at the gate below, and who, with several of his men, was standing on the bastion which rose beside the gate. "Look out, sir; the Pandies may be trying to get round there. Wait for me, sir, before you fire."

"All right," answered the ensign in command, "we're ready here. Do you keep a sharp look-out too; I shan't fire till they are close."

Seeta's faculties were in the highest degree of tension. She was perfectly calm, and Grace ever after remembered the serene look, the almost smile, with which she gazed into the darkness below her. She had scarcely appeared to notice the discharges of artillery which echoed round the buildings of the fort: and the growing light of the conflagration falling on her face, showed it glowing and confident, with her beautiful lips parted, and her small pearly teeth glistening within them. Suddenly, she seized Grace's arm and said, "Don't you hear them—the elephant bells clashing?"

"She's loaded wid a shell," said the sergeant, "and the fuze is cut for the gardin. But, bedad, boys, I don't see that a round shot over it would do harm; she's able to carry that, an' more. In wid it, min, and ram it down well." And the sergeant took another look down the piece, and was satisfied that the aim was correct. The glare of the fire was now shining on the gun, and upon the lawn of Cyril Brandon's garden; and the sergeant could see all there clearly.

Yes! nearer and nearer came the bells, and suddenly some torchbearers appeared in the road behind Cyril's house, followed by a motley crowd of native foot soldiers, carrying bright matchlocks, and running at a steady pace. Then they dashed round the corner of the house, followed by an elephant, in the howdah of which some one was sitting.

"Be jabers," cried the sergeant, who was looking along the gun, "it's the gineral of the Pandies! If that baste 'ud only stand still now, for a minnit, I'd have him. Steady, all of yez, and mind when I say Fire."

The elephant was still. Some one in the howdah was talking to men who had been through the house and cottage. The figure was dressed like a man, but the features could not be distinguished, though the light of the many torches and of the conflagration showed the whole group distinctly; and two men with torches were evidently obeying signs, for no words could be heard, to fire the houses.

The sergeant, however, had got his aim perfectly. "Fire!" he cried, and the men ran to the parapet of the bastion to see the effect. The bursting of the shell hid the object for a moment; but an instant after, they saw the noble beast totter and fall, and there was a heap, from the bottom of the howdah, flung out on the grass.

At the same time the guard fired a volley from the bastion below, and perhaps with some effect, for the distance was within easy Enfield range; but there was no need to fire again. Every man on the lawn had fled, and the now decreasing blaze of the conflagration left the lawn in darkness.

"I hot 'im, boys, so I did," cried the sergeant exultingly, as he saw the effects of his shot. "Ah! be me sowl, but you're the best old girl I iver handled," and he patted the breech of the howitzer; "an' I hope yez seen it too, Mistress Brandon? Bedad, it's she that doesn't faint, lads, at the crack of a gun; and if it waren't clane agin orders, we'd give yez three cheers, ma'am, so we would."

Yes, Seeta had seen the shot; and early in the morning,

Buldeo and Luchmun Singh ran down to the lawn, and saw the bloated, shattered body of Máma Jumeela lying beside the dead elephant and its driver. The jackals and hyenas had already been busy with it, while vultures sat grimly on the trees around, waiting their turn.

"I wish it had been Azrael Pandé," said Buldeo, as they took the gold ornaments from the woman, and a heavy bag of money from her waist; "but his time may come."

CHAPTER XLIII.

"THE STILLING OF THE STORM."

THROUGHOUT the night, the frightful tumult continued. The evil rabble which always follows a military camp threw off all restraint, and plundered at their will, sacking the deserted bungalows of officers, or the shops of traders in the bazaars, and in many places causing fresh fires to break out. Shrieks and cries came from all quarters to the fort; but it was impossible to render aid to sufferers, or indeed to take any measures for local tranquillity until the morning should break, and show what could be done. The Brigadier's precautions had often been sneered at, but the issue had proved the wisdom of his foresight. The outbreak might be renewed at any time since the first bursting of the storm; and had there been no preparation, what could have been done in an emergency like the present, with no provisions laid in, and no quarters prepared? Who could have surmised that one regiment would be faithful? Had both suddenly risen when all were off their guard, and Christian men, women, and children were scattered in their houses over the wide cantonment, many must inevitably have perished; and even the English soldiers might have been overwhelmed, or forced to retire from Noorpoor. If the native troops had then seized the fort, who could have driven them out of it? or if such a measure as an attack on it had even become necessary, how enormous would have been the sacrifice—how precarious the success! Never in their existence, perhaps, had those in the fort felt more perfect security, or had been more grateful for protection.

One by one the officers of the regiments that had mutinied, dropped in and told their tale: how the commander and the adjutant, and a few native officers, had gone from company to company in the lines, and adjured the men to be steady; how they had been jeered, taunted, and threatened, until the regiment formed into a mass on the parade, and marched away. And how, strange to say, none of the English officers had been hurt, though at the last, to drive them off, the men fired—if not at them, at least near enough to them to give a significant hint of what was intended if they should persevere in attempting to hinder their designs. As to Captain Hobson, he, too, had appealed earnestly to his men, and as he thought at first with some effect; but as they wavered, one man, a notoriously violent character, had suddenly ridden at him, and wounded him severely in the chest and shoulder. Others were following up the action of their comrade: when, seeing that they could barely save their lives, he had called to Temple, and escaped as I have related.

"Those two shells, and the loyal —th, saved us," said Hobson, as he was having his wound dressed, and was telling his story; "but when my horse was staggering from loss of blood, and we saw the regiment forming, we thought it was all up with us, till we knew their officers were with them; then only we felt we were safe."

And never were gladder sounds heard in Noorpoor than the bugles of the —th, as at daylight the regiment marched steadily upon the parade ground, from the cover of the gardens beyond, headed by their brave commander and other officers. The Brigadier, and many who were with him, hurried down from the fort to give them a hearty reception, and hear how the night had passed with them, and truly it had been an exciting one. They had beaten the recreant regiment out of the limits of the cantonment, and inflicted some loss upon it as long as there was light; but when the moon set, they could see no longer, and it was evident from the shouts of men, the neighing of horses, and the clashing of elephant bells, at a little distance, that they had effected a junction with the Nawab's forces, which had been drawn up to receive them. The faithful regiment had suffered but little loss; one English officer had been slightly wounded by a bayonet-thrust in his arm; but none of the rest had been hurt, and among the men, the casualties were slight considering the nature of the service they had performed. Never was there a fitter opportunity for reward, and the Brigadier, on his own responsibility, distributed a month's extra pay to all present through the night, with an immense increase to his popularity. Some of the men, however, had gone with the mutineers. On the other hand, more than an equal number of the faithless regiment, with several of its native officers, had remained, who met their comrades in undress, and implored to be received into their ranks. Nor were the cavalry all gone, for nearly a hundred men and some native officers, came from their lines and submitted themselves to the Brigadier's orders. Thus Noorpoor became actually stronger than before; and the positive gain by the flight of the disaffected was a relief to all, beyond conception.

Cyril Brandon had been doing his duty too, in another quarter. After he had passed through the gate he made the best of his way to the police lines, where he found Noble with the men, and was welcomed with a shout of delight. But it was too late to save the Kucherry and the treasury. A guard of the mutinied regiment had been upon it that day: and at the signal, they had at once fired the building, loaded the treasure, fortunately of no considerable amount, on the tumbrils, and made off towards Futtehpoor. As this was beyond doubt, Cyril and his companions betook themselves to the gaol, which was full of prisoners in the last degree of excitement. Fortunately it had been in charge of police only, who were faithful, and violence within had been repressed. An attempt had been made by the mutineers to dislodge the guard, but they had resisted stoutly, as the bodies of several dead Sepoys lying near the gate attested.

The varying nature of the night's engagement prevented any renewal of the attack, and Mr. Brandon's reinforcement of some fifty men placed the security of the building beyond question. All night long, therefore, he and Mr. Noble had watched, not knowing what was occurring, till nearly daylight; when two of the Sikhs who had volunteered as spies, brought the welcome news that the mutineers, with the Nawab's forces, were retiring upon Futtehpoor.

Meanwhile, poor Seeta had passed a very woeful night, for of Cyril there were no tidings. She had herself watched the tower whence the events I have recorded had been witnessed, and where she saw Mr. Mostyn: but not her husband. Then she had sought Mr. Mostyn, and inquired of him; but he could tell her nothing but that Cyril had been with them, and he had suddenly missed him; and he went with the distracted girl everywhere he could think of to seek him, but he was not to be found. Could he have gone to the Kucherry with Noble, and both perished there? For Mr. Mostyn had seen the flames of the building soon after the mutiny had broken out. To ascertain anything definite during the night was impossible: and, making over Seeta to his wife's and Grace's care, he went to renew his watch with the Brigadier and the rest on the high cavalier; and as he looked through his glass at the —— as they crossed the parade after daylight, and saw that neither Cyril nor Mr. Noble was with them, his heart sank within him. What could he tell Seeta?

It had been a hard, a weary night for Seeta to bear. "Why did he leave me alone?" "Why did he go?" "Will they bring him to me?" "O, let me go and seek him!" Such piteous cries, mingled with choking sobs and prayers, neither her two friends nor good Mrs. Pratt could soothe; for in truth they all feared the worst, and could only console Seeta to the best of their ability and pray with her. So she sat, tearless and silent, with a white, seared face, only moaning a little now and then, but patient, though scarcely understanding what was said to her. They said afterwards, as they thought then, that had Cyril's body been brought in, she would have died, without speaking.

And perhaps she would; but there was joy in store for her. We know that at daylight Buldeo and Luchmun Singh had gone down to the house, and they had not returned. Seeta, who had been restless in the octagon room, had gone up to the terrace overhead, and Mrs. Mostyn followed her, for the fresh morning air was delicious. They saw Seeta looking earnestly at the lawn, and presently, the figures of the men moving about. Then Seeta had descended quickly to her oratory, and before they knew what she was doing they saw her, dressed in her boy's clothes, hurry down to the gate, and run down the slope, accompanied by the rest of her Rahtores, who had been on guard with the English soldiers. Mrs. Mostyn and Grace were now in the utmost alarm; but who could recall her? Buldeo and his companion had met her as she descended. Not heeding the ghastly heap on the lawn, or the dead lying about, she cried to them all, "If ye are men, come and look for your lord, with me;" and the party pressed on.

We know, however, that Cyril was quite safe; and that he could depend upon the police. So, leaving the brave old Darogah at his post, he thought he might as well see what had happened at or near his house, for he had heard the report of guns from the tower. I do not think he was even in any particular hurry: and as Seeta turned round the house from the lawn, she first saw Muff, who came barking and leaping on her, and then Cyril, strolling along leisurely, with a cigar in his mouth.

"Why did you leave me, O why did you leave me?" she cried as she touched his feet. She could say no more, for he thought she would have fainted from excess of joy; and he supported her into the cottage, and laid her down upon the divan, while the old Brahmin and his wife, who had gone down with Buldeo, brought her water.

"O, I will thank God! I will thank God, Cyril," she said, when she could speak, "who has saved you all. I will go to Him as a little child, and He will not be angry with me, He will not turn me away. But do not leave me again, Cyril; never, never leave me. I should have died last night when the tumult continued, but for my prayers. O, never leave me again! If you go, even into battle, take me; I will not fear; but alone I am a coward indeed. Promise me this, Cyril; O my darling, do not deny it!"

Cyril knew his wife spoke the truth. "No, I will never leave you again," he said fervently. "There may be rough work, but you are best with me. I could not help myself yesterday, for there was no time to call you, and indeed I was quite safe."

Then he went out to give directions for the lawn to be cleared of what lay there, and Buldeo showed him what remained of the horrible woman who had come for Seeta. It was with a thankful heart that Cyril knew his wife to be safe.

"Does she know of this?" he asked.

"No, sir," replied Buldeo. "We did not like to tell her, but Luchmun Singh and I washed the ornaments, and have put them away safely above. What could have brought the Máma Sahiba here, sir?"

"Her own folly and wickedness, I suppose," said Mr. Brandon, looking up to the tower. "She did not know that you were watching her?" Cyril did not choose to gratify Buldeo's curiosity in regard to the woman. When he returned to Seeta he asked her whether she knew who had been killed; but she did not. "I was too anxious then to care or think who was in the howdah," she replied. "I thought it was one of the Nawab's officers, and that they would burn down the bungalow and my cottage; but the sergeant prevented that; and I saw the elephant fall, and something thrown out of the howdah. What was it?"

"Máma Jumeela," he answered; "so be thankful that you have one enemy the less. How true the dancing girl was, Seeta; we must reward her somehow."

"Yes," she said absently, "we must reward her." But she was shuddering at the horrible danger she had escaped. Who could have helped her had she remained in her cottage? who could have helped Mrs. Mostyn or Grace? All of them must have perished miserably, or been reserved for a fate far worse than death; and how blessed was safety under such thoughts!

There was to be a special thanksgiving service by the chaplain on the ensuing Sunday, in the hall of audience, the "Dewan-i-Am," usually the public room of the soldiers, which was to be specially arranged for the occasion; and as all the Christians of Noorpoor were in the fort, it was preferable to have the service there, to attempting to use the church, which, though entire, had been wrecked by the camp plunderers, and the seats and altar damaged.

Seeta knew that this ceremony was to be performed, and very timidly she asked Cyril whether she would be admitted. "Suppose I should go," she said with a wistful face. "Many native Christian women will go, and I could be with them; no one would know me."

"And why not go with Mrs. Pratt and the Mostyns?" he asked. "Go! of course you can go. Our churches are open to all; and where prayers are publicly read, the place is God's temple, for the time. I am sure Mrs. Pratt and your friends will take you, and if they don't, I will. O Seeta, I am so glad that you can think with us now."

She said nothing, but buried her head in his breast, and sobbed like a little child, a weary child perhaps, seeking what had not yet been fully developed to her. "O, if you will but take me, Cyril, just for once, that I may pray to the God who brought you safe to me, I should be quite happy. Indeed, I would not make Him angry, for I would pray to Him only as a child, and I know He is very pitiful." When Cyril told them, dear old Mrs. Pratt and Mrs. Mostyn and Grace said Seeta should sit with them, and do just as she liked; nor did they think her less a Hindoo than ever; but they felt the girl's high aims of gratitude and love in all their force, and were content to wait their effects.

Seeta joined Mrs. Mostyn and Grace in their own rooms on Sunday morning, and Mrs. Mostyn, as she welcomed her with a kiss, gave her, in her own name and Grace's, a pretty prayer-book, bound in ivory plates, with a clear bold type. None of them could speak very much, and Seeta was trembling, but not excited. She was simply dressed in a white muslin saree, without ornaments of any kind; and as they entered the hall, Seeta put aside her sandals, as she always did, and walked up to their seat with bare feet.

The hall was a fine specimen of Pathán Gothic, the groins of its arches rising to meet octagons which supported the small domes that formed the ceiling. All the principal portions of the walls and roof were profusely decorated with arabesques in stucco, and had been now washed and cleared, from the bats and swallow's nests which had before disfigured them. The open apertures of the clerestory let a flood of light upon the centre, which fell in long slanting rays. Below, the wall was solid, but broken with bold niches and recesses in archways: and but for the light above, the interior would have been gloomy. On the daïs at the end, where the king, or local ruler, had been wont to sit of old, a carpet was spread; and there was a table with a pure white cloth, and the silver vessels of the sacrament upon it: a slightly elevated reading-desk had been put up at one side, and there were rows of forms for the soldiers, and chairs for the officers and their wives.

When the group entered the church, and proceeded to their seats, we may well believe that the presence of Seeta attracted no little attention: and there was a good deal of indignant sniffing on the part of some ladies present, at the unwarrantable intrusion, as they expressed it, of a "black woman," a heathen, into a place of Christian worship; but Seeta sat between Mrs. Mostyn and Grace, somewhat retired, and covered her face with her saree; nor did she feel nervous, for kind looks from Mrs. Hill and Lucy Home, and Mrs. Pratt, not to mention the sympathy of her friends, and the hearty approval of Mrs. Mostyn and her husband, gave her a calm confidence she had little expected to possess. I think if she had followed her own instincts she would have gone forward at once, and fallen prostrate before the table, and there prayed in her own simple fashion; but nobody she saw did that, and she followed the service which she had often read in a humble reverent spirit, with her heart swelling with gratitude in a kind of silent ecstasy, which she had never before experienced; and at the prayer for peace and deliverance, in time of war and tumult, and perhaps most of all at that supplication in the litany to Him "that despiseth not the sighing of a contrite heart," she could hardly restrain her emotion. Perhaps she could not follow all the service, for its length, and the changes in it, bewildered her; but she saw that passages had already been marked for her by the loving friends who best knew her thoughts—knew how full her heart was of devotion that as yet she could only think, but not express; and they watched the silent soft tears dropping gently from her eyes, while her reverent glances were now and then upraised, and her lips moved to her thoughts. They all noticed, too, that by chance one of the rays from the clerestory fell on her, and surrounded her as with a glory all the time she sat.

It was a fine service too, for the church harmonium had been saved, and brought up, and the Canticles and the Psalms of the day were chanted. Mrs. Pratt played the instrument, and some of the soldiers and their wives formed a strong steady choir. Then the sweet music and the blended voices ascended among the domes and fretted ornaments of the roof, and multiplied the sound till the effect to Seeta was wellnigh overpowering; and there was one hymn which she knew, and in which Grace whispered to her to join, and Seeta did so, her full rich voice being heard over many around.

Perhaps of good Mr. Pratt's sermon Seeta did not understand much, for indeed that excellent divine's delivery was none of the plainest, and was monotonous besides; but others understood it, practical and seasonable as it was, warning all to be ready should they be called, reminding them of those who had already suffered violent deaths elsewhere, and had comported themselves like true Christians, and exhorting all present, especially the thoughtless among them, to live in humble reliance on Him whose mercies had been already so signally proved.

When he had finished, most perhaps went away; but there were many that remained for the after service, and in their turn went to the table and took the bread and the wine. Could Seeta have gone with Grace and prayed there, she would; but there was a gulf fixed between them, which Seeta could not pass, and she could only watch the ceremony with earnest interest and eyes dimmed with tears.

Perhaps the wonder and admiration which blended with the conciousness that she had attended Christian worship and thanksgiving, had prevented her feeling to its utmost extent the impressive ceremony she had witnessed. As she reached home, she went into her little oratory, took the ashes from the sacred fire as usual, and touched her forehead reverently with them, and then prostrated herself before her little altar. There was only one silver image of Krishna on it, that her grandfather and Aunt Ella had confided to her with earnest injunctions for its worship: and now it seemed to blink at her sleepily with its sapphire eyes, and she cried to it in the words of her own liturgy which she had by heart. But after a time those prayers seemed to her cold and comfortless: and instead of them there came up involuntarily in her heart, the Christian wail, "O God, merciful Father, that despisest not the sighing of a contrite heart, nor the desires of such as be sorrowful," and she felt that, through God's mercy, "the craft and subtilty of the devil or man had indeed, for her, been brought to nought," and that she was safe —safe from the horrible violence that had been intended. And I think, as the Hindoo girl rose and sought her husband, to tell him of her gratitude, that there were few in Noorpoor that day who felt more deeply than Seeta, how merciful the Lord had been to all.

CHAPTER XLIV.

SEETA'S KINSFOLK.

WITH what agony the old banker of Shah Gunje and Aunt Ella had heard the common rumours of the mutiny at Noorpoor, I dare not attempt to describe; for it was reported that all the English had perished—that the soldiers and their officers, with all the ladies and children under their protection, had sallied from the fort, and surrounded by both the infantry regiments and the cavalry, and by the guns and forces of the Nawab, had fought bravely for a whole day, but had been slain in heaps: and that by the evening, none had survived.

Coupling this with the results at Jhansy and Cawnpoor, which were known to be true, and had been written to him circumstantially by his correspondents, Narendra gave the fullest credence to what he had heard, and was bowed to the earth by grief. As to poor Aunt Ella, she threw dust and ashes on her head, and sat moaning piteously, refusing to be comforted, and helplessly rocking herself to and fro, rejecting all food. For if the news as regard the English was horrible, that in regard to Seeta was still worse. She, it was stated, with a young English lady, the Judge's sister, had been carried off by the Nawab, and placed in his zenana; that Seeta had been immediately made a Mahomedan, and forced to eat cow's flesh, and that after hers and the English lady's seclusion, no more had been heard of them. No wonder poor Aunt Ella was like to die, as the news was brought to her by her servants; and even the priest could give no cheering hope or comfort. If it had happened, the catastrophe was too terrible, and the agony of grief too profound for human comfort; and indeed Narendra and his friend thought that, were the dear old lady to expire in one of her frantic paroxysms of suffering, it would be a merciful release to her. "Ram! Ram! Ram!" was suspended or forgotten; and in its stead there were cries for "Seeta! O, better she were dead;

better a thousand times she had perished with her husband, than live a polluted life as a Mahomedan slave."

Were then the English really to perish, or had they already perished everywhere in the north? In the south indeed, all was quiet and safe as yet; but the banker's letters from Poona and Hyderabad were by no means satisfactory. At Nagpoor the retainers of the old Bhóslays were conspiring to re-establish the family; and even in Bombay there was alarm and mistrust. When, I say, all this bad news and a great deal more was constantly arriving, and, as he believed for a time, Noorpoor had fallen, Narendra, well-wisher as he was to the English, might truly despair. He had not a word with which he could combat the now open-mouthed rejoicings of the evil-minded at Shah Gunje nor the advice of specious friends, that he should at once wind up his affairs and proceed to Benares, where he would be safe; but the old man was yet steadfast and brave, and remained. He had no doubt, in his own mind, that all the present evil would pass away in time, and that when the moonsoon ceased, the English from the south and west, would advance and drive the rebels from the prey on which they were now gorging themselves; but of all in Shah Gunje, though many had hopes, there were few perhaps, except Wamun Bhut, who could think with Narendra. So the old man had been hopeful and even confident till the reports from Noorpoor came, which broke him down for the time, entirely. Cyril Brandon dead, and his darling child carried away into pollution! I try to realize what the intensity of the sufferings of these two loving hearts must have been under this conviction, while it lasted, and am beaten back by my own thoughts, which cannot follow theirs.

Nor was this the only trouble which came upon the goldsmith's house. As he heard of the mutiny at Noorpoor, with all the exaggerations which went to Shah Gunje, Rajah Hurpál Singh, setting aside his habitual indolence, saw it was time to strike in. Some Sepoy mutineers from distant stations, had joined him in numbers sufficient for his purpose. His own levies were ready for plunder, and he advanced at once to secure his share of the Noorpoor province. It was a scramble in which the strongest and most active would get most; and Shah Gunje was not likely to be overlooked. With Ram Das, the Rajah had carried on a secret correspondence for some time past; and that wily person had already marked those from whom the largest contributions could be best levied. Among these it was not likely that Narendra would escape; and when the Rajah, with a force of several thousand men and artillery, suddenly attacked

Shah Gunje, putting the few police that guarded it to flight or to the sword, and hanging the unfortunate Tehsildar, who was the head local authority, Ram Das accompanied the conqueror, and assessed the contributions to be levied.

It was by no means his policy to exact too much from Narendra, for he had another and more effectual object in view, that of seizing the whole of his business and property for himself; and the Rajah's demand on the banker for ten thousand rupees was at once paid, partly in cash, and partly in bills on Benares and Mirzapoor, which were easily negotiable. Perhaps if Ram Das had known of the banker's secret treasure vault, neither he, nor the Rajah, would have let him off so easily; but he did not know, and none of the banker's establishment knew it except the Rahtores, now absent at Noorpoor, whose fidelity nothing could corrupt. Nevertheless Narendra was far from easy, and dreaded the unscrupulous character of the man in whose power he now remained.

If Ram Das could not discover the treasure, he could at least trace outstanding balances, and debts due from persons around the district; he could also discover the condition of accounts at Mirzapoor, Oomrawuttee, Bombay, Poona, and other agencies; and it was a miserable piece of ingratitude in one of Narendra's most trusted clerks, to direct Ram Das where to find books and papers relative to these matters. For Narendra himself was now a prisoner in his own house, inhabiting Seeta's old room, where the memories of her added perpetually to his other griefs; and Aunt Ella had been removed to one of the rooms in the upper corridor, on an occasion when, roused to fury by the conduct of Ram Das, and for the time forgetting her miseries, she had assailed him with reproaches, and abuse; declared that he was murdering her brother as he had murdered Huree Das, and that she would have her revenge on him when the English returned. What the reply of Ram Das was, I need not record, certainly neither temperate nor decent; and in spite of the old lady's sanctity, she was taken upstairs struggling, and kicking violently, but helpless against her detestable persecutor. Worse than this, the sacred fire which she had tended since she came to her brother's house was allowed to go out, and could not be lighted again without a special ceremony: and thus the cup of the dear old lady's misery was full; so full, that her mind was, for the time, a strange chaos and jumble, which affected her speech in a very peculiar and distressing manner, and rendered her quite insensible to solace, even the little that her brother—for Wamun Bhut's visits were now interdicted—could afford her.

There were others too in the town as badly off as Narendra, or perhaps worse. Small bankers and money dealers, whose means were narrow, weavers, provision dealers, copper-smiths and brass-smiths, grain merchants, cloth merchants, in short all trades that ministered to the social wants of the place; farmers, landholders who lived there, and generally all persons from whom contributions could be exacted, even of the smallest amount, were forced to give them. I say forced, for the Rajah and his courtiers sitting in the public court of the Tehsildar who had been hanged, amused themselves for several days with their own peculiar methods of ingenious extortion: that is, by laying out people in the sun with their hands and feet tied to tent pegs, piling stones on their chests, and—— But perhaps I need not specify all the modes of torture which, as the people could not help thinking, did not exist in the days of the English. There were not many Mahomedans in the town, but with them, some of the Hindoos had a long existing feud, and now was the time to pay off old scores. So the Rajah, who hated Mahomedans, sent for a pig and had its throat cut in the Mosque, and its blood smeared on the arches and pulpit, and the place wholly defiled. Nor, as the Mahomedans thought, had the English ever done anything like this. Why, it was not many months ago, since Mr. Brandon had given a grant in aid of their school, and with this it was to be enlarged and new books bought; and he had examined the boys and given them a feast of sweetmeats, because they had pleased him; and these things were not forgotten. But they were all helpless now.

Nor were the villages round Shah Gunje much better off than the county town. Ram Das and his agents were particularly active as revenue collectors, and there was no escaping the screw that was put on for payments in advance, of the coming year's collections. And but too many suffered heavily by this, being obliged to sell their cattle and family jewels, under their value, to extortionate money dealers. Well, I need not perhaps tell of more miseries; but the anarchy and disorganization of the rural districts was as complete as if there never had been any English. It was a practical return to the rule of old times.

> The good old rule, the simple plan,
> That those do take who have the power,
> And those do keep who can.

And the wonder was, if it was wonderful, that the change was the effect of but a few days. And marauders, plunderers, and thieves without number, sprang up in all directions, and there was no more peace abroad.

But peace did come to the banker and Aunt Ella after some days; a peace so entire, and so blissful, that all the other troubles they had suffered, and were enduring, went by them as on the wind. The very day after the thanksgiving service at Noorpoor, Buldeo and one of the Rahtores, accompanied by one of Narendra's treasure carriers, who was with the agent at Noorpoor, left that city with special despatches for the banker; and other bankers of Noorpoor availed themselves of the opportunity to forward letters to their own correspondents at Shah Gunje. Seeta, indeed, would have written at once after the mutiny to her grandfather, to assure him of her safety; but one of the Nawab's first acts had been to stop all the posts, to drive away the runners, and to prevent the garrison of Noorpoor having any communication with the world outside; and thus Seeta was obliged to wait till the agent considered the despatch of the men tolerably safe. All of them knew secret paths to Shah Gunje through the woods and forests, the inhabitants of which they did not ordinarily fear; but now, every man's hand was against his neighbour, and the utmost circumspection was necessary. But in the end, the intelligence and courage of the men triumphed. Their last resting-place had been the lonely temple cave at which this tale opened, and it was with the utmost caution that they entered Shah Gunje in the evening. Buldeo, not knowing the secret ways of the house, was sorely puzzled how to deliver his precious packet; but at length, one of the women servants who knew him, led him up from the back yard by a small staircase; and with a cry of delight, he laid the parcel at the old man's feet. "They are well," he exclaimed, "well and safe; not one of the English has been harmed, and they are stronger at Noorpoor than ever!"

Narendra had looked up, wistfully at first, from the bed on which he was lying. He did not know Buldeo's face, or had forgotten it: but he remembered the high cracked voice, at the trial, and starting up he received the packet without speaking, and opened it with trembling hands. Then, too, Aunt Ella, now far more gaunt than before, hearing a strange voice, tottered in, supporting herself on her staff: and when Buldeo touched her feet reverently, and pointed to Narendra, she saw that he had a letter in his hand, and was trembling very much, but his face seemed full of triumphant joy. As he saw her, he stretched both his arms out to her; "Ella! sister! they live," he cried, "they live! come and listen." But the revulsion and the joy were too much for the dear, loving old heart; it seemed to stand still, as her features quivered, and she would have fallen to the ground, but for the strong arms of Buldeo, who supported her, and laid her gently down.

It was long before she recovered, and indeed at one time they all thought—for her women had come to her—that she had died; but her breath came to her by gasps, and when she had swallowed a little water, she looked up imploringly, and raised herself, though she could not speak, and was shivering. "Dead? All dead?" she gasped.

"Not dead, Ella," said Narendra, "nor yet harmed," and he spoke very slowly that she might understand gradually, "but safe, sister, safe! Look! here is Seeta's letter; here is Mr. Brandon's. Look! O! how shall we thank the gods!"

Dear Aunt Ella! It was only very gradually that the blessed truth, the assurance of safety, broke upon her mind. She wept; she laughed; she put the letters to her breast and hugged them; to her eyes, which now rained tears, and covered them with kisses. She stretched out her arms to her brother, and fell upon his neck and sobbed, and wept and laughed by turns as though she were distraught. O! joy that had come to them both! so full, so complete, so indescribable that it were profanation to attempt to define it, for we know what they had endured even for those few short days, which had wellnigh wrung life out of both their hearts.

And when they were calmer, Narendra read the precious letters they had received, again and again; for Seeta's was full and descriptive, and Brandon's tender and grateful that all were safe. "Take good heart," he had written in conclusion, "we are not only safe, but more powerful here than before, now all are loyal and true. Tell this to every one in Shah Gunje, and be thankful with us, that the storm of 1914 has passed over us without injury. Soon, perhaps, we may have forces to act against rebels, and the old peace will ensue." Nor did they doubt his hearty, cheering words, and they seemed to ring in their ears as though the writer himself had been there with them and spoken them. All night they sat with Buldeo, and heard what had happened, and how Máma Jumeela had died; how bravely the —th had fought, and how safe and strong the fort was, with the English "sojers" in it. As the day broke Aunt Ella could no longer restrain herself; new life and new strength seemed to have come to her, and without telling her brother, who had fallen into a sweet sleep, she took her staff and went to the temple as was her former wont; and Wamun Bhut found her prostrate before the image in the sanctum, weeping, but crying out her thanks, and, after a while, heard all the glad tale from her lips. When she returned, she found Narendra writing answers to the letters, for Buldeo was anxious to be gone, and had betaken himself for the day to his hiding-place. "He would come at night," he said, "for the despatches." As to Aunt Ella, I think the old ejaculations recommenced with unusual fervour, and as she saw the tally on her wall increase, she was more than ever convinced of the favour she had obtained from "Ram."

Meanwhile at Futtehpoor there had been a good deal of trouble and excitement. The ex-Havaldar Goor Bux, in his capacity of "Colonel," had, under his professional knowledge of guns and gunnery, furbished up several of the Nawab's old cannon, long disused and rusty, but still tolerably serviceable if leisurely fired. He dare not interfere with the mutineers, who were often at variance with each other, one party pressing an immediate march to join the Nana, or the Ranee of Jhansy; the other admitting the wisdom of the ex-Havaldar's advice to stay where they were and move only after the rains were over, and he promised them enough to do if they would stay.

As to the Nawab, he was but as a straw floating hither and thither on the stream. He was out of favour with both his wives, though one was relenting. He had lost Máma Jumeela, his chief confidant and adviser; he had not secured Missy Mostyn, nor been able to give Seeta to Azráel Pandé, who, after the excitement of the mutiny and his bitter disappointment that no English blood had gone to the "Mother," had resumed his old incantations, and rarely appeared above ground; and when he did, was moody and savage, and with difficulty restrained by his associates. Some men of the mutinied regiment had volunteered to go into Noorpoor and stir up the loyal regiment; but two had been detected and seized by the men of the —th, another had been apprehended by the police hiding in the town, and these were summarily tried, and blown away from guns, after the prevailing custom of the time.

When the "Colonel's" preparations were complete, he marched out from Futtehpoor with the Nawab's forces, and tried to establish a siege of the fort; but he succeeded very badly with the old guns and hammered shot, and the garrison were always active and vigilant, and well protected by the guns of the fort and the cover of the station, and occasionally made vigorous sorties against the earthworks which represented the enemy's batteries, and on one occasion captured one of the guns which the "Colonel" was not able to get away in time. Thus, therefore, constant skirmishes were going on, in which Brandon and

Mr. Noble and their stout police took an active part, defending their special post of the gaol, for which purpose they were amply sufficient. Nor was Seeta ever left behind now. No matter how great the exposure, or the fatigue, the active girl shared all; and the care of her person became, as might be expected, a point of honour to the men. Very often the English soldiers and the loyal —th asked to be allowed to follow up the rebels to Futtehpoor, and even to take the place from which such constant annoyance was experienced; but the Brigadier was cautious, and was quite satisfied by their conduct in protecting the fort and the cantonments.

But the Nawab thought he was wasting time in these ineffectual attempts to take Noorpoor, and when Rajah Hurpál Singh's successes and heavy collections of money were reported to him, he resolved to act vigorously. Sending the Moulvee Sahib in one direction, he took another himself, driving out what few police they found, establishing their own agents, and issuing proclamations that in virtue of the Nawab's appointment from the Emperor, he had become proprietor of the Noorpoor district, and all men were to obey him. Perhaps these proceedings are not worth record, for they afforded little contrast with the effects of those of Rajah Hurpál Singh, already mentioned: and if the Nawab, in some slight degree, was more careful of the people than the Rajah, in essentials perhaps there was not much to choose between them, or the anarchy that they created.

If it had not been for the constant skirmishes, and the occasional harmless whirr of a rough round shot over their heads, the garrison of Noorpoor would have been even duller than they actually were. No news came from without, and even the native merchants' despatches, of which Baba Sahib always collected the particulars, had grown dull and unimportant. Either their correspondents had become accustomed to the change, or there were events in progress of which they dared not write. The soldiers were, perhaps, the most content, for they had books, cricket, and all the games and amusements that could be devised for them, and they even got up a play and concert, at which our dear Mrs. Mostyn and Grace, and Cyril, and Captain Hobson, who looked very interesting with his left arm in a sling, assisted skilfully and well, and at which Seeta was present in a quiet corner.

As to the rest of the society, perhaps, the less I say about it the better; people penned up as they were, are liable to petty jealousies, fluctuations of parties and opinions of each other, which even a common danger does not prevent; and I think that our set was the happiest, because it did not trouble itself with its neighbours' affairs, and held its own with modest dignity, and courtesy to all.

CHAPTER XLV.

"FAITHFUL UNTO DEATH."

Life in the fort was gradually becoming very irksome; and even the excitement of occasional skirmishes had passed away, for the Nawab and his army had been making a triumphant progress through the district, and were at a considerable distance, with no apparent intention of returning to Futtehpoor. He was watching the actions of Rajah Hurpál Singh, whose retainers had attacked a party of his levies, and the indignation, both of the Nawab and the Moulvee, was at its height when the priests of the Mosque at Shah Gunje came to the camp with lighted torches in their hands, and wearing grave-clothes, while they threw ashes on their heads, and demanded justice for the defilement of the Mosque at Shah Gunje. "You are the representative of the King of Kings," said the chief delegate, "who has entrusted all of us to you; and we look for justice on the Kafirs who have done this wrong. In the time of the English such tyranny would have been impossible; and last year they even gave us an ample donation. Come and avenge this insult to the Faith, else we will beg our way to Dehly, and tell our injuries to the King of Kings! Dohai! Dohai!"

The Nawab was sorely distressed and puzzled. When such things had happened in his own estate, as they had done, he had left matters to adjust themselves, or had only interfered if he felt strong enough. But this had been the deliberate insult of a rival—one with whom the old feud was not dead—one against whose power his warlike progenitors had done stout battle. Was it come to his turn now to do the same? Certainly, he could not avoid or evade the quarrel which had been forced upon him; and yet the commanders in his army were Hindoos. Colonel Goor Bux and Azráel Pandé were Brahmins; the Soobadar Major of the —st, whom he dare not dismiss or offend, was a Brahmin also. Most of the Sepoys who had mutinied were Brahmins and Rajpoots; all likely to join Hurpál Singh if they had any temptation to do so, or to go to the Ranee of

Jhansy. And if they went, what was to become of him? His own local levies, undisciplined and worthless, he well knew could be beaten any day by the English troops at Noorpoor. Futtehpoor might be taken, and he himself become a wretched fugitive. All this passed like a flash before his troubled mind, while the delegates from Shah Gunje without his tent, were waving their torches in the bright sunlight, and throwing handfuls of dust into the air, crying "Dohai! Dohai!" and calling upon God and the Prophet for justice!

The Moulvee—who had been sitting in the Nawab's inner tent drawing up proclamations, and writing eloquent despatches to the King of Kings, giving florid descriptions of how the province had been taken possession of in his Majesty's name—hearing the tumult, now came forward, and soon learned the truth; and his ardent zeal for the Faith became suddenly inflamed.

"Can you hesitate, Dil Khan," he exclaimed, "as to what you should do, with the cries of these true believers ringing in your ears? March at once on Shah Gunje, and exterminate these infidels: or give me some of your men, who will fight with me for the Faith, and let me go. Deen! Deen!" he shouted, throwing down his turban and striding into the agitated crowd bare-headed, with his right arm upraised, and his pocket Koran held aloft. "Deen! Deen! let those who will follow me for the Faith, swear on the holy book to die rather than justice should fail. Let us away, my sons, and revenge this insult?"

Nor was his fanatical cry without effect. What true Moslem present could refuse it? So, from all quarters of the camp, the Mussulman warriors rushed forward, and the men of the cavalry became infected, and in a short time the Moulvee had a thousand fanatics around him, to whom, standing on a low mound of earth, he delivered a short sermon or address on the delights in paradise which awaited any who might become martyrs; and was answered by hoarse cries of "Ameen! Ameen!"

To check this tumult, the Nawab was perfectly helpless; and perhaps he regarded with a secret pleasure, not only the absence of the Moulvee, but his employment in a dangerous duty which he himself had chosen. The recovery of Shah Gunje, and the district of which Hurpál Singh had possessed himself, was a most important measure in regard to the consolidation of his conquest; and the promise of an estate to the saintly man, should he succeed, added much to the fervid zeal by which he was actuated. I need not, perhaps, detail the events which followed. Suffice it to say, that on the third night, the surprise of Shah Gunje was complete. Rajah Hurpál Singh, indeed, was not there; but his lieutenant was taken and hanged, his men routed and many slain, and in the excitement of victory, the fierce Moslem fanatics slew a cow in Wamun Bhut's pretty temple, overturned the idol, smeared its face with blood, and defiled the place as completely as the Mosque had been defiled before. Then the Moulvee issued a proclamation that no Hindoo was to appear with caste marks on his forehead, that bells must not be rung, nor conch shells blown, and that on any breach of these orders, every temple in the town would be blown up. I am almost tempted to translate the holy man's report of the victory to the Nawab, which was drawn up in his most grandiose and scholarly manner; but the quotations of Persian and Arabic are too numerous, and perhaps my readers would not be interested in so notable an example of Mahomedan fanaticism in its worst form.

If the capture of Shah Gunje did not directly concern characters which belong to this history, it might very well have been omitted altogether. Even now, I notice the event only as an effect of the times; how religious animosities, which had so long slumbered, awoke in many localities, and entailed terrible sufferings and indignities upon the people—becoming prominent and distressing parts of the anarchy which prevailed. If the excesses of Hurpál Singh's soldiers had been great, those of the Moulvee's were worse; and the wily Ram Das, making a handsome "nuzzer" or offering to that great person, was allowed to share his confidence, and direct exactions as before. Thus, the situation of all at Shah Gunje, and the riotous conduct of the excited Mahomedan soldiers, and the Moulvee's intolerance and exaction, became more and more unendurable.

Meanwhile, as I remarked at the commencement of this chapter, life in the fort at Noorpoor was becoming more and more tiresome. Party spirit, to some extent, had risen higher, and all kinds of amusements were obstructed by small jealousies. There were days when all dined together at the mess, where those whom it pleased to do so, saw favouritism in cuts of mutton, wings or legs of fowls, and special bones in the curries. Or, if they dined at home, matrons declared that the meat grew worse and worse, and the distribution of joints was shamefully partial and exclusive. Such small discontents were at first but as little clouds rising out of the distant horizon, and disappeared for a time; but again they gathered thicker, and sometimes broke in small peals of thunder.

There were two other causes, also, that helped to disturb the serenity of the female inhabitants: one was our poor dear Seeta's visit to the church on that memorable occasion; and the other the piano in the "ladies' room," on which every one seemed to wish to play at the same times of the day. On both these questions, party spirit and battles of "the sets" ran uncomfortably high; and though most frequently neutral, yet the gentlemen were not without bias, and were obliged to fight their wives' battles, warmly enough, sometimes. I think if I had the power and ingenuity of Mr. Trollope, I might find materials enough for a very spicy detail of male and female doings and sayings during this period, and of the many pretensions to the fair hands of Miss Mostyn and Miss Lucy Home, and their results; and even of attentions to poor Miss Clay, a rather antiquated spinster who resided with her sister, Mrs. Mowbray, of the —th. These, I say, with occasional brushes with the Pandies outside the walls, by way of sensation, are very tempting materials, but as I am not Mr. Trollope, I regret I cannot avail myself of them on this occasion, and must pursue the tenor of the history I am recording.

"I really can't stand this any longer, Philip," said Mrs. Mostyn, as she went into his den, as he called it, a small antechamber of the old palace, "those women are too bad—so unladylike!"

"Why, what's the matter now, Rose, anything new? I'm really tired of the scrags of mutton battles, and the drumsticks in the curry, and the brown of the rice pudding," replied Mr. Mostyn. "What's the matter?"

"No Philip," cried his wife, "it's not scrags of mutton, or curry bones, or rice puddings—it's spite! What do you think I heard two *ladies* say just now, quite loud enough for me to hear, and evidently intended for my ears, I'm sure? Now you'll never guess, though you are a Judge."

"I can't imagine, Rose—about Seeta? for I see some of them hate her."

"Not exactly, Philip; but, just think, they said that Grace was a governess, and that's why she taught a 'black woman' like Seeta, and gave lessons to that stupid Lucy Home."

"Well," said Mr. Mostyn, laughing, "I don't see any harm in that; and if Grace had been a governess, I'm sure I shouldn't be ashamed of her, nor would you."

"Oh, it's not that, Philip; but see the spite of it. It's just like their sneering ways and speeches, and I should like to box that Mrs. Smith's ears ten times a day," she replied, with a stamp of her foot. "What do you think my lady did? Just after she had shot her arrow at me, Grace came in with some music in her hand, and I know wanted to practise; but Mrs. Smith, if you please, just seats herself on the stool, and begins to strum some horrible quadrilles and waltzes—all wrong, too—and there she is still, and poor Grace fit to cry. Won't you come and speak to the wretch?"

"No," said Philip. "It is insolence, I know, but we need take no notice. I will tell Smith privately to caution his wife, and I know he hates her tongue as much as you do."

"Very well," said Rose, with a little pout, "do as you like; but if I were a man——never mind," she continued, "it's not worth notice; but can't we get rid of them all by going to our own house? Mrs. Smith can't go to hers, for it was burnt; but ours is all right. We went down yesterday morning with Mr. Brandon and Seeta, and the flowers are really lovely. And then you know all is quiet; there has not been an alarm even for more than a month."

"Yes," he said, "I think it's a capital idea. We have enough police for a night guard, and I need not ask the Brigadier; besides, I am really not well, and the change will do me good. Pooh!" he continued, as if assuring himself, "and we shall be right under the guns of the fort. There was an attempt there once, which I think the Nawab's rascals have not forgotten, and will not repeat. I'll see the Brigadier about it presently. And now go away, wifie; I am really very busy with my report, and all these dreadful statistics, and don't you mind Mrs. Smith."

The Brigadier had no objection. He only suggested caution, and that it would perhaps be better to sleep in the fort the first few days at any rate, and this was done. Early every morning, the ladies walked down to their garden, and every evening they came up in their tonjon. Sometimes Seeta was with them, sometimes not. She liked to be alone more than usual. She had her own troubles of mind which she dare tell to no one—no, not even to Cyril or Grace, though both suspected them, but would not speak about them to her as Mrs. Pratt did.

Were the foundations of the old Hindooism—the grand citadels of the Vedas and the "Bhugwut Geeta," the metaphysics of Patánjula, giving way? Sometimes Cyril thought they were, and Mrs. Pratt, who knew a little about them—but not much—thought so too! yet only sometimes, for Seeta's defence was strong and subtle. She had been an apt scholar of Wamun Bhut, one of the best disputants of the Vedantic Brahmins of the Noorpoor province against the materialist Poouránic sectarians; and she had all his arguments by heart, and often became fierce over them; while, finding she had grown rusty in some respects, she had lately almost neglected her English, to regain what she had lost. If Mrs. Pratt or Cyril had been as deeply versed in Hindoo theology as Seeta was, they might have had many a fervid battle; but, to all her learning, they could only oppose the simple truths and faithful realities of their own belief. Nothing of dogma was ever mentioned; only a Saviour's atonement for sin, His present help in all trouble, and faith to realize His gracious promises. It was truly a type of stormy waves beating against a rock, for Seeta grew fond of these arguments: fonder and fonder, as it appeared to Grace and Cyril, who did not encourage, and indeed avoided them. But Mrs. Pratt did encourage them, and rejoiced to hear them. The dear old lady argued from Seeta's persistence, that the good seed had taken root; but whether it had fallen among thorns, or in a dry and barren place, or in rich and fruitful soil, who could as yet tell? Who, indeed? Certainly not the Hindoo girl herself, who, with prayers and cries, when she was alone in her oratory or sitting in the oriel window looking over the lake, besought to be led aright.

Simple-minded and unworldly herself, Mrs. Pratt found Seeta equally simple in regard to all temporal matters. Mrs. Pratt knew she was wealthy; but Seeta seemed to have no idea of the value of her wealth or its use to others. She had committed all to her grandfather and her husband; "and, should I have a child," she said modestly, "it would inherit all."

"No," said Mrs. Pratt, "I am sure it could not. Only a Hindoo could inherit from a Hindoo—at least I think not—and you can't make a will as we can. Why not ask Mr. Mostyn about the whole matter, and take his advice? It appears to me, that at least there would be great litigation for your property, my dear, if you have any relations."

But, except Ram Das, Seeta knew of none.

"But my child would inherit the English property; no one could keep him out of that," said Seeta, as if driven into a corner; "that has nothing to do with Hindoos."

"My darling," said Mr. Pratt, as the colour rushed into her face, "it needs some one you believe in to tell you the truth about that. Has yonr husband never said anything to you on the subject?"

"O yes, mother" (Seeta always called Mrs. Pratt mother), "he has, many times! but"—and her face flushed in turn—"he never mentioned about England. O, I should like to see my son an English gentleman, like his father! Why should he not be?" she added proudly, as she saw an incredulous look on the old lady's face. "He would be a Christian—the Honourable Cyril Brandon."

"Now you will be angry with me, my child, if I tell you the truth," returned the old lady; "but, sooner or later, some one must do so, and Grace cannot. Will you hear it from me?"

"What is it?" asked Seeta, much agitated. "Let me put my head on your breast, and I shall not be afraid."

"Faithfully then, and as if I were truly your mother, I will tell you," continued Mrs. Pratt. "By English law and Christian custom, if you had a son as you are, he could not inherit except what was specially given him. He would have no rank and no name; he would, indeed, be illegitimate."

"But I am married," she cried, starting up, with her eyes blazing. "Cyril told me I was, and Narendra, and Wamun Bhut. I have not been living in sin, mother. O, do not say that—I should die!"

"No, darling: by the rites of your faith you are Mr. Brandon's wife, and as such we have taken you to our hearts and love you. But the English law does not recognize that. Your rites are not ours, Seeta."

"Then if I were married to him by Mr. Pratt," she gasped through her sobs, which were coming heavily and fast, "should I be truly his wife, by your law and ours?"

"Yes, Seeta, you would; but Mr. Pratt could not marry you to Mr. Brandon while you are a Hindoo."

"God help me! God help me!" was the girl's bitter cry, as she threw herself once more on the dear old lady's breast. "God help me, for I know not what to do!"

"And He will help you, my sweet child, if you cry to Him," returned Mrs. Pratt, sobbing in her turn: "no one ever turned to Him in doubt or difficulty like yours, and sought Him in a child's spirit with an earnest heart, that He did not direct. No matter what you say to Him, He will hear. Do you believe that? But," continued the old lady, as Seeta clung convulsively to her, "let no worldly care or thought influence you, or come between you and God; put them all away when you go to Him. I know all your trials, my darling, and I would help you more if I could; but the message to you, must come from Him, not from one like me. Now dry your tears and be hopeful, and brave as you always are, and I am sure you will do right."

I dare not say what effect this conversation had upon Seeta, nor tell of the mighty struggles that were going on in her gentle loving heart; and I think it would be profanation to attempt to describe them. To outward appearance, indeed, she seemed even gayer than was usual with her! and it was only Grace and Cyril who felt, in some degree, that a crisis in her fate was at hand. Nor did Seeta omit to consult Mr. Mostyn. As a child might go to a father, so she did to him one day when be was alone; and told all her anxiety, not of her faith, but of her condition in life. Need I say that Mrs. Pratt's opinion was confirmed? Mr. Mostyn did not even tell Rose of this consultation: he only said, "I wish Seeta were baptized and married;" and Rose Mostyn echoed the wish. "O! that she were," she said; "our pet would be so happy, and Cyril even more than she."

How pleasant it was now for all! The old occupations were resumed with enjoyment after their long suspension. The splendid "Erard," which had been covered up with a heap of blankets, was in excellent tune, and the friends enjoyed their reading, and their music and drawing, with their old spirit and skill. All alarms from without had passed away: and the advices to the merchants of Noorpoor, which arrived from Dehly, told of the immense English force that besieged the city, which the Sepoys could now barely hold, and which would soon be stormed. We who heard this news, remember the intense excitement of that time; the turning point of that awful struggle; and hoped and feared by turns as to its decisive effect upon the Sepoy war, into which the widely scattered events had changed.

From without, however, no intelligence came to Noorpoor, except from Shah Gunje, to which Buldeo had again penetrated, and brought back letters from the old banker and Aunt Ella.

"We are weary of oppression," wrote Narendra to Mr. Brandon; "all classes are sighing and praying for the English to return. Our temple has been defiled by the Moulvee, and the people here, and all through the country, are yearning for you. When can you come to help us? A thousand men would follow you, and I have money enough for all. As to myself I am a prisoner, and Ram Das has appropriated all my books, and carries on the business in his own name. The Moulvee and the Nawab have decided the suit in his favour; but I am not disturbed by that. Once you come again, all he has taken will return to me: and if it is lost, what matter? Only come soon, come soon!"

"And we will go, little one," said Cyril cheerily; "I have a plan in my head already, and, my darling, we will drive out the rebels, and Aunt Ella shall have her temple again, and cry 'Ram!' as much as she pleases."

"Dehly is taken!" cried Baba Sahib in an ecstasy of delight, as a few mornings after, at daylight, he called Mr. Brandon out, "Dehly is taken! O! thank God, sir, thank God! An express came to Poorun Mul Mahajun in the night, and here is the printed paper which came with it; which Poorun Mul sends with his compliments and congratulations. Thank God, sir, that the tempest of 1914 is spent at last."

Cyril could hardly read the little slip of "Extra." But there was no mistake. After six days of hard fighting the city had been won on the 19th of September. The "Asylum of the World" was a helpless fugitive! As soon as he had told Seeta, Cyril ran to the Judge's house, showed the paper to him, and then went up by the water-gate—where the guard cheered him as he read it to them—to the fort to tell the joyful news to the Brigadier; nor was it long before the guns thundered out a Royal Salute, the most glorious that those who listened to it had ever heard. A joyful thankful day, indeed, was it among the weary residents of Noorpoor; and even petty bickerings and jealousies seemed to be forgotten.

"Let us have a small dinner, Rose," said Philip Mostyn to his wife. "Let me see: the Brigadier and the two commanders, Hobson, and Wharton of the artillery, and Noble; just ten. We can manage that, and I will write to them all."

It was the day after they had heard the glorious news from Dehly, and all were in the highest spirits. Seeta no less than the others, for Cyril had told her that he should soon now put his plan in execution, and she should see Narendra and dear Aunt Ella once more.

So there was a pleasant party at the Judge's; and much talk and speculation ensued at dinner upon what might be going on elsewhere. After the ladies had retired for a short time, the gentlemen joined them in the drawing-room, and the piano was opened and the music began as usual. Never were the parties in better voice, for their good spirits gave them unusual energy; and it was a treat to sing there after so long. Seeta had listened for some time, sitting in Grace's boudoir which adjoined the drawing-room; and she had gone home to dress for the night ride with Cyril, for the patrols were still continued. She changed her clothes and went up on the terrace of part of her cottage, and was sitting by herself thinking much, when Buldeo suddenly called to her from below, "Come down! come down! I have seen them! Quick, lady!" And almost as he spoke, looking towards the shrubbery near the road, she saw distinctly a body of men moving silently and rapidly. In an instant she was flying down the steps with her utmost speed and up the gravel walk to the Judge's house. Entering by the back, she ran on through the house, and burst into the drawing-room, where Grace and Cyril were singing the old "Dimmi che m' ami, ancor." All looked strangely at her for a moment; but terror was in her face, she was out of breath and could only cry out, "Fly! get to the fort, the rebels are on us," when shouts arose outside, and a volley was fired through the windows, shattering the glass and frames, and knocking plaster from the walls.

No one, then, went about without arms; and there were loaded guns, revolvers, and swords in the corners of the room; each snatched his own weapons, and as yet no one was harmed. If it had been possible, the officers would have held the drawing-room till succour should reach them from the water-gate; but it was not to be done, the attacking party had at once fired the thatch in several places, and the blaze spread over the garden, increasing every instant. "Look to the ladies, gentlemen," cried the Brigadier sharply; "we must cover them." There was now a great clamour without, for the Judge's police guard and Cyril's, with the Rahtores, had struck in manfully; but they were too few to stop the attack at once.

Cyril was supporting Grace, who had clung to him; and Seeta, whose presence of mind seemed to be rising, also put her arm round her, and led her on. Mr. Mostyn and one of the other officers hurried on Mrs. Mostyn. They had already got down the steps, and Cyril was following, when Azráel Pandé, more terrible to look on than ever, his eyes staring, and his livid shattered face convulsed with passion, sprang suddenly on him from a corner of the verandah, with his spear. Cyril parried the thrust, and made a cut with his sword in return, which was caught on his spear by the Dacoit, when at that instant a chance shot struck Cyril in the right arm, and his sword dropped. He was entirely at his enemy's mercy. "Jey Kalee Mata!" shouted Azráel. "Dog of a Feringee! No escape now for thee," and as he drew back his deadly weapon to strike, Cyril heard a cry—it was not a scream—and Seeta had rushed before him, receiving the blow in her breast. Then Captain Hobson, who had tried to save Seeta, or, as he first thought, Cyril, plunged his sword into the ruffian's heart, who, writhing impaled upon the weapon for an instant, fell to the ground and was despatched, if indeed he lived, by Buldeo, with repeated thrusts of his own spear.

It was all the work of a moment, and while other combats

were going on in the verandah and in the garden, and Luchmun Singh and the Rahtores, with the police, were striking in with their war cries, Cyril stood for a moment stunned and bewildered. His right arm was pierced and nearly useless: but he tried to raise up Seeta, while Grace Mostyn, who had not lost her presence of mind, was endeavouring to staunch the blood with her dress and her handkerchief. Then Hobson and Buldeo gently took up the wounded girl between them, and carried her down the steps, Cyril following, and Grace holding her hand. For a moment Seeta's eyes opened, and she said to Grace, faintly, "Run, save yourself—let me die here," and again relapsed into insensibility. So they carried her down the garden, till they were in some degree safe; then Buldeo undid his waistcloth, and they put Seeta into it, and with some others carried her on gently to the water-gate, where Mr. Mostyn, his wife, and others were preceding them.

As the officer at the gate saw the outbreak of the disturbance at Mr. Mostyn's, he had dashed down with half his men to the rescue; but he was too late. Dismayed by the death of their leader, and by the loss they had already sustained from the spirited defence of the officers and the guards, as well as from several discharges of grape which the watchful sergeant had fired at the crowd on Mr. Brandon's lawn, now perfectly distinct under the glare from his burning house, and Seeta's cottage, the rebel Sepoys and their companions fled in confusion; and with the English guard covering the retreat of the party, in a few minutes the gate was entered and closed. Except a few hurried mournful words, no one spoke, as the sad procession wound up the path to the tower, lighted by the blazing houses, little heeding the rattle of musketry, and the guns from the cavalier, which showed that the attack on the Judge's house had been a fein for a more serious and obstinate one in front, than had ever occurred before.

END OF PART THE THIRD.

PART THE FOURTH.

CHAPTER XLVI.

"A CROWN OF LIFE."

SEETA was not dead: though as they looked at her, again and again, as they moved slowly on, they thought her spirit had passed away. Grace, whose marvellous composure astonished them, and Mrs. Pratt, who hurried to the tower, with poor old Bheemee distracted by grief, undressed her and washed away the blood, and wrapping her, as well as they could, in one of her own garments, admitted Cyril and Dr. Home, who, with another surgeon, were in attendance. As yet Seeta had been quite insensible; but the dressing of her wound roused her a little, and she opened her eyes, and looked around her; but she did not recognize those about her, and only murmured plaintively for water, of which, when Bheemee gave to her, she drank freely, but again relapsed into unconsciousness.

"Is there any hope, doctor?" asked Cyril; it was all he could say then.

"I fear not," replied Dr. Home. "I fear not! Poor thing, poor thing. But we cannot judge yet. I have seen worse wounds, from which men have recovered; but she is so slight and delicate, and the injury is so near her heart. We can only do our best, Mr. Brandon. Would she take any stimulant? It might revive her, and we could judge her case better; as she is, I fear that she may sink at once."

"I will try," he replied; and he held what Dr. Home gave him in a glass to her lips. "It is medicine, Seeta," he said, "to do you good; try and drink it, my darling; try!"

She understood what he said, and endeavoured to raise herself, stretching out her hand for the draught; but Cyril's arm trembled from the effect of the wound, and he made a sign to Grace, who took the glass from him; and as Seeta's fingers closed about it, directed it to her lips, and they saw that she drank nearly all.

"That will do! that will do! brave little soul that it is," cried the Doctor, wiping his eyes; "but, bless my heart, you are wounded too, Mr. Brandon! and while she lies quiet let me dress your arm: it must be very painful. I see, I see," he continued, as he examined the wound; "the ball has gone through, and you are saved the pain of its extraction; and the bones, too, are yet sound and safe; but there is a good deal of laceration, and you may be thankful that the limb will be as good as ever by-and-by."

Grace and Mrs. Pratt still watched, and after a little, Mrs. Mostyn came in; but she seemed almost hysterical, and Mrs. Pratt told her that she had better go and lie down: and Mr. Mostyn, who was at the door, took his wife away. Her condition, indeed, forbade the risk of any undue excitement: and the scene at the house, though she did not then know of Seeta's wound, had wellnigh overpowered her. Cyril even implored Grace to go with her; but she refused gently; and Mrs. Pratt, who fully estimated her calm strength of mind, and usefulness, asked Cyril not to press her, and he did not. Who, indeed, had loved Seeta better, or in whom did the poor sufferer trust more, than in these two loved friends?

What a night it was! No more attempts were made upon the water-gate, for the assailants had already sustained heavy loss from the gun in the tower, and from another gun on a bastion not far off; but in front there was cover, and the rebels, who were evidently bravely and skilfully led, made the most of it in charging the loyal —th repeatedly, and inflicting considerable loss on them, nor was it till the regiment began to be sorely pressed, and even appeared to be losing heart, that a company of English soldiers, with another in reserve at the main gate, were sent to their aid. Indeed it had been difficult to restrain the men, who were clamouring to be led against "the Pandies," and to help the brave —th. The succour was welcomed with a shout and a cheer which dismayed the rebels; yet they made a last charge, and were met by the Englishmen in the same spirit as Dehly had been won, and Lucknow relieved by Havelock and Outram; and when the reserve also struck in, the rebels fled, suffering heavily from showers of grape from the guns that commanded the parade. Then it was clear the attack was abandoned.

Although all those with Seeta listened with throbbing anxious hearts to the tumult of the action, yet she did not appear to be conscious of its progress, nor of the sound of the heavy guns which were now and again fired. She seemed to be sleeping quietly, though she breathed heavily; and Dr. Home, who came in every now and then to feel her pulse, said it was stronger than he had even hoped for. So they waited and hoped. For some time the blaze of the houses had lighted up the room with a bright red glare; but that gradually faded, and at length died out in fitful flashes, and they had lighted candles which, shaded from her eyes, only threw a dim light over her. None of them spoke except in whispers; but the draught had to be repeated, and Grace, who had asked Seeta several times whether she could take it again, motioned to Cyril to speak to her.

"Seeta, my darling—little one," he said gently, and using all his old terms of endearment, "drink again what Grace gives you."

The girl was roused at last as she heard the voice she loved best on earth, and tried to turn to it, but she put away Grace's hand, and looked at her husband. The sweet eyes were full of intelligence and love, so earnest, so wistful, so entreating, and Cyril thought her sensible now, and taking the glass from Grace's hand, put it to her mouth. She drank again, and sighed; but she would not release her husband's hand, and he sat down by her side, while the same earnest look continued and a faint smile played about her lips. It was as if, till then, she had not known that he lived.

"Saved! saved!" she muttered at length. They were the first intelligible words she had spoken. "O, I thank God! I thank God!"

"Yes, darling," he said, "we are all safe, and here are your friends; can you speak to them?"

She looked round, and put out her hand to Grace, who, with Mrs. Pratt, was sitting on the floor beside the low bed, but she could not speak yet; she could only look at them, silently by turns, as a dog would at one it loved, and the great brown eyes seemed, for the time, full of warm soft light.

"Saved! saved!" she said again more distinctly. "It is as I wished—only to die—for Cyril!—my lord!—my darling, look at me!"

"I am here," he said, "Seeta, close to you."

"I thought—I thought," she continued shuddering, "that he who had the spear—ah! save him! Look! he strikes!"

"There is no one, Seeta; do not fear, my pet—only your Grace, and mother, and I." But she did not seem to know them yet, and lay quiet, keeping her husband's hand in both of her own, close to her heart. The rest seemed to refresh her, and presently she asked for water very distinctly; and Bheemee, who had been sitting moaning without, rocking to and fro, brought her silver cup full of cool lemonade, which Dr. Home had ordered; but she put away the old woman's hand; and would only take it from her husband. Then she drank long and easily, and looking round, said to them, "I see you all, my darlings, now, but I have a great pain here. What has happened? Ah! I remember—but you are safe—all of you, Cyril?"

"All of us, Seeta," answered Grace, kissing her; "after that man was killed, we were safe. Ah! I thank God you know us again, my darling. Now you will soon be well, and we will all nurse you day and night, and God will heal all your pain."

"Yes," returned the girl, with the colour flushing to her white cheek, "He will heal my pain, and I trust Him now——I always thought I could go to death—like Savitri—and it is very near now, I think——I seem to understand——what puzzled me so—better, I think. O Cyril, what is this?" and she looked at the bandage on his arm. "You are hurt!"

"Not much," he said. "You saved me, darling, and Hobson killed him when I was helpless."

"Dead!" she said faintly. "Dead? may God forgive him!"

"Do you forgive him, Seeta?" said Mrs. Pratt, "and from your heart? He said, 'forgive your enemies.'"

"I do," she returned firmly. "Why was he my enemy? What had I done to him? O pray for me, mother; pray that the kind, good God may take a little child."

Then the dear lady knelt down, and prayed. Many a dying bed had she prayed by in her long life; many a wavering, fainting Christian soul had she soothed to its last rest. But this was very different; the firm strong faith, the pleading as a little child, the perfect trust in One, whom she knew only very dimly—seemed to be growing triumphant now, over all doubt and fear and pain—and the dear lady prayed. Often broken were her words by sobs and tears, often faltering; but the few simple expressions she used, were, she knew, understood by the sufferer who had asked for them, and she saw, too, that Seeta's lips moved, while her hands were clasped together over Cyril's. She was praying——

Then there was silence; and they looked with wonder on the beautiful face, now smiling and full of joy, the lips parted, and the soft dewy eyes looking up in reverence and hope.

"My lord!—my Cyril!" she said at length, in her own language, but very faintly, as she turned her eyes full upon him. "I would live for you if—if—it might be; but the Lord is calling me, and I cannot stay—— Do not sorrow for me, Cyril, when I am gone——only forgive your wife that she was careless, negligent often, and so ignorant. But O, my lord, I loved you, my darling, and I would have done better if—if—I could, but I knew nothing. And you will tell them of all that has happened—— They will not forget me, Cyril, never; their little Seeta will be in their minds till they die, and Aunt Ella must not grieve—she must only remember the girl who loved her and played with her. You must go to them, Cyril, and tell them this—promise me you will, and tell Wamun Bhut that I loved him too."

"I will," he said, in a choking voice, "if—— O Seeta, the Lord God will surely spare you to me, and we will go together to them. Keep a strong heart, my pet."

"No," she said, more faintly, "it cannot be. He is calling me now. 'Come to me,' he says, 'all ye that are heavy laden——'" And for a while she seemed wandering, and strange snatches of her Sanscrit prayers were mingled with lines of simple Christian hymns she had learned. Thus they sat and listened wonderingly, and saw that a change was passing over her face. Then Dr. Home came in and felt her pulse, and shook his head.

"It is fluttering now," he said to Cyril. "I can do no more, poor thing—poor child—she will soon be at rest."

The morning was now breaking, the roar of the night tumult had ceased, and all was still. High up into the grey night clouds, a stream of crimson light had leaped suddenly, and was fast changing into gold below, and the still, placid lake reflected the gorgeous spectacle in all its brilliancy.

Seeta was breathing heavily, but seemed to have no pain, and she only sighed now and then. Suddenly, and as though the vivid light had roused her, she raised herself a little, and stretched out her hands, and said the Vedantic invocation to the sun, which is called Gáyatri. It seemed as if she would have repeated the hymn also, but she had no strength, and as she fell back she cried faintly, "Cyril! Grace! kiss me. Mother! He calls me again!—Listen! And there are the bright flowers of heaven!—Lord!—I come!" As they put their arms under her to support her she smiled, and sighed once, and as the glory of the sun rested on her face, her humble, loving spirit had passed away for ever.

"The life will not depart," said Bheemee, "unless ye lay her upon the earth!"

"It is gone," replied Mrs. Pratt. "She is at rest with God. Look how beautiful she is! Let us pray!" and she prayed that those who had seen Seeta die might, when their time to die came, pass away in the same humble, faithful, child-like spirit.

Afterwards Cyril went out and sat down on the terrace where the gun was. He had cut one long tress of Seeta's hair, and laid it at his heart. The guard were there, and the honest fellows were crying, many of them, for they had heard what had happened, and they did not speak. Cyril was stunned and bewildered with the grief that had struck him so terribly and so suddenly. All he could realize was, that Seeta had gone; gone to her eternal rest in God, surely believing, and trusting to the last; and her noble act of devotion had saved him. At such times those who have their part in the household tragedies which happen every day around us, cannot realize much beyond the fact of the bereavement; and that, stunned as the mind feels, is borne passively, perhaps even calmly. The aching void is hardly felt then. Below, lay the ruins of the once pleasant houses, with the embers of the fire still smouldering; and on his own lawn, and in the garden, as well as about the Judge's house, many dead bodies were lying. It was a strange thought and impulse, but one Cyril acted upon immediately. "Come with me," he cried to some of the Rahtores and Buldeo who, with several of the police, were below the bastion, and he went down to them, and they followed him to the water-gate.

"You are not going out, Mr. Brandon?" said the officer on duty. "Some of those scoundrels may be lurking about. At least, take a few of the men with you."

"No," said Cyril, "I am much obliged, but you would be blamed, and I have my own stout fellows with me. I have been watching for some time from the tower, and have seen no one."

Then he went on, direct to the Judge's house. Some jackals slunk away through the bushes in the garden, and half-gorged vultures flew up heavily into the trees. As he ascended the steps of the verandah the body of Azráel Pandé lay before him in a pool of blood: the staring, glassy eyes glistening in the light, and the foul, livid, shattered features, with the same look of hate and defiance on them, which he remembered as the fatal spear had been raised against him.

"Search him," said Cyril to the police. "See if there are any papers on him;" but they seemed to hesitate from dread.

"I did not fear him living, and I do not fear him dead," said Buldeo, as he stepped forward and began to unfasten the waistcloth about the body of the Dacoit; and, assisted by the Sikhs and others, it was soon stripped. Around the waist was a long leather bag, almost filled with gold coins; another similar bag held rubies, and a smaller one a number of fine pearls and unset precious stones.

"Ah! he cheated us out of these, sir," said Buldeo, as he turned out the contents. "They belonged to the Dacoity at ——, and here are the diamonds and the rubies which he told us were for the shrine of the Mata in Calcutta. Yes, he was a thief, too."

There were no separate papers; but tied to his back there was a cloth case, which Buldeo handed to Mr. Brandon, in which was a Sanscrit book; and opening this, Cyril found some letters and other documents between the leaves, which he took out carefully and put into his own handkerchief. There was nothing else, and after leaf after leaf had been turned over, Cyril rose to go. As he flung the book down, one of the police would have taken it up, but Buldeo prevented him. "That is the 'Gurúra Poorán,'" he said, "from which the Maharaj there used to summon his devils. It should be burnt. Hrrám, Hrrám, Hrrám! I hear it still! Fling it into the fire yonder, friend, or it will do us harm. And now, master, the last search follows. If Azráel had any secret in the world, it is there;" and he took up the robber's quilted packet, and began to unrip it strip by strip. At last he came to two papers folded up, one in Persian, one in Hindee, which he handed to Cyril; but he did not abandon the garment till every stitch of it had been unripped, and every part explored. "Now, sir, believe me; whatever he had most secret, is in your hands. Come away!"

Cyril took one look through the drawing-room, which was entire. There he had been singing with Grace when Seeta burst in through the folding doors; and on the piano, which had escaped—for the fire had not affected the strong terraced roof, and the folding doors were only partially burnt—was the old duet, "Dimmi che m' ami," smoke-stained, certainly, but entire. "I will keep this," he said to himself, "in memory of the night." And, with his men, he returned to the fort.

Baba Sahib was there already, and had brought his wife and other Brahmin women, and the professional dressers of the dead, who were busy with the last sad rites, and wailing and moaning as was their custom. The room was no place to go into, and even to his faithful old friend, Cyril could say but little. Baba Sahib knew it must be so, and respected the grief he could not console. And Philip Mostyn came, too, and wrung his friend's hand. What could he say? What could any one say then? All there was to go through must be done. "Rose and Grace will come to take leave of her," he said; "I will find out when they are ready inside."

The women had dressed Seeta's head with garlands of flowers, and clothed her in one of her simple white muslin garments; and as she lay, looking like a wax figure, and with a beautiful but strange wondering look of the majesty of death on her sweet face, even the professional women sitting around her seemed to be awe-struck, and were silent; and when Mrs. Mostyn, Grace, Mrs. Pratt, Mrs. Hill, and Lucy Home came in, all stood up respectfully. I think they were as much awed as the others had been, and, for the most part, were silent too; but Grace and Mrs. Mostyn were sobbing bitterly, and would have knelt down and kissed the dear sweet face, only that Baba Sahib's wife prevented them.

"She has been purified for her death," she said to Mrs. Pratt, who, she knew, understood her, "and no one can touch her now!" But they each took a garland from her, and silently passed out, weeping.

Meanwhile, a pyre had been prepared below on the margin of the lake, close to the water-gate, and Seeta was taken up and carried thither on a bier and laid upon it. The English soldiers had saluted the bier as it passed, and Cyril and Mostyn, Mr. Noble, and several others followed the mourning women who were chanting the litany and hymns for the dead. Baba Sahib and many Brahmins, bare-headed, met them, and as the last sad wail arose, the pyre had been lighted.

"Enough!" said Philip Mostyn; "you have done all you could, Cyril, come away!" And, supporting his friend, he led him from the mournful spectacle.

"I must see," said Cyril, as they went up to the tower, "what the papers I have found contain. My strong impression is, that they will throw light on my poor Seeta's death. I cannot rest, Philip, till I have examined them. Come and help me."

There were two, as we know. One was a bond or acknowledgment from Ram Das, banker and goldsmith, for the sum of seven hundred and fifty rupees, dated the — August, 1855, and it had been increased by another item of one thousand, of which some payments were recorded.

"Ah!" said Mr. Mostyn, "this is important indeed! Let me see! that was the day after the murder of Huree Das, I think, but I can refer to my notes of the trial. I have no doubt, now, that Ram Das was the instigator of that horrible affair."

"Yes!" said Cyril, who was thinking, and much agitated, "but this has the Nawab's seal to it," and held it up, though his hand was shaking.

"Give it to me," said his friend, "you are not fit to read it." And he read what I thus translate. Notwithstanding bad grammar and worse spelling, the purport was quite intelligible:—

"In the name of God, the most clement and merciful.

"I, who am the Nawab Dil Khan Bahadoor (he had omitted his new dignities), covenant and promise to Colonel Azráel Pandé Bahadoor, to give to him the sum of five thousand rupees, and the villages of Zynabad and Seetapoor, of the Talook of Noorpoor, of the annual value of rupees four thousand seven hundred, and all the lands and rights pertaining thereto.

"*Item.*—And for this grant, the aforesaid Colonel binds himself to attack the Judge's and Brandon's houses at Noorpoor, and to bring to me unharmed, Missy Mostyn, the sister of the Judge aforesaid, and to kill the Judge, and Brandon, and all other Feringees, men and women and children, that may be in the houses aforesaid, and in the fort of Noorpoor, when my brave army has stormed and taken it.

"*Item.*—And in regard to Seeta Bye, I, Dil Khan Bahadoor, make no claim. She is to be the 'Colonel' Sahib's slave, and he is at liberty to do as he pleases with her.

"Written with my own hand, in my camp at Ryna; sealed by me, with my own seal; and signed by me,

"DIL KHAN."

Cyril ground his teeth. "If I could—— God help me," he cried; "this is no time to talk of revenge. Yes, Philip, there are two palankeens down there in my garden, abandoned. Think of what they escaped! Yes! she is at rest, now, my sweet darling!" he continued, sobbing, "and these hellish conspiracies are at an end, for her."

Philip Mostyn was much moved. He knew that Cyril had saved his sister, for he had seen some of the fight, and how he and Seeta had protected her. "Horrible! horrible!" he said. "But I cannot bear to think of what Grace escaped; I only know what she owes to you, and to her who is gone."

"Nay!" said Cyril, calmly; "not to me, but to Hobson—who saved us all. For this," and he pointed to his wound, "had made me helpless; and there was no one else near. But for him, I had died with her."

CHAPTER XLVII.

"SHAH GUNJE."

SOME weeks had passed, wearily and sadly. At the moment and, indeed, for many days after Seeta's death, Cyril Brandon had been stunned by the loss of one who had grown to be more his companion and friend than he had ever believed possible; and now, ensued the aching void, which there was nothing to fill up. He missed Seeta at every turn, and in every occupation she had shared with him. At first, their lives had not had much in common, perhaps; but the ardent nature of Seeta's mind had already overcome many hindrances to more perfect communion. In her indefatigable studies she had been chiefly guided by Grace Mostyn, whose serene and delicate feeling had been reflected in her pupil. It was almost unaccountable to Cyril and her friends, how much, and how rapidly, Seeta had learned during the last four months; how much her capacity had been enlarged, and her sense of comprehension vivified by her enthusiasm in her new pursuits. She had, indeed, but one incentive to exertion: the desire to be, what she felt she ought to be, as Cyril's wife. Not the mere Hindoo girl, whom no one could know but her husband; but one who, in time, might take her place openly in the world, and of whom he should never be ashamed. And it had seemed to Grace and her sister that this might come to be; but that it would necessarily be impossible so long as Seeta retained her Hindoo faith and her customs.

Would she ever relinquish them? That, indeed, had been a subject of anxious discussion between all who loved Seeta; but even Mrs. Pratt, whose education and experience as a missionary gave her more weight and perception than Mrs. Mostyn or Grace, had hesitated to make any decided attempt at conversion. Seeta's mind was not yet prepared for the change. She could not throw off caste. She could not dissever herself from her old associations and her deep love for those who remained at Shah Gunje. She could not at once abandon the old belief in which she had been reared, and the deep and often grand metaphysical arguments by which it was supported. Before these, the simplicity of Christian truth had, at first, indeed, appeared childish, if not contemptible; and yet how they had perceptibly grown upon her! How they were urging her on to take one final, irrevocable step, we already know in part, but not entirely.

Nor is it needful for me to lay bare the struggles of that loving, pious heart more than I have already done in these imperfect pages. Such struggles, even in Christian hearts yearning to feel the truth, are often long and terrible; how much more, then, those of a heathen, with intellect and education powerful enough to understand it, and yet with every consideration, before held most sacred and precious, not only to be risked, but abandoned entirely for a new faith, and altogether new affections and associations. If she renounced Hindooism, she should be a stranger in her grandfather's home. She could not eat with them, or live with them, at all, as she had used to do. They might reproach her, and refuse to see her; and Wamun Bhut, her revered preceptor, would be grieved to the heart. Her old associates would despise her, for she knew how Christianity was esteemed among them—nay, how she had esteemed it herself, hardly a year ago. If Cyril died—and he might die before her—and she were a Christian, who could receive her, when her caste was gone? No penance, no fine, no entreating of the guild, or the Brahmins at Benares, could restore what she had designedly given up. She must live alone, as an outcast: and if she died, who would even bury her?

I say these and a thousand other thoughts were daily passing through Seeta's mind, as the time went on, and the weakening of the old bulwarks of her faith was progressing; and, perhaps, in this respect, Seeta is only a type of thousands and thousands of her own countrymen and women, who feel the truth, and who, until some unforeseen crisis in their lives arises, dare not make the final plunge which not only severs them from all they love, honour, and respect in life, but makes them social outcasts—utterly despised and rejected by their people, even to the refusal of a cup of cold water. Too many among us blame the hardness of the heathen, and call their belief in their own faith by very ugly names; but I think the utmost bound of charity needs to be extended to them when we think on—if we can at all estimate—the force of the reality of struggles like Seeta's. And yet they who watched by the dying girl in that memorable night, knew how near she was in faith to God, in whom she trusted as a child. Would she ever have accepted baptism? They could not tell, for none had dared to ask. They had been content to watch the mental struggle, and to comfort and encourage Seeta as well as they could.

Yet towards becoming a Christian, the advantages, in a worldly point of view, appeared by far more decided than in continuing as she was. Mrs. Pratt had put Seeta's position before her more plainly than any one, except Cyril himself, who had never concealed it. As a Christian, he would marry her by Christian rites. No one could then deny her right to social rank and position. She might go to England, and visit Lady Hylton. She might even, if Cyril's brother died, be a Lady Hylton too, honoured and respected. If she bore children to her husband, they would no longer have a stigma of illegitimacy according to English law; and had she not of her love, of her faith and constancy, cast her lot with a Christian? So it would seem to be her duty to belong to her husband's faith: to abandon all else, loving and venerating it, never so much. Had she any right to refuse what she knew her husband would hail with delight? Then she and Grace would be indeed sisters, for Mrs. Mostyn had said playfully one day, that she and Mrs. Pratt must be her godmothers. All this Seeta knew, yet it had not dazzled her, not helped to still the tempest in her heart, in which no worldly motives were engaged. Yet the crisis was nigh, and a few, a very few days perhaps, would most probably have decided the question, which was solved otherwise, now, and for ever.

Baba Sahib had taken upon himself the duty of writing to Narendra and his sister, and he enclosed a note to them, only a few words, from Cyril. What could he say who could find no comfort himself? But little indeed, except to bear bravely what had befallen them all. I think one of their greatest comforts at Shah Gunje was to think that they were not forgotten by Cyril; but Aunt Ella was in sore trouble on many accounts. Seeta had not been purged from her offences against caste. If she had only gone to Benares at once, when Huree Das died! If, indeed! Then she would have returned like unto Aunt Ella herself, and this little history had never been written. It was some comfort to know that Baba Sahib and the guild at Noorpoor had managed the cremation, and performed all needful ceremonies; and Wamun Bhut would see to the rest. Altogether perhaps, at first, Aunt Ella was more resigned to the sad occurrence than it appeared likely she should be. The one great dread that Seeta should become a Christian was at rest; there was nothing to prevent her soul resting in peace, and perhaps the long continuance of rigid asceticism, and the painful attempts to discern the end of her nose, had blunted the old lady's feelings of humanity and love not a little; at all events as regarded outward observances or demonstrations. But few perhaps knew, how often, as she rose in the night to bathe in cold water, to sit in wet clothes, and to repeat her "Ram, Ram, Ram," natural feelings would have their bent: and as the sweet child who had grown up before her, the tendrils of whose love had clasped themselves round heart, came to her in spirit and seemed to caress her—Aunt Ella felt them clinging there still, and wept passionate floods of tears—unknown to all besides. I think, too, that Narendra, wise as he was in worldly matters, thought, after a while, more gently of the bereavement than at first. Seeta, once part of his daily life, had been gradually separated from it. Latterly that separation had become wider, and it would never have surprised the old man to hear that Seeta had become a Christian; indeed, he was so satisfied of Mr. Brandon's honour, that news of such a change in his wife's faith would almost have been welcomed, as assuring him of more perfect accordance in their lives. It is probable that poor Seeta might, in this respect, have overrated the effect of home influences; and her own determination had been to see them once more ere she came to a final decision on the most momentous crisis of her life.

Buldeo, as before, had carried the letters to Shah Gunje. He found the old man submissive and patient, waiting, as he said, a turn in public affairs. Ram Das seldom left Shah Gunje: he had appropriated all the apartments on the lower storey of Narendra's house, sat in the old banker's seat, and transacted all the business; but he had not discovered the banker's hidden hoard, and the correspondents and agents had declined to remit the balances they held without direct orders from Narendra, which he refused to give; so except the gathering up of moneys that had been lent in the district around, Ram Das had indeed derived little benefit. Thus he was daily tantalized by the consciousness that large, very large sums of money which belonged to Narendra, were beyond his reach—at least for the present; and the hope that there should be "no English" was perhaps passing into a dread that that hope might not, after all, be fulfilled.

Around, and within Shah Gunje, the people were beginning to rouse themselves against the Moulvee's oppressions, which indeed were grievous in many ways, and hard to bear. Not only were the tribe of swash-buckler soldiery, who attended him, violent and unruly, but the farmers and landholders began to find that demands upon them for instalments of revenue in advance, were increasing in amount, and were levied with even greater cruelty than before; and they had sent word to Narendra that if Mr. Brandon would only come, they could muster enough men of their own to drive the Moulvee out of

Shah Gunje, and hold the town and district for the English. In his letter therefore to Mr. Brandon, Narendra, after some kind words of comfort to him on Seeta's death, pressed him to come quickly. "I have money enough to pay the men that will assemble," he wrote, "and they will be many; and when, you deliver us from oppression, your name will live gratefully for ever in all our hearts."

Indeed, it appeared a most opportune time, in which good service might be done by an active movement with the assistance of the people themselves! They only wanted a leader, and Mr. Brandon felt assured that not only would Government approve of action against the rebels, but would sanction any expedition necessary for the purpose. Money he could not burden himself with; but Narendra would provide funds, and Buldeo had assured him that without his proceedings becoming known, he and the Rahtorés could lead him to Shah Gunje by secure but unknown paths through the forests. Nor was Mr. Brandon less anxious to secure Ram Das, whose original crime could, he considered, be brought home to him in the evidence which the search of Azráel Pandé's body had furnished, and there would be more procurable if he could only get to Shah Gunje. There were several accounts in Azráel's handwriting found among his other papers, all pointing to transactions with Ram Das, which had begun about the time of the murder of Huree Das, but which could only be perfectly understood by an examination of the goldsmith's books. Buldeo had often been examined as to the antecedents of the affair at Gokulpoor, but he was consistent in declaring that he knew nothing. He had been absent on an errand to a village, and had rejoined Azráel at Shah Gunje, and the gang at the waterfall, only on the day the Dacoity was committed. He had heard certainly that a banker had come to the waterfall, and brought money; and that two of the scouts, Sumbho and Govinda, had accompanied him; but whether he was Ram Das, or not, he could not tell. "If I could only find out where these two men are," he said, "we should know all: but they disappeared when the Docoity was discovered and Azráel was apprehended, and must have fled from the country."

Buldeo's brother, Foorsut, had long since joined him; and was now one of Cyril's most active spies. He had not known of the intended attack on Noorpoor, or proposed abduction of Seeta and Miss Mostyn. The Nawab and his army were at Ryna, watching Hurpál Singh; and Azráel had remained in his retreat, growing more and more wild and uncontrollable.

Even Goor Bux had given him up, and left him with three men to take care of him. One morning, however, after one of his most fearful nights, Azráel and the others had suddenly left Futtehpoor, desiring him to remain; and there he had waited many days, till at last the Sepoys returned, one of them being badly wounded. They told him the army had been repulsed at Noorpoor, and they had seen Azráel killed by Captain Hobson and Buldeo, just as he was on the point of seizing Seéta. There had been great hope that the surprise of Noorpoor would be complete, and there were palankeens provided by Azráel to carry away some of the ladies; but the attack had failed, and there was great discontent in the army in consequence. After their comrade died, Foorsut therefore was free to act for himself, and had brought away Azráel's property, such as it was, and given himself up. Then he and Buldeo, who could never rest for more than a very few days at a time, went out occasionally to bring in news, the last of which was, that the armies of the Nawab and Hurpál Singh had fought together, and that Hurpál Singh had the worst of it, and had returned to his castle; but that the Nawab's Sepoys were mutinous, and wanted to take him to Jhansy or Cawnpoor, and that he was helpless in the hands of Colonel Goor Bux, who now did as he pleased.

"I am quite clear, Philip, it will be the best thing to do," said Cyril to Mr. Mostyn one day, not long after Buldeo and his brother had returned from their last expedition as scouts; "and if we carry Shah Gunje, of which I have little doubt, the whole country will be with us. Baba Sahib is entirely of my opinion, too. It is quite impossible to remain here with all that has happened so fresh in my memory, that every day seems a repetition of the same horrible scene. Indeed, I try not to complain, Philip; but you can hardly put yourself in my place, and feel what I do. If I succeed, I may win some credit, and if I don't come back to you, there will be only one more gone, who tried to do his duty."

"And were I in your place, I would do the same, Cyril," replied his friend. "I know you won't be rash, and you must always remember that you have others to think of at home, as well as yourself. But you won't go alone?"

"No, Philip; Temple will come with me, and I shall leave Noble in charge. Hobson would have come, also, but his wound is not healed, and while the nucleus of his regiment is here, the Brigadier says he must stay; and he is very sorry about this. Twenty-five volunteers from his men were called for, and we shall have as fine a set of fellows with us as men need to have."

So it was settled that they should go; and it was with a lighter heart than he had had since Seeta died, that Cyril Brandon took leave of Mr. Mostyn and Grace, and other friends; and as the small party assembled at the gate at dusk one evening, the English soldiers and the officers all came out and gave him three hearty cheers, and wished him a safe return. Poor Mrs. Mostyn had been much affected, and could hardly speak to him; but Grace, though her tears were falling fast, told him to go and do his duty, and prayed that God would keep him safely.

"If I do return," he replied earnestly, "I shall be very thankful; and if I do not, I cannot leave you without again telling you how deeply grateful I feel for all your love and affection for my dear wife, even to the last, a feeling which will only increase with time;" and so he left her.

What a pleasant march it was! The sense of freedom, the open country, the absence from that almost unbearable atmosphere of petty squabbles and jealousies, gave the companions new heart. Cyril's wound was almost healed, and he had regained the use of his hand and arm, which was at one time rather doubtful. The first night they rested at the Gáo Mookh, under the trees, where the tents had been pitched months before. The Incherna was now a considerable body of water, and plunged into the chasm with a dull, sudden roar, sending up clouds of spray. How true had been his poor Seeta's augury! A brief term of happiness, and as it seemed nearest the highest fulfilment, yet to be dashed away! Next morning they plunged into the forest below, by a rough path, and making as rapid marches as possible, reached the foot of the glen, at the head of which was the temple, and the waterfall, with which this tale commenced.

The place on which they encamped was an open level spot, close by the stream, a short green sward, which looked indeed like a meadow. All around were lofty rugged hills, which seemed to close up the amphitheatre, leaving only room for the stream to escape under a lofty precipice. And then the place was perfectly free from observation; nor was there any village much nearer than Shah Gunje, which was about seven miles distant.

"O that I were free!" cried Narendra, as Buldeo came to him that night with the message from Cyril; "that I might go at once to meet him; but I must seem more than ever to be a prisoner. Tell him that all are ready, and he will meet a thousand men to-morrow night at the waterfall. He need not delay; let him bring them on at once, while their blood is hot. Let him send a party to release me, and I will soon be with him."

On the afternoon following, Cyril and Temple, with the Rahtores and his orderlies, moved cautiously up the glen, by the margin of the stream, and after a rough scramble the little piece of sward under the waterfall was reached. They were the first there, and had time to admire the extreme beauty of the spot, now glowing under the orange rays of the setting sun, which shone directly upon it, lighting up the gaunt arms of the old peepul tree, and the precipice and fall, with golden light. Round the tree, flocks of paroquets and wild pigeons were wheeling, as they settled to their night's rest; and down the glen, pea-fowl were screaming as they flew from side to side of the stream.

"This is the place whence we went to the Dacoity at Gokulpoor," said Buldeo. "It is an old rendezvous of ours; and look, there are the crucibles in which Azráel melted the gold and silver. No one has been here since, for our marks have not been disturbed;" and he pointed to a few twigs arranged in a peculiar manner at the entrance to the temple.

Presently the sun went down and the night fell, and the sound of a village horn was heard far away in the distance. "That is the signal," said Buldeo; "that is Bulram Singh's horn; and he will be here with his two hundred clansmen." Bulram Singh was the old friend of Cyril, that we know of, and with him were allied most of the petty chieftains of the Noorpoor district. Nor was Buldeo mistaken, for in a short time they heard a body of men descending the path which led to the temple, and Bulram Singh hurried on to meet the two friends, who stood at the entrance to receive him. Heartily embracing Bulram Singh, who was sobbing like a child, Cyril bid him be of good heart, and if all were like him, the district would soon be cleared.

"They are all coming, sir," he replied; "all that we need. There will be a thousand men or more here to-night. Then we will take you on silently."

And it was a strange wild scene, when, as there was no room for the men, leader after leader came down the path, and introduced by Bulram Singh, presented the hilt of his sword: and when all were there, some one lighted a torch, and the glare spread over the bronzed determined faces of some fifty men, petty landholders, heads of villages, all of whom Cyril had known before. Truly they seemed in earnest.

"My friends," he said, "I could not come sooner, for I was wounded, and my arm was helpless; but I am among ye at your own call, and we will free ourselves from the tyranny from which all are suffering. Keep together and do not speak, let no one fire a shot. Ye all know the place. One half go with me, another with my friend here, whom ye do not know, but whom I know to be brave and true; and now—for no one can hear it here—one cheer for the English, 'Jey Koompani Bahadoor.'" And it was heartily answered by all, and taken up by the masses of men above, ringing through the air till Cyril feared it might be heard far away.

"The horses and horsemen are come," said one of the Sikh orderlies as he came up; "and we are all ready, sir!" and with another shout of "Jey Brandon Bahadoor," the leaders moved on, followed by Cyril, and Temple, who was wild with delight and excitement. "Quite dramatic, isn't it, Brandon?" he cried; "what a scene for a play!"

When they were close to Shah Gunje, there was another short halt; nothing seemed to be stirring within the town. The gates were shut, but there were gaps in the wall which were not guarded, and, entering by them, the surprise was complete. Cyril, who knew the town and needed no guide, had sent Bulram Singh with Temple, who took him direct to the local court-house, whence some sounds of music were proceeding. The Moulvee, in fact, had been holding one of his nightly revels; and the party rose in confusion as the young Englishman and his companions entered. Then there was a short *mêlée*, and the Moulvee rushing at Temple with a shout of execration, was shot by him as he advanced, and all the rest were soon sabred or overpowered.

"You should have left him to me, sir," said Bulram Singh; "I had marked him for my own, but I was too late."

"Yes, too late, my friend," replied Temple; "but you were busy enough, I think," as he observed his bloody sword. "Well done, well done!"

Meanwhile Cyril had advanced on the dear old house he remembered so well. There was a strong guard at the gate, but ere he could pass the chowke, he heard a clamour within, and many of the guard ran out crying, "Treachery! treachery!" The fact was that Buldeo, with several of the Rahtores, had been admitted from behind by the women-servants: had gained the inner court, and while Ram Das, who slept there, was being bound by two of the men, the remainder attacked the guard from within, and put them to flight, with terrible use of their heavy swords. The rest was completed by Cyril's men, and as he entered the old court he saw the tall figure of the banker standing on the steps with his arms outstretched, crying to him to come, for he had once more saved his life and his honour. "And you are safe, you are safe," he said again and again, passing his hands over him. "O thanks be to God who sent you!" and Aunt Ella too was close behind, who threw her arms about Cyril's neck, and wept and laughed hysterically, and cried her thanks incoherently, till her brother drew her away, trembling as she was, and bid her be silent.

"And Ram Das?" asked Cyril; "he has not escaped, I hope?"

"No, sir," said one of the Rahtores who stepped from within. "He tried to strangle himself with his hands, but we tied them up with his turban, and he is quite safe. Come and see him."

Yes, he was quite safe, writhing on the floor, with an expression of malignity on his evil face, which Cyril thought even Azráel's had not surpassed; but he did not speak.

Presently Temple came in, full of praises of Bulram Singh and all who had been with him. "A few of the rebels have escaped," he said, "but we have a good many prisoners, for I could not kill the wretches who had put grass in their mouths and were crying for quarter; but a good many are dead. Every gate is guarded, and I am glad to say we have only a few wounded. Who would have thought these rustics would have fought as they did?"

"They only wanted you to lead them, sir," said Narendra gracefully, "and may God bless you both. Many there are who will come to kiss your feet to-morrow."

Then they sat talking of the past almost till the day broke; sadly indeed, but very lovingly. "It is strange, Mr. Brandon," said Narendra, as Cyril lay down to take some sleep, "that our darling had always an idea she should die for her husband; and in this her belief was fulfilled to the last. So let her live in our memories as one whose devotion saved you, and whom God spared the misery that ruffian had intended for her."

Next morning the town was like a fair. The people from villages around brought in garlands of flowers, and laid them at Mr. Brandon and Temple's feet. The dancing girls of Shah Gunje dressed themselves in their gayest apparel, and spreading carpets in the chowke, danced and sang ballads in Cyril's praise which they had often sung before, but never with more spirit and applause. Then as the old English flag was once more hoisted amidst the shouts of the people, and garlands were hung on the staff, and cast at its foot, all felt that the English were in authority once more, and there would be peace. Before daybreak a party of cavalry and the Rahtores had been despatched with two of Narendra's clerks to Gokulpoor, where the books and papers of Ram Das had been seized and brought in; and before evening of a busy day, order had been quite restored. The treasury of the district was found to be full, for the Moulvee had intended to take away what he had collected himself; and as a head local authority was needed, Bulram Singh was appointed by Mr. Brandon, and was accepted by the people with joy. As to the guild of goldsmiths, they went in an abjectly penitent body to Narendra's house and besought him to resume his authority; and in all respects there was rejoicing that day in Shah Gunje such as had never been remembered before, tempered, as it might well be, to those in whose memories the recollection of the dead was fresh and vivid.

CHAPTER XLVIII.

THE NAWAB'S TERROR.

The next few days were a busy time. Not only had the exactions made from the people to be repaid, but the new levies to be, in some degree, organized and fitted for service. Some of the old police had proved unfaithful, and had gone over to the Nawab or Rajah Hurpál Singh; but many had been true, who now joined Mr. Brandon, and assisted him in his new formation. Bulram Singh and another landholder provided four guns, the two lightest of which were prepared for active service; the others were to be left at Shah Gunje with Temple, who, Narendra declared, must be his guest till his tents could arrive. As to Ram Das's connection with Azráel Pandé, the books captured furnished ample proof of their mutual transactions, and were therefore sealed up, to be opened only when the case should be tried by Mr. Mostyn. Ram Das himself made no admission whatever; he preserved a sullen silence, and was removed to the guard-room of the court-house till he could be sent to Noorpoor.

So far all was settled at Shah Gunje; and Baba Sahib, who had been unable to remain inactive at Noorpoor, accompanied by several of the native clerks, soon tried to make his way to Shah

Gunje, and to take his part in the work with his usual zeal. Under his assistance, an effective administrative establishment was speedily constructed; those who had hidden themselves in terror from the Moulvee, now rejoined the service; and public business was in such active progress that Cyril could no longer delay, for the opportunity was admirable. Hurpál Singh had gone to join another rebel Rajah at some distance, with all his levies. There were already rumours of the advance of several English armies, and since Dehly had fallen, and the English had recovered strength, it was becoming evident to all waverers that now was the time to assume a loyal demeanour.

Leaving Temple therefore, with directions for every emergency, Mr. Brandon pressed on through the country, not only delivering the people from petty local oppressors, but re-establishing the authority of Government soundly and satisfactorily; and it was a great assurance to him to find how deeply the people rejoiced in the return to old laws and customs. They might be hard; they might be unsympathetic; but they were just. They furnished personal and general security, and the tyranny of the strong over the weak was at an end. Cyril's progress was indeed almost a triumphal procession. At every village he was met by the women, singing hymns, bearing water-pots and garlands, and waving trays over him in which were lighted lamps and offerings. Where there were musicians they played before him, as at a marriage feast. Here and there some slight resistance was encountered, or there were little skirmishes; but they did not hinder the main object of the tour, which was effective and encouraging.

From Noorpoor, too, the news was satisfactory. Mr. Noble, with Hobson, a native assistant, and some volunteers from the police and the Sepoys, had made two successful sallies, and beaten the Nawab's posts out of several considerable places in what had been Mr. Noble's portion of the district. Then the Brigadier himself had made a forced march upon the greater part of the Nawab's army, and forced it to retreat; for while men were stirring around them, it was no easy matter to hold the English soldiers in an inactive position; and on a good opportunity occurring, they were treated to a dash against the Pandies, and enjoyed it. There was no denying, however, that the Nawab's army was still strong; and for the present it was not deemed advisable to attack Futtehpoor, or to show how few soldiers could be spared for fiell operations. But the rapid re-establishment of the civil power was a contingency for which Nawab Dil Khan had not been prepared; and the practical exposition of it to which Mr. Brandon resorted, was as unexpected as it was very decidedly unpleasant.

It was quite within the province of the Commissioner of the district, in the latitude of action which all civil authorities then possessed, to offer a high reward for the Nawab's apprehension; and a proclamation, in the local vernacular language, was put in circulation, to the effect, "that Nawab Dil Khan Bahadoor, of Futtehpoor, having wantonly rebelled against the English, attacked Noorpoor, with the intention of destroying all the English there, and carrying off certain ladies; taken possession of British districts, plundered their treasuries, and in several instances (detailed) put to death the local officers in charge of them"—and with much more to the same purport, which need not be particularized—"was therefore a rebel: and that for his apprehension" (Baba Sahib's opinion being, that the words "for his head" should be added) "the sum of five thousand rupees was offered, with a free pardon—unless they had committed murder—to all who might apprehend him, and bring him to Noorpoor."

No sooner was this written, than Buldeo and Foorsut, ever ready for any desperate enterprise, volunteered to attach copies to the very gates of the Nawab's fort; and they performed this feat in the most approved Dacoit fashion. Foorsut well knew the secret staircase from the well, and led Buldeo up by it at night, till they fairly entered the Nawab's hall of audience, and stuck one of the papers against the wall in a conspicuous place, with others against the gates outside; and no doubt the practice of their old profession had very considerably conduced to their success.

While the brothers were returning to Mr Brandon's camp, great was the consternation at Futtehpoor. As he awoke in the morning—for the Nawab, after his defeat, had returned to his castle some days before—the proclamation was brought to him by an attendant, who, when he entered the hall of audience early, in order to sweep it, had found the document stuck against the wall, over the Nawab's customary seat, and was horribly alarmed. Nor was the Nawab less so. There was no doubt of its authenticity. The seal of the Commissioner of the Noorpoor Province was attested by the "Cyril Brandon" of the Commissioner himself, about which there could be no mistake whatever. Everybody knew those bold yet delicate characters. Above all thoughts which now peculiarly disturbed the Nawab, were two: first, the conviction that his deed of promise to Azráel Pandé had fallen into Mr. Brandon's possession, and could be used against him. All he might urge in extenuation was, the fact that the writing had been extorted from him by Azráel, who had gained access to him as he slept, and holding a dagger to his heart, had forced him to write as he dictated. But as, unfortunately, no one could prove this, it might not be believed. Then the secret entrances to his castle had been discovered by some one, and Dil Khan felt that at any moment, even Mr. Brandon himself, pistol in hand, might come up the staircase and slay him. It was of little avail, for comfort, that the Nawab directed the archway opened by Azráel Pandé to be re-closed: the horrible proclamation became an actual terror, which possessed him night and day and scared away sleep; a terror which no one could comfort, no one mitigate. It was as if the words of his wife, the "Star of Women," were becoming true; that he would be a fugitive, and that in the hour of his trouble no one would help him.

Help him! Who was there to do so, now? Colonel Goor Bux had long ago taken all military authority out of his hands. He, the Soobadar Major of the rebel —th, and the Rissáldar of the cavalry, did as they pleased, took what money they pleased, and spent it as they pleased. Indeed, it was hard for them, except by largesses, to hold their men together, in the face of the news from Dehly, and other news too, which followed fast and thick. They were already thinking, and more than thinking, of deserting the Nawab and following the rebel armies to Jhansy, or elsewhere. And, if they left him, what chance was there of meeting, even for a day, any onset by the Brigadier, or even by Mr. Brandon, whose levies were driving all before them? No more ghastly fiend—Ghoul or Jinn—could even the sorcerers of his faith have called up from the realm of spirits, than this horrible proclamation. Comfort, he had found none. One wife had already betaken herself to Dehly, to prepare the way, as she said, for her lord's reception by the "King of Kings." The other, more faithful, and secure in her local influence, had told him that she should remain and claim the protection of the English; and urged him, with many prayers and tears, to do the same. But the Nawab was, alas! too far—too deeply committed—for that; and the proclamation, staring him in the face as it lay before him, forbade a thought of surrender. There was only one alternative, it seemed—to rejoin his army, then lying at the frontier of the Noorpoor province, and to lead it, yes, to lead it to Jhansy to join the Ranee! "Colonel" Goor Bux would, he knew, coincide with him in this, as their best course; and now he had no other adviser. The Moulvee was dead; all his schemes were dead. The province of which he had assumed the rulership was a phantom to the Nawab which was melting away. Máma Jumccla was dead. Azráel Pandé was dead: but his fearful secrets were not dead, and there was the proclamation which told its own story in proof of them. For five thousand rupees any one might betray him, and lead him away captive to Noorpoor, where a traitor's doom awaited him—a parade of white faces, a loaded cannon, or the hangman with a rope!

Could he contrast this with what he might have been, had he remained steadfast to the English, and not shiver to his very marrow? His ancestral dominions safe, and increased by his generous friends! Honours and congratulations showered upon him. Visiting the Brigadier and Mr. Mostyn, with the certainty that he had aided Mr. Brandon or Mr. Noble—that he had beaten away the rebels from his gates—would have been very different to what he must endure now, if he went as a mean suppliant for his life! I say, with all these miseries gnawing at his heart, it could hardly be otherwise, than that the Nawab followed the course of escaping from present dread, rather than that of meeting those whom he had enraged; and one morning, riding at early dawn from his castle, they heard a few days after, at Noorpoor, that his whole force had left the province, and was on its way to one of the head-quarters of the rebel army.

Then, indeed, the district was once more free, though, as yet, not entirely, of rebel influences; and gradually the posts were re-established, and news came in from many parts, which told them at Noorpoor what had been done elsewhere, and what was doing in the great war, and set their hearts at rest as to the final issue. Very gradually Cyril Brandon had worked round towards Futtehpoor; and when his camp was within a few miles of the castle, he received a letter from the Khánum Sahiba, the "Star among Women," praying to be taken under English protection; that the Nawab had gone away—where, she knew not—and that no Sepoys nor any army were there—no one, in fact, in charge of the place but her own personal retainers, who were true to the English, as she was herself, and had been from the first. There was no doubting the sincerity of this profession; and as Baba Sahib had ascertained its correctness from other sources, Cyril marched at once to the castle, and was admitted to the hall of audience, at a door of which, behind a screen, sat the poor lady weeping, and unable to speak much; but, consoled by Mr. Brandon, was not as yet entirely in despair. At her request, Cyril continued certain of the civil officers in local employment, and the household, who were faithful to their mistress, remained as before. But a proclamation was issued, that the Nawab's estate was under attachment, and that authority in it belonged to the Commissioner of Noorpoor until the pleasure of Government was made known.

"There are two men whom I have had a long time in confinement, Mr. Brandon, in one of the secret dungeons, who entreat to be taken to you," said the Kotwal of the town; "they tell me they were Dacoits, with one Azráel Pandé who was their leader. They do not know whether he is alive or dead; but they can give you important information about him, and about the Dacoity at Gokulpoor. Will you see them? They have been well cared for, but secreted by the Nawab for about two years; I infer, therefore, that they were of some importance."

See them? Of course he would see them! Why, this was another of the wonderful events of the time! and Buldeo was sent with the Kotwal to bring the men. In a short time Buldeo returned, crying and laughing like a child. "They are Sumbho and Govinda," he exclaimed; "so long lost! Ah, they will tell you all about the murder of Huree Das, at last!"

As he spoke, the men entered, their heavy irons clanking as they moved, and fell down before Cyril, who was in the hall of audience. They were pale from long confinement and inaction, and dazzled by the light of day; but they were perfectly collected, and told their story with simplicity and truthfulness which could not be mistaken. We know all about that sad matter already, and need not recapitulate it. These men were the two scouts whom Azráel had employed: who had brought Ram Das to the waterfall at night, had heard his proposal and Azráel's acceptance of it; who had returned to Gokulpoor with him, and, assisted by him, had concealed themselves behind some cotton bales, and opened the gates for the Dacoits when the time came. Thus, all was revealed which had lain hid so long! What a strange, painful drama it had been! with only Seeta's life shining out of the gloom, as it were, a vision of a bright jewel in a horrible dream.

They were longing at Noorpoor to see Cyril, and he had arranged to be with them at Christmas. Mr. Mostyn had already had a new roof put upon his house, and it was quite habitable and comfortable; but Cyril's was still a ruin. Do we remember the previous Christmas? It will not, I think, have been forgotten; and the conversation between the friends, and many other circumstances which then happened, when Seeta was there too, and they all began to know her. Well, a year was gone—a year of tumult and horror. But though one victim had been claimed, the evil shadow of Sumbut 1914 was already departing, and though the weird year must inevitably fulfil its character of blood, yet it would be that of cruel enemies, who had brought retribution on themselves for many a dastardly act of murder; and not the blood of those whom Azráel Pandé had doomed when he made his address to the Thirty-fourth at Barrackpoor. All of them were safe now, except such as might fall in the ordinary course of war. No more helpless women and children, thank God, would perish in hideous massacre!

As Cyril Brandon rode into Noorpoor early on Christmas morning, did he remember his last ride by that road, and his companion then? I do not think he had forgotten either; but the last wound was open, and bleeding still, and Grace Mostyn was but as a sister. He was a good deal changed, too, in many respects. More resolute, for the exercise of independent action and responsibility involve, or perhaps beget, resolution—more confident in himself, and more thoroughly imbued with a knowledge and conviction of the value of her who had so miserably perished in saving him. Would they have forgotten her? Not so, he thought; nor was he mistaken. Seeta's memory was very precious among her friends, and their conversation often turned upon the strange incidents of her life, and her last act of devotion and love.

Yes, it was a very affectionate, pleasant meeting, a very happy one I might say, though the reminiscences to Cyril Brandon were inexpressibly painful, and they grew upon him day after day, more than was good for him. He could not walk through his garden, or see the blackened ruins of Seeta's pretty cottage, he could not be in the drawing-room of the Judge's house—without remembering the sudden burst of Seeta from the dining-room, while her sudden piercing cry to escape seemed to ring in his ears; nor could he go down the steps in front, without having the whole scene of that horrible night repeated. It was almost worse at first if he went up to the fort; but after a few days he felt he had rather live where Seeta died than be always with the Mostyns, with whom his presence seemed, he thought, to be a sort of constraint. And he could be freer to do his work, too, by himself. With Grace Mostyn, so long as Seeta lived, he had been on the terms of a brother with a sister. Now that was changed, for the object of common interest and love no longer existed, and the heart which had once resisted temptation was now stronger than ever, entrenched, as it were, behind a rampart of grief, which, though neither morbid nor intrusive, could not at once give way.

Noorpoor was not a gay station, by any means, that Christ-'as; indeed, I hardly care to write how dull it was. Some of residents had gone to their bungalows in the cantonment; a whose houses had been burnt, remained in the fort with igadier and his staff. Noble came in to eat his Christmas r with the Mostyns. All were thankful, no doubt; but ss prevailed, for even petty squabbles had departed before vant of exciting causes, and the absence of home news. And that, when it came at last, was an event never to be forgotten. Months had passed since those beleaguered in Noorpoor had received letters. Now there was news of children, of wives, of parents, of friends; some joyful, some sorrowful, some painful and hard to bear, but better than the suspense which had existed before; and they heard too, often, of the exertions that England was making for all, and how the evil tidings of rebellion and massacre had been received.

Cyril's letters were very varied. There was at first a complaint about his brother's health; but in the latter ones there was much anxiety both on his mother's part and on his sister's. They were now at Cannes, and had taken a villa there for the season, that is, from November till March. "Mentone was thought too relaxing, and John does not like it," wrote Lady Hylton. "The place is too quiet for him. Here, at any rate, we have plenty of friends, and he can get as much riding as is good for him; and really it is very pleasant, though *I am* anxious, because the doctors plainly told me, and told him, that he *must not* risk another winter in England. If we were only as little anxious about you; but I am comforted by what —— tells me, that you are not in the disturbed parts of India, and will not be affected by the mutiny of the Sepoys. If I thought you were, I am sure I should never sleep," etc., etc.

The last of his mother's envelopes, a fortnight later, was of a different nature. I need not quote the whole of it; but between her thoughts that the news she had received was true, and the increasing evil tidings from India, poor Lady Hylton had written in evident anguish. "I received the enclosed by the last mail," Lady Hylton wrote, "and you can only estimate faintly, how it has distressed and grieved me. Whether the writer's insinuation that the native connection you have formed is a permanent one, is true or not, I have no means of judging. An old friend, ——, who knows Indian customs well, says it cannot be permanent, and that temporary *liaisons* are only too common; but, O, my dear son, that any scandal of this kind should be spread about you, cuts me to the heart, and I cannot bear it. I dare not tell the matter to Augusta, and when I mentioned it to your brother, he flushed very much, and said he would not write to you, but I might, as it would have more effect. O Cyril! I have *so* trusted you since you left me, and never, never have I heard a word about you that grieved me. I can bear all this horrible news that comes, for I know you will do your duty wherever you are; but if this abominable scandal be true, it will break my heart." From his brother, too, there were a few lines:—"Mater will tell you all about me, and I suppose I must submit to live here till spring to please her and the doctors. As to Augusta, she is perfectly happy, and indulges in as many flirtations as she conveniently can. You will see that some very particular friend of yours has written to mother about what you confided to me. Do satisfy her, like a dear fellow, for I foresee that she will be miserable if you don't—and that by return mail. Take care of yourself; and I think if you can get a lick at those Pandies, you won't let it pass. Somehow or other, I don't feel a bit anxious about you."

Cyril looked at the envelope enclosed in his mother's letter. The postmark was Calcutta, and the handwriting of the direction he did not know; but the enclosure was very different. There were the peculiar spiky characters of Mrs. Smith, which it was impossible any one could imitate, and the purport of the letter was such a strange, spiteful mingling of truth and falsehood, piety (after Mrs. Smith's fashion), and irreverence, that I am almost tempted to copy it as a curiosity of literature, but I refrain for many reasons. Possibly there are some of my readers who, hating "black people," might enjoy Mrs. Smith's opinion of them, and I should appear to pander to such. There was also a digression upon the morality of Indian females in general, and poor Seeta's in particular, which is too prurient to be sufficiently decent to transcribe, and which, of course, was written in "the very strictest confidence."

Cyril was reading this in the octagon room when Philip Mostyn entered, who saw at once the angry flush on his friend's cheek, and in conjunction with the pile of English letters on the table, thought it might be some family matter; but Cyril undeceived him at once. "Read that," he said, "about my poor girl. I found out Mrs. Smith once before, and, like a fool, forgave her; but she shall not escape me this time. Think, Philip, what agony it has been to me to read that, here where my darling's pure spirit passed away."

Philip Mostyn read the letter slowly, and Cyril saw the

tears well up in his eyes as he did so. "She would have forgiven her as she did the ruffian who murdered her, Cyril," he said at length, solemnly. "If Seeta were alive, I should say nothing; but as she is gone to rest, I plead for her, that this infamous tissue of lies should be forgiven, though it may not be forgotten."

Cyril looked out through the oriel window towards the placid lake, blue and crisped by the slight breeze that blew across it, and, far away, the hills were dimmed in the soft haze. He did not speak for some time, but the appeal from his friend, so tenderly given in her name, had not been lost upon him. "For her sweet memory's sake, Philip," he said at last, "which should not be blurred, even by a thought—God help me—I do forgive this. I had thought of sending it to the writer's husband, but——" and he took the letter and tore it into the smallest fragments, which fluttered down to the water in a white shower. "Let it pass now—now that my darling is at rest."

CHAPTER XLIX.

THE RANEE OF JHANSY.

WHEN the Nawab Dil Khan and his army arrived at Jhansy, the British forces, under Sir Hugh Rose (Lord Strathnairn), were sweeping all before them to the southward, while Madras troops, under General Whitlock, were carrying war further to the east into the territories of the Rajah of Banpoor and the Nawab of Banda. From the north-west, strong columns were pursuing a flying enemy down the banks of the Jumna towards Kalpee; and others were already assembling from the eastward for a last attack upon Lucknow. Thus while this tale does not, as I have before said, profess to give the history of the period which historians have provided, it seems needful to mention in some part, and briefly, what was being done to hem in the rebel Sepoy army and its allies; and among those operations, Jhansy was soon to be the scene of one of the most brilliant achievements of that very exciting period of the war.

It does not appear to me that Nawab Dil Khan had in any degree improved his position by the march to Jhansy. He had been carried thither by his fears rather than his hopes. Behind him he saw disgrace and ruin, nay, even death, which there was no apparent means of escaping; before him—well, his "Kismut" or fate, whatever that might be. I have before said that the Nawab was no warrior; he had no experience of leading armies or of fighting battles; and he had already seen that a mere handful of British troops, English and native, had been able to drive his own forces from a strong position, and that his few guns had been saved with difficulty. There was no good accord between the leaders of his forces; and, as it neared its destination, the mutineers of Noorpoor had separated, the majority, under the Rissáldar and the Soobadar Major of the —th, preparing to join the Nana Sahib's army which lay at Kalpee, under Tantia Topee, who was preparing to support the Ranee.

"Colonel" Goor Bux and the Nawab therefore, with the guns and the irregular levies, duly arrived at their destination; and the former was heartily welcomed; for there was no doubt that he was a brave and efficient officer, practically acquainted with his professional duty, and as such needful to the Ranee in case her strong fort should be attacked. But Dil Khan had no qualifications to make him welcome; nor indeed had he rank or wealth to help her cause in any way. He had notoriously failed to hold his ground in the Noorpoor district, through which British armies were now sweeping with resistless force; but he had brought some guns, of which perhaps she had enough already, and as he presented the hilt of his sword to the undaunted woman, and offered his poor services against their mutual enemies, the English, the tone of his reception did not encourage him.

The Ranee, Lukshmee Bye, a Mahratta Brahmin, had no affectation of personal concealment; and she sat daily on the seat, or Guddee, of her deceased husband, receiving reports, giving directions, hearing petitions, and comporting herself as a brave and determined woman had need to do in her position. In appearance she was fair and handsome: with a noble presence and figure, and a dignified and resolute, indeed stern, expression, which appeared to have usurped the place of the peculiar softness which, when she was younger, and had good hope of a prosperous life, had distinguished her. Dil Khan could hardly understand the sometimes dreamy, sometimes fierce expression of her beautiful eyes. She had bade him be seated apart, as she was engaged with others; and that presently, she would converse with him.

Dil Khan felt himself very lonely in that busy place. No one came to speak with him; people passed and repassed, and the men with silver maces scowled at his own mace-bearers as though they had no business to show themselves there. For a time a burly Mussulman, with a strong black beard and coarse hands, who looked like a truculent butcher, but who declared himself to have been a "Doctor" under the English, came and sat by him, describing how all the English, men, women, and children, had been taken out to a garden and killed, many by himself: and how he had hacked at the "Kafirs" till his arm was tired, and sent many, most perhaps, of the seventy-five who perished, "to hell." The Nawab remembered the sweet ladies of Noorpoor, and had often noticed many of the fair English children there: and as he heard the grim, hideous recital of the doctor, he, rebel as he was, in his heart thanked God that he had slain none such as they. There were not many Mussulmans present. The majority of those who came to make their obeisance were Hindoos of various castes, none of whom noticed him: indeed, most seemed to regard him as an interloper who had done nothing, could do nothing, and whom the Ranee Sahiba did not want.

Perhaps there never had been a time since he left Futtehpoor when remembrances of its former peace and security came home so vividly to the Nawab's mind. As he closed his eyes he could see, as if from his seat in the oriel window, his gardens and rich sugar-cane fields, and the blue hills beyond, soft, and dreamily glowing in the sun. He could hear the music which played over his castle gate at stated times of the day, and came up softly through the courts and halls. He missed his familiar gossips, the town Moulvees, and some of the bankers and landholders, who used to drop in and chat with him. Then there was peace, now there was war; but he had won no glory, did not seem likely to win any, and was to all intents and purposes a fugitive. He had promised himself to go to Dehly to salute the "King of Kings" sitting in pomp upon his throne, as his ancestors had done: now he had to salute an "Infidel" Ranee, whose rank was not as high as his own. The English had, of course, attacked and taken his domains. Could he now win them back? Could this Ranee help him? Ah, no! not now that the English seemed stronger than ever, with tens of thousands of English soldiers fresh from their country. It would be all the Ranee could do to keep her own: and, indeed, there appeared little chance of that, if what his servants told him were true. As he thought of these things, sitting alone in the great hall of the Ranee's palace, tears, very bitter tears, welled up in his eyes, and there was a painful lump in his throat which would not subside; but at last his turn came, and a mace-bearer, roughly to his perception, told him to "get up," that the Lady Ranee would allow him to speak with her, and conducted him to the Royal daïs, by which he seated himself, having again offered the hilt of his sword as a Nuzzur, or offering, which the Ranee touched lightly with her soft, beautiful hand.

"Be at your ease, Nawab Sahib," she said, in good Hindee, for she affected not to speak the courtly Oordoo, though she understood it perfectly. "Tell me about yourself. I have often heard my lord husband speak of your gallant father. What have the English done to you that you are here with me, their enemy, and have left your fair domain? Where are your children?"

"I have no children, lady," he replied, sadly. The Ranee had touched a painful chord in the man's feelings. "I have no children."

"I see," she continued. "Then they, the English, would not let you adopt, and you are like me?"

"I did not ask them, lady."

"Nay, then, by the holy Mother Gunga!" she exclaimed, sharply, "thou hadst no wrong done thee. Was it not greed of power that led thee on to rebel, not loss of honour?"

"I fought, as my forefathers did, for the Faith, and for the 'Asylum of the World,' who conferred rank and my own province on me," returned Dil Khan, doggedly.

"A poor reed to lean on, Nawab," she said, scornfully; "a poor reed; a flickering torch, which has gone out with an evil stink, and will never be kindled again. Ah, sir! with no wrong to redress, with no honour lost, with your faith pledged to those for whom your ancestors fought and had served; with a fine ancestral castle and estate—methinks it was a traitor's part to leave them for a phantom. Had I been like thee, the red flag of the English, which their Lord Sahib gave to my husband, and which has been soaked in English gore, had now been flying from the fort above us; and I, weak woman as I am, would have fought for them. No harm should have come near them that I, Lukshmee Bye, could have prevented. I would have taken those Englishwomen and their babes to my breast and held them there, truly and safely; while their husbands should have kept them and me against all enemies. Yes, I would have done this, Nawab, if they had been true."

"Yet all who are here—died—were slain--lady——"

It was perilous ground to tread upon; but the Nawab's spirit had risen. He had never before been so addressed or reproached by a woman. If he were a traitor, she was a vindicative murdcress.

"Slain? Yes," she exclaimed, with her eyes flashing and her lips quivering, "I was childless, like you, and spared none—no, not one! Do you know the history of our house? No? Well, listen. We declared for the English when their power hurled back the Mahrattas of the Dekhan. They had crushed Dehly, and that high station they could not maintain. We of Jhansy might have lost all then; but the English of that time were just and merciful, and continued to our house all it had gained. We were honoured by them, and we were loyal. We loved the English; we hoisted their flag over our own; and it would have been there now, had their old justice been continued to us. My dear lord died, and he had no children. I asked and pleaded, in his dying words, to adopt a boy who should inherit what had been once freely given; but this was refused; our little petition was rejected. The English, with all the empire of Dehly belonging to them, refused to continue what they themselves had once granted to us freely and generously. But these men now are not like their former princely heroes; they are a mean, covetous race; farming our country from their Government, seizing every scrap of land, every rupee of revenue they can, to swell their enormous gains. When we heard of Nagpoor and Sattara, we were touched for the fate of our royal houses; but we said, in our simple, blind confidence, 'These great acts cannot affect us, for we have been loyal and true, and the English flag flies from our towers.' And yet—and yet—they did not spare us. They offered me and mine a pension. A pension! I say it was an insult: mean, cruel, and deliberate. Should we have honour if we were pensioned? Should we have self-respect? I tell thee, no! I would rather have shaved my head and wandered on foot as a poor Bairagin, begging my way from shrine to shrine all over Hind, denouncing these English as tyrants and oppressors, than taken the crumb they flung to me—as to a dog. But there was one thing that came into my heart instead—one thing for which I waited, Nawab Sahib—we could have revenge; and therefore I had them slain. They were ruling where I ruled; they were collecting my money, they were changing the old customs of my people, they were corrupting our priestly caste.

"There came once, before Sumbut 1914 began," she continued, in a lower tone, "a holy Brahmin, a man who recited the 'Mysteries of Kaleo Mata,' who told us the truth; yea, in this hall he told it fearlessly. He had wandered many years preaching the same; but my husband's heart turned not toward him. But when he came to me, in my gloom and misery, and told me what the English had done—what they were doing, what they purposed to do to all Hind—to sweep away all royalties, and all caste—I, a Brahmin woman, lone and childless, joined my tears and my prayers to his. He cried, 'There shall be no English! Kalee Ma'a has given them to us, that she may drink their blood.' And when the time came and the signal, all here died—every one. Not in war, with honour, but like sheep, victims of a sacrifice to the 'Mother.' I say one and all they died, and their blood flowed, and their English flag was dipped in it, and hangs black and stiff on the walls. Dost thou understand now, Nawab, why they were slain?"

"I had the same Brahmin with me, lady. His name was——"

"Do not mention it, sir," she exclaimed, moving her hand impatiently, and seeming to shudder. "He comes to me when I call, and asks for blood. All the rites he taught me call for blood—well, the 'Mother' may have it still, and take mine in the end; but death is sweeter than dishonour; and if I win, Khan Sahib!—if we, the Mahrattas, win, there may be a Péshwah at Poona, though there will be no Emperor at Dehly. Now go, sir; your quarters are allotted to you, and the duty of your men. For yourself, you will receive the daily rations of your rank while you stay."

"I expected to have heard Azráel's cry of 'Hrrám! Hrrám! Hrrám!'" said the Nawab to Goor Bux afterwards. "Is she, too, mad, like him? Thirsting for blood?"

"It is not her wont," replied the "Colonel." "The people speak of her as gentle and loving once; but the English have wronged her deeply, and she has thrown away her scabbard. Sometimes she weeps floods of tears; but more frequently she is, as you saw her to-day, brooding over her wrongs and her revenge, gloomy and vindictive, a very tigress at heart; so, beware of her!"

Lukshmee Bye was not long in suspense. On the 23rd March, 1858, as Sumbut 1914 had just closed, the English army she had heard of so long, encamped over against her fort, drove in all the outposts, and the siege commenced. "Colonel" Goor Bux knew very well what English guns were, and English shells and shot; and though his own material of war was indifferent, he fought his battles with the devotion of a good soldier, worthy of a better cause and fate. No hiding for any one now; and Dil Khan began to see and feel what English war in earnest meant. A portion of the wall was allotted to him to defend, and he did his duty doggedly, for there was no shelter, and no retreat. The English guns came nearer and nearer; and the wall crumbled away under the storm of shot, while almost every gun on the fort walls was by turns dismounted or disabled. "No matter what we lose," said the Ranee's officers, "if we can but hold the place till our friends relieve us; then, between two fires, our turn will come, and they cannot escape us." Night after night, Lukshmee Bye watched from the highest tower of the fort; but there was no signal. Had they left her to perish?

Not so; they were doing their best to save her. Twenty thousand men with twenty English guns, were marching upon Jhansy with all practicable speed. The Ranee herself had at least ten thousand within the fort, and the plan of the battle had been deftly arranged. While Tantia Topce was attacking the rear of the British position, the Ranee's troops were to sally in their front; and with a throbbing but exulting heart Lukshmee Bye sat waiting for the blaze of the fire which was to prove that her succour had arrived. Nor was she disappointed. As her friends crossed the Betwah river, a bright light shot up into the sky, which confirmed every hope, and arroused her for the first struggle near the town, in which she should strike in, leading her men to victory!

But this was not to be. A veteran intelligence, far superior to any she could command, was directing the siege: and the rebel plan was frustrated by a daring movement, of which there are few examples in war. While the siege operations progressed as usual, a body of 1200 men, all that were available, were posted by night on the road to the river, and as the rebel columns came up, the battle began. For a time the struggle was fierce; but the result was never doubtful. Not only was the rebel host defeated with the heavy loss of 1500 disciplined men dead on the field, but with that of all its guns, and chased away till the exhausted troops could follow no further. Then the siege of Jhansy was pressed more closely than before.

On the third of April, 1858, the town was stormed, and the English troops had taken up their position in a part of the place, preparing for the final assault on the fort on the morrow. Had the Ranee any hope? Perhaps the messengers she sent for terms might have told her there was none, had they returned; but there were few spared at Jhansy when the past was remembered; and when no messengers returned, she knew their fate.

Nothing now but flight. Some devoted men still defended the walls of the rock fort, who said they would die there to cover the retreat of their beloved mistress; and through the night of the 3rd of April the English shells rained upon that part of the town and fort which the enemy still held. By daylight, all must be decided, and there was no hope of defence now.

Was Dil Khan to stay or to fly? He seemed to be so stupefied by what was passing around him, by the noise of the crashing fire, and by the sight of the hundreds, nay thousands, of dead and dying wretches; by the sight of English faces within the walls—that he was passive in the hands of his servants, who were watching what might be done; and there were already rumours that the Ranee would fly. They had the Nawab's horse saddled, and he himself sat, with his loins girded, praying to be led out of that hell of shot and human suffering.

At last, while yet much of night remained, one of the gates in a secluded part of the fortifications was opened, and a sad procession issued forth. The Ranee and her sister, or companion, dressed like men, with a few of her own chosen retainers, rode silently from the portal, into the gloom beyond, and were followed by Dil Khan and such of his men as could escape. No one spoke, except in whispers, and the gate was closed and barred as the last man passed out. It was to be a ride for life that night, for the English cavalry patrols of the 14th Dragoons, and the Hyderabad contingent, were everywhere vigilant; and to meet any of them, was to ensure certain death. How these were evaded, was never ascertained; but the Ranee had perfect guides, she was a fearless rider, and she pressed on at a rapid pace into the rough, jungly country, in which her best safety lay.

But not without pursuit: for the fact that she had fled was soon known to the cavalry patrols from the crowds of soldiers who were now escaping from the doomed city, and who were being pursued and sabred in all directions. One of these patrols fell upon the Ranee's track; and at one time she was in sight upon her grey horse, attended by a few followers; but the pursuers had already ridden twenty-one miles; their horses were exhausted, their officer badly wounded, and the gallant Hyderabad cavalry were obliged to abandon what they could not continue, and Lukshmee Bye escaped.

In that hot frightful night, Dil Khan fared badly. He kept up with the Ranee for some time, with a few mounted followers, who dropped off gradually, one by one. His own fat, pampered horse, splendid indeed to see as he caracoled in a procession, was in ill condition for such a ride. Again and again the Ranee and her retainers called to him to come on, but in vain: and at last he found himself abandoned by all. Then he lost his way in some jungle, and wandered about till it was daylight. It seemed that he had ridden back towards Jhansy; for as he ascended a low hill, he saw the rock fort at only a few miles distance, and the red ensign of England fluttering in the hot sunlight from the highest tower of the citadel. Jhansy then was no place for him, unless he gave himself up; and then—— Ah, there was no hope, no refuge now! None but in God! And the miserable man dismounted from his panting horse, and spreading his waist-band on the ground, knelt down mechanically to perform the morning prayer of his faith. He was wearied out, physically and mentally, and parched with thirst. As he lay down after his prayer, he fell into a troubled sleep, and mocking visions of his quiet castle, his gentle wife, and of the fierce Dacoit, seemed to come to him; and the very "Hrrám! Hrrám! Hrrám!" of his unholy rites rang in his ears.

Suddenly his horse neighed, and he awoke: and raising himself up on his arm, he saw that a body of cavalry, scouring the country for the escaped Ranee, were upon him. He drew his sword, but the blow he made at the first dragoon was parried, and a moment after he was laid low by a sabre thrust, and sinking at his horse's feet, died without a groan.

It was evident that he was a man of rank, and he might have been saved had the English officer been near. But there was no quarter given at Jhansy, and Dil Khan had asked for none. He had died, like a soldier, with his sword in his hand. Then his body was searched for papers, and perhaps for valuables also. But he had carried nothing on his person. All he possessed was in the saddle-bags of poor Mótee, who was led off, and duly entered in the ranks of Her Majesty's Dragoons. The papers found were of no consequence, further than to tell who he was, and after a time, Mr. Brandon received official intimation of the Nawab Dil Khan's death.

I need not follow the fortunes of the Ranee of Jhansy, who has no other connection with this tale than as regards the Nawab. But she joined Tantia Topee, again defeated at Koonch, and in the subsequent operations proved to be the most untiring, and perhaps the ablest of the rebel leaders who captured Gualior, and obliged its ruler, Sindia, to fly. But her triumph was of short continuance; and in the successful attack upon the rebel army at Gualior, on the 17th of June, she, and her sister, or companion, were slain, being dressed like men, in a charge made by the 8th Hussars, of which event Sir Hugh Rose wrote: "One most important result was the death of the Ranee of Jhansy, who, although a lady, was the ablest and bravest military leader of the rebels."

CHAPTER L.

PARTING.

It was no time for delay at Noorpoor; and when the Christmas week had passed, and the greetings of the new year had been exchanged, Cyril left his friends for his district work, which, indeed, needed all his time and ability. His official communications had been re-opened, and his nomination of young Temple as an extra assistant commissioner confirmed. Nor was Baba Sahib forgotten, for the same despatch brought his appointment as "extra assistant" also; while the eminent services all had rendered to Government at a most critical period, were impressively recorded in a State minute forwarded to Cyril by his friend, whose letters on a former occasion we know of, and for which the high official tendered his sincere apologies. "Nothing, my dear Brandon," he wrote, "vexes me more than that I should have been so misled as to consider them as much necessary for the public welfare as your own; and from our mutual friend, Mostyn, I now know the truth, and the miserable catastrophe that ensued, in which, believe me, you have my very sincere sympathy."

I have said before, that the week preceding January, 1858, had been a dull one; very dull, to all or most of our friends. There was no music, for the piano was found to have been warped by the heat of the conflagration of the Judge's house, and was, for the time, useless, and was to be sent home for repair. Even had it been in order, I think those who would have sung to it were out of tune also, for no attempt was made to renew the old pleasant practices; and though other pianos were offered, none were accepted. The memory of the dangers all had escaped had not passed away with victory, now everywhere progressing. But Sumbut 1914 would yet die in blood, according to the old weird prediction a hundred years before.

As to poor Grace, she longed to be away. How much she had been distressed by offers which she was obliged to refuse, all through that weary time in the old fort, I will not reveal;

nor is it fitting to mention those who had made pretensions to her hand. Was it because of objection to her successive admirers, or did the reasons for her refusals lie deeper? If they did, and I believe they did, she saw no hope. Cyril Brandon was kind, and even affectionate; but Grace saw that time, a long time, perhaps, would be needed to reconcile him to the loss of one whom they had both loved so dearly; and she could only hope, dimly, indeed, but yet hope. There was, however, no apparent opening for any change by absence from Noorpoor. Mr. Mostyn had again pressed his wife and Grace to go to the Hills for the ensuing hot weather, but in vain; nor was the condition of the country sufficiently settled in the direction they would have to travel, to warrant such an undertaking as a long journey; nor, truly, was Mrs. Mostyn herself equal to it, so they remained. And as Cyril Brandon left them, it was with the certainty that they should meet again.

Perhaps I need hardly follow Cyril Brandon into his district occupations. They had not changed, nor had his habits of hard work and assiduity, which have been already recorded. There was much to repair, some still prevailing lawlessness to overcome, and sullen minds to be reconciled to the existing necessities of the time; but there were few who could resist the influence of his genial nature and true popularity. Firm, just, and devoted to the best interests of the people he ruled over; confident, yet deliberate in his acts and judgments, he was at once loved and respected by the loyal, while his name was a terror to evil-doers. The secret of his success, if it can be called one, lay in his true sympathy with all classes, and his ready attention to all demands on his time and patience. Many an old feud had broken out afresh, many a dispute, long ago settled, had been renewed fiercely in the confusion that had prevailed; many a family litigation for lands or divisions of inheritance, which had slumbered for years, had been revived so long as might made right, and all had to be re-adjusted.

Those only know who have experienced them, how deeply and distressingly such disturbances of public feeling and security as had occurred affect the rural population of India, and how obstinate are the prejudices and antipathies which have to be reconciled or overcome; and yet, in some respects, Cyril Brandon found himself gaining a truer and deeper knowledge of the real opinions, dispositions, and requirements of the people, than in previous years of smooth, eventless progression which, too often, had concealed festering sores beneath. Mr. Brandon could see very plainly that the discontent, in many localities, had had real ground of existence, and that the present experience he was gaining would be most valuable aid towards a new settlement of many disputed points; but while he removed all the causes of discontent which lay within his powers, the fuller and more complete re-organization could only be effected under orders from the Government, which, at present, too deeply occupied by the emergent political affairs of the time, would not be able, for several years to come, perhaps, to bestow the requisite attention upon his own province, one of many, which had been too long neglected.

So he worked and worked: making notes for the report which he would submit when the season was over, obtaining facts, and the opinions and counsels of the most respectable and influential people of the country, adding his own practical suggestions of relief and amendment of administration. But I do not know that many of my readers will care to follow dry details of Indian administration, though they form the soul, as it were, of the vast body they regulate; and it would be well for all if they engaged a deeper share of sympathy and interest, or the English people at large cared to understand, or sought to understand, how, with a few assistants such as we know of—Cyril Brandon, like scores of others, governed hundreds of thousands, or, perhaps even millions, with a province as large as Wales or Scotland, or one of the divisions of Scotland; and how an aggregate of such men rule the vast population of India, and endeavour, and, it may be hoped, succeed, in securing its good will, and in some, but in rarer cases, its affection. I do not mean to put forward Cyril Brandon as perfection. He had his faults and shortcomings, his struggles, and, in some respects, prejudices to overcome; his regrets that he had left so much undone, and that, after all, he could do so little: but I wish him to be understood as one who had devoted himself to his work; who, while seeing many serious faults in native character, yet was able to recognize many sterling qualities; as one whose good will, and practical unostentatious benevolence, attracted and secured the love of those he governed—a love which often smoothed away difficulties which, in other indifferent and less sympathizing hands, might have been wellnigh insurmountable.

And I wish him to be distinguished from those who, having no sympathy with the people they rule over, are haughty or supercilious, uncourteous in address and demeanour, forbidding and scorning confidence, entrenched behind native clerks and ministerial officers, and rarely seeing, therefore, with their own eyes, or hearing with their own ears. Such men despise native acquaintance, and make no friends. How should they? Many are excellent officers and administrators of routine duties; but they are those who, some one wisely said, know natives only "when they are trying them, or taxing them," and therefore seek no further than to know, and believe in, the worst points of their character. Such men cannot alter, or be altered; but there are many, I trust, who may read these lines, that may not be ashamed to follow Cyril Brandon's example in professing a faith in the people they govern, which leads to kindliness and courtesy of speech and of manner. Time was, when any one in India known to say his prayers, was sneeringly and scornfully called a "New Light," as a term of reproach; but men now-a-days say their prayers more openly than they used to do, and are not reproached, nor would be afraid if they were.

So, after this fashion, I may hope, perhaps, that no false shame or bitter prejudice, may come between their immediate rulers, and the people whom they govern, on the part of the English nation; and that there may be many, if not all, who do not hesitate to belie the reproach of the great Edmund Burke, that "young men govern India without society and without sympathy with the natives: an endless, hopeless prospect of new flights of birds of prey ever passing before the eyes of the people!" I will hope, too, that the illustrious examples of Elphinstone, Metcalfe, Munro, Malcolm, and a host of others whose names are still household words, invoked when evening lamps are lighted, or sung in the early morning, when the "two women are sitting grinding at the mill"—may be perpetuated.

But it is not the pride of competitive examination that will do this. It is the manly, simple, kindly minds, which may not be very learned, and need not be: but which, like those of the men I have named, can divest themselves of narrow prejudice, and enter into the feelings and desires of the people without losing their independent thoughts, or positions as English gentlemen.

In his present anxious work, the help of Seeta would have been invaluable to Cyril Brandon. For who, better than she, knew the real wants of the people? And who could lay them before him more freely, or so truly, and so lovingly? Often, during the unquiet period at Noorpoor, had they discussed these matters, and looked hopefully to the time when, the local troubles past, they could carry on reform freely. As Seeta's mind had expanded and grown in dignity of comprehension, how eloquent an advocate had she become of education of all grades and classes! She had vowed to build and endow a school-house for girls at Shah Gunje; she had a hundred plans in her thoughts of establishing schools for girls and boys in different towns; and truly the hope of directing them was a constant joy! Well, all that was dead and past now; and in the daily life—the studies—the pleasant chatty evenings—the morning ride, and the "bit of shooting"—with all the protection against lapsing into self, were dead to Cyril also; and the void, which nothing could fill up, was very painful to bear. Even poor little Muff could not forget; and often, as Cyril sat outside in the evening, the fond creature would run into the tent, look round, and return whining, as if asking—as indeed it seemed to be—where his dear mistress was gone!

Mails, and letters from home, came now with their accustomed regularity. Lady Hylton had made no further allusion to the anonymous letter; but she was evidently looking for some explanation of it. This Cyril had given, fully and without reserve, in the letter which he wrote in reply to his mother's; and her answer to that would come soon. Cyril blamed himself much, that he had not written at first explicitly to his mother; but in truth, he feared her repugnance to his having married, what she would call, a heathen, and whilst informing his brother of what he had done, looked hopefully for the time when Seeta should become a Christian, and that he could marry her by the rites of Christian faith. I think he felt too, in a great degree, how difficult, if not impossible, it would have been to reconcile his mother to what he had done, in any case at least not for a long time; and could she, indeed, ever be brought to believe what Seeta really was, unless she saw her? So there had been struggles in many ways, but these, too, were past. In regard to his brother's health, the news was favourable; more so than his mother expected: and they should return to Hylton in the summer, with good hope that the threatened danger was past.

So work went on, patiently and unremittingly, and there was so much to arrange and reorganize, in every county of his province, that Mr. Brandon was hardly sufficient for the task. Perhaps in the rains he should have more leisure, he thought, and should enjoy the society of his friends; but that was not to be. As the hot weather began, both Mostyn and his wife seemed to give way. Mrs. Mostyn did not gain strength after the birth of her child; and during the rains, and confinement in the fort, Mr. Mostyn had suffered from frequent attacks of low fever, that showed a chronic form, over which medicine had no power; and his strength did not rally. Dr. Home, and another skilful surgeon at Noorpoor, had sat in judgment on Mr. Mostyn's case: and their verdict was, that an immediate return to England was imperative, both for Mrs. Mostyn and himself, and it was clear it could not be delayed. If they went at once, they should avoid the monsoon, and they should reach the Mediterranean by May, and pass the summer in England. Mr. Mostyn had only returned home once since he came out, during a period of nearly twenty years; and the sudden break-down in his health was a warning which could not be overlooked. He felt that he had not the strength to sit daily at his work, or to write elaborate judgments upon appeal cases, or to compile the statistics of his department; and he knew from the example of many friends, that a visit to 'the Hills' was only a temporary expedient, which was useless in his own case. But if he felt anxious about himself, he was doubly anxious about Rose and Grace, who were both weak, and looked like ghosts of their former selves.

Such events are the common lot of those who serve in India. A sharp fever, overwork, constant and increasing debility, a deranged liver, or any one disorder, in fact, that shows when health previously so good, and so equable in all seasons, gradually breaks down, and cannot be locally repaired—separates husbands and wives, parents and children, lovers and friends, with a terrible and distressing promptitude and certainty: and Cyril Brandon, after hearing from Mr. Mostyn and his wife, as well as from Noble and Mostyn, that his friend's health was seriously giving way, was hardly surprised by a sudden summons to come and say good-bye, for they must leave Noorpoor in a few days.

And he went from his camp to visit them, and was much concerned and distressed to see what he found to be the case; for there was no question that the change was imperatively necessary. Philip Mostyn's hollow eyes and gaunt frame were proofs of his sufferings: and he could hardly believe that such havoc could have been made in the appearance of the two ladies. It was, however, no easy matter for them all to part, who had been so closely bound together by many ties. I think, if it had been possible for Cyril to have obtained leave, he would have gone with them; but that was not possible to any but those who had to fly India for their very lives' sake—and he was well and strong; able yet to do his duty, and indeed determined to do it until he had arranged everything to the satisfaction of Government.

The last important criminal case which had been tried by the Judge, was that of Ram Das of Gokulpoor, for having incited the murder of Huree Das. I need not enter into particulars of this trial, further than to state that the evidence supplied by his account books, by the bond and memoranda found on the Dacoit's body, by the two approvers who had been released at Futtehpoor, and the evidence of several servants who had seen the approvers with their master the day before the Dacoity, and the night it occurred—proved ample for his conviction. Mr. Mostyn had sentenced him to be hanged; but this had been commuted into transportation for life to the Andaman Islands, then newly established as a penal settlement; but I question whether the miserable wretch thought the mercy extended to him was any real boon.

Cyril went to see him at his own request; and if it were any satisfaction, heard from his lips a confession of his crime, and an acknowledgment of the justice of his sentence. There were a few requests as to provision for his wife and children by Narendra, and Mr. Brandon gave his assurance that he would do what he could for them.

A few days passed, and I have no heart to write of them. In many respects they were very painful, in others hopeful to those concerned. Philip and Rose longing to see their children, and for health for all. Grace—well, hopeful too, perhaps, in her heart, though it had no utterance even to her sister. And so the last evening came, and the friends were sitting in the verandah while the ladies were preparing themselves for the night march. Philip Mostyn was giving his last directions, and he had gained Cyril's consent to inhabit the house so long as he had need of it.

"We shall meet in England, I am sure," said Philip. "It will not do for you to remain longer than you absolutely need after the regular furloughs are opened. I am sure, too, that your mother and brother need your presence, and it will be such a comfort to them. But I will write my own impressions of your brother's health when I see him, and you must promise me —promise us all," he continued, as Mrs. Mostyn and Grace came out in their travelling clothes, "not to delay here on any consideration, when a way home is open to you."

"I do promise, promise you all, dear friends," replied Cyril, "as far as I can, not being at present a free agent. I do indeed yearn to see them; and after you are gone, what have I here to keep me but my work? And you can explain so much to my mother and Hylton about what has happened; much that I *could* not write, and which will come from all of you more naturally and more forcibly than from me, that I am sure I need say no more on the subject. All I would have them believe is, that I did no wrong, and that I was true; and it will be a relief to me, greater than I can tell, when I hear that you have been to Hylton. Will you all promise me to go?"

"Indeed, indeed, we will," cried Mrs. Mostyn earnestly through her tears; "and we will be true to you and to Seeta, as you will know hereafter; won't we, Grace? and I will write, too, everything. I am sure Grace, for one, will not let me rest till I do, so you may quite trust us."

Poor Grace could not speak then, for her tears, and many thoughts were wellnigh overpowering her. But I think, as Cyril took her to her palankeen, and bade her farewell, telling her, with a choking sob, that he could never forget her kindness and love for Seeta, and should miss her presence sadly, there was, in his lingering clasp of her hand, more comfort than she had dared to hope for.

Then, "God bless you! good-bye! good-bye!" from all, and they were gone.

CHAPTER LI.

"THE TENDER GRACE OF A DAY THAT IS DEAD."

THEY had a safe passage home, and Cyril heard regularly by every mail, of the great and rapid improvement of all their healths. Philip Mostyn wrote that he felt nearly as strong as ever: and as for Rose and Grace, none of their friends could believe that they had suffered from the climate, and the anxieties of the mutiny and war in India. But he gave a very poor account of Lord Hylton, with whom they had stayed a month at Hylton Hall after his return from the South of France. "England is evidently no place for him," wrote Mr. Mostyn by the September mail; "and your mother and sister begin to be most anxious about him and for your return to them; but I have explained to them how impossible it is for you to get leave, except under the most emergent necessity, and that, I may safely say, has not come yet, so far as your brother is concerned; indeed, the medical opinion is, that another winter in the South may restore him to health. I must not conceal from you, however, that he is weak, and was obliged to go home several times, during the glorious partridge shooting, in which I, old Indian as I am, fairly took my part; and he actually shivers at the thought of an English winter. So he had better go at once, and I fancy your next letters will tell you of their proposed journey southwards.

"I have had many conversations with him about Seeta. Poor fellow, he was deeply moved by all I told him about her, and your mother and sister no less so by what they were told by Rose and Grace: but they have said little to me on the subject. It was very difficult for any of us to make Seeta's character known to them as we knew it; and I think, on reflection, that you will understand this. Nothing, however, now disturbs their grateful, loving remembrance of her last act of devotion to you, which preserved you to them: and it is only their ignorance of the people, and the almost impossibility of causing them to understand what Seeta had become, and was becoming, that at present obscures their perceptions. All the memorials of your poor girl that Grace has kept, her little notes and exercises, her marks in Grace's books, and her own sketches of Seeta, have done more to make them think of her as you and we all wish them to think, than anything we could say, or you could have written: and I am sure they will come to our opinion at last. You see I have expressed myself frankly, but it was due to you that I should do so. At first, I will not say that there was not coldness, and even some aversion on your mother and sister's part to mention Seeta: but this did not last, and I rejoiced to find, before we left them, that love and admiration had gained places in their hearts, and were abiding there. For the present, therefore, you must be content that so much has been gained.

"A good deal of the feeling and prejudice that did exist may be traced, I am sure, to the impressions which late events have left upon the minds of most persons here, who know nothing of the people of India as you, and I, and others know them: and who believe them, all or most, to be like the monsters who committed the massacres at Cawnpoor and elsewhere. These sad impressions will disappear in time; but at present it is almost hopeless to try to overcome them."

If Cyril Brandon at first resented the doubts of his family on the subject of Seeta, he could not, on mature reflection, refuse to feel the weight of his friend's remarks; and in his letters to his mother, he forbore mention of the subject further than by reference to those who had been her best friends. Nothing, in his case, could have been more opportune than the return of the

Mostyns to England. The Judge's high position in India, the refinement and delicacy of Rose and Grace, were warrants for the respectability of Seeta's position and character, which no letters from himself could have supplied; and the devotion of the last act of her life, which was now so fully made known, would, he knew, leave its fruits in the loving retention of her sweet memory. In writing to his mother, he could assure her at last, confidently, that he was fully determined on coming to her as soon as he possibly could: certainly by the close of the next year, when he would have finished the work in hand. The rest could only be fulfilled when he saw them face to face, and could tell them much that would ratify all that his dear true friends had prepared them to hear from himself. How deeply grateful Cyril felt to them, and most especially to Grace, I think I need not mention to those who, in these pages, have followed his character.

As the time passed, Cyril Brandon found what he had hoped for—a healthier spirit rising among the people. There was no further clinging to the memories of old rulers and old systems of government. Those that had appeared on the scene, during the troubled times of Sumbut 1914, had been the cause of wide-spread misery and disappointment everywhere; and wherever mutiny and rebellion had existed, all enterprise had been checked, and all mutual confidence and security impaired, if not destroyed. The strange prophecy that the rule of the Koompani Bahadoor was to last only a hundred years, had, indeed, been literally fulfilled; for, on the first day of November, 1858, the gracious proclamation of Queen Victoria was issued at Allahabad, by the Governor-General, Lord Canning, and fell like oil upon troubled waters. The Company was, indeed, dead: but the Queen of England and her Government lived; and the first publication of its official existence, and determination to rule justly and mercifully, was accepted from high to low with a reverential confidence that those estimated best who watched its effects.

Meanwhile, the war was dying out; and, before the close of 1858, what remained of the rebel army had been driven across the Raptee, in Oudh, into the jungles of the Terái of Nipál. There perished the Nana, Azim Oolla, his detestable adviser, and a host of other chieftains and rebel officers, among whom, it was supposed, was Rajah Hurpál Singh, of whom no distinct account was ever heard. The able historian of the Sepoy War* tells the details of these events with admirable vigour and perspicuity: and such scant notice of them as I could venture

* Sir John Kaye, K.S.I.

to give here would, I feel, be out of place, and presuming. I have no further occasion to notice the rival native powers in the Noorpoor province. Both had perished as rebels, and their possessions were justly confiscated. But while the fortifications of their castles were blown up, the Palace of Futtehpoor was preserved, and the wives of the miserable Nawab allowed to dwell in it, while they received a liberal provision from the estate for their lives, and most of the old household, who had taken no part in the rebellion, were pensioned.

Mr. Brandon had visited Shah Gunje on many occasions during his various tours, and, although his first visit after Seeta's death had been inexpressibly painful to him, and to Narendra and Aunt Ella, he had found them more resigned, perhaps, than himself, and they had entreated him not to grieve for that which had no remedy, and had been the will of God. Nor were the good priest's exhortations less impressive in their homely wisdom and earnestness.

Aunt Ella could, indeed, say little, for her mind was much turned now from the affairs and affections of the world, which, to her, were dead. "If I could have seen a child of my darling's before I died," she said to Cyril, "I should have been very grateful; but that was not permitted, and my best consolation is, that she died pure in her solemn faith, and that the ceremonies for the repose of her soul are regularly performed."

Narendra, however, was very different, and with him the priest. "We would fain have seen her take her place among your people," they had said, "for she had gone out from among us to you, and by no means could the purity of her caste have been preserved." They knew, too, from Cyril, how near she had been to a final profession of the Christian faith; and what would have raised her to honour, would have been, to them, no degradation.

On one occasion of a visit, the banker had submitted to Cyril a statement of Seeta's property, which was very considerable, and urged him to take possession of it, as he had an undoubted right to do; but he would receive nothing, and told Narendra and the priest of Seeta's wish to found and endow schools in Shah Gunje for girls and boys, and a foundation for the support of poor and helpless persons. Narendra gladly accepted the alternative, as a solution of all the difficulty; and, by a proper deed, all that she could dispose of was devoted to these purposes, and invested in public securities, the income of which was to be administered by a local board of native gentlemen and merchants. Cyril himself drew the designs for the school houses, and when they should be complete, he promised to come and open them himself.

Although his brother had taken their old villa at Cannes for the winter, Lord Hylton did not write to Cyril regularly, but his mother and Augusta did, and there was an increasing tone of sadness and anxiety in their letters, as the season advanced, which foreboded no relief. A return to England for summer was very questionable, if not impossible. The last visit had done no good—indeed, positive harm—and the medical adviser had suggested Switzerland, or Arcachon, as by far preferable. There was no positive alarm in their letters, for that was slow, perhaps, to come, in the case of one so precious to all; but, as Cyril thought, if there was any good hope of that entire restoration to strength for which all prayed, why was there not assurance of it, in place of continued uneasiness about debility and loss of spirits and appetite?

Once his brother had written pleadingly: "If it were not for your assurance that you will come to us this year, I think, dearest Cyril, I should go down fast; but that keeps me up, though I am wretchedly thin and weak, and even a short ride tires me out. Mind, I would not have it said of you, that you abandoned your work before you had completed it! that would distress me far more than that I did not see you; but Mostyn writes to me that your leave will soon be open, and, if you can, *do* get to me before Christmas. I should be very, very thankful, and so will Mater and Augusta. Where I am to go for this summer is not decided, but I think it little matters where, and I prefer Switzerland to Arcachon. I dare say we shall settle at Lausanne, and eat grapes at Montreux when they ripen. We know all about Seeta now, and her memory lives with us *very* preciously. I know it will gratify you to hear how much mother and Augusta talk to me now, of all that Grace Mostyn told them: and, but for her, how little should we ever have known of the truth! We can only think, how unutterably lonely you must be without her."

It was a hard wrench to Cyril; but by the September mail from Europe, the tidings of Lord Hylton were at last alarming. He had revived much at Lausanne, and had been able to enjoy yachting on the lake, with some English gentlemen who had formed a club there; and the gentle exercise and excitement appeared to be the very best remedies he had tried. But one day, in a severe squall and heavy sea, he had been completely drenched and chilled, and his cough, which had almost gone, had returned with great violence, accompanied by spitting of blood. They were all to proceed at once, or as soon as he could be moved, to Mentone; and the Mostyns had promised to meet them there, as a winter in the south of France had been recommended for Mr. Mostyn, who had suffered considerably from the winter he had passed in England; Lady Hylton now adjured Cyril to fulfil his promise, and the necessity of doing so admitted neither of doubt or delay. He therefore sent in his application for leave on urgent private affairs, and wrote to his mother that he had done so, and would leave India by the November mail if possible.

There was little time in which he could pay even a flying visit to all his old friends; but it must be done; and his first care was for Shah Gunje, where Temple's tents were pitched for him in the grove near the temple. As soon as his leave had been granted, Cyril had written to Narendra that he should come and bid him and Aunt Ella farewell; and to Temple and Baba Sahib to assemble all the principal people, that he might take leave of them. But Baba Sahib and Narendra, with Bulram Singh and others, determined it should be no empty leave-taking, and they drew up an address, on rich gold-spotted paper, illuminated after a quaint and beautiful manner; and the people from towns and villages around crowded into Shah Gunje to sign it, till nearly two thousand signatures were obtained; and Narendra had a handsome silver case made for it, by one of his head workmen, and a salver, on which it was to be delivered. The school-rooms were ready, too, and the scholars were entered who were to learn there, and would be presented to Cyril at the ceremony.

How much all had endured through the past terrible year, I think we know in part, yet not all: but how deeply suffering had united them to each other, ruler and ruled, that farewell ceremony proved beyond any doubt. Early after his arrival, Narendra and Baba Sahib, with a deputation of the chief people, had gone to the tents, and requested Mr. Brandon to come to the schools at noon, when all would be ready to receive him. I do not think much was said beyond this, for the hearts of those who brought the message were too full to speak much then; and, indeed, Cyril felt as if he should be glad when the ceremony of leave-taking was over. At the time appointed, he and Temple rode down to the town, and as he looked at the schools, Cyril was gratified to observe how skilfully his pretty Gothic design had been understood and executed. In a niche over the principal entrance was a tablet of white marble, with the inscription in English, Hindee, and Persian:—

"These school-rooms, for the education of the boys and girls of Shah Gunje, were the gift of Seeta Bye, wife of the Honourable Cyril Brandon, Commissioner of Noorpoor. Begun 1858; finished 1859."

The rooms, which opened into each other by folding doors, were large; but the space within was full to overflowing. Cyril could hardly bear to look around him, for there were few dry eyes in the assembly: and those of the persons who met him to conduct him to the daïs that had been constructed, were sad too; but there was little delay in the proceedings, which were opened by Baba Sahib with a simple speech, requesting permission to read the address they had all prepared. "I cannot trust myself to speak much," he said, nervously, "but I may be able, I hope, to read this, sir, though it is to bid you farewell;" and he read what had been written, often in quivering tones, and with tears dropping from his eyes, to the end. I need not, perhaps, translate the whole, but there were a few passages that I cannot withhold.

"What can we say? You were like a parent to the people: a kind and merciful parent; for in the troubled season of Sumbut 1914, you, regardless of danger to yourself, came to us when we were suffering more than we need relate now, and purged this district from rebels, Dacoits, and gang robbers, and not a trace of them remains. For this protection, and for our present security, we are deeply, very deeply, grateful to you.

"We, who are the servants of Government in this district, as also all the people, well know what your conduct to us has uniformly been: and know, also, that your kindness to us has never failed. You have taken care of us, as of your children. Were we to relate how you have exerted yourself for us, we should never make an end of it. You heard the complaints of the poor; and, as flies to honey, all classes gathered and mingled together without apprehension in your Court: but we never heard or saw that you were impatient or used harsh expressions to any one. Your perfect knowledge of our language assured complainants, for they knew they were understood, and were contented; and never, on any occasion, have we seen that even the meanest was treated with indignity, or affronted.

"Now you are departing from us; and we know that you would not go unless you had sore need to see your illustrious family. Be it so. Wherever you go, may God prosper you and keep you safely. Our hearts are full, and we can say no more. If you return to us, we shall be grateful to God who will send you; if not, you will not be forgotten; and from this time your name will be sung with praise as our women grind at their mills, and light their lamps.

"Now our last request is this: that as you have bestowed so many obligations and so much love upon us, we, to show our gratitude to you, have signed this humble address, which indeed is unworthy to present to you, save as an expression of our affection and devotion; and we pray that you may be pleased to accept it from us, and to keep us in your remembance always."

Cyril tried to reply; and as his old friend stood wiping his eyes, and sobbing like a child, said as much as he found words to utter. All his remembrances of Shah Gunje and his love for Seeta, rushed upon him so vividly, and so distressingly, that it was difficult to arrange words in his mind to assure those who heard him of what he felt; but they seemed to understand intuitively what he was thinking of, as he mentioned the last gift of one whom he had loved and honoured as his wife, and in whose name the schools they had used that day, for the first time, had been erected and endowed. Then he thanked them for their love to him, and their obedience and loyalty, and told them that if God willed, he would return to them again.

It was poor comfort perhaps, and they believed he would return if he could; but nothing could repress the passionate outburst of grief which ensued as he ceased speaking, and said "Farewell," asking them not to forget him.

"We will not forget you," cried hundreds: "never! never!" and as he descended from the daïs, the people crowded about him, kissing his hands, his feet, his clothes, or reaching forward their hands that they might touch him: and so they followed him to Narendra's house, and left him there.

There was not much to say perhaps, and the old banker was, too much affected to speak more than a few words. His adopted son was present, and Cyril felt that he had chosen well in the fine intelligent young man who was introduced to him, and who bent before him while he put his hands on his head. At last Narendra said, "Leave us, Mr. Brandon, for this parting is too bitter and painful for us all to be long maintained. Write to me of your welfare, and I will write to you myself, as long as God spares me. We have one memory in common which can never fade, and for all your love to her, and your confidence in me, I am most grateful. I hope to hear soon of your marriage, sir, for you ought not to remain as you are; and if you should choose Mr. Mostyn's sister, I shall be happy to think that you have as your wife one who so loved our darling. For the rest, I will take care of all your people. Buldeo and his brother will belong to my guard, and had better stay with me now. Your Sikhs are well provided for already. Now come and see Aunt Ella, but indeed she will hardly be able to speak, and you will forgive her. But take my blessing, Mr. Brandon; once more, and for the last time, I think, I commit you to His care before whom there are no distinctions."

Poor Aunt Ella! she clung to Cyril, sobbing and gasping hysterically, but could not speak, though she tried hard to do so: and it was merciful, perhaps, that she seemed to swoon away, and then Cyril left her to the care of her women. After that came the farewell to the good old priest, Wamun Bhut, and to many friends who had assembled in the court-yard. All that Cyril took away with him was Seeta's old "tumboora," which, as he went once more to the upper room, he saw standing in the corner where he had first seen it, and when she sang to him the sad old Hindee ballad we know of.

"This day's work will be a lesson to me, Brandon, that I shall never forget," said Temple, as they sat alone after all were gone away. "Would that I possessed the love of the people as you do!"

"It is easily and simply gained," replied Cyril. "Be just, be patient, be firm and true: be always accessible and courteous, never forgetting your position, and they will love you. They are almost like children, you see, easily led, when once they have given their faith."

In the morning ere the day broke they had parted, for Cyril had to hasten back to Noorpoor. He could not see the oriel window so dear to him, but a lamp was burning in the room which seemed to twinkle like a bright star.

There was a similar ceremony awaiting him at Noorpoor. Equally moving and equally grateful to him were the words of the address, but I do not think I need to repeat the details. Then came farewell dinners at the messes, and a public dinner at the Brigadier's, with speeches in his honour at all, and hearty wishes for his safe journey home and speedy return. Perhaps Captain Hobson would have gone with Cyril; but he was then raising a new regiment, and he was thinking, too, what a pretty and comfortable wife Lucy Home would make him, while, to all appearance, her opinion of him, as a possible husband, was in exact consonance.

After all, had Cyril Brandon been as popular among his own people as he was among those he had ruled? Perhaps not.

Certainly not as popular as Mr. Mostyn, and there were reasons which strike me for this, which I will not withhold. Philip Mostyn was always present, and his genial nature could not be resisted; Cyril Brandon was for the most part absent in his district, and who knew or cared what he did there? As a keen sportsman he was popular with the youngsters who went to his camp on hunting parties, but they did not constitute society. Of the rest, many, perhaps most, sneered at Cyril's care, nay affection, for the people he ruled over. They professed not to be able to understand how an English gentleman could so much identify himself with "the natives," how in fact he could bear with them at all, much less make friends of them. And perhaps it is too often the case, that entire unsympathy causes such characters as Cyril Brandon's to be almost universally misunderstood, and perhaps often misrepresented. They have, however, their reward, as Cyril Brandon had, who did not hesitate between the affection of his people, and the opinions of the ever-fluctuating and varying society of the station, carrying away grateful remembrance of the love and gratitude of the one for his life, while the other faded altogether out of his memory.

The last day came; and very early in the morning Cyril walked down the Judge's garden to his own, and past the ruins of his house and Seeta's cottage to the shore of the lake under the water-gate, where a little altar to Seeta's memory had been erected. There was no inscription on it but the word "Seeta" in English and Hindee letters, and the date of her death. Out of the top grew a plant of the sweet basil or toolsee, which was still carefully watered and tended by the old Brahmin and his wife, who, on the part of Narendra, performed the necessary ceremonies, and lighted a lamp in a niche of the altar every evening. The lamp had gone out, for the night was past; and as Cyril sat down near the little memorial the sun rose, and flashed upon the quiet lake, the town, and the grim old fort above, in a rich golden glory. There were many, many sweet memories rushing into Cyril's heart, of one gone to her rest, which were not put back, as he prayed for help and direction in his future life. He might return, but he felt an almost consciousness that he should not; and as he looked around for the last time, he stepped forward and broke off a branch from the plant, which was to be treasured safely. Then he went up to the octagon room in the tower, but there was nothing there now but the flowers which Seeta had planted near the entrance, and of which he gathered a few blossoms. The pet birds had been long ago sent to Shah Gunje, and were safe. So he took leave of all that would never be forgotten. Never!

* * * * * *

"I am only a competition-walla," said Noble, as he bid Cyril good-bye in the evening, "and I admit I have had my conceits and strong prejudices; but I am pretty well cured of them, Brandon, and I have grown to be of your opinion as to the people whom I used to sneer at: and though I can never attain your popularity or the love they bear you, yet I, too, will try to follow your example, and you need be under no apprehension that all you have done and projected, will fail in my hands. Yes, you have been right all through: and I hope you will forgive the petulance with which I used to speak of the people as 'niggers,' and think, as by Jove I used to think, that the only way to manage them was not certainly to gain their affections. I often think how patient you have been with me, and indeed, Brandon, I will not fail now."

"And you will succeed, too," replied Cyril. "I, for one, have faith in any one who has faith in himself, and I leave everything in your hands with perfect confidence. If I can help you in any matter you have only to write, and I hope you will write in any case. Now, good-bye! Come, Muff, we must go!"

"Good-bye, and God bless you, Brandon," said Mr. Noble. Cynic as he was, tears rose to his eyes as he turned away when Cyril's palankeen disappeared out of the gate, attended by some sorrowing servants, who followed their kind and generous master till he had passed beyond the boundaries of the cantonment.

CHAPTER LII.

"CLOSING SCENES."

I KNOW few more lovely spots on earth than Mentone, soft and grand by turns; a rare combination of mountain, wood, and sea—ever varying in tint and expression, in light and shadow, and in the aerial effects of its soft, sweet, dreamy climate. It was nearly Christmas, yet gardens were gay with flowers; the air was laden with a perfume of orange and lemon blossoms, of roses, of violets, and tuberoses, and was as soft and warm as a mild English spring. Those who live there have their prejudices as to situation, and there are as strong advocates for the west bay as for the east; but to me the latter is the most lovely. The Monarch "Berceau," with its naked limestone precipices, rising out of the grey olive woods, and its broken ridges declining till they end in the glowing "Rocher Rouge," which forms the eastern horn of the bay; the picturesque old town hanging to the rock on which it is built, and the rows of hotels, pensions, and villas, bright and cheerful, backed by dense olive woods, are reflected in the blue sea: and, above all, the grand masses of the rocks of St. Agnese, and the high sharp peak of the "Gran' Mondo"—at this season capped with snow—form pictures of ever-varying and trancendent beauty, perhaps above all other localities of the Riviera.

Near a window in a villa, on the very skirts of the olive woods, situated above the line of hotels, and so as completely to overlook them and command an unbroken view of the bay, the town, and the ranges of mountains, up to Monaco, lay Lord Hylton, now weak almost unto death. The bright sun is shining into the room, and the air is deliciously soft and balmy as it comes through the partly opened casement: yet the dear invalid is closely wrapped in blankets, and he seems to shiver as he draws his hand across his face.

"Are you cold, dear?" asks his mother anxiously, who has been sitting near him reading. "Shall I shut the window?"

"No, mother," he replied; "I was not cold. I was only thinking—thinking whether I should last till Cyril comes. I feel so weak, to-day—so weak, mother!"

Lady Hylton turned away her head to hide her tears. Ah! he was weak indeed, and there was no hope now. Last year there had been a rally, and, when they arrived from Lausanne, Lord Hylton had revived again for awhile; but worse symptoms had set in, and kind Dr. B—— had warned them all that the end was now inevitable, and was only a question of time.

"He will come, darling," she replied. "Do not fear. This is his mail, and there are letters from us waiting at Marseilles, directing him what to do; but he cannot possibly arrive for three days yet, so you must be patient!"

"I will, mother," he said, with a resigned sigh. "But O, I yearn for him, more than I can tell, except to God; and there are so many uncertainties, too. Even at the last they may have said to him in Calcutta, 'You are of too much use, we cannot spare you.' Indeed, I can't help thinking of all these contingencies, and then he seems to fade out of sight altogether."

"But you must not think of them, my pet; you must believe

he is to come, as he will come, I am certain. Why, Mr. Mostyn said, only this morning, that he had seen his leave in orders by the last Gazette, and that Cyril's hurried letter from Benares ought to satisfy you."

"I will try, mother," he said, more cheerfully. "And now read on; I was dozing when you read last, and you must go back a page or two."

It was very quiet and peaceful everywhere; a few flies were buzzing about the window pane; without there was a slight, very slight, rustle or sigh of the woods; the tall cypresses before the house waved very gently, and the low murmur of waves lapping the shore, came up soothingly. The bay was blue and bright, and the old brown city seemed to be asleep in the sunlight, while above it were the faint blue distances of the land and the ocean. Lady Hylton was reading softly, and the only sounds that broke the silence were the grand and loving words of a portion of Jeremy Taylor's "Holy Living and Dying," which was Lord Hylton's favourite book now.

"He will come from the sea, there," said Lord Hylton, in a dreamy whisper, as if to himself, as he pointed in the direction of Monaco; and as he turned, apparently to watch, he fell unconsciously into a soft sleep, like a child's, while his mother sat by him.

"Ah! thank God for this," said his mother; "he will be better when he wakes." As she rose softly to close the window, she looked out for a moment, and saw a tall bronzed man, with a large beard, and a little grey Skye terrier running before him, walking up a path from the road below. She could not see the features, and said to herself, "Some tourist, perhaps, but I hope he won't come here for the view, for Hylton must not be disturbed." And she was sitting down again, when a strong footstep was heard on the gravel without, and a tall figure passed the window rapidly; Lord Hylton started from his sleep, and, as the man crossed another window, stretched out his arms and cried, "Cyril! O Cyril, come to me!"

He was right. Another moment, and Cyril, who had entered by the open hall, as he had caught a glimpse of his mother's face at the open window, crossed the drawing-room with his strong firm step, and, while his mother clung to him, in a burst of tears, he knelt down by his brother and threw his stout arms about him in a gentle loving embrace.

Lord Hylton could not speak, but his thin white hands were caressing his brother's bronzed face, passing through his thick curly beard, running through his hair, while his tears were falling silently and rapturously on the strong brown hands. What a contrast there was, between the brothers! one full of health, energy, and vital power; the other so wasted, so feeble, and yet his cheeks and eyes flashing with unwonted brilliance. "Cyril! Cyril!" was all he could say, as again and again he leaned his head on that broad breast. "Mother, I do thank God that I have seen him."

Then Augusta came in, who had been on an errand in the town, and threw her arms round Cyril, who still knelt by his brother's sofa. "And you passed me in the street, you bad boy," she said, "and would not even look at me, though I stared ever so hard. I was sure it was he, mother, though I dare not speak to him. And are you Muff?" she continued to the little fellow, who was humbly trying to attract notice by sitting up and begging. "Come, you are a pet, indeed!" and Muff jumped into her lap, and kissed her after his own doggish fashion. And so they sat, while Lord Hylton listened to Cyril's account of his voyage; but he could not speak much, for the excitement had brought on his terrible cough, and Cyril saw, only too surely, that there was no hope of life.

Augusta had written a hurried line to Mrs. Mostyn, "Would they come to dinner, for Cyril had arrived, and they were like themselves, to him?" The Mostyns had rooms in the great pension below, and, in truth, Grace, who had been sitting at the window, had seen Cyril and Muff pass up to the villa, and had run to tell her sister. They were not likely to stand on ceremony, and they came up and joined the party gladly. How much had they all to say! while the poor invalid sat up, and listened with a quiet, smiling, thankful face, more like his own, they all thought, than they had seen for a long time past.

So days and weeks passed, happily, though the dark shadow was hanging over one of them, plain to see by all. For a long time—for several weeks, indeed—Cyril's presence had seemed to give his brother new vigour; and Cyril's tales of his Indian life, of the period of the mutiny, and of the official work, had a charm of novelty and freshness in which he revelled. Nor was Seeta omitted; but I think she was mentioned with some reticence by all. The joy they felt on having Cyril among them seemed, for the time, to have dimmed the recollection that, but for her devotion, they had never seen him. This, however, was only at first; and presently, to Cyril's great relief and joy, they came to speaking of her as she deserved, and as he and the Mostyns had best hoped. Then there were pleasant excursions to Gorbio, to St. Agnese, to Sospello, and Bordighera, all within the day, for they dare not leave Lord Hylton long; and one evening he asked them to sing to him, as, indeed, Grace and Mrs. Mostyn had been in the habit of doing, for he loved to hear their rich voices blending together in sweet harmonies. They had been taking new lessons while they were in London, and their performance was wellnigh perfect now.

One evening Cyril went to his room, and brought the old copy of the duett we remember, with the last sad night on which it had been so fearfully interrupted. Grace had not asked for it, and flushed to her clear bright forehead, as he unrolled the yellow smoke-stained music, and spread it before her on the piano. I will not say that he had not pain in the effort he had made: but he had overcome it, for she was very dear now, and he thought she looked grateful, as she took up the old worn copy and looked over it. "Dimmi che m' ami, ancor." Their voices were trembling, and Rose's accompaniment was far from steady; but Lord Hylton listened with a delight he could not conceal. "Sing it again," he said; "I like it best of any you two have sung to me." And they did so, more steadily, perhaps, now the ice was broken.

Yes, it was the old, old story once more. Why should I conceal it? Told to each other one evening, among the grand old olive trees behind the villa, mutually believed with not a doubt or fear, and with only poor, happy Muff as a witness. How beautiful Grace was now! more womanly, more perfect in form, more graceful, and yet with none of her charming, gentle, gracious manner disturbed or altered. Lord Hylton had been urgent with his brother for a long time to declare himself to her, for he had early seen that there was no real impediment; and as to Augusta, she had wormed out Grace's secret long ago, and teazed her brother—not by telling it, indeed, but by urging him to give her to her as a sister. Lady Hylton was, perhaps, not so enthusiastic at first; Cyril, she thought, though she did not say it, ought to see more of English society than Mentone afforded, and take his choice more deliberately. And yet, after all, whom did she know like that sweet, tender Grace Mostyn, so fitted to adorn any station in life? And thus the dear old lady took Grace to her heart, and loved her as a daughter.

Most likely they would have waited, as Grace desired, till their return to England; but Lord Hylton was now becoming nervous and impatient that the marriage should take place in his presence, while he had strength to witness it; and that time was now fast drawing to a close, for Dr. B—— had warned them all, and not less his patient, that all worldly matters should be set at rest, for that the final parting was very near. "It must be, and that soon, dear Cyril," Hylton had said, after one of the kind doctor's visits. "He has been telling me that all earthly things should be settled, so that I can look up to God without a thought save of His mercy. And indeed, Cyril, to know—to feel that you and dear Grace were happy, would be the crowning joy of my poor life. As you did not refuse my prayer to come home to me, so you must not deny me this last great satisfaction and blessing. Since you came, I seem to have lived years with you in unreserved confidence, and I know and respect all your thoughts; but this is one of my last requests."

Could Cyril refuse such an appeal, backed as it was by his mother and sister, and Rose, whose dearest wish, long, long ago entertained, was now to be fulfilled? It was quite impossible; and Grace, too, yielded to the general combination against her. So, one day, Lord Hylton was carried in a hammock down to the little church by the sea, placed in an easy-chair by the altar, and was able to follow the ceremony which united them with a grateful, satisfied heart. It was a quiet affair, altogether; Augusta and three mutual friends were bridesmaids, and Charles Graham, a fine young fellow, to whom Augusta was engaged, acted as best man to Cyril. Even the poor invalid was cheerful and joyous in his quiet way, and at the *déjeûner*, after the ceremony, raised himself, and said a few grateful words, while he drank to the health of those most dear to him. Lord Hylton was happy now; happy and content that in this, his last act in life, he had done his duty.

They went away on a short excursion for a fortnight along the quiet towns of the Riviera; and when they returned, Cyril was shocked to find so much alteration in his brother. It was only what he had been told to look for, but when the reality came, it was inexpressibly painful. Lord Hylton had no desire to live, his two last wishes had been mercifully accomplished, and his release from weakness, which had become constant pain, would be welcome. And one evening, towards the close of April, the pure humble spirit passed gently away. Reclining by the window, in the place where he had first seen Cyril, he had been looking with dreamy eyes over the sea and town, and had murmured something which Cyril could not hear; but an old thought had come back, and pointing to the sea he had said, "There, there. Thank God!" And Cyril had raised him a little, and put his head on his own breast. Once or twice Lord Hylton looked up gratefully and smiled, as he pressed the hand he held; then there was a slight shiver, and a sigh, and he was gone!

They laid him to rest in the little quiet cemetery, which is shaded by trees above the town, and where all the last offices were fulfilled. There was no need to remain at Mentone, and they separated for a time. Lady Hylton and Augusta went direct to England under the charge of Charles Graham, and the Mostyns travelled with them; while Cyril, now Lord Hylton, took his wife to Italy, and returning home by Germany, met them all again at the grand old home of his ancestors, Hylton Hall.

I need not dilate upon his new life. We know what he was in India, and though England does not bring him into that close, and, if I may say it, fatherly connection with the people and their interests that his Indian office did, yet he finds much to do. He is very hospitable, an active magistrate, and a thorough sportsman, which are acceptable qualities in his county, and the compliment of his appointment as Deputy-Lieutenant in his brother's place, was at once paid to him. When he took his seat in the House of Lords, his eminent services in India were mentioned warmly, and he continues to be looked up to as an authority in Indian questions, in which he has few rivals there. On these questions he speaks fluently and persuasively, and not without a certain weight and authority which his experience has given him. Perhaps, when he has had more experience of English politics, he may become an English statesman, but that is yet to come. It was gratifying to him to receive the order of the Star of India, and a high pleasure to know that in the same grade had been included the name of his old faithful friend and constant companion, Baba Sahib. When his furlough had expired, Lord Hylton was obliged to resign the service to which he had belonged; but to do so was a hard wrench, the pain of which has not, I know, passed away, nor indeed will ever completely leave him; and it would not surprise me to hear that some day he took Grace back to India for a cold weather tour, and paid a last visit to the people in whom he trusted, and with whom he so lovingly parted.

If you, gentle reader, wish to know his views of Indian policy, I must request you to read Her Gracious Majesty's proclamation in 1858, in which he is a true believer. He sees what has been done for the advancement of the people in education, and, indeed, in every other respect, and watches carefully what is doing. He has, however, one anxiety which he trusts will pass away; that the doctrines of the Manchester school may lead to a greater local expenditure than the true public interests warrant, and that a too profuse expenditure may lead to additional burthens on the people which would be resented, and endanger the popularity of the Government. He would therefore prefer that the public expenditure should be strictly kept within the income, now so largely increased and increasing, so as to leave a surplus in every year for any possible and unforeseen contingency.

Lord Hylton (may I still call him Cyril?) hears constantly from his old friends, and the news of his marriage gave much and genuine delight. Narendra, who gave a great feast in honour of it, has insisted upon sending Grace a magnificent waistbelt or zone of the purest gold, made in almost invisible joints, with a richly chased clasp, almost too heavy for her to wear. Aunt Ella has sent her a valuable cashmere shawl and a necklace of pearls which her husband thinks were Seeta's; and every six months or so comes a box full of pickles, curry paste, the dear Aunt's famous vermicelli, and "Pápurs," with other condiments. Both still enjoy a green old age, and are very happy, for Aunt Ella is less ascetic, and more natural now. Narendra's adoption has satisfied every one, even Aunt Ella, and the business is greater than ever; and Temple knows, for he is a trustee, though Lord Hylton does not, that the "grand old man," as Temple calls him, has invested five thousand pounds in the names of each of the three children that have been born, and should more follow, they will, he thinks, be equally well provided for. "I never shall forget his honour in regard to Seeta," he said to Temple; "and all I am worth could not repay his tender love for her and for us."

Grace's, Lady Hylton's, character has been much developed by her position, and her beauty still fascinates all who see it. In her sphere she is ever truly the lady—bountiful, kind, gentle, hospitable, and truly benevolent. Perhaps there is a certain reticence about her which she has never lost, and that she does not wish to be known to all with whom she is necessarily thrown in contact; but to those whom she does know, she is the most charming of their friends. Sometimes old Lady Hylton stays with her son, sometimes with Augusta, whose husband is a magnate in Scotland, and I am bound to say that dear grandmamma is most popular among her grandchildren.

The Mostyns paid a last long visit to Hylton Hall, and Philip heartily enjoyed shooting with his old friend. Soon afterwards they returned to India, but not to Noorpoor; for

Mr. Mostyn has obtained one of the very highest judicial stations: and they are looking forward with hope to a speedy and final return home.

* * * * * *

And is Sceta forgotten? Not so. Come, I will show you a picture. Look well on it, and if you can realize the group in your mind, it is one that is, I think, both touching and beautiful!

There is a room which is known at Hylton Hall as my Lord's study; but which Cyril calls his "den," hung round with Indian trophies of the chase, and Indian arms and hog spears, the addresses in their silver cases, and many sketches, and finished drawings of Indian landscapes and figures. Now, as I gently open the door, we see that two figures are standing before the fireplace, looking up to a picture which hangs on the wall above them. It is a large, masterly drawing in water colour, of a fair Indian lady, simply dressed in white muslin drapery. Below its rich frame is another oval frame made like a large locket, and lined with crimson velvet, in which are a long tress of wavy, deep brown hair, almost black, but which, where the light falls, shows a tinge of bright gold. With it, there is a small withered branch of a sweet-scented Indian plant, and some dried flowers tied up with ribbon, of which we know.

Those who are looking at these objects are Grace, Lady Hylton, whose beauty is great, but not greater than that of the picture, though of a very different character. The tall strong figure beside her, with the brown curly beard and handsome manly features, is her husband, and a pretty child, a girl of three years old, with a profusion of curly golden hair, is clinging to her mother's skirts, while an old grey Skye terrier, now infirm, licks her hand, and she cries, "Me look, mamma! Rosey look!" till she is taken up. Then her mother opens the case, and smiling, though her eyes glisten with tears, turns to her husband and says, "The leaves are sweet still, Cyril, as sweet as ever."

"Yes, darling," he replies, "as sweet as her memory is to us both." And he draws her to his heart close—closer—while she rests her head on his breast, and Rose strokes her father's face, for it is graver than usual. They are fond lovers still, you see; and we need look no more. Come away! There is no happiness on earth that is wanting to them, but their thoughts are ever with the dead as they look on these memorials, for it is the tenth anniversary of Seeta's death. Hush! Come away! and let me close the door, gently, lest we disturb them!

Forgotten! Ah, no! for at the little altar—far away—Brahmins offer flowers and sing hymns to-day. And many a girl lays a garland there and prays to the sweet spirit, whose death she commemorates!

THE END.